W9-AMP-849

Stephen McCranie's

SPACE BOY

VOLUME 6

Written and illustrated by
STEPHEN McCRANIE

DARK HORSE BOOKS

President and Publisher **Mike Richardson**

Editor **Shantel LaRocque**

Assistant Editor **Brett Israel**

Designer **Anita Magaña**

Digital Art Technician **Allyson Haller**

STEPHEN McCRANIE'S SPACE BOY VOLUME 6

Space Boy™ © 2020 Stephen McCranie. All rights reserved. Dark Horse Books®
and the Dark Horse logo are registered trademarks of Dark Horse Comics
LLC. All rights reserved. No portion of this publication may be reproduced
or transmitted, in any form or by any means, without the express written
permission of Dark Horse Comics LLC. Names, characters, places, and incidents
featured in this publication either are the product of the author's imagination or
are used fictitiously. Any resemblance to actual persons (living or dead), events,
institutions, or locales, without satiric intent, is coincidental.

This book collects *Space Boy* episodes 76–92,
previously published online at WebToons.com.

Published by Dark Horse Books
A division of Dark Horse Comics LLC
10956 SE Main Street | Milwaukie, OR 97222
StephenMcCranie.com | DarkHorse.com

To find a comics shop in your area,
visit comicshoplocator.com

First edition: March 2020
ISBN 978-1-50671-400-4
10 9 8 7 6 5 4 3 2 1
Printed in China

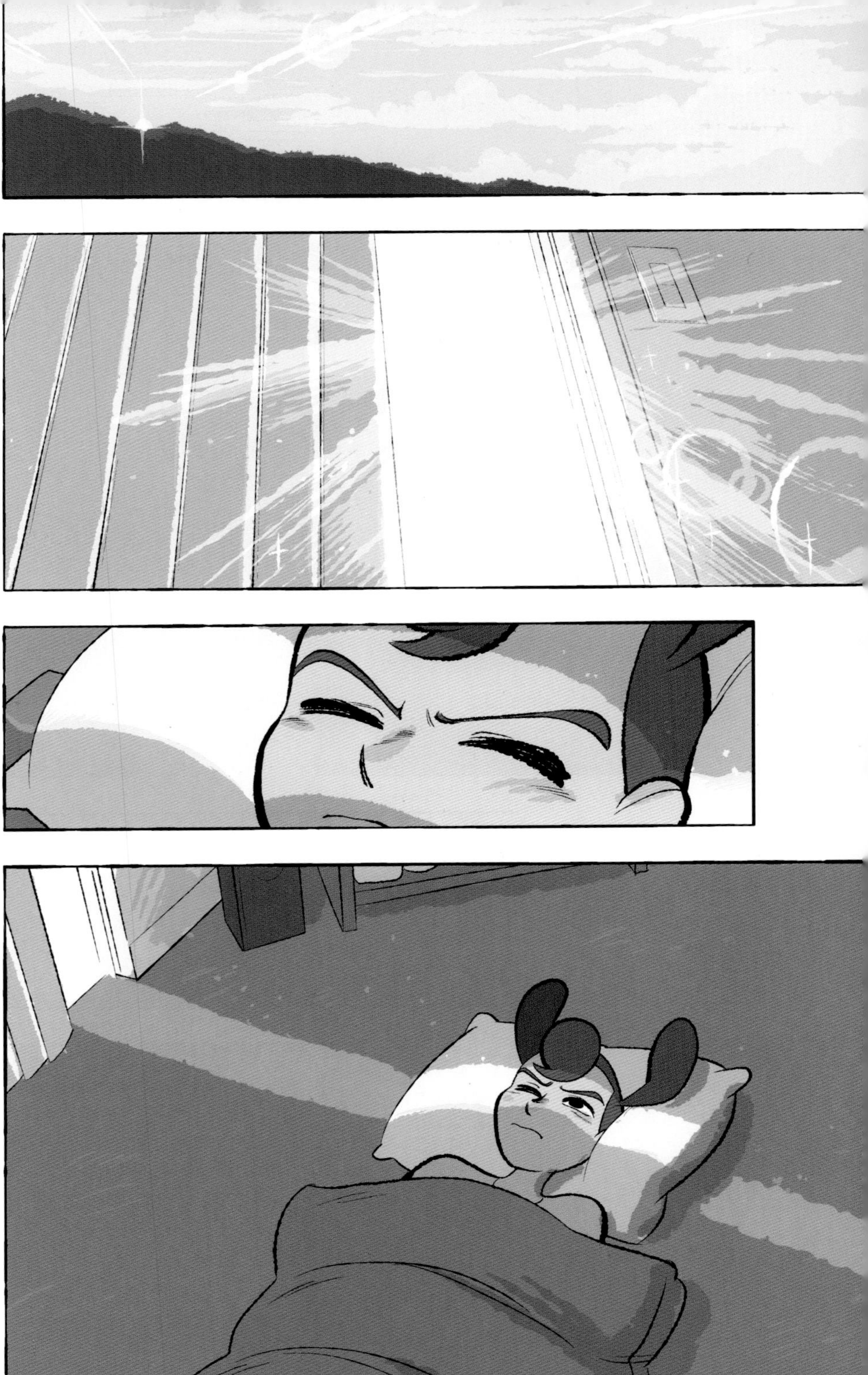

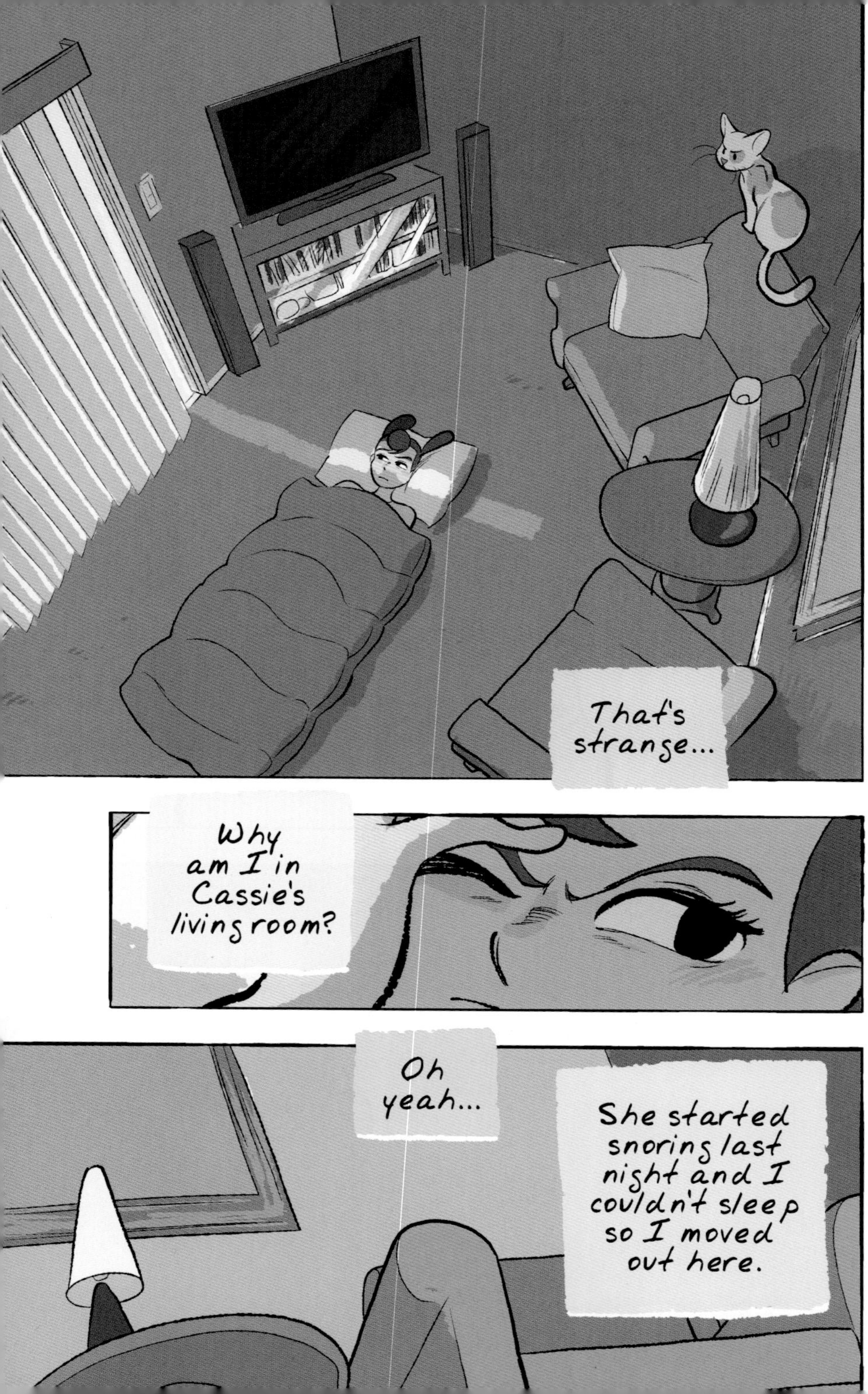

That's strange...
Why am I in Cassie's living room?
Oh yeah...
She started snoring last night and I couldn't sleep so I moved out here.

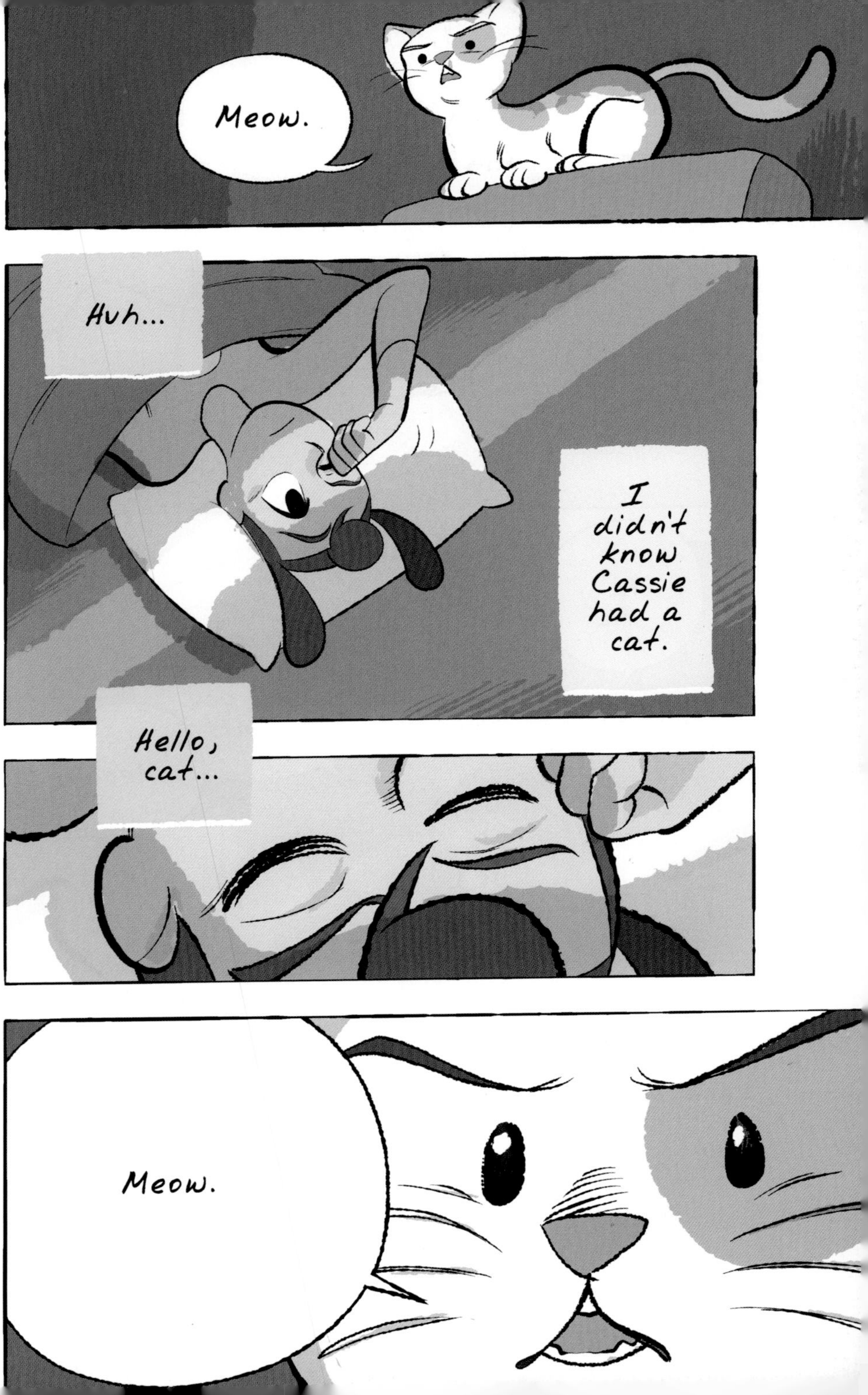

Meow.
Huh...
I didn't know Cassie had a cat.
Hello, cat...
Meow.

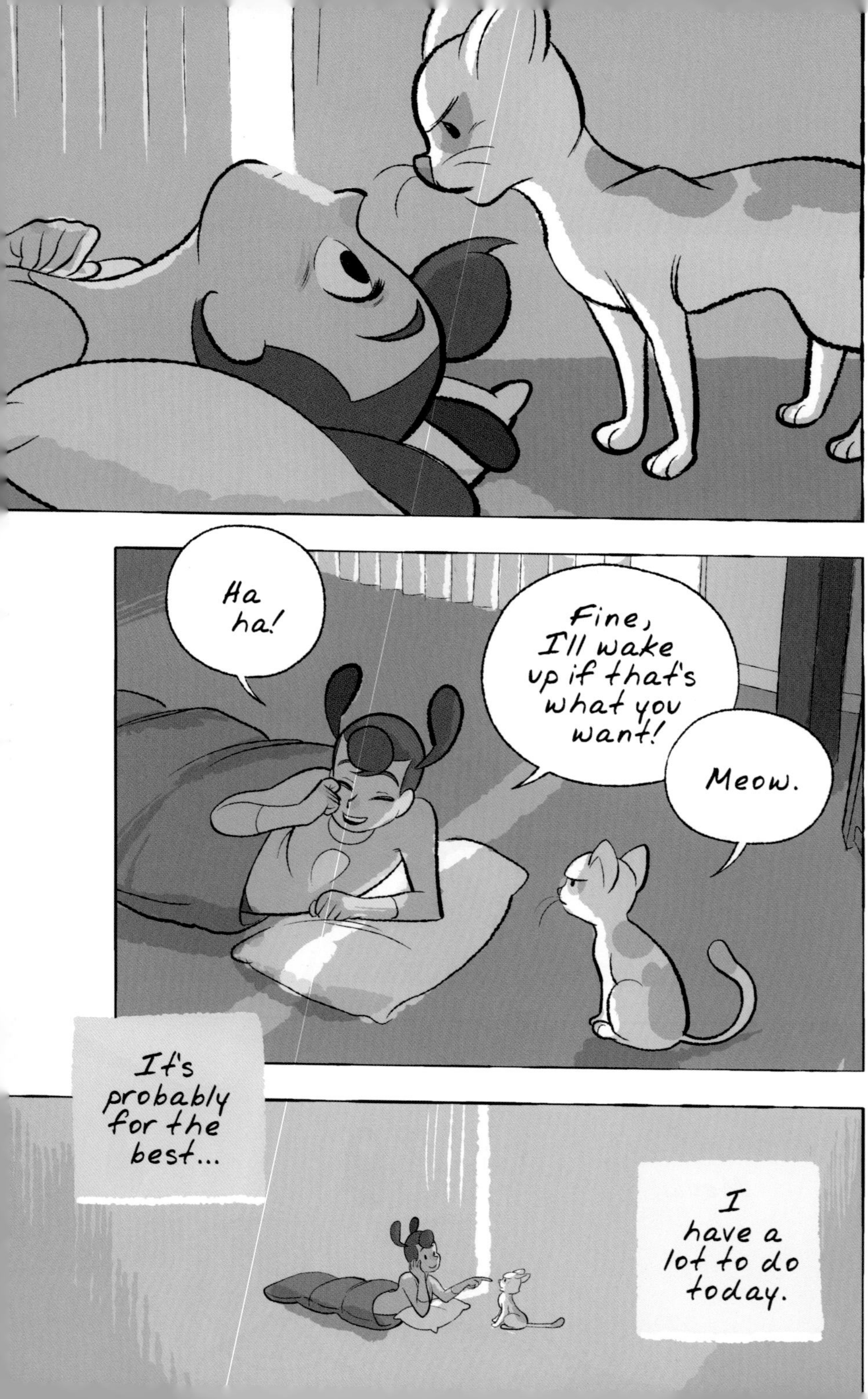
Ha ha!
Fine, I'll wake up if that's what you want!
Meow.
It's probably for the best...
I have a lot to do today.

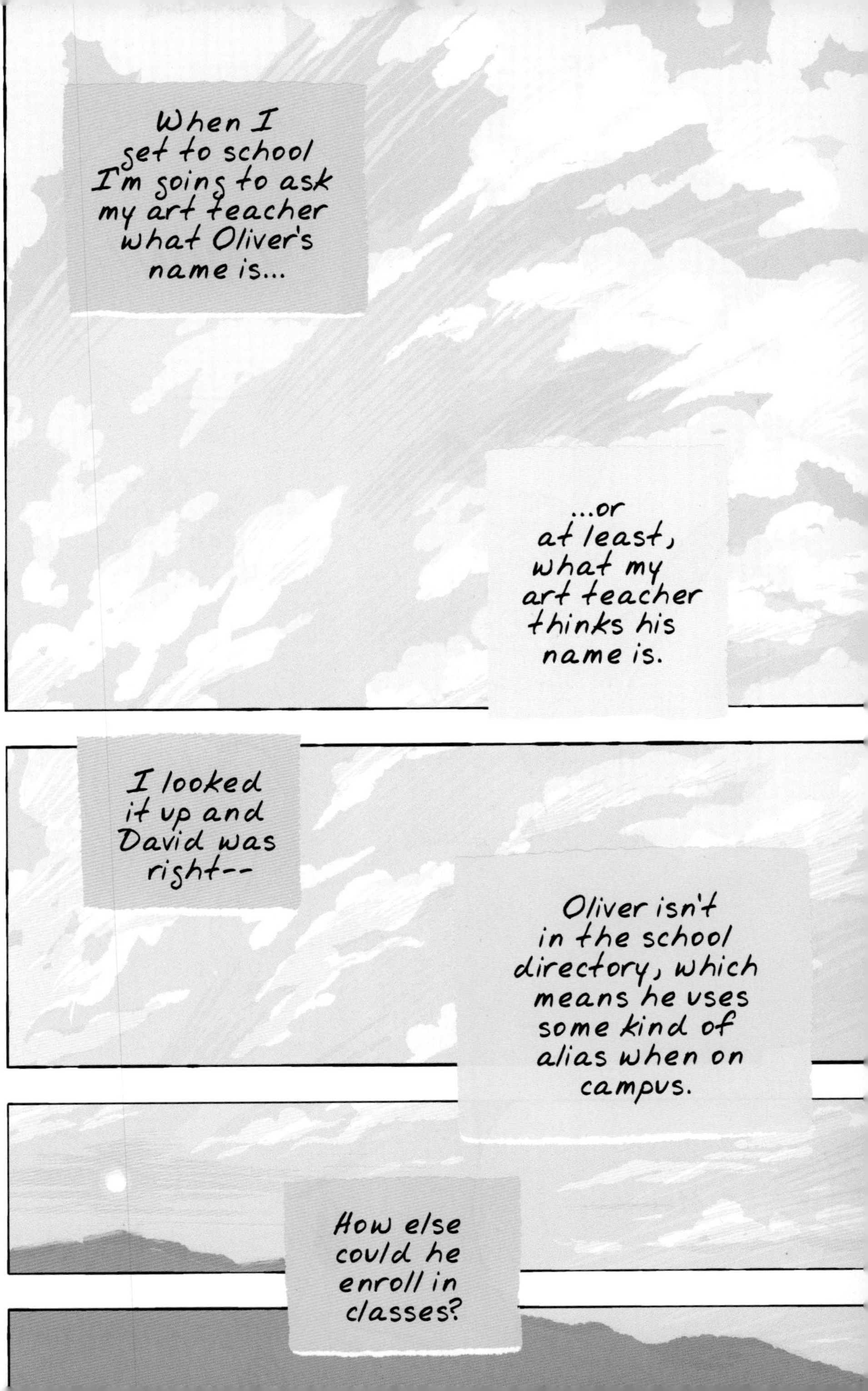
When I get to school I'm going to ask my art teacher what Oliver's name is...
...or at least, what my art teacher thinks his name is.
I looked it up and David was right--
Oliver isn't in the school directory, which means he uses some kind of alias when on campus.
How else could he enroll in classes?

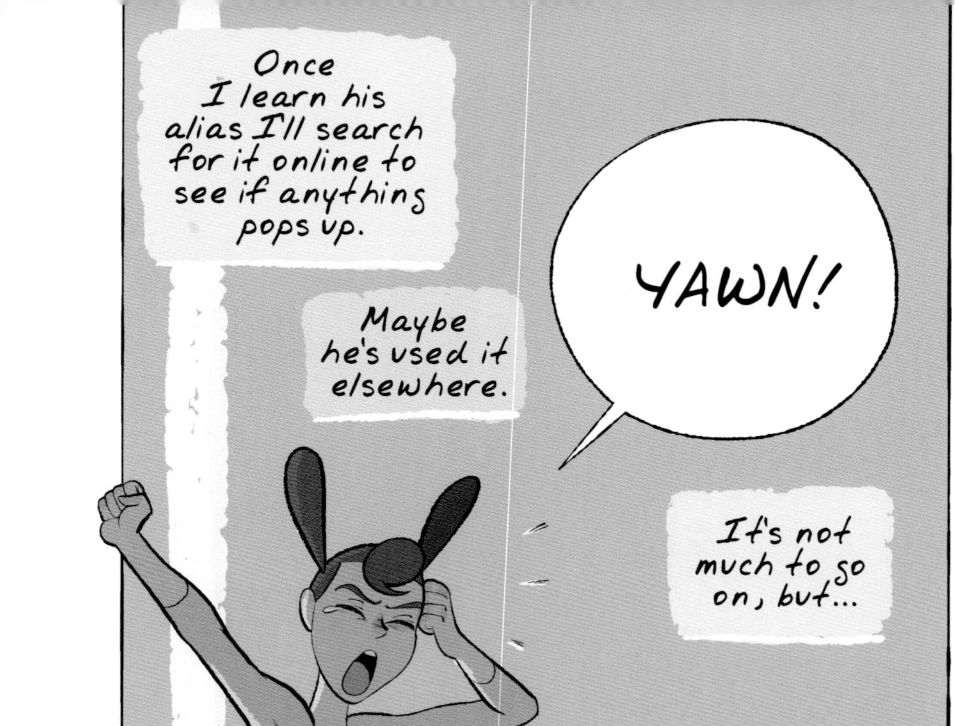
Once I learn his alias I'll search for it online to see if anything pops up.
Maybe he's used it elsewhere.
YAWN!
It's not much to go on, but...

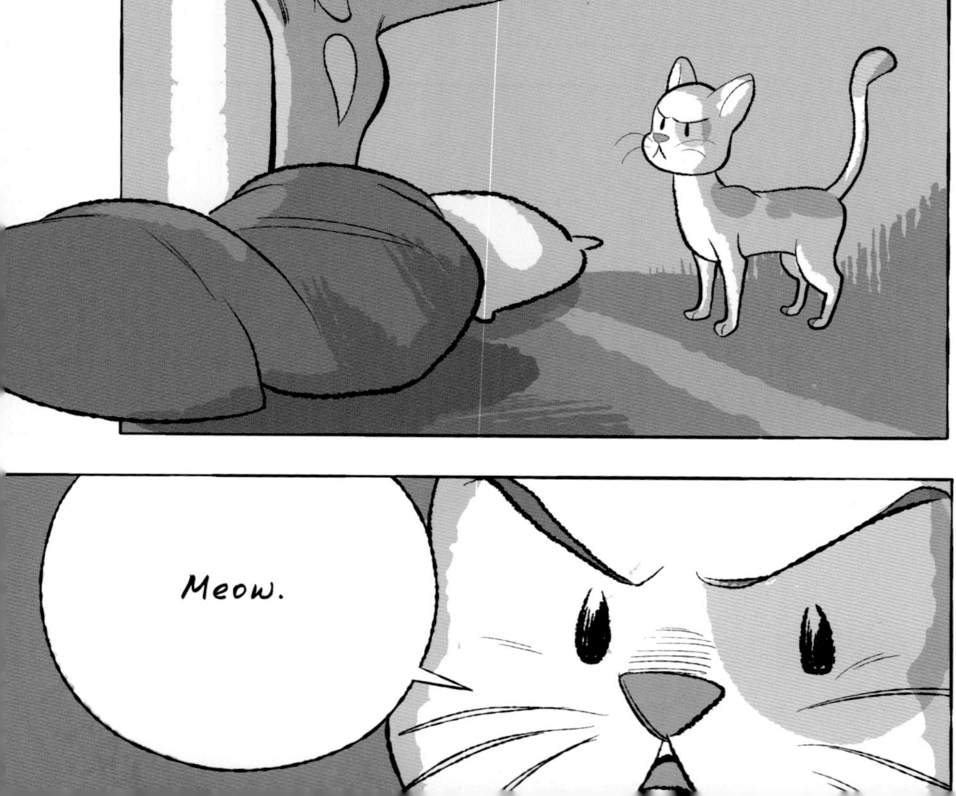
Meow.

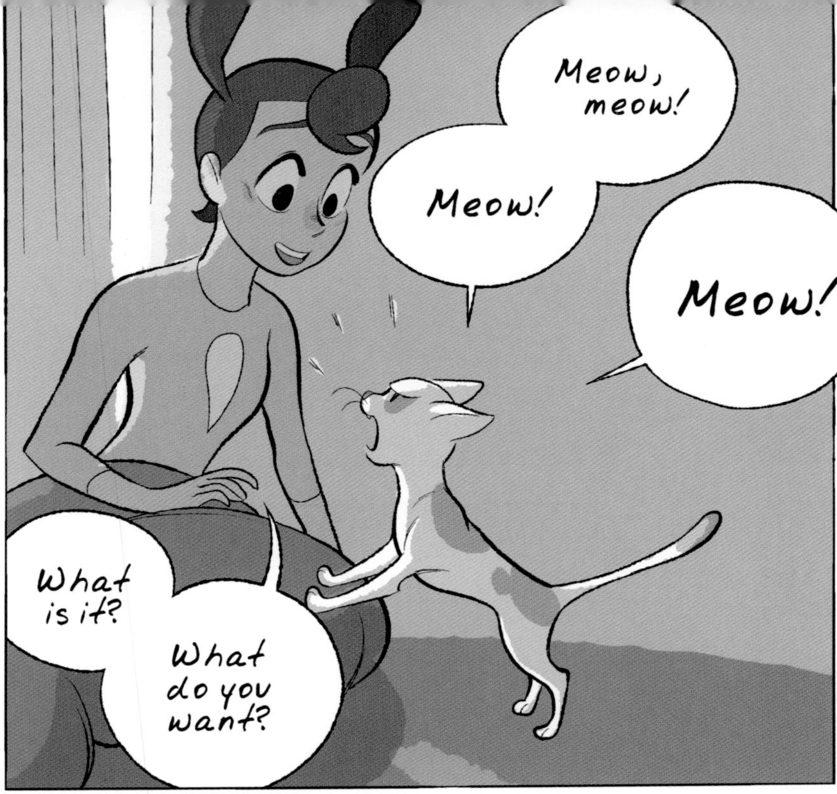
Meow, meow!
Meow!
Meow!
What is it?
What do you want?

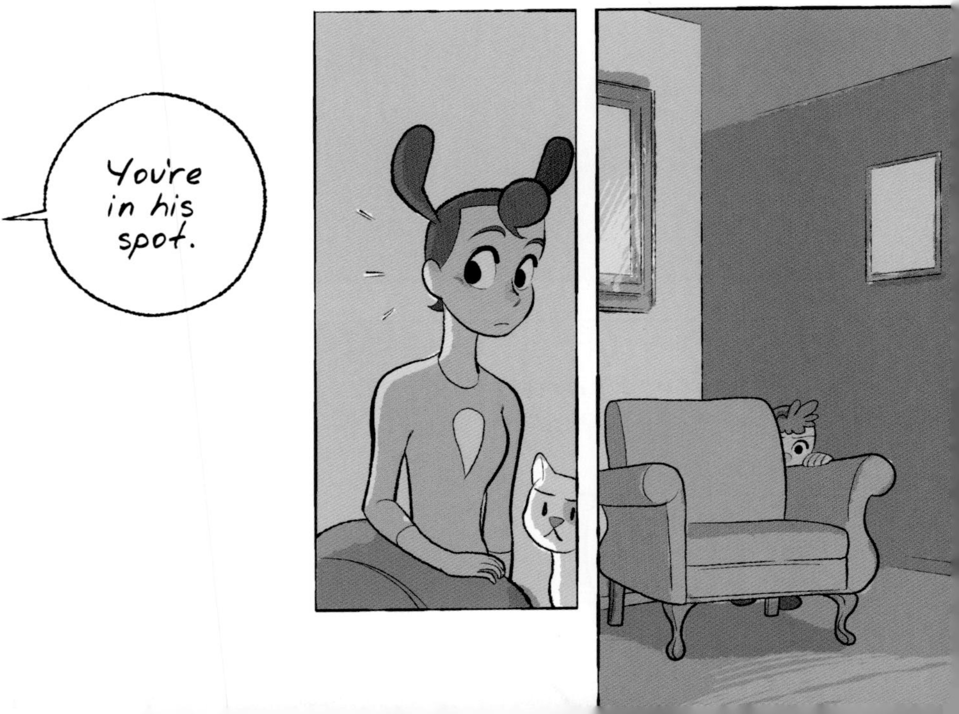
You're in his spot.

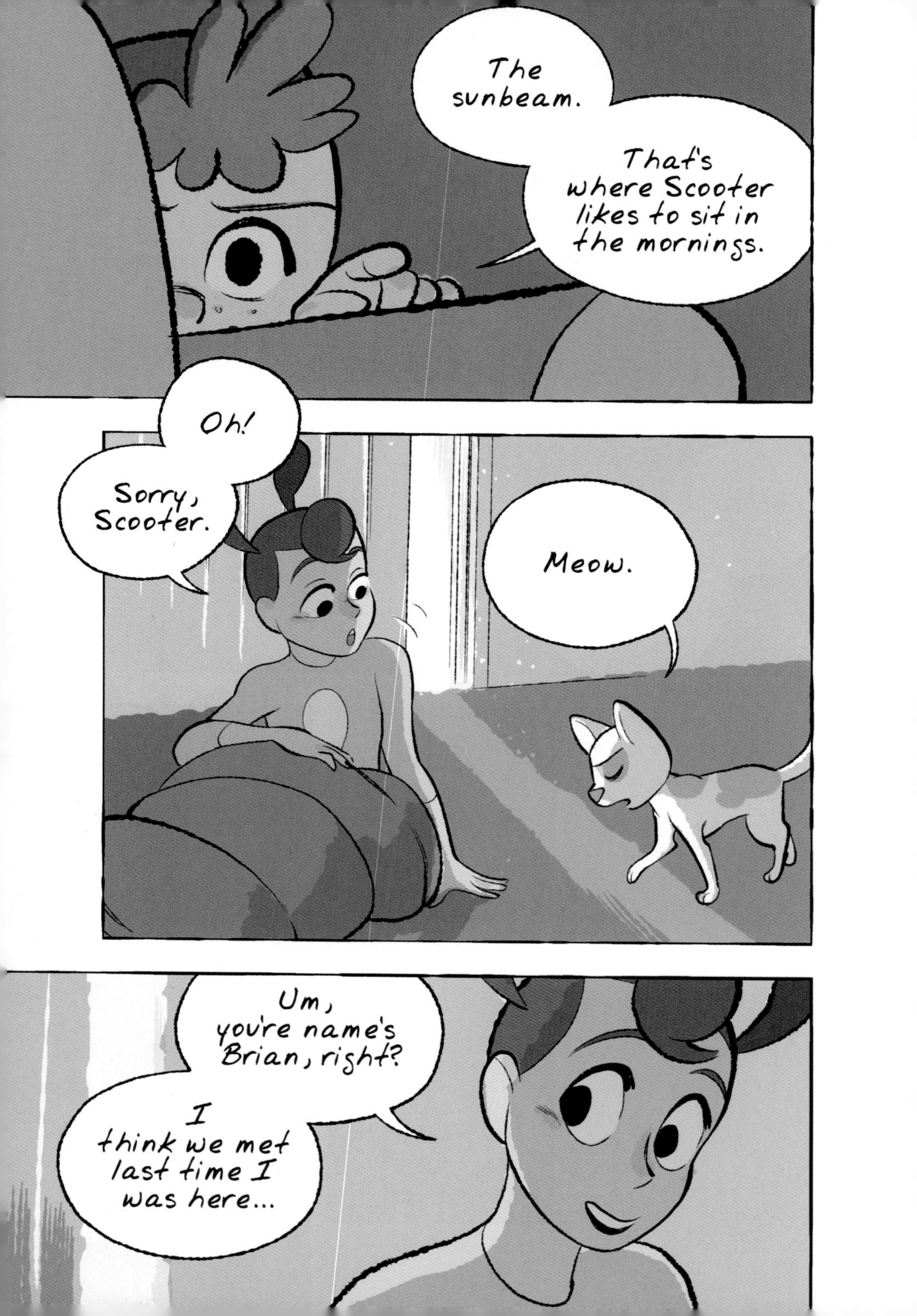
The sunbeam.
That's where Scooter likes to sit in the mornings.
Oh!
Sorry, Scooter.
Meow.
Um, you're name's Brian, right?
I think we met last time I was here...

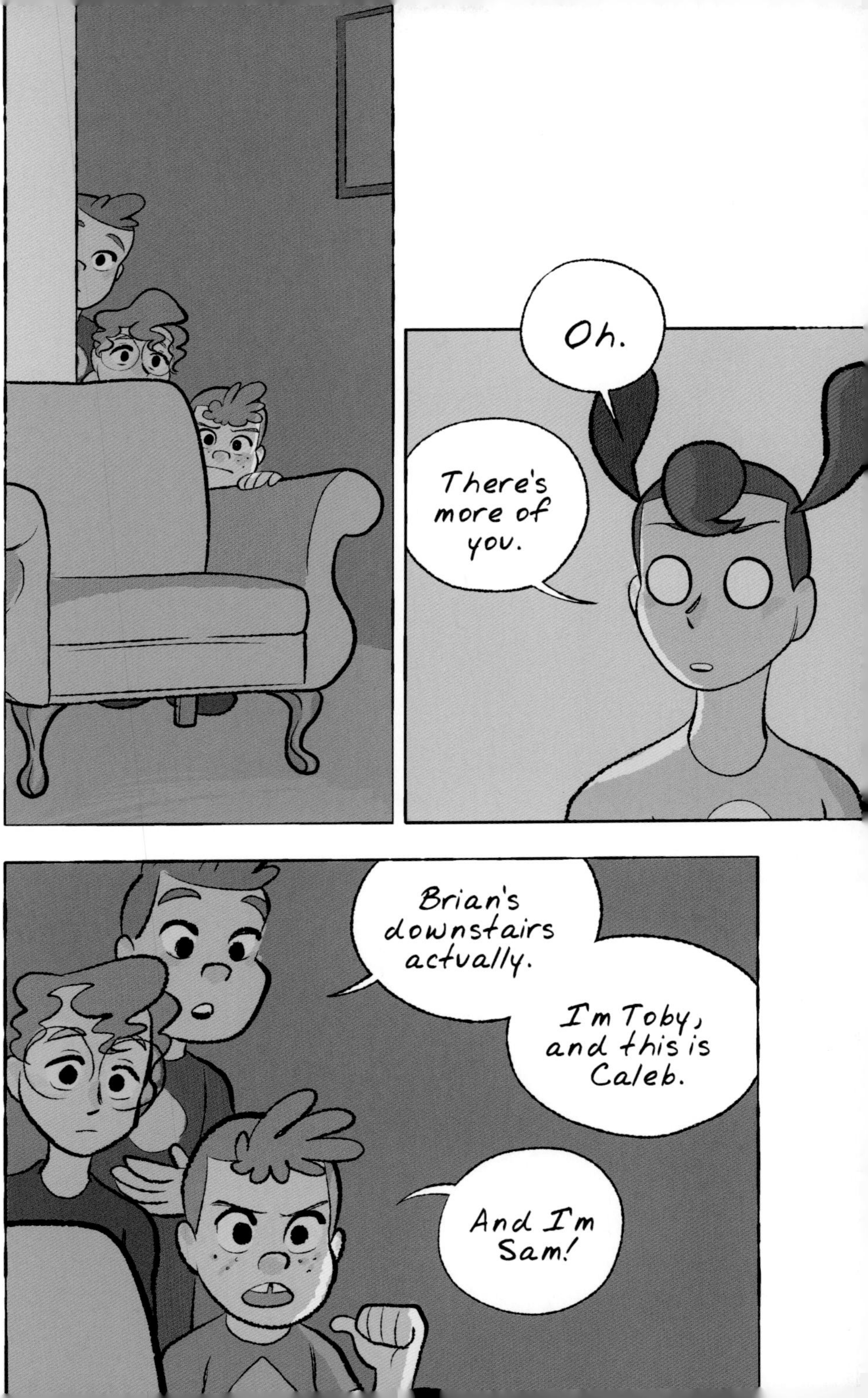
Oh.
There's more of you.
Brian's downstairs actually.
I'm Toby, and this is Caleb.
And I'm Sam!

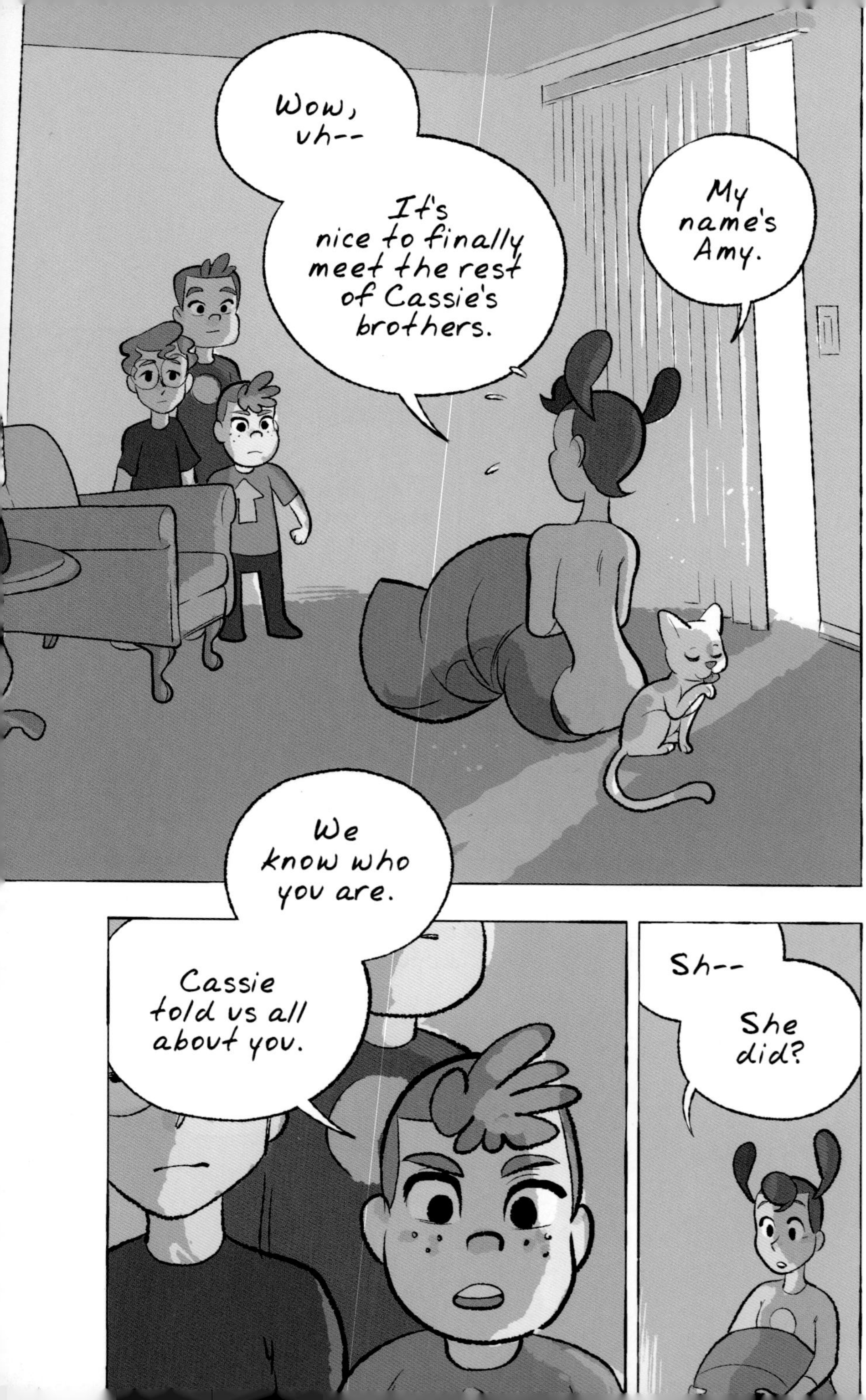

Wow, uh--
It's nice to finally meet the rest of Cassie's brothers.
My name's Amy.
We know who you are.
Cassie told us all about you.
Sh--
She did?

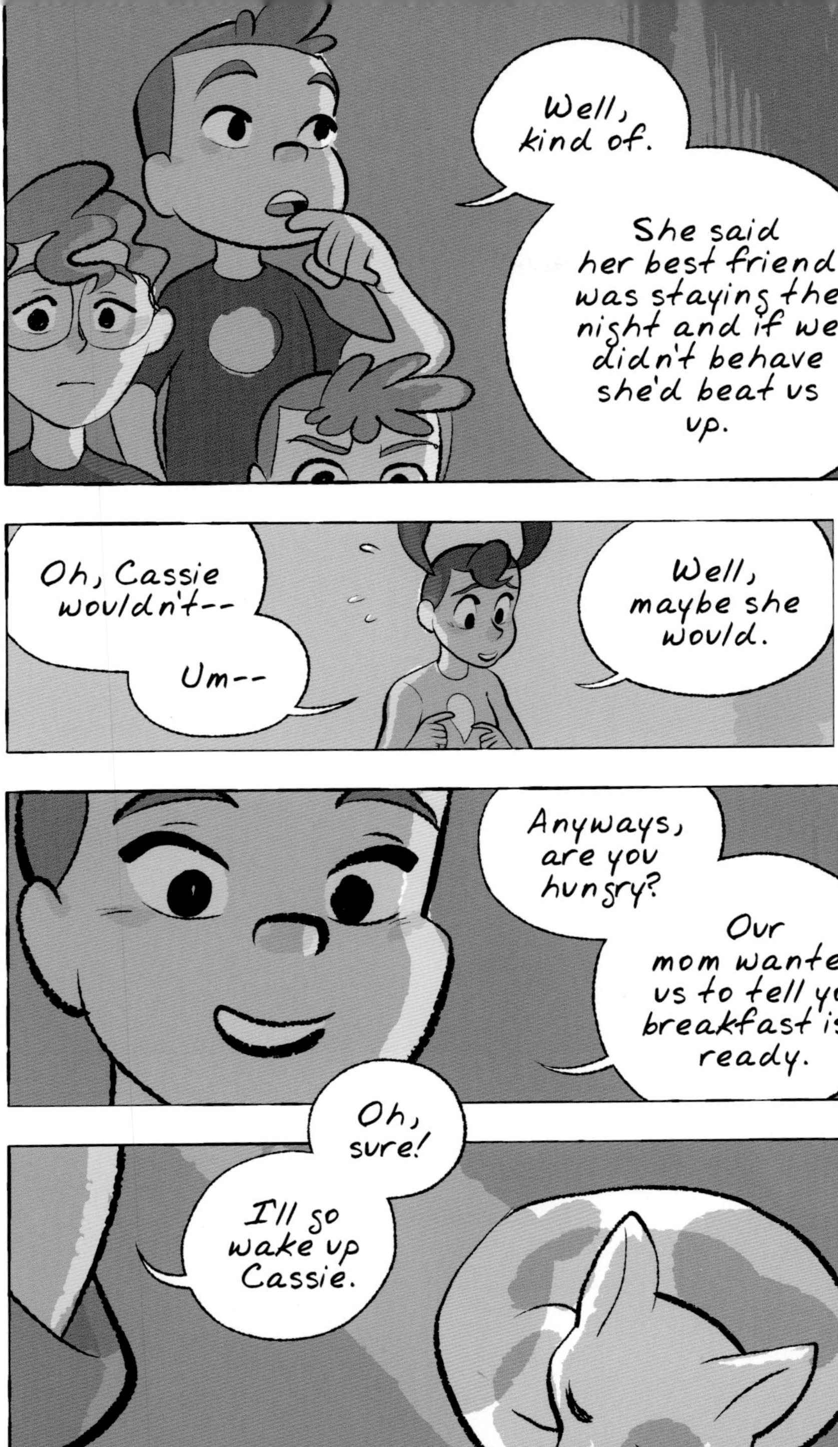
Well, kind of.
She said her best friend was staying the night and if we didn't behave she'd beat us up.
Oh, Cassie wouldn't--
Um--
Well, maybe she would.
Anyways, are you hungry?
Our mom wanted us to tell you breakfast is ready.
Oh, sure!
I'll go wake up Cassie.

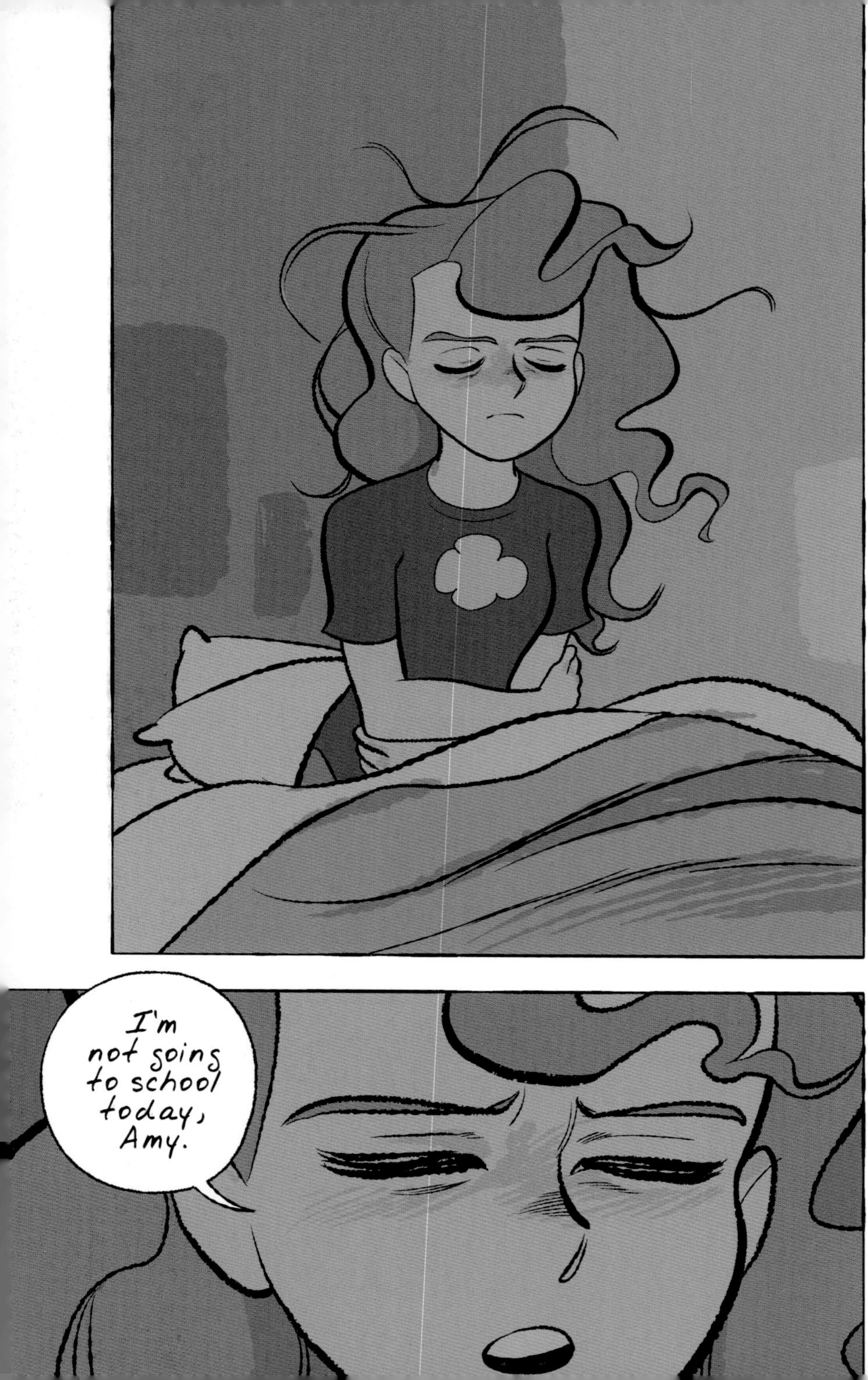
I'm not going to school today, Amy.

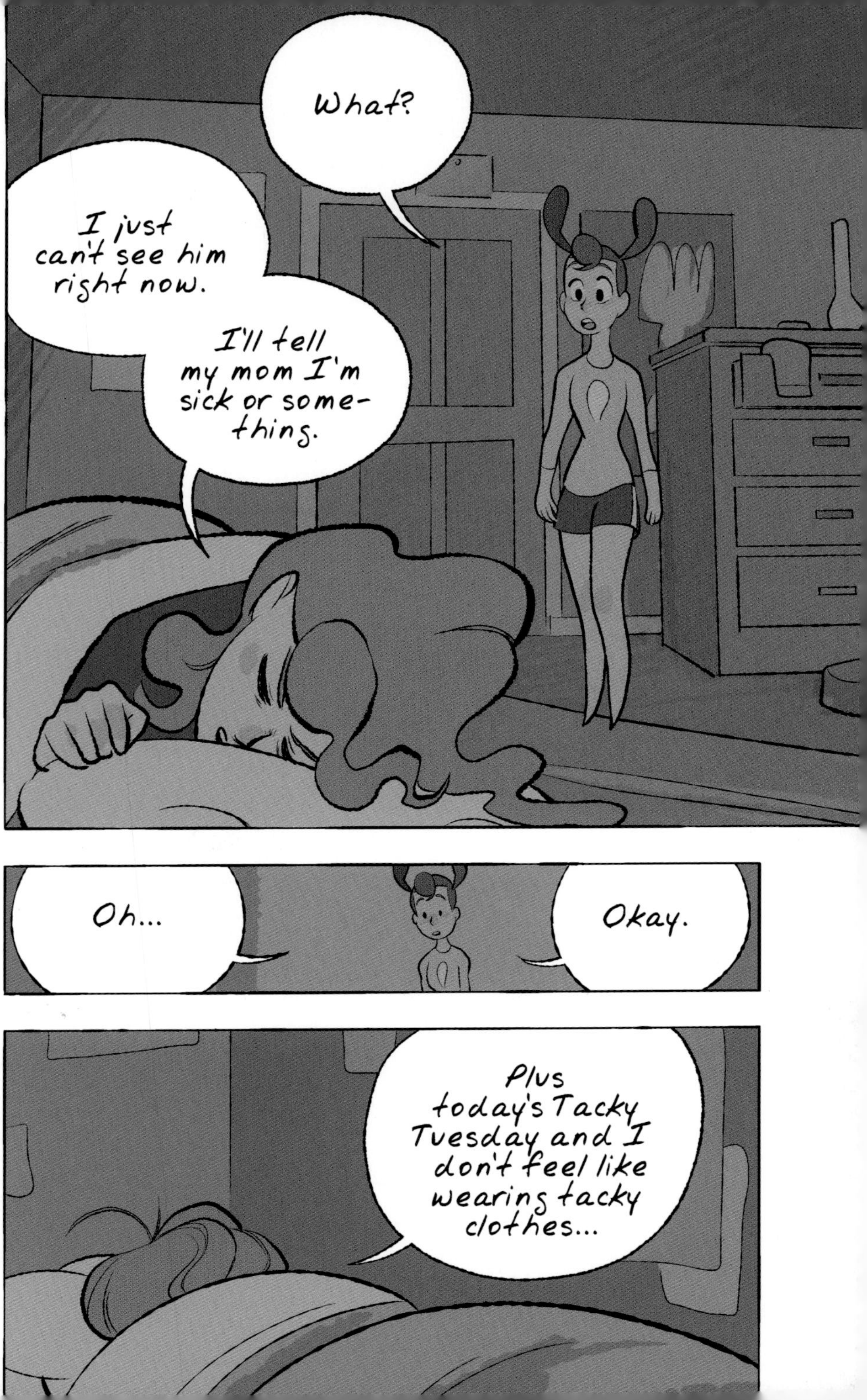
What?
I just can't see him right now.
I'll tell my mom I'm sick or some-thing.
Oh...
Okay.
Plus today's Tacky Tuesday and I don't feel like wearing tacky clothes...

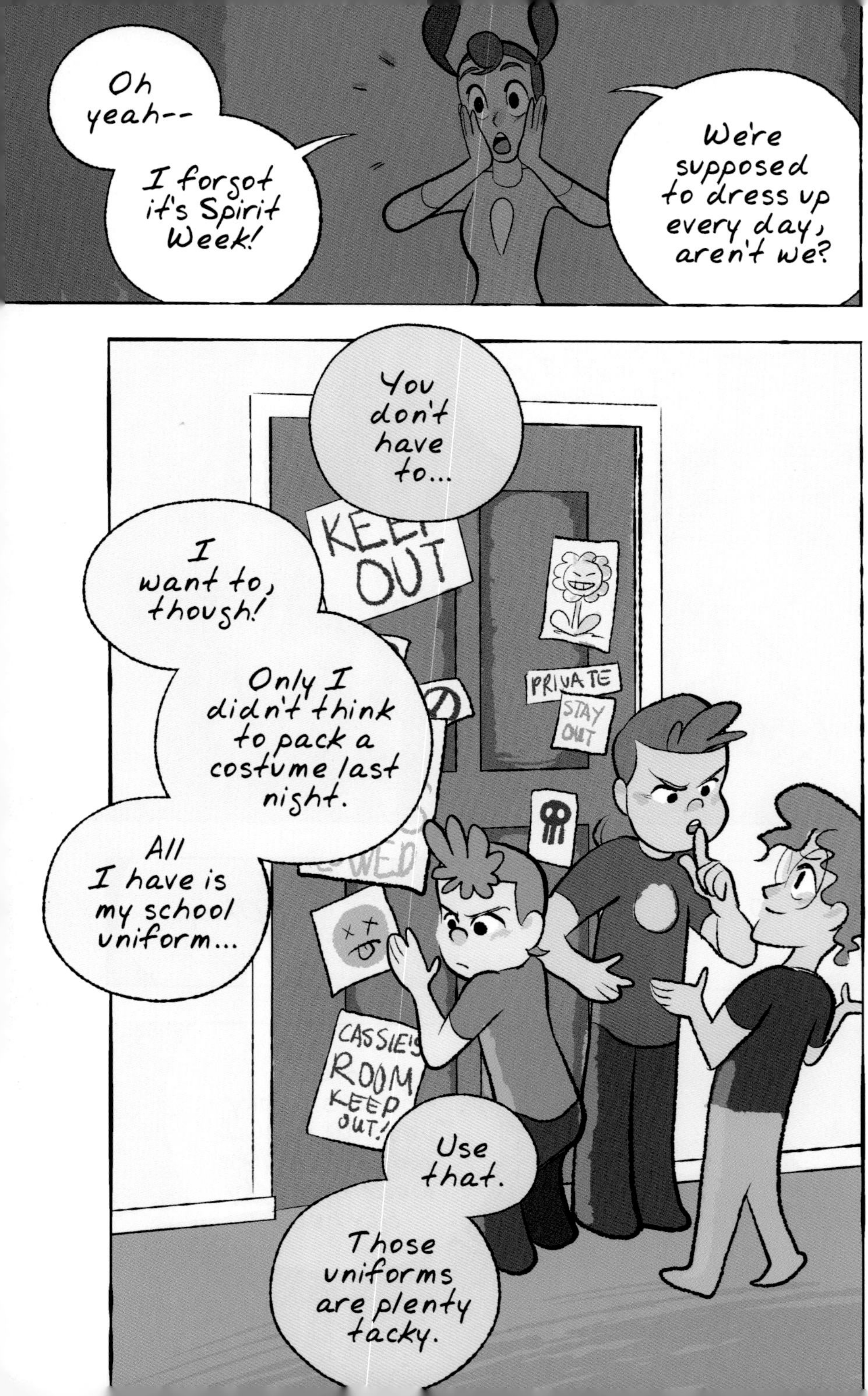
Oh yeah--
I forgot it's Spirit Week!
We're supposed to dress up every day, aren't we?
You don't have to...
KEEP OUT
PRIVATE
STAY OUT
I want to, though!
Only I didn't think to pack a costume last night.
All I have is my school uniform...
CASSIE'S ROOM KEEP OUT!
Use that.
Those uniforms are plenty tacky.

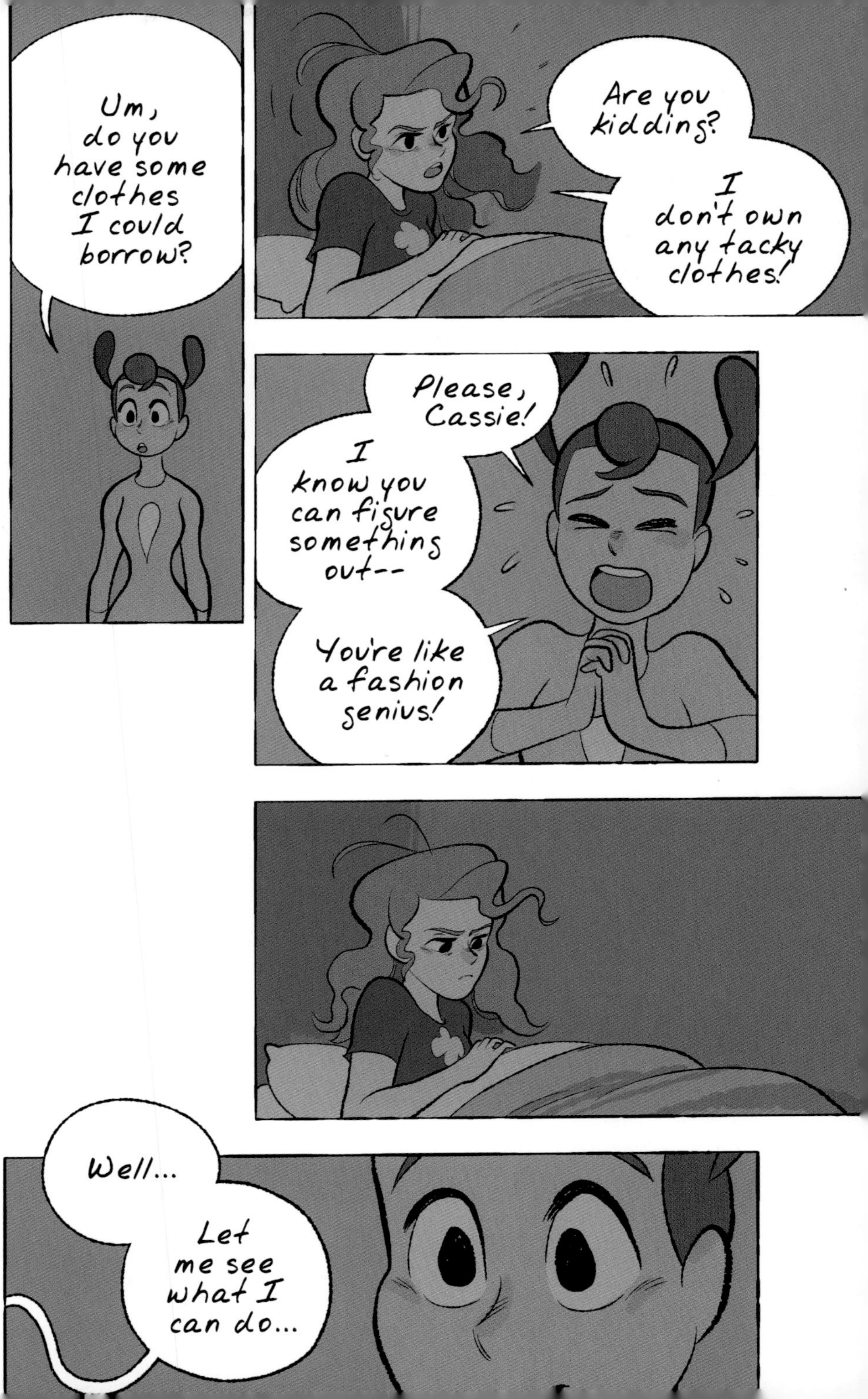
Um, do you have some clothes I could borrow?
Are you kidding?
I don't own any tacky clothes!
Please, Cassie!
I know you can figure something out--
You're like a fashion genius!
Well...
Let me see what I can do...

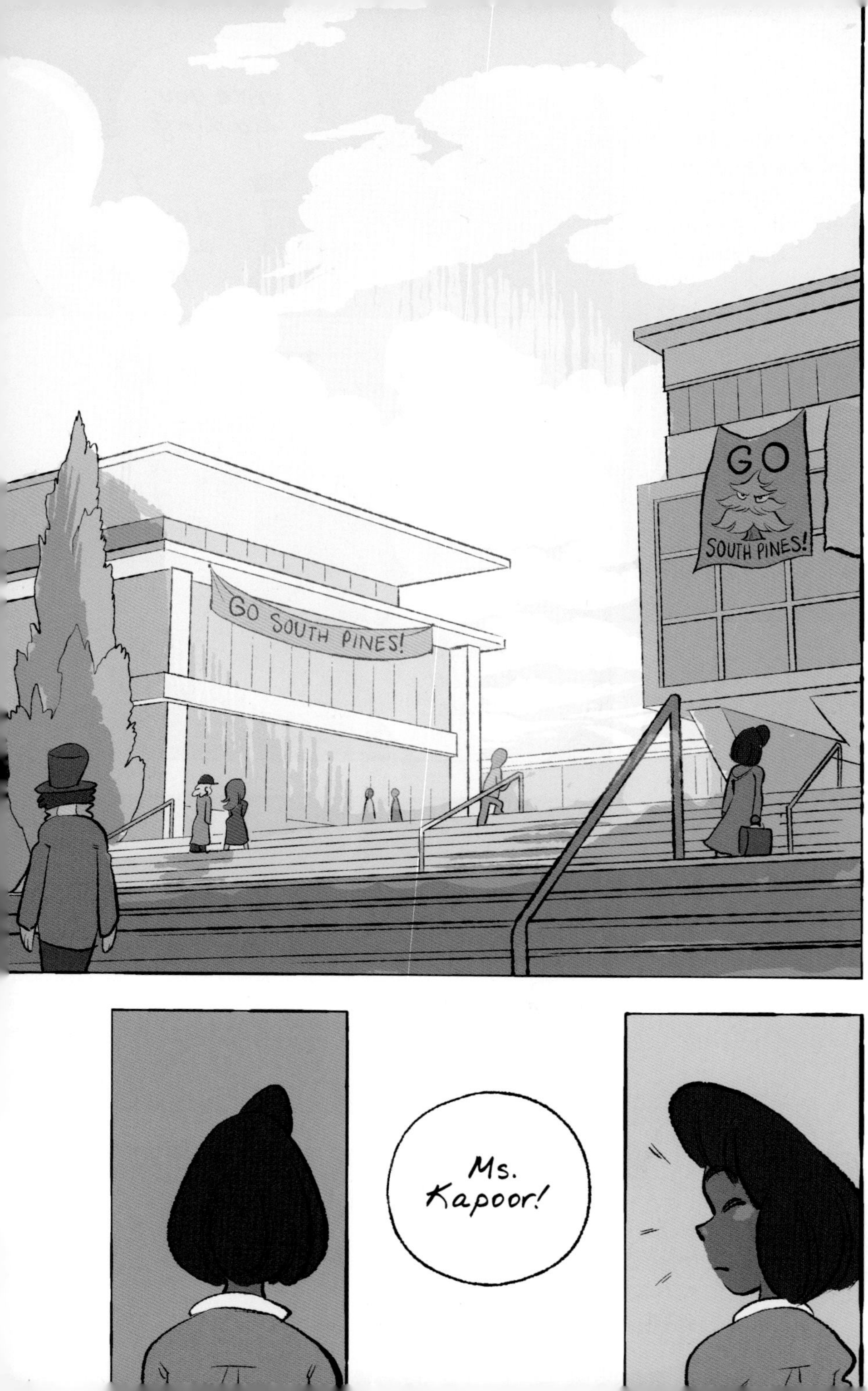
GO SOUTH PINES!
GO
SOUTH PINES!
Ms. Kapoor!

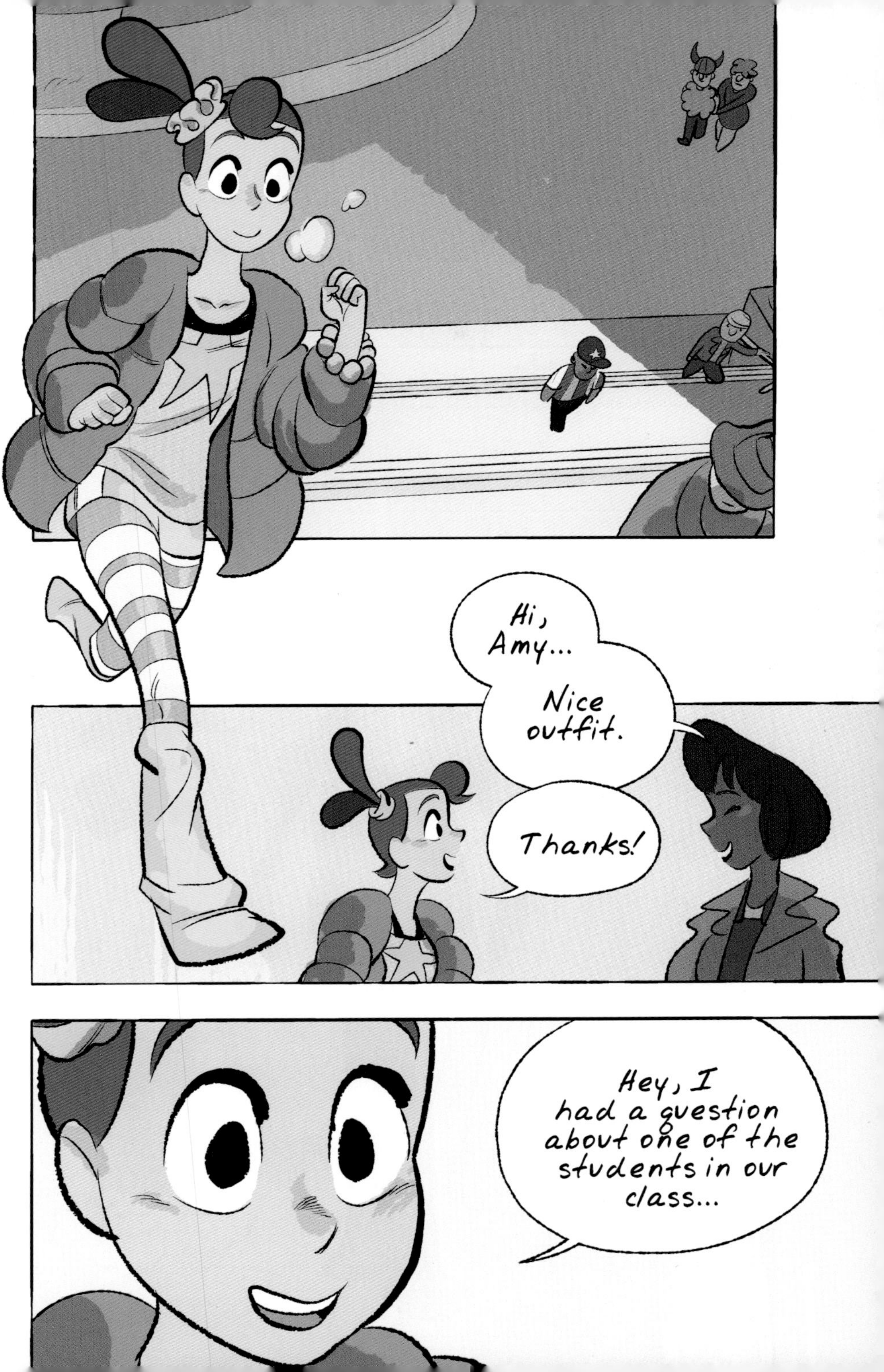

Hi, Amy...
Nice outfit.
Thanks!
Hey, I had a question about one of the students in our class...

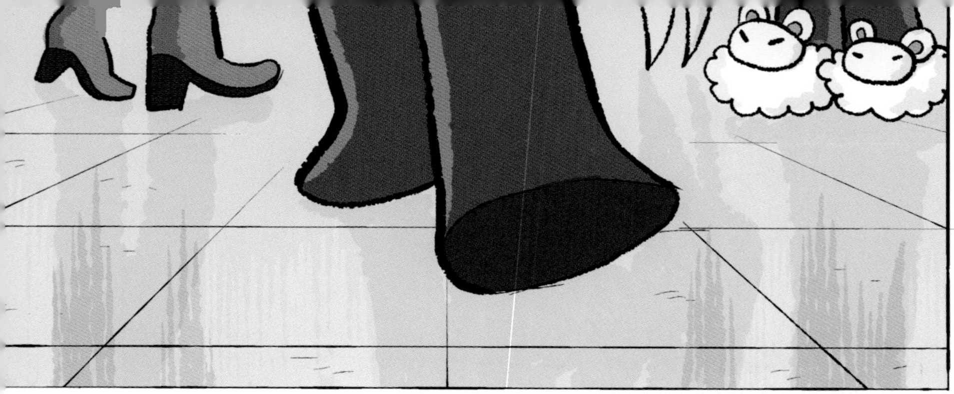

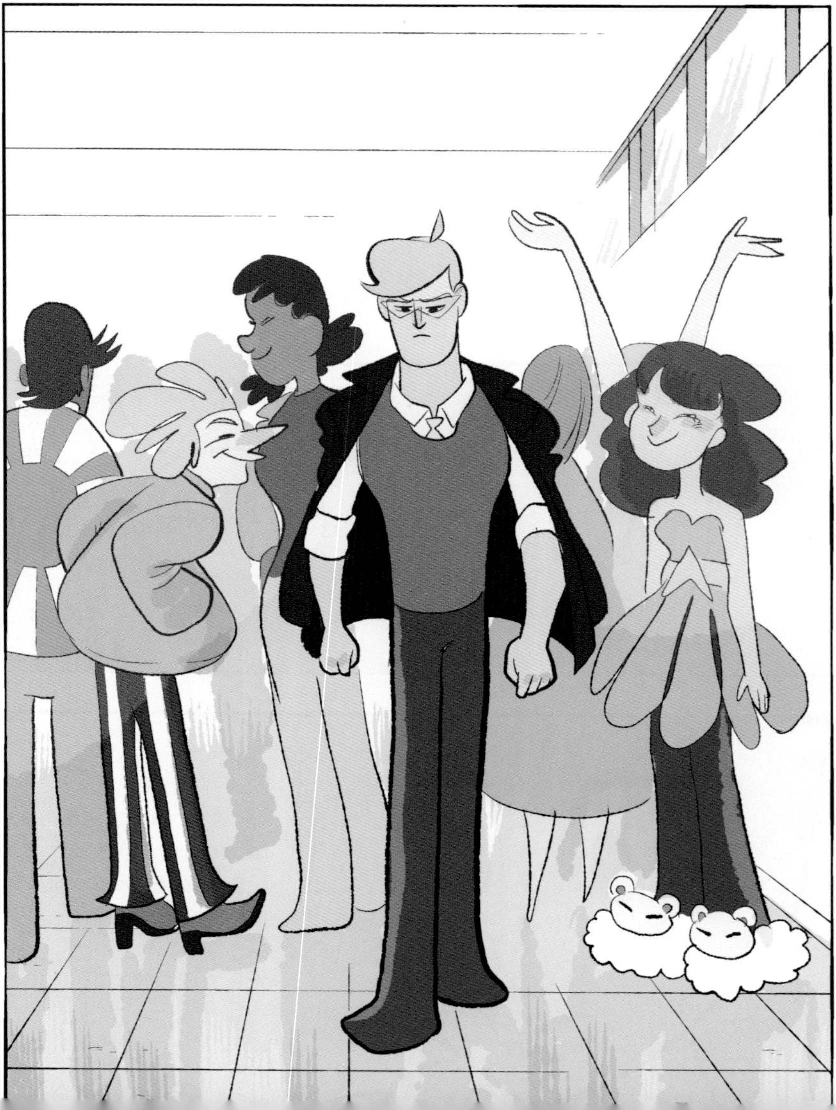

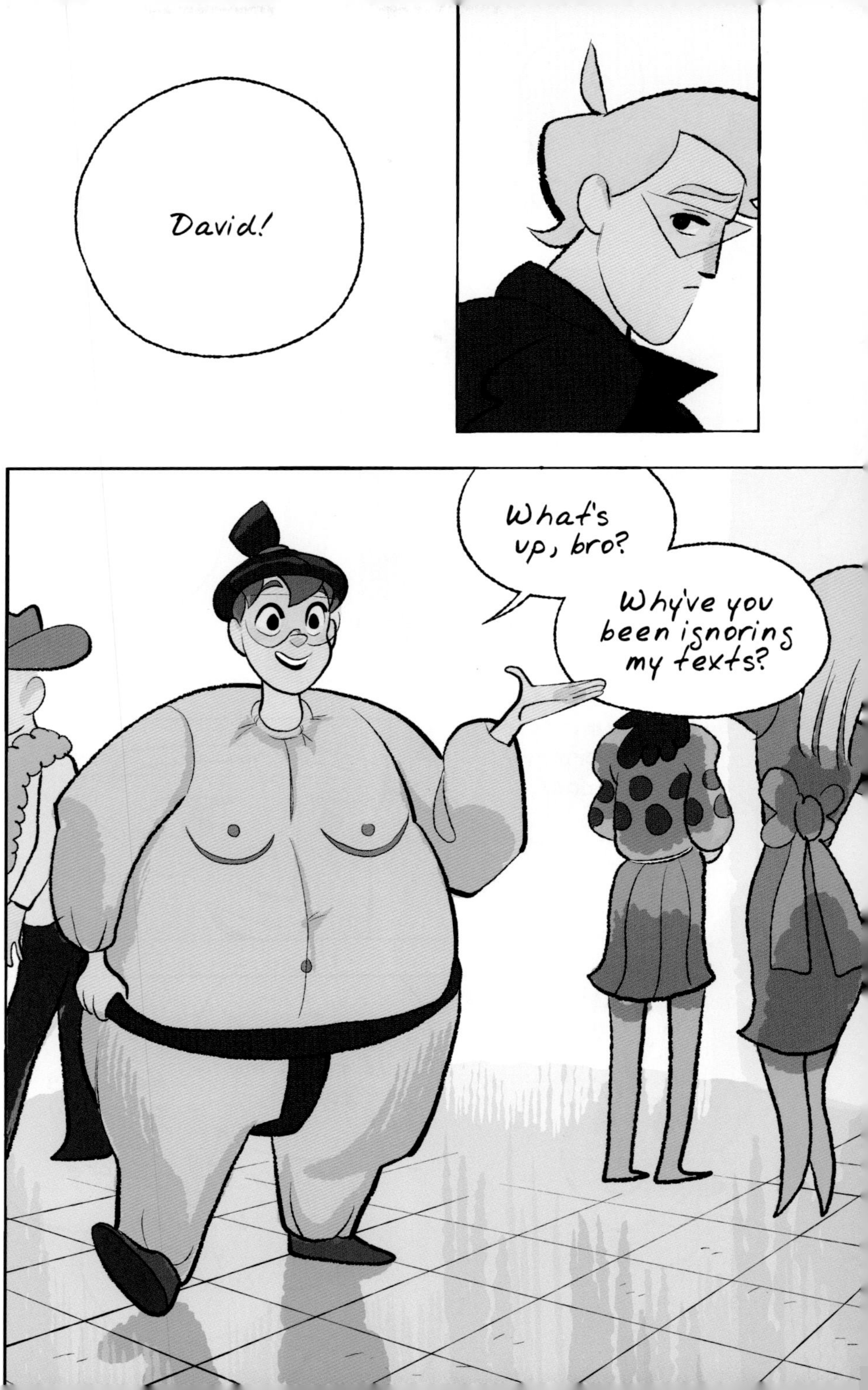
David!
What's up, bro?
Why've you been ignoring my texts?

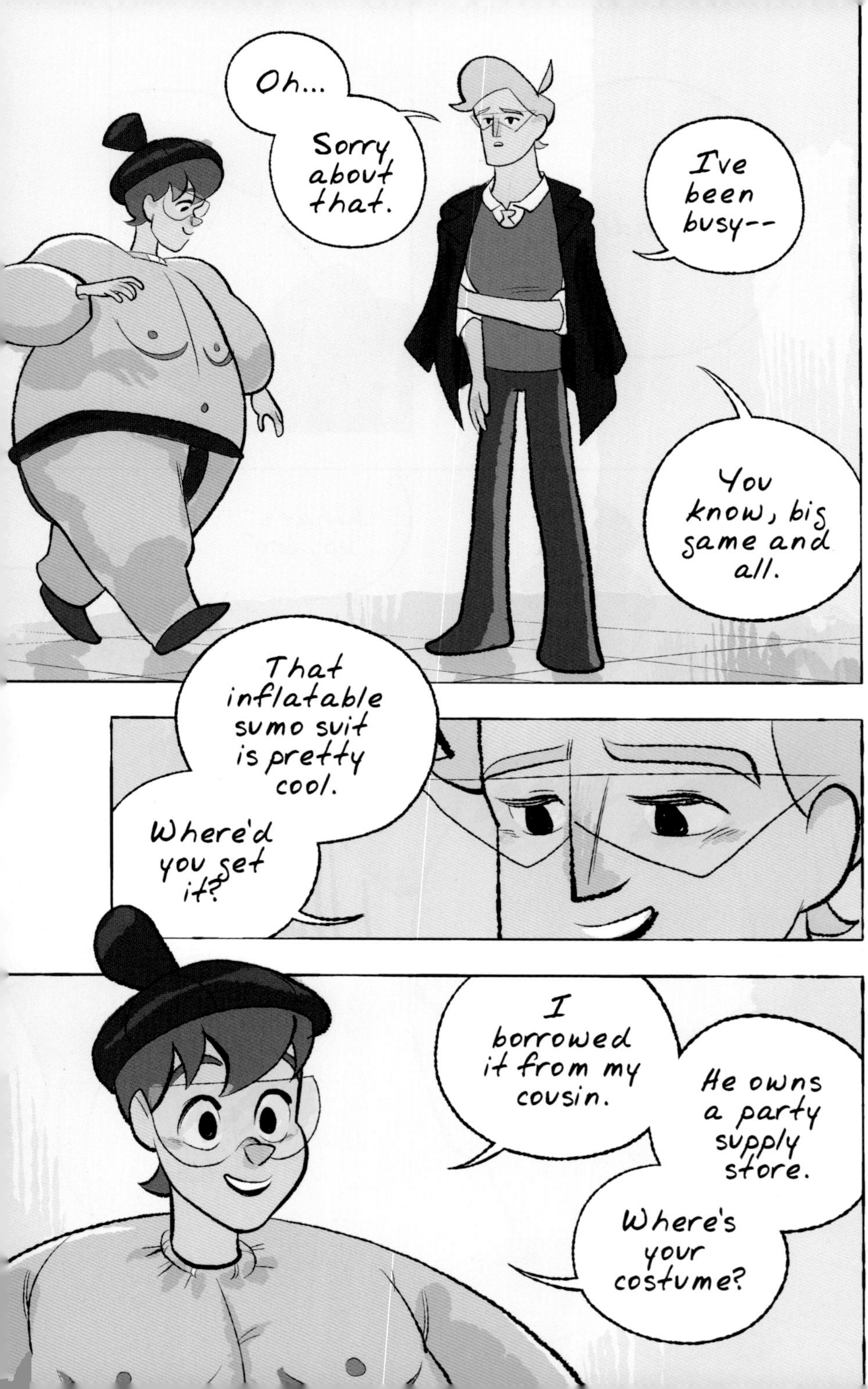
Oh...
Sorry about that.
I've been busy--
You know, big game and all.
That inflatable sumo suit is pretty cool.
Where'd you get it?
I borrowed it from my cousin.
He owns a party supply store.
Where's your costume?

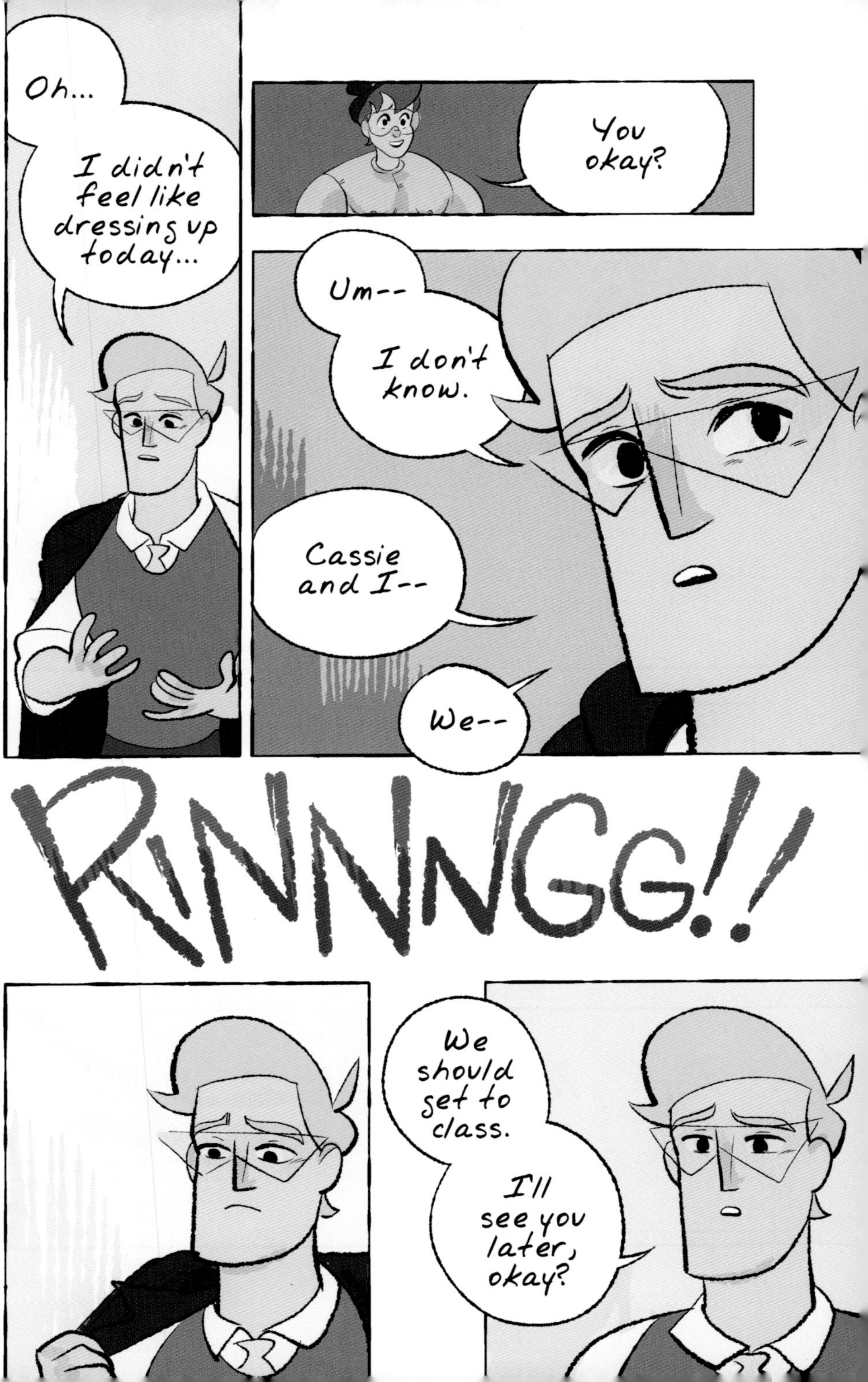
Oh...
I didn't feel like dressing up today...
You okay?
Um--
I don't know.
Cassie and I--
We--
RINNNGG!!
We should get to class.
I'll see you later, okay?

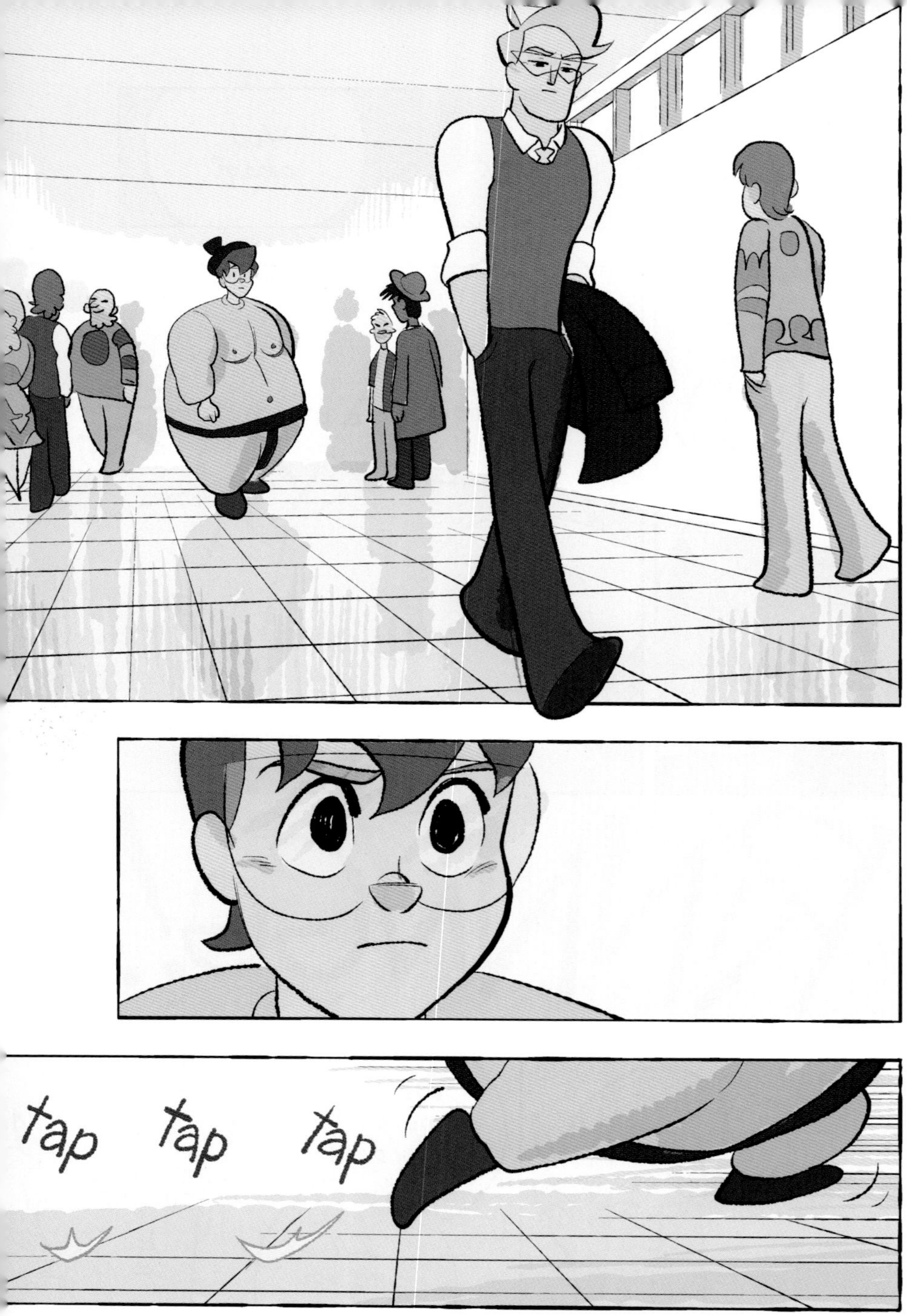
tap
tap
tap

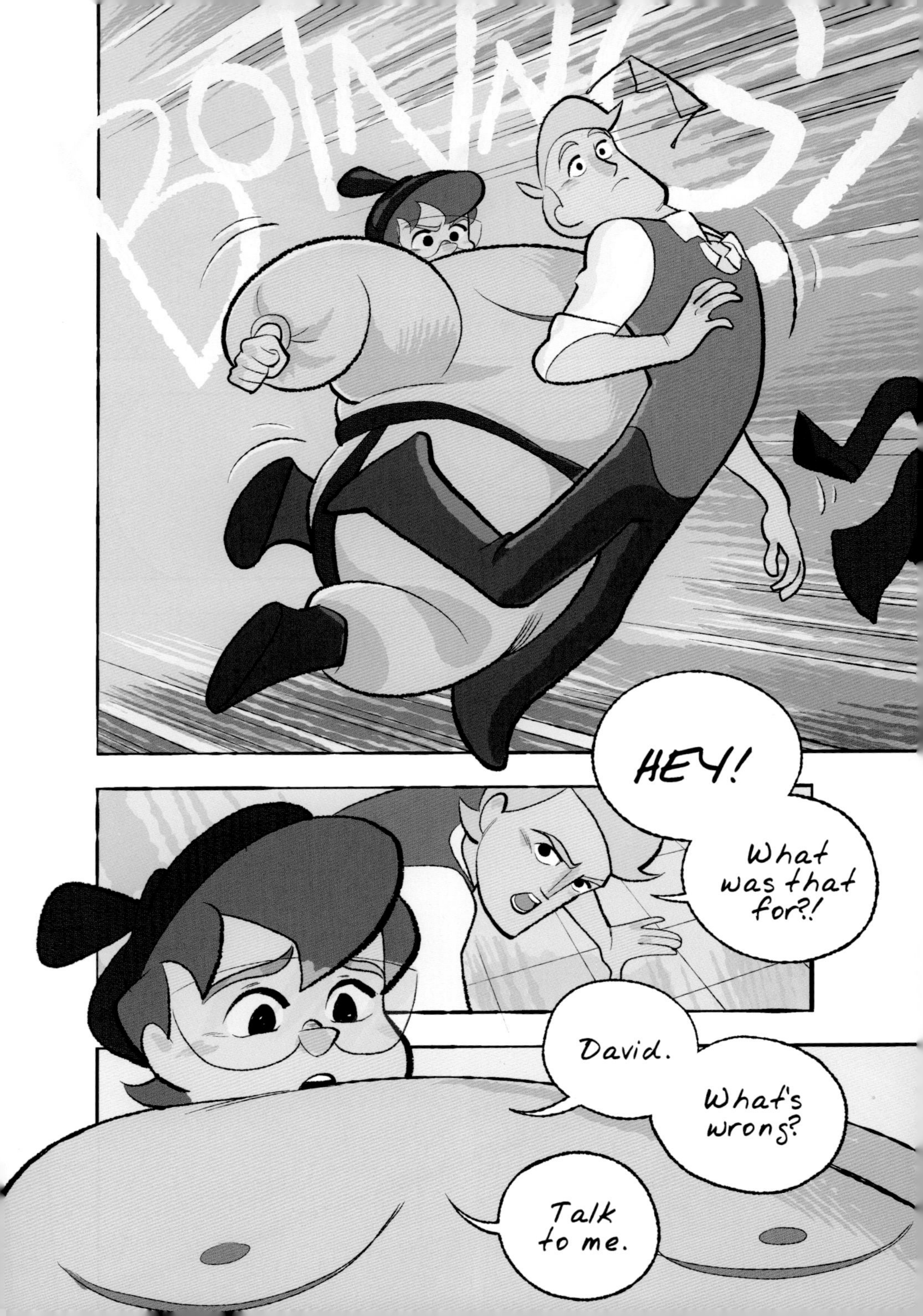
HEY!
What was that for?!
David.
What's wrong?
Talk to me.

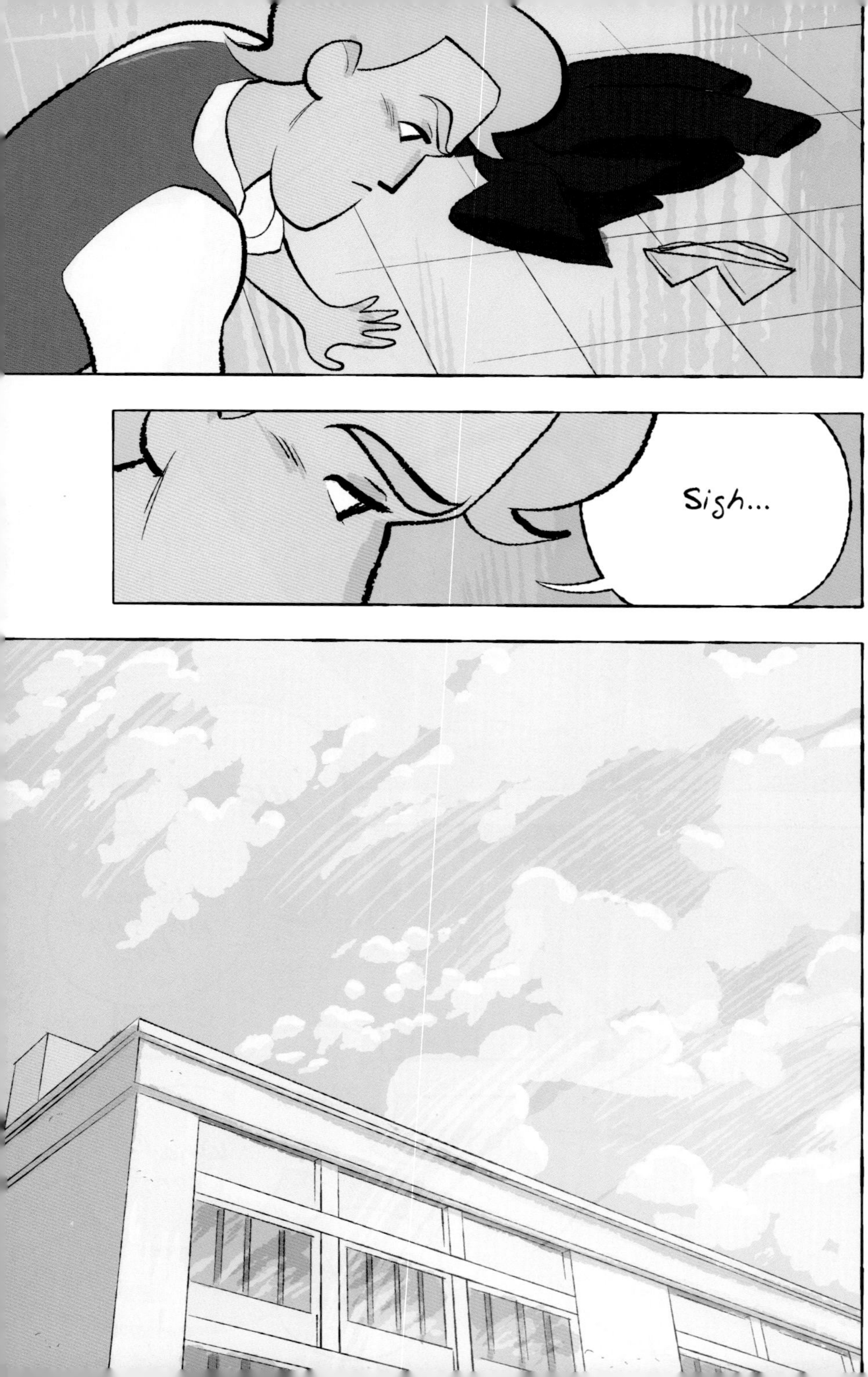
Sigh...

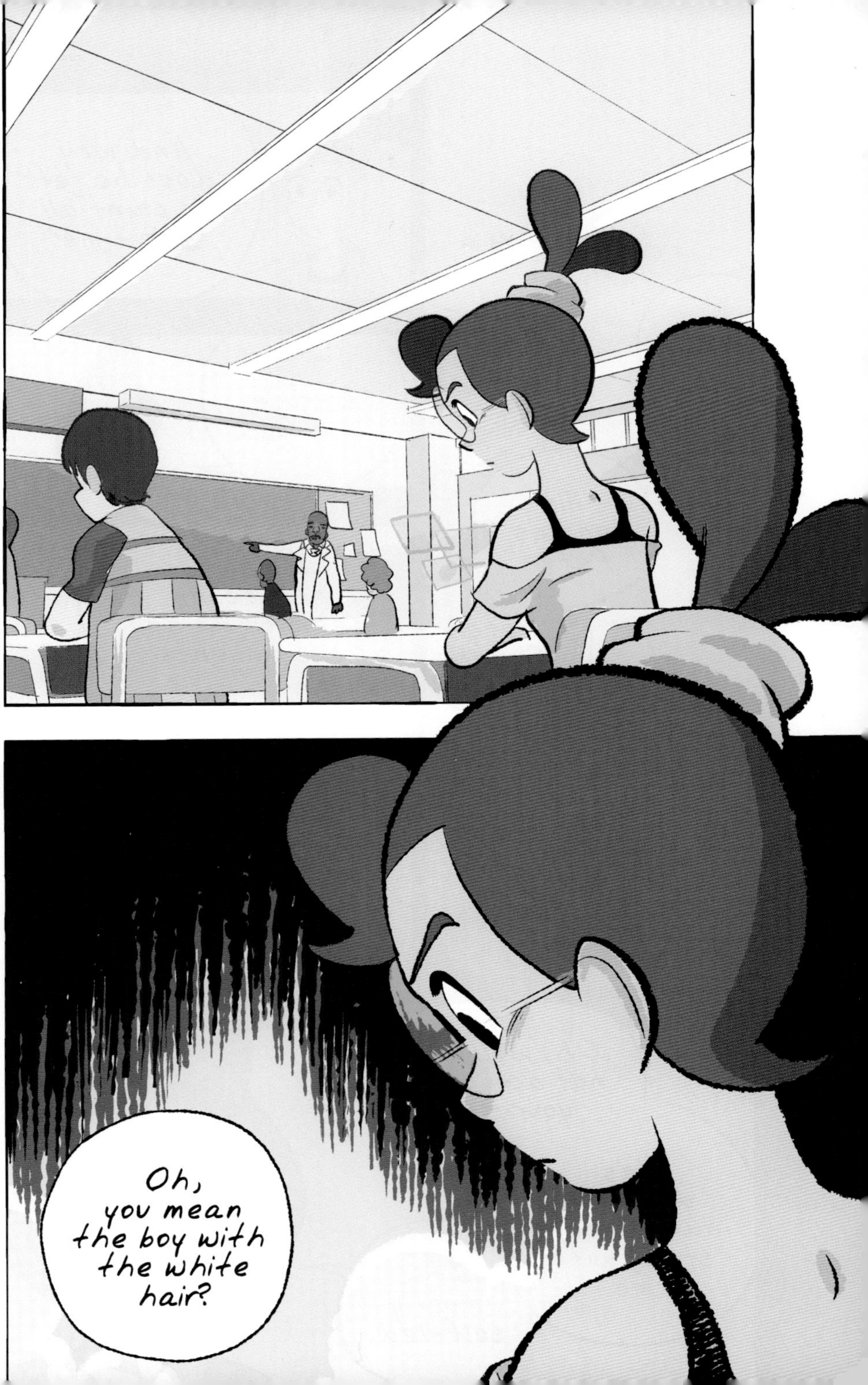
Oh, you mean the boy with the white hair?

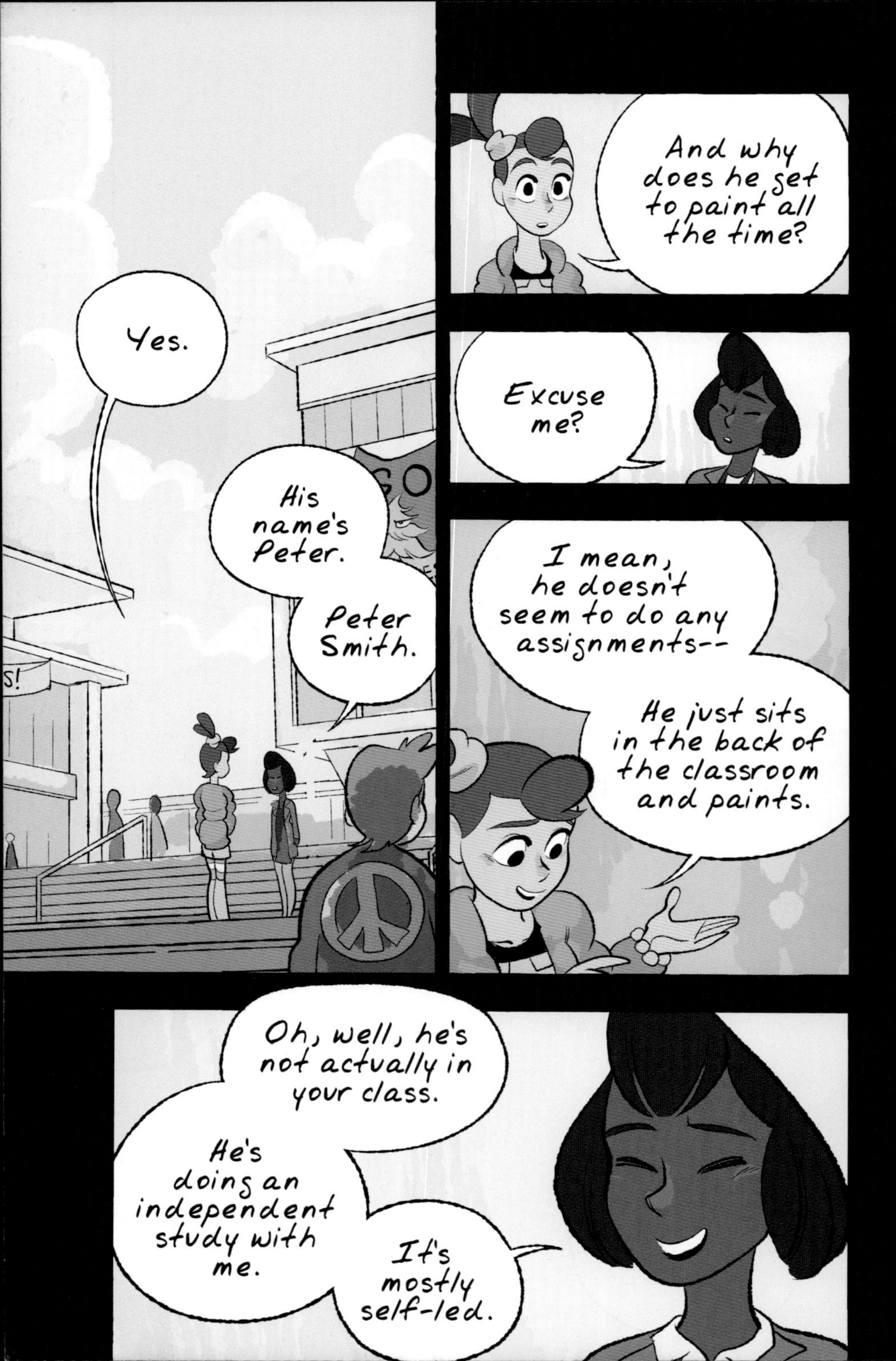
Yes.
His name's Peter.
Peter Smith.
GO
And why does he get to paint all the time?
Excuse me?
I mean, he doesn't seem to do any assignments--
He just sits in the back of the classroom and paints.
Oh, well, he's not actually in your class.
He's doing an independent study with me.
It's mostly self-led.

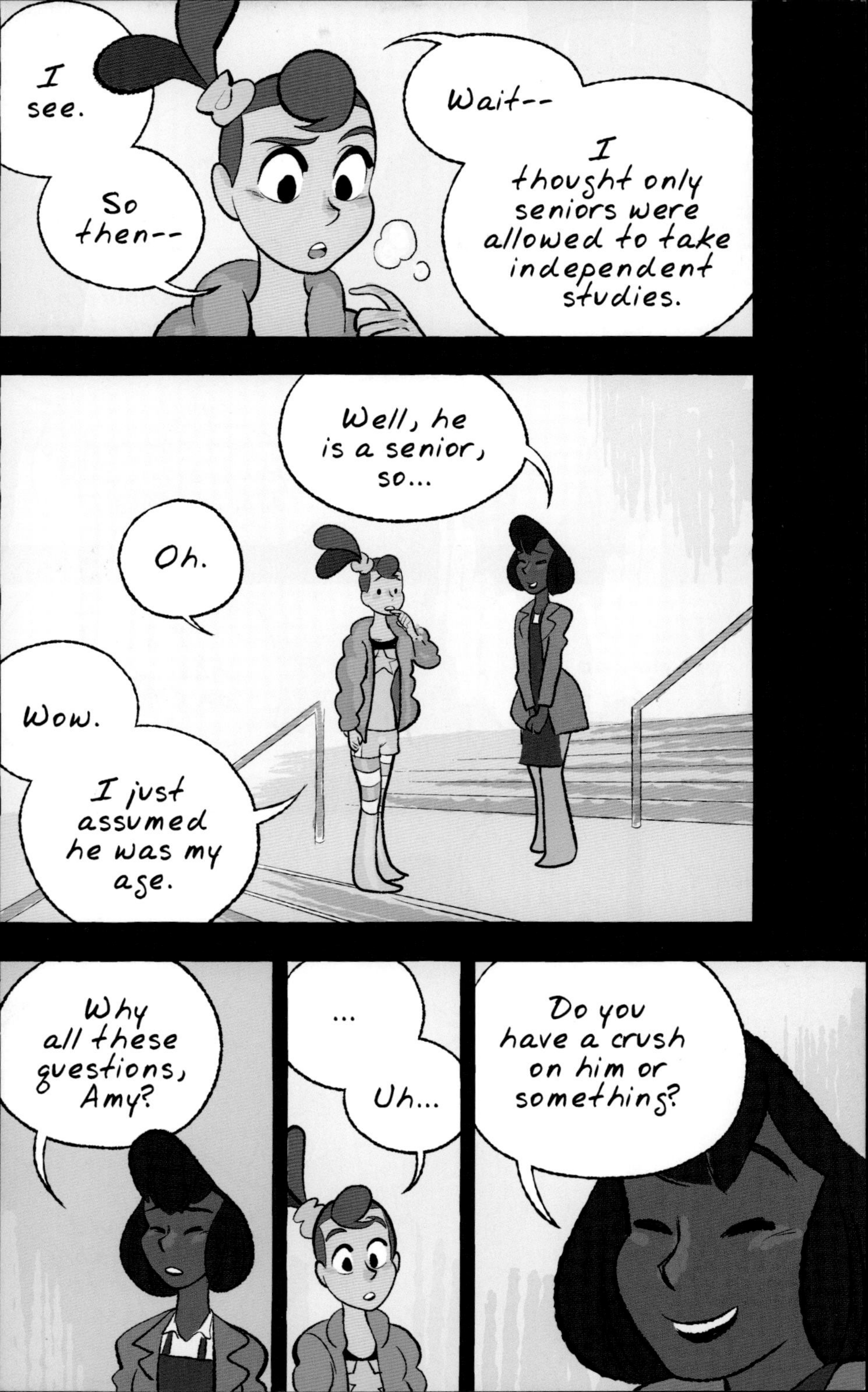
I see.
So then--
Wait--
I thought only seniors were allowed to take independent studies.
Well, he is a senior, so...
Oh.
Wow.
I just assumed he was my age.
Why all these questions, Amy?
...
Uh...
Do you have a crush on him or something?

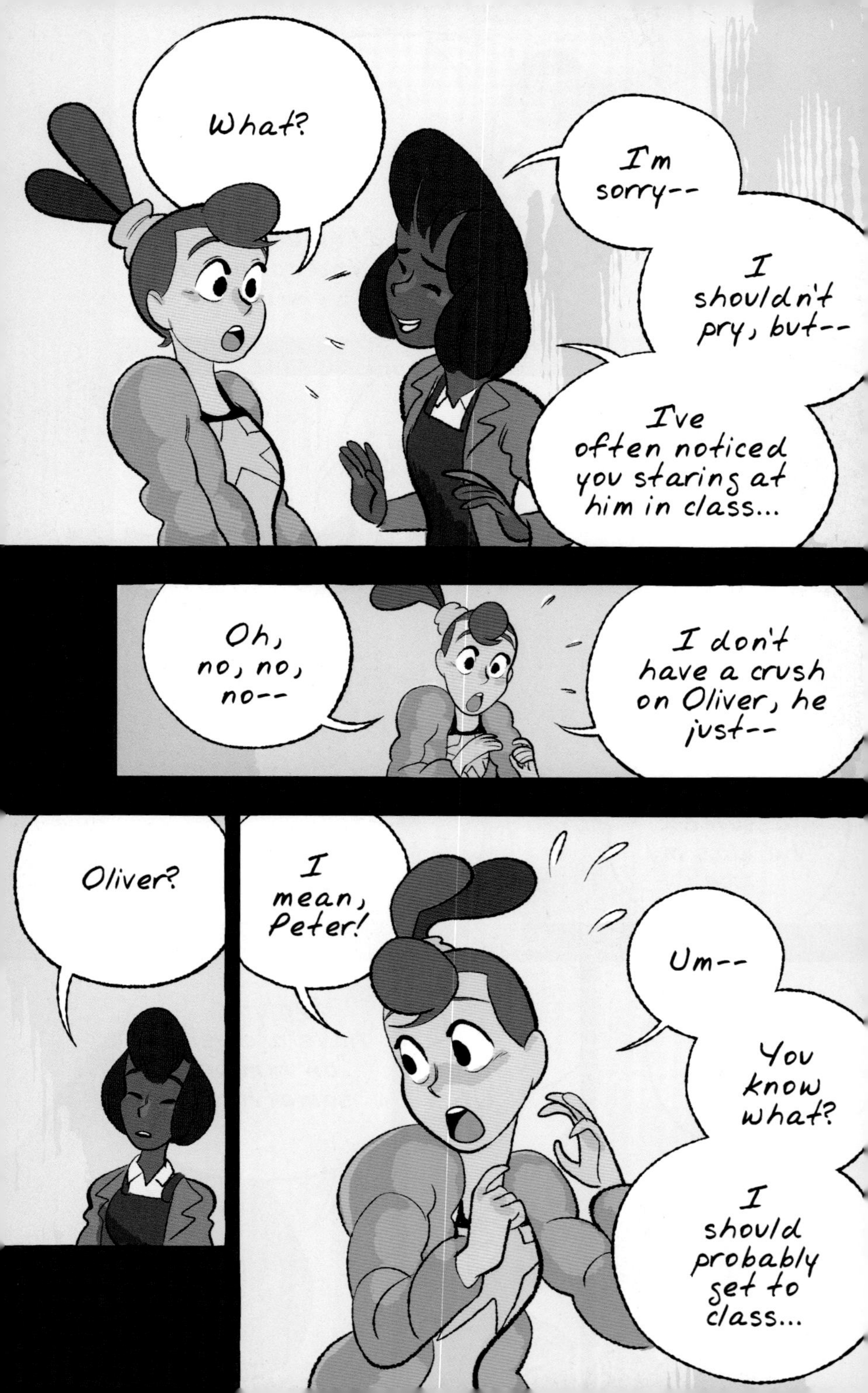
What?
I'm sorry--
I shouldn't pry, but--
I've often noticed you staring at him in class...
Oh, no, no, no--
I don't have a crush on Oliver, he just--
Oliver?
I mean, Peter!
Um--
You know what?
I should probably get to class...

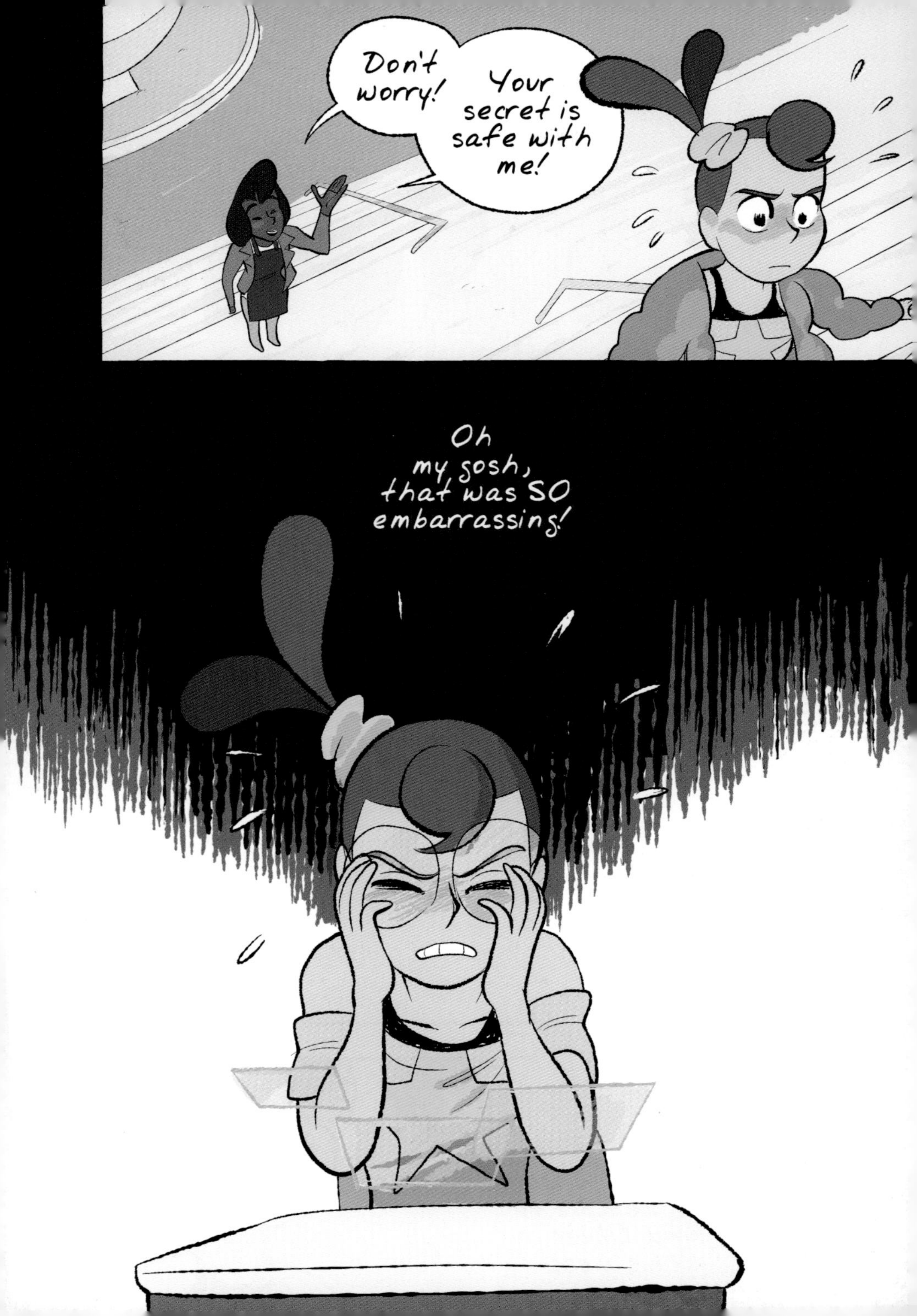
Don't worry!
Your secret is safe with me!
Oh my gosh, that was SO embarrassing!

But at least I know Oliver's alias now...

type type type

Q Peter Smith

450,000,000 results.

Peter Smith ...ia.com/wiki/petersmith ...is a professor of the university ...lien from the ground ...uctic

Wow, there's millions of Peter Smiths online.

There's no way I'll be able to find Oliver in this mess.

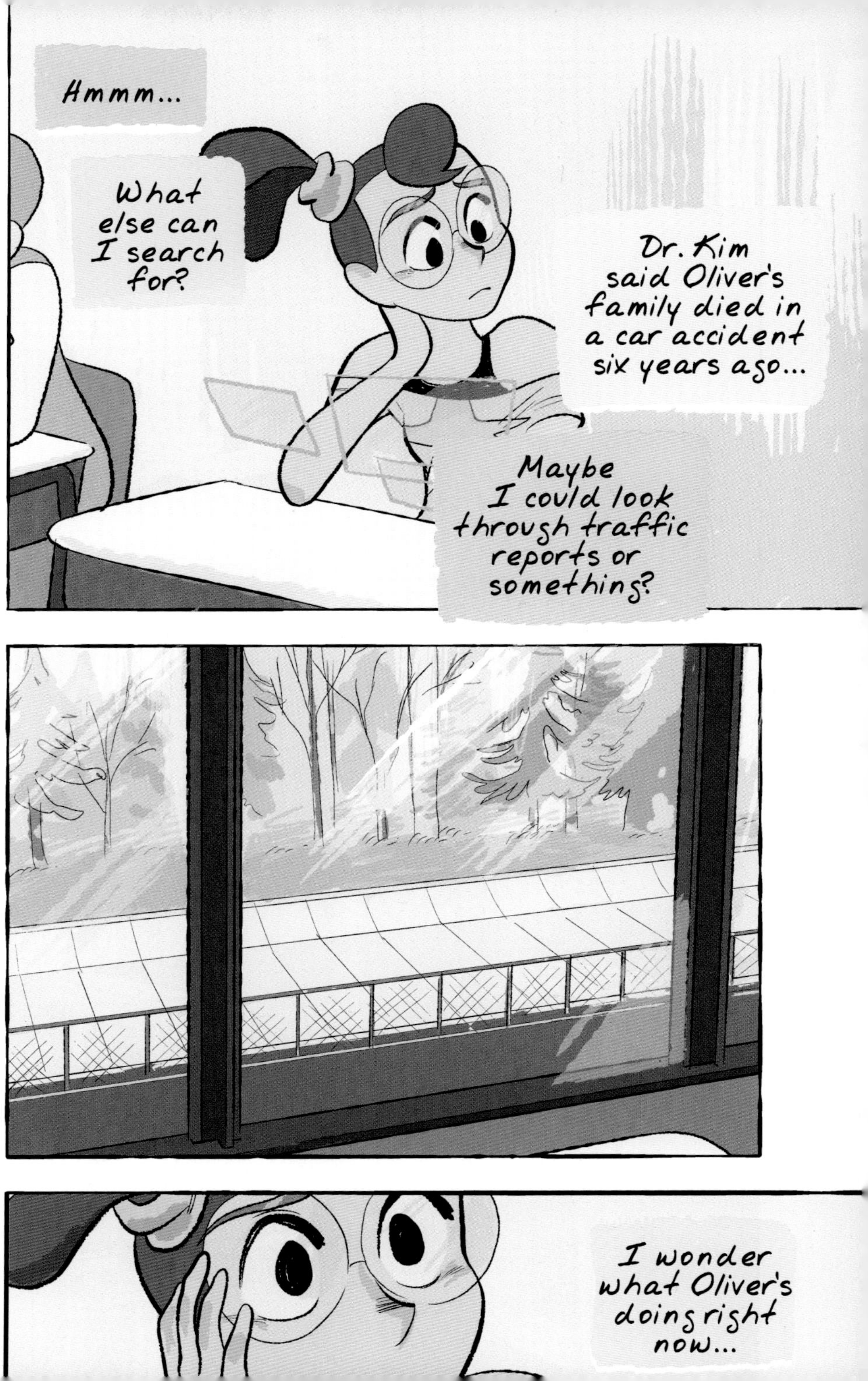
Hmmm...
What else can I search for?
Dr. Kim said Oliver's family died in a car accident six years ago...
Maybe I could look through traffic reports or something?
I wonder what Oliver's doing right now...

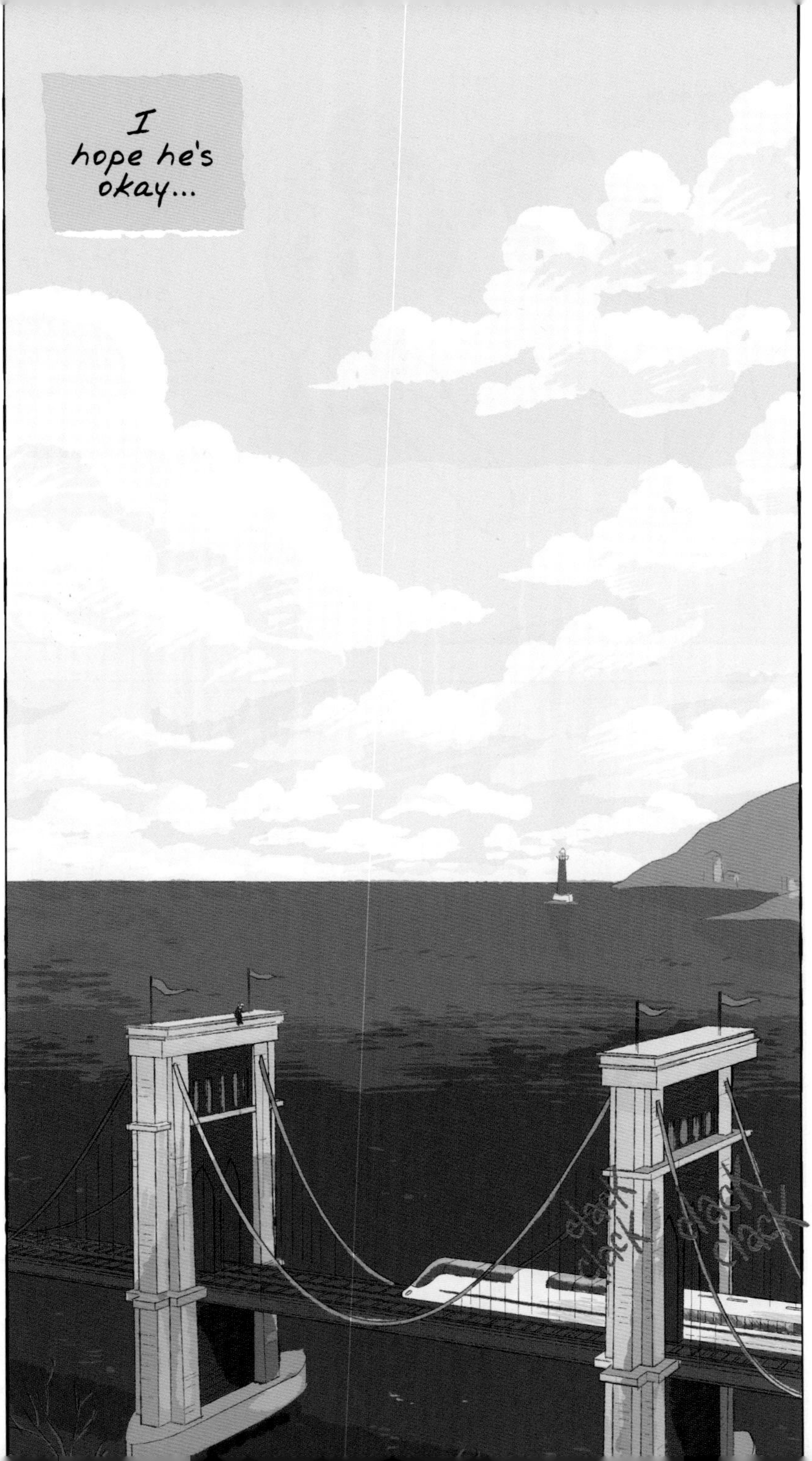
I hope he's okay...
clack clack
clack clack

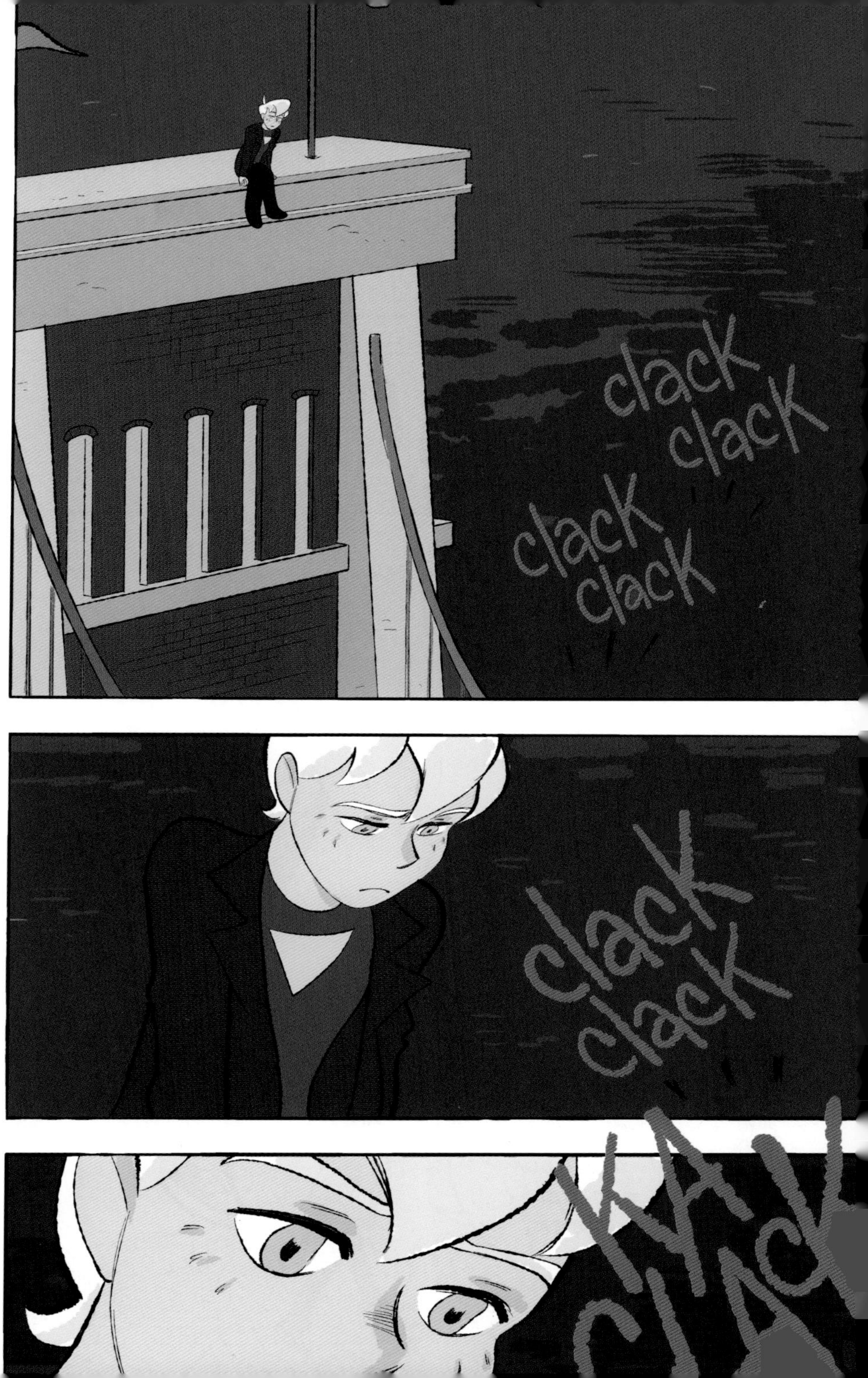
clack
clack
clack
clack
clack
clack
KA
CLACK

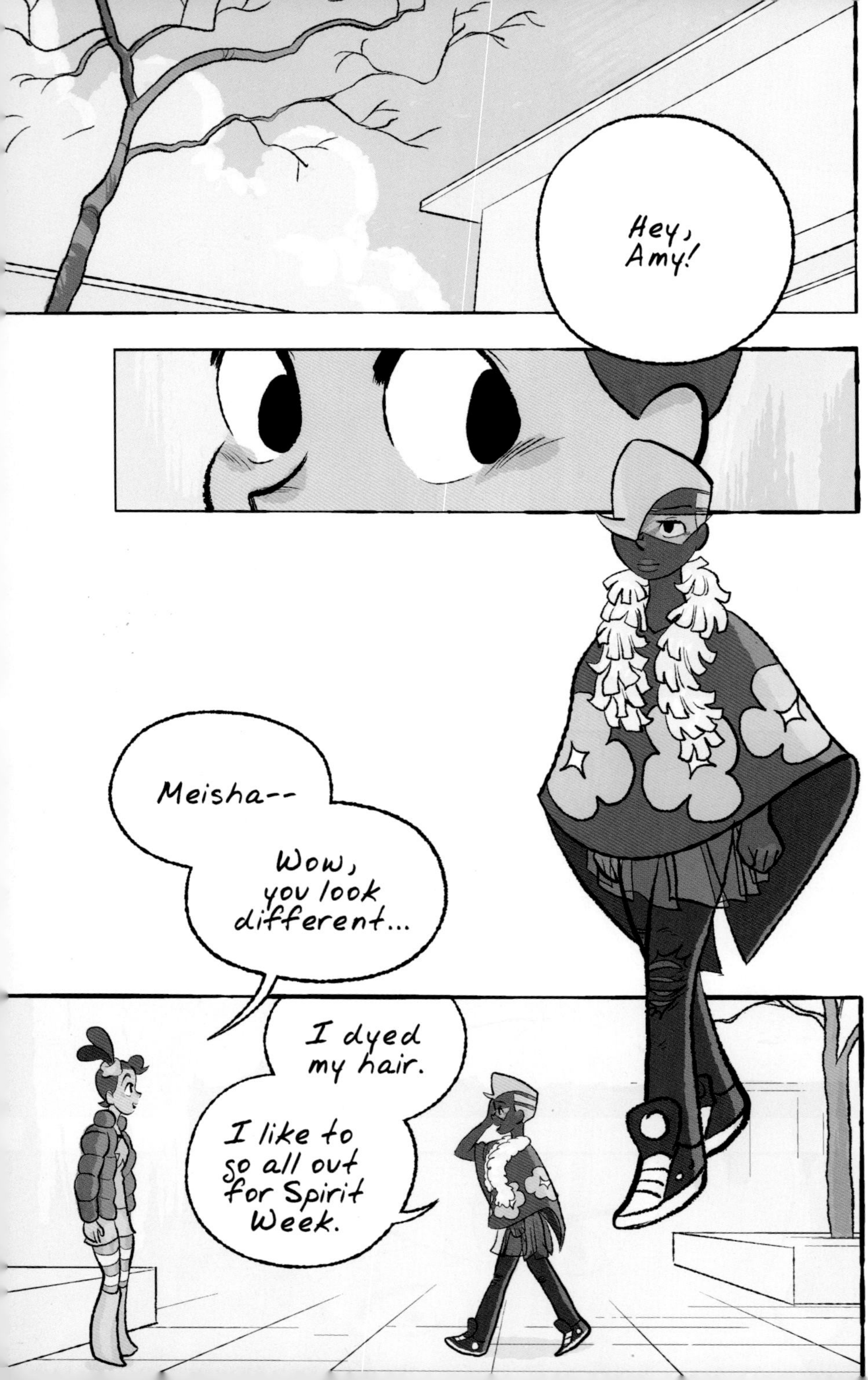
Hey, Amy!
Meisha--
Wow, you look different...
I dyed my hair.
I like to go all out for Spirit Week.

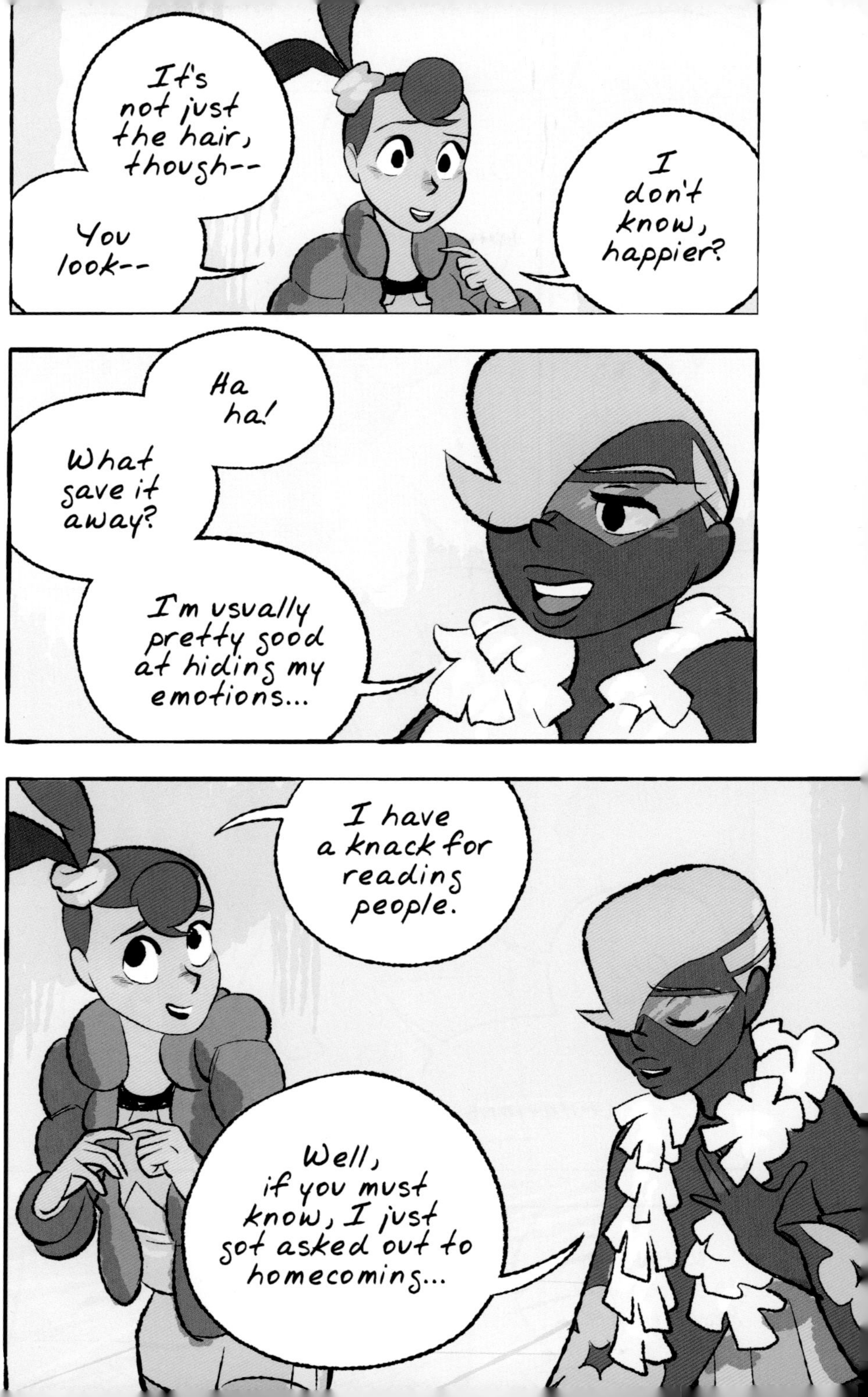
It's not just the hair, though--
You look--
I don't know, happier?
Ha ha!
What gave it away?
I'm usually pretty good at hiding my emotions...
I have a knack for reading people.
Well, if you must know, I just got asked out to homecoming...

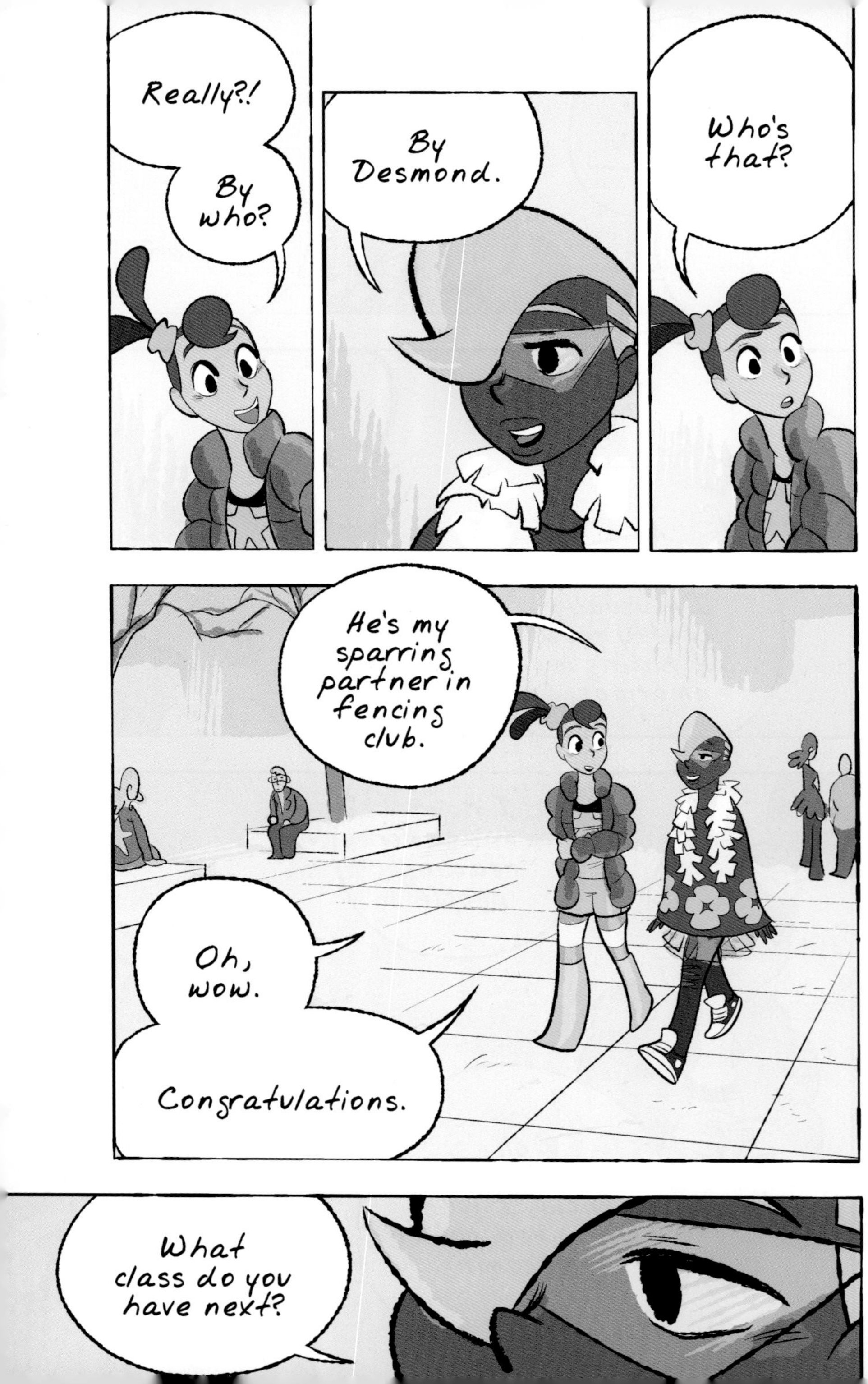
Really?!
By who?
By Desmond.
Who's that?
He's my sparring partner in fencing club.
Oh, wow.
Congratulations.
What class do you have next?

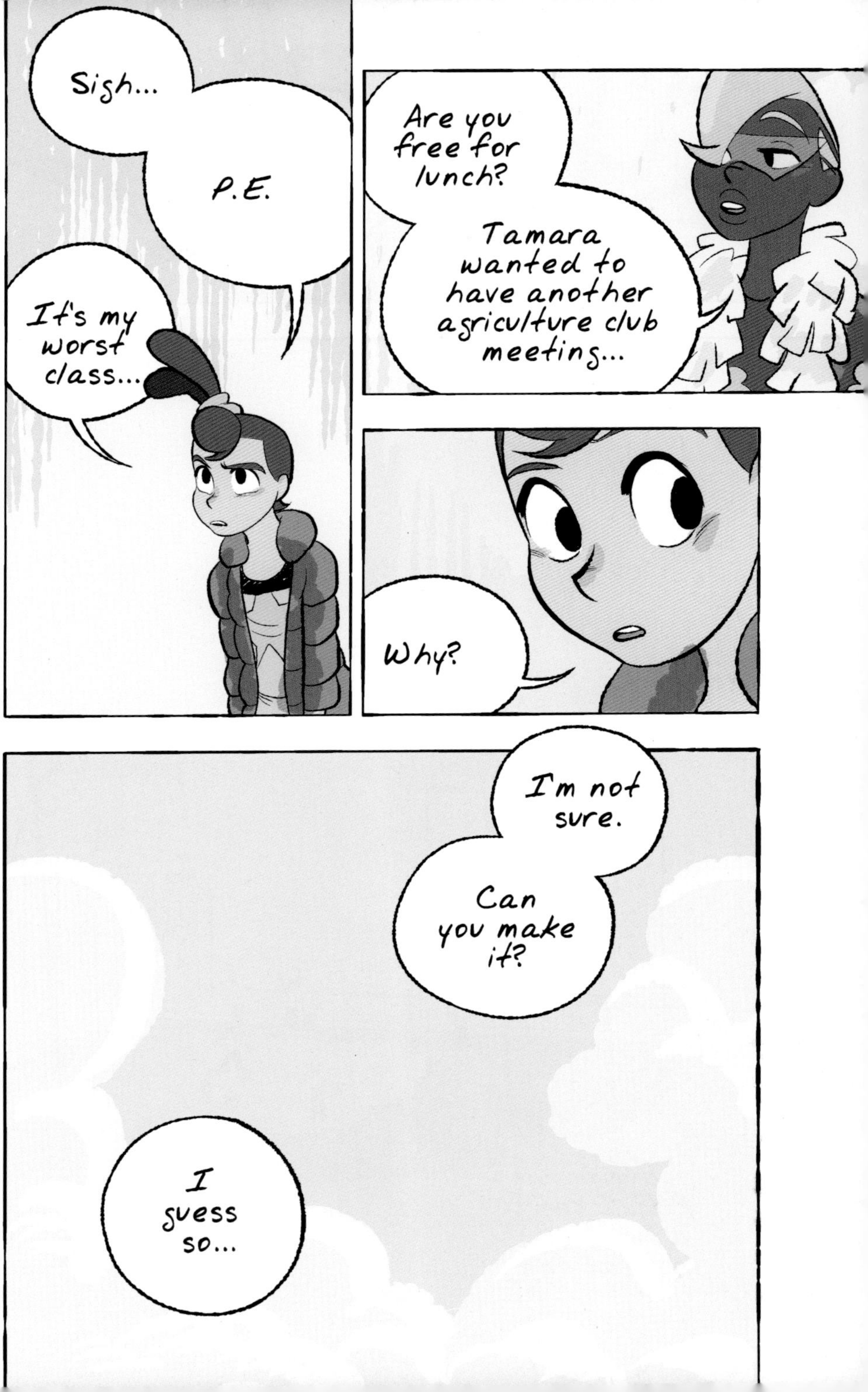
Sigh...
P.E.
It's my worst class...
Are you free for lunch?
Tamara wanted to have another agriculture club meeting...
Why?
I'm not sure.
Can you make it?
I guess so...

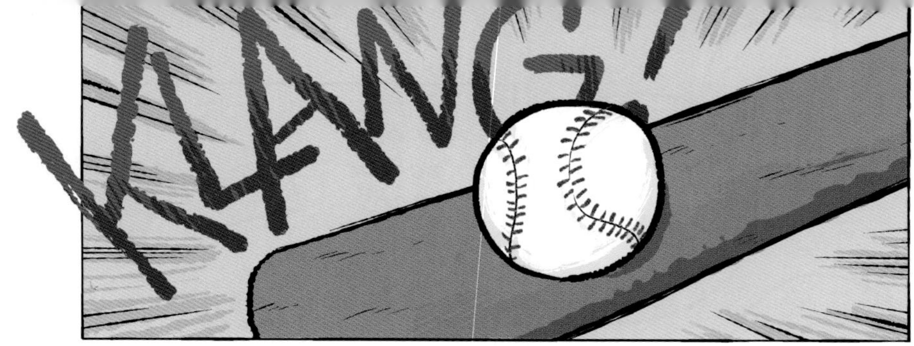
KLANG!

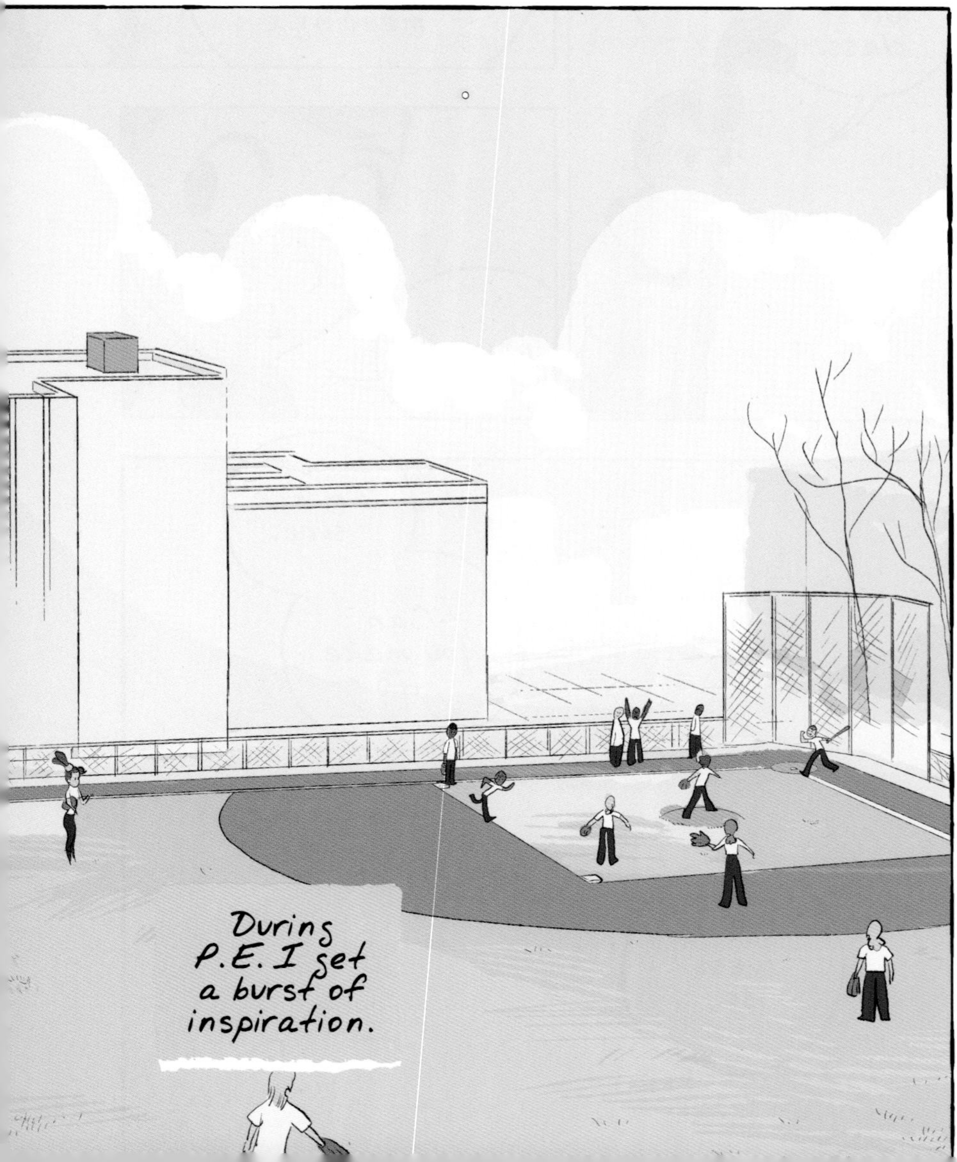
During P.E. I got a burst of inspiration.

I remember Oliver saying once that he got expelled for setting something on fire...

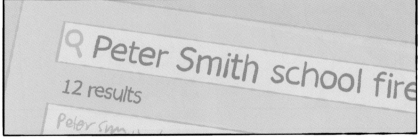

Q Peter Smith school fire

12 results

Peter Sm...

There we go!

That brings it down to only twelve results!

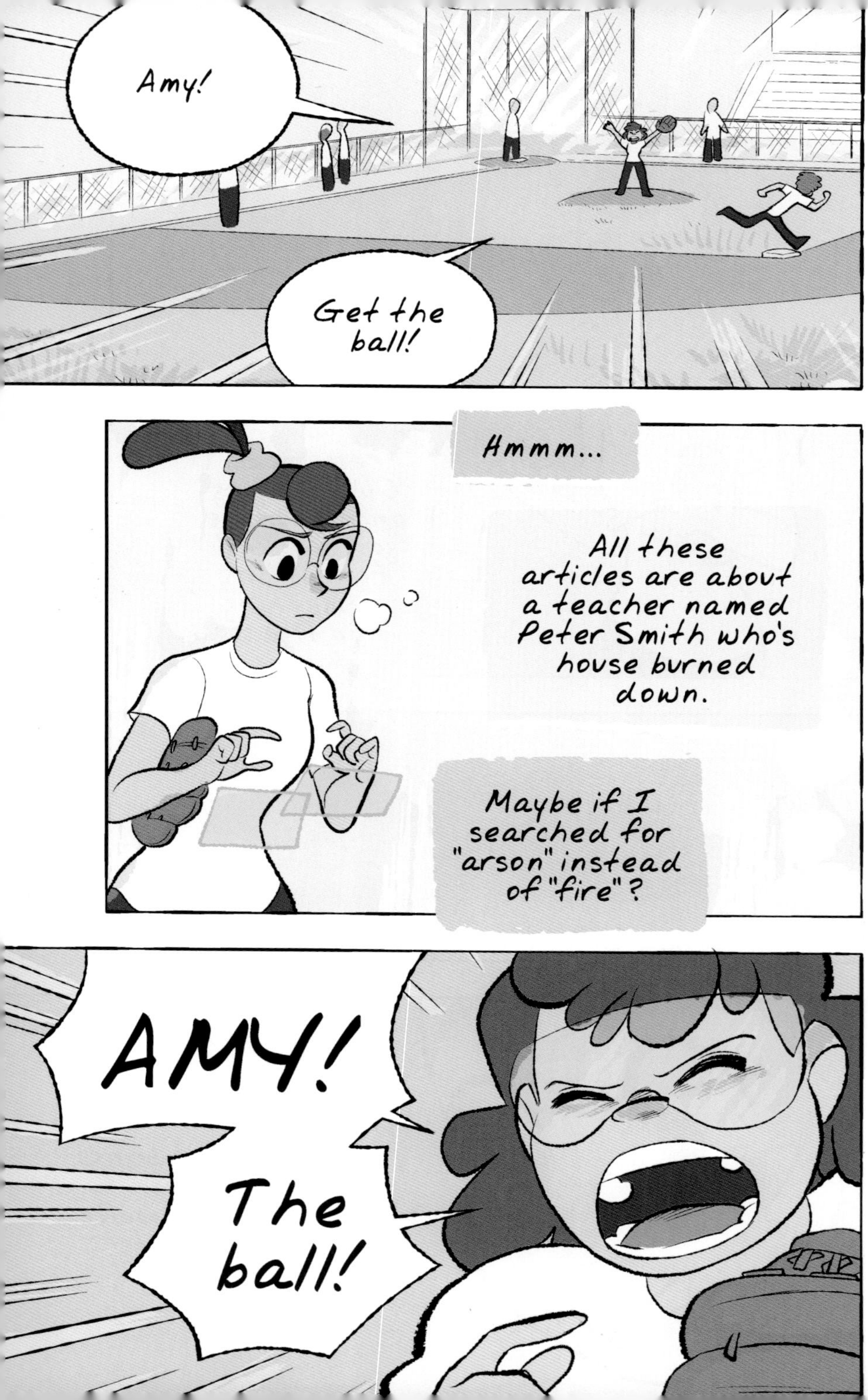
Amy!
Get the ball!
Hmmm...
All these articles are about a teacher named Peter Smith who's house burned down.
Maybe if I searched for "arson" instead of "fire"?
AMY!
The ball!

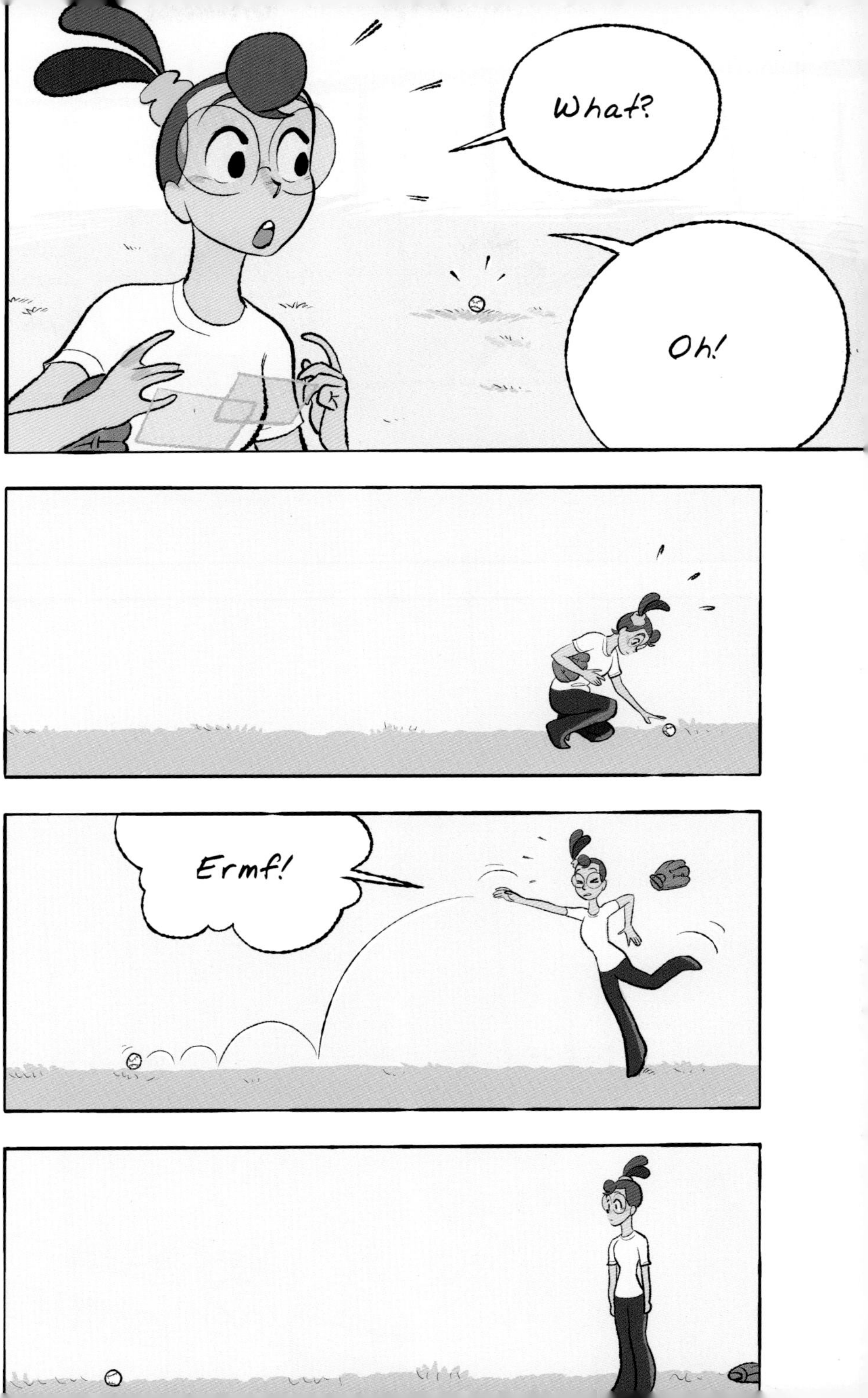
What?
Oh!
Ermf!

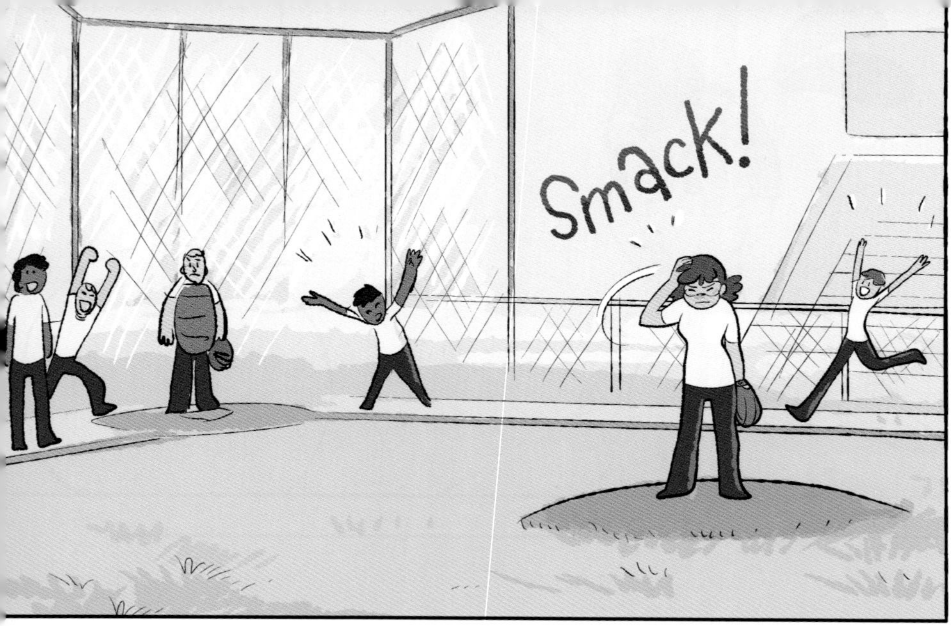
Smack!

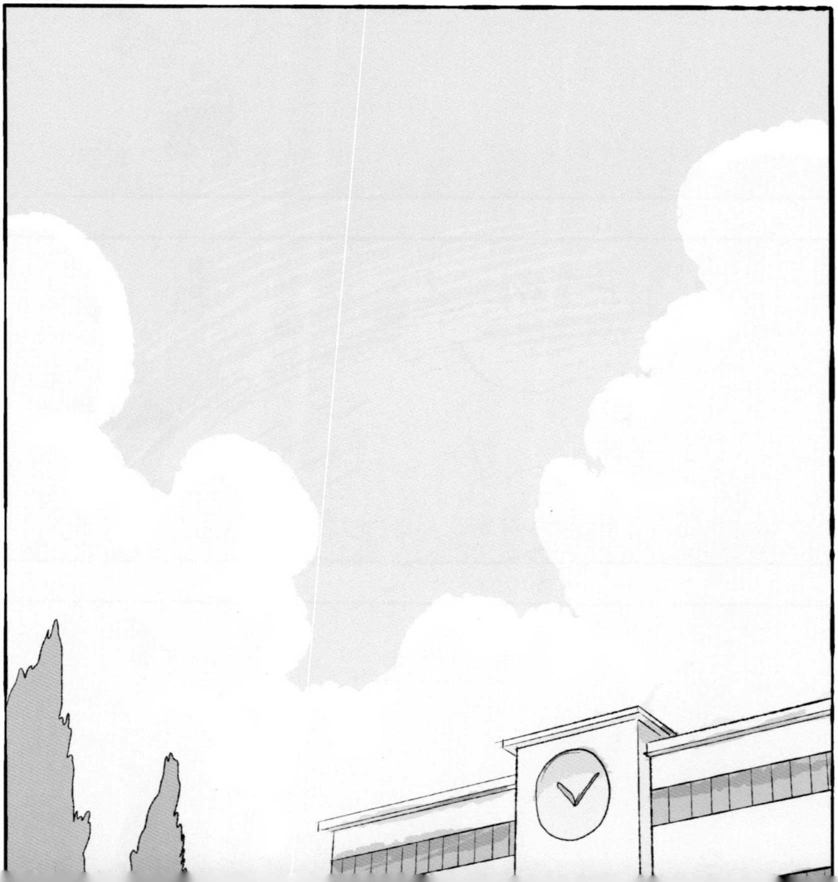

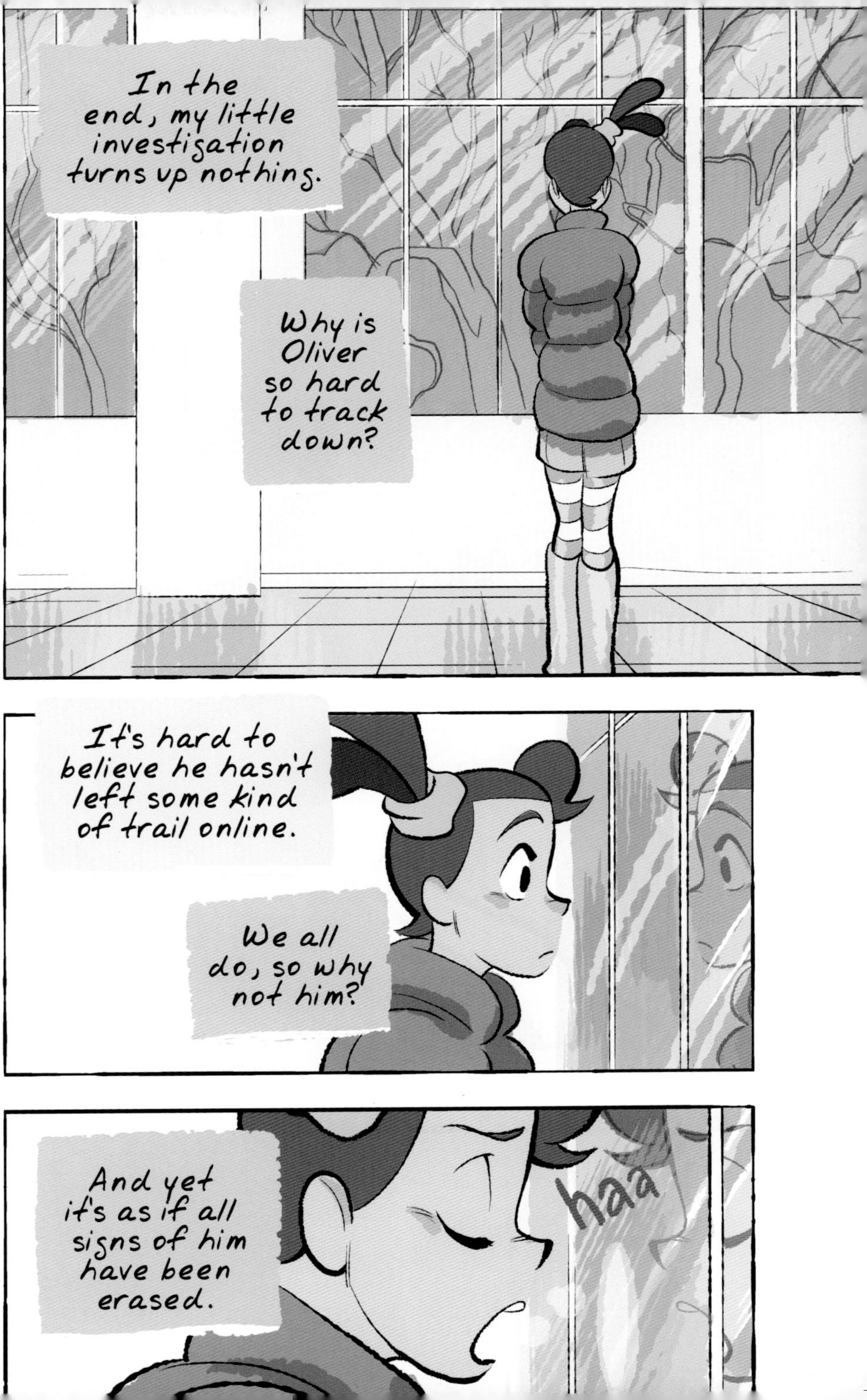
In the end, my little investigation turns up nothing.
Why is Oliver so hard to track down?
It's hard to believe he hasn't left some kind of trail online.
We all do, so why not him?
And yet it's as if all signs of him have been erased.
haa

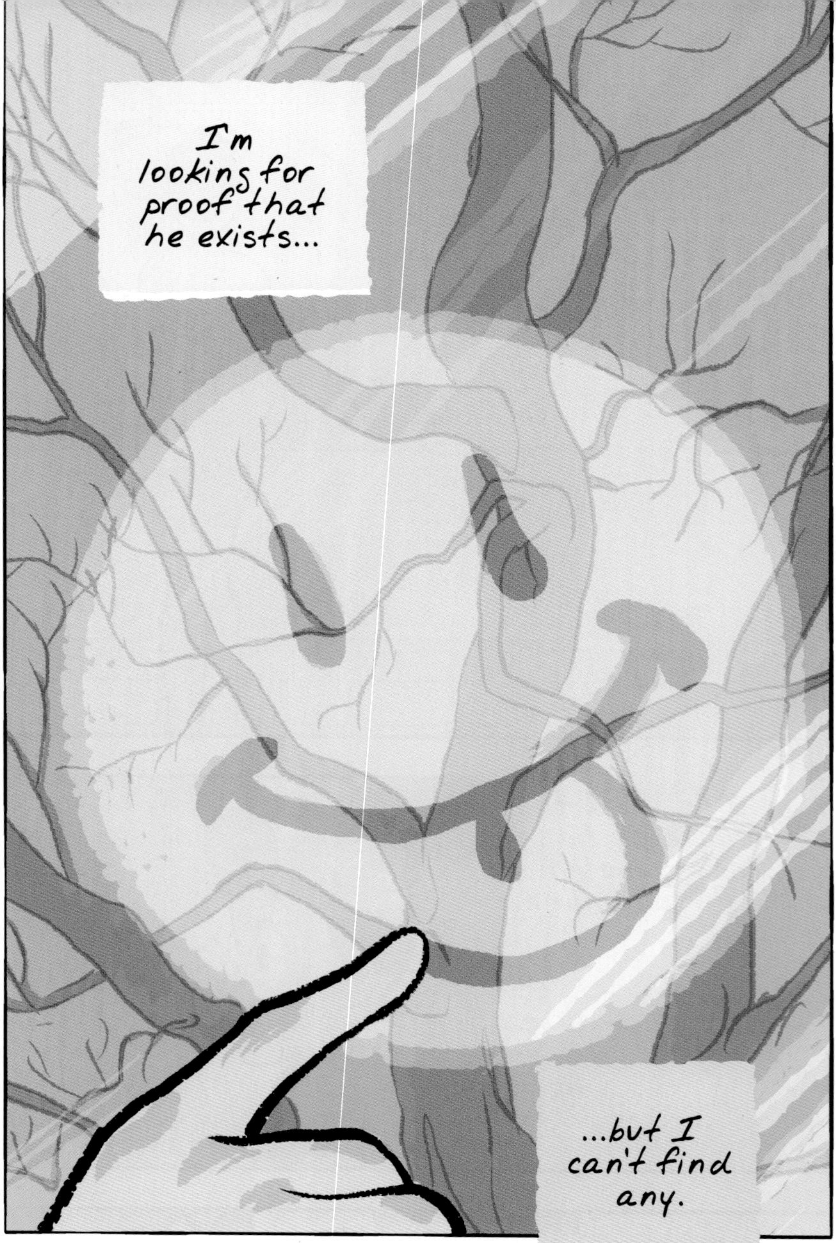
I'm looking for proof that he exists...
...but I can't find any.

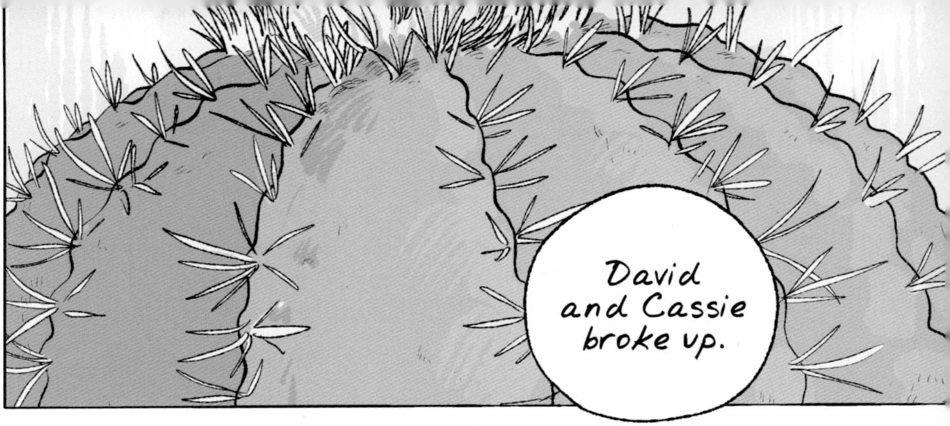
David and Cassie broke up.

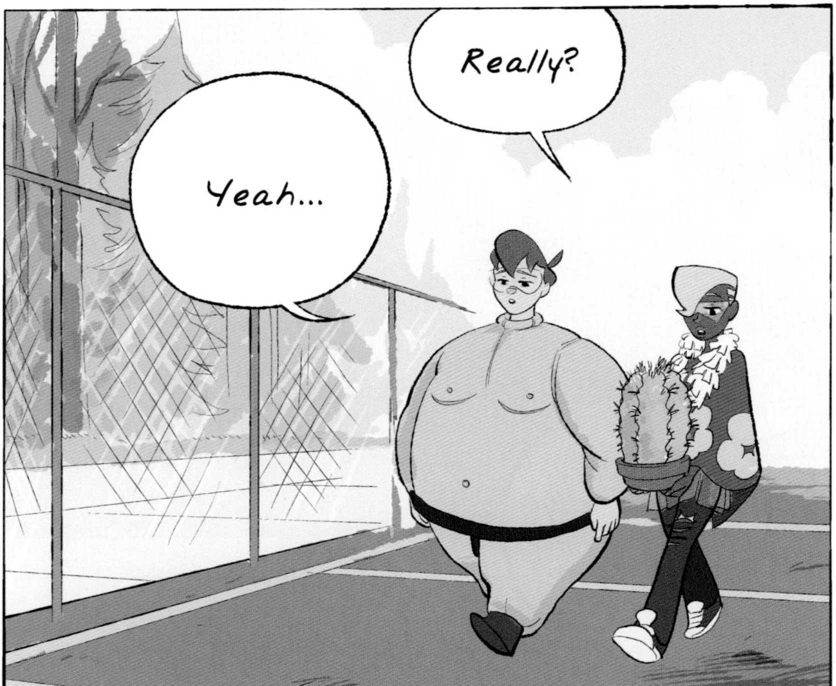
Really?
Yeah...

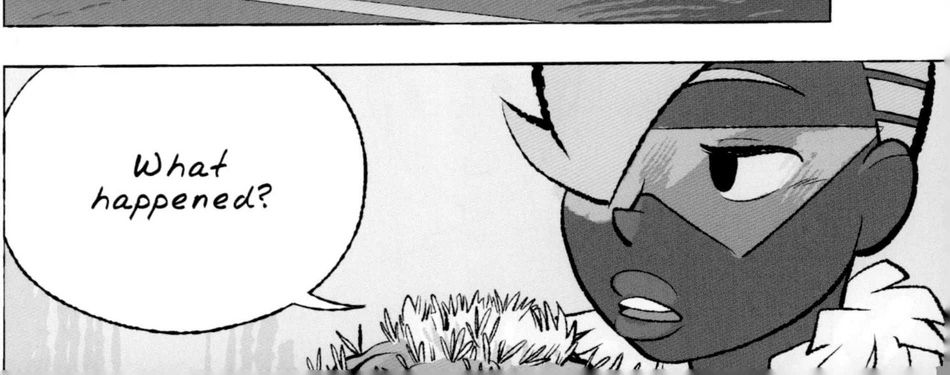
What happened?

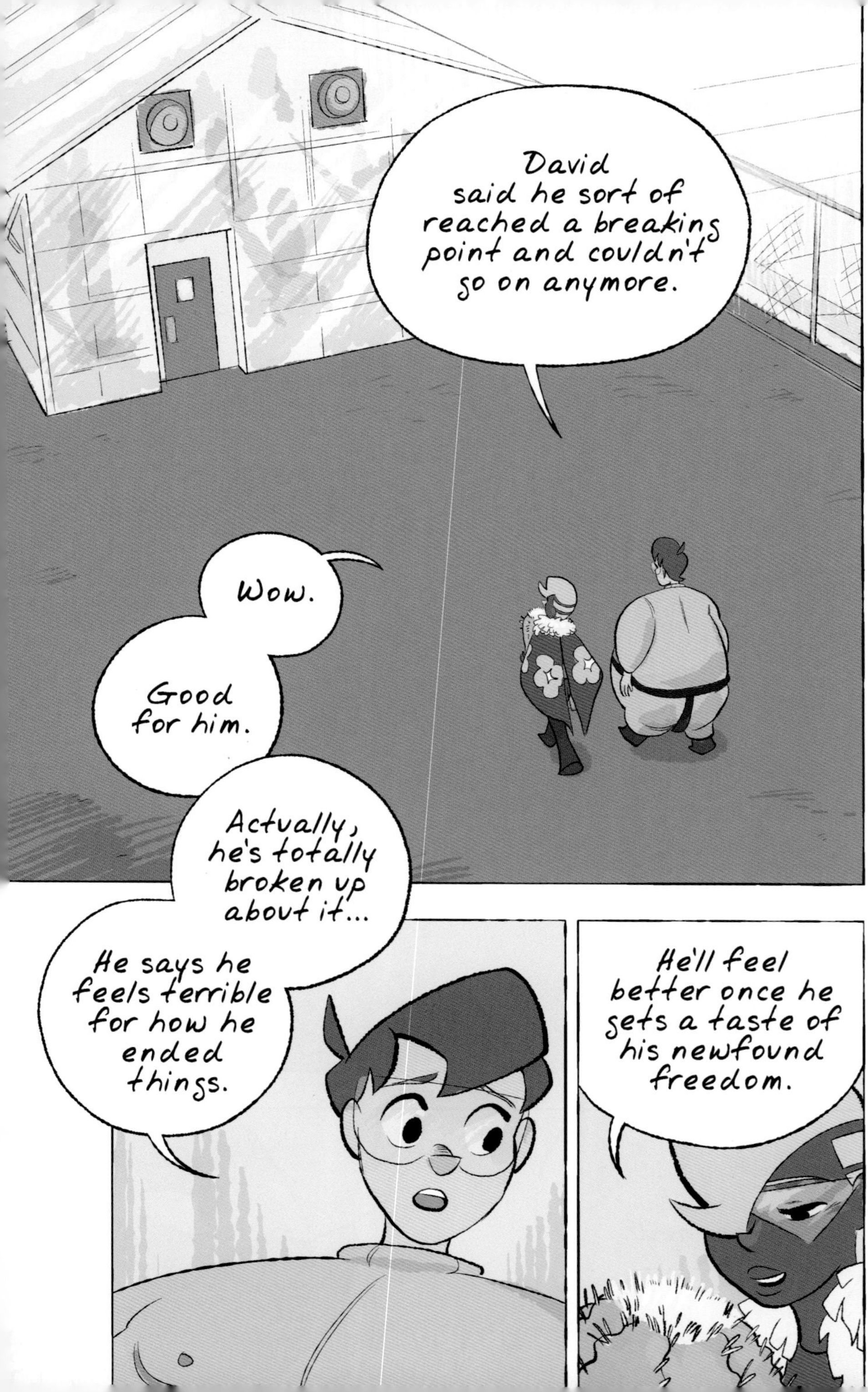
David said he sort of reached a breaking point and couldn't go on anymore.
Wow.
Good for him.
Actually, he's totally broken up about it...
He says he feels terrible for how he ended things.
He'll feel better once he gets a taste of his newfound freedom.

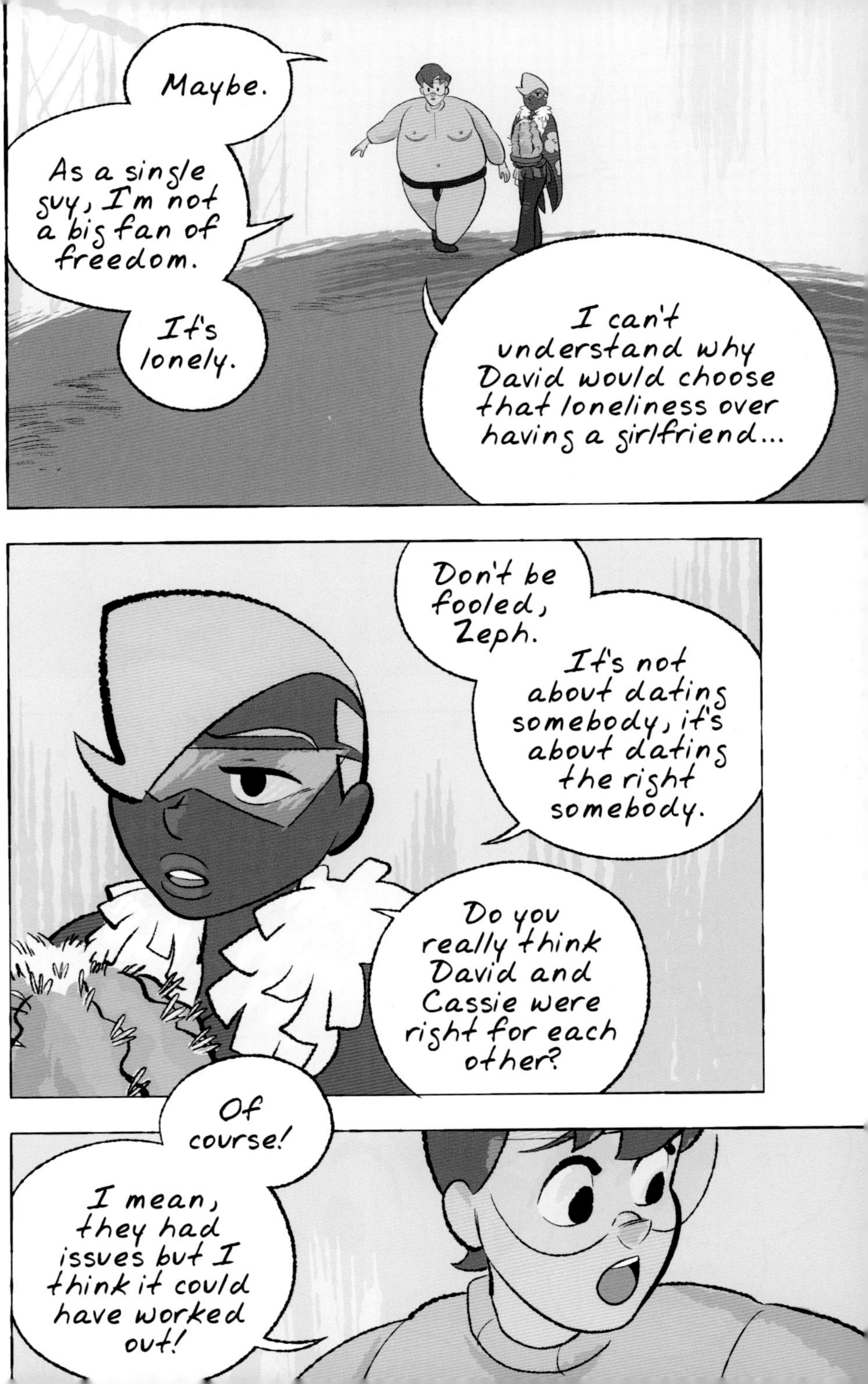

Maybe.
As a single guy, I'm not a big fan of freedom.
It's lonely.
I can't understand why David would choose that loneliness over having a girlfriend...
Don't be fooled, Zeph.
It's not about dating somebody, it's about dating the right somebody.
Do you really think David and Cassie were right for each other?
Of course!
I mean, they had issues but I think it could have worked out!

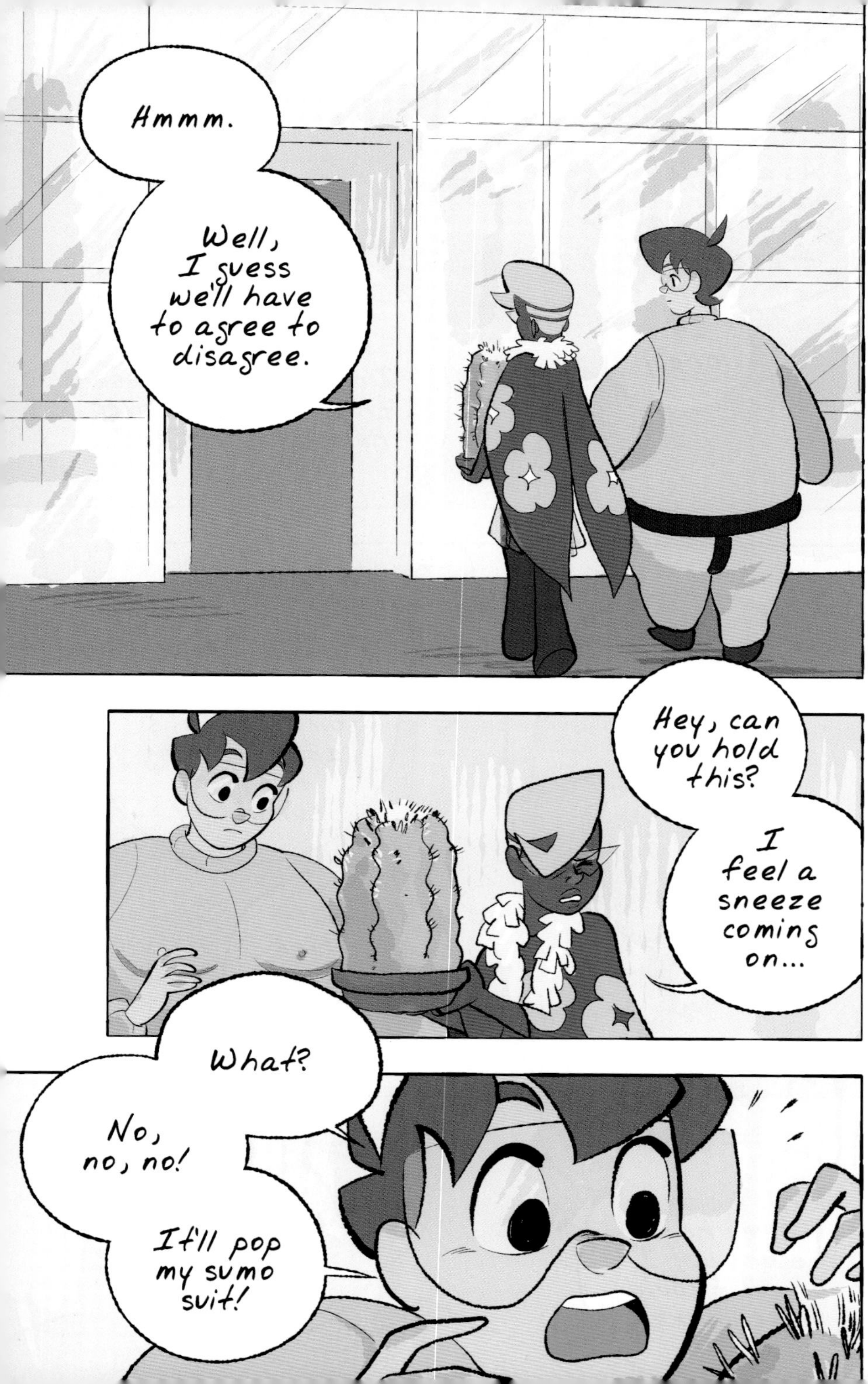
Hmmm.
Well, I guess we'll have to agree to disagree.
Hey, can you hold this?
I feel a sneeze coming on...
What?
No, no, no!
It'll pop my sumo suit!

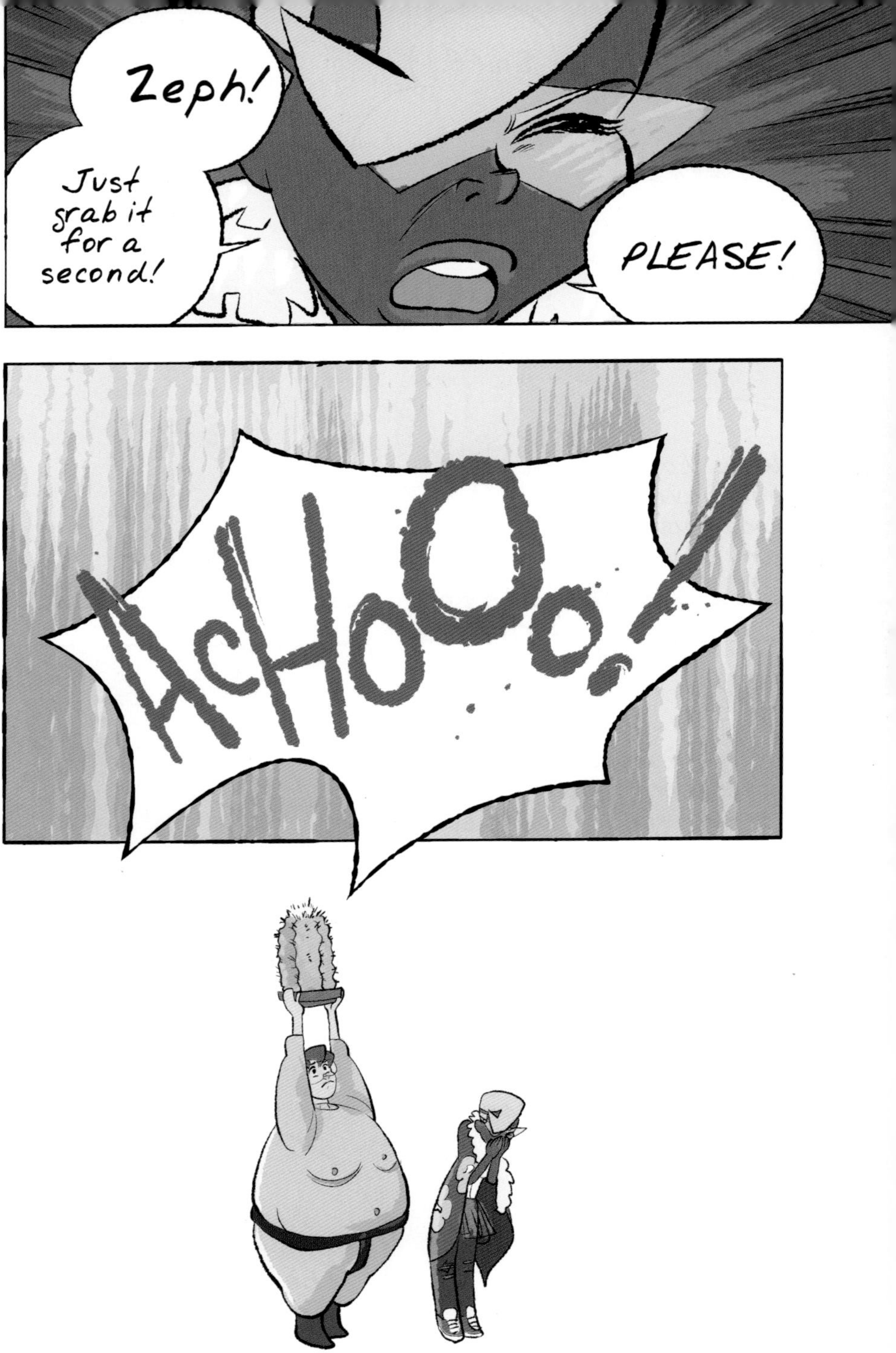
Zeph!
Just grab it for a second!
PLEASE!
ACHOOOO!

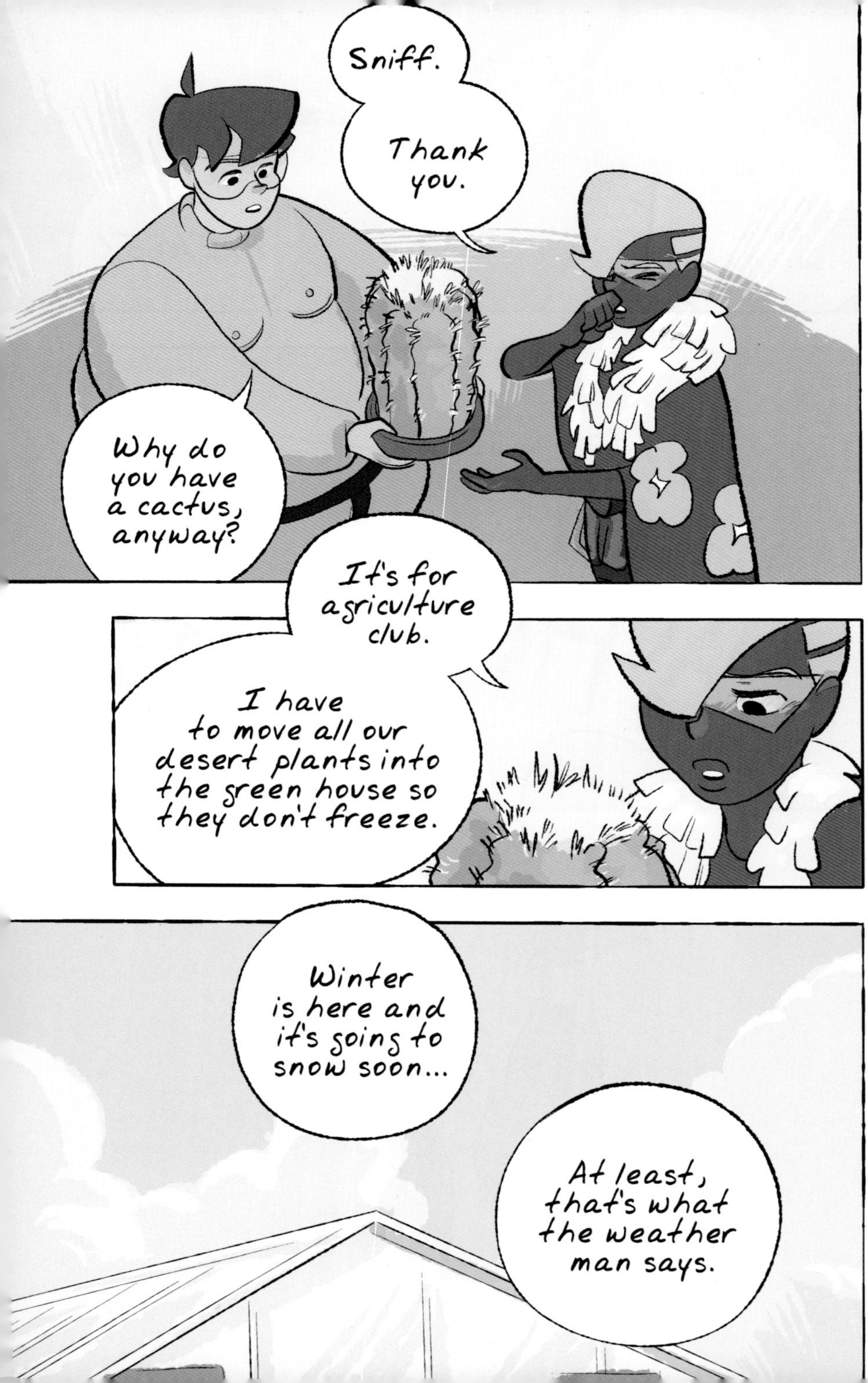
Sniff.
Thank you.
Why do you have a cactus, anyway?
It's for agriculture club.
I have to move all our desert plants into the green house so they don't freeze.
Winter is here and it's going to snow soon...
At least, that's what the weather man says.

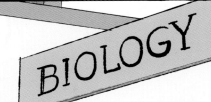

BIOLOGY

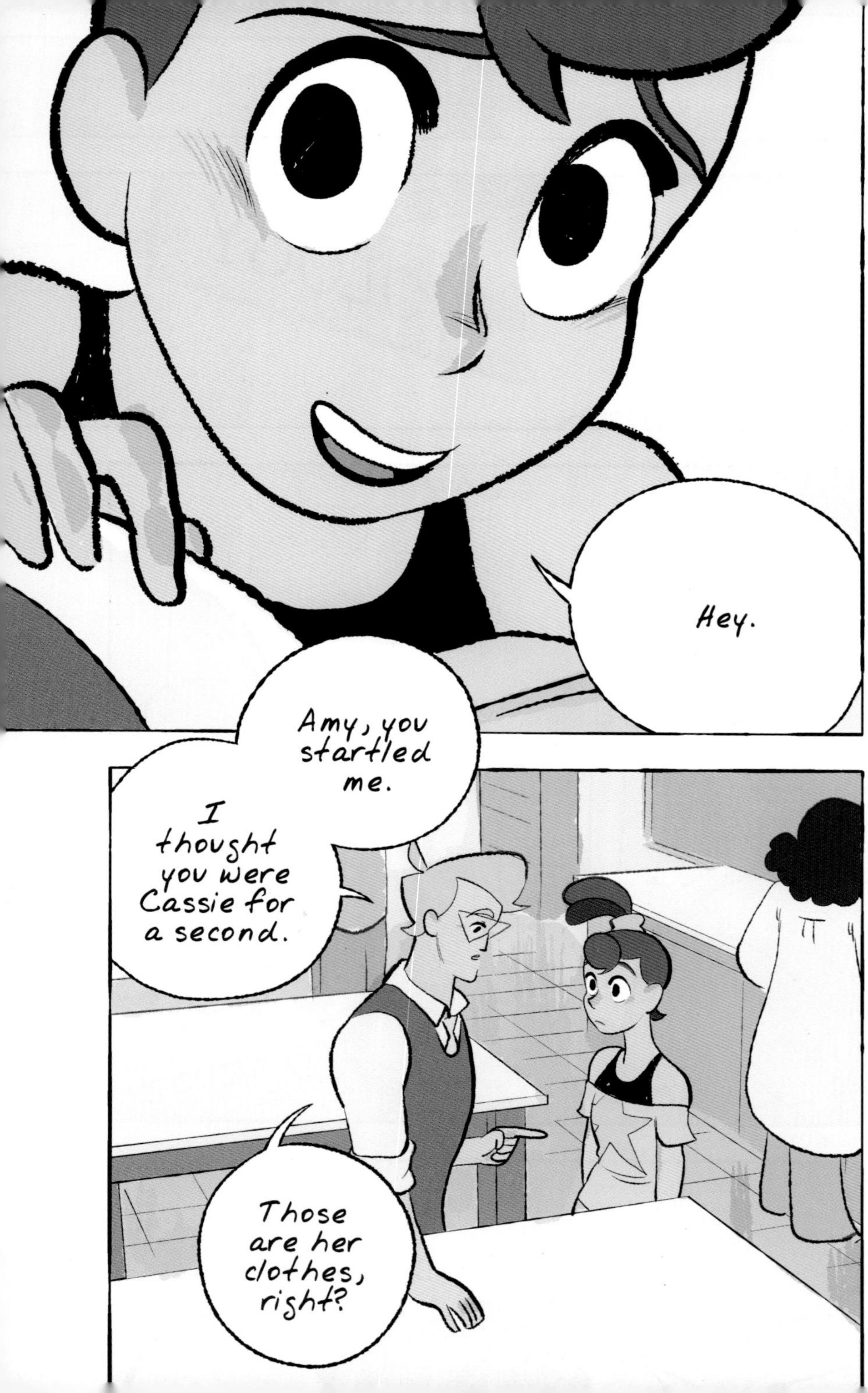
Hey.
Amy, you startled me.
I thought you were Cassie for a second.
Those are her clothes, right?

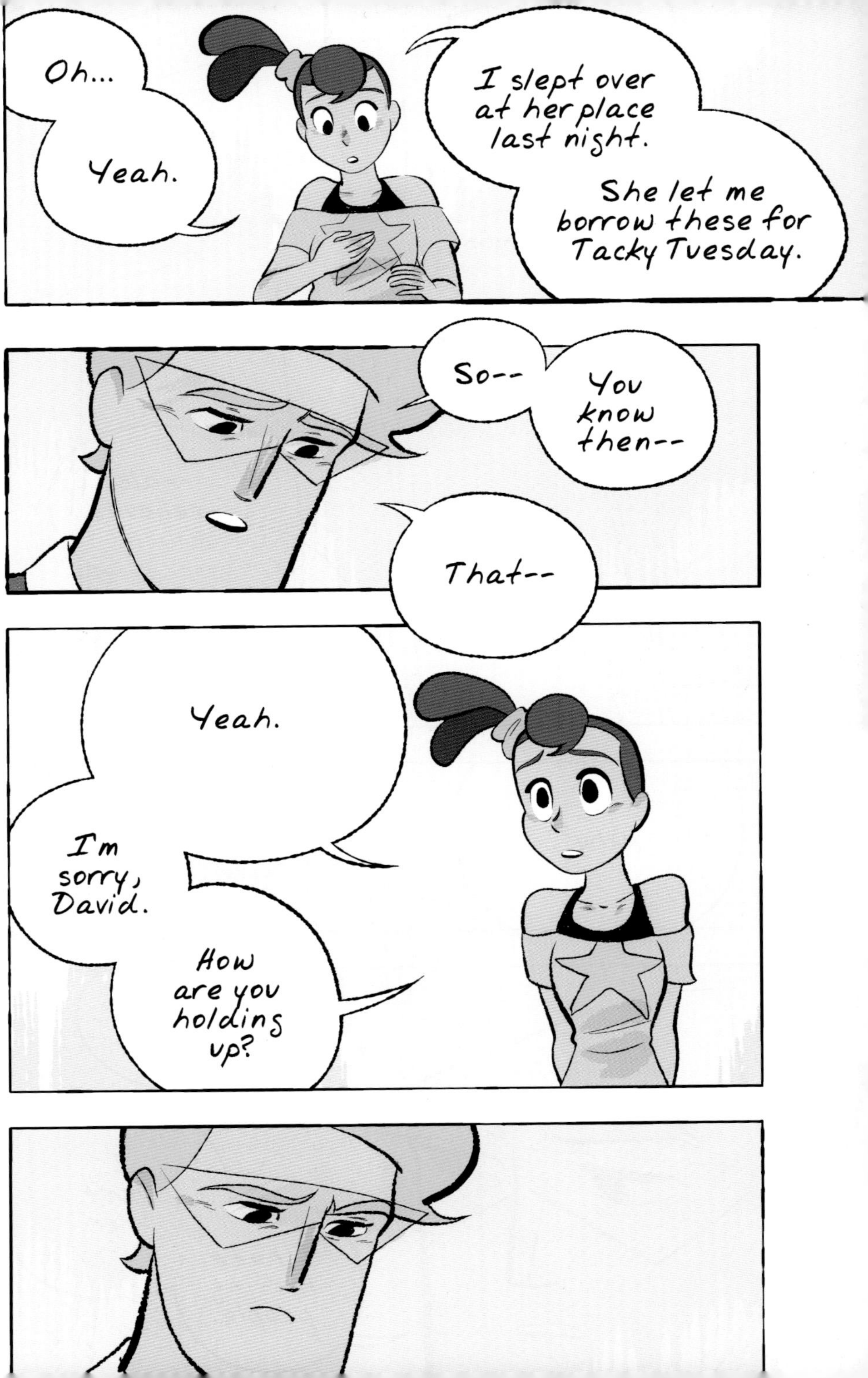
Oh...
Yeah.
I slept over at her place last night.
She let me borrow these for Tacky Tuesday.
So--
You know then--
That--
Yeah.
I'm sorry, David.
How are you holding up?

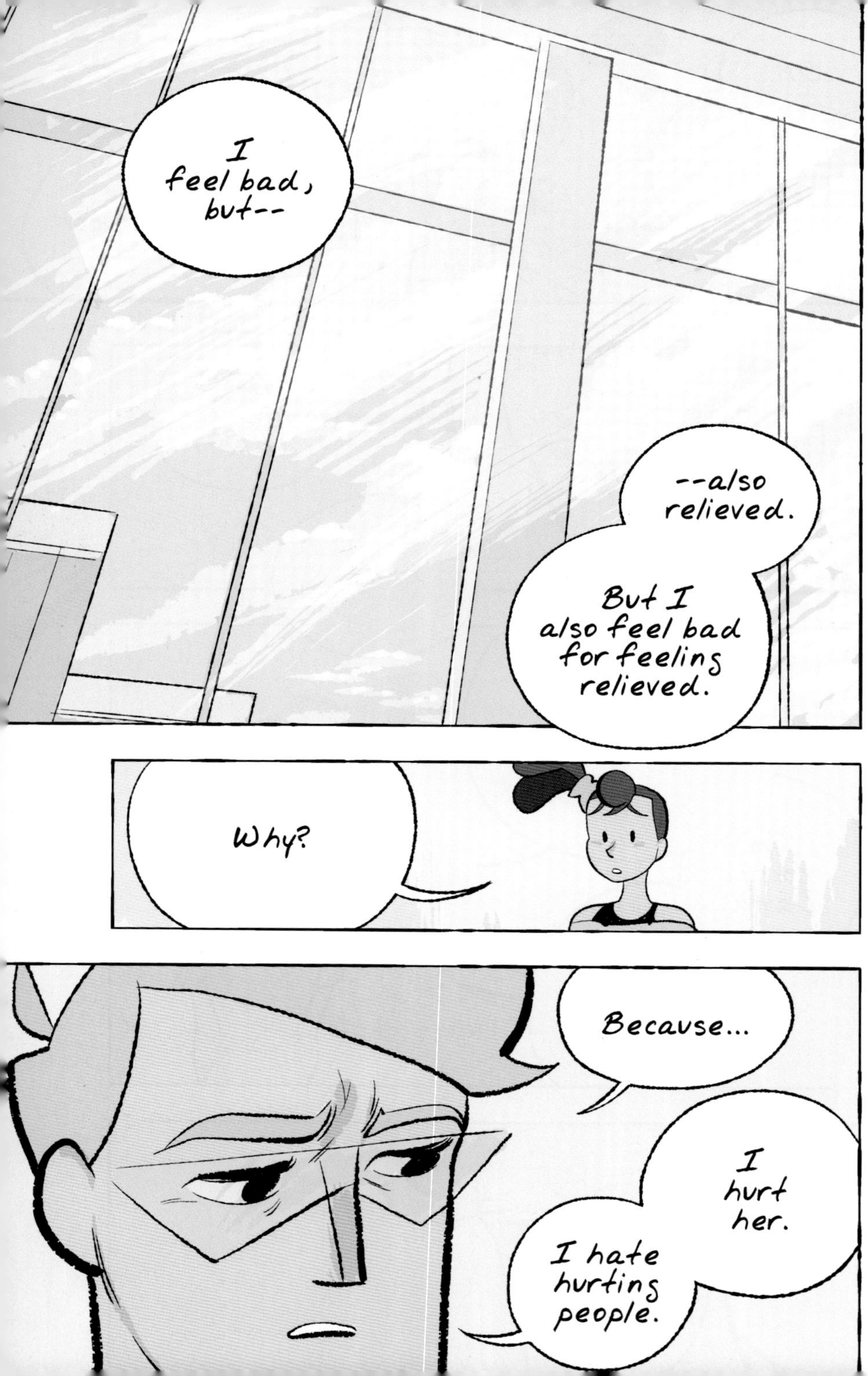
I feel bad, but--
--also relieved.
But I also feel bad for feeling relieved.
Why?
Because...
I hurt her.
I hate hurting people.

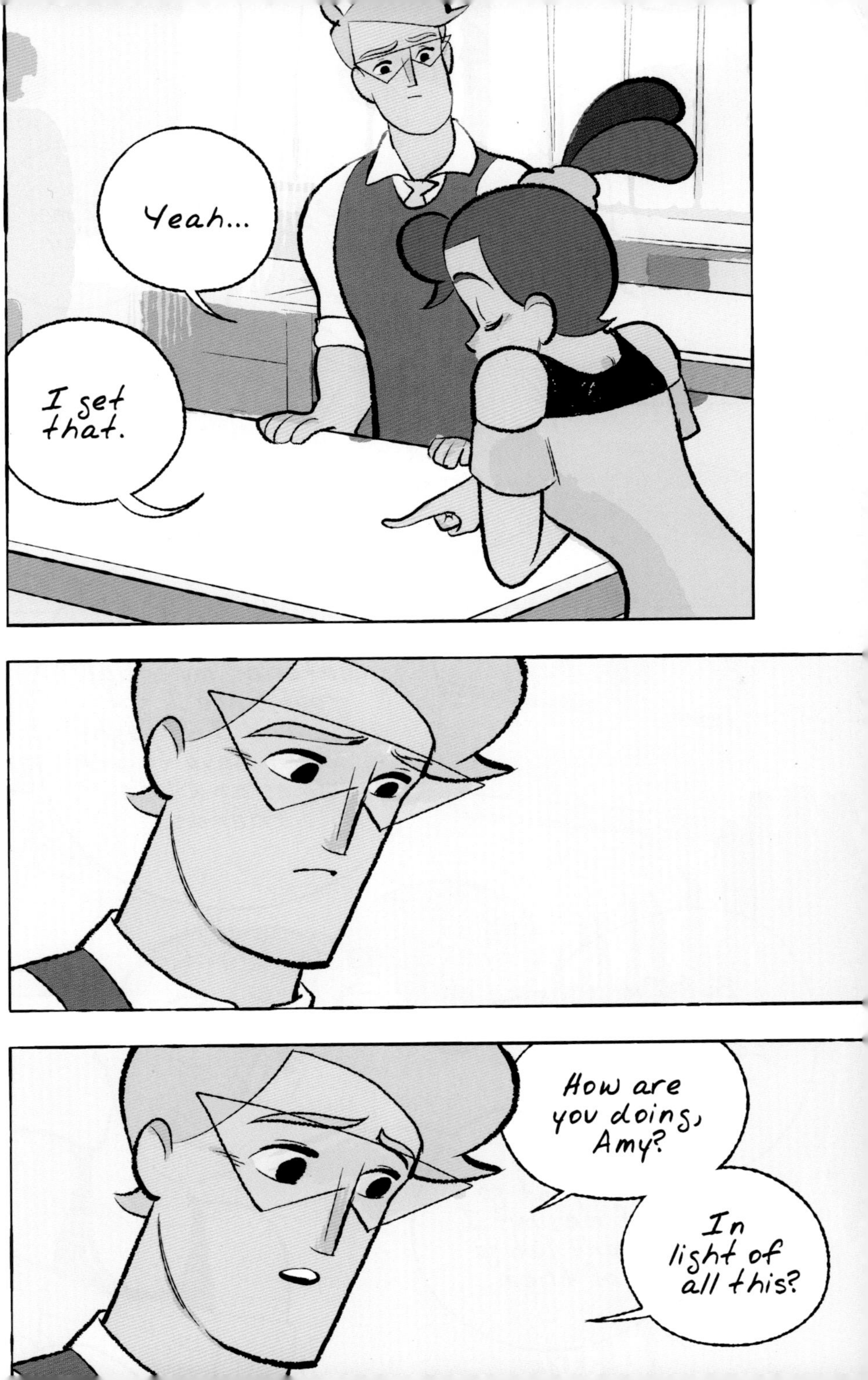
Yeah...
I get that.
How are you doing, Amy?
In light of all this?

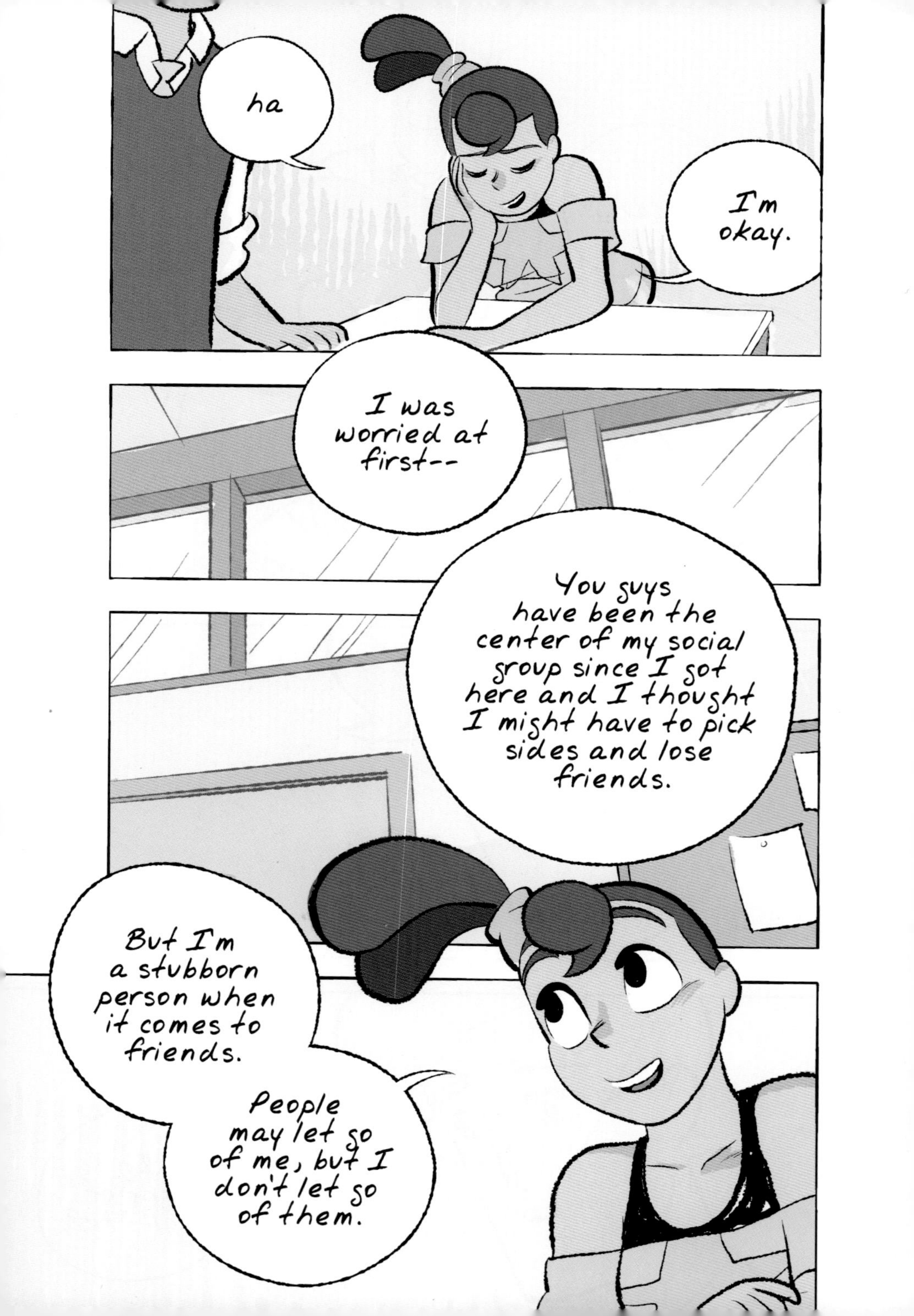
ha
I'm okay.
I was worried at first--
You guys have been the center of my social group since I got here and I thought I might have to pick sides and lose friends.
But I'm a stubborn person when it comes to friends.
People may let go of me, but I don't let go of them.

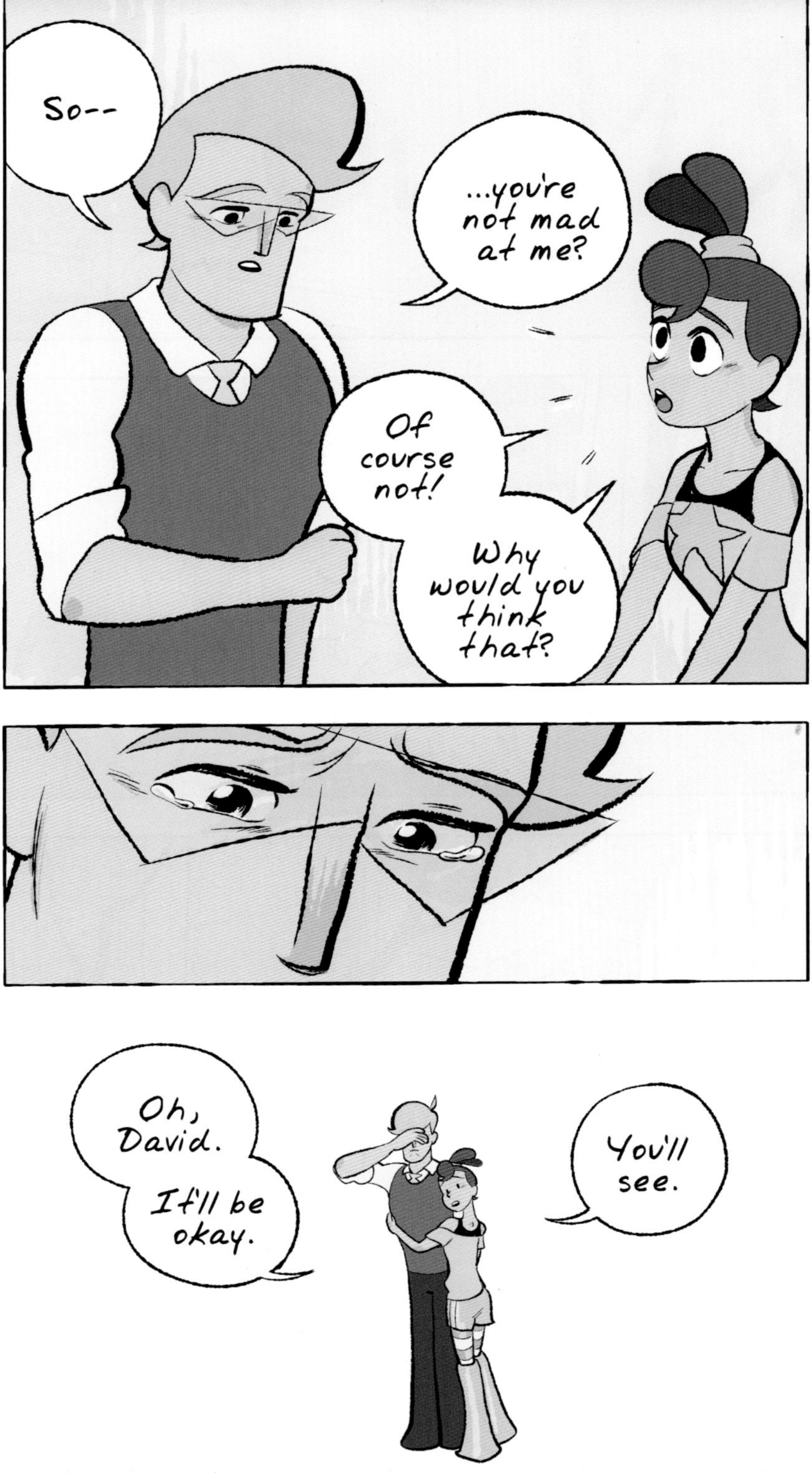
So--
...you're not mad at me?
Of course not!
Why would you think that?
Oh, David.
It'll be okay.
You'll see.

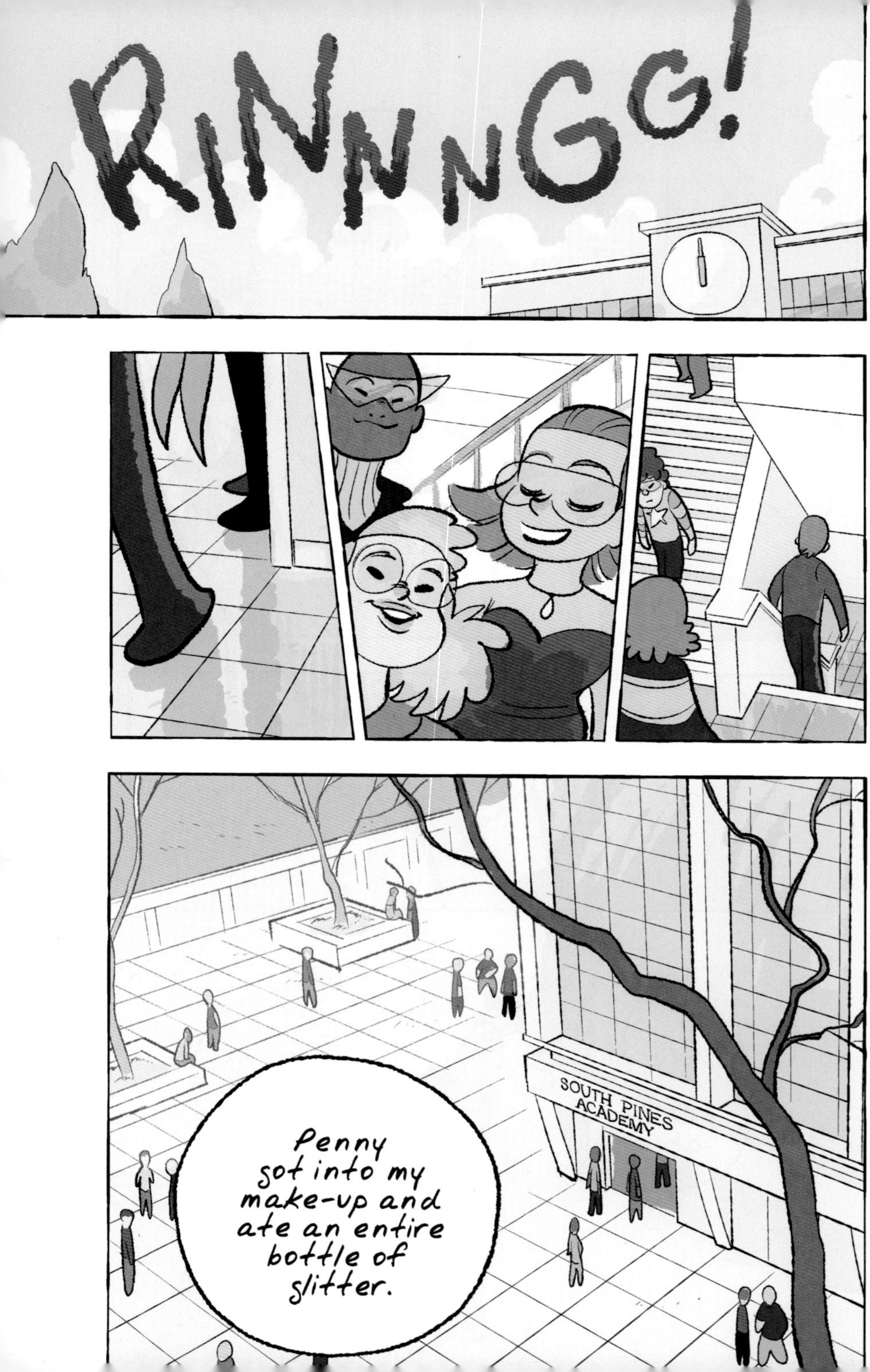
RINNGG!
SOUTH PINES ACADEMY
Penny got into my make-up and ate an entire bottle of glitter.

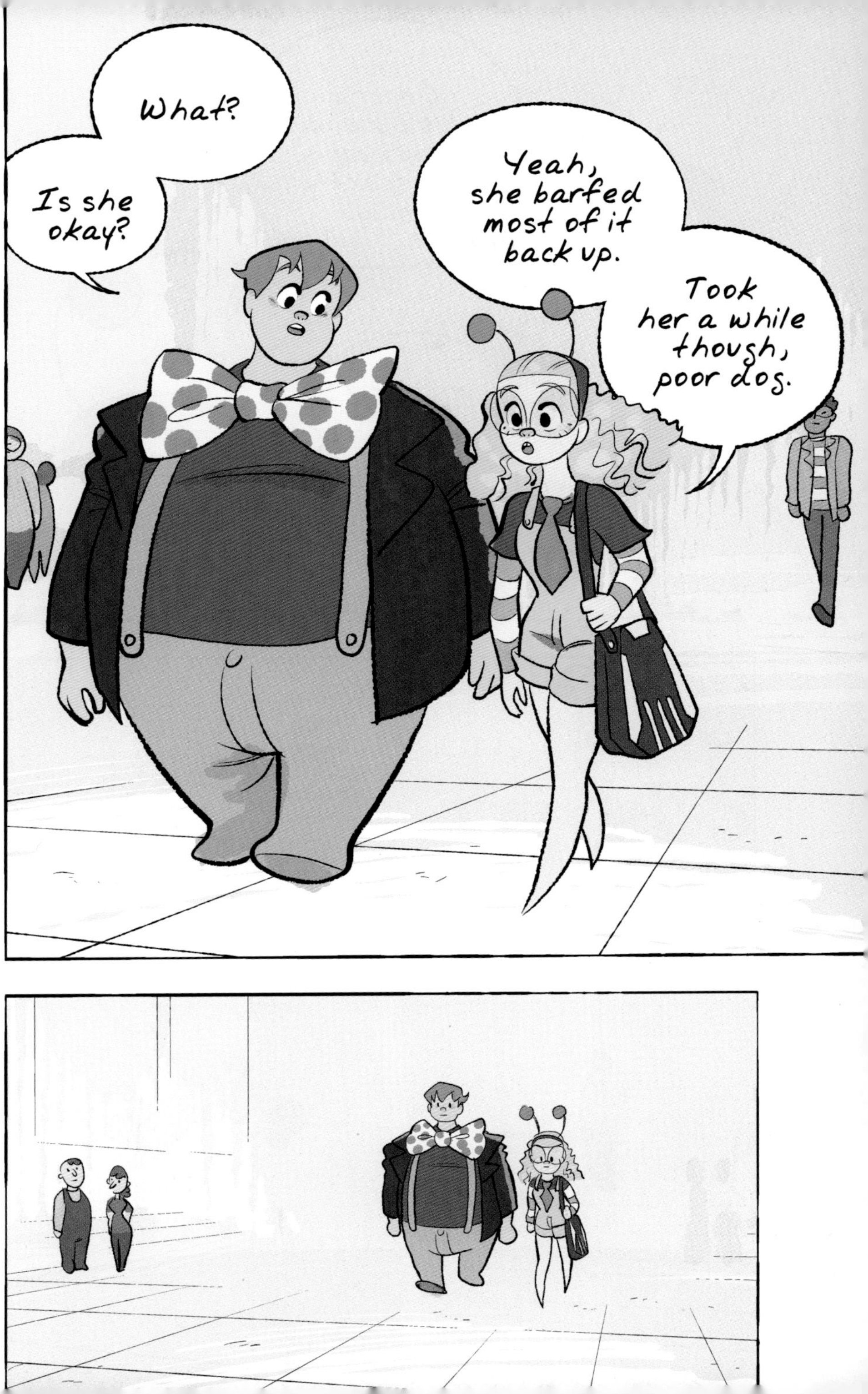
Is she okay?
What?
Yeah, she barfed most of it back up.
Took her a while though, poor dog.

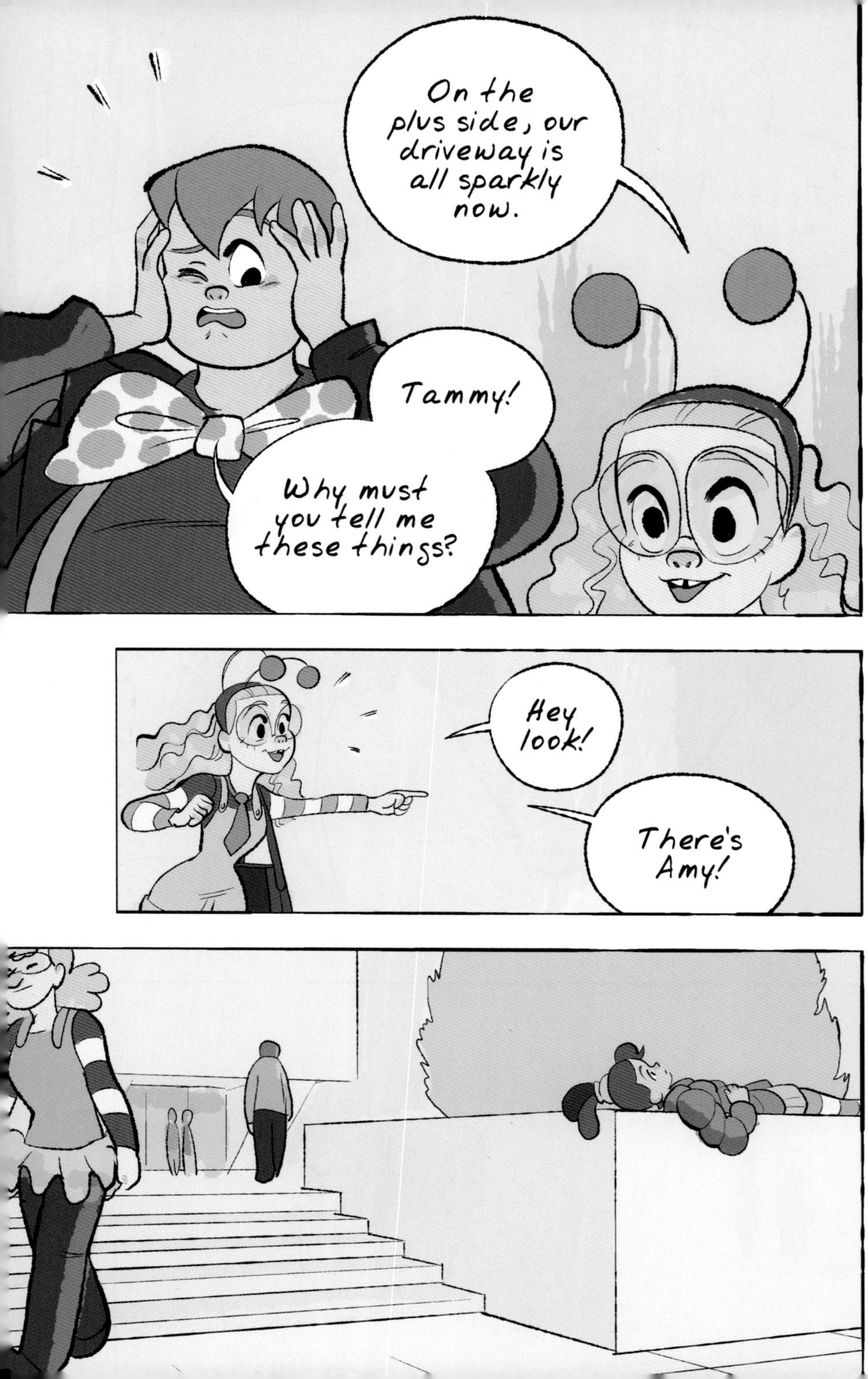
On the plus side, our driveway is all sparkly now.
Tammy!
Why must you tell me these things?
Hey look!
There's Amy!

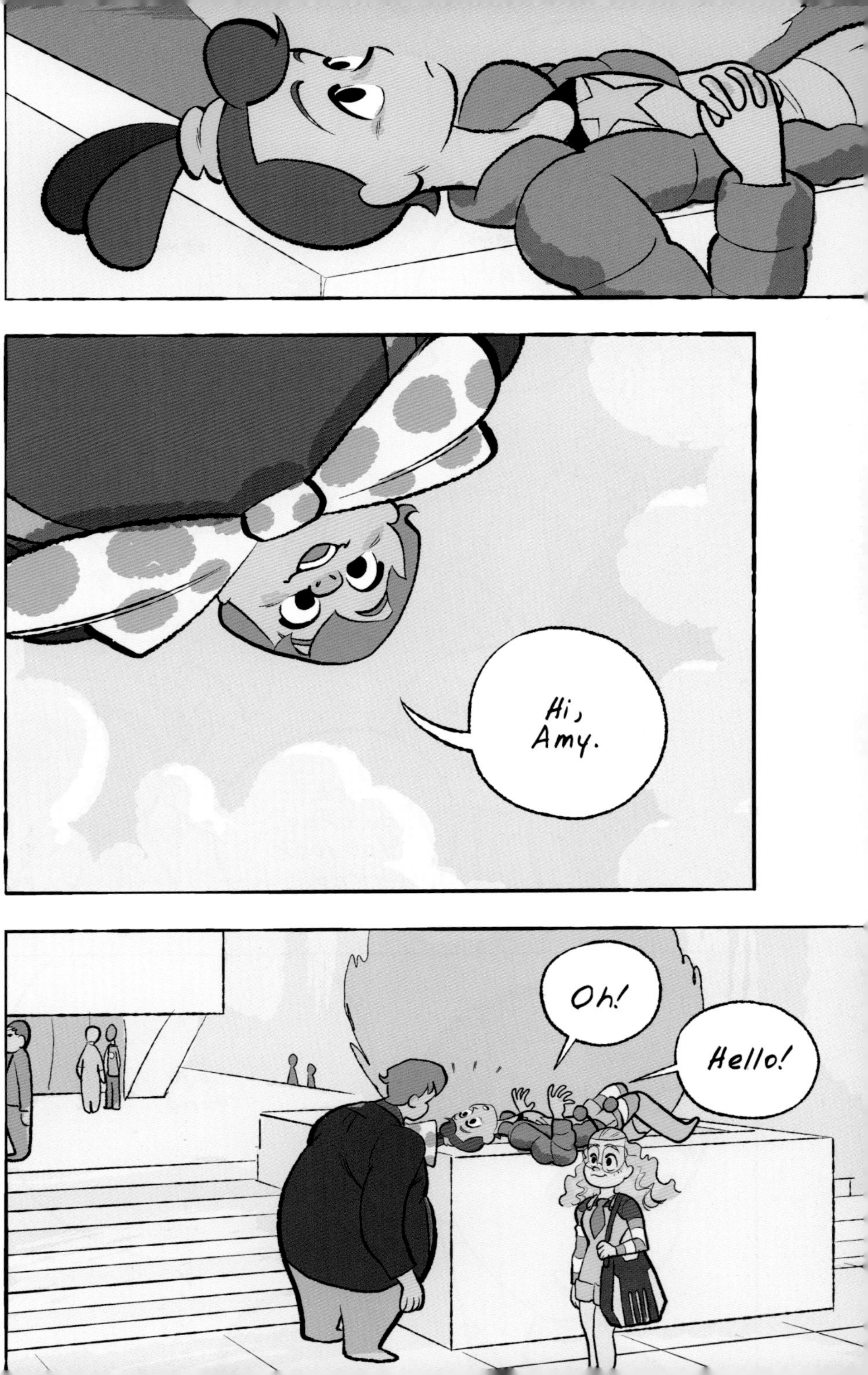
Hi, Amy.
Oh!
Hello!

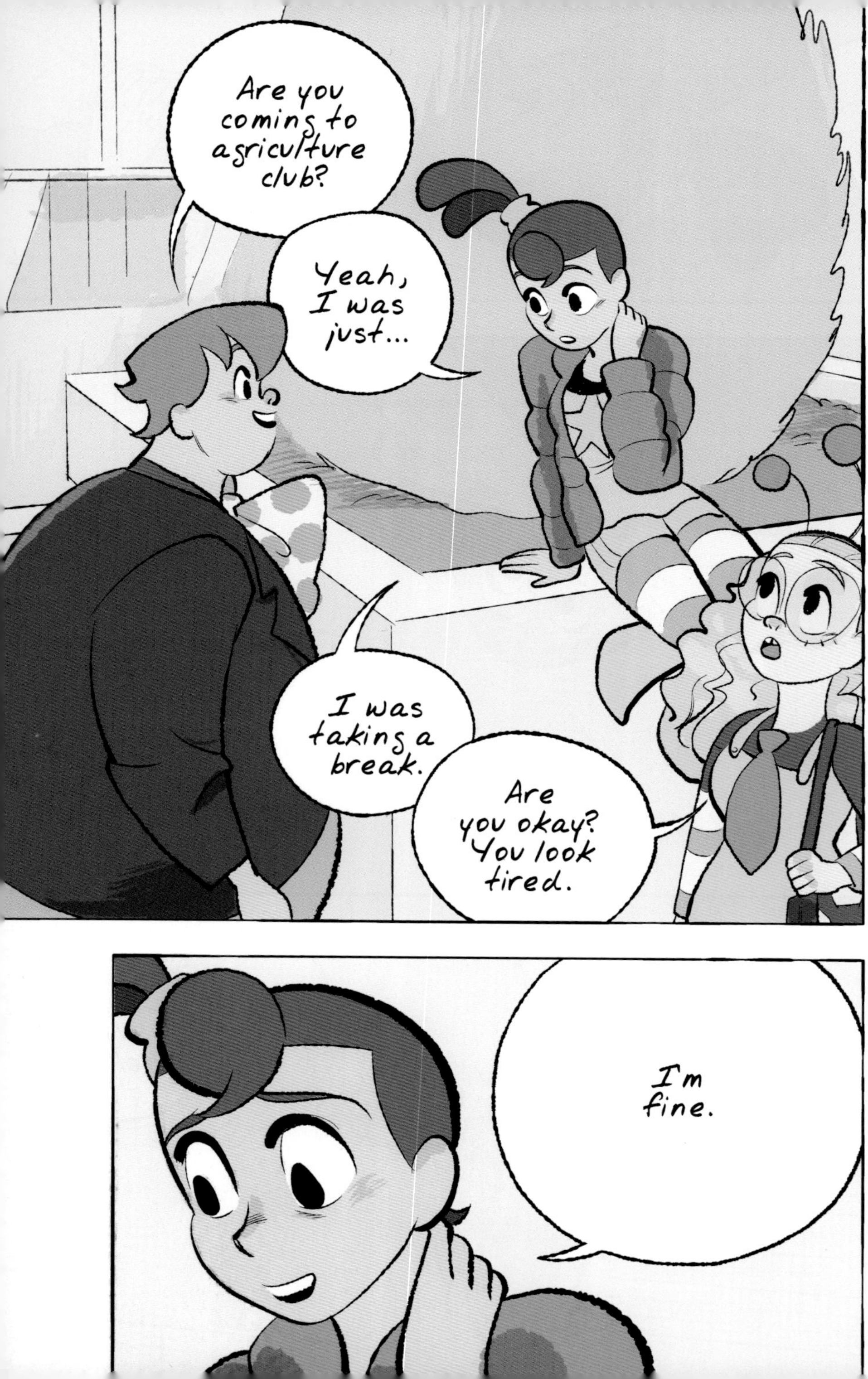
Are you coming to agriculture club?
Yeah, I was just...
I was taking a break.
Are you okay? You look tired.
I'm fine.

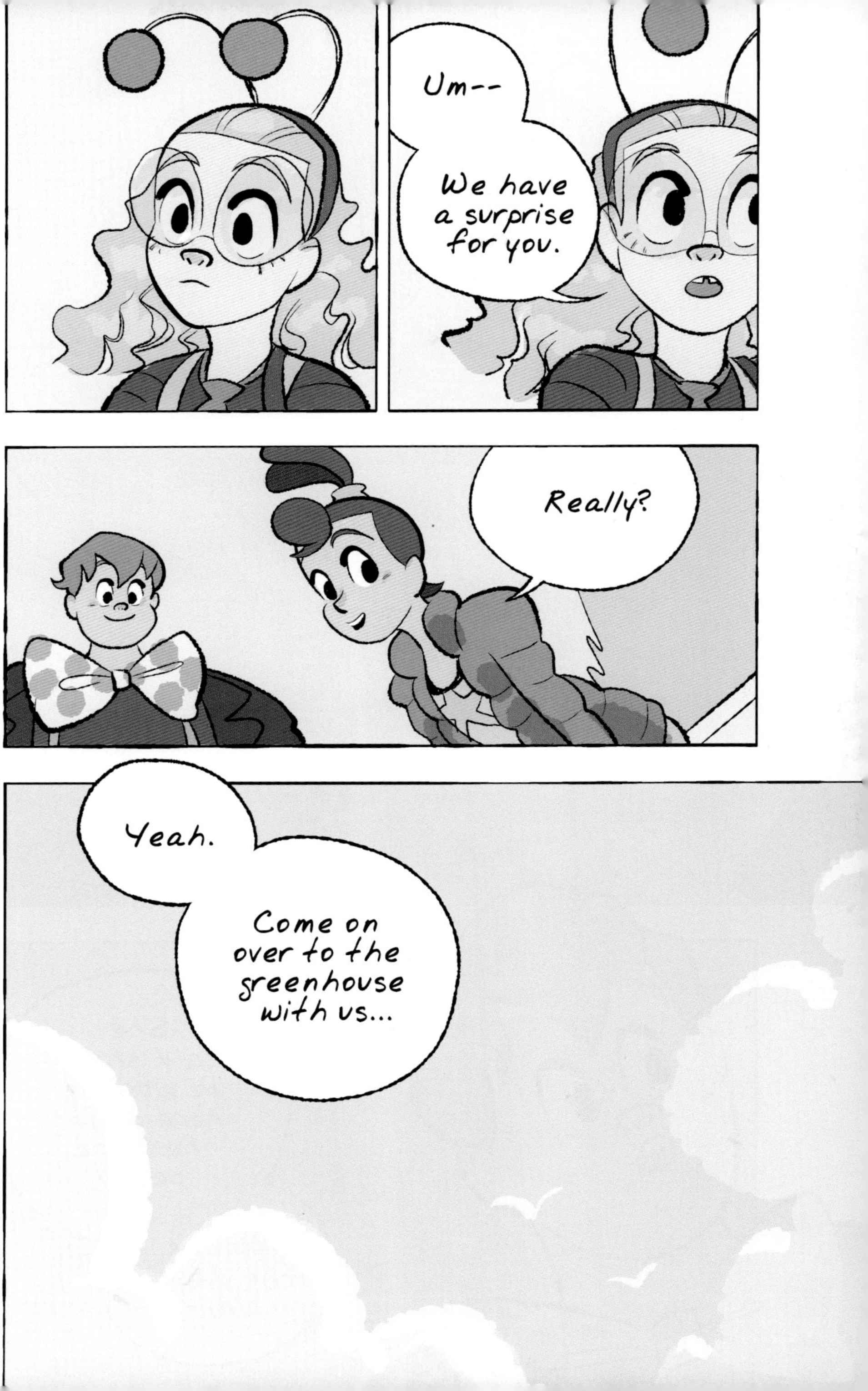
Um--
We have a surprise for you.
Really?
Yeah.
Come on over to the greenhouse with us...

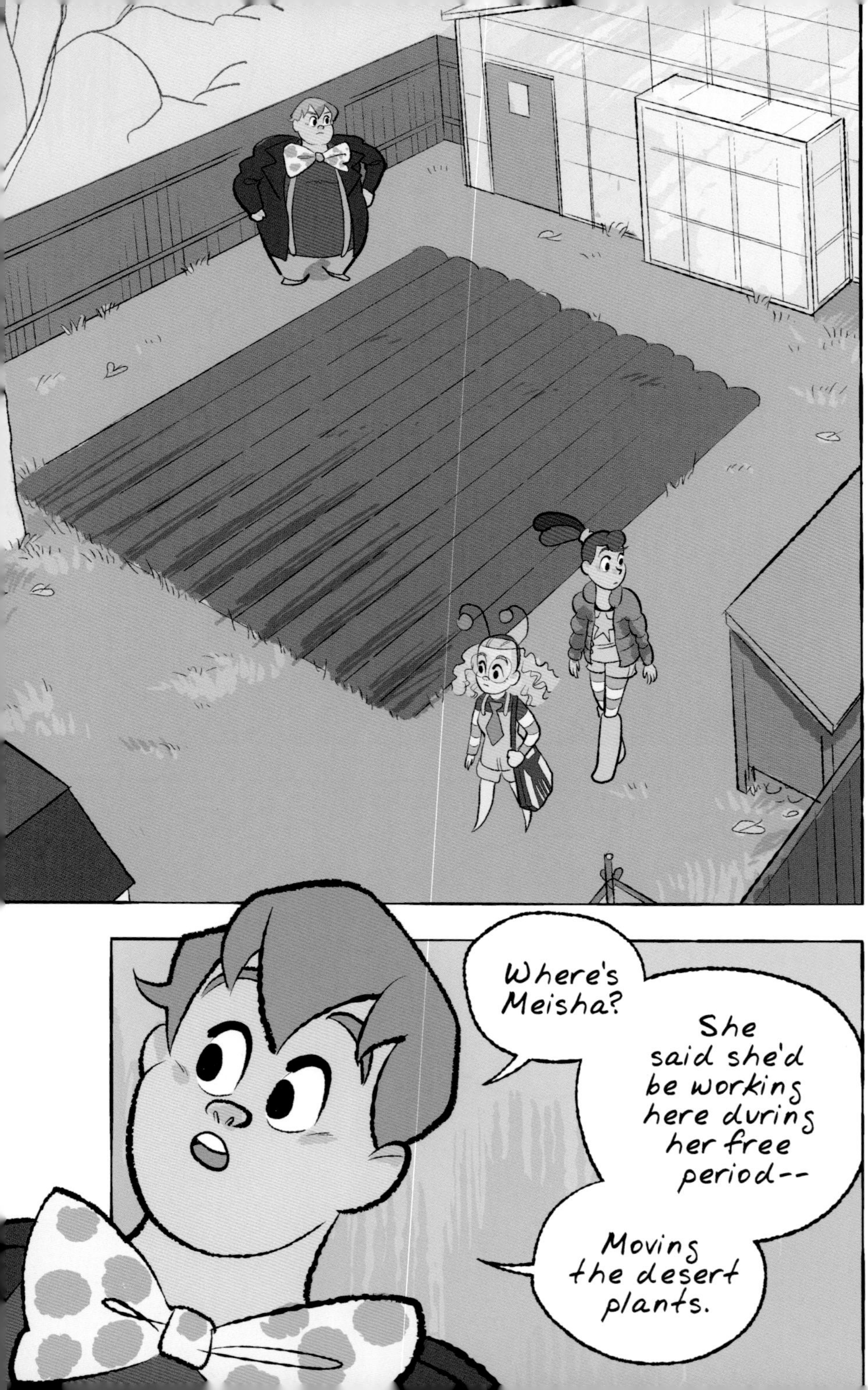
Where's Meisha?
She said she'd be working here during her free period--
Moving the desert plants.

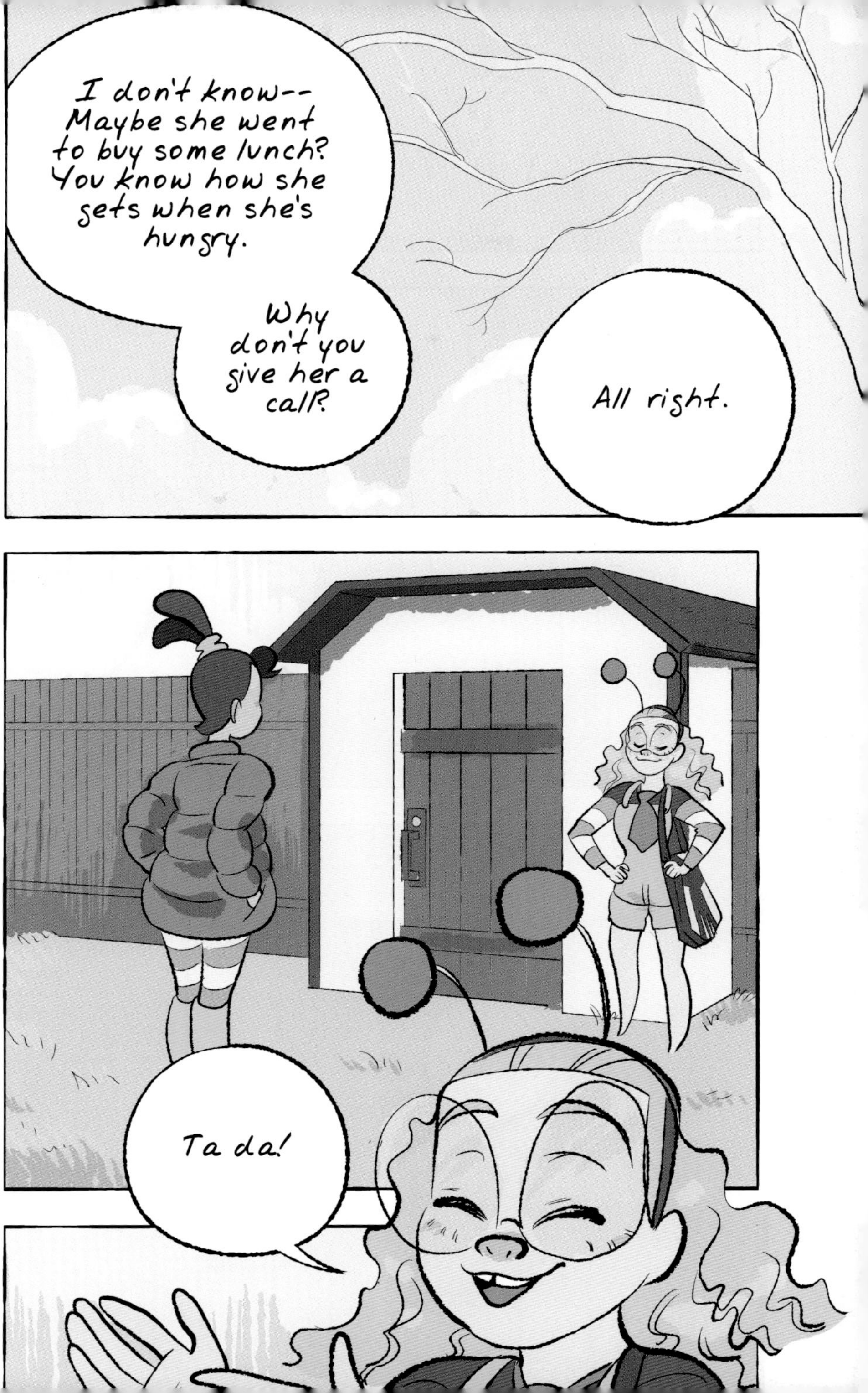
I don't know-- Maybe she went to buy some lunch? You know how she gets when she's hungry.
Why don't you give her a call?
All right.
Ta da!

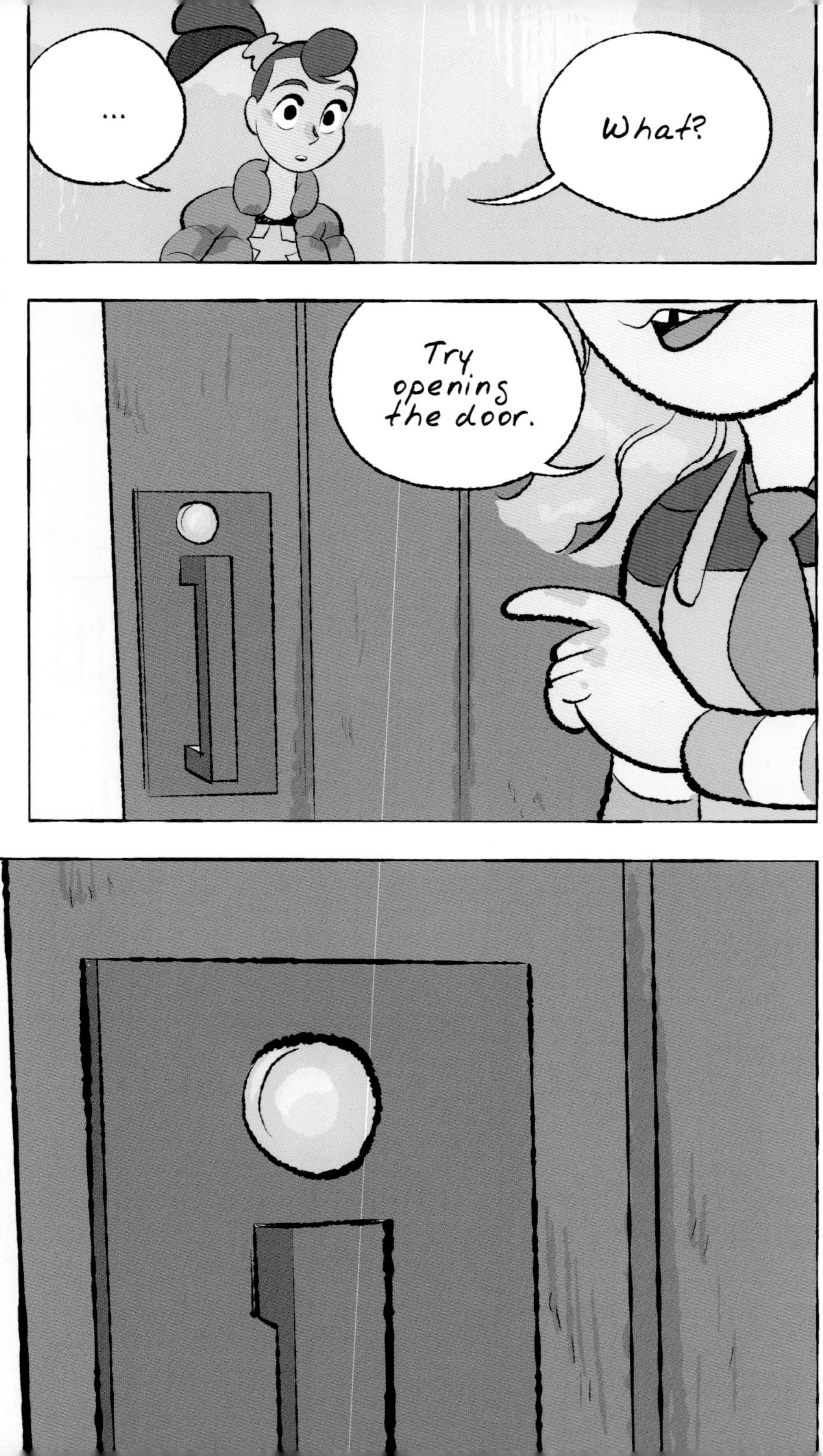
...
What?
Try opening the door.

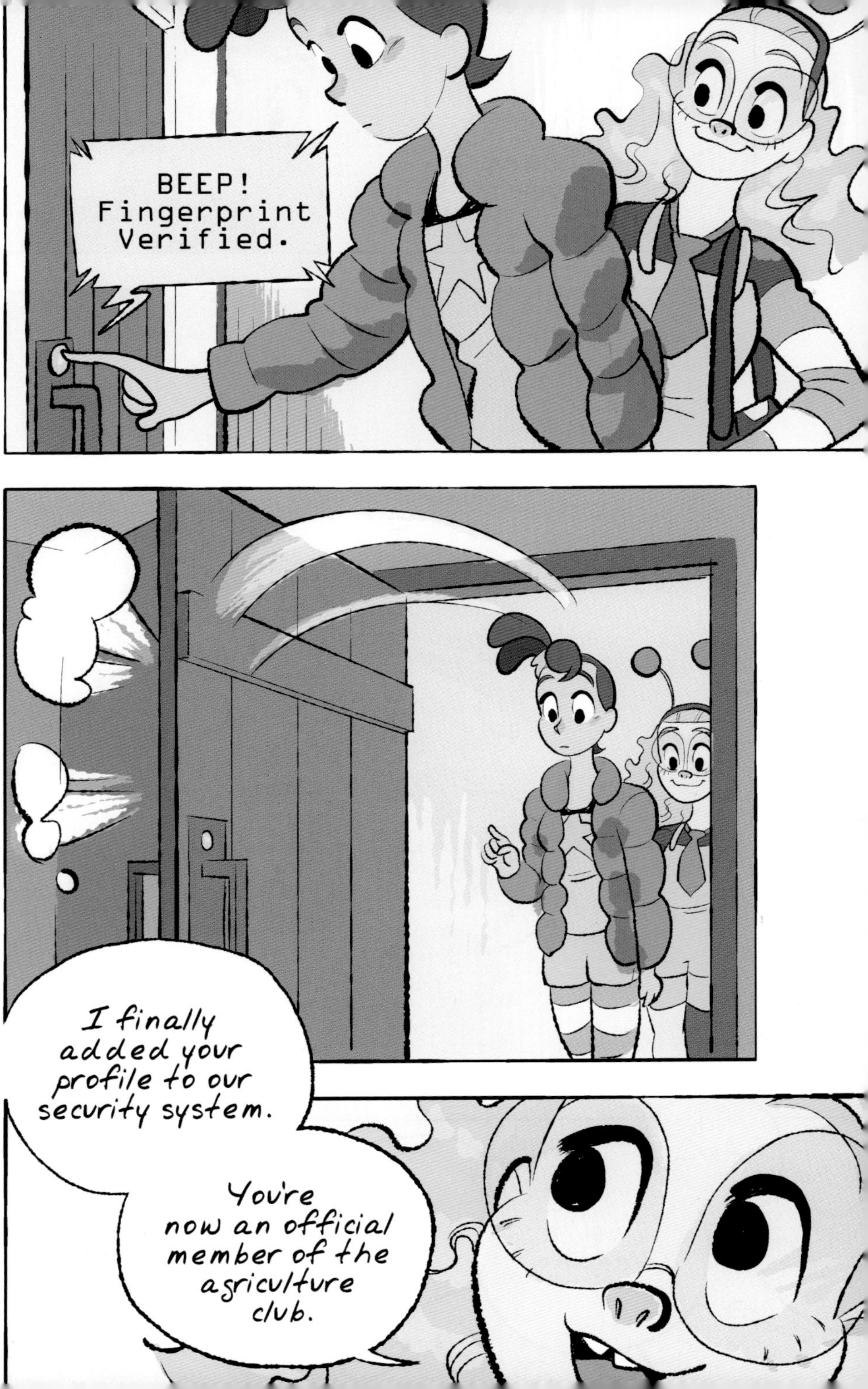
BEEP! Fingerprint Verified.
I finally added your profile to our security system.
You're now an official member of the agriculture club.

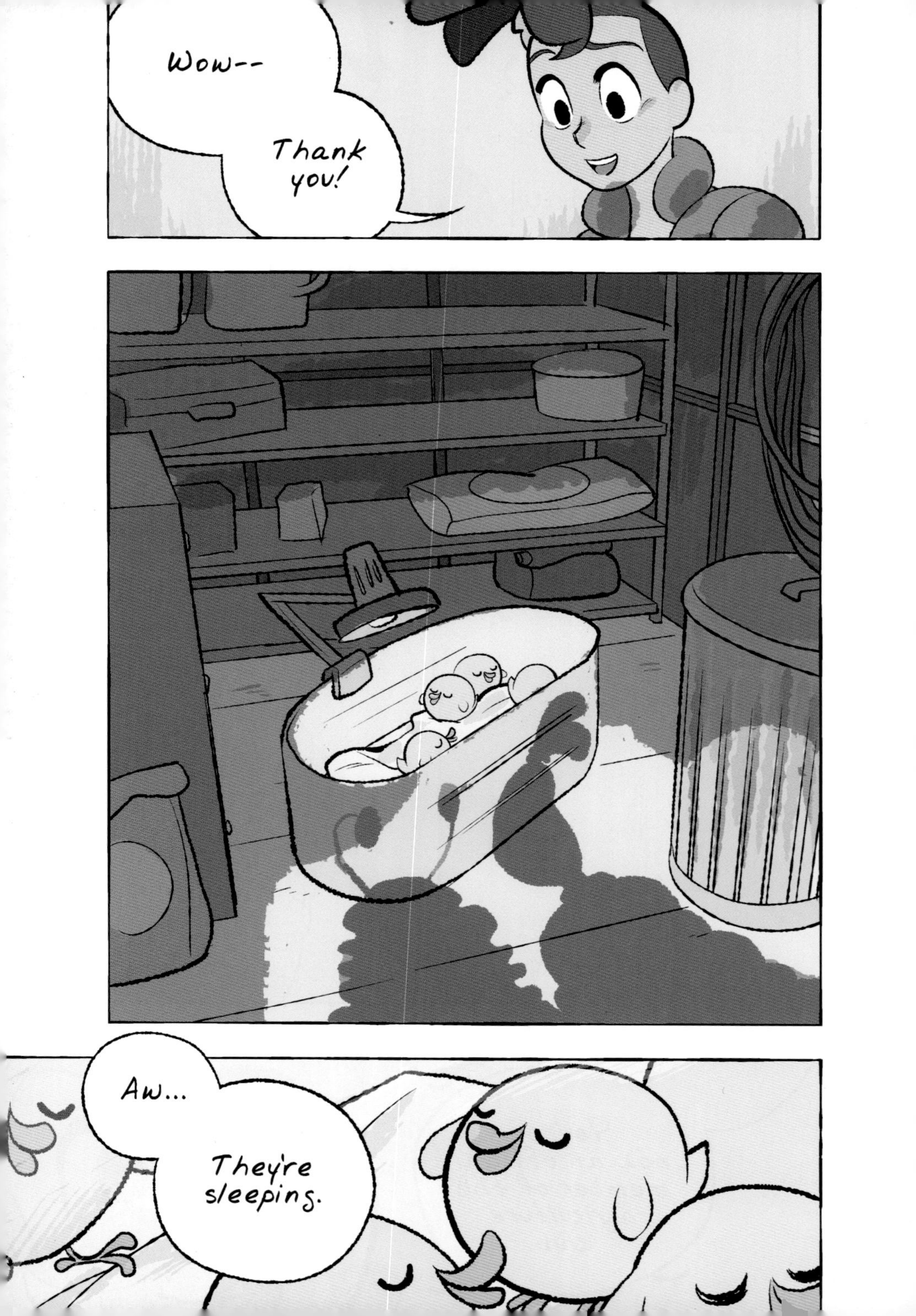
Wow--
Thank you!
Aw...
They're sleeping.

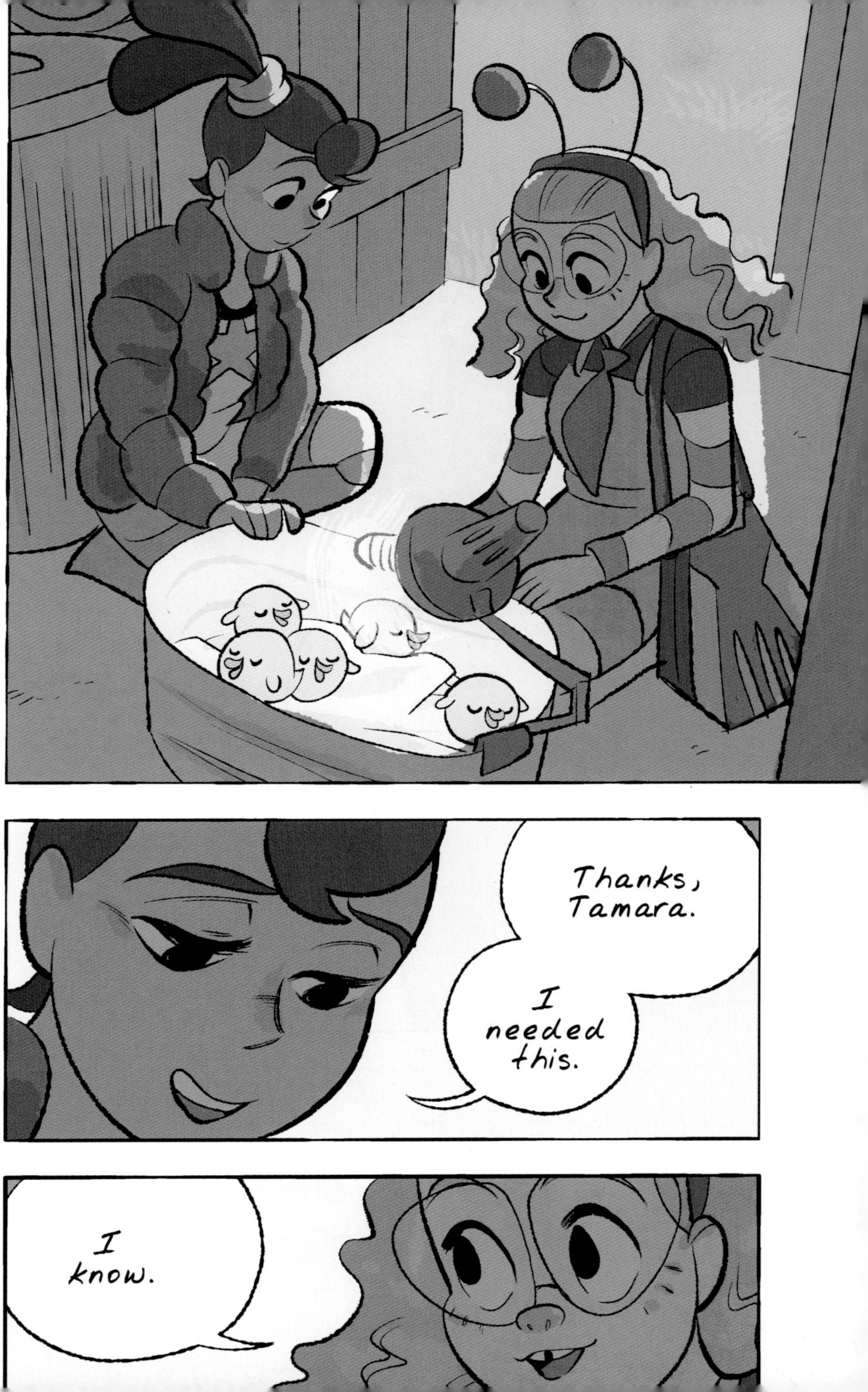
Thanks, Tamara.
I needed this.
I know.

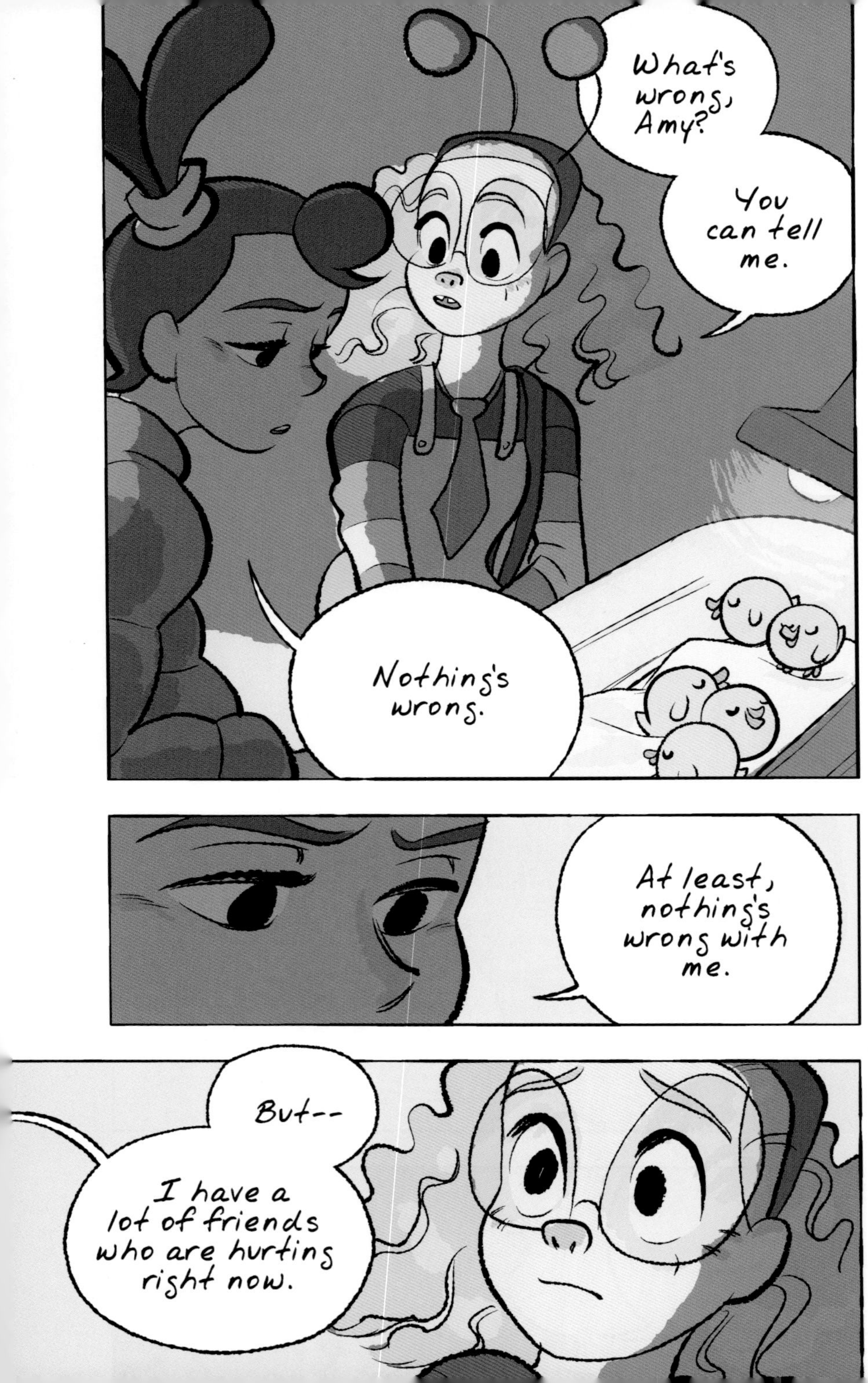
What's wrong, Amy?
You can tell me.
Nothing's wrong.
At least, nothing's wrong with me.
But--
I have a lot of friends who are hurting right now.

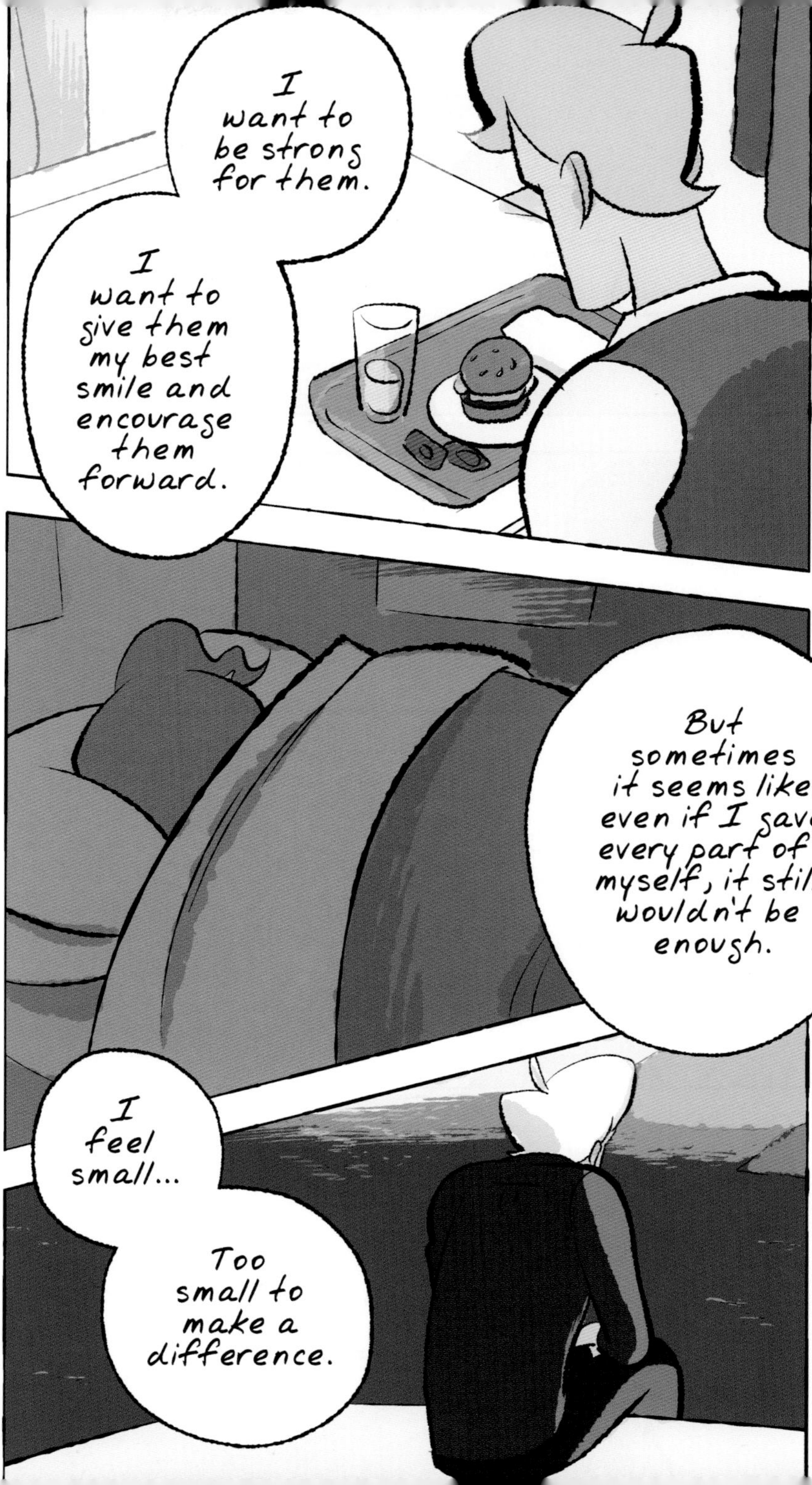
I want to be strong for them.
I want to give them my best smile and encourage them forward.
But sometimes it seems like even if I gave every part of myself, it still wouldn't be enough.
I feel small...
Too small to make a difference.

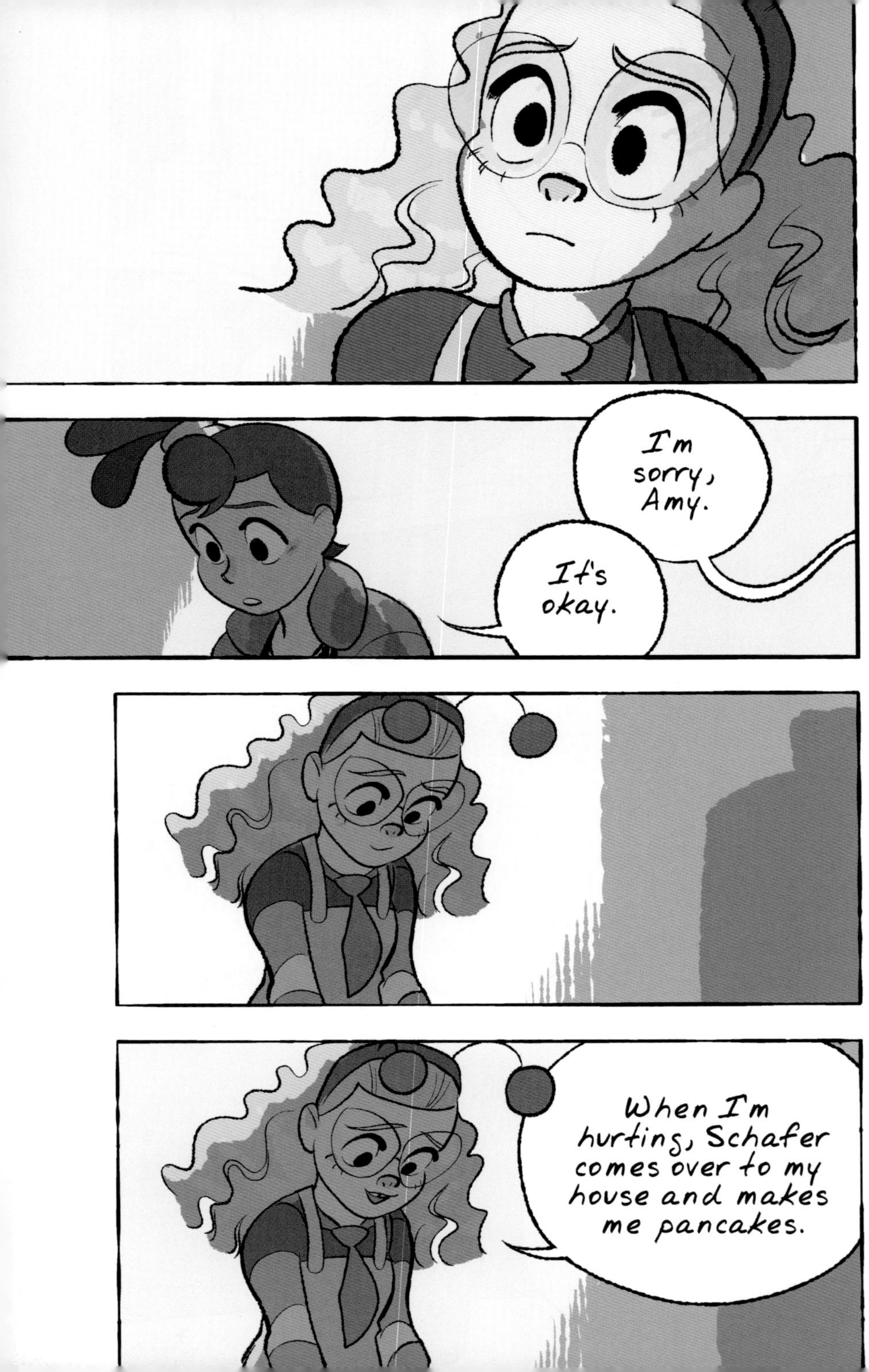
I'm sorry, Amy.
It's okay.
When I'm hurting, Schafer comes over to my house and makes me pancakes.

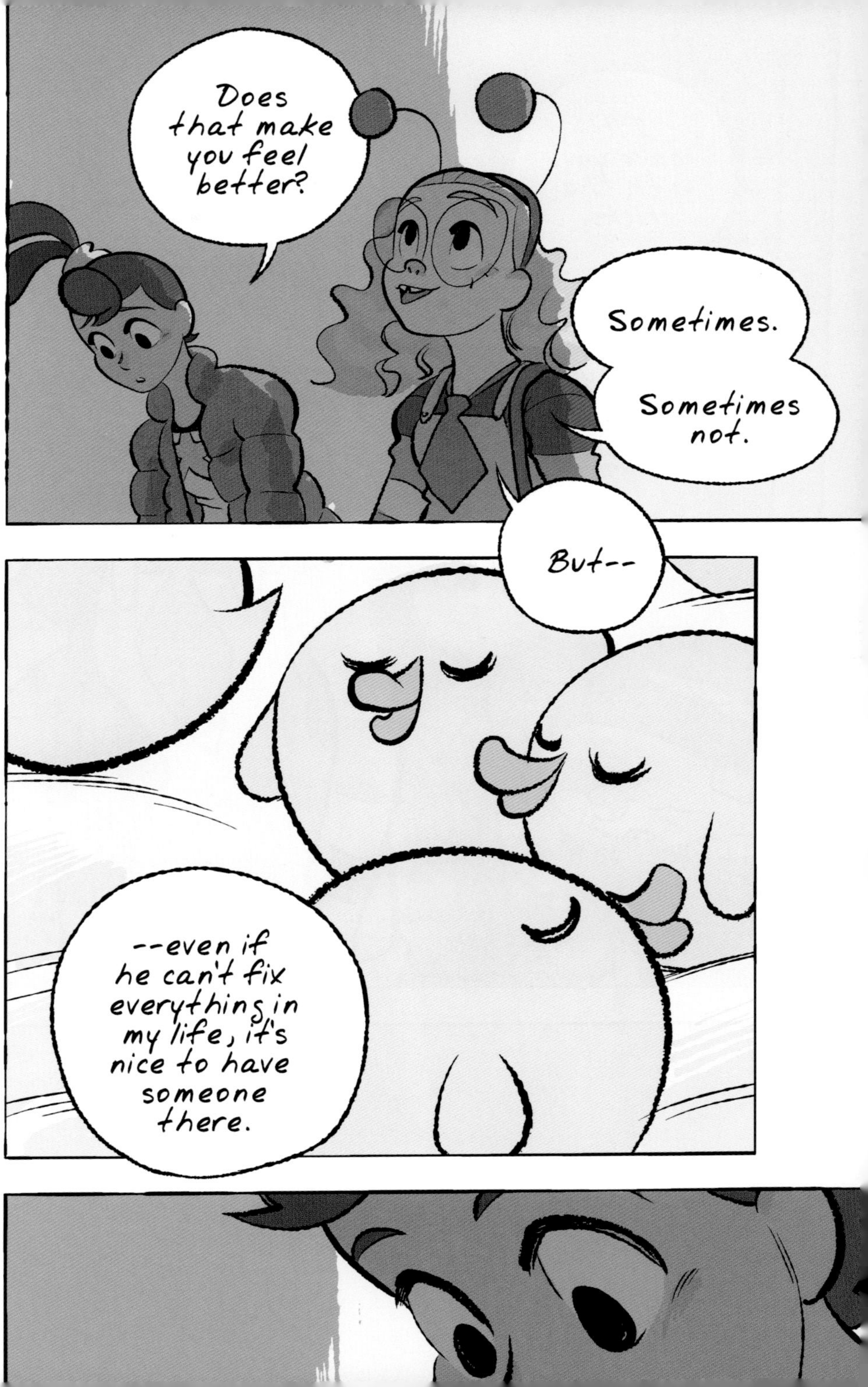
Does that make you feel better?
Sometimes.
Sometimes not.
But--
--even if he can't fix everything in my life, it's nice to have someone there.

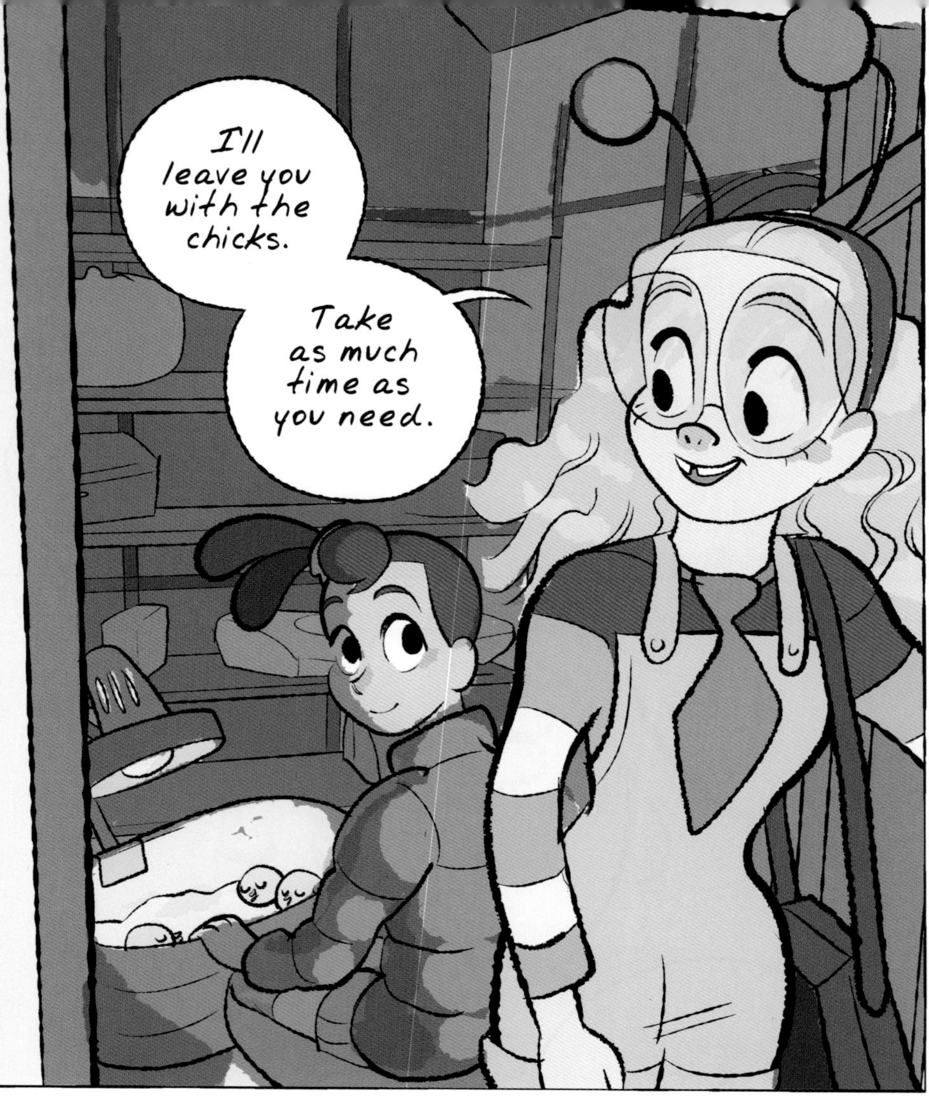
I'll leave you with the chicks.
Take as much time as you need.

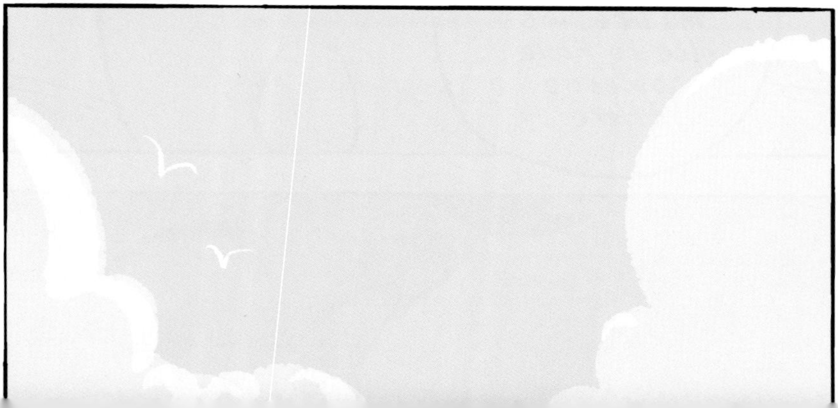

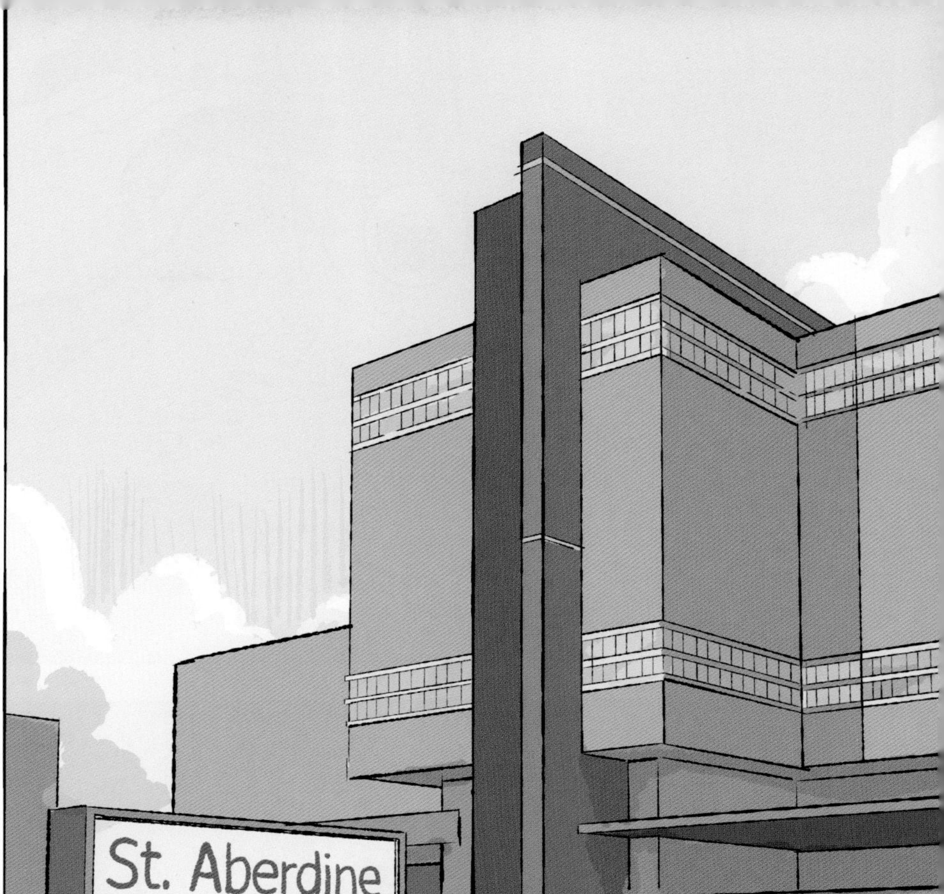
St. Aberdine
Memorial
Hospital

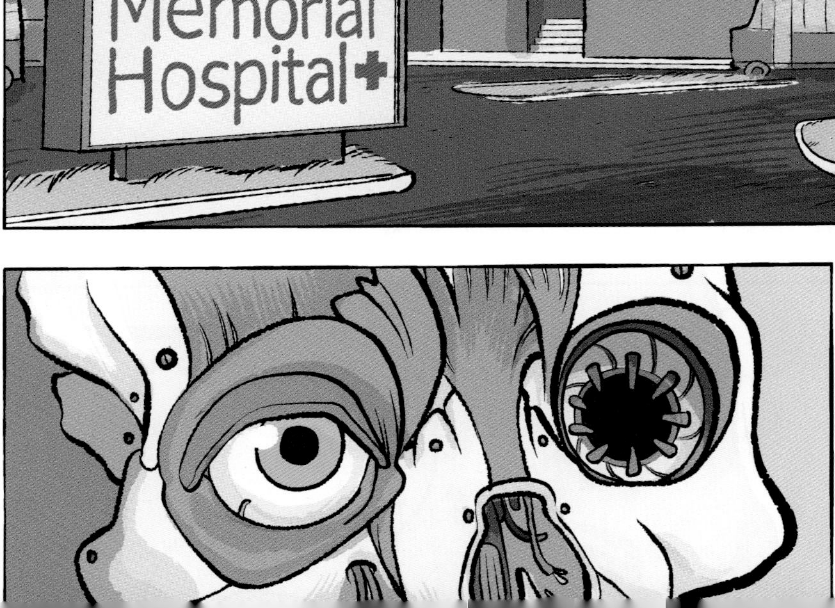

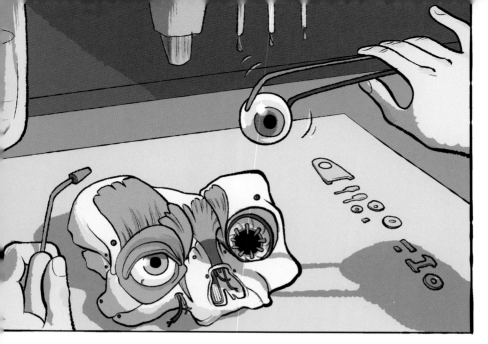

RINNG

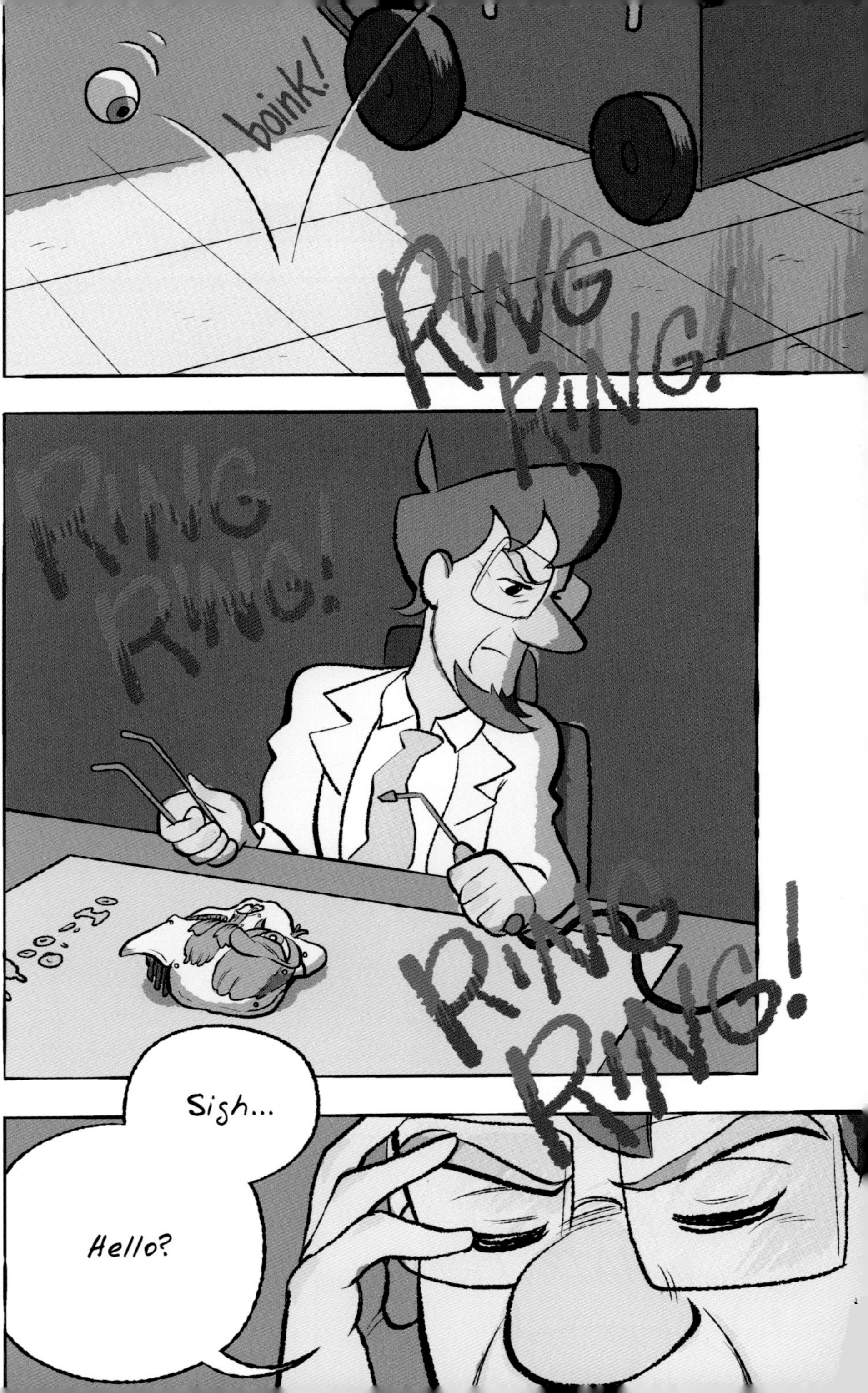
boink!
RING RING!
RING RING!
RING RING!
Sigh...
Hello?

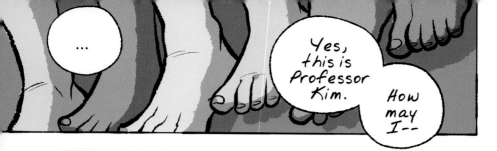

...

Yes, this is Professor Kim.

How may I--

HE WHAT?

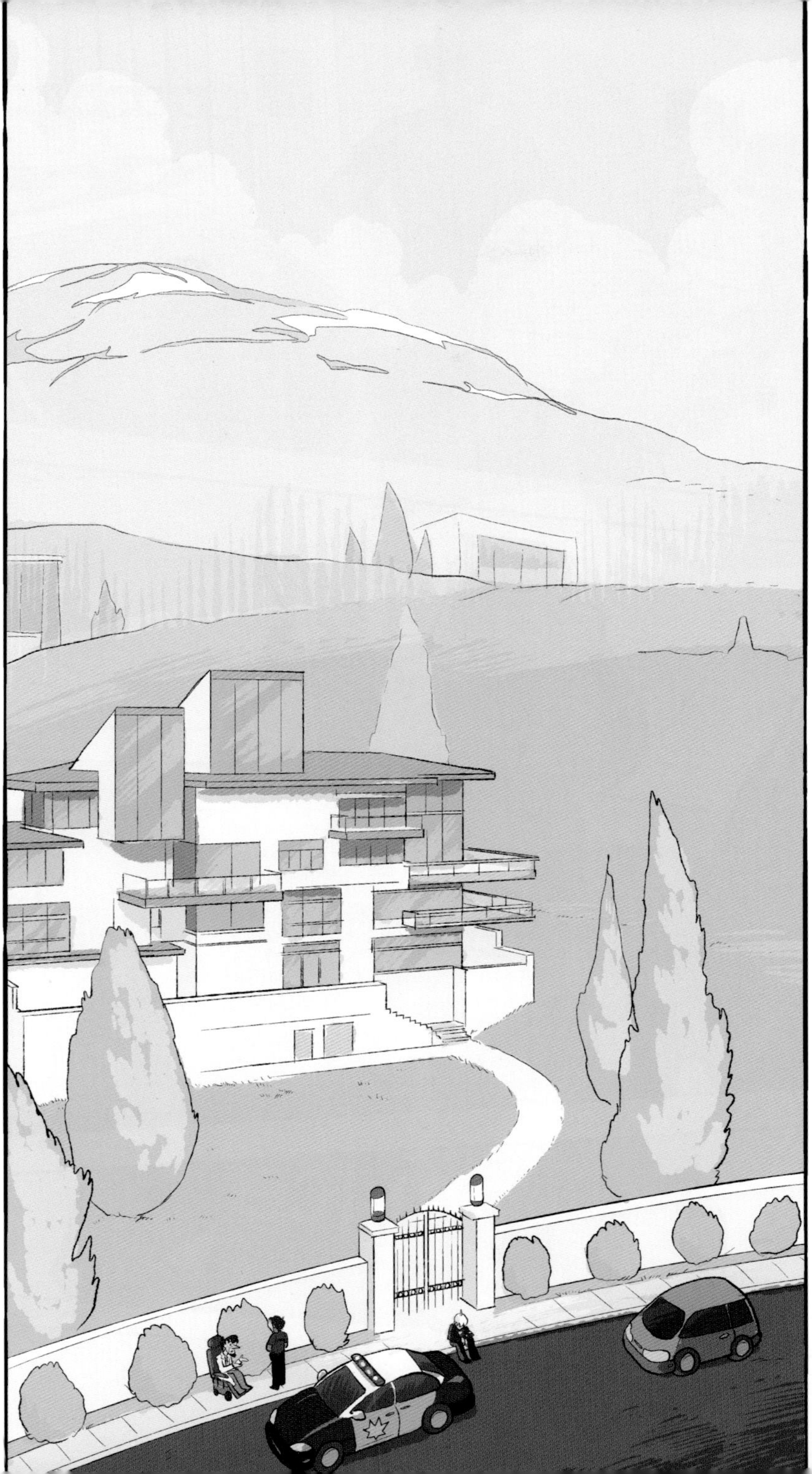

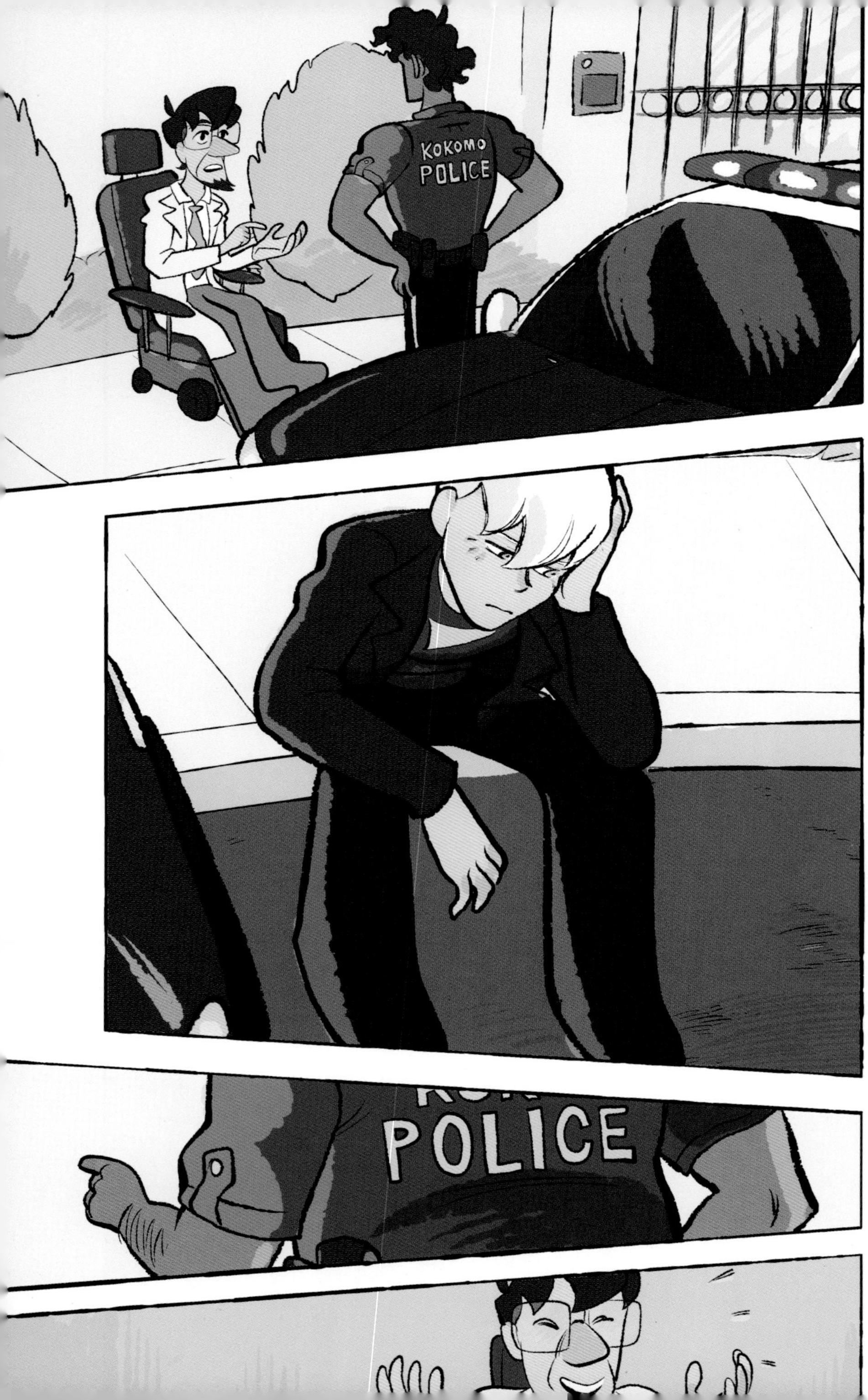
KOKOMO
POLICE
POLICE

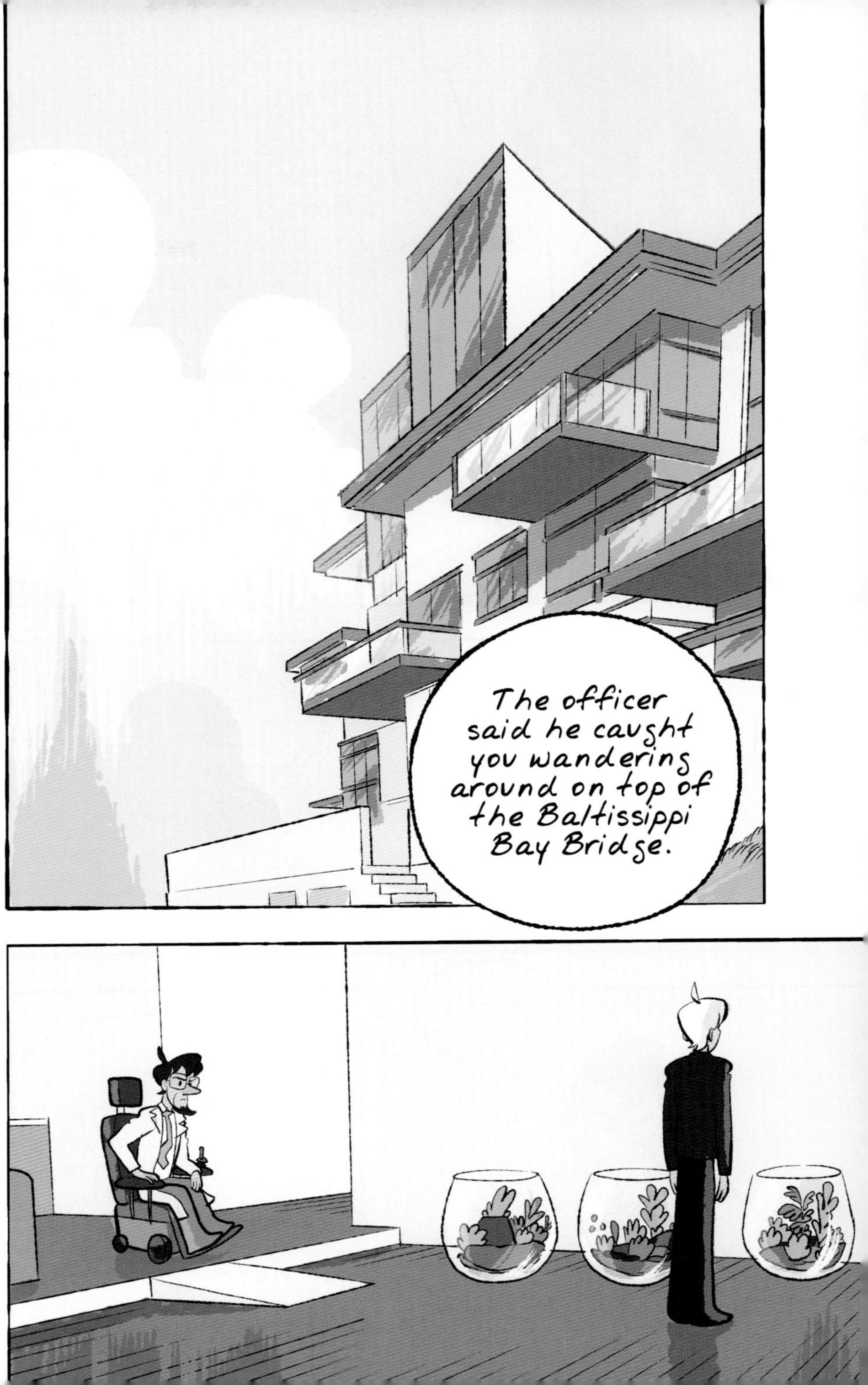
The officer said he caught you wandering around on top of the Baltissippi Bay Bridge.

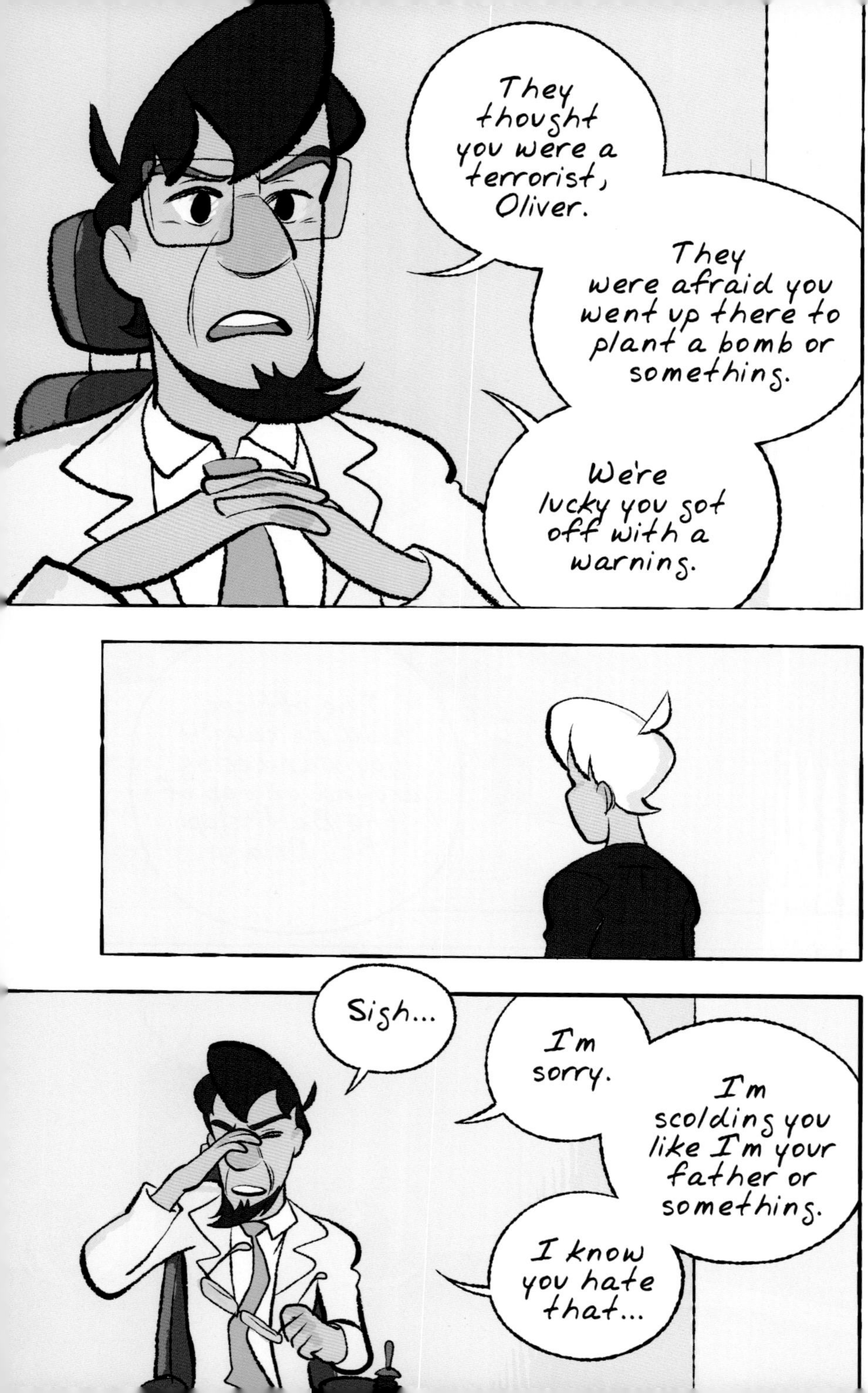
They thought you were a terrorist, Oliver.
They were afraid you went up there to plant a bomb or something.
We're lucky you got off with a warning.
Sigh...
I'm sorry.
I'm scolding you like I'm your father or something.
I know you hate that...

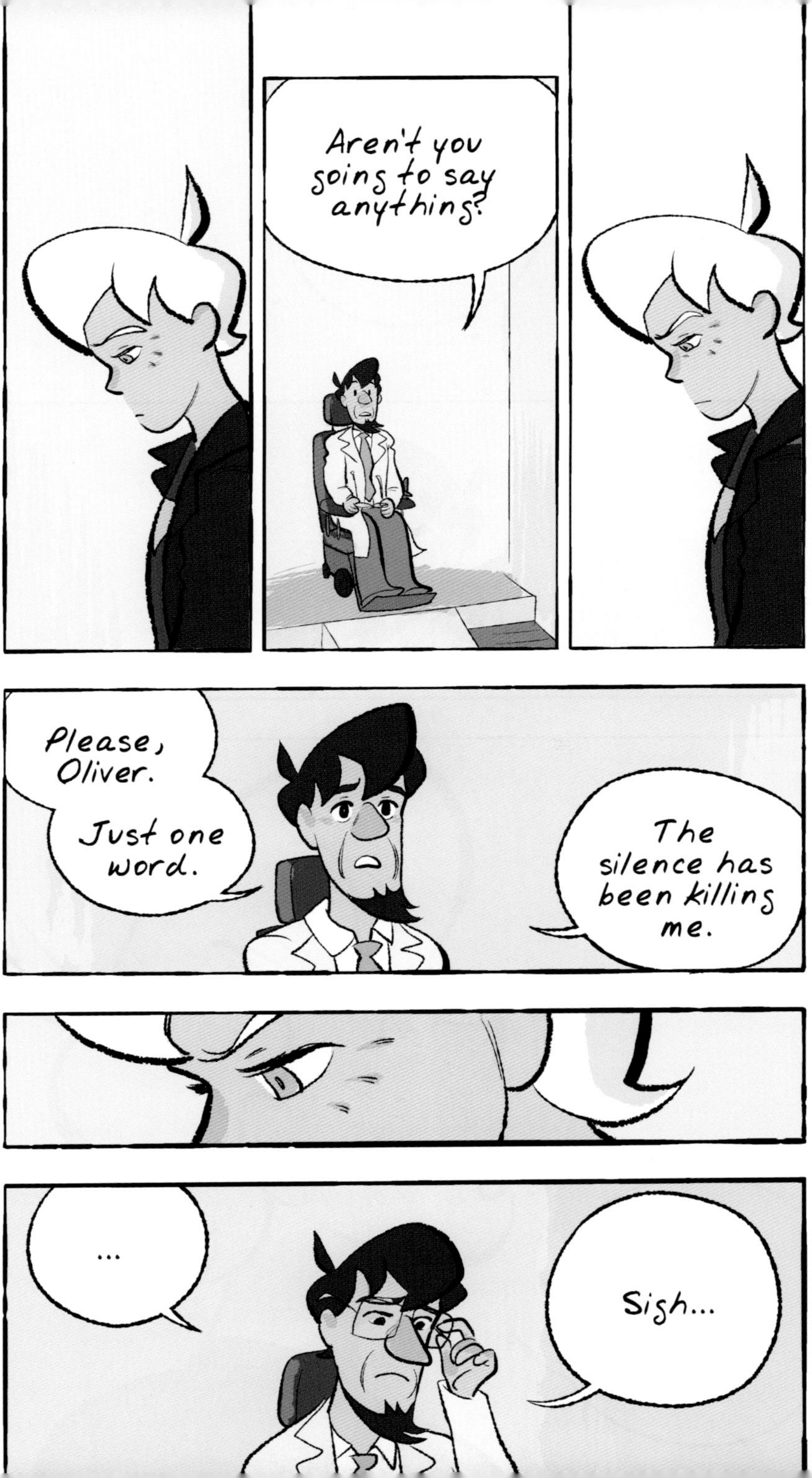
Aren't you going to say anything?
Please, Oliver.
Just one word.
The silence has been killing me.
...
Sigh...

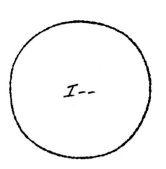

I--

I want to leave Kokomo.

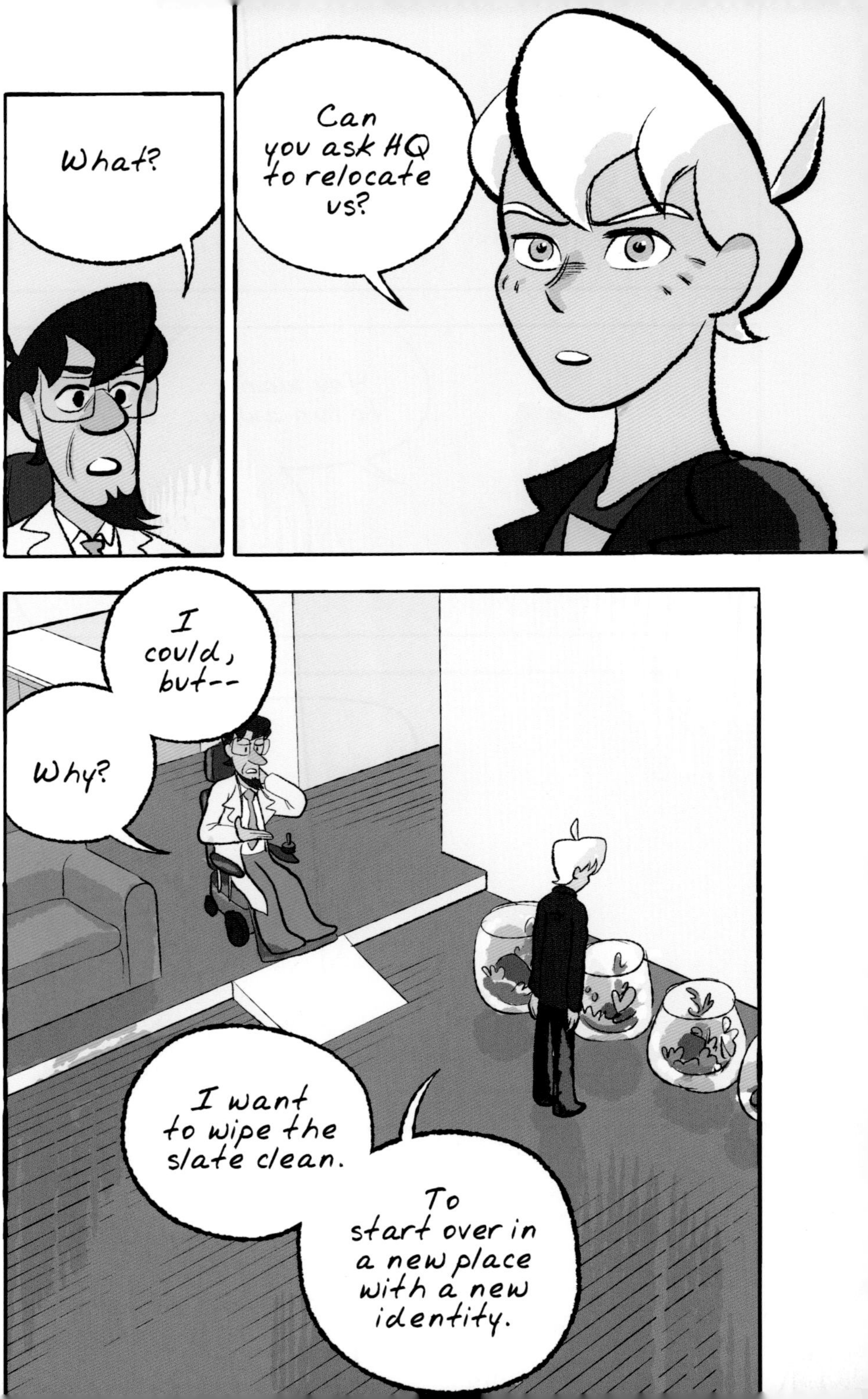
What?
Can you ask HQ to relocate us?
I could, but--
Why?
I want to wipe the slate clean.
To start over in a new place with a new identity.

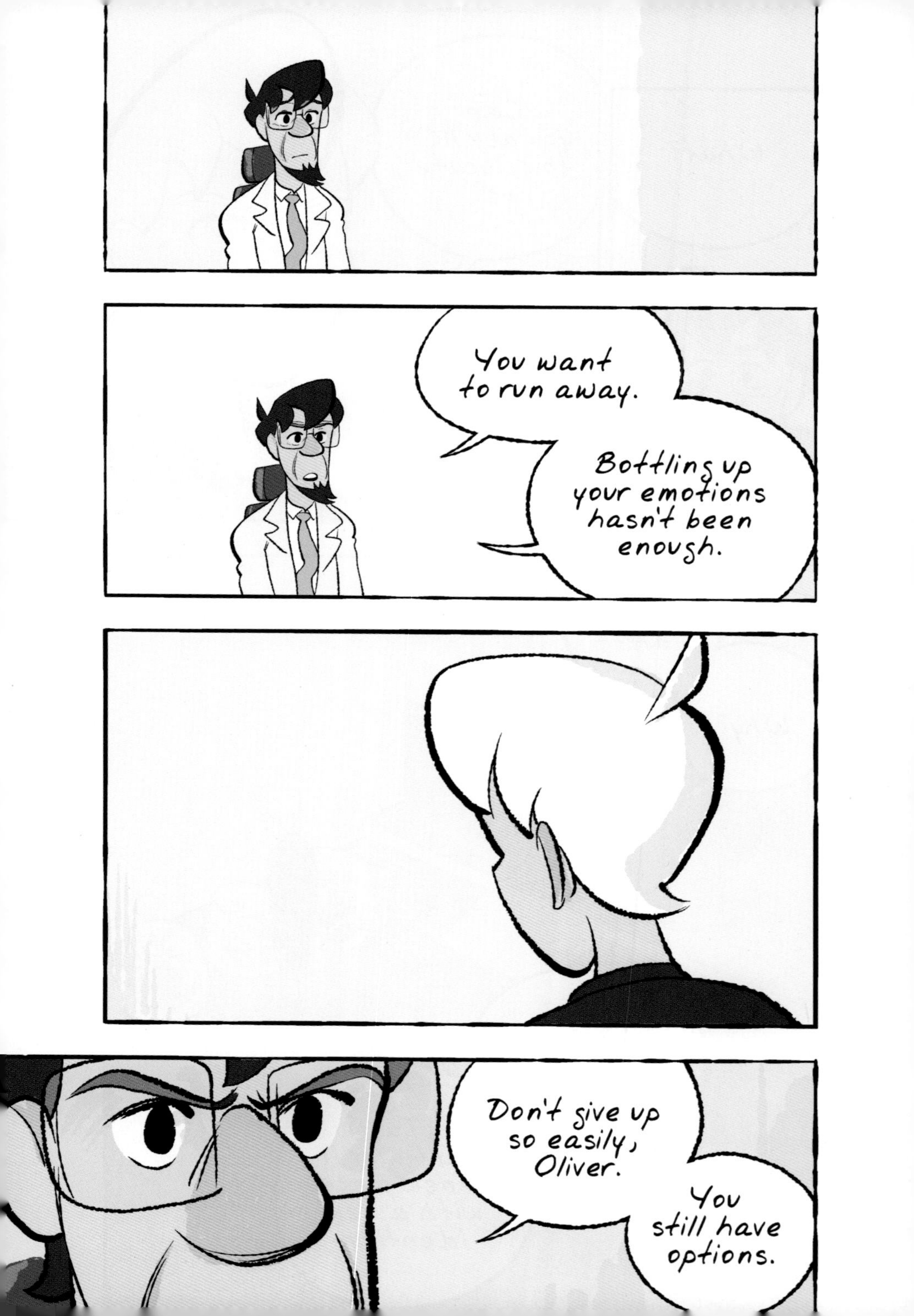
You want to run away.
Bottling up your emotions hasn't been enough.
Don't give up so easily, Oliver.
You still have options.

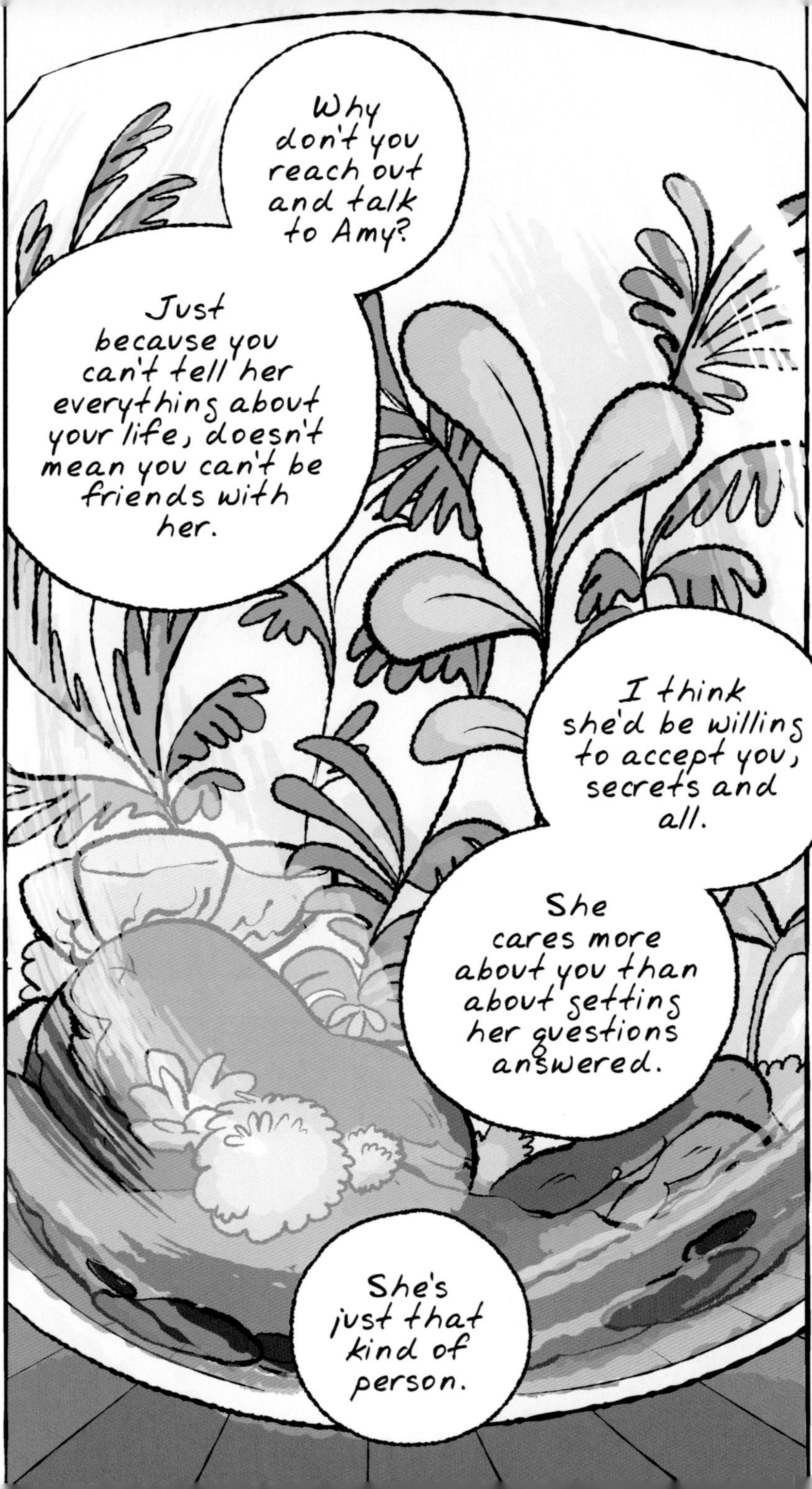
Why don't you reach out and talk to Amy?
Just because you can't tell her everything about your life, doesn't mean you can't be friends with her.
I think she'd be willing to accept you, secrets and all.
She cares more about you than about getting her questions answered.
She's just that kind of person.

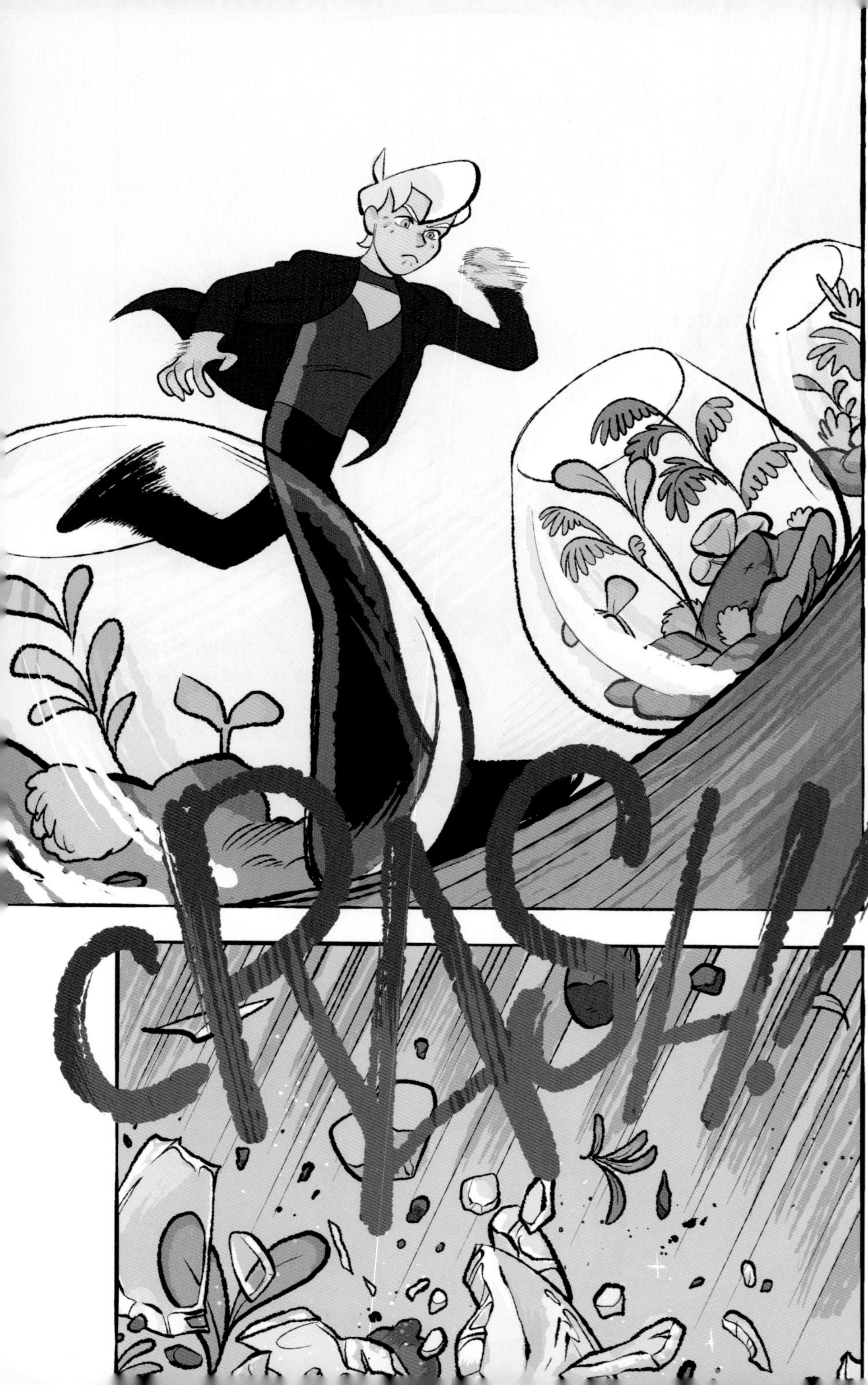
CRASH!!

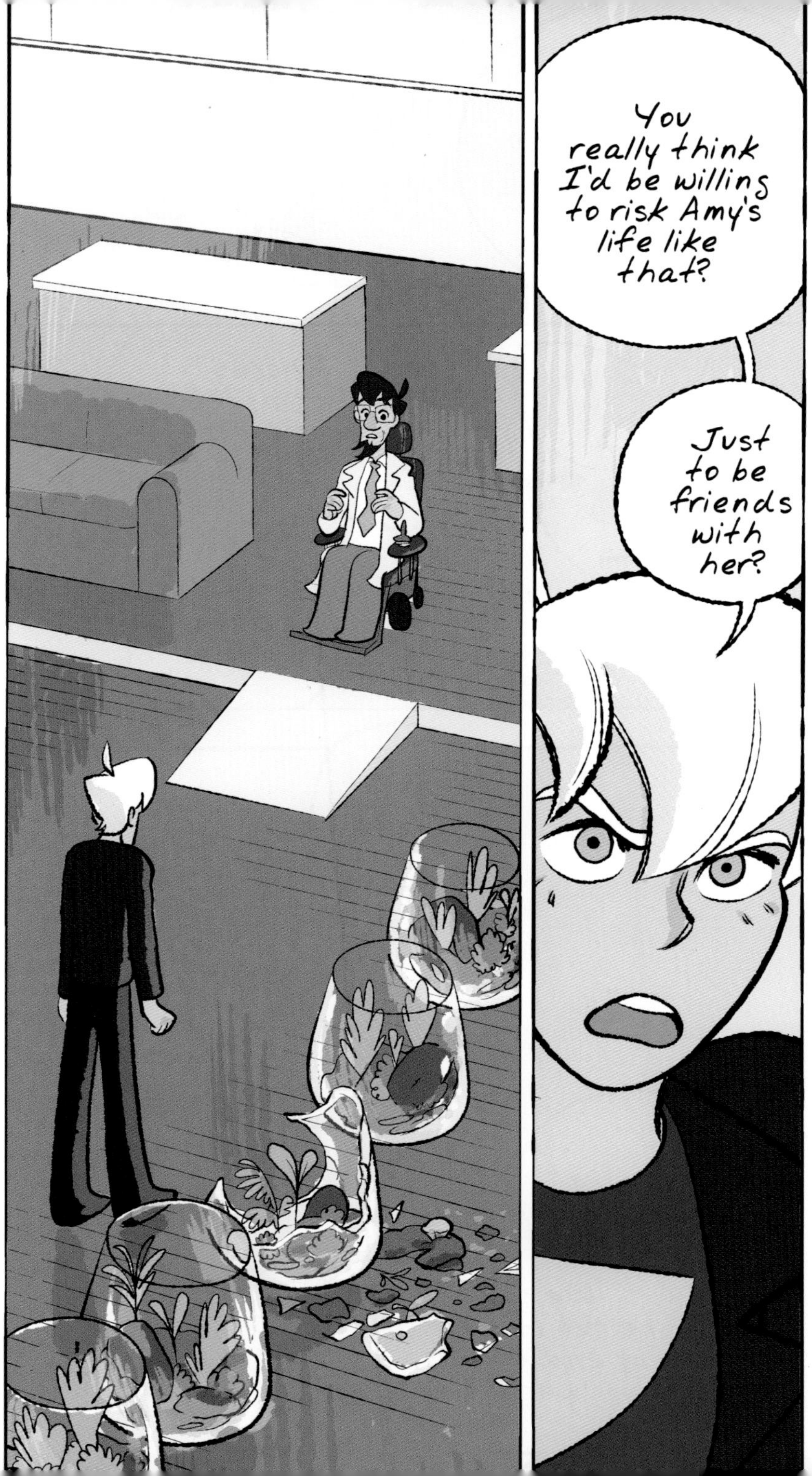
You really think I'd be willing to risk Amy's life like that?
Just to be friends with her?

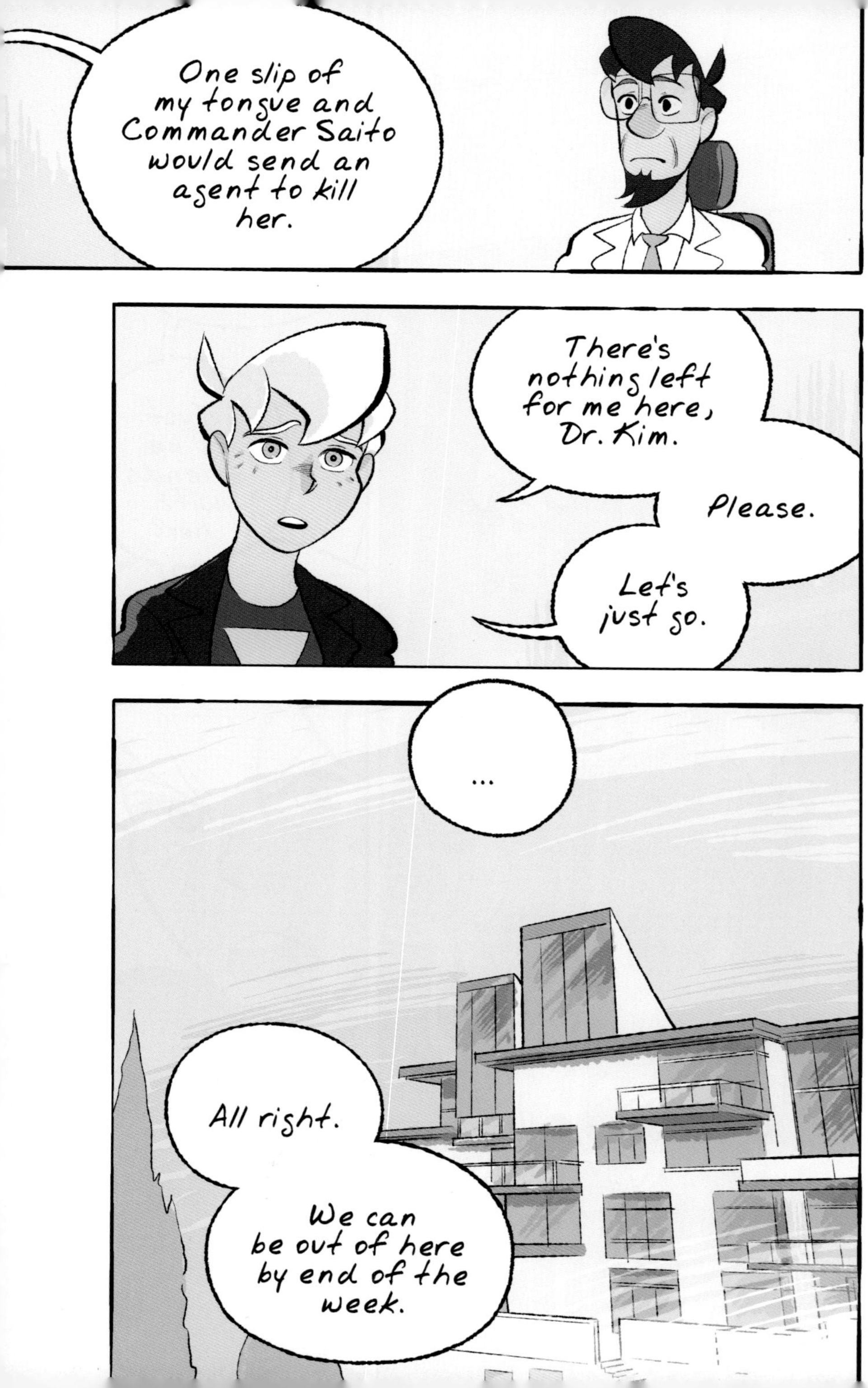
One slip of my tongue and Commander Saito would send an agent to kill her.
There's nothing left for me here, Dr. Kim.
Please.
Let's just go.
...
All right.
We can be out of here by end of the week.

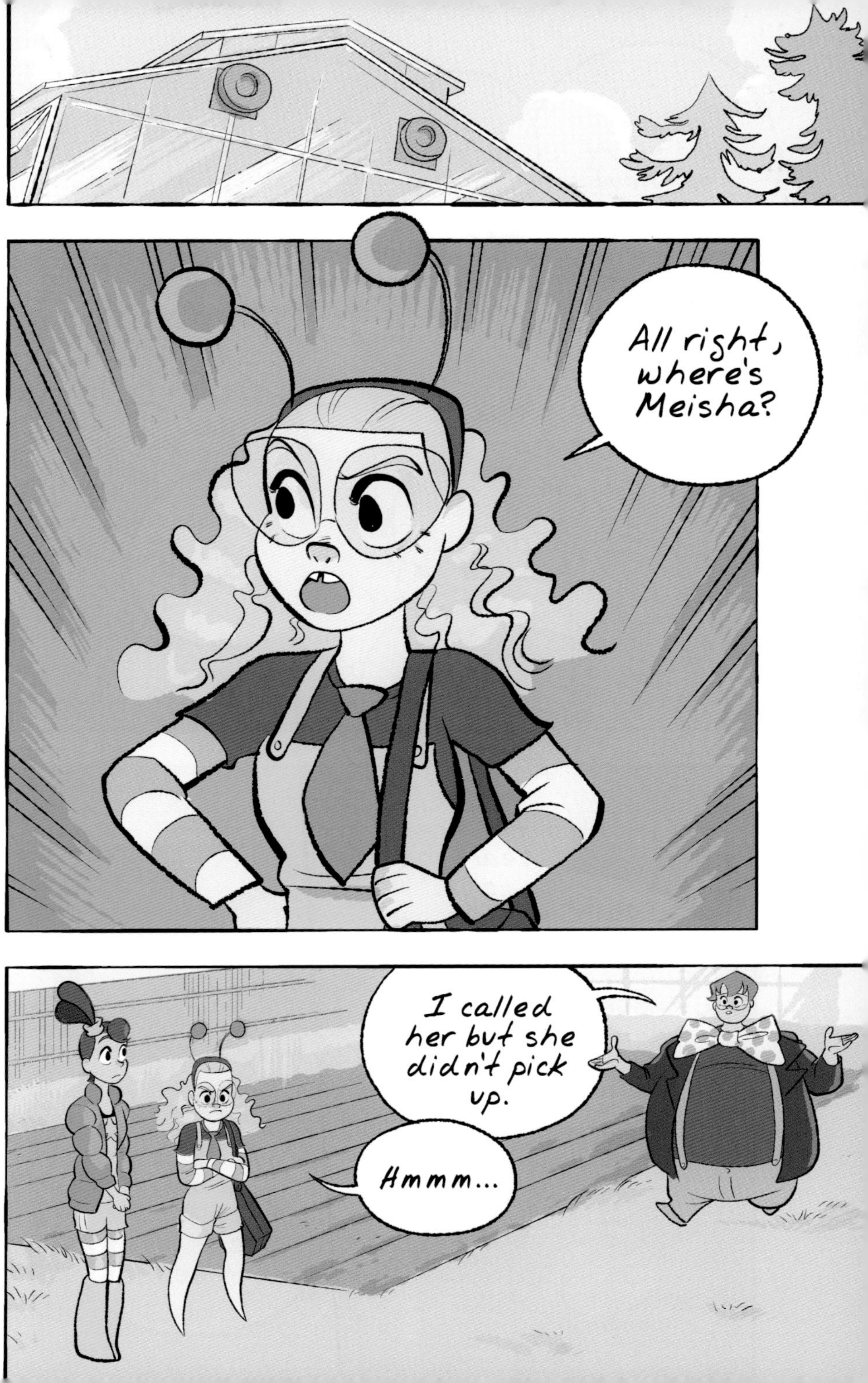
All right, where's Meisha?
I called her but she didn't pick up.
Hmmm...

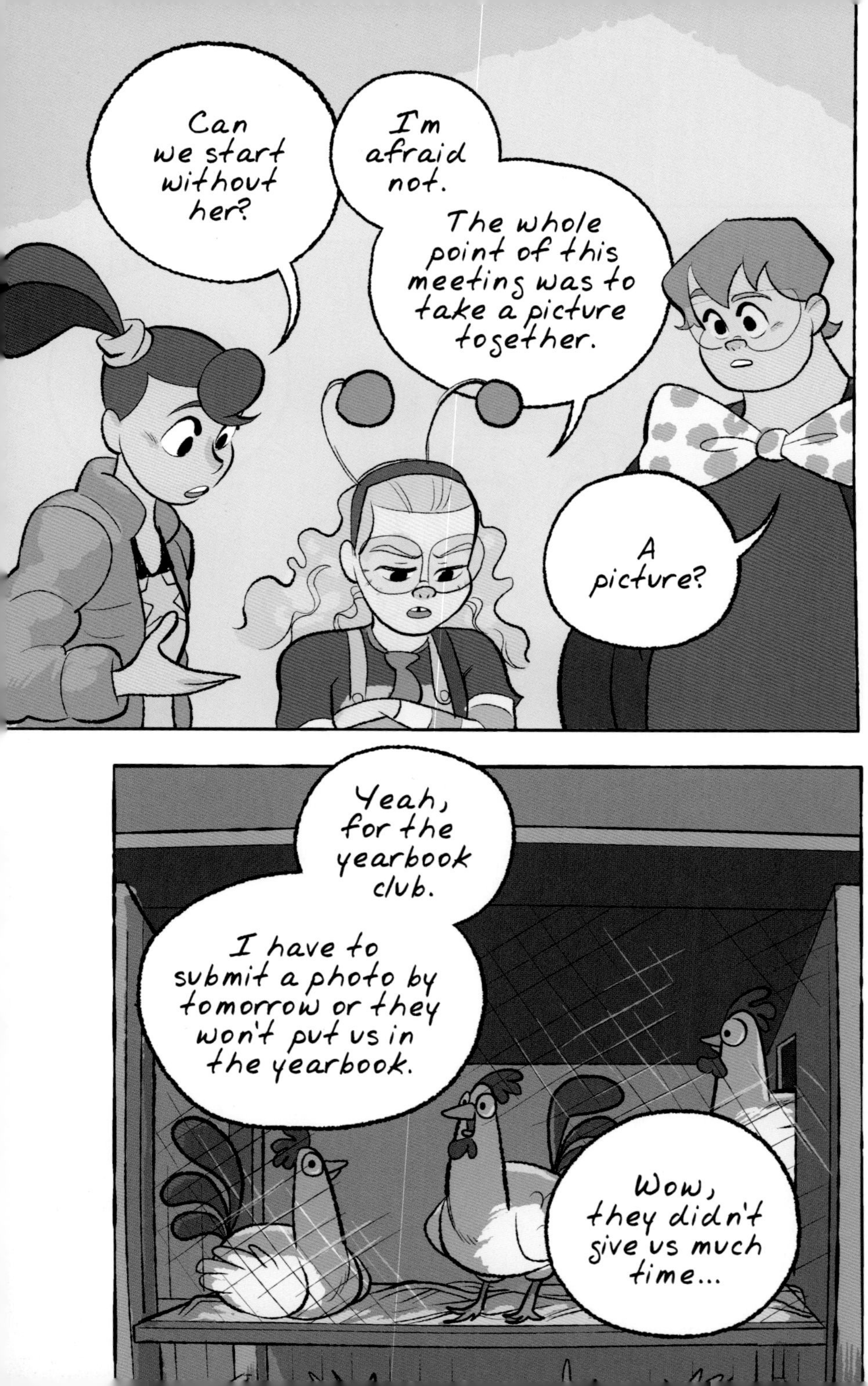
Can we start without her?
I'm afraid not.
The whole point of this meeting was to take a picture together.
A picture?
Yeah, for the yearbook club.
I have to submit a photo by tomorrow or they won't put us in the yearbook.
Wow, they didn't give us much time...

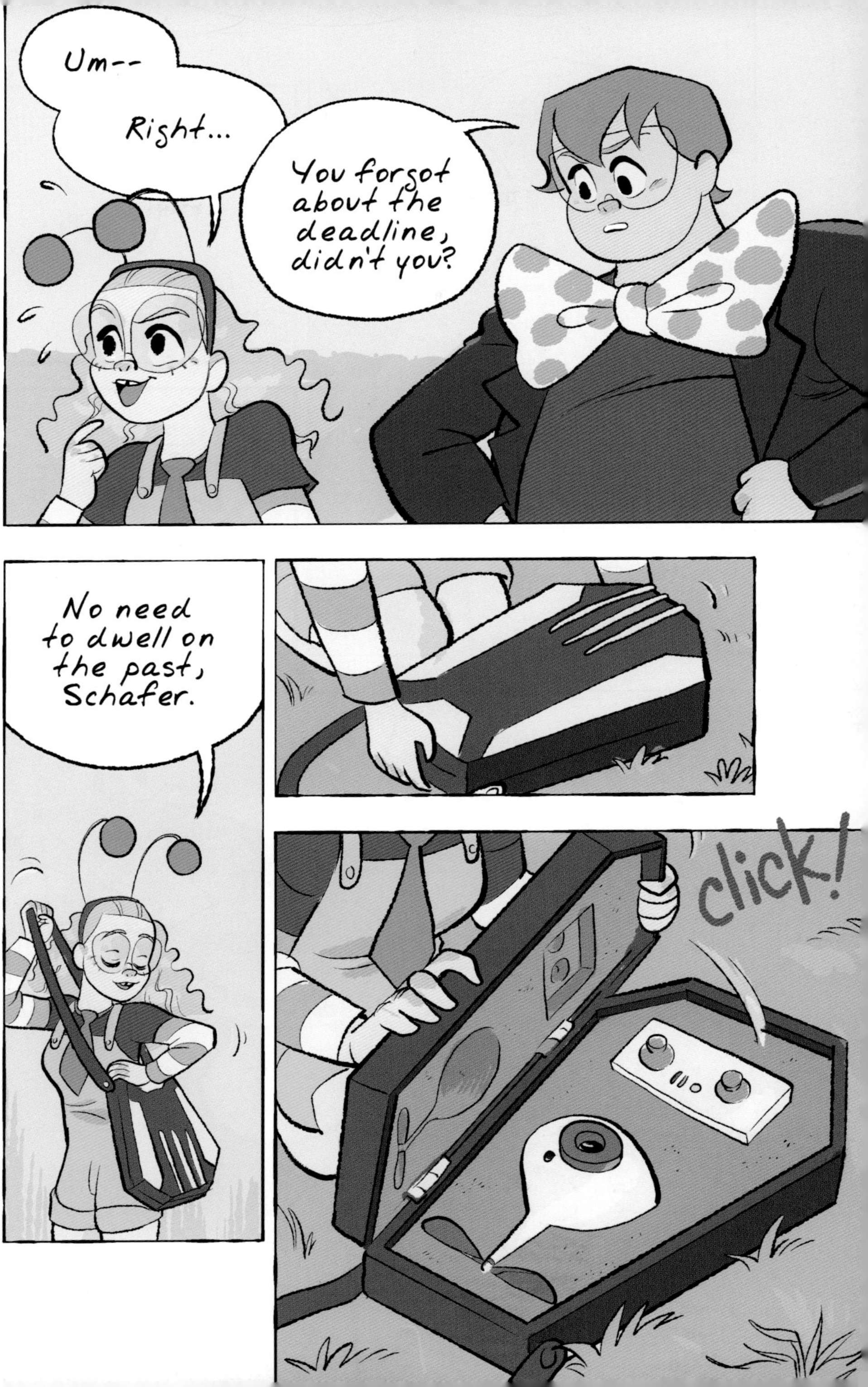
Um--
Right...
You forgot about the deadline, didn't you?
No need to dwell on the past, Schafer.
click!

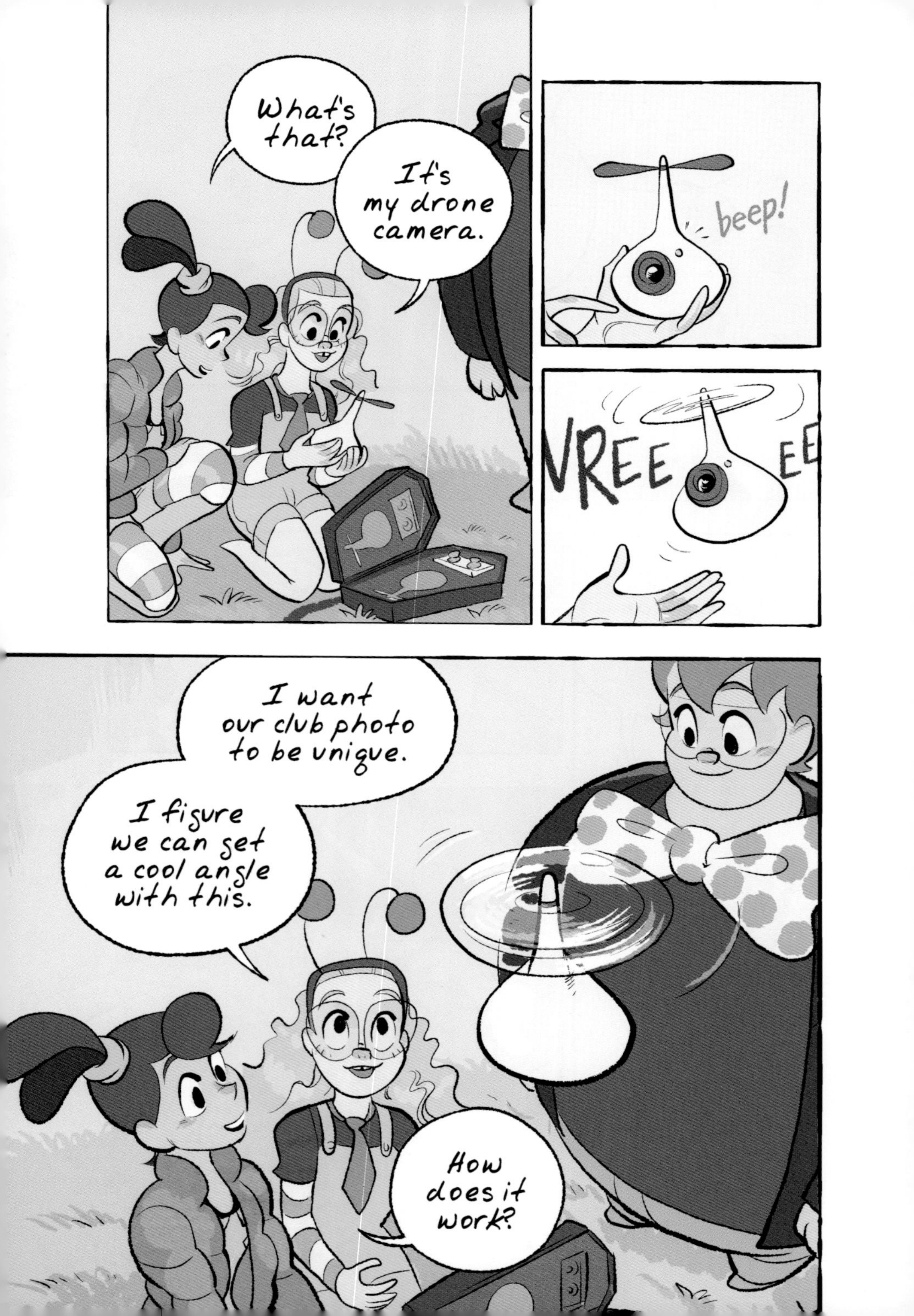
What's that?
It's my drone camera.
beep!
VREEEEE
I want our club photo to be unique.
I figure we can get a cool angle with this.
How does it work?

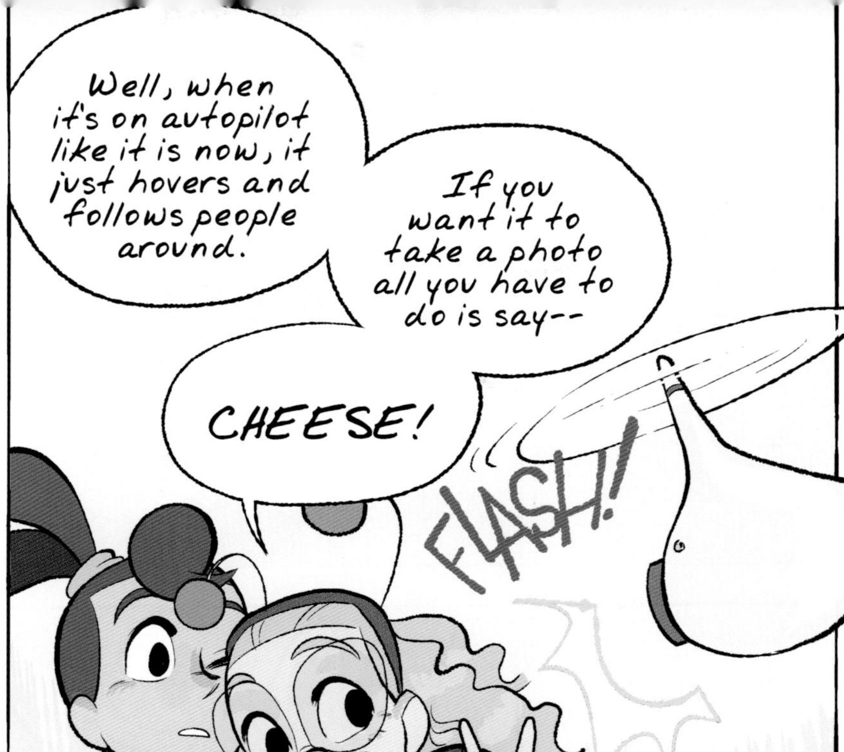
Well, when it's on autopilot like it is now, it just hovers and follows people around.
If you want it to take a photo all you have to do is say--
CHEESE!
FLASH!!

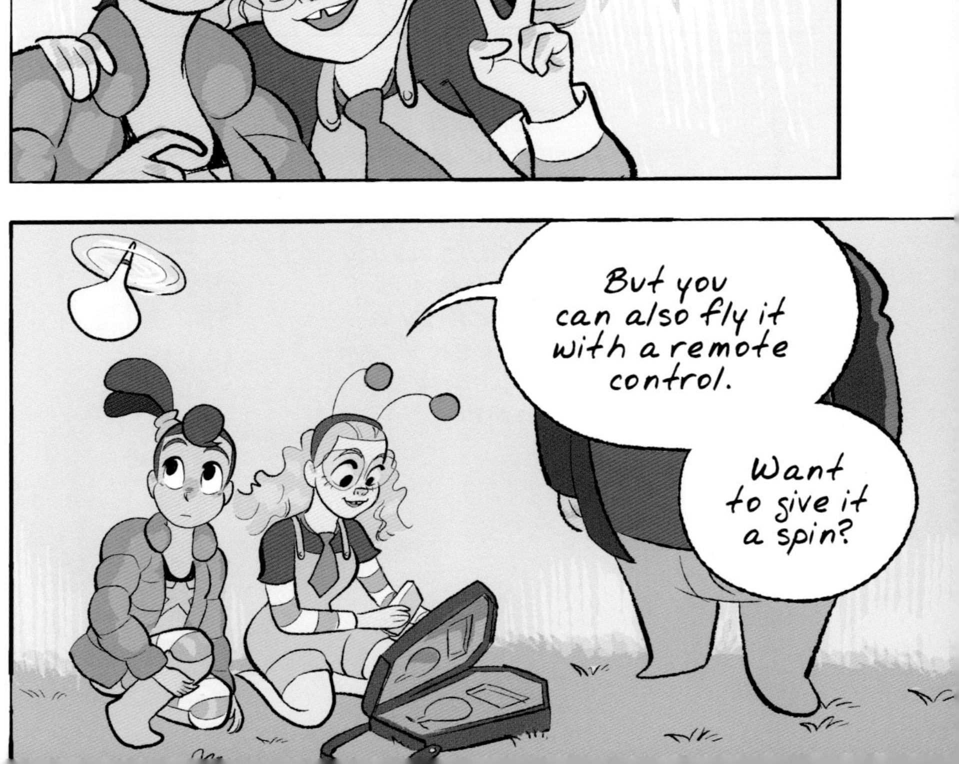
But you can also fly it with a remote control.
Want to give it a spin?

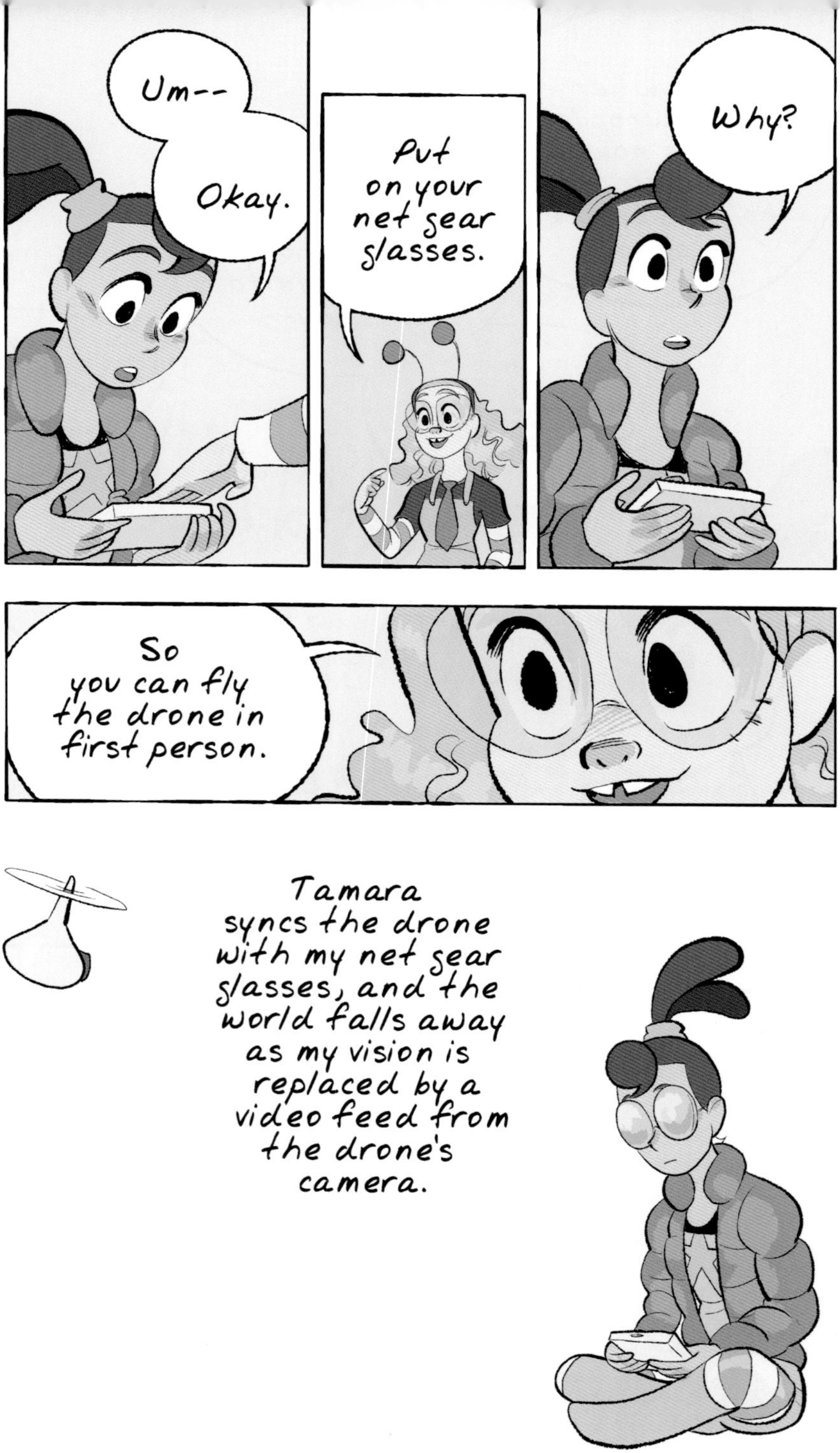
Um--
Okay.
Put on your net gear glasses.
Why?
So you can fly the drone in first person.
Tamara syncs the drone with my net gear glasses, and the world falls away as my vision is replaced by a video feed from the drone's camera.

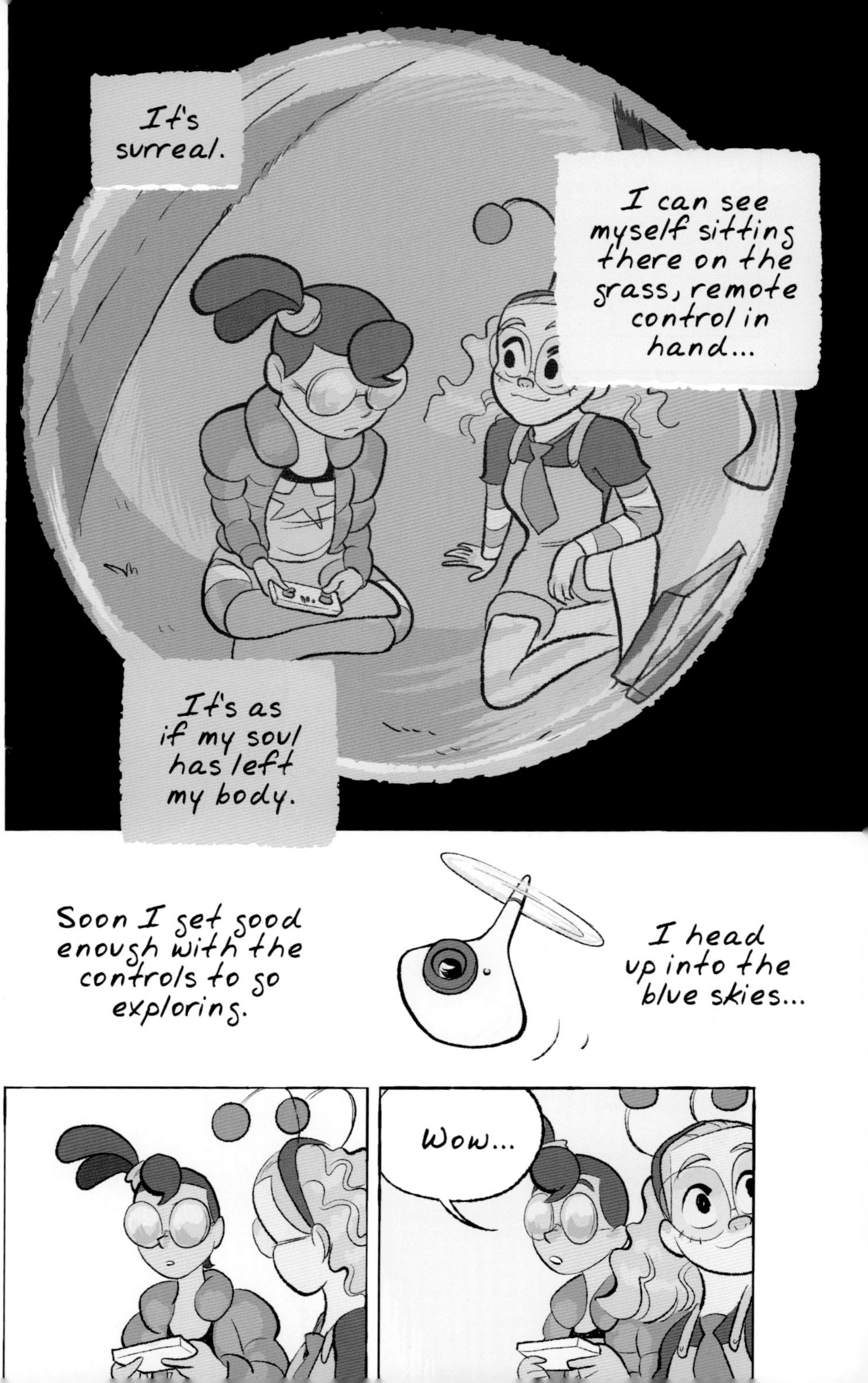
It's surreal.
I can see myself sitting there on the grass, remote control in hand...
It's as if my soul has left my body.
Soon I get good enough with the controls to go exploring.
I head up into the blue skies...
Wow...

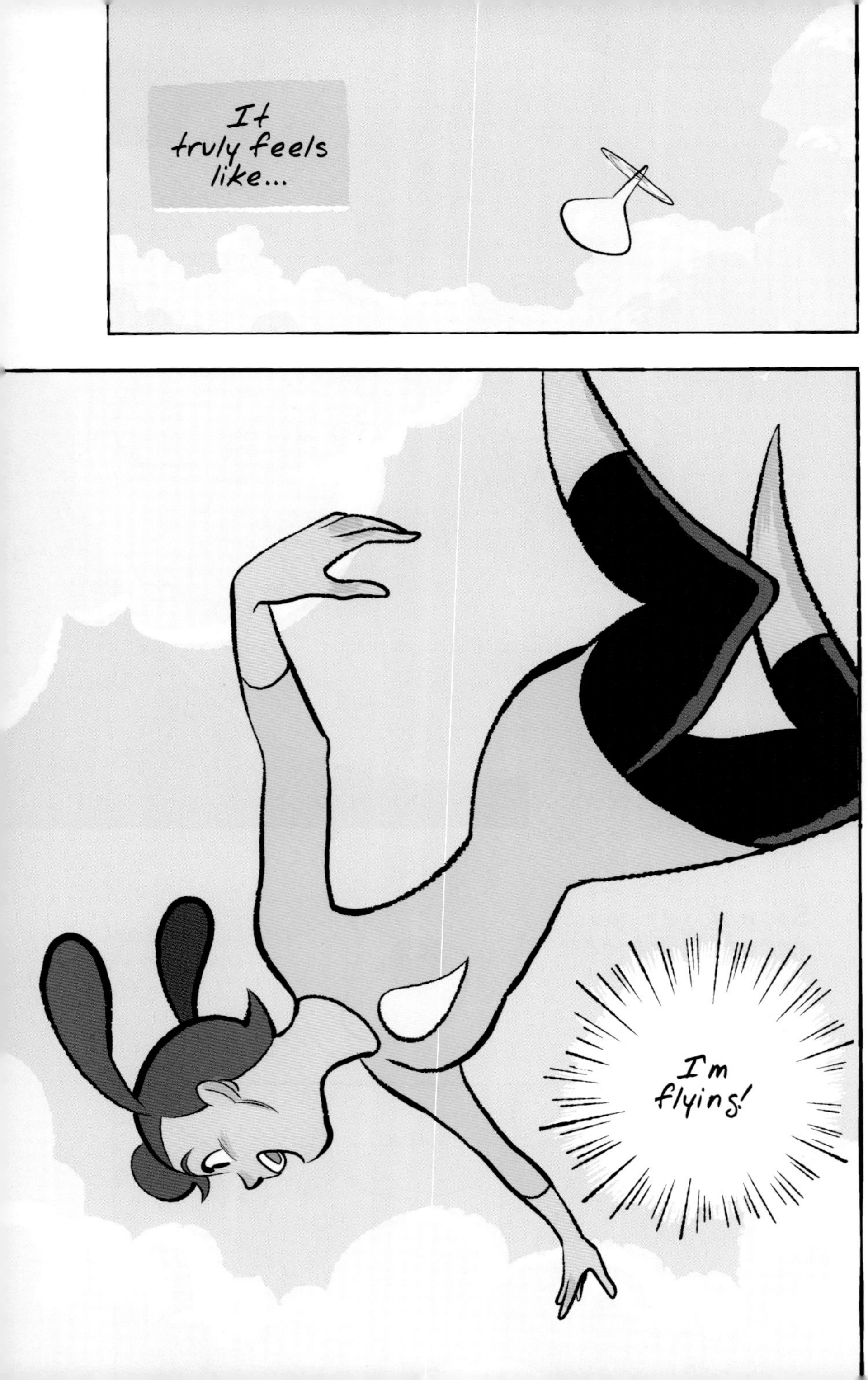
It truly feels like...
I'm flying!

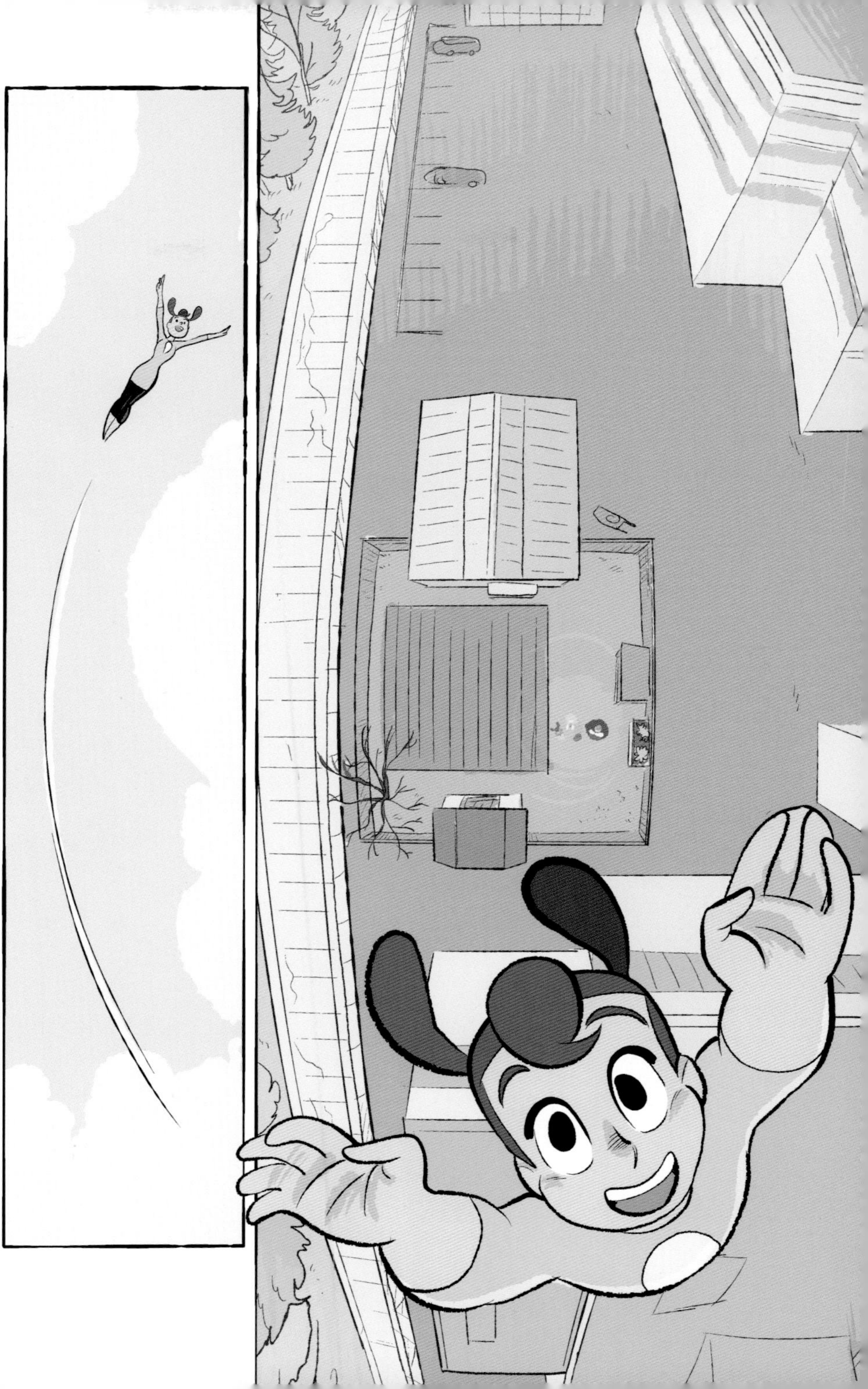

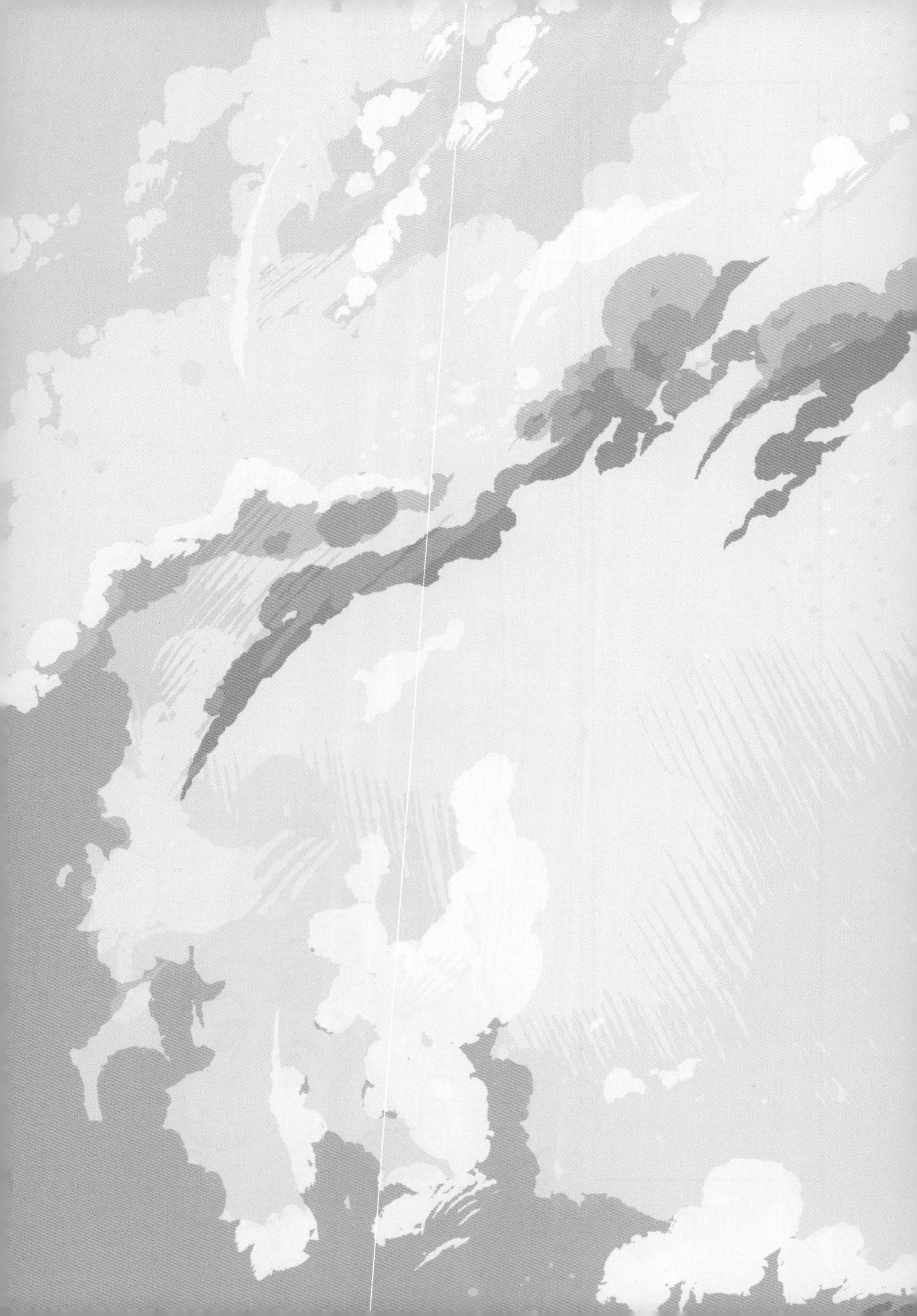

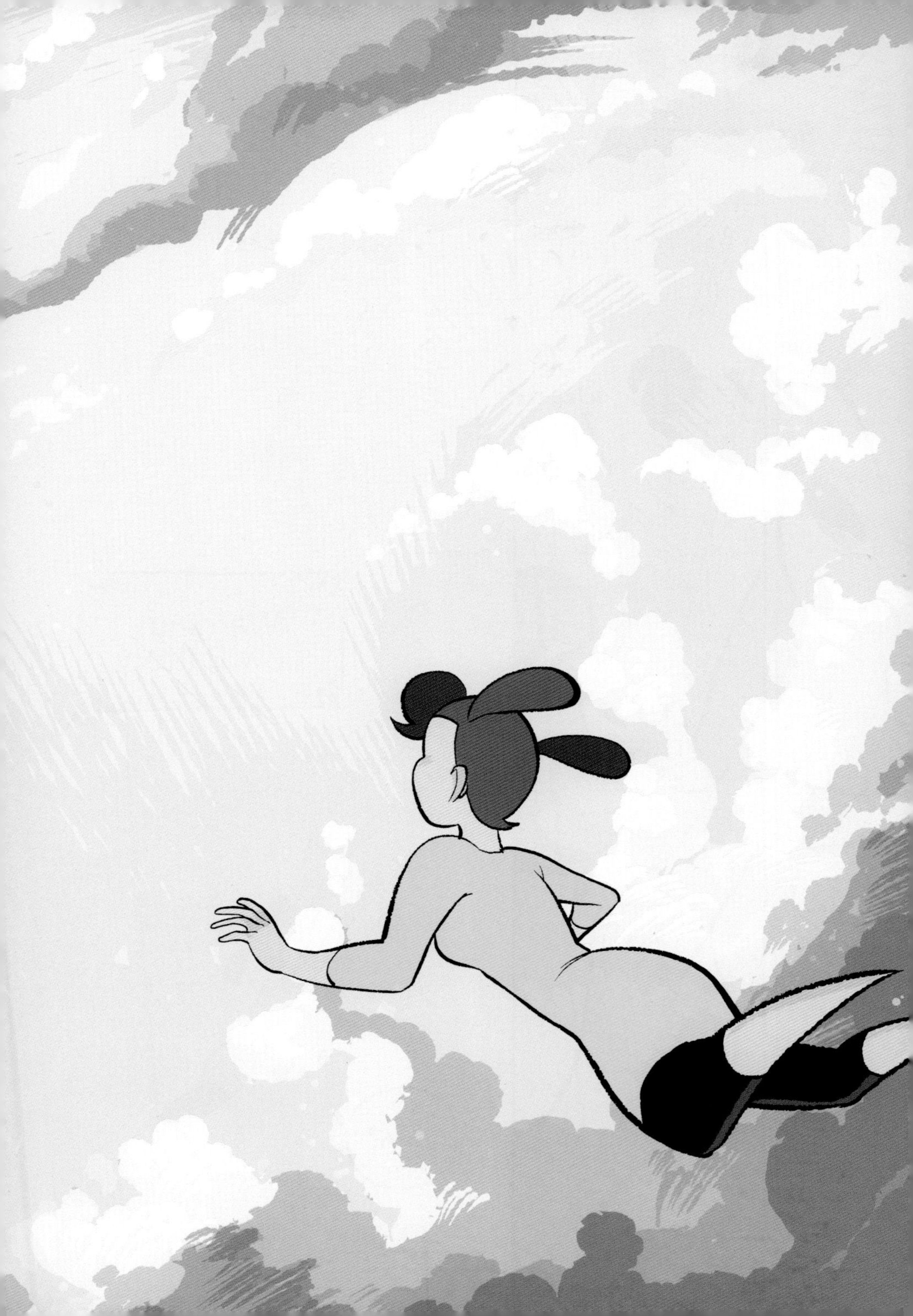

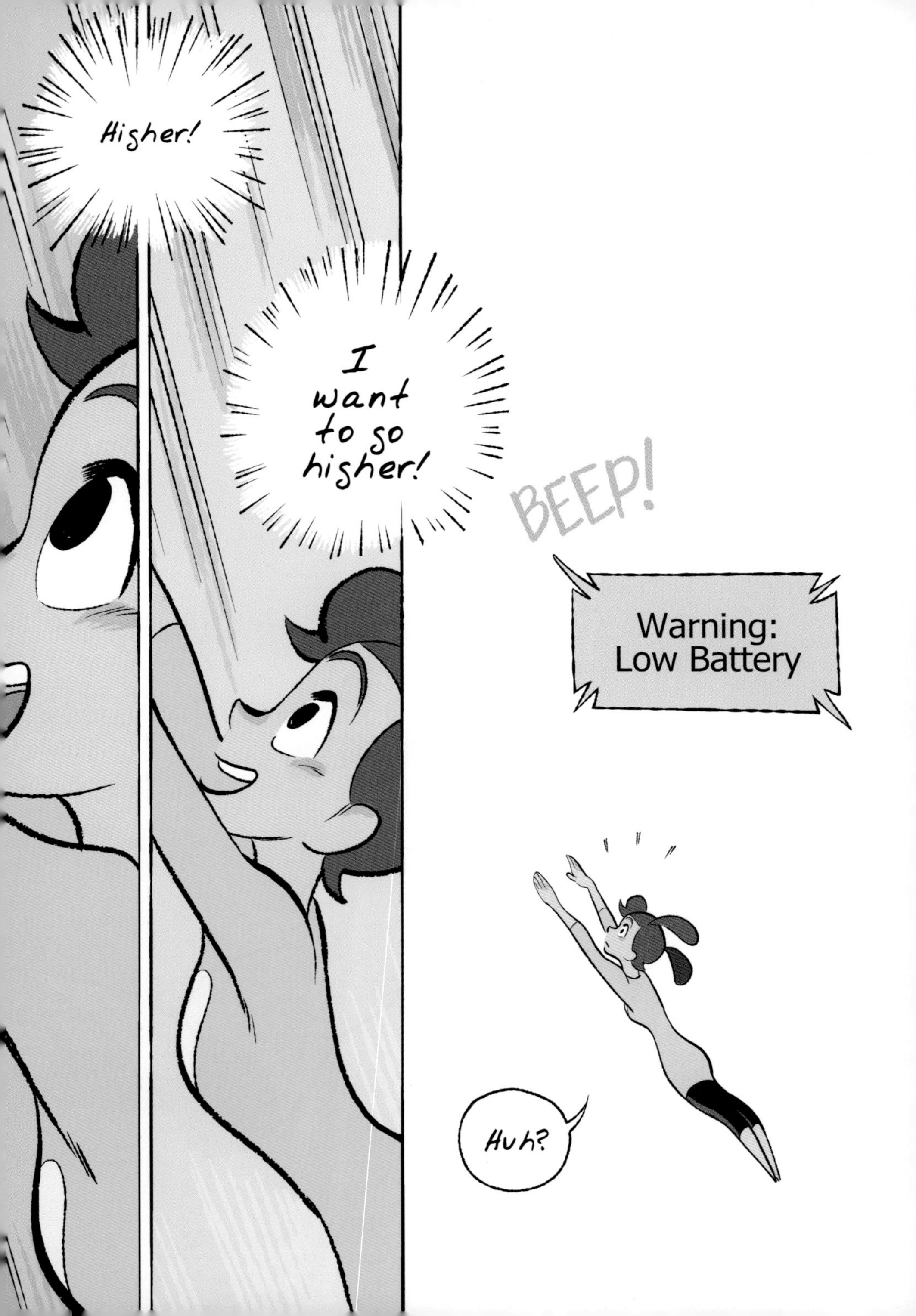
Higher!
I want to go higher!
BEEP!
Warning: Low Battery
Huh?

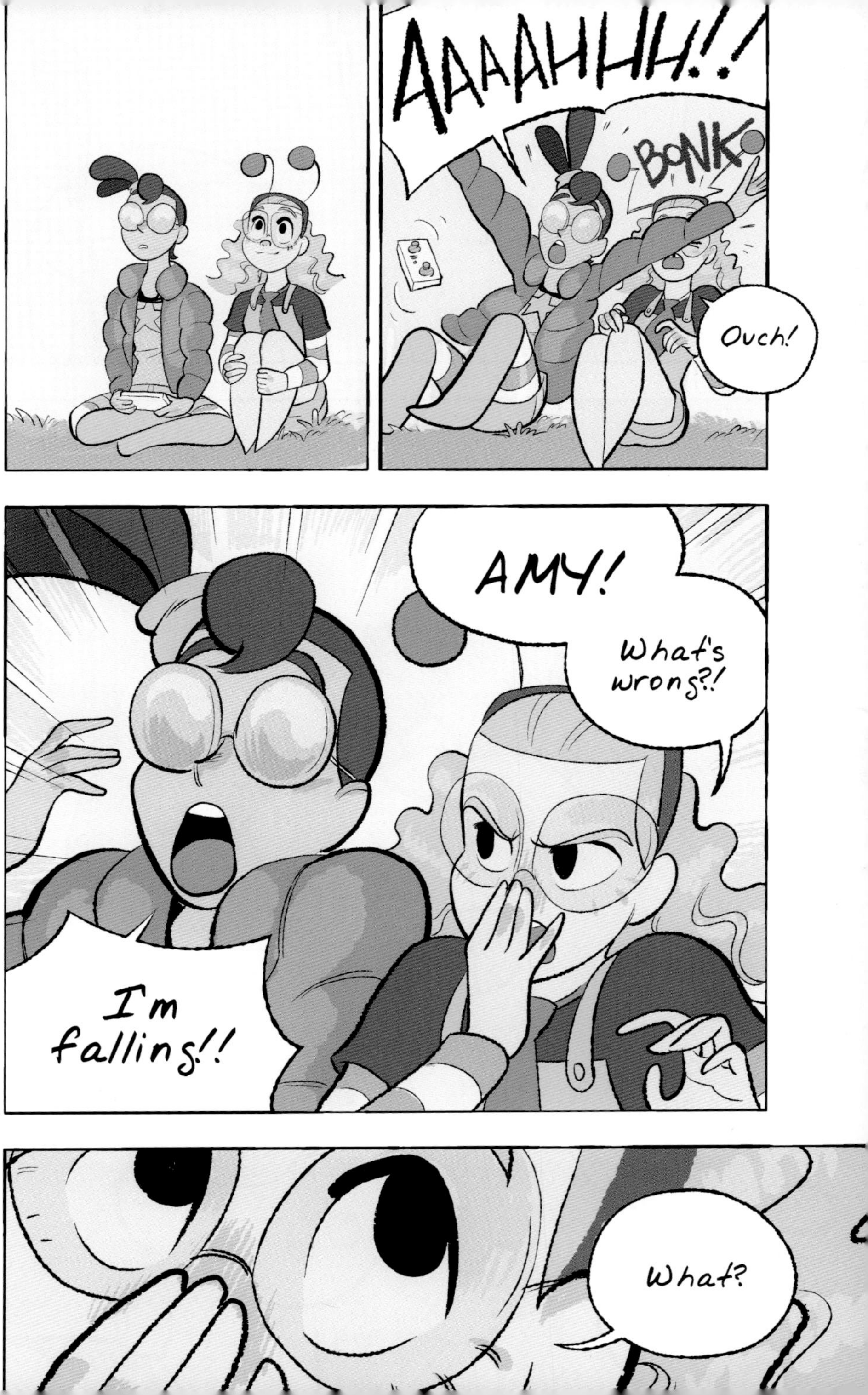
AAAAHHH!!
BONK
Ouch!
AMY!
What's wrong?!
I'm falling!!
What?

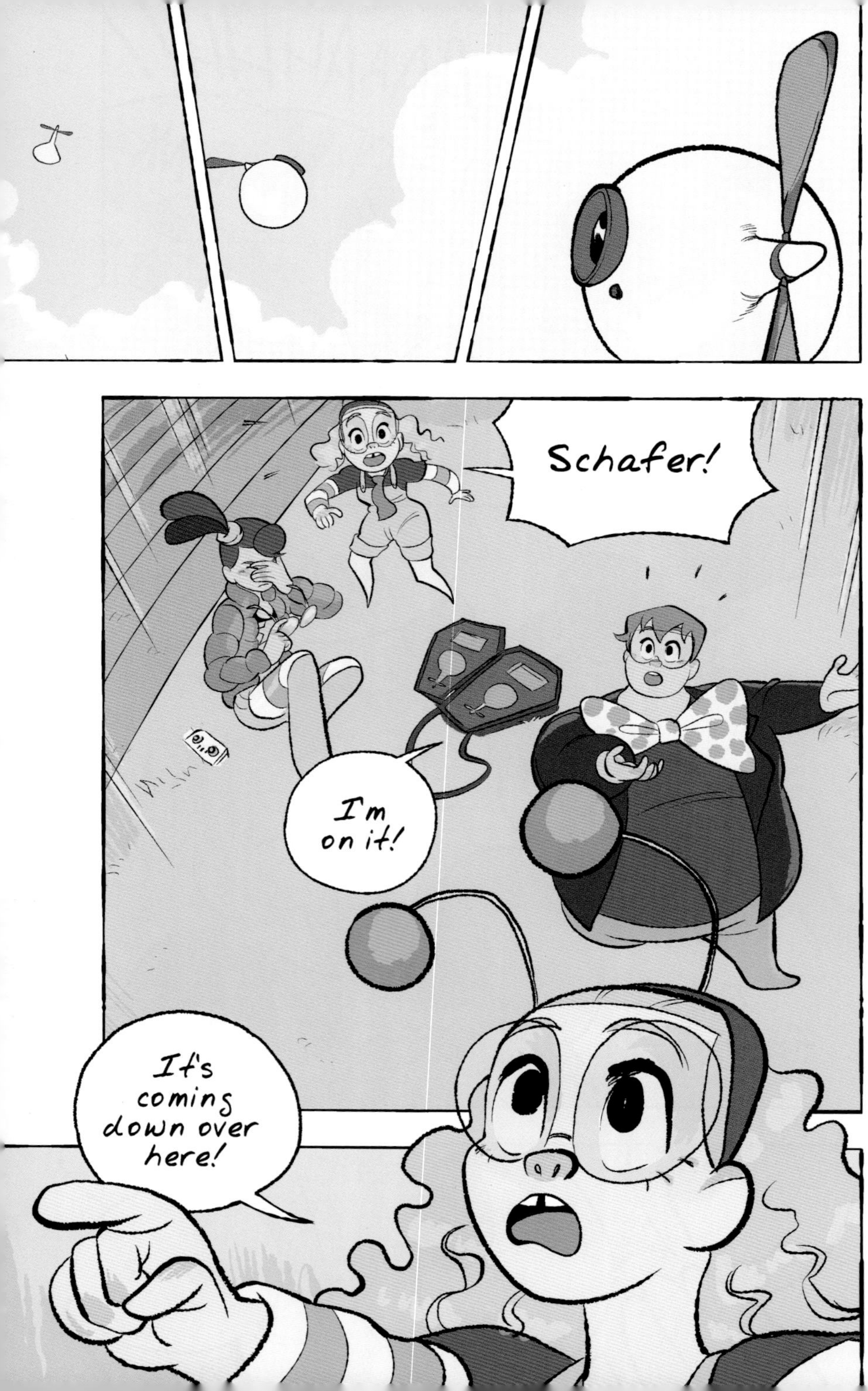

Schafer!
I'm on it!
It's coming down over here!

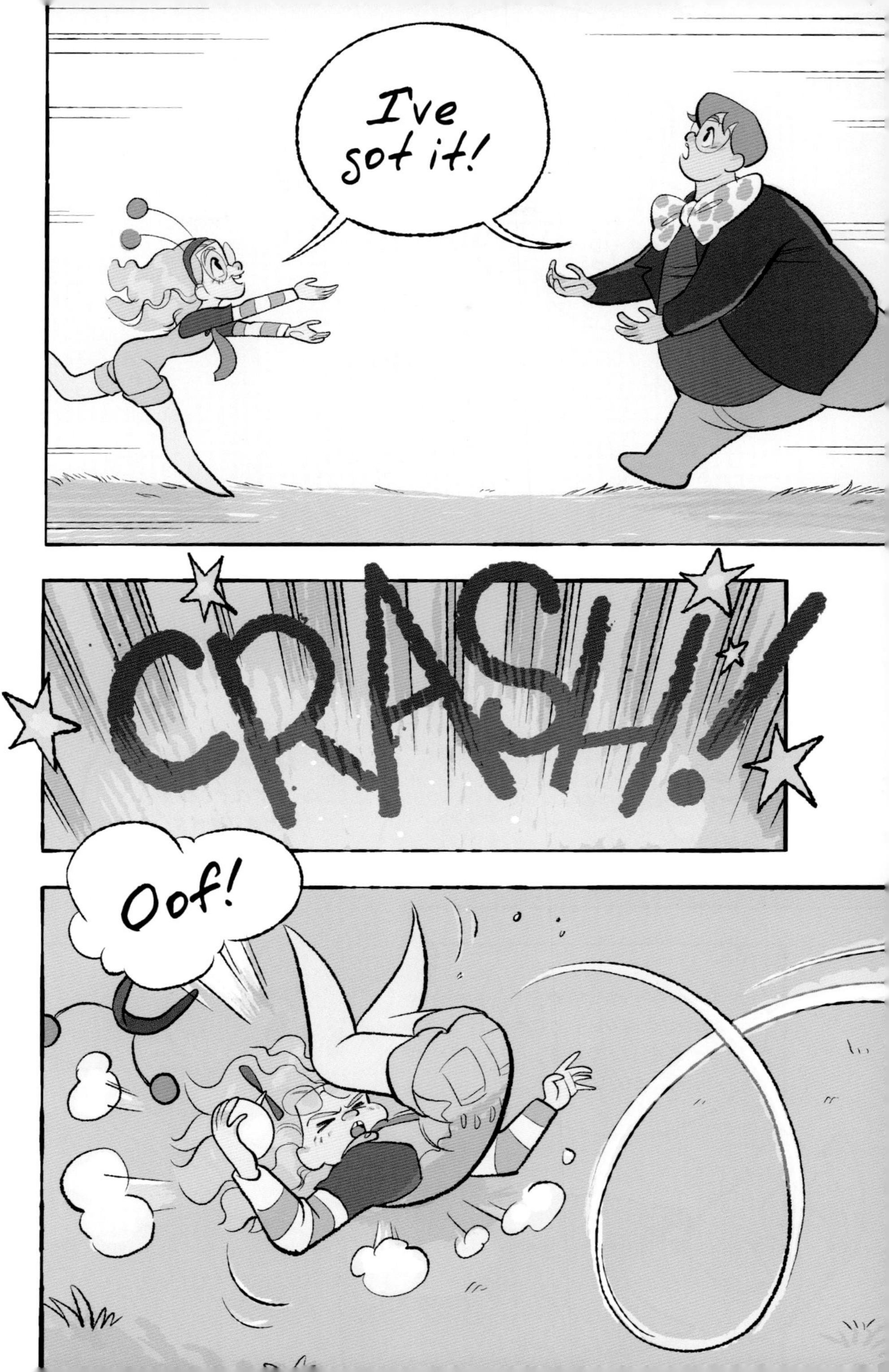
I've got it!
CRASH!!
Oof!

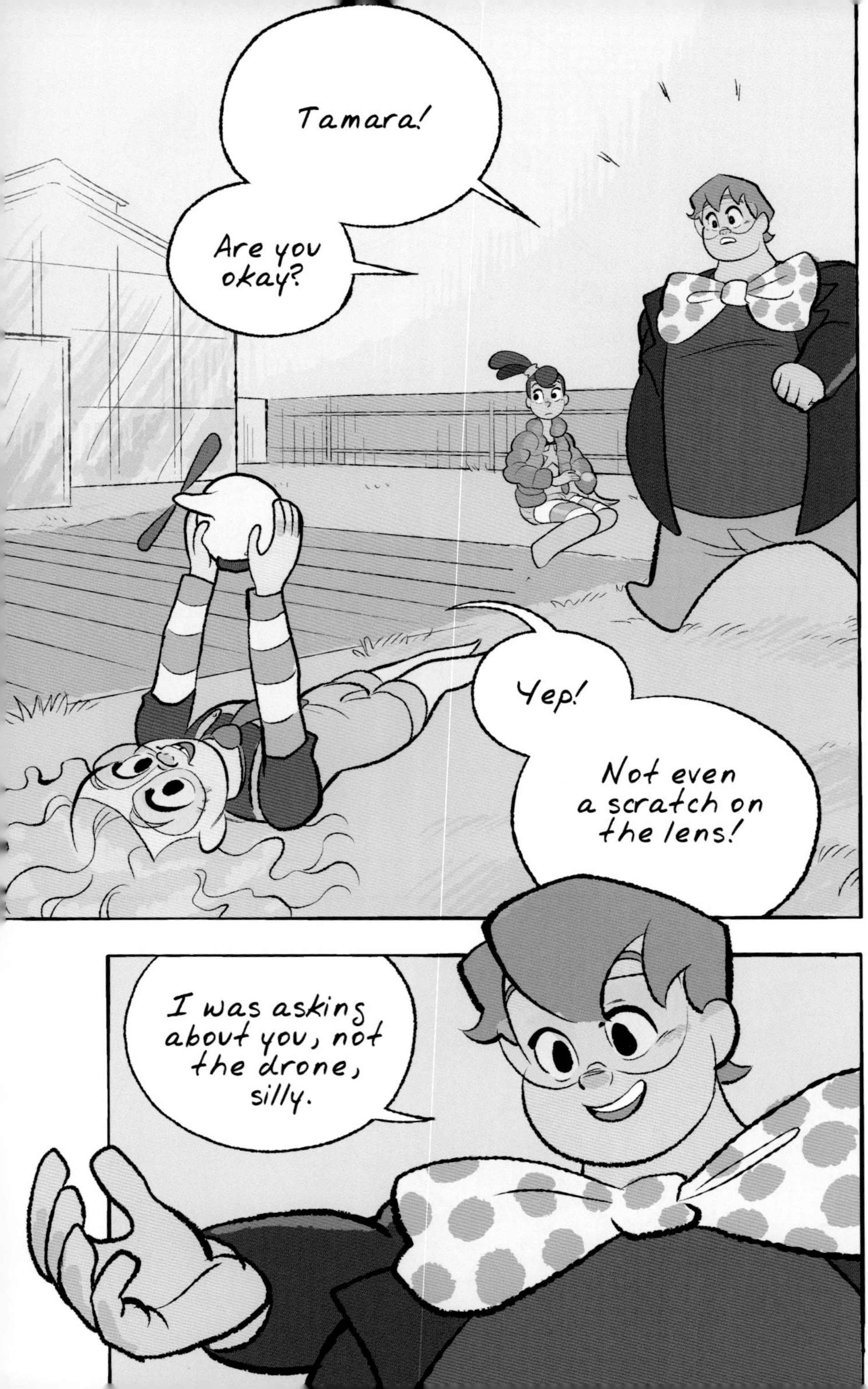
Tamara!
Are you okay?
Yep!
Not even a scratch on the lens!
I was asking about you, not the drone, silly.

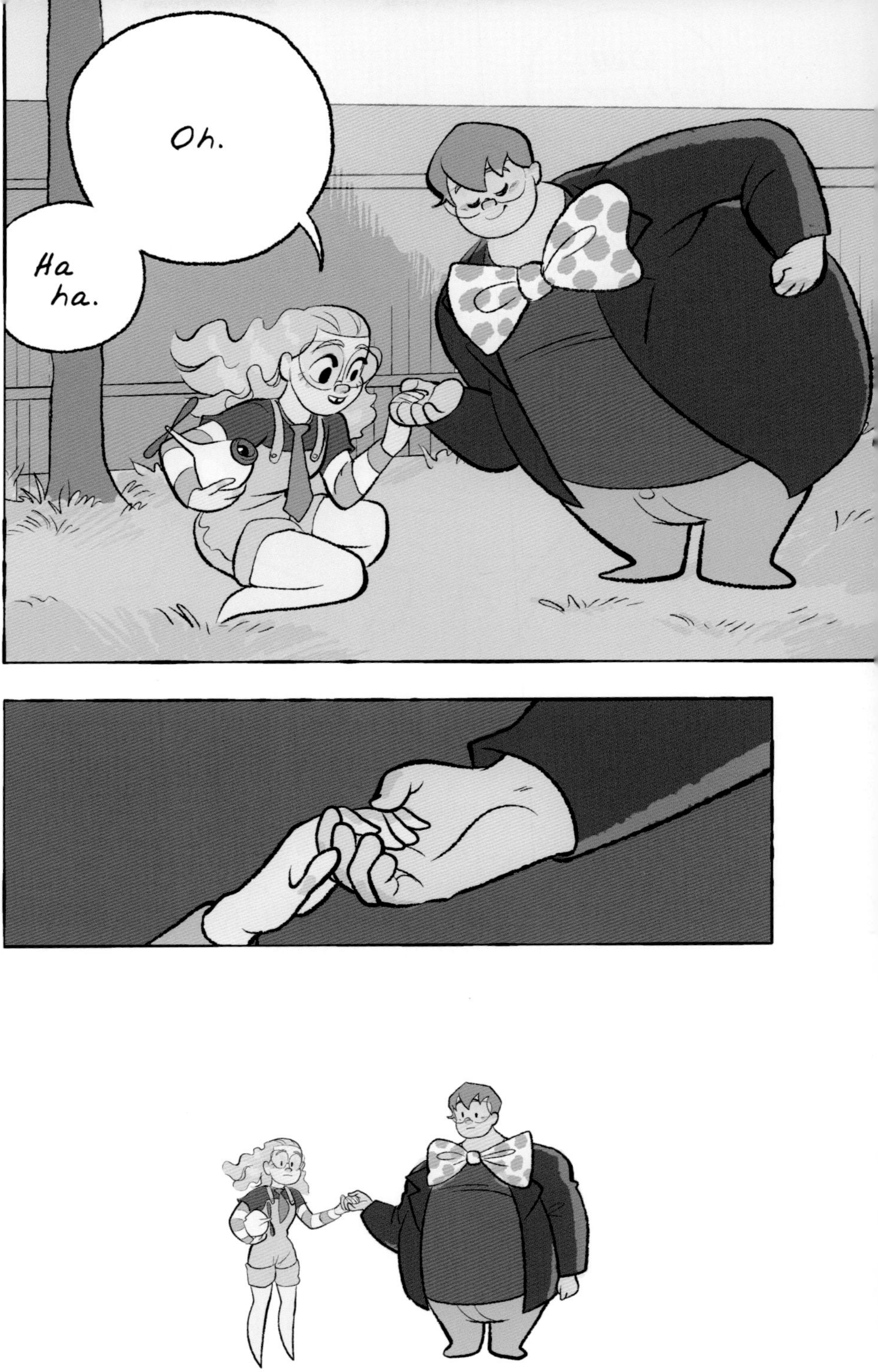
Oh.
Ha ha.

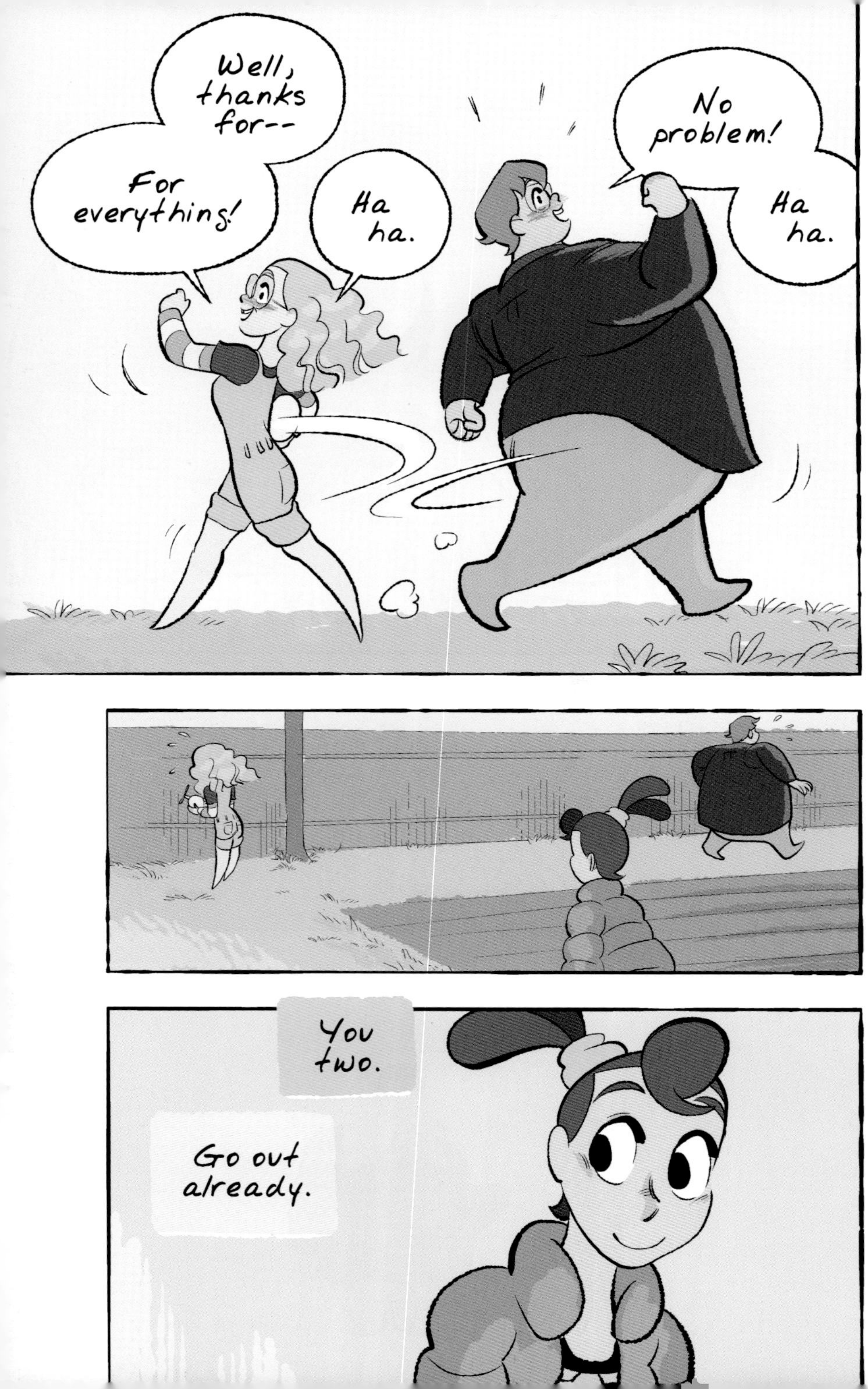
Well, thanks for--
For everything!
Ha ha.
No problem!
Ha ha.
You two.
Go out already.

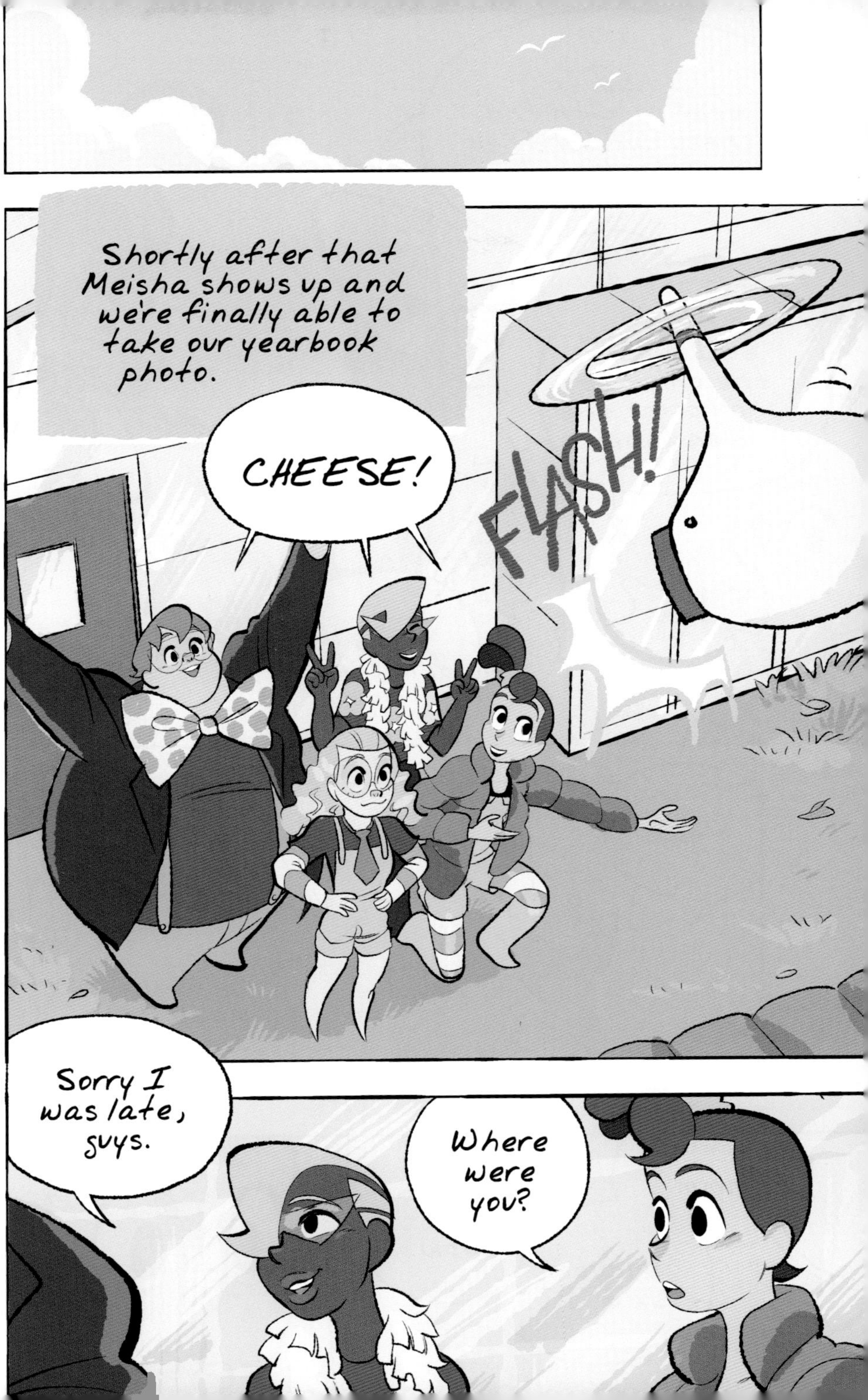
Shortly after that Meisha shows up and we're finally able to take our yearbook photo.
CHEESE!
FLASH!
Sorry I was late, guys.
Where were you?

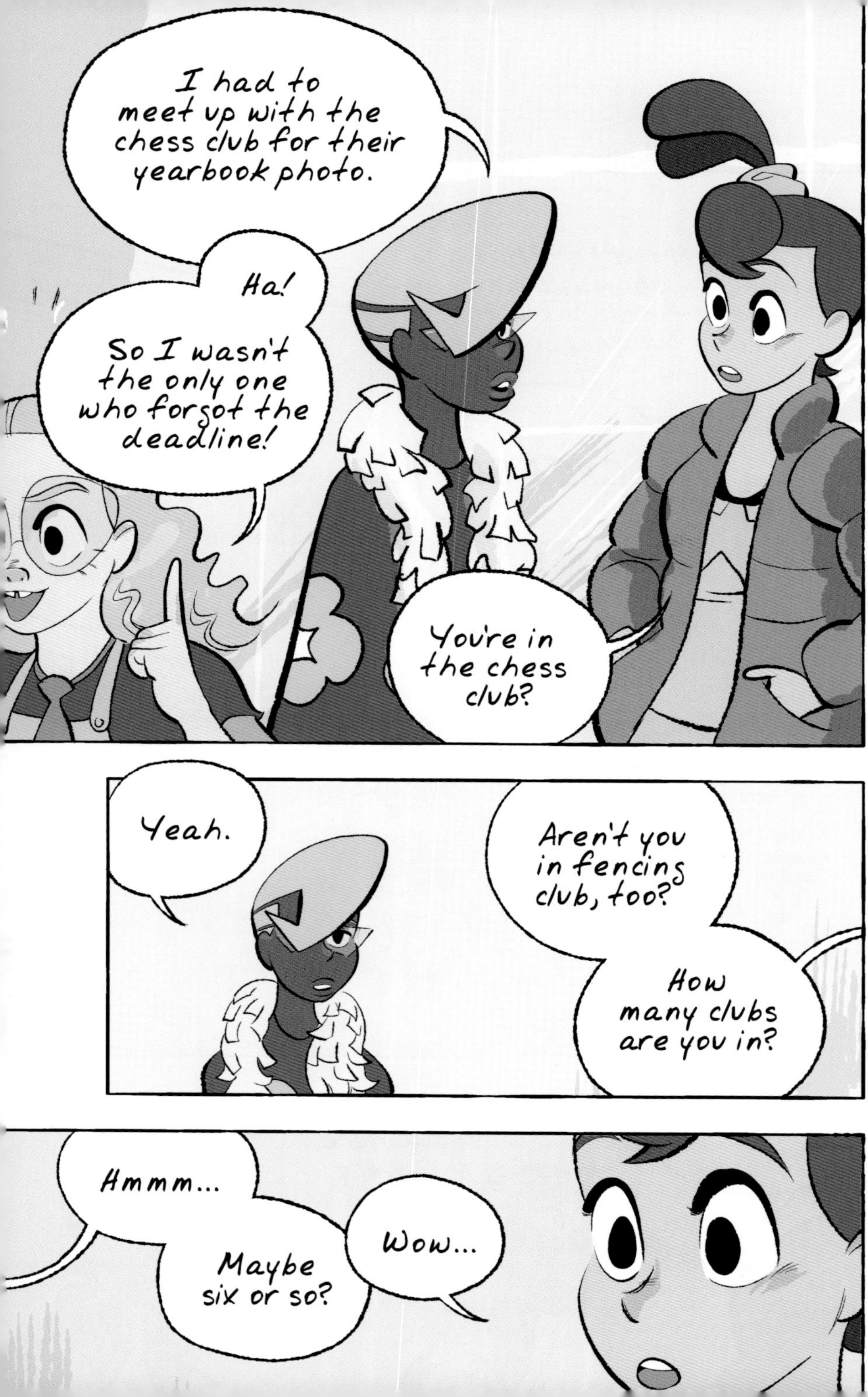
I had to meet up with the chess club for their yearbook photo.
Ha!
So I wasn't the only one who forgot the deadline!
You're in the chess club?
Yeah.
Aren't you in fencing club, too?
How many clubs are you in?
Hmmm...
Maybe six or so?
Wow...

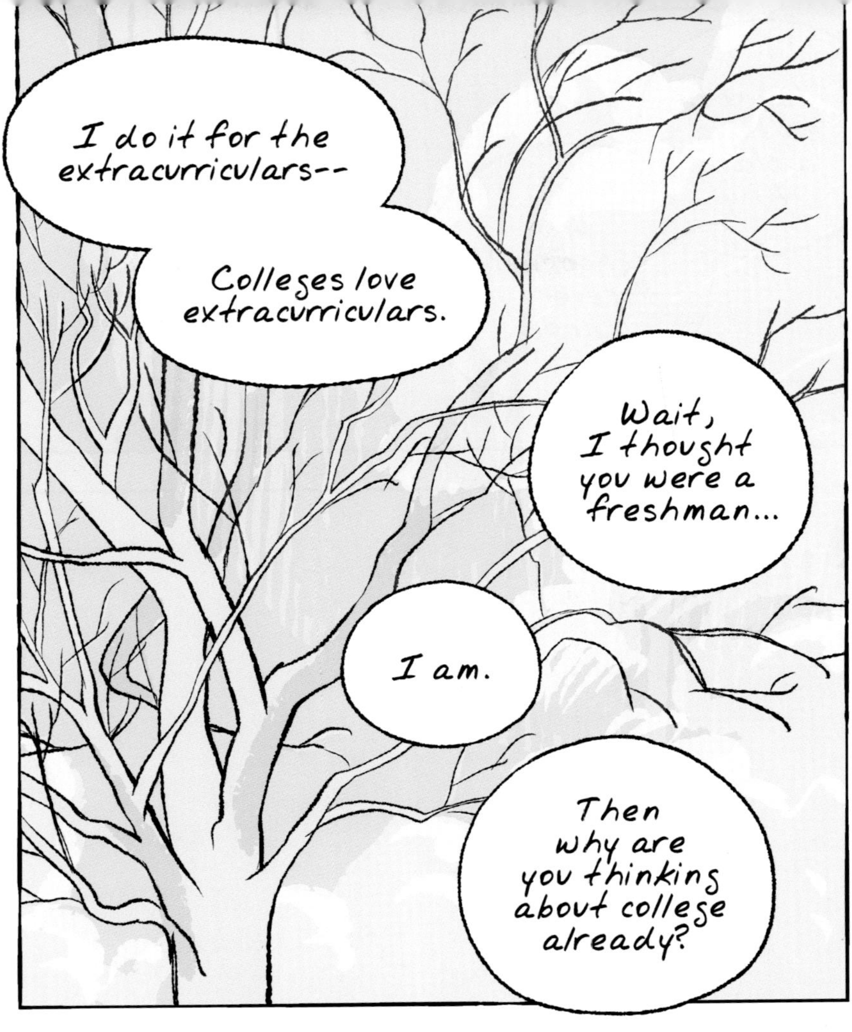
I do it for the extracurriculars--
Colleges love extracurriculars.
Wait, I thought you were a freshman...
I am.
Then why are you thinking about college already?
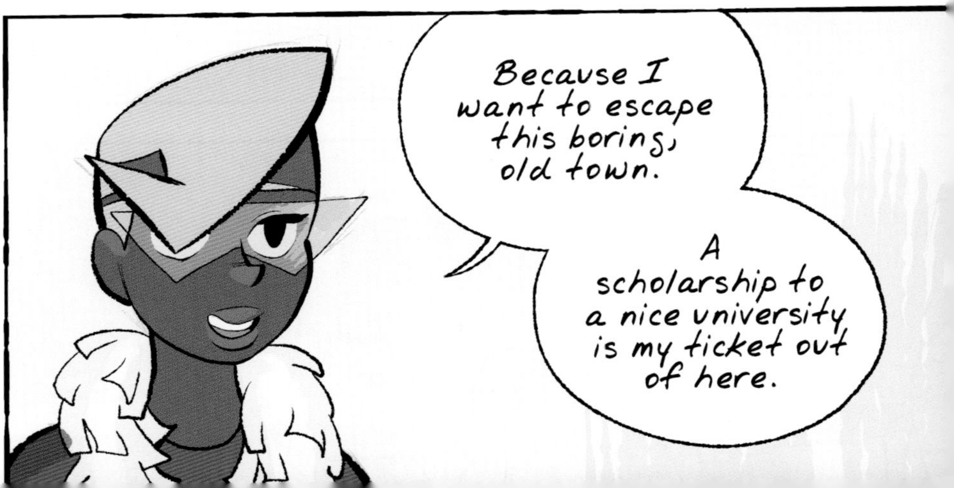
Because I want to escape this boring, old town.
A scholarship to a nice university is my ticket out of here.

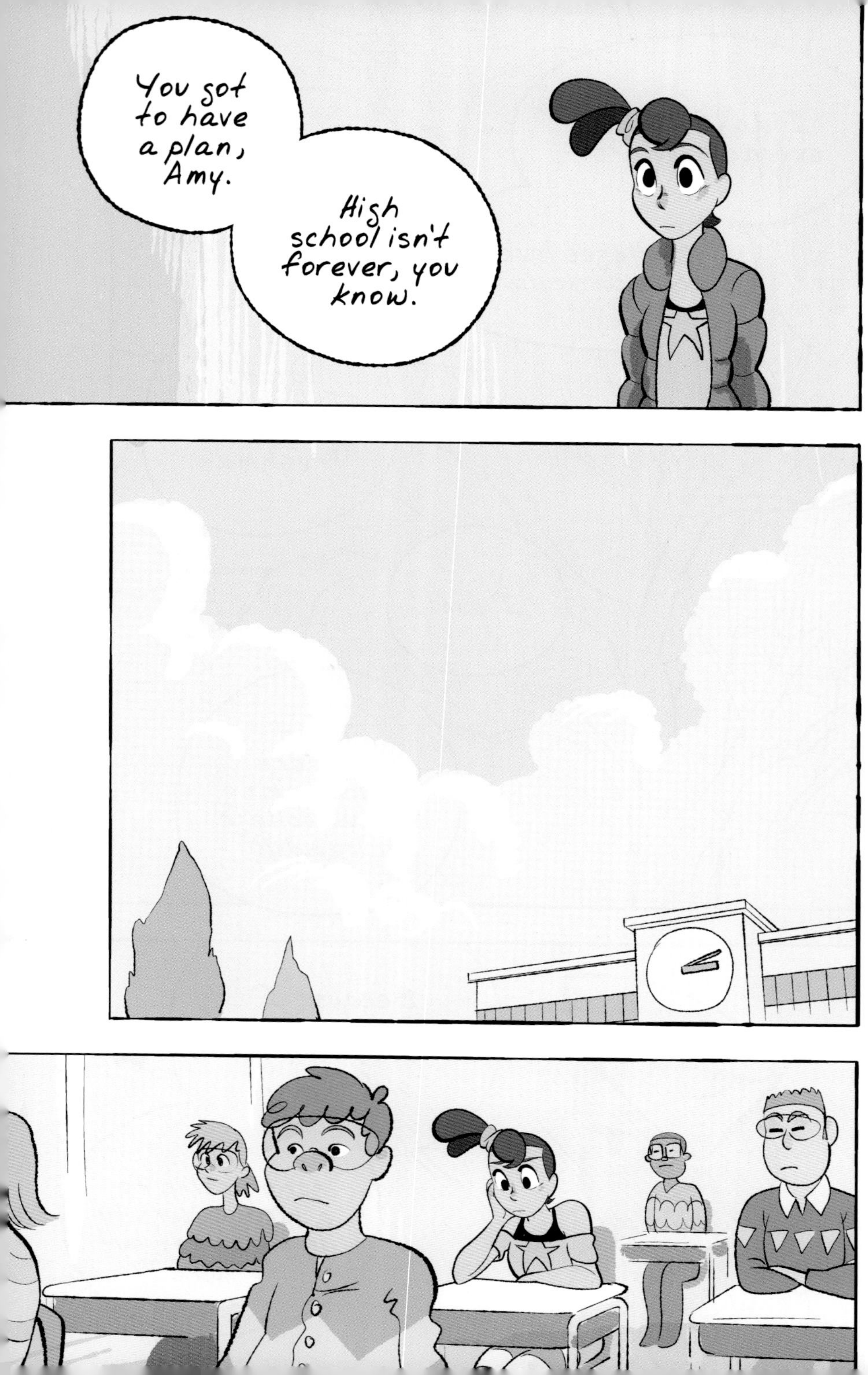
You got to have a plan, Amy.
High school isn't forever, you know.

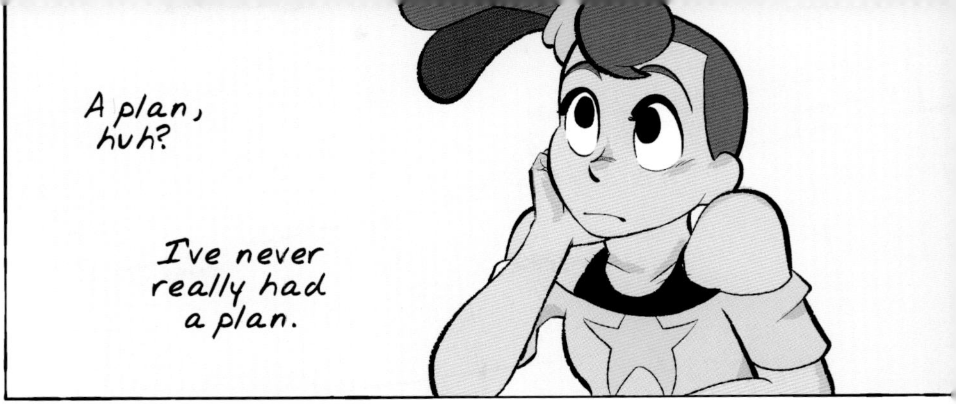
A plan, huh?
I've never really had a plan.

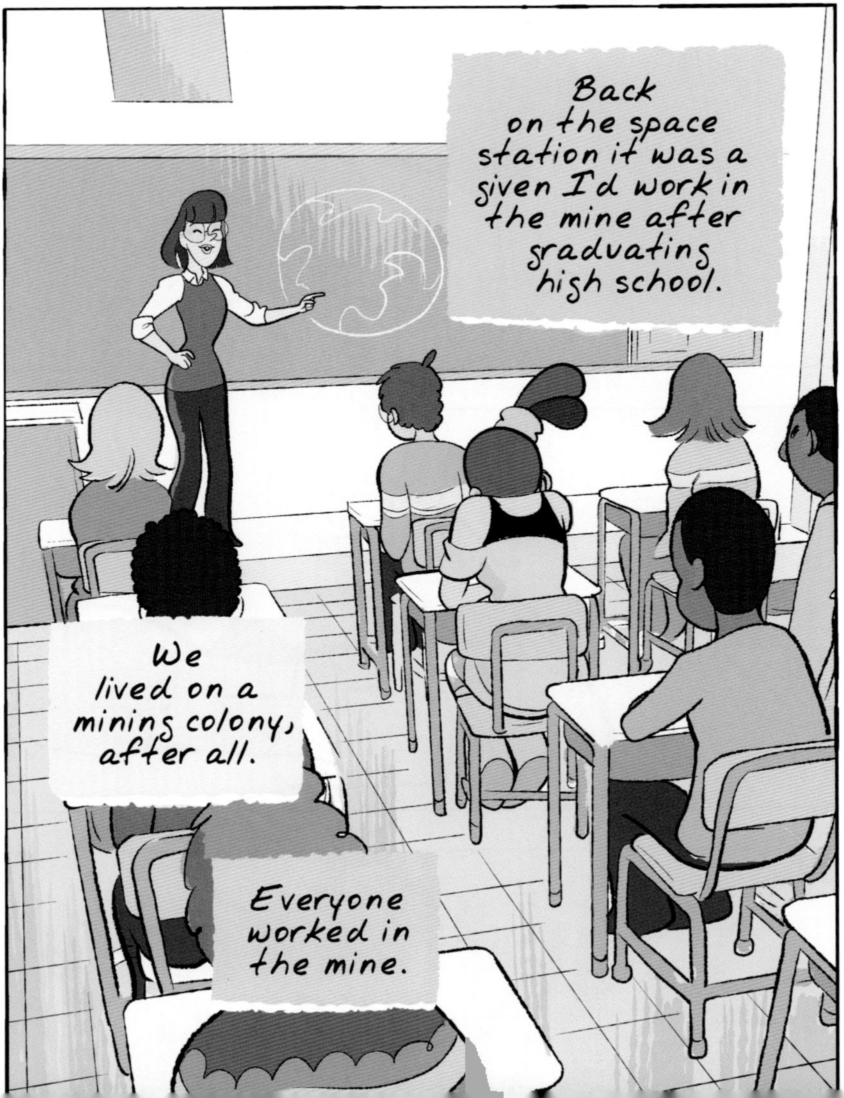
Back on the space station it was a given I'd work in the mine after graduating high school.
We lived on a mining colony, after all.
Everyone worked in the mine.

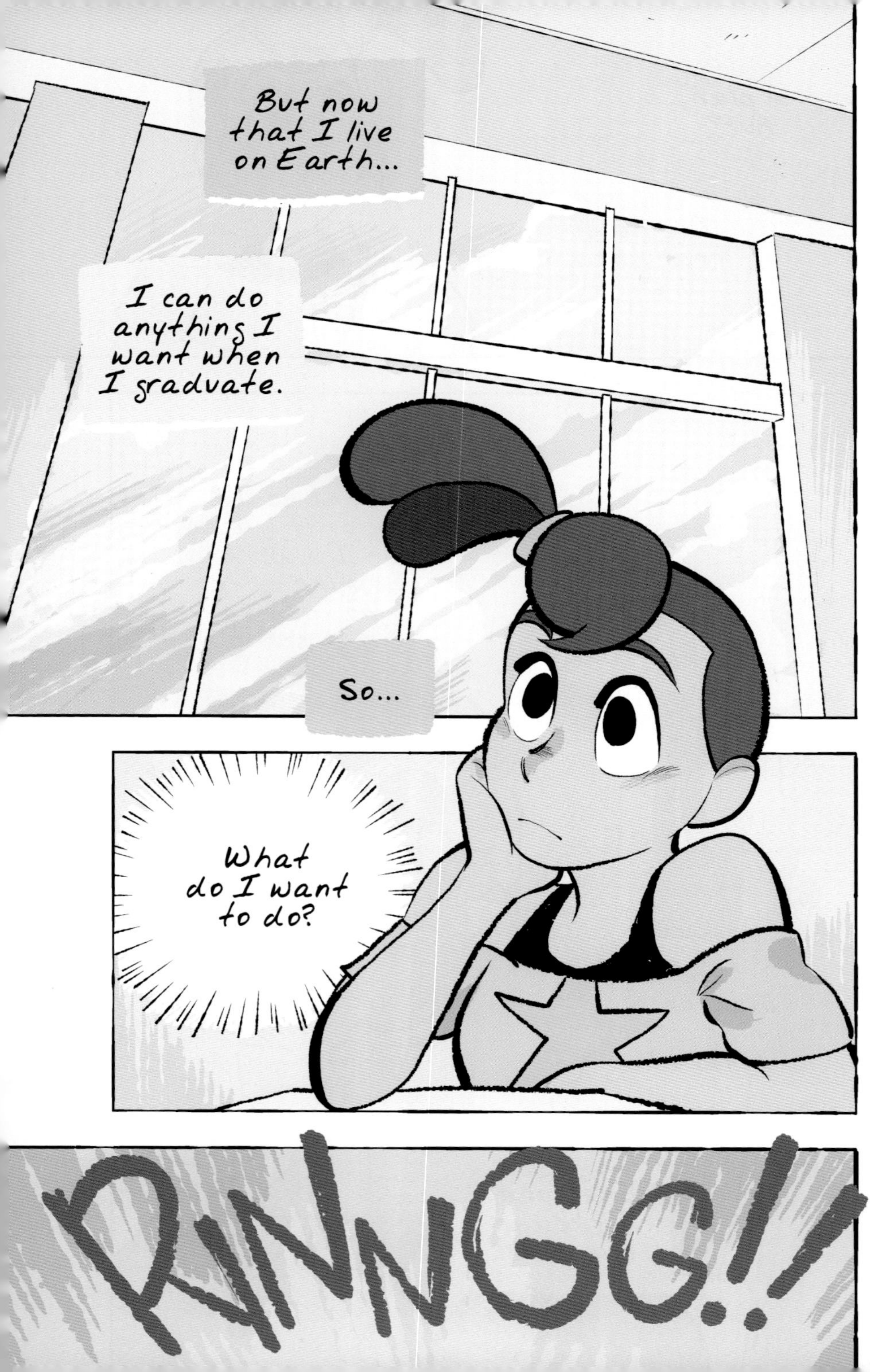
But now that I live on Earth...
I can do anythin g I want when I graduate.
So...
What do I want to do?
RINNGG!!

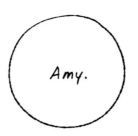
Amy.

Could I talk to you for a minute?

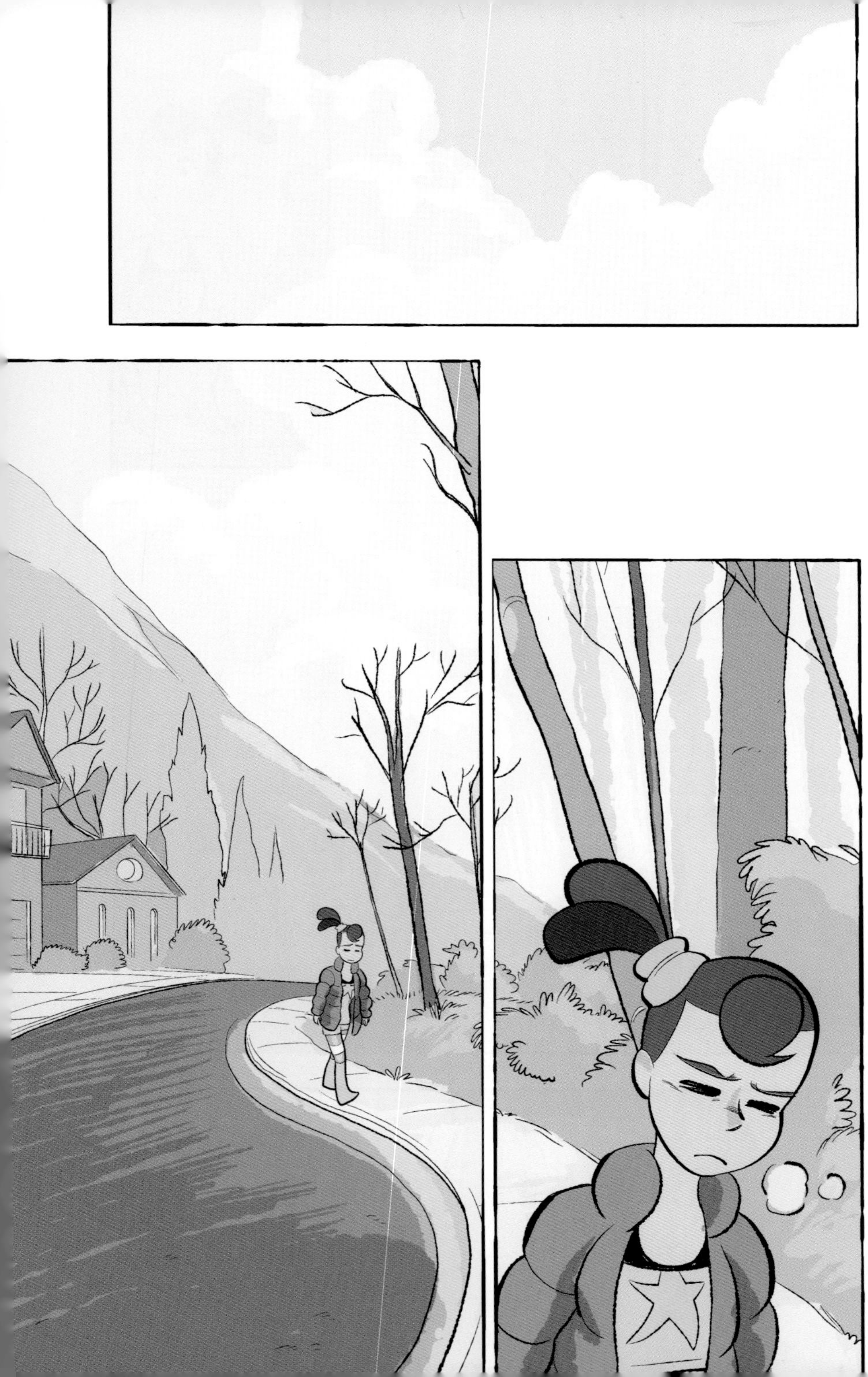

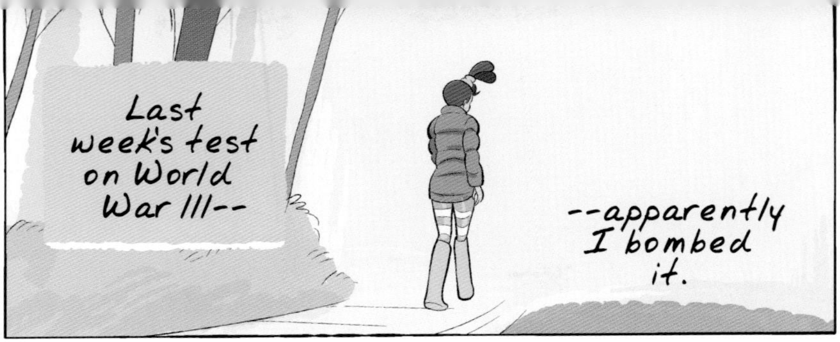
Last week's test on World War III--
--apparently I bombed it.
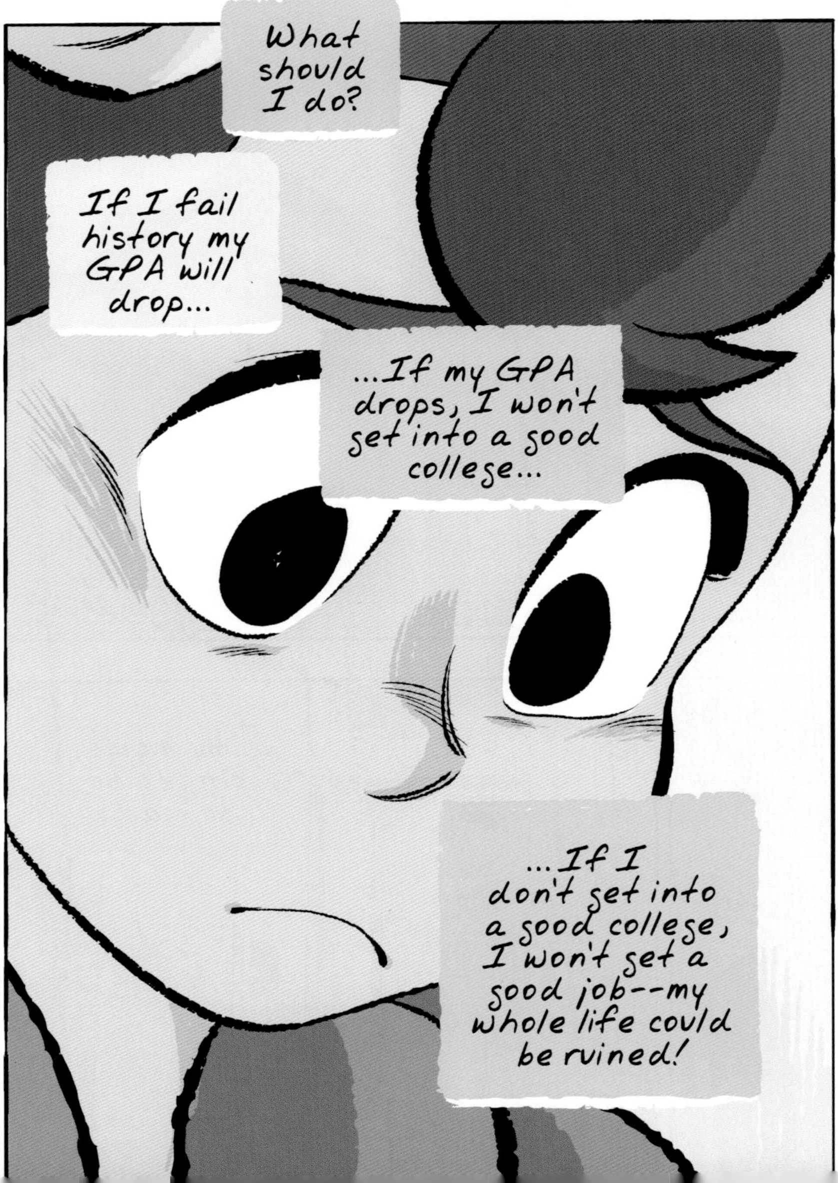
What should I do?
If I fail history my GPA will drop...
...If my GPA drops, I won't get into a good college...
...If I don't get into a good college, I won't get a good job--my whole life could be ruined!

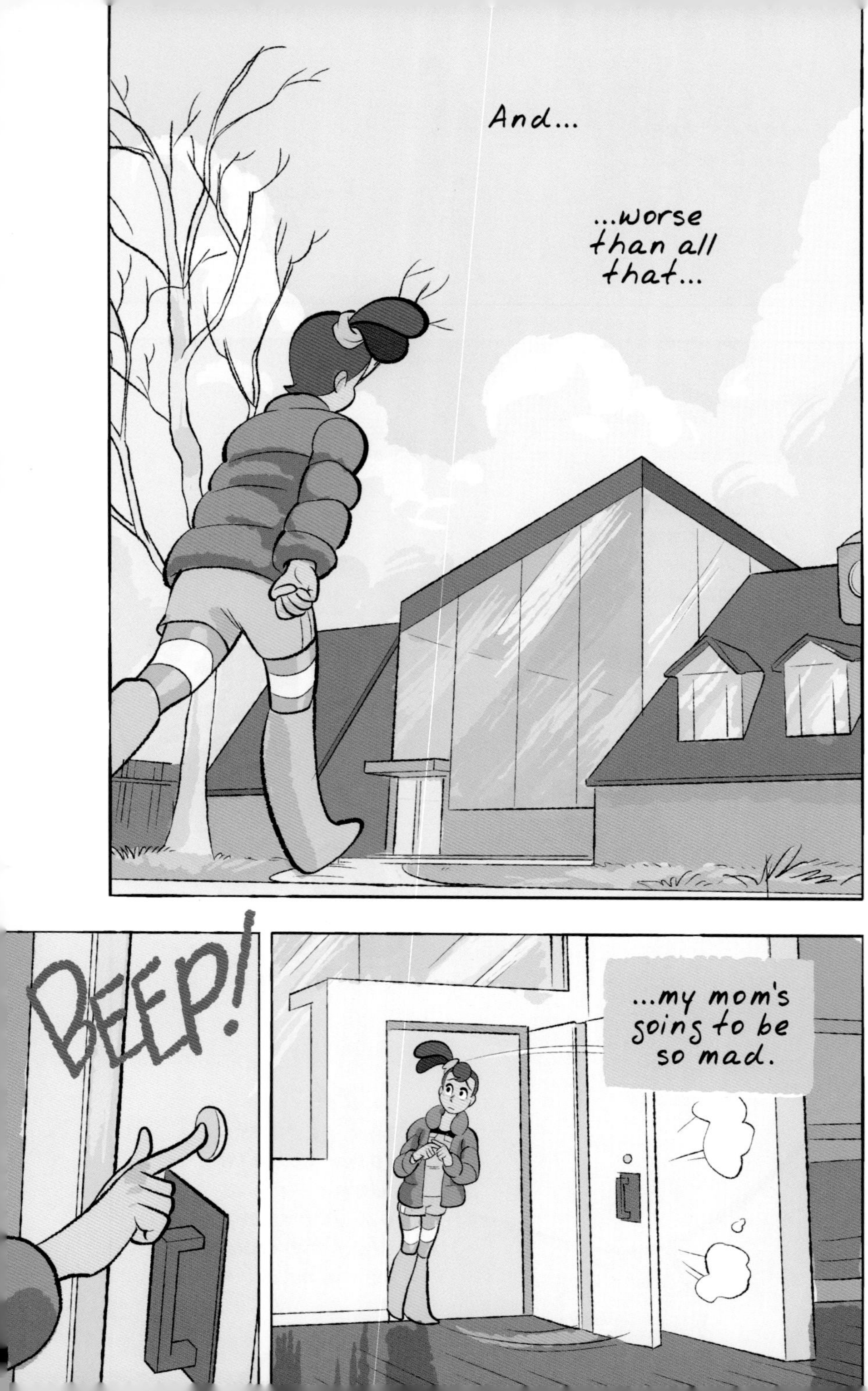
And...
...worse than all that...
BEEP!
...my mom's going to be so mad.

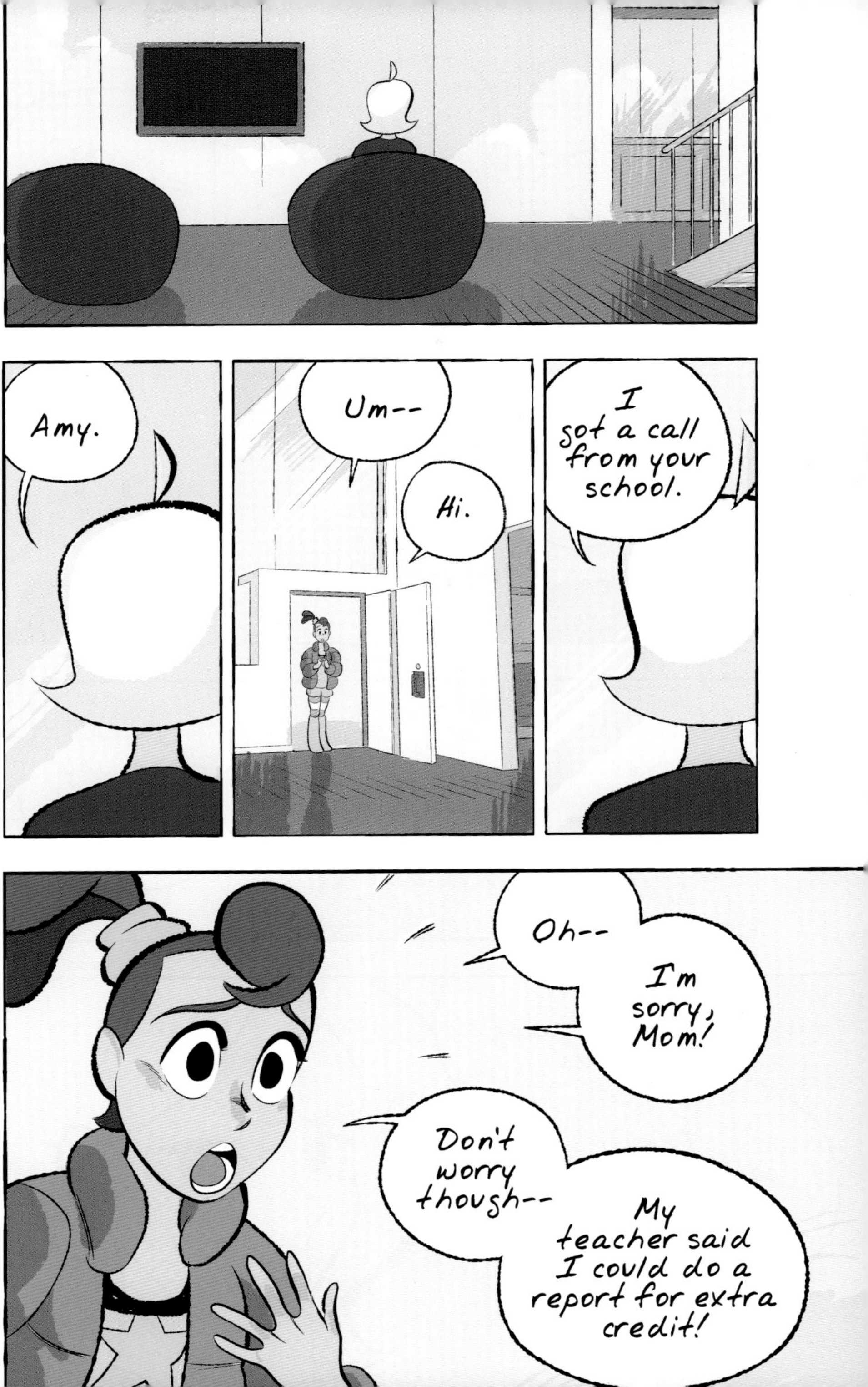
Amy.
Um--
Hi.
I got a call from your school.
Oh--
I'm sorry, Mom!
Don't worry though--
My teacher said I could do a report for extra credit!

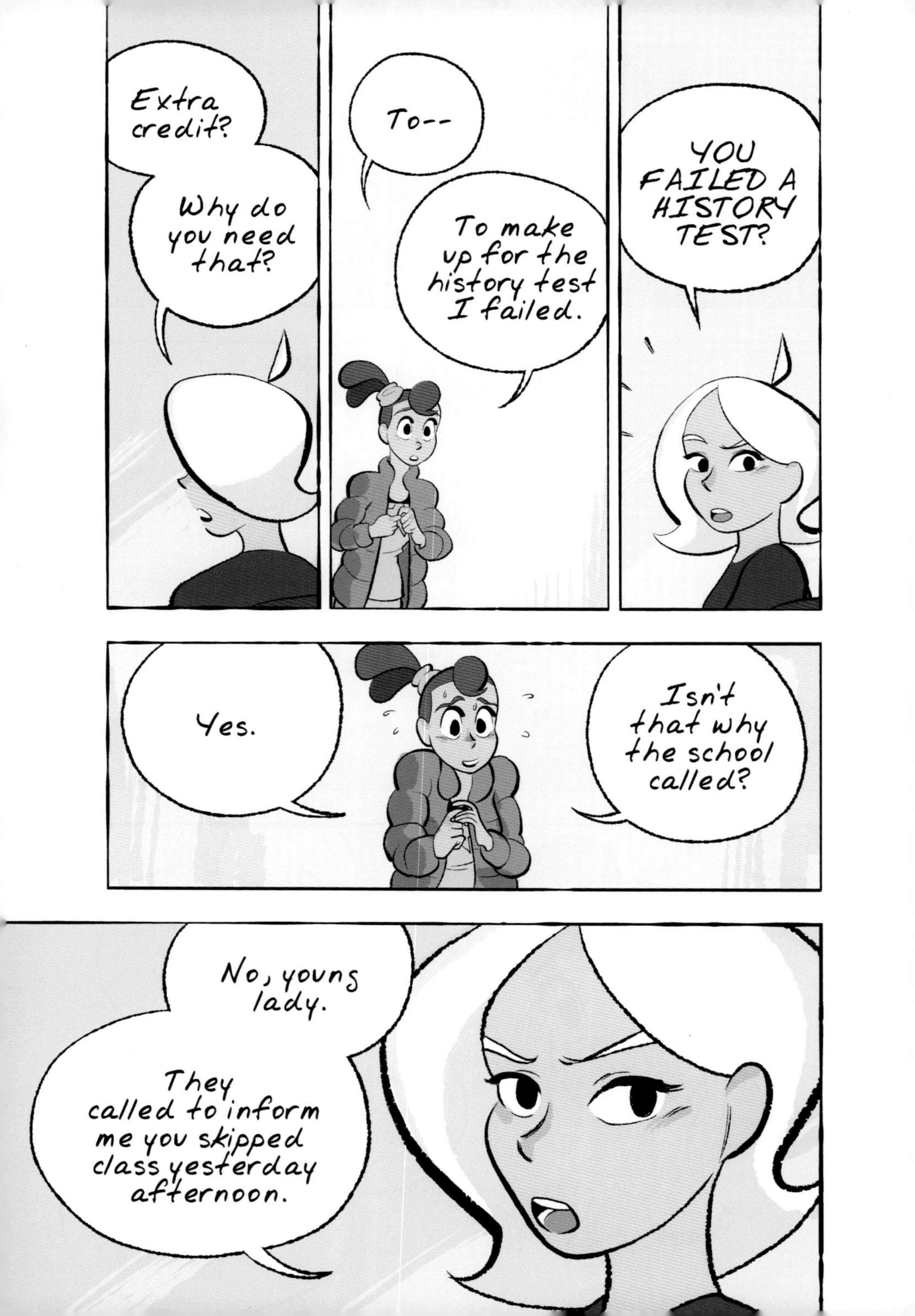
Extra credit?
Why do you need that?
To--
To make up for the history test I failed.
YOU FAILED A HISTORY TEST?
Yes.
Isn't that why the school called?
No, youns lady.
They called to inform me you skipped class yesterday afternoon.

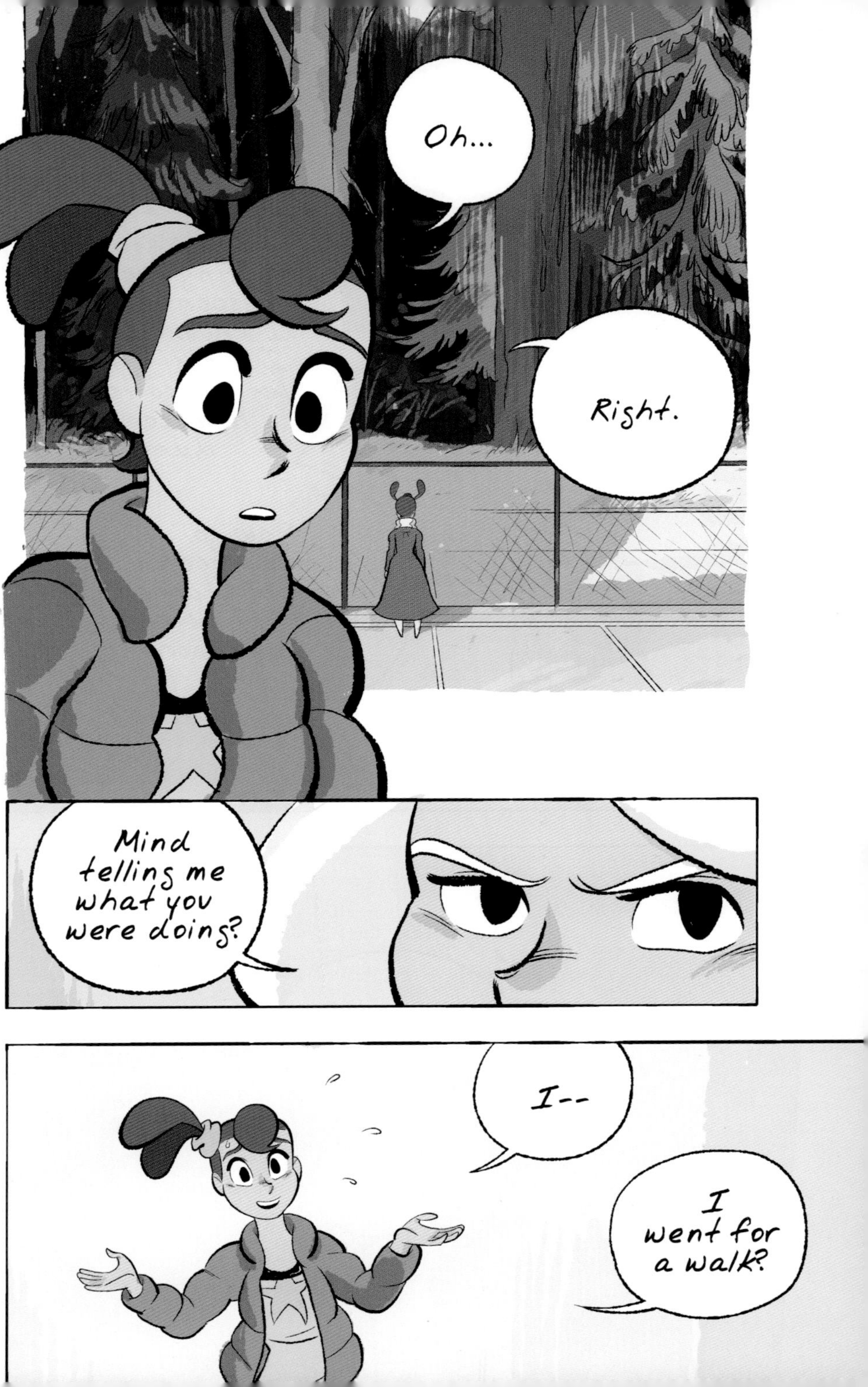
Oh...
Right.
Mind telling me what you were doing?
I--
I went for a walk?

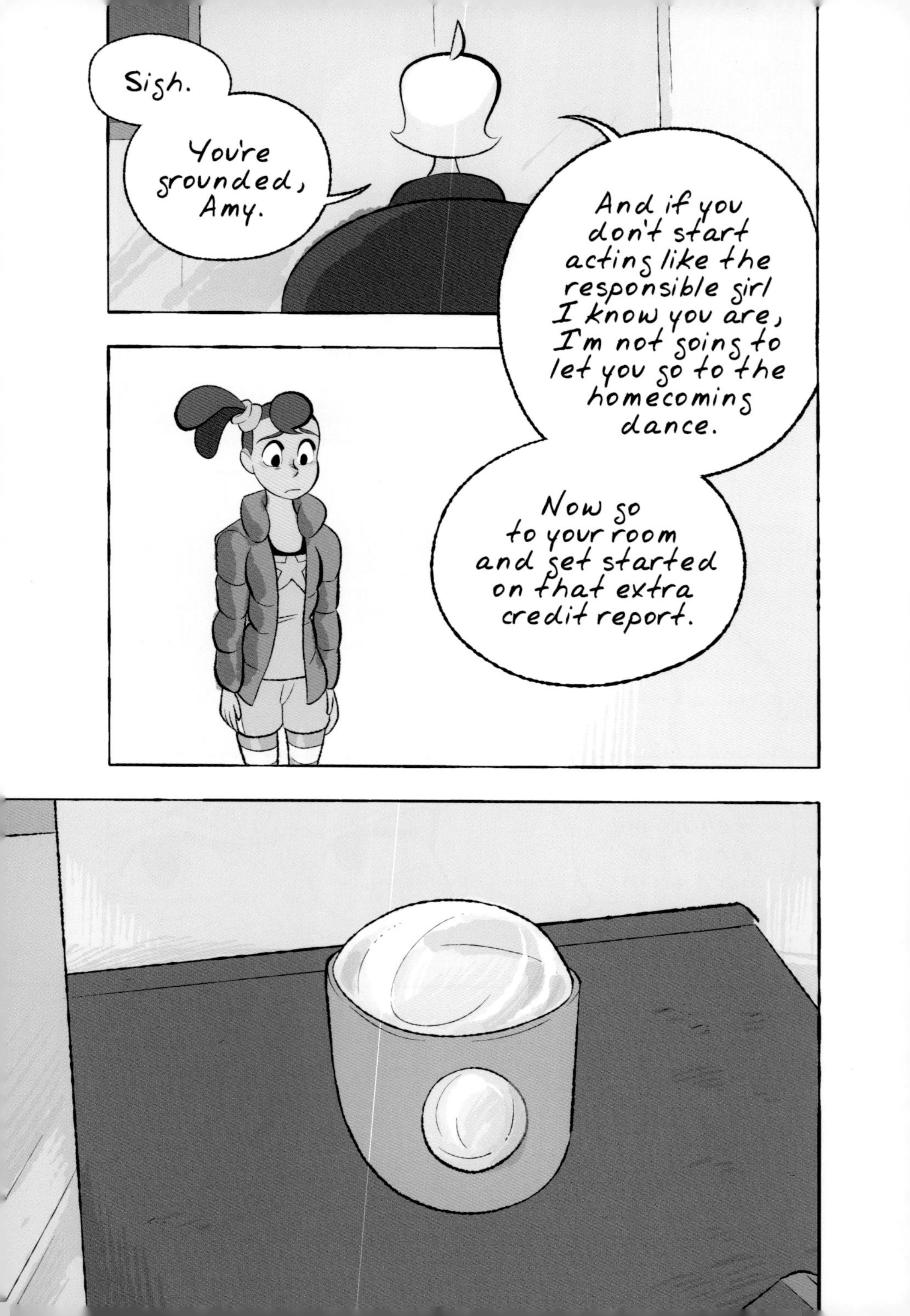
Sigh.
You're grounded, Amy.
And if you don't start acting like the responsible girl I know you are, I'm not going to let you go to the homecoming dance.
Now go to your room and get started on that extra credit report.

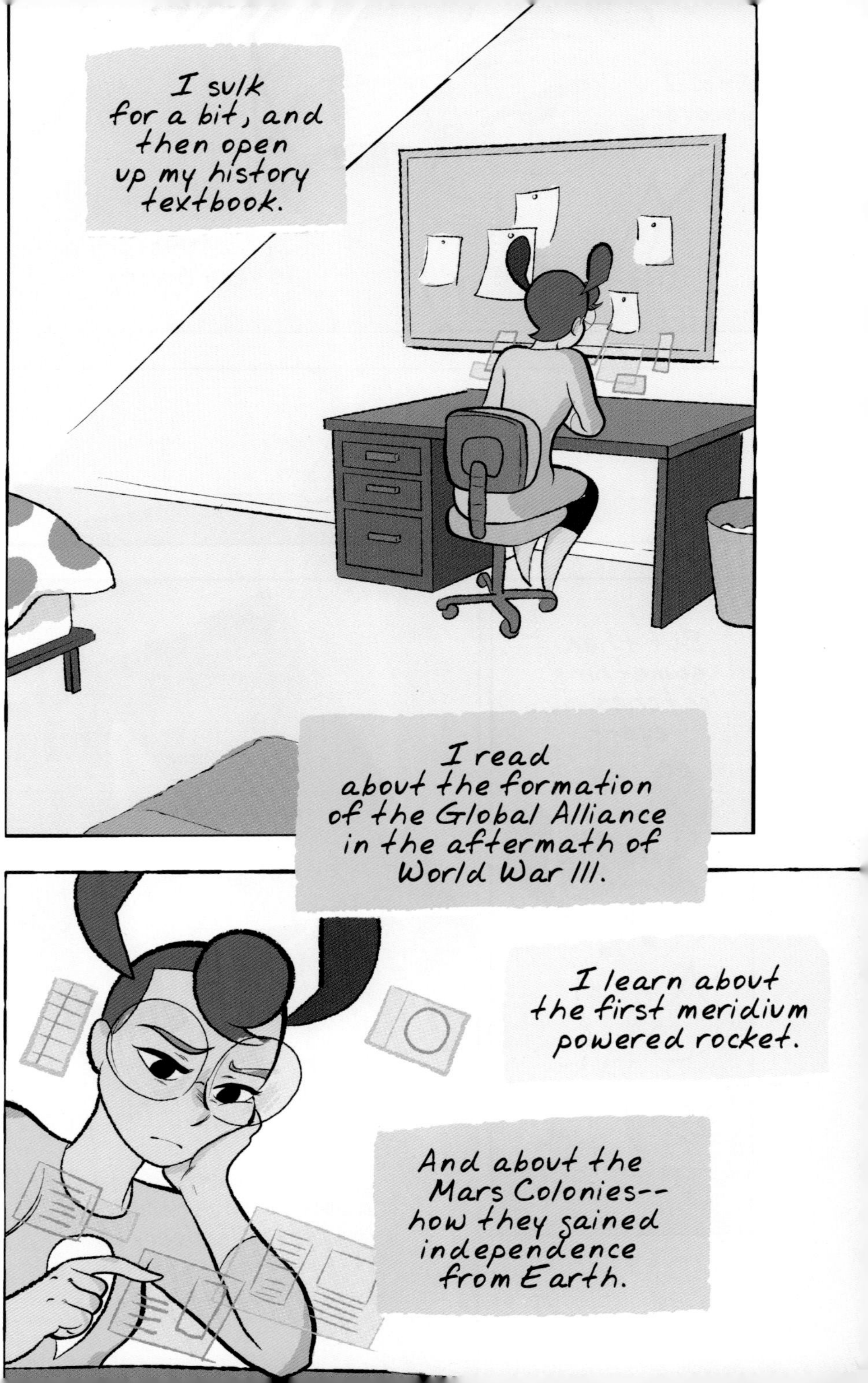
I sulk for a bit, and then open up my history textbook.
I read about the formation of the Global Alliance in the aftermath of World War III.
I learn about the first meridium powered rocket.
And about the Mars Colonies-- how they gained independence from Earth.

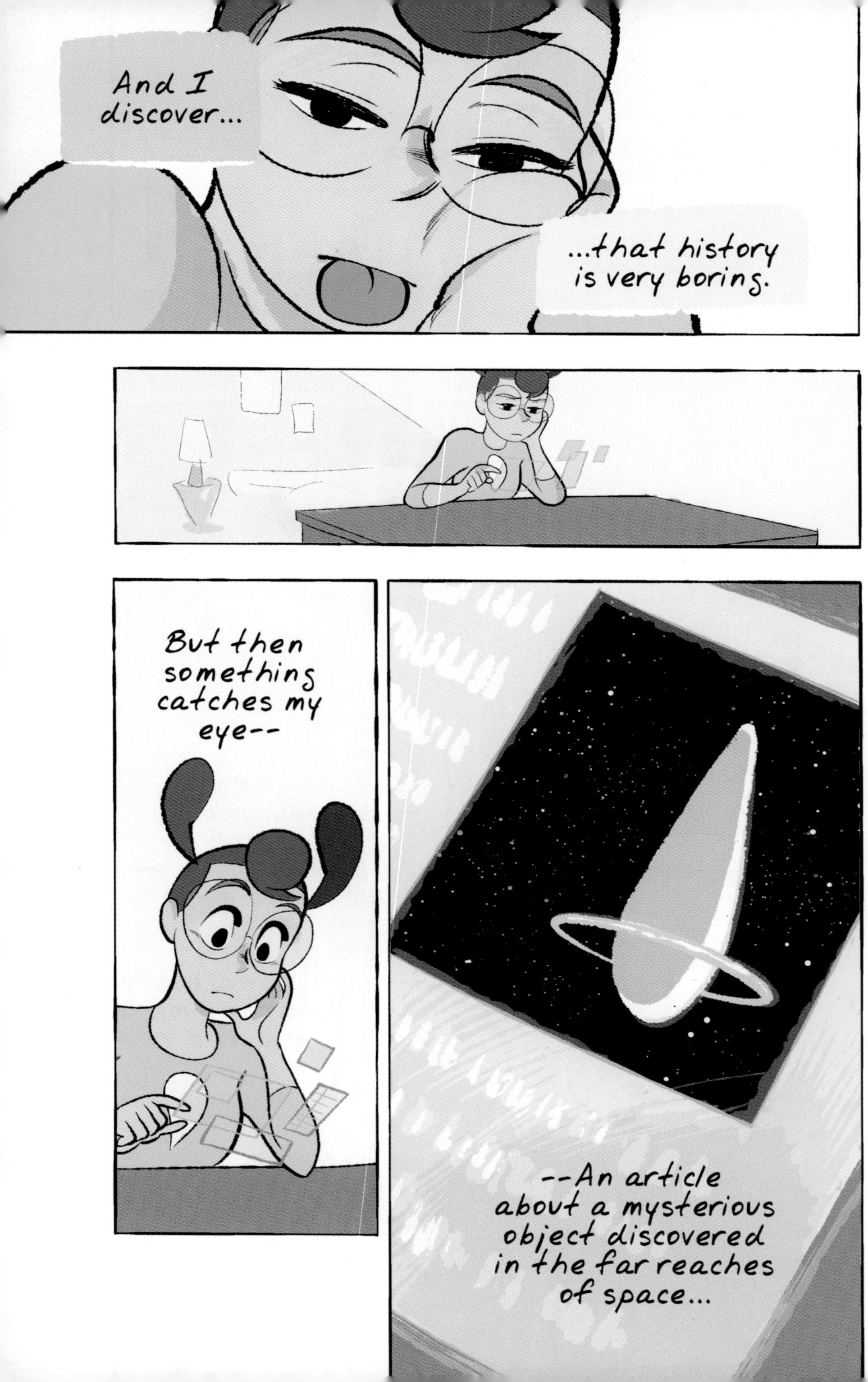
And I discover...
...that history is very boring.
But then something catches my eye--
--An article about a mysterious object discovered in the far reaches of space...

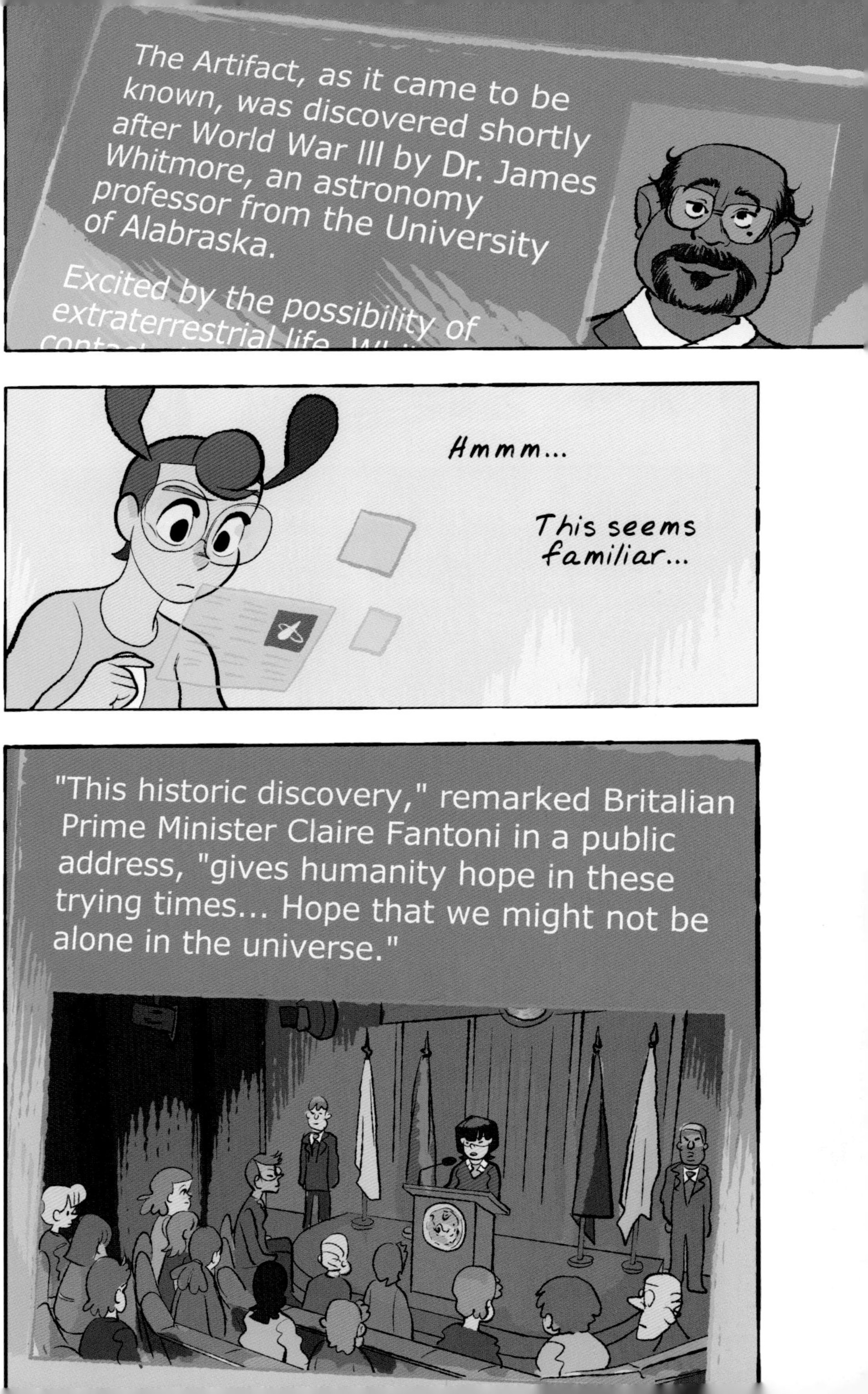
The Artifact, as it came to be known, was discovered shortly after World War III by Dr. James Whitmore, an astronomy professor from the University of Alabraska.
Excited by the possibility of extraterrestrial life,
Hmmm...
This seems familiar...
"This historic discovery," remarked Britalian Prime Minister Claire Fantoni in a public address, "gives humanity hope in these trying times... Hope that we might not be alone in the universe."

A week after Fantoni's speech, the Vietnamerican government announced they were working on a probe capable of making the 322 year journey to the Artifact.

Fearing what might happen if Vietnamerica were to reach the Artifact first, many other countries followed suit--announcing similar projects of their own.

"A race is afoot," declared the Newark Times, "And the prize is the Artifact, and whatever treasure of alien technology it might contain."

In February of 3026, Vietnamerican counterintelligence caught a Cubanian spy trying to sabotage their probe.

Tension mounted and many feared another war would break out.

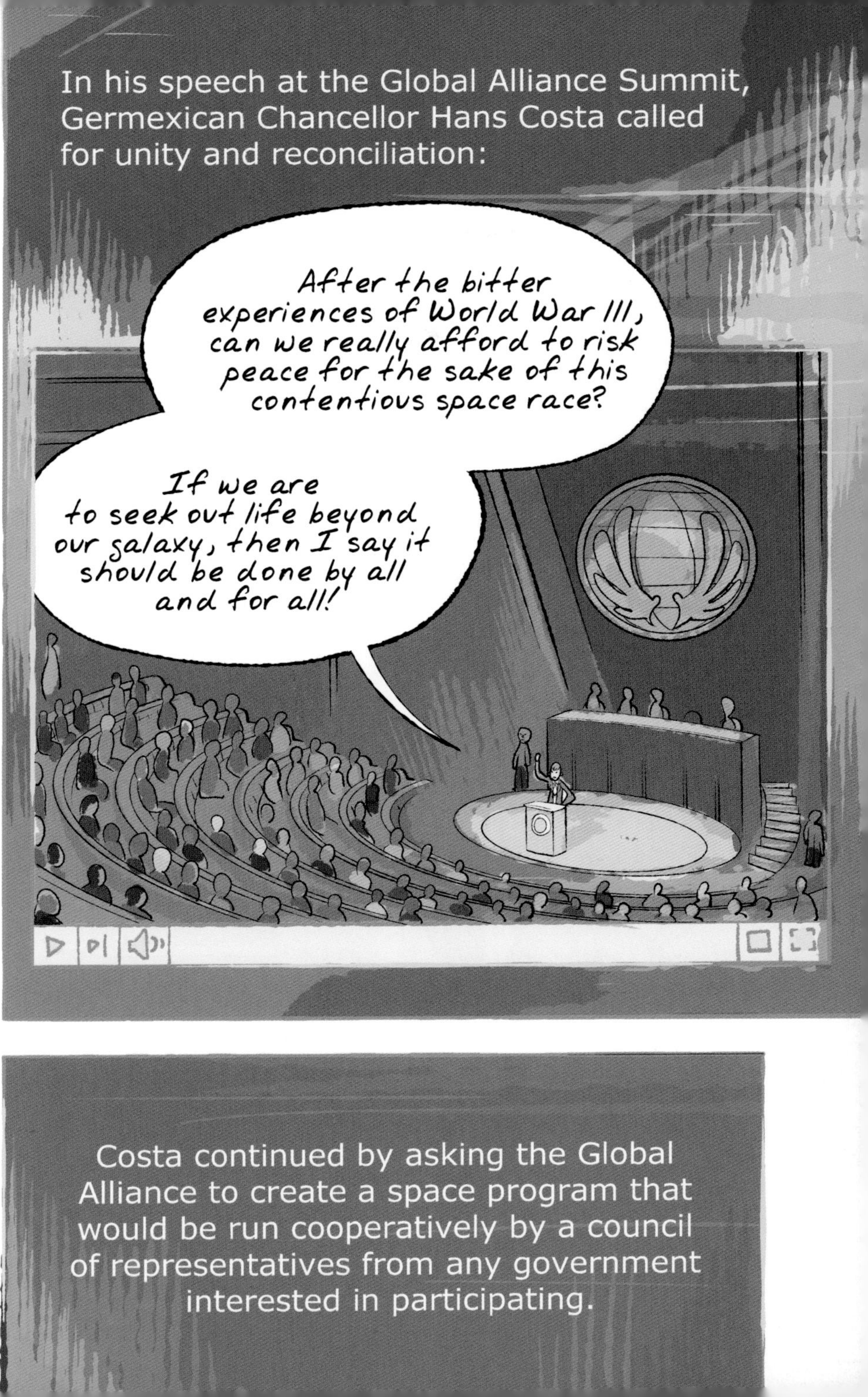
In his speech at the Global Alliance Summit, Germexican Chancellor Hans Costa called for unity and reconciliation:
After the bitter experiences of World War III, can we really afford to risk peace for the sake of this contentious space race?
If we are to seek out life beyond our galaxy, then I say it should be done by all and for all!

Costa continued by asking the Global Alliance to create a space program that would be run cooperatively by a council of representatives from any government interested in participating.

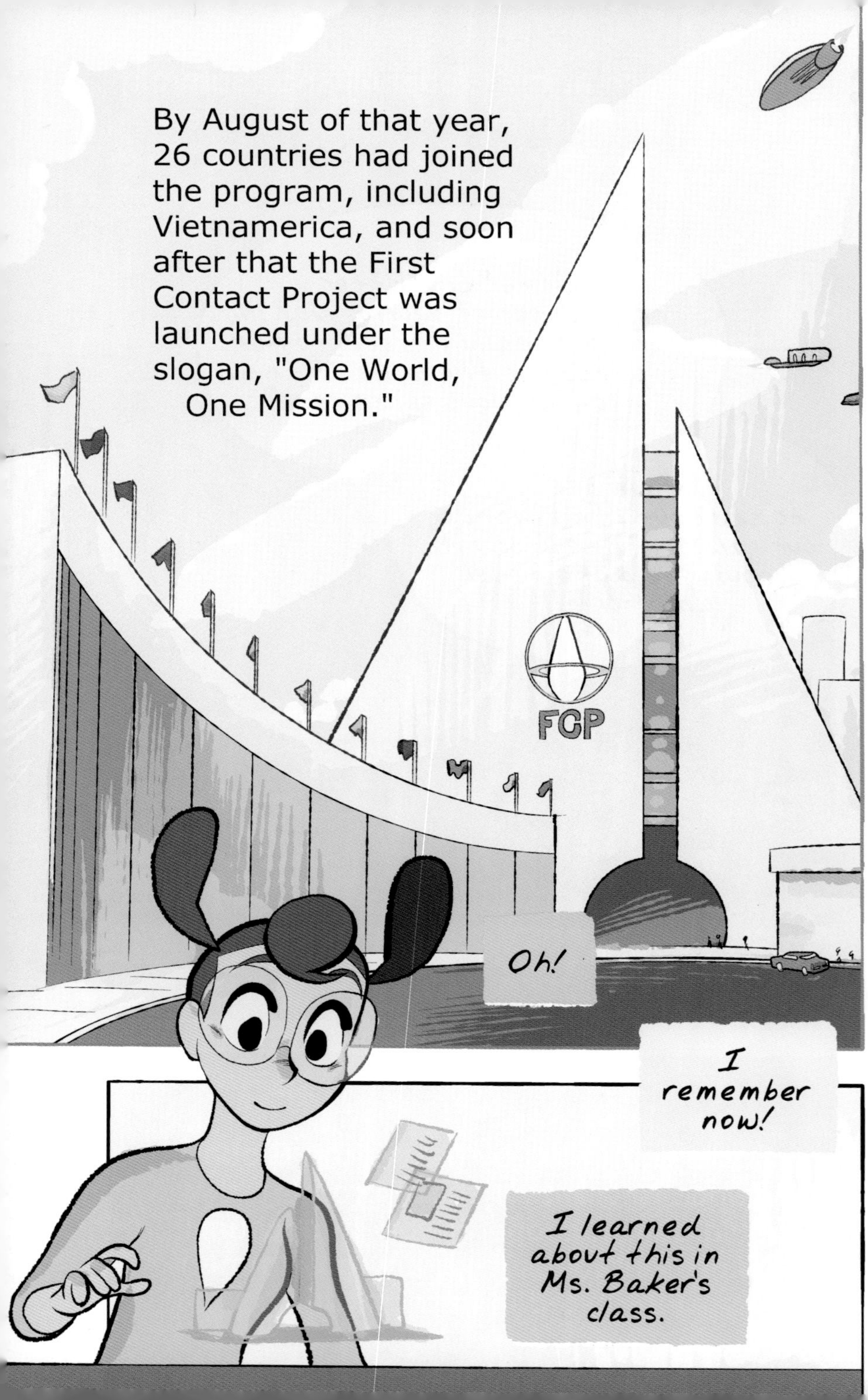
By August of that year, 26 countries had joined the program, including Vietnamerica, and soon after that the First Contact Project was launched under the slogan, "One World, One Mission."
FCP
Oh!
I remember now!
I learned about this in Ms. Baker's class.

Didn't they build a giant spaceship or something?

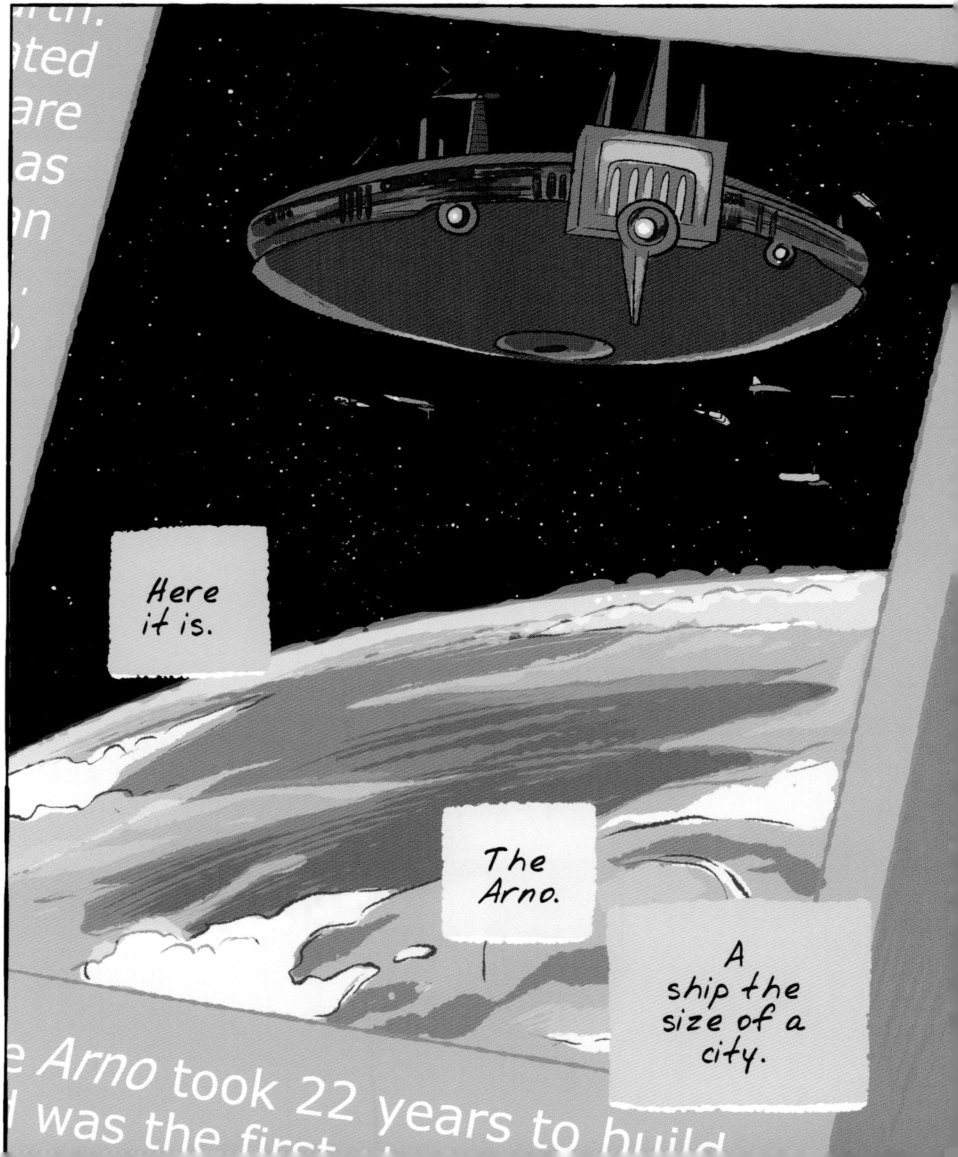
Here it is.
The Arno.
A ship the size of a city.
Arno took 22 years to

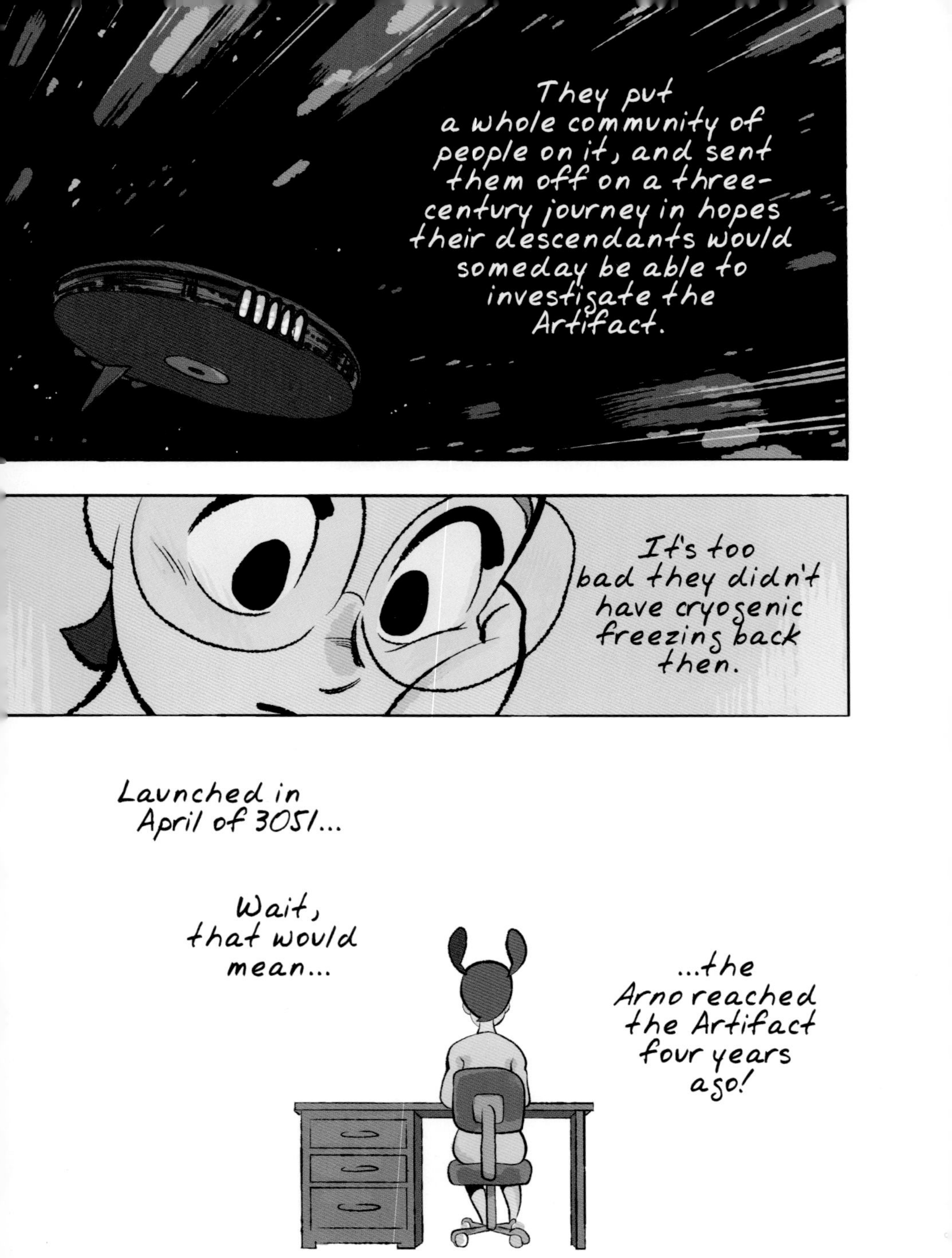
They put a whole community of people on it, and sent them off on a three-century journey in hopes their descendants would someday be able to investigate the Artifact.
It's too bad they didn't have cryogenic freezing back then.
Launched in April of 3051...
Wait, that would mean...
...the Arno reached the Artifact four years ago!

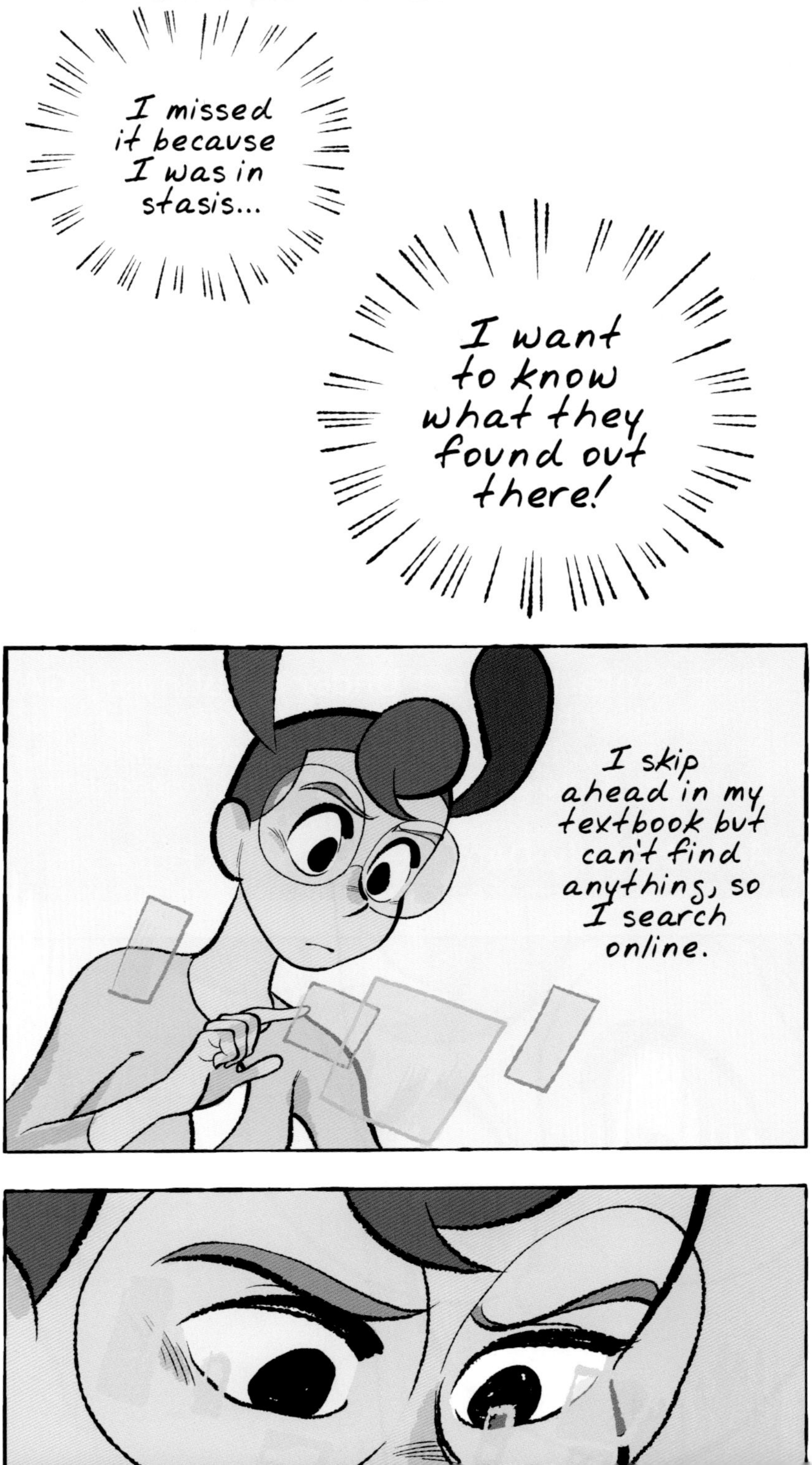
I missed it because I was in stasis...
I want to know what they found out there!
I skip ahead in my textbook but can't find anything, so I search online.

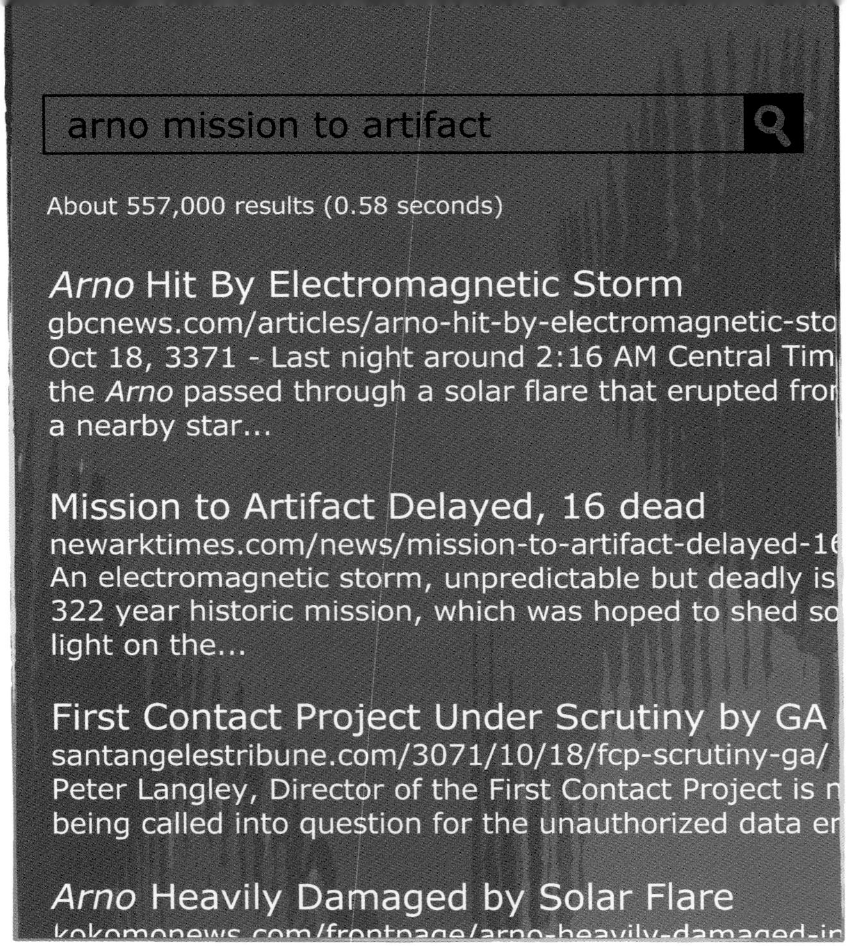

Arno Hit By Electromagnetic Storm
gbcnews.com/articles/arno-hit-by-electromagnetic-sto
Oct 18, 3371 - Last night around 2:16 AM Central Tim
the *Arno* passed through a solar flare that erupted fror
a nearby star...

Mission to Artifact Delayed, 16 dead
newarktimes.com/news/mission-to-artifact-delayed-16
An electromagnetic storm, unpredictable but deadly is
322 year historic mission, which was hoped to shed so
light on the...

First Contact Project Under Scrutiny by GA
santangelestribune.com/3071/10/18/fcp-scrutiny-ga/
Peter Langley, Director of the First Contact Project is n
being called into question for the unauthorized data er

Arno Heavily Damaged by Solar Flare
kokomonews.com/frontpage/arno-heavily-damaged-in

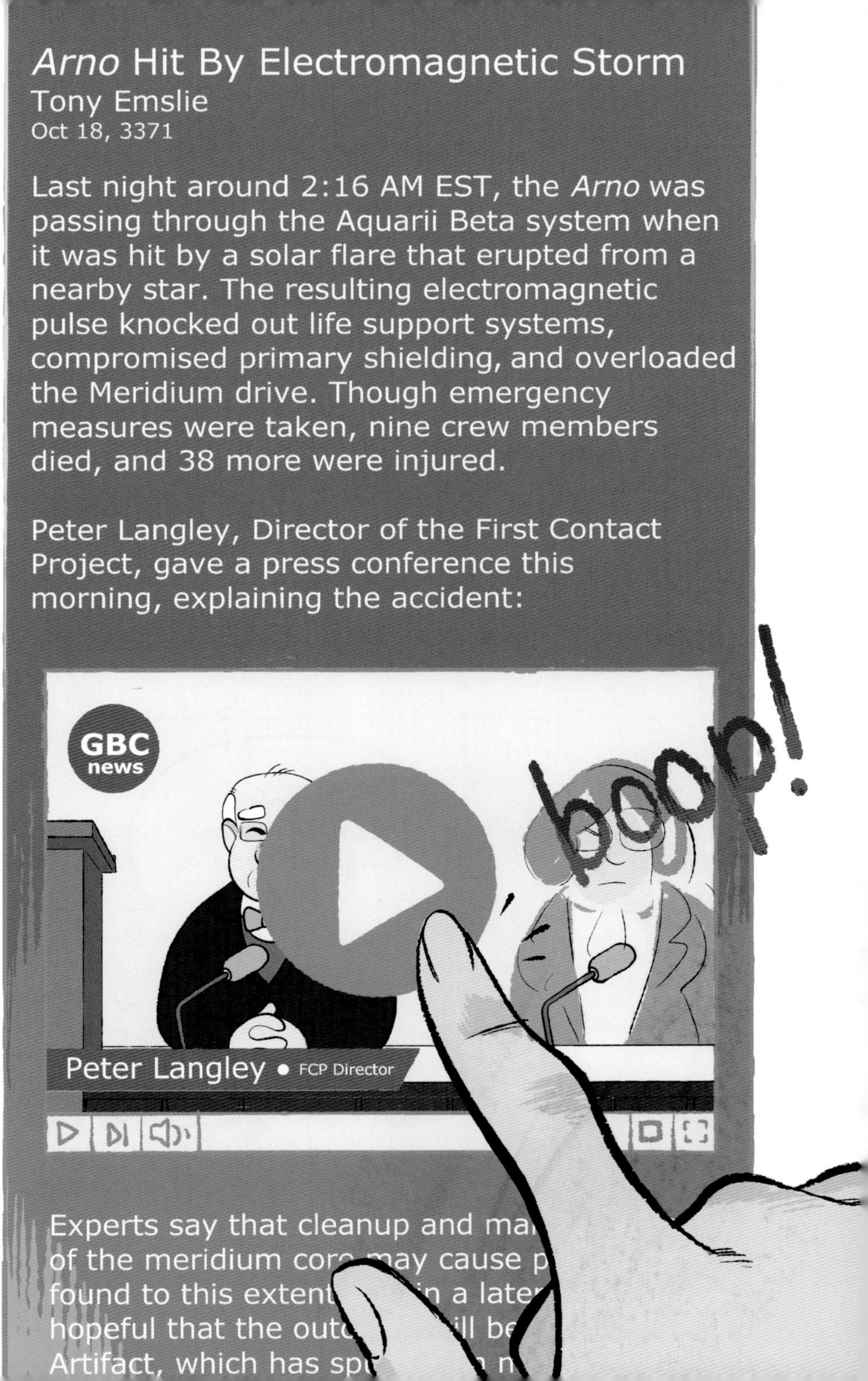

Arno Hit By Electromagnetic Storm
Tony Emslie
Oct 18, 3371
Last night around 2:16 AM EST, the Arno was passing through the Aquarii Beta system when it was hit by a solar flare that erupted from a nearby star. The resulting electromagnetic pulse knocked out life support systems, compromised primary shielding, and overloaded the Meridium drive. Though emergency measures were taken, nine crew members died, and 38 more were injured.
Peter Langley, Director of the First Contact Project, gave a press conference this morning, explaining the accident:
GBC news
Peter Langley • FCP Director
boop!
Experts say that cleanup and ma
of the meridium cor may cause p
found to this extent n a late
hopeful that the out ill be
Artifact, which has sp n

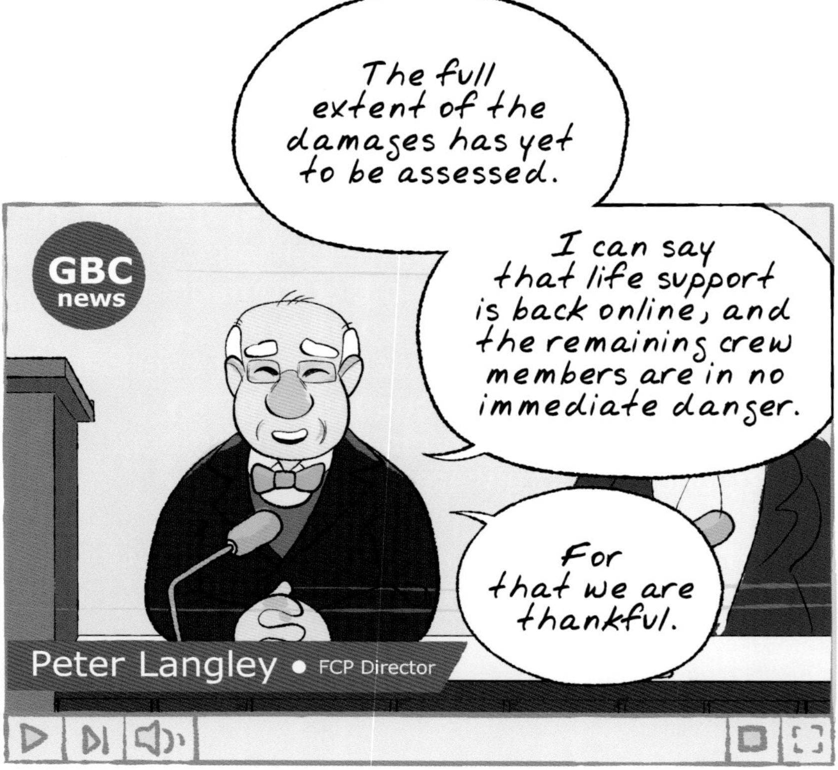
The full extent of the damages has yet to be assessed.
I can say that life support is back online, and the remaining crew members are in no immediate danger.
For that we are thankful.
GBC news
Peter Langley • FCP Director

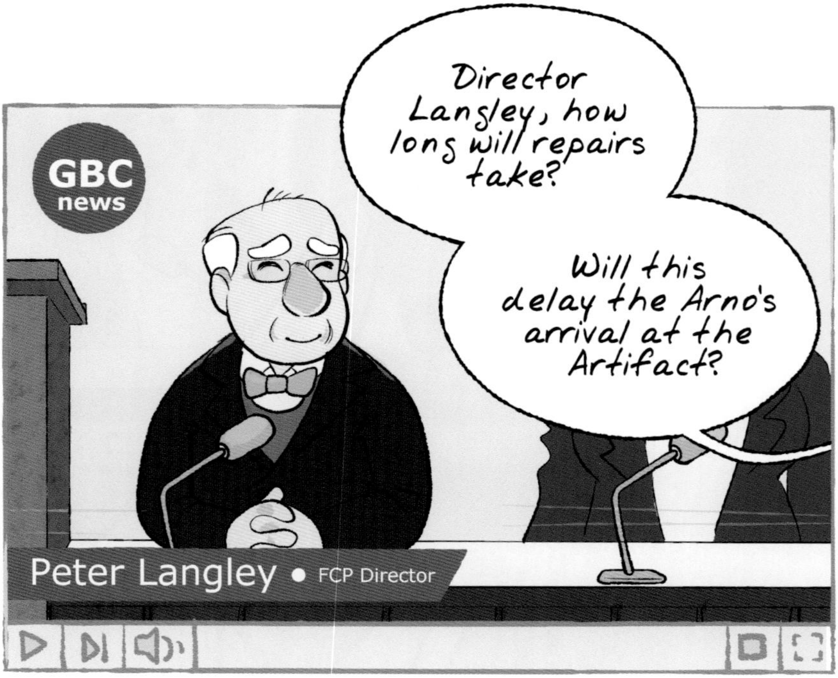
Director Langley, how long will repairs take?
Will this delay the Arno's arrival at the Artifact?
GBC news
Peter Langley • FCP Director

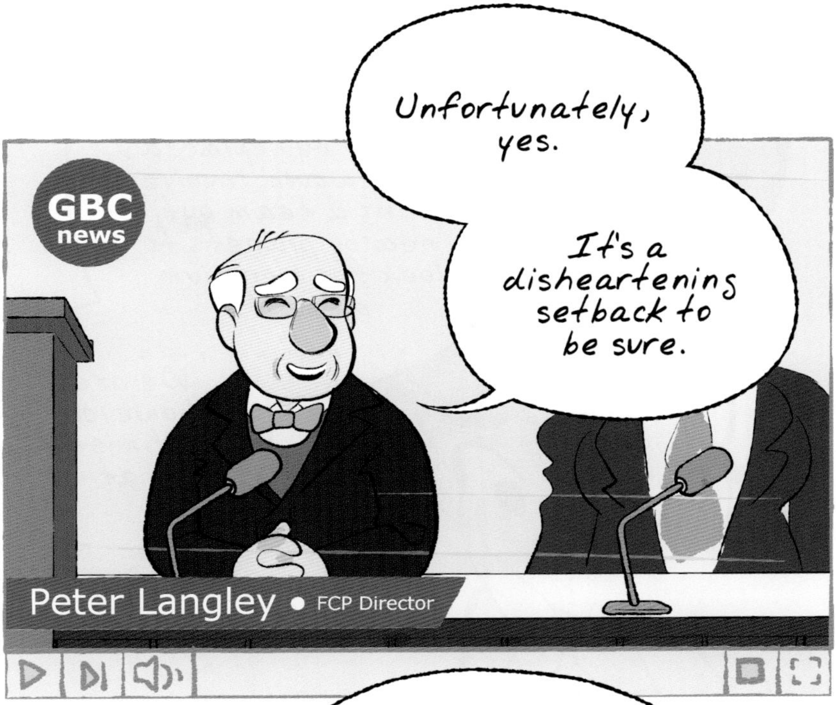
Unfortunately, yes.
It's a disheartening setback to be sure.
GBC news
Peter Langley • FCP Director

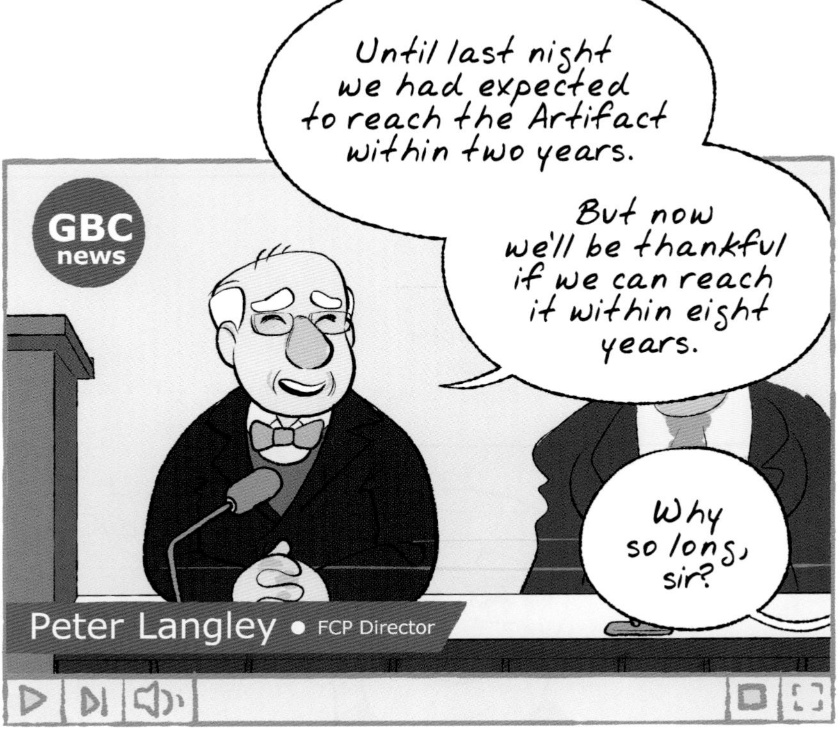
Until last night we had expected to reach the Artifact within two years.
But now we'll be thankful if we can reach it within eight years.
Why so long, sir?
GBC news
Peter Langley • FCP Director

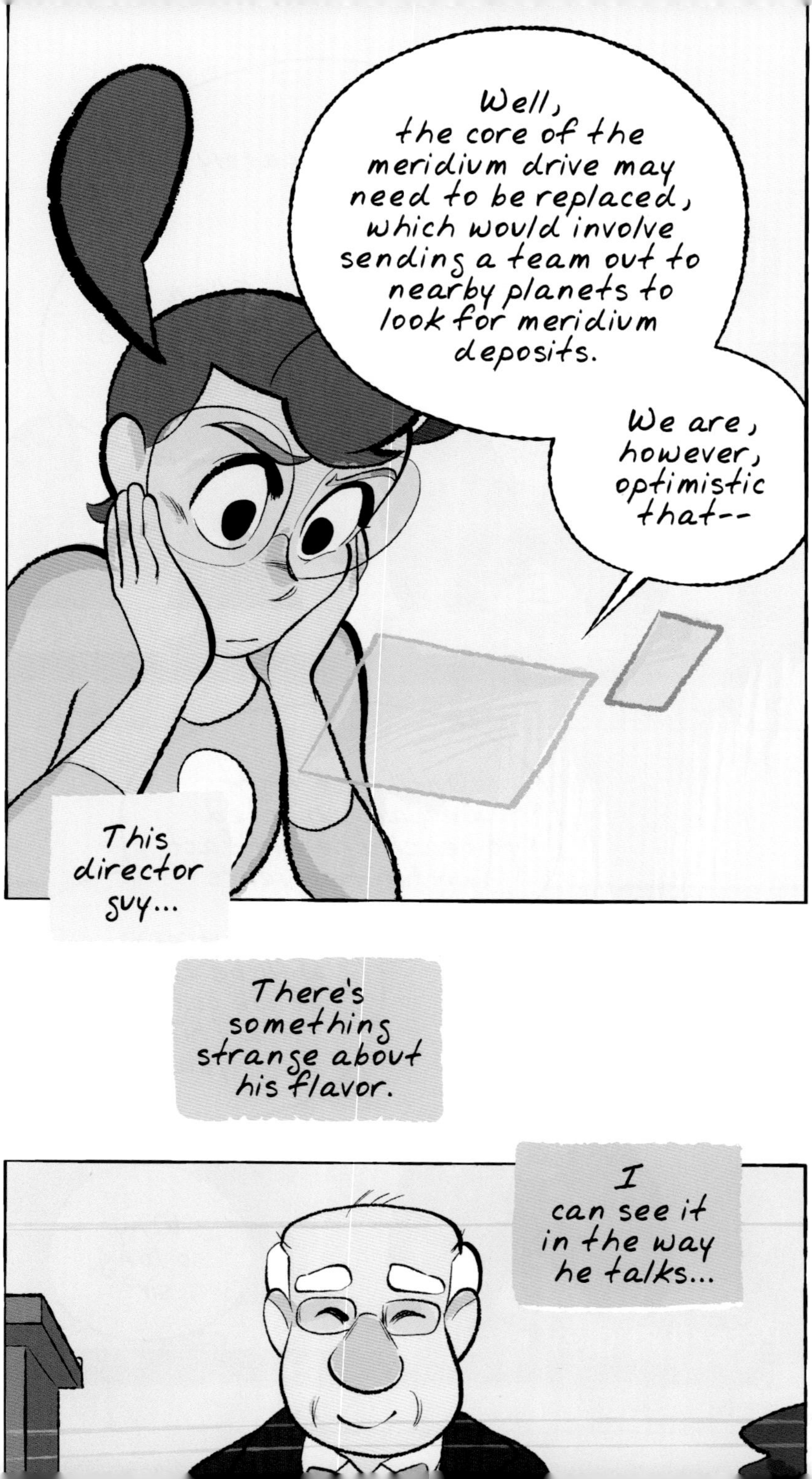
Well, the core of the meridium drive may need to be replaced, which would involve sending a team out to nearby planets to look for meridium deposits.
We are, however, optimistic that--
This director guy...
There's something strange about his flavor.
I can see it in the way he talks...

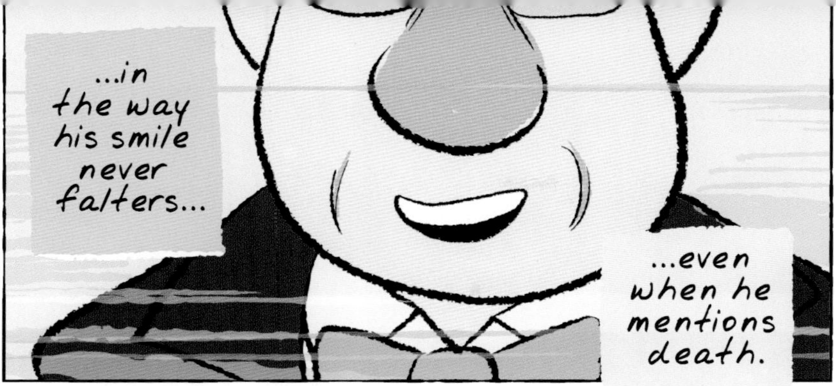
...in the way his smile never falters...
...even when he mentions death.
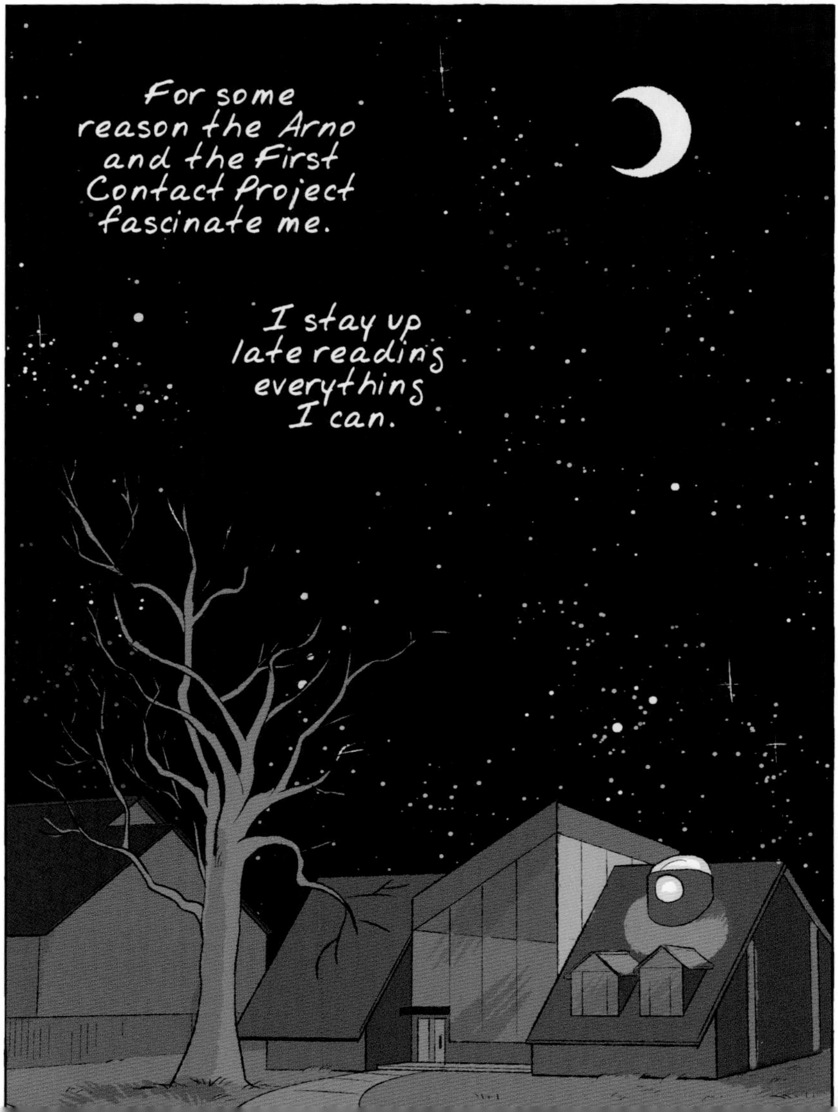
For some reason the Arno and the First Contact Project fascinate me.
I stay up late reading everything I can.

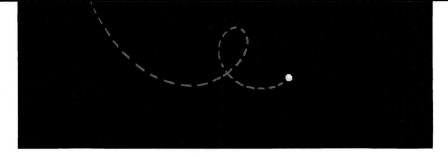

Z

KNOCK
KNOCK

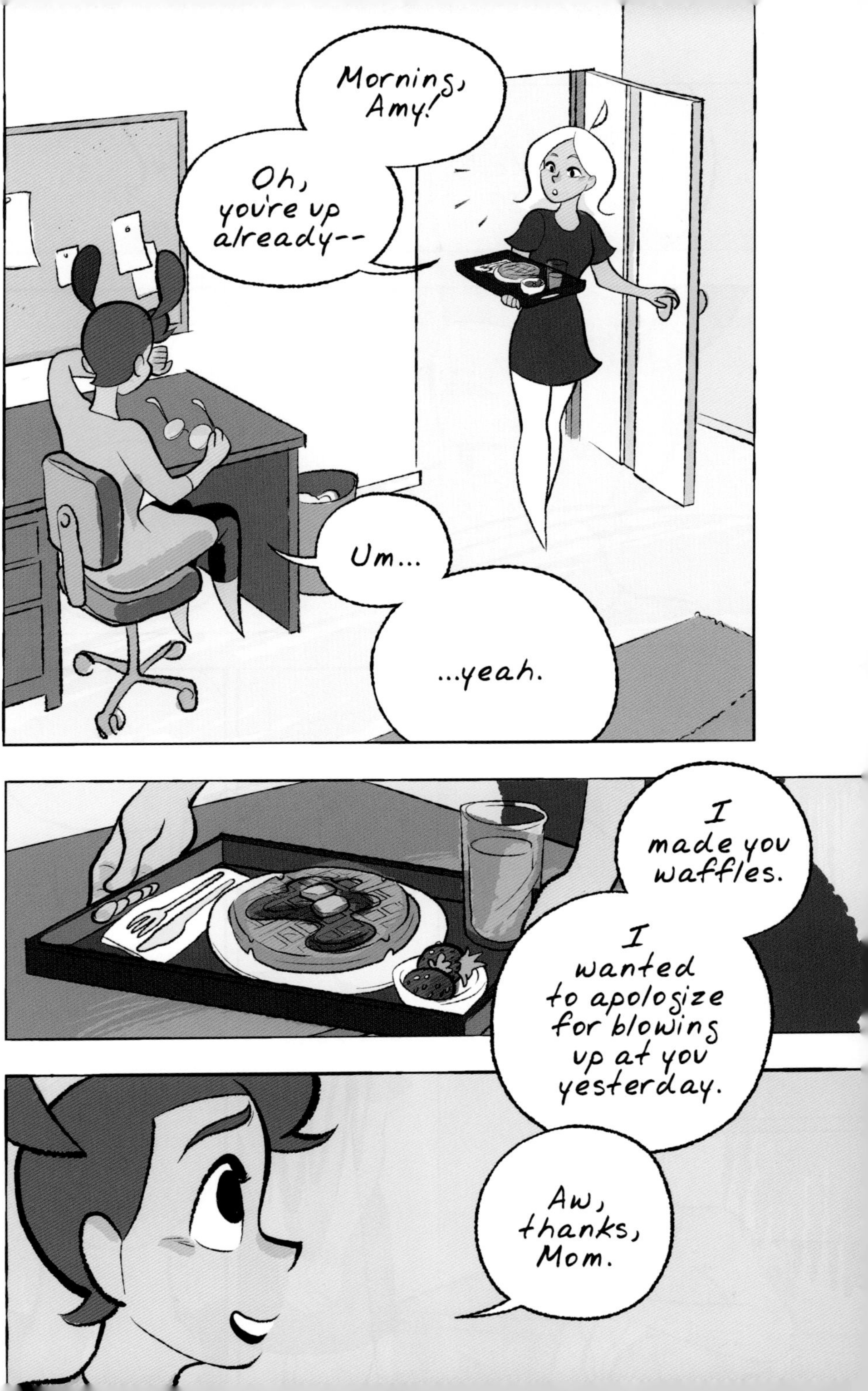
Morning, Amy!
Oh, you're up already--
Um...
...yeah.
I made you waffles.
I wanted to apologize for blowing up at you yesterday.
Aw, thanks, Mom.

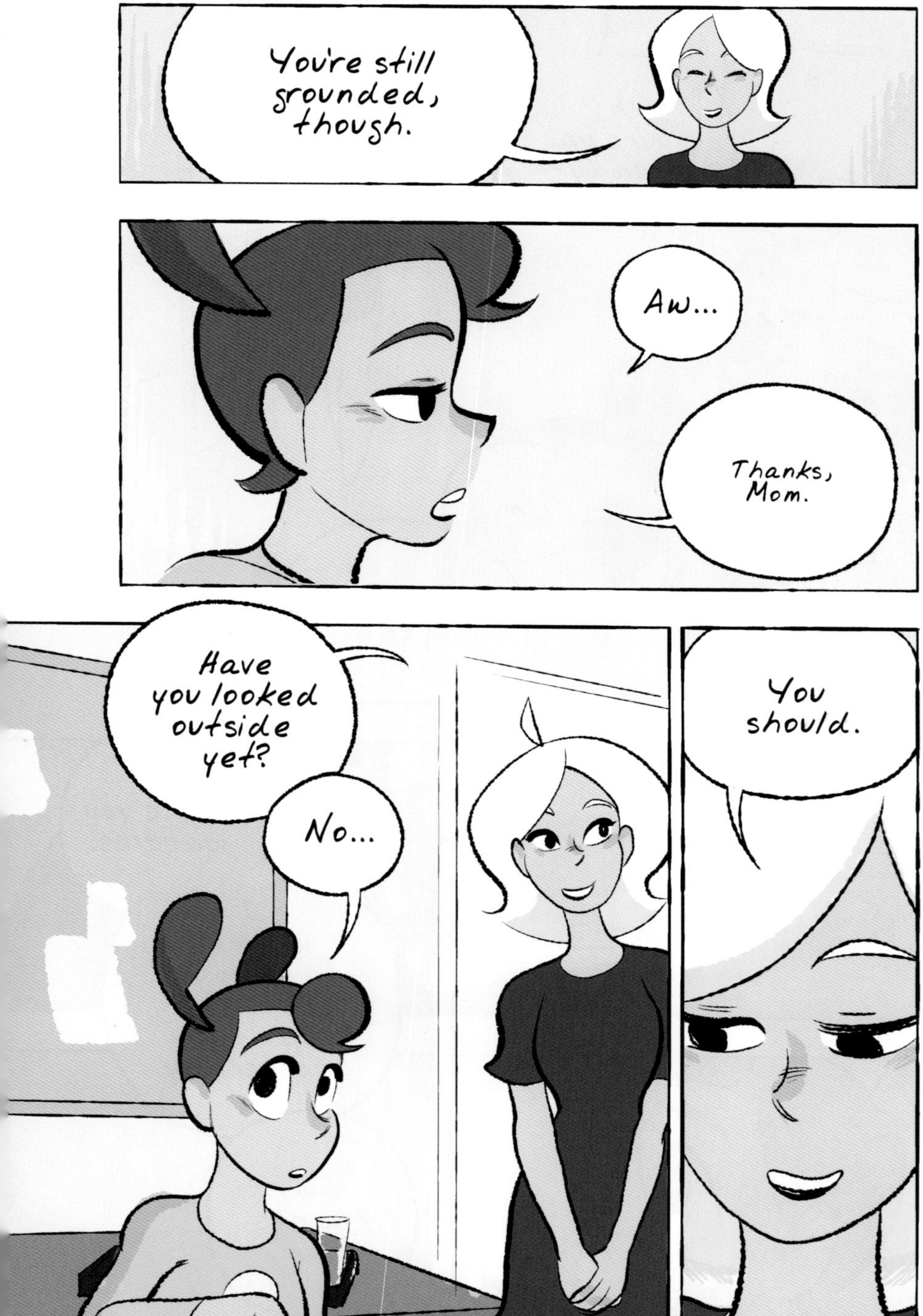
You're still grounded, though.
Aw...
Thanks, Mom.
Have you looked outside yet?
No...
You should.

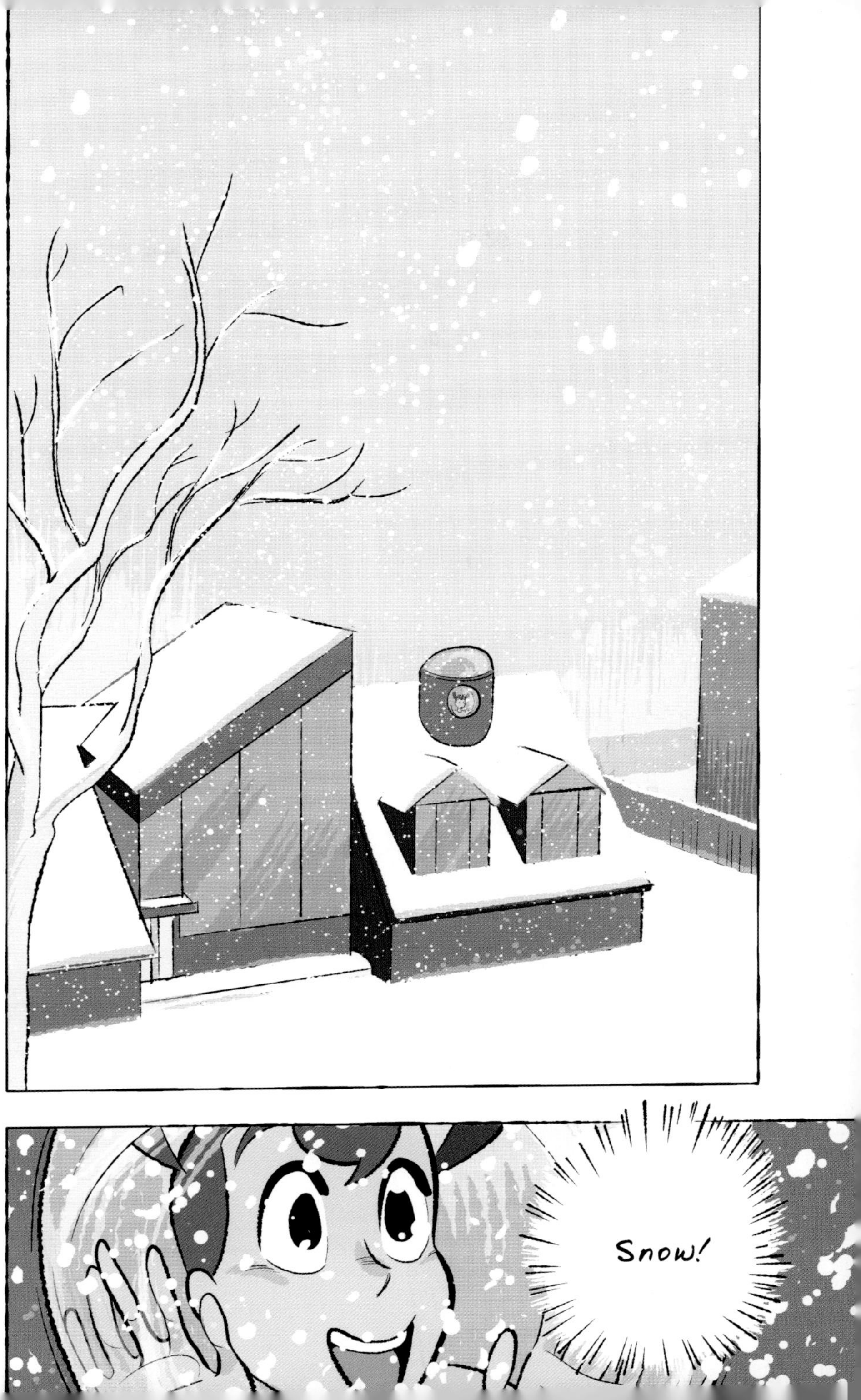
Snow!

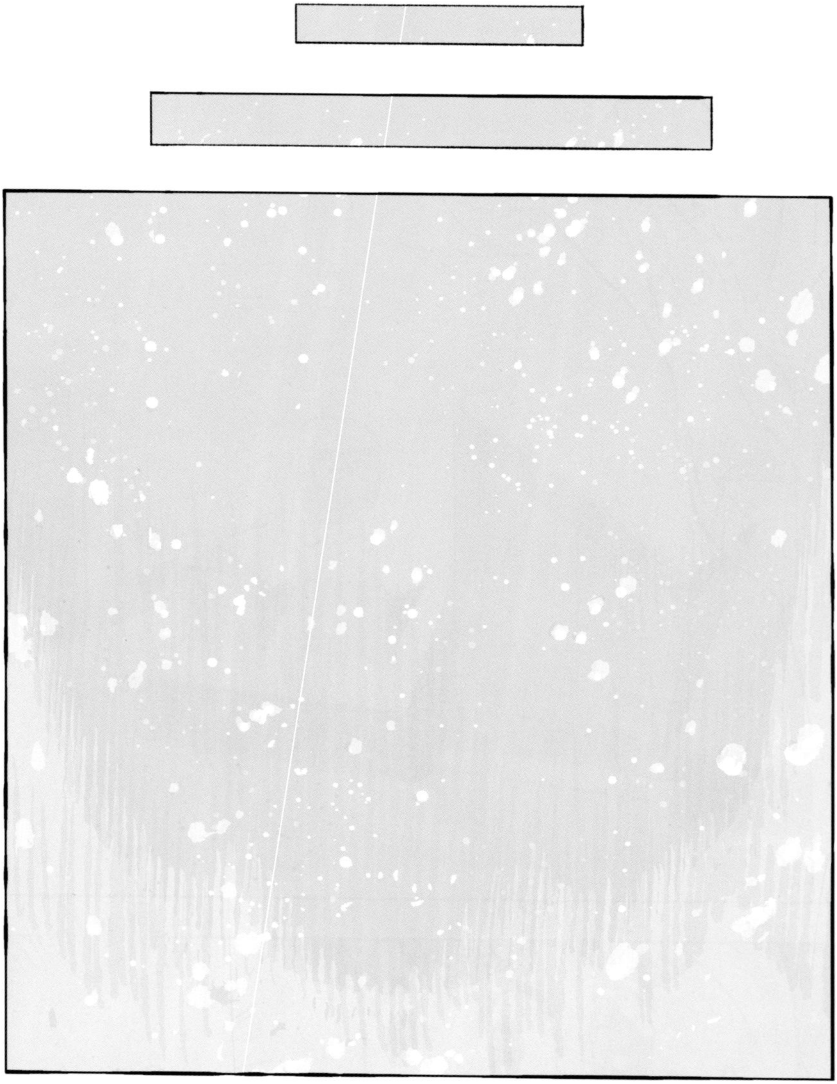

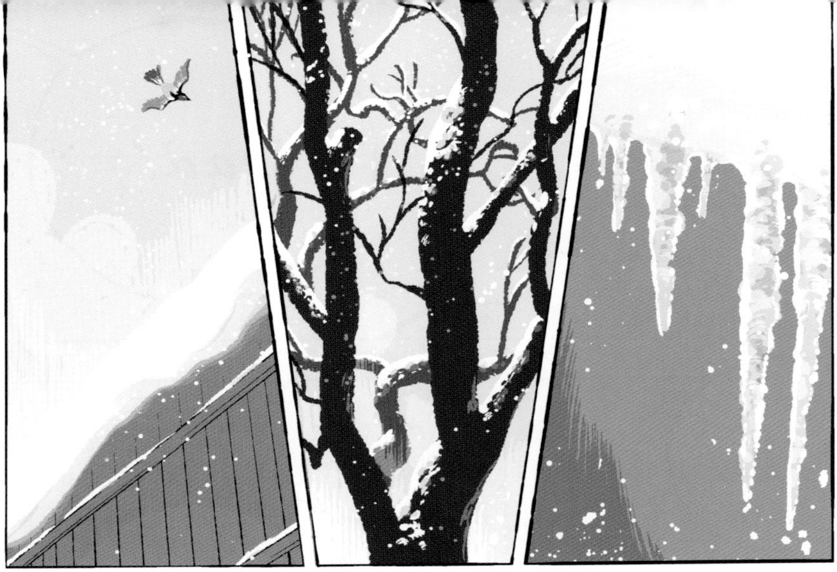
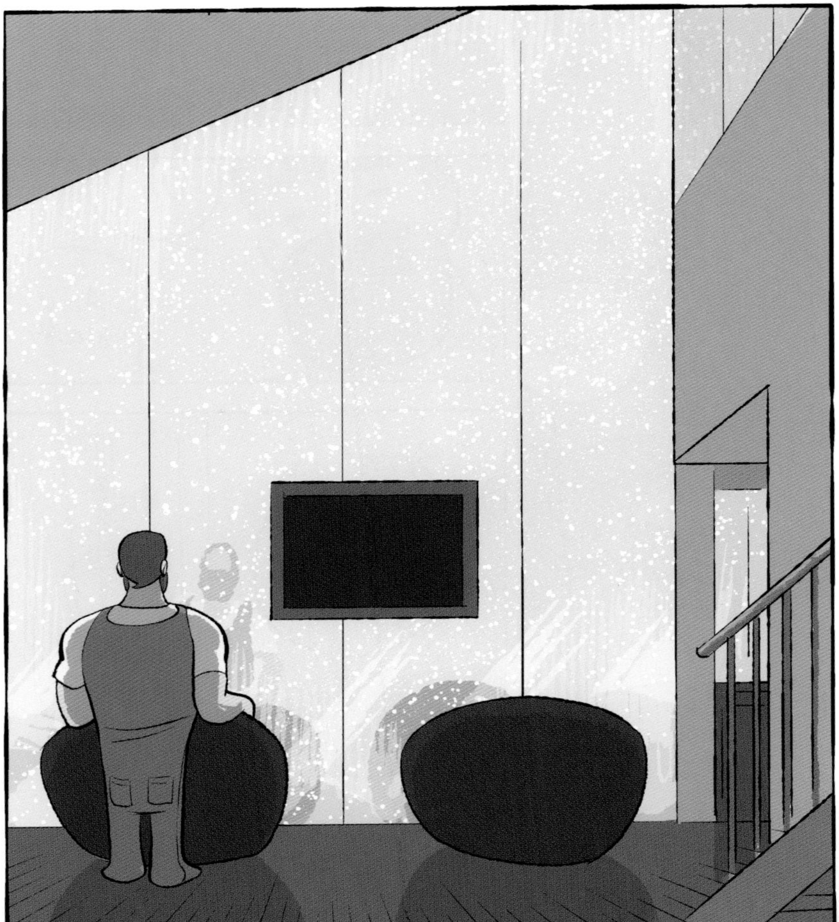

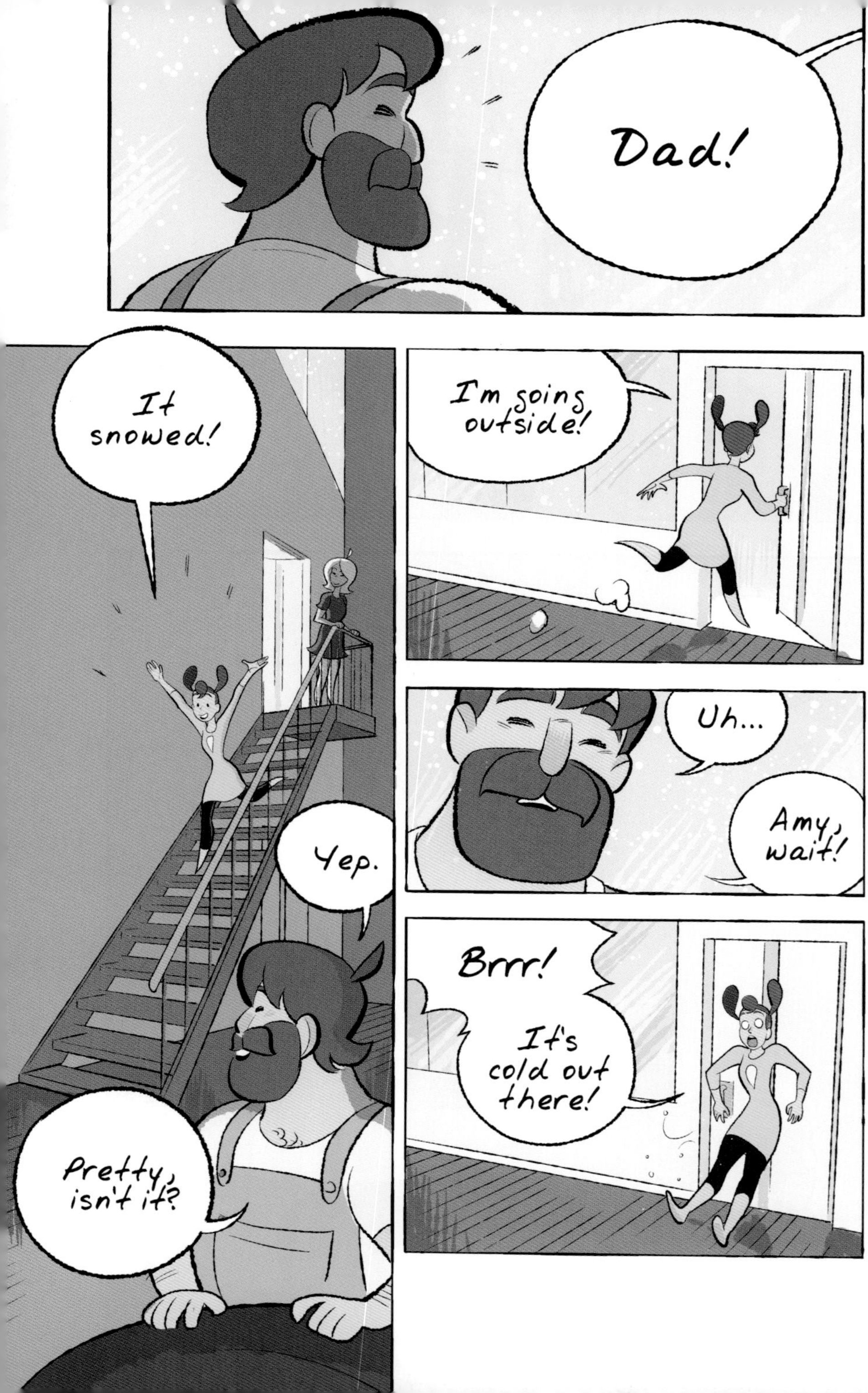
Dad!
It snowed!
Yep.
Pretty, isn't it?
I'm going outside!
Uh...
Amy, wait!
Brrr!
It's cold out there!

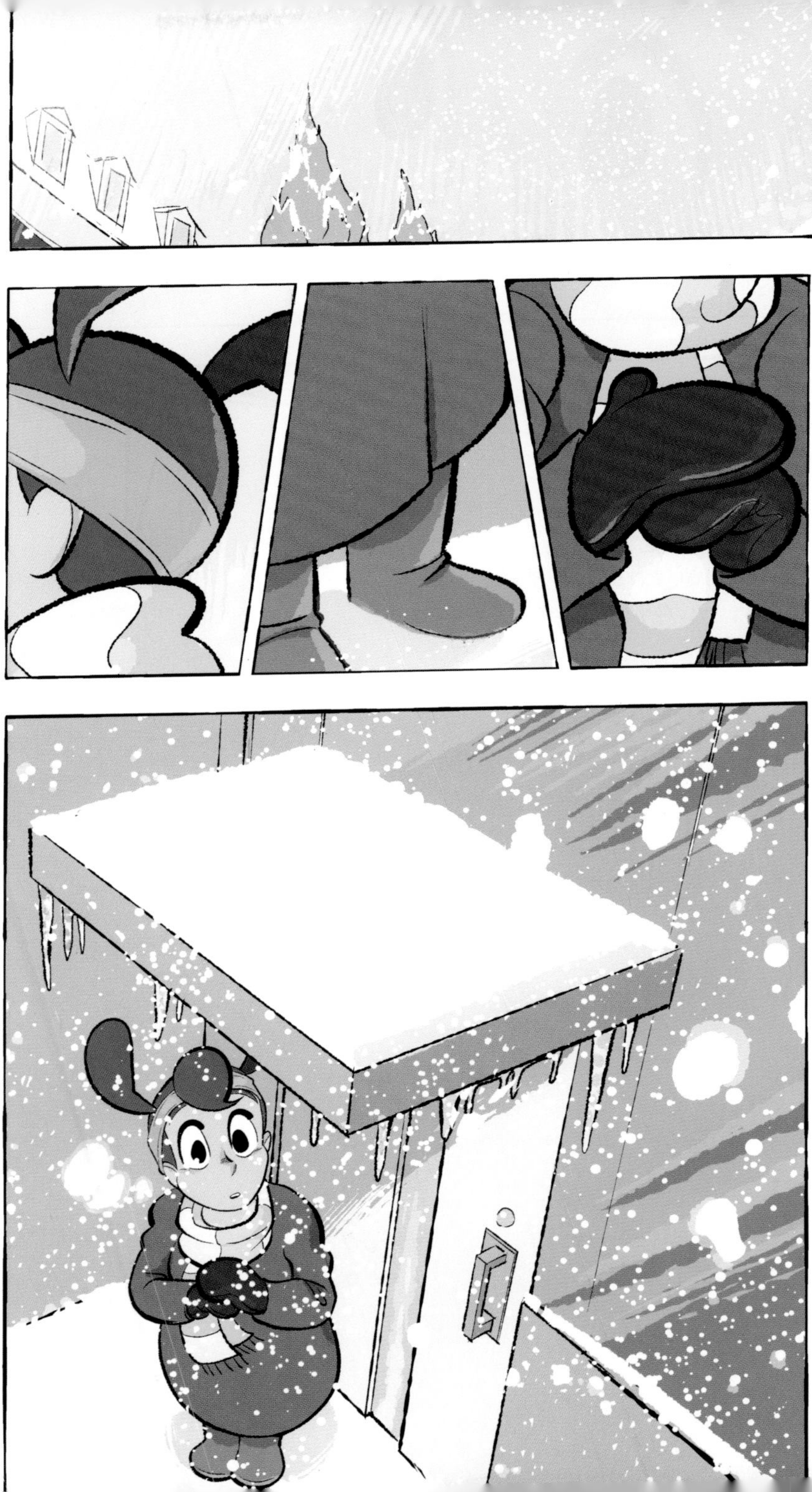

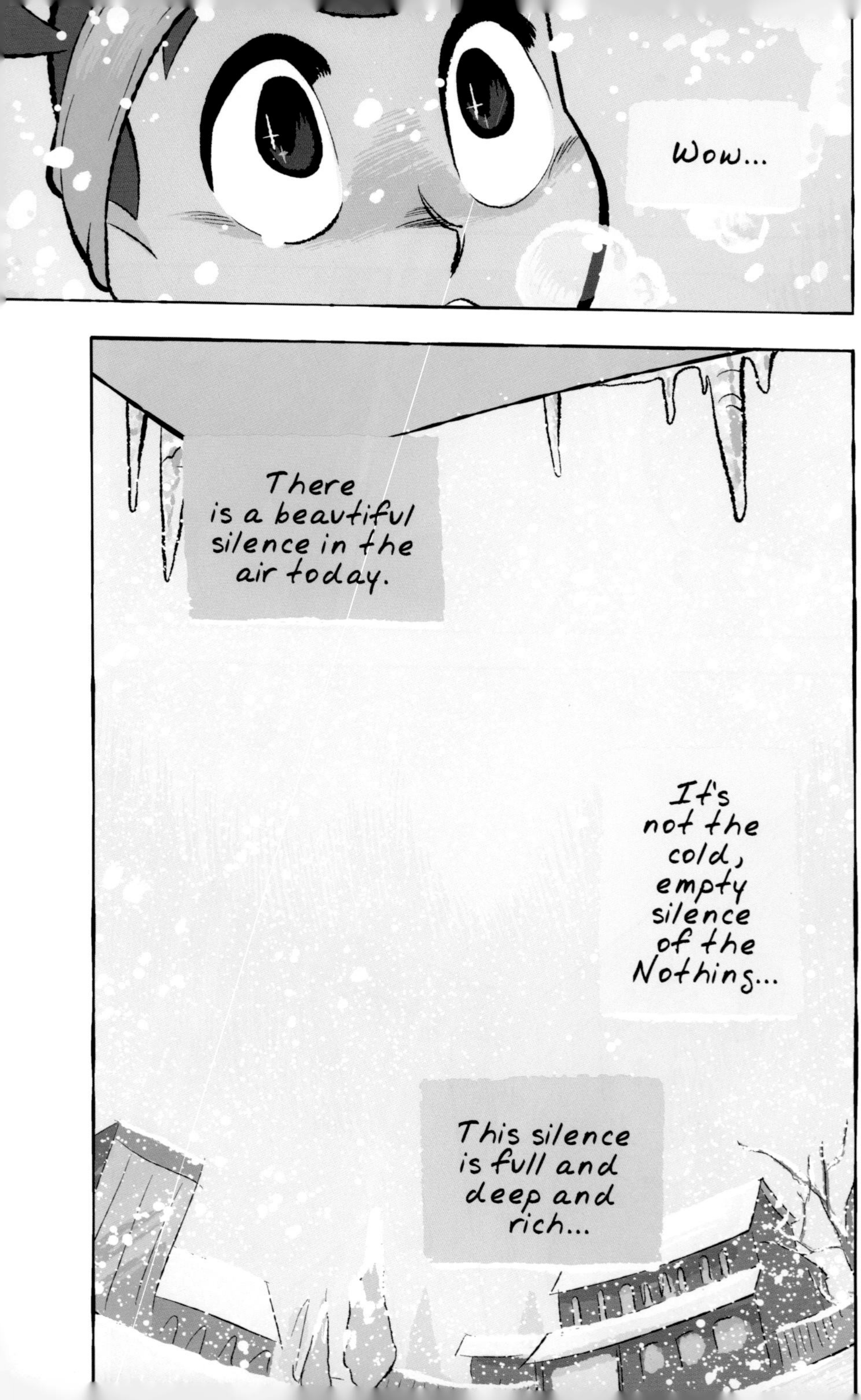
Wow...
There is a beautiful silence in the air today.
It's not the cold, empty silence of the Nothing...
This silence is full and deep and rich...

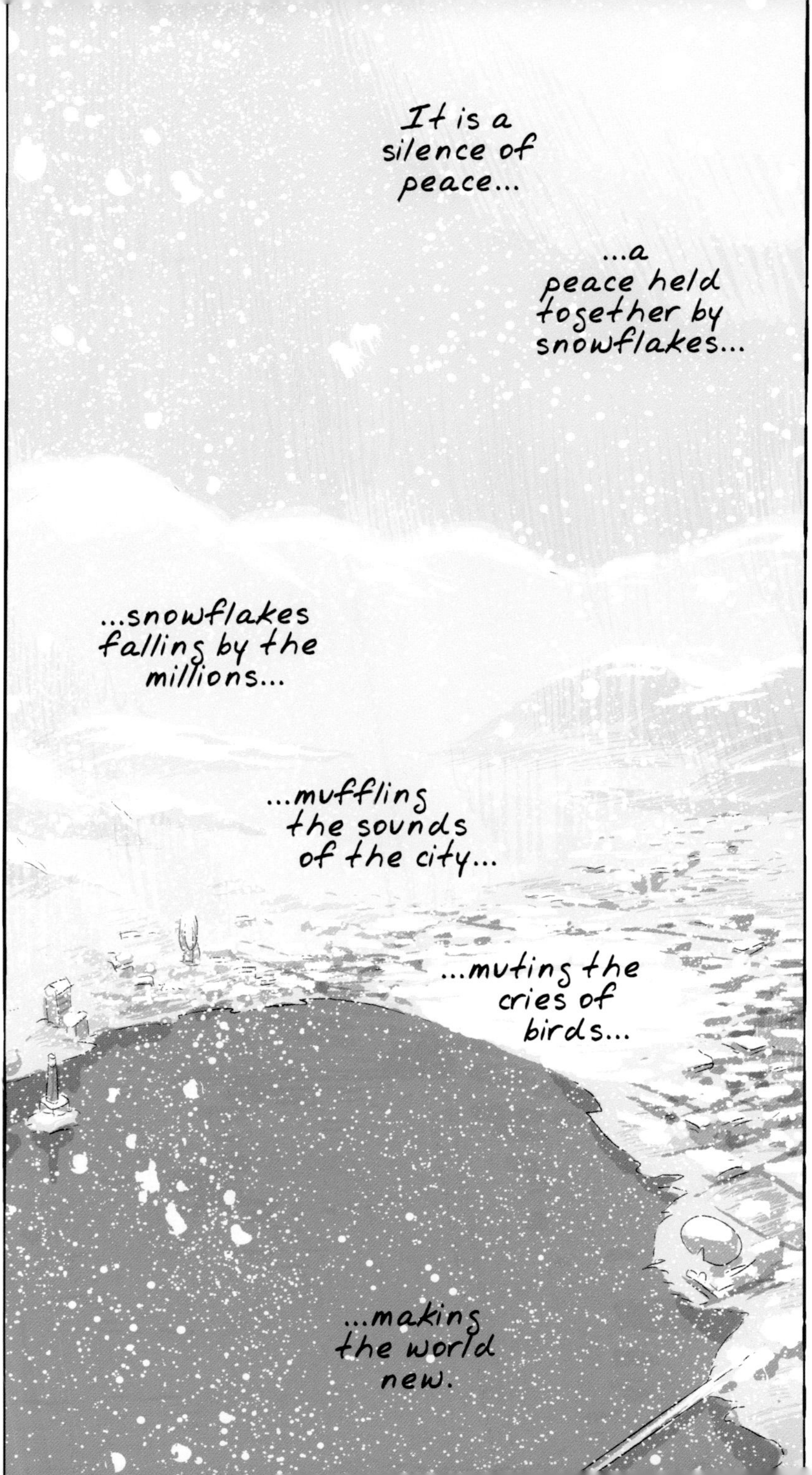
It is a silence of peace...
...a peace held together by snowflakes...
...snowflakes falling by the millions...
...muffling the sounds of the city...
...muting the cries of birds...
...making the world new.

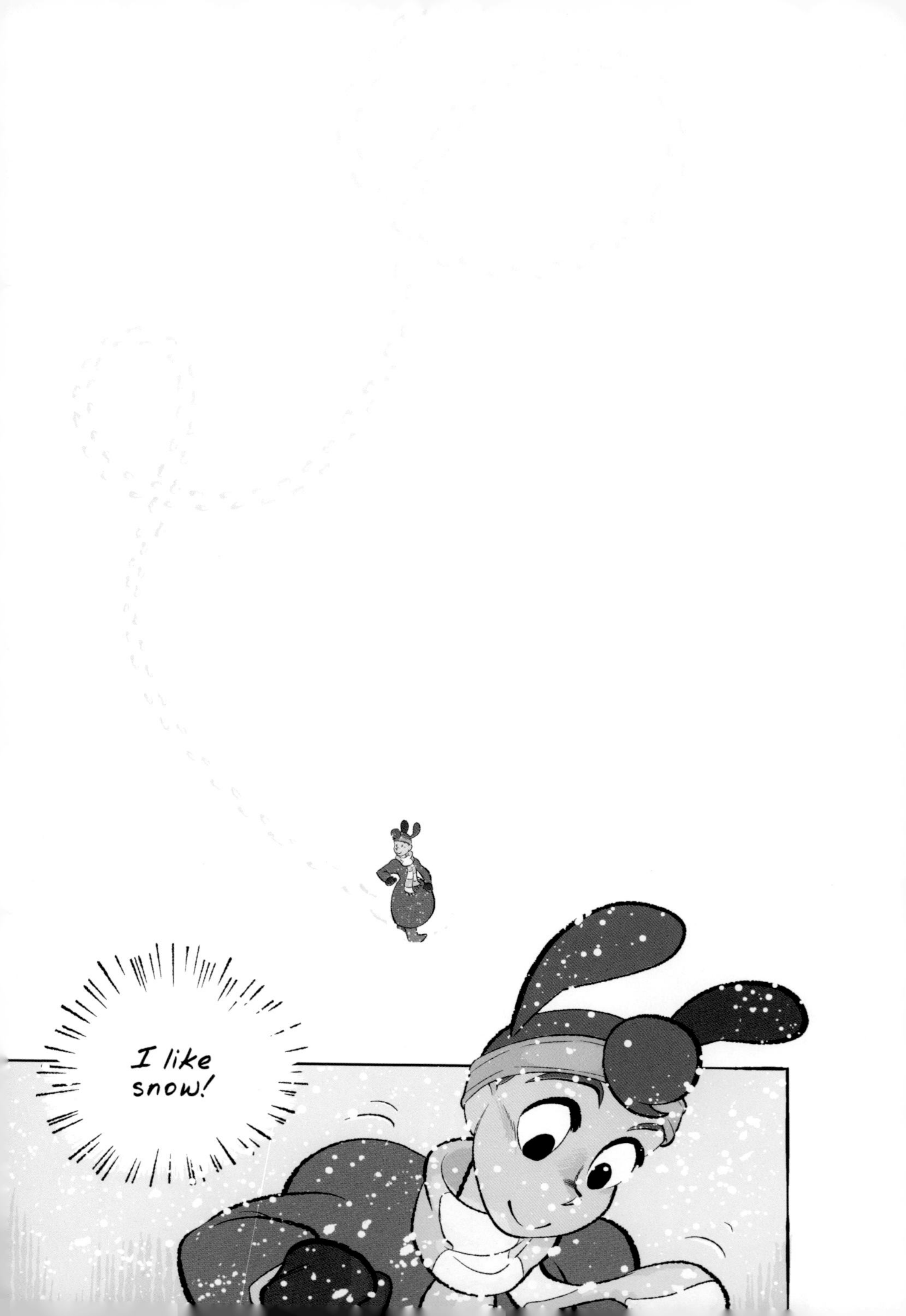
I like snow!

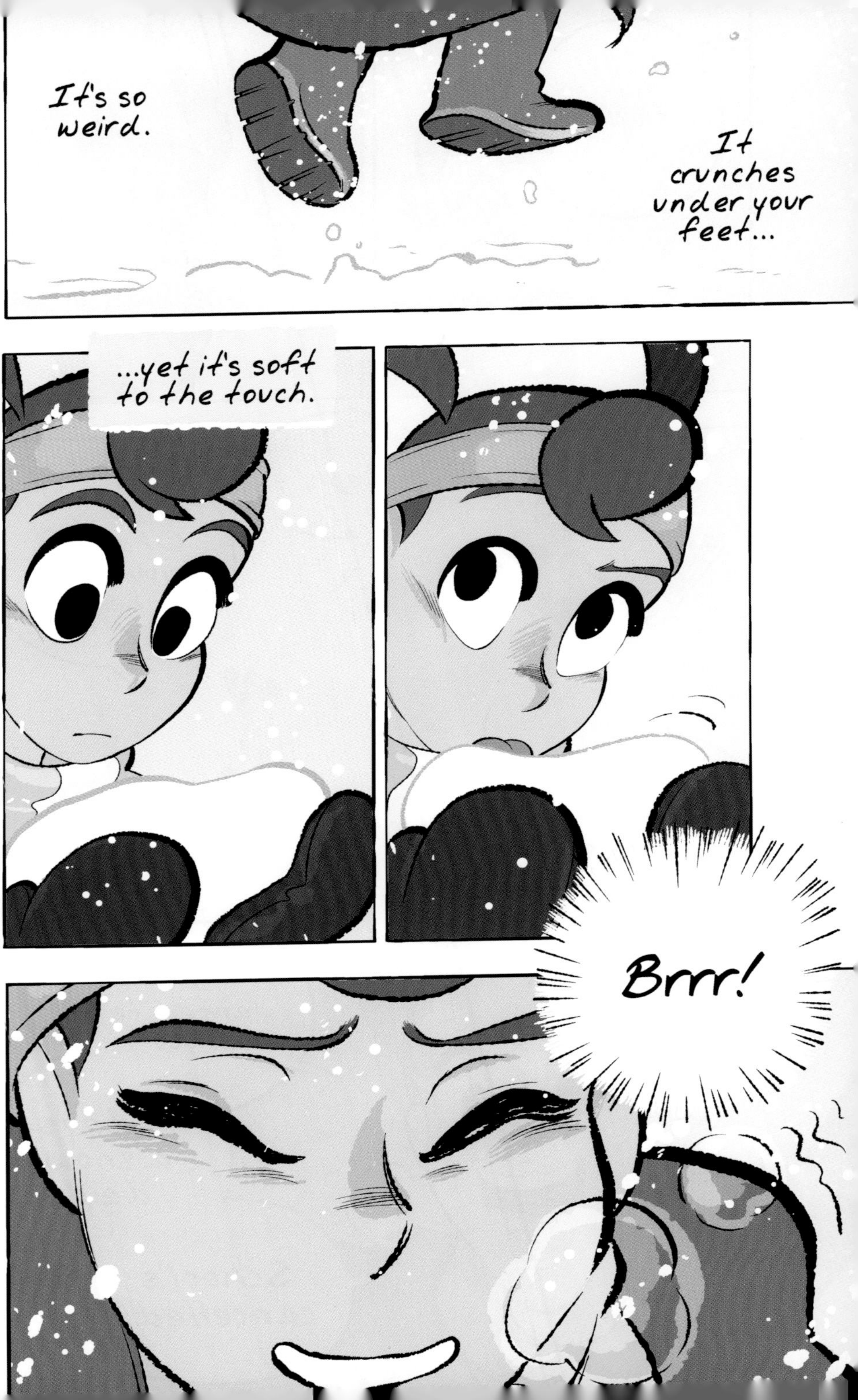
It's so weird.
It crunches under your feet...
...yet it's soft to the touch.
Brrr!

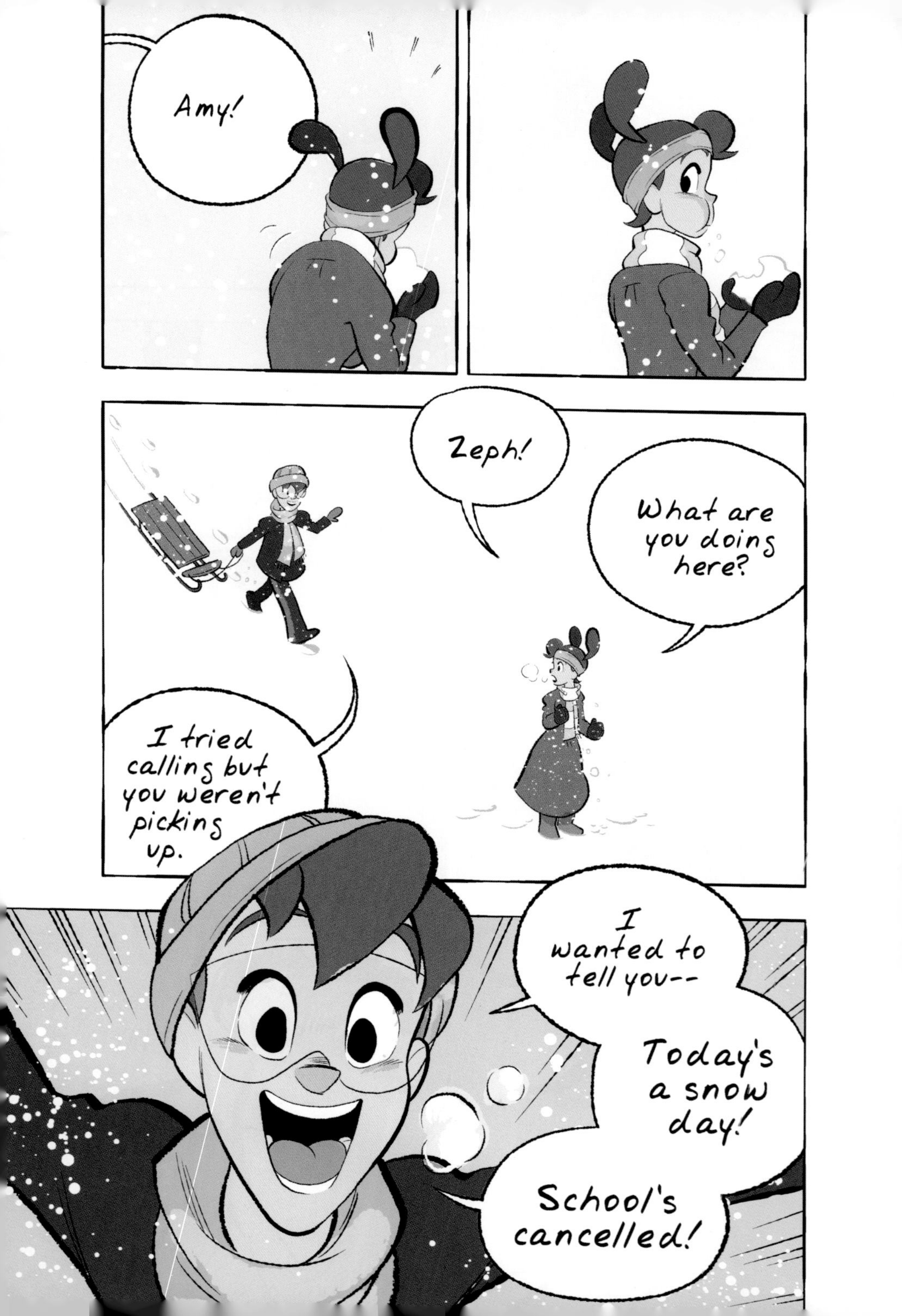
Amy!
Zeph!
What are you doing here?
I tried calling but you weren't picking up.
I wanted to tell you--
Today's a snow day!
School's cancelled!

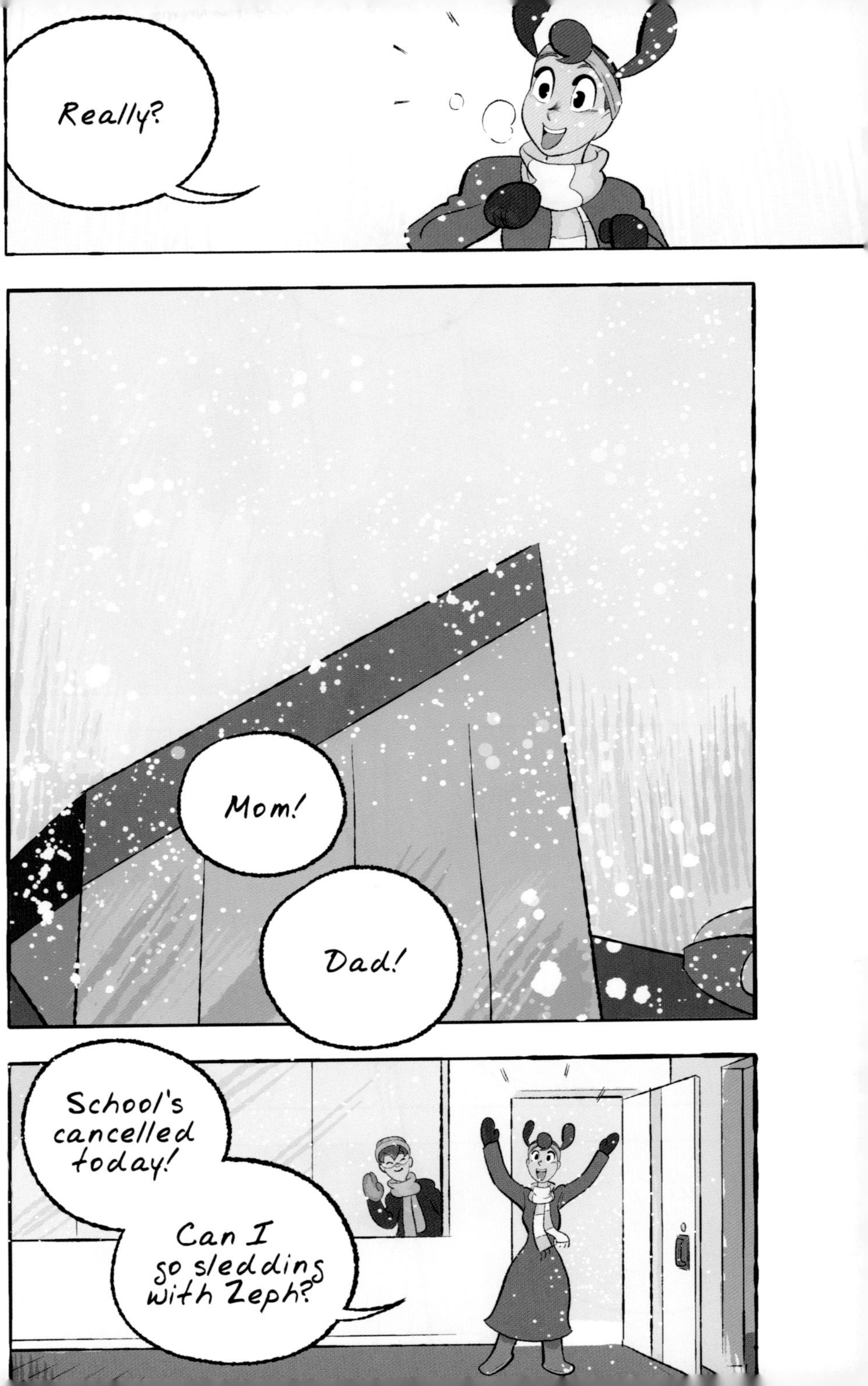
Really?
Mom!
Dad!
School's cancelled today!
Can I go sledding with Zeph?

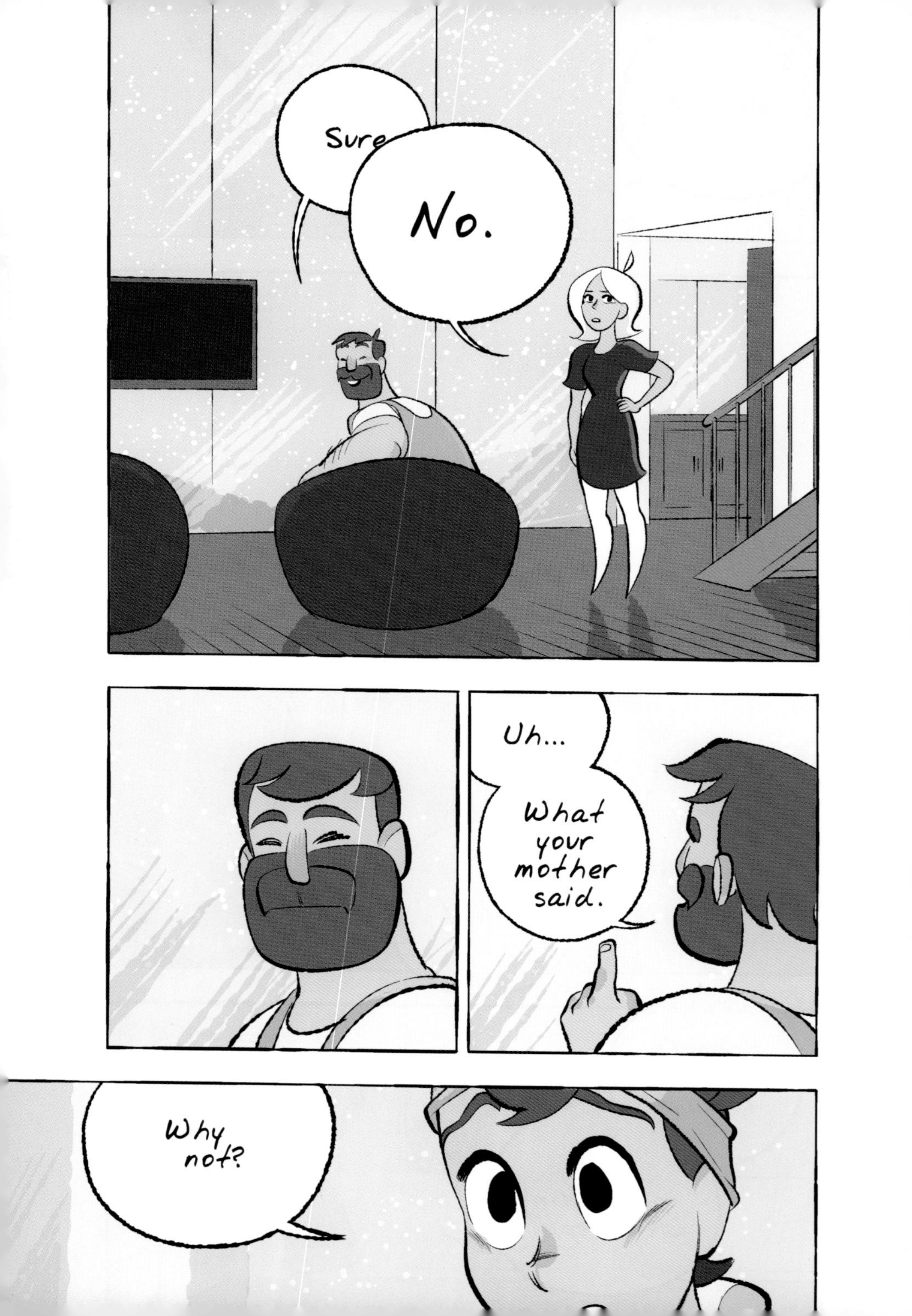
Sure
No.
Uh...
What your mother said.
Why not?

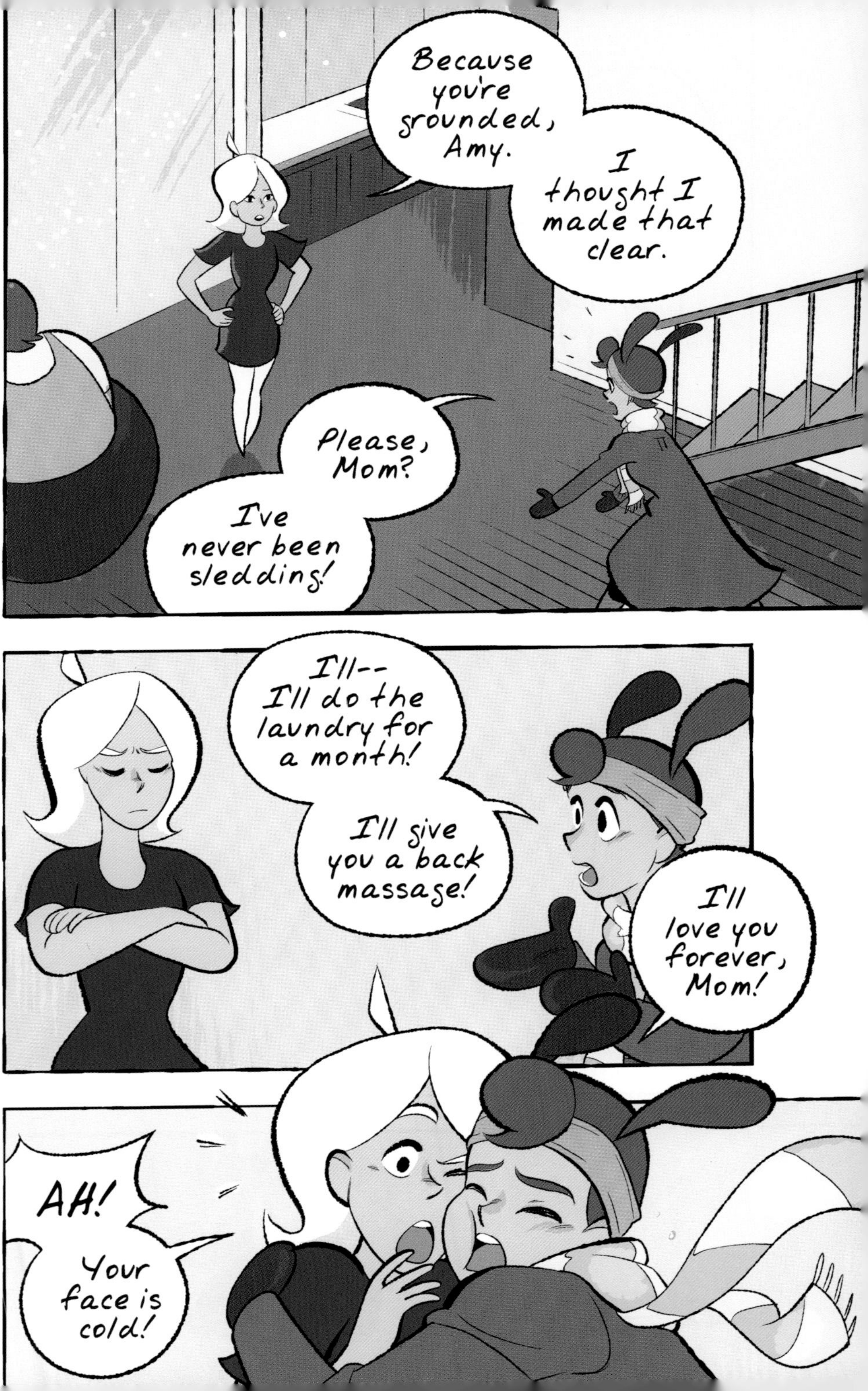
Because you're grounded, Amy.
I thought I made that clear.
Please, Mom?
I've never been sledding!
I'll-- I'll do the laundry for a month!
I'll give you a back massage!
I'll love you forever, Mom!
AH!
Your face is cold!

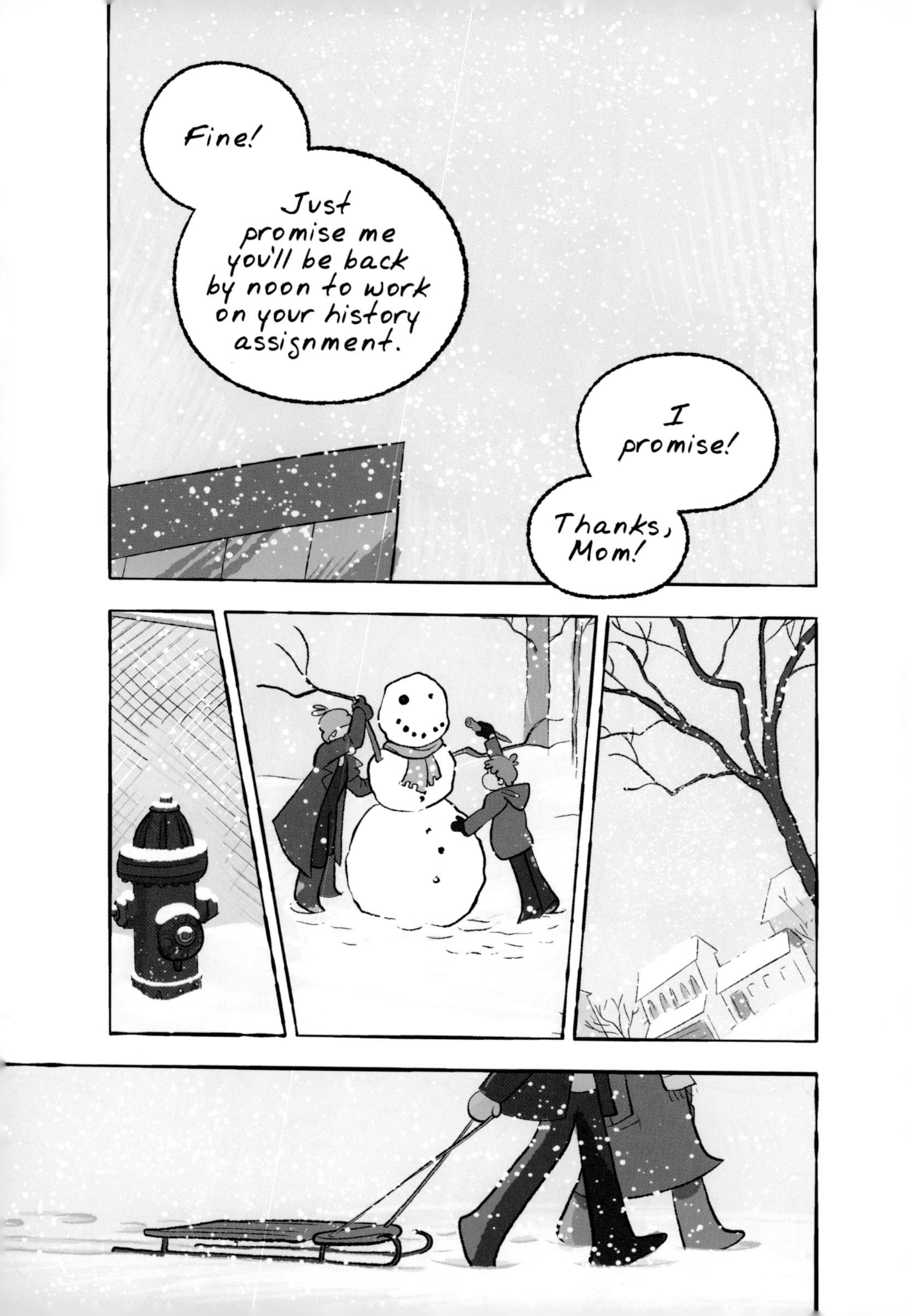
Fine!
Just promise me you'll be back by noon to work on your history assignment.
I promise!
Thanks, Mom!

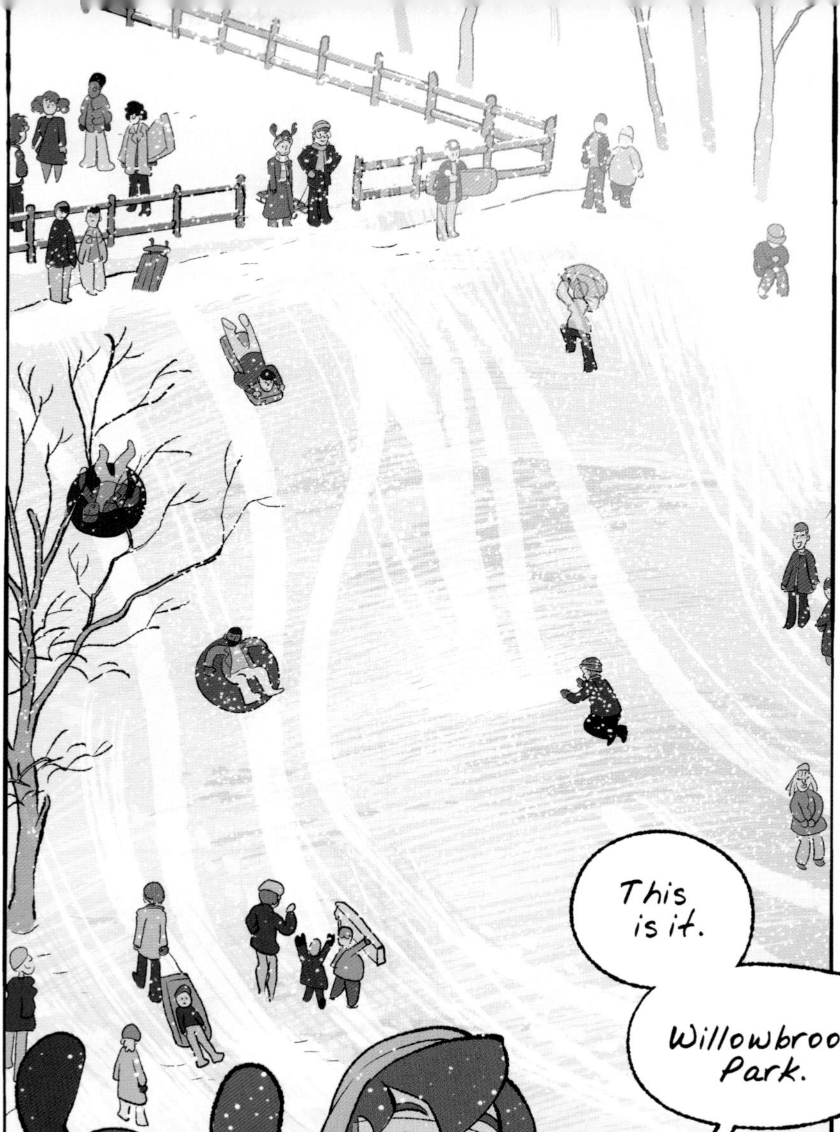
This is it.
Willowbrook Park.

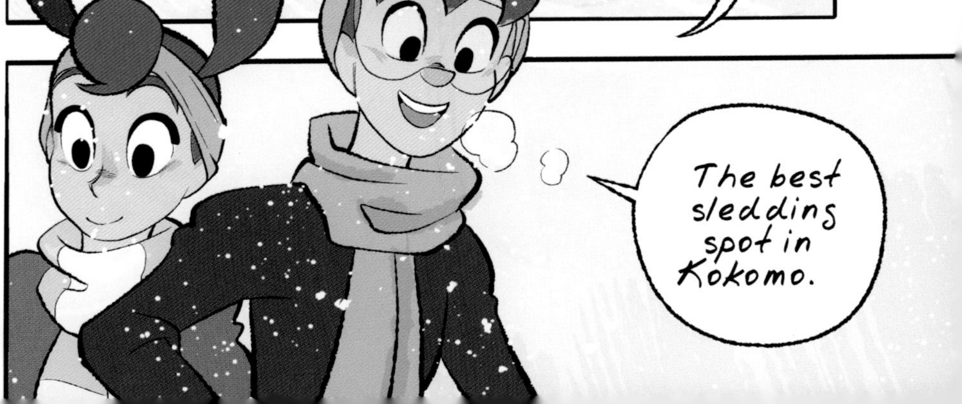
The best sledding spot in Kokomo.

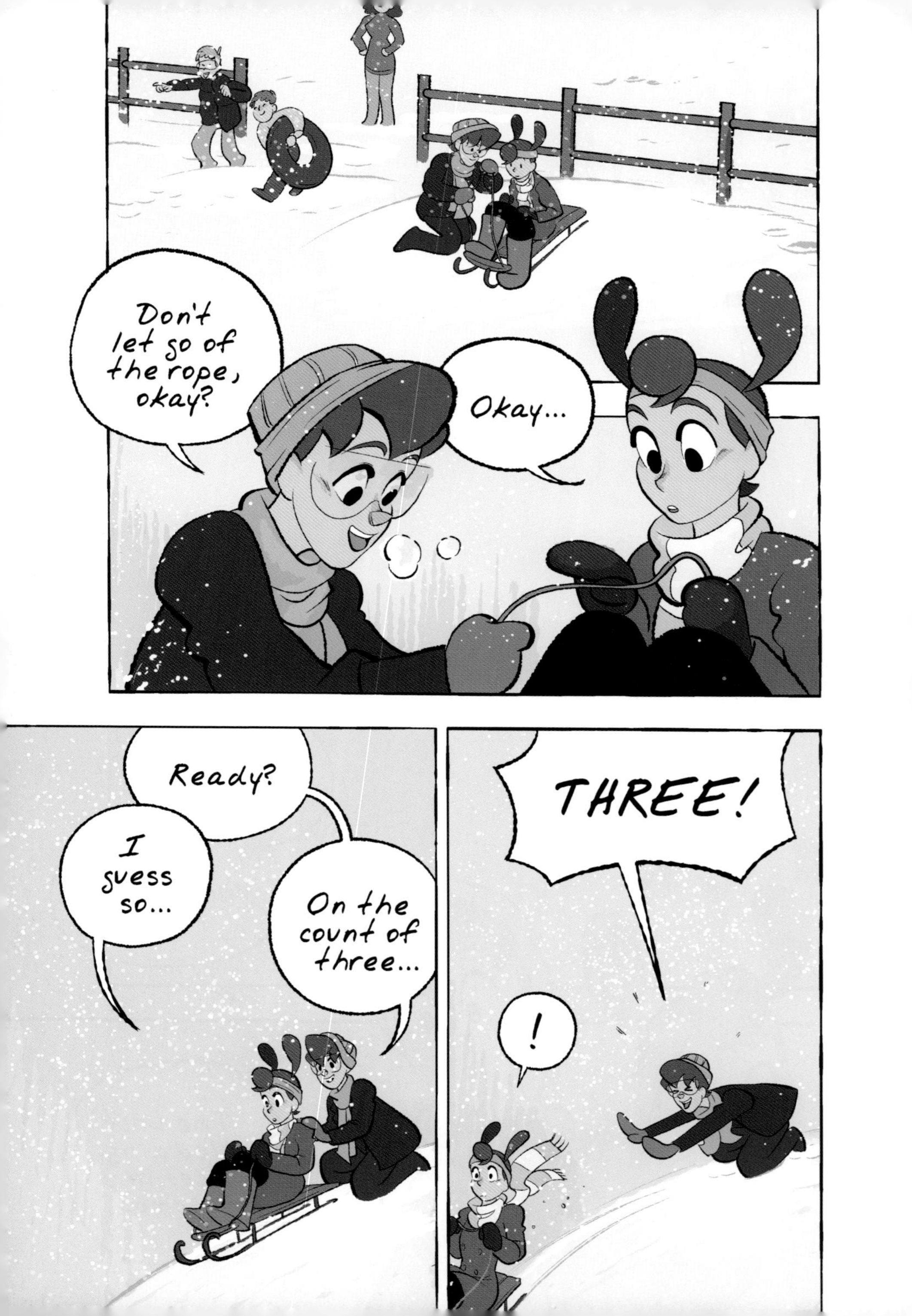
Don't let go of the rope, okay?
Okay...
Ready?
I guess so...
On the count of three...
THREE!
!

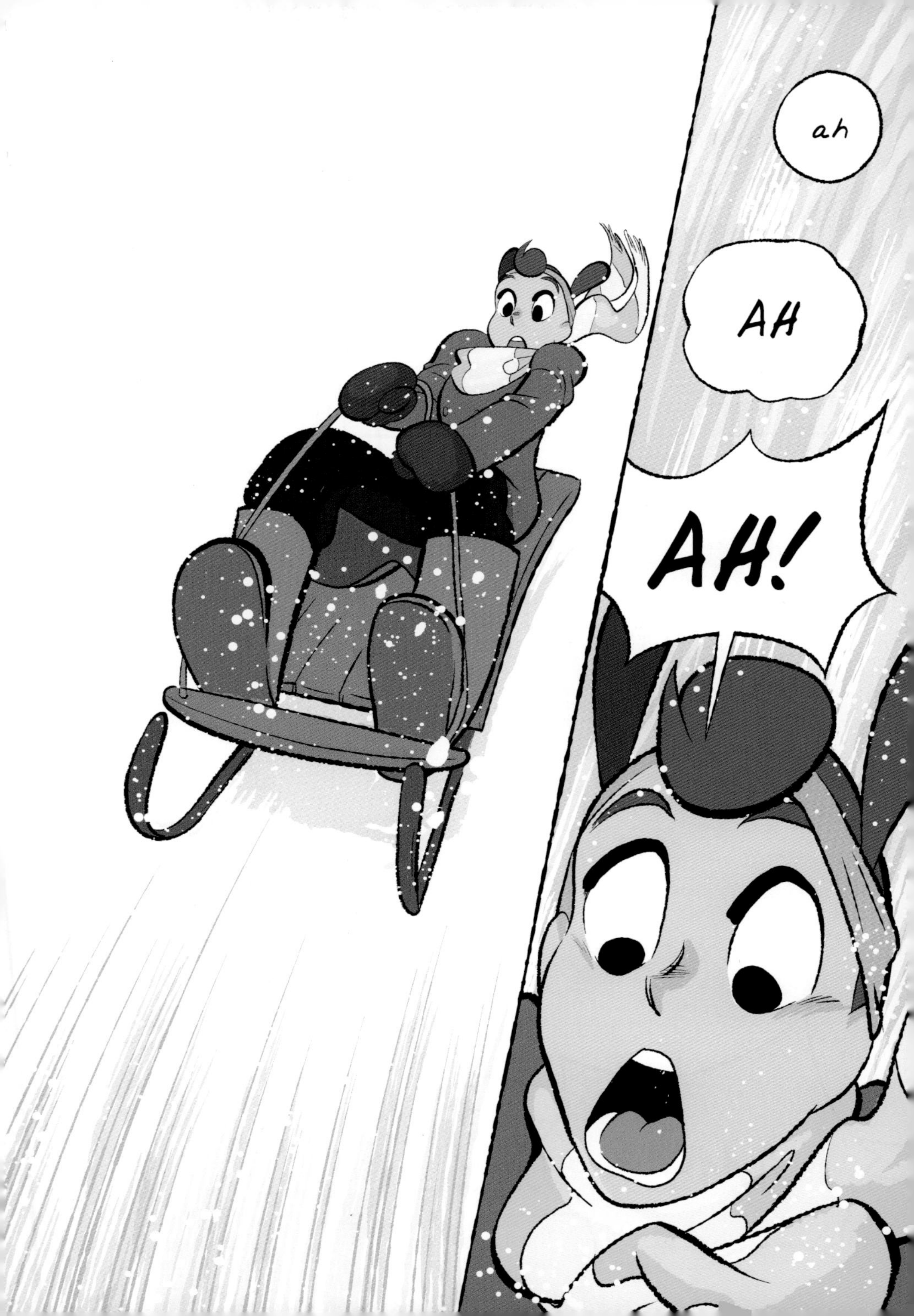
ah
AH
AH!

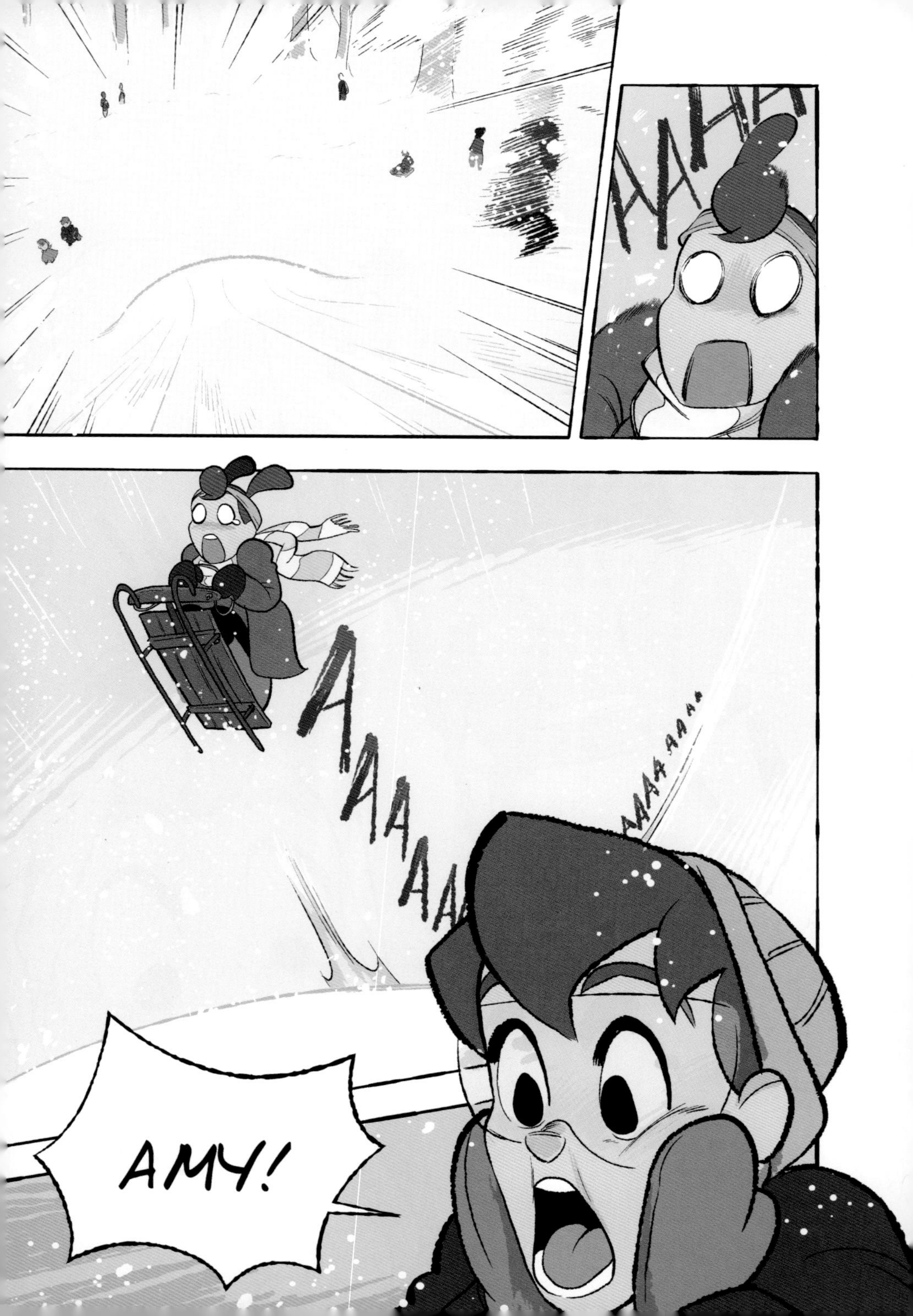

AAHH
AAAAAAAAAAAAaaaa
AMY!

Amy!

GOSHARE
UALLRIGHT?
IMSOSORRY
IHADNOIDEA
HATRAMPWAS
FREISHOULD
HAVE--

That was fun!

Let's do that again!

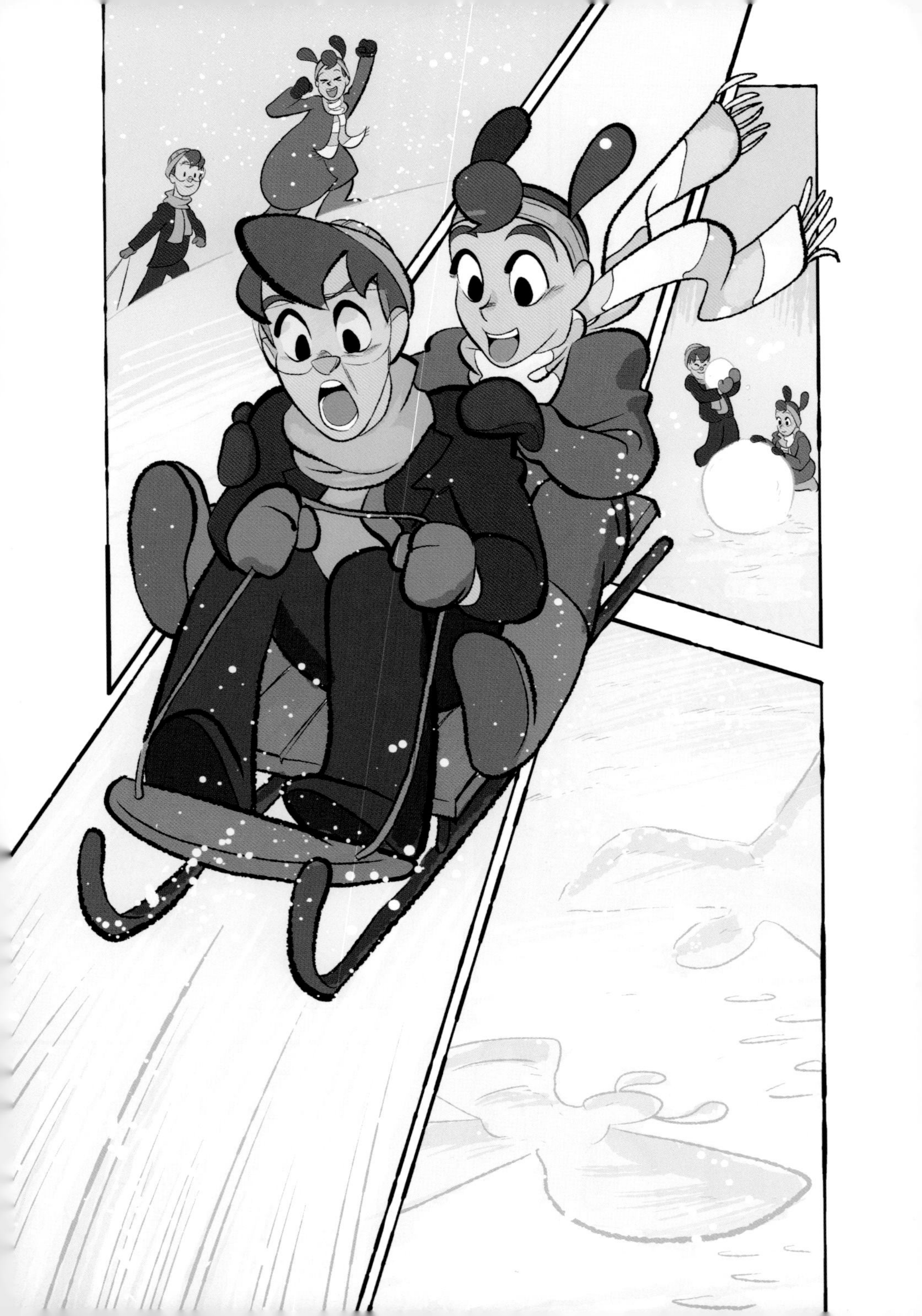

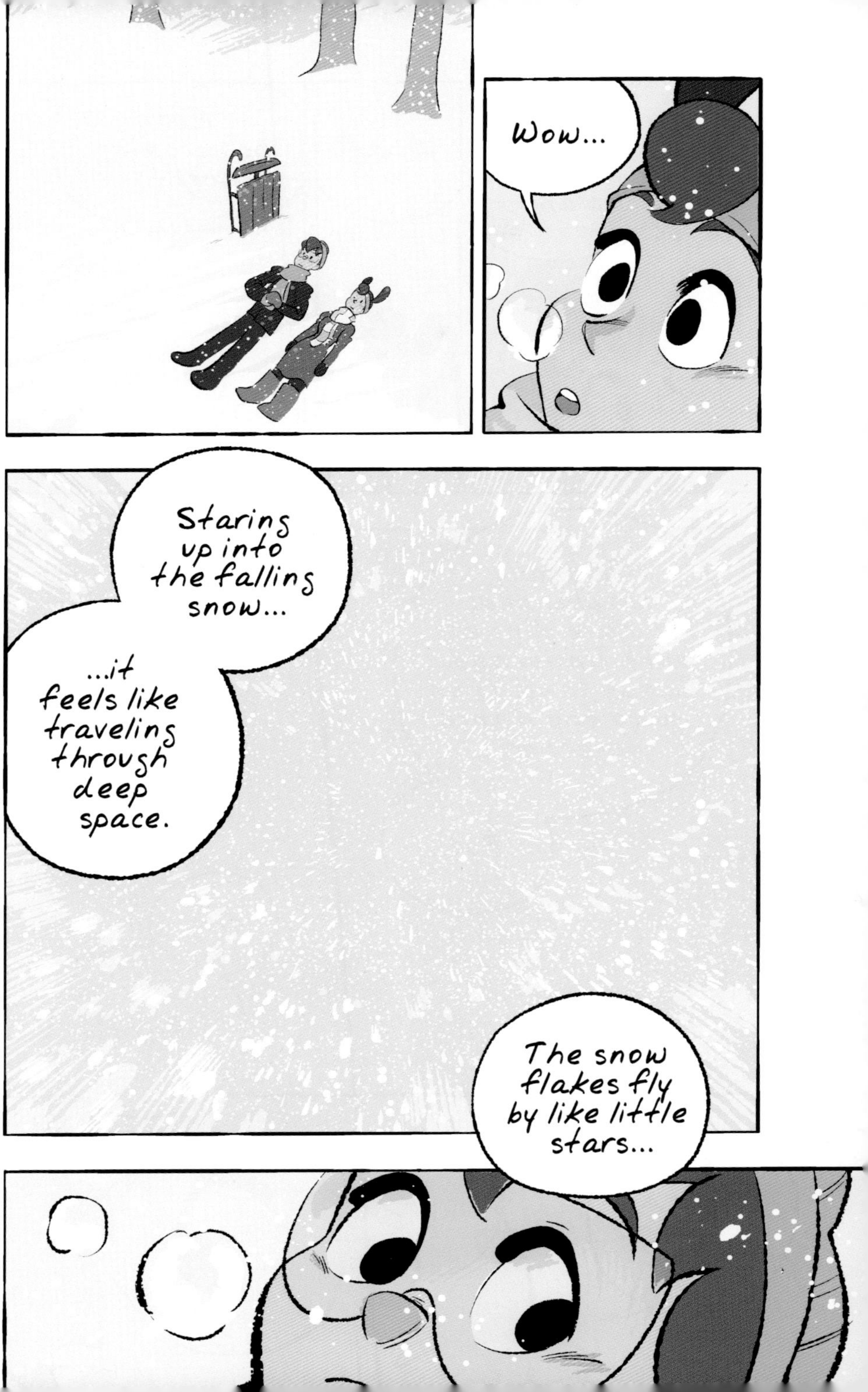
Wow...
Staring up into the falling snow...
...it feels like traveling through deep space.
The snow flakes fly by like little stars...

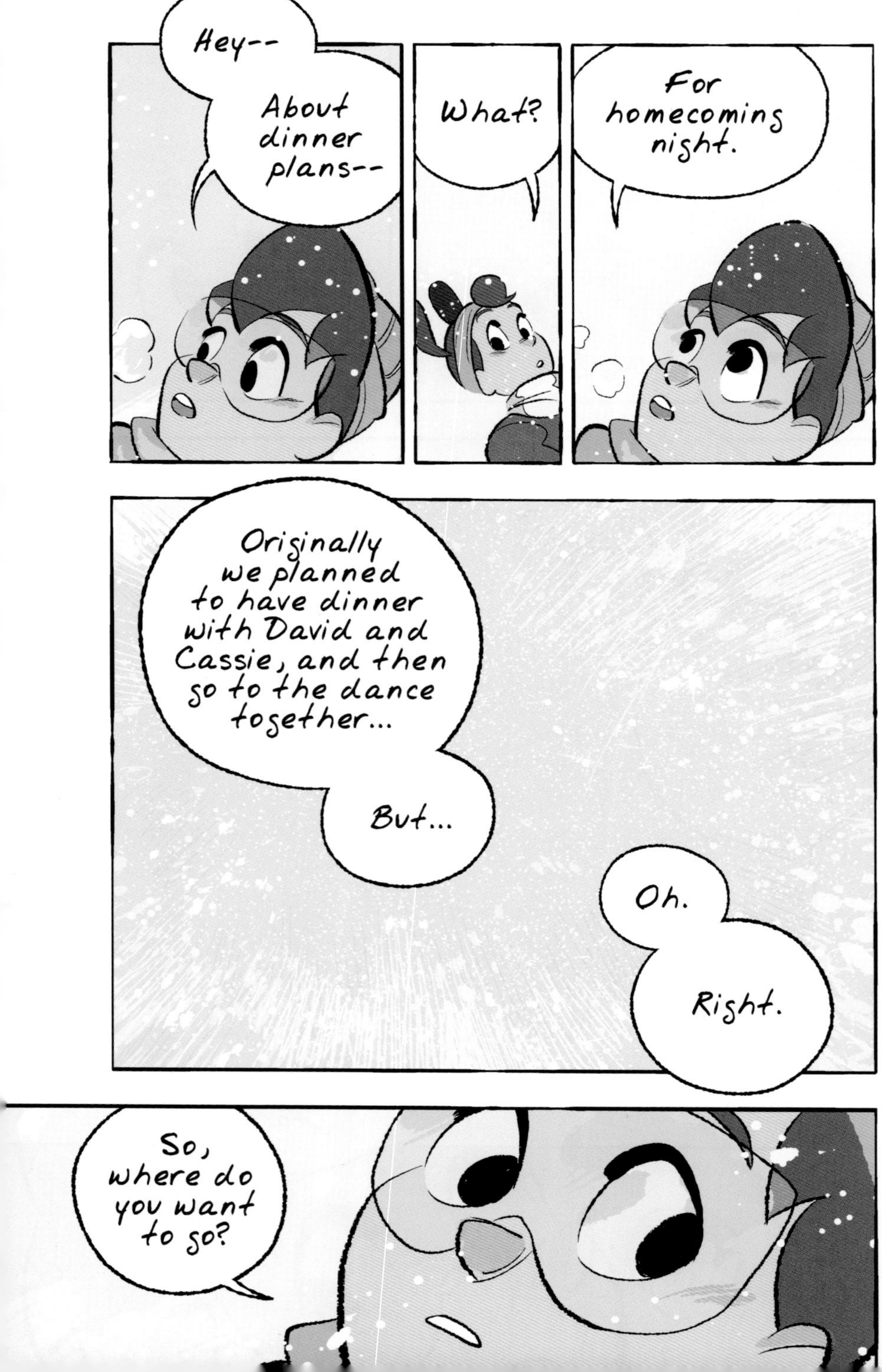

Hey--
About dinner plans--
What?
For homecomins night.
Orisinally we planned to have dinner with David and Cassie, and then so to the dance together...
But...
Oh.
Risht.
So, where do you want to so?

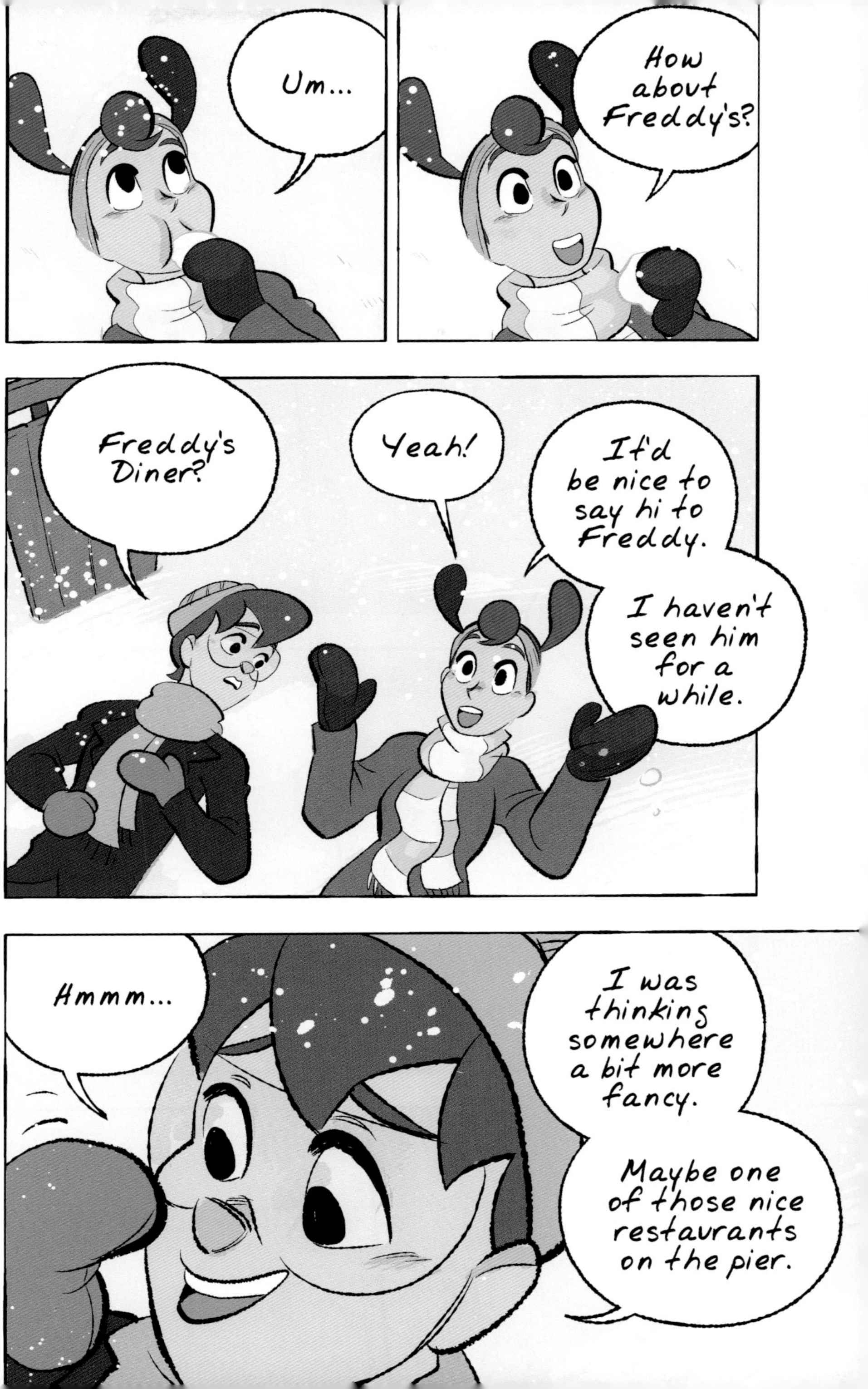
Um...
How about Freddy's?
Freddy's Diner?
Yeah!
It'd be nice to say hi to Freddy.
I haven't seen him for a while.
Hmmm...
I was thinking somewhere a bit more fancy.
Maybe one of those nice restaurants on the pier.

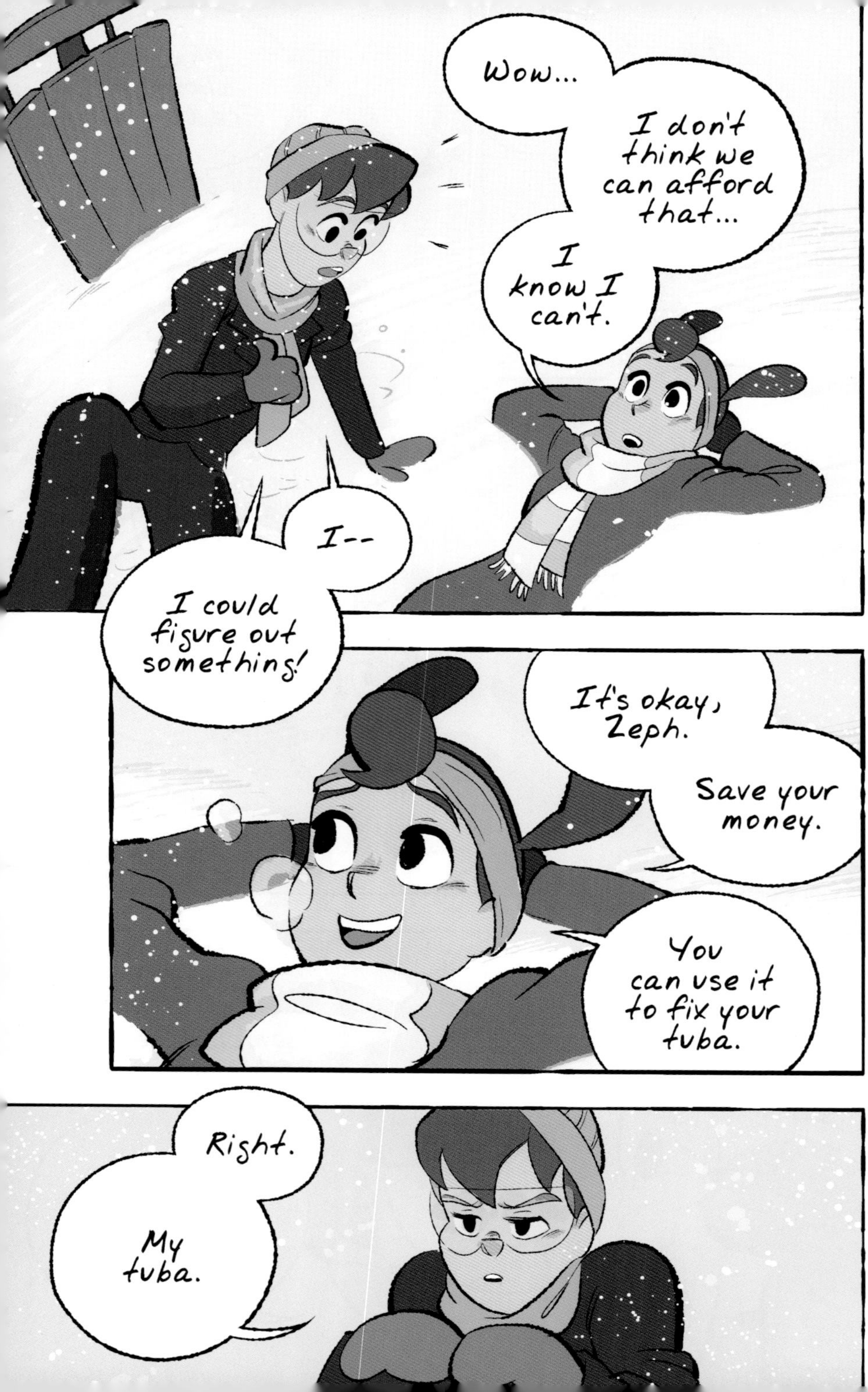
Wow...
I don't think we can afford that...
I know I can't.
I--
I could figure out somethins!
It's okay, Zeph.
Save your money.
You can use it to fix your tuba.
Risht.
My tuba.

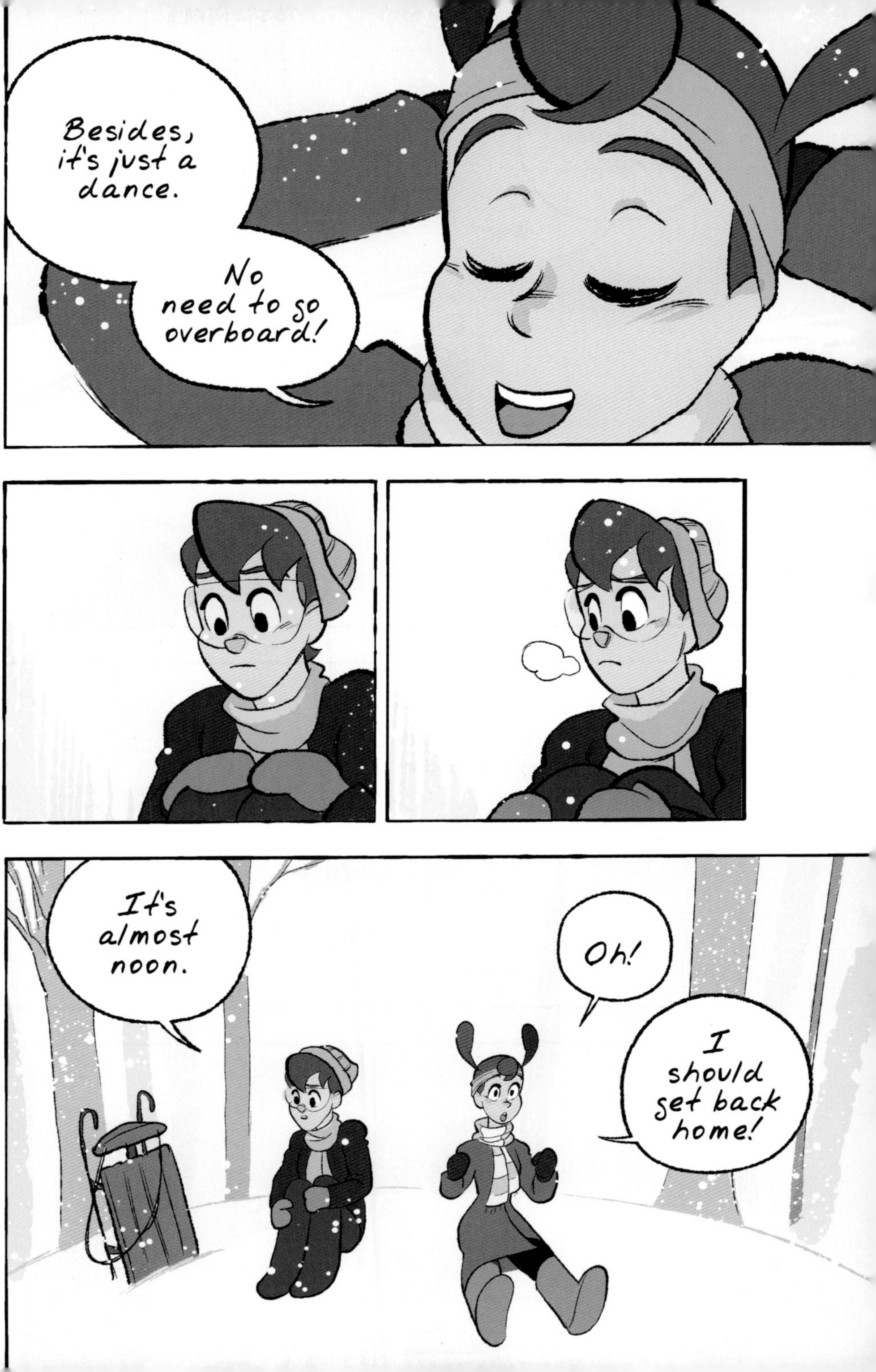
Besides, it's just a dance.
No need to go overboard!
It's almost noon.
Oh!
I should get back home!

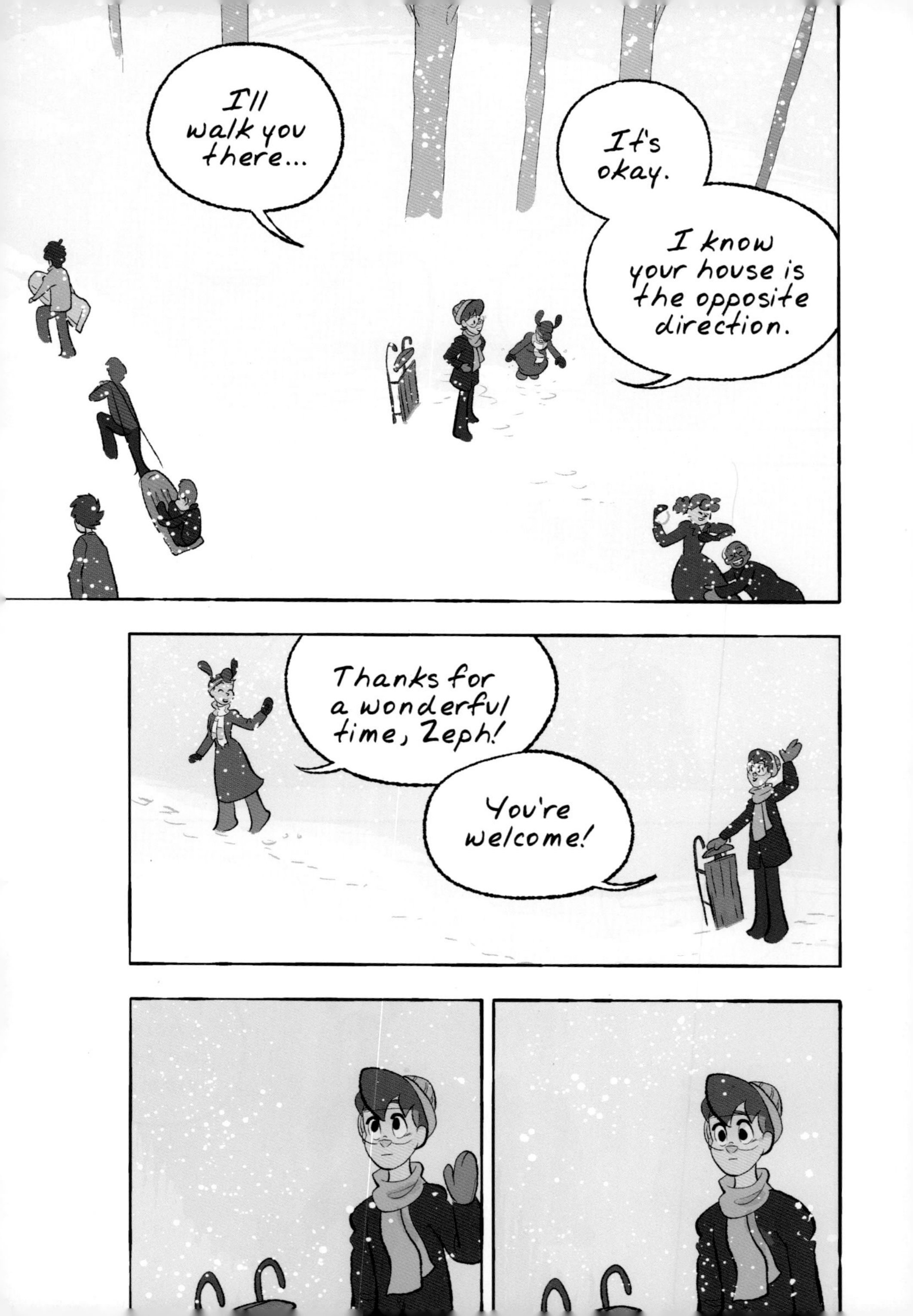
I'll walk you there...
It's okay.
I know your house is the opposite direction.
Thanks for a wonderful time, Zeph!
You're welcome!

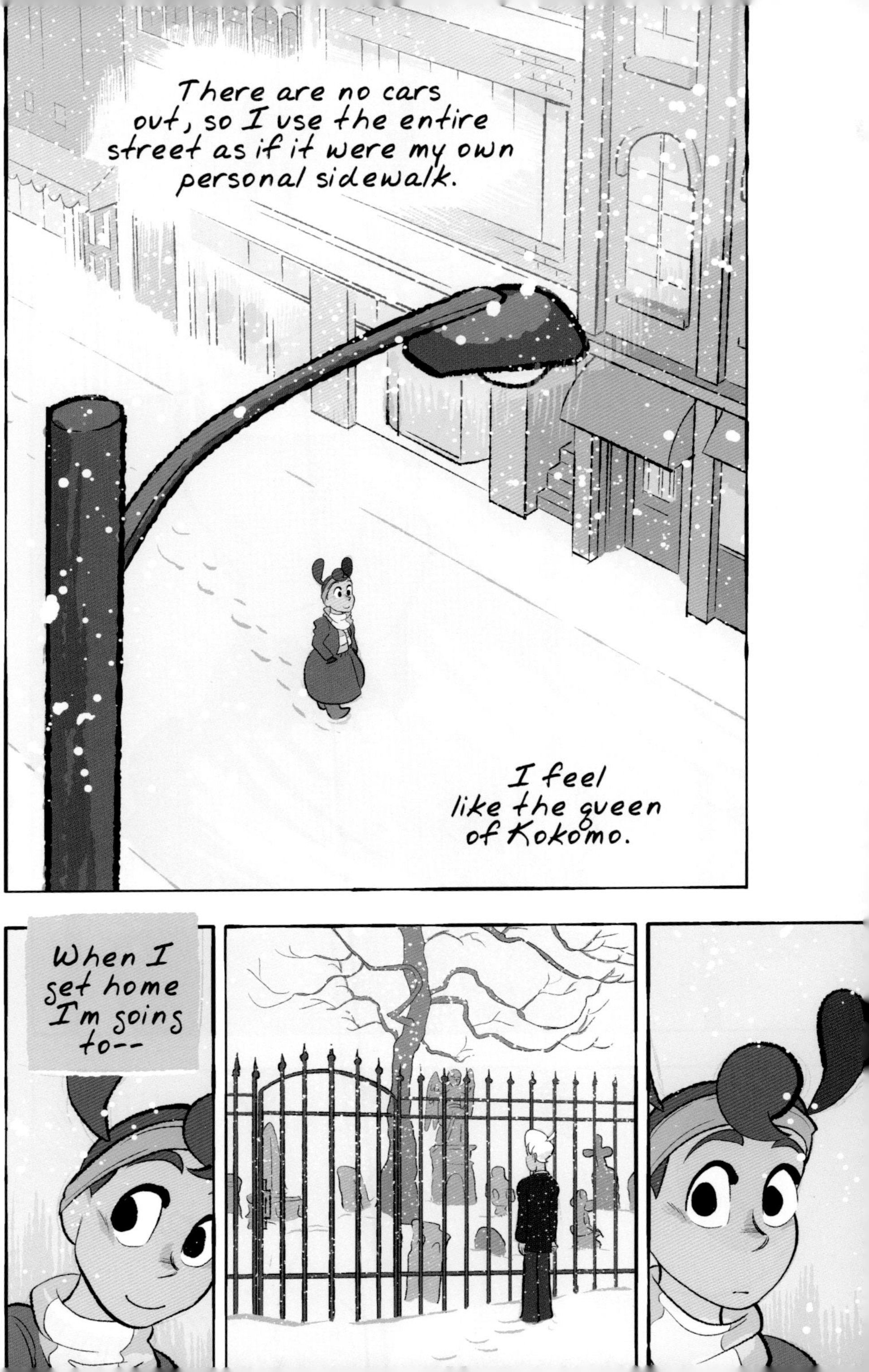
There are no cars out, so I use the entire street as if it were my own personal sidewalk.
I feel like the queen of Kokomo.
When I get home I'm going to--

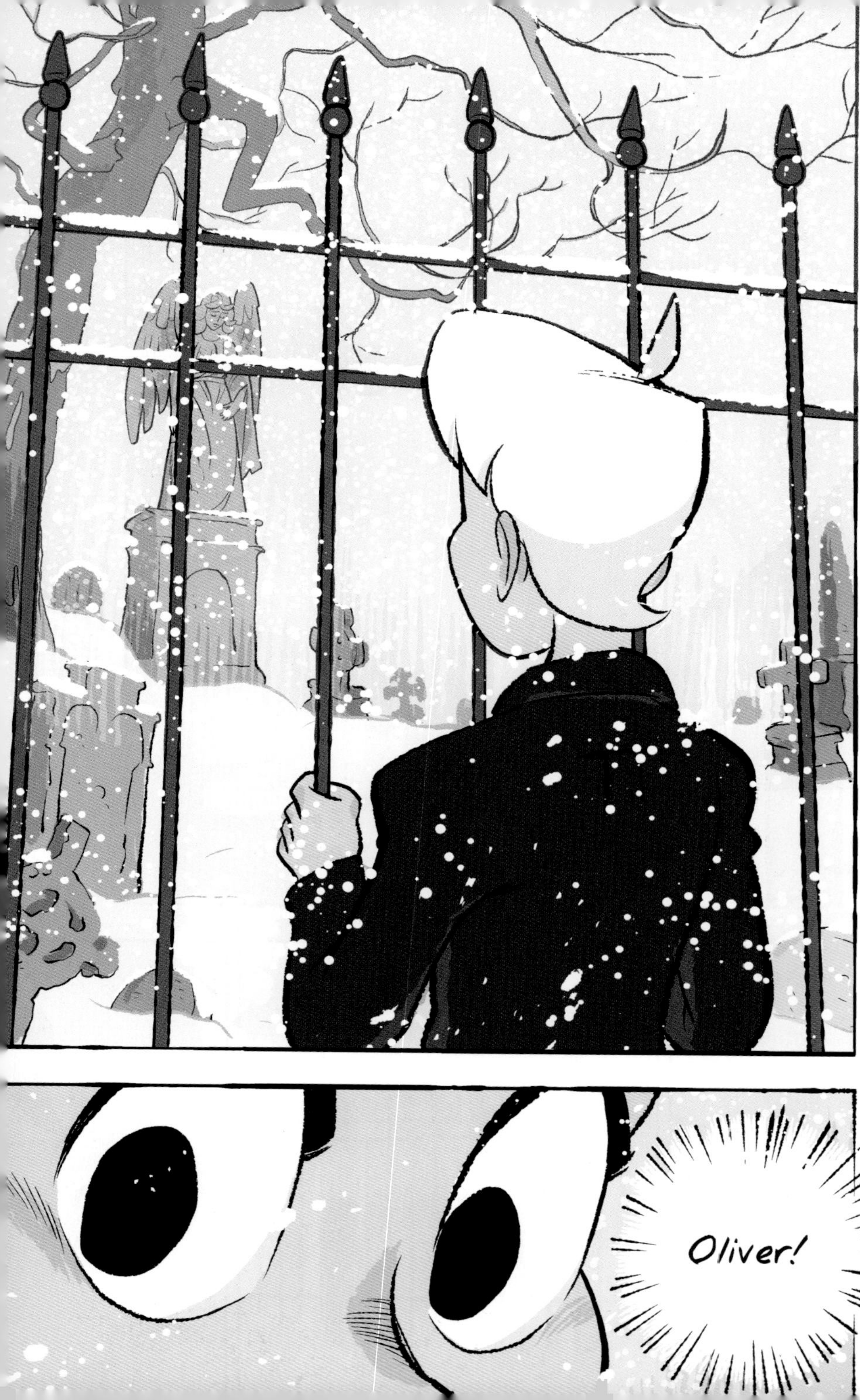
Oliver!

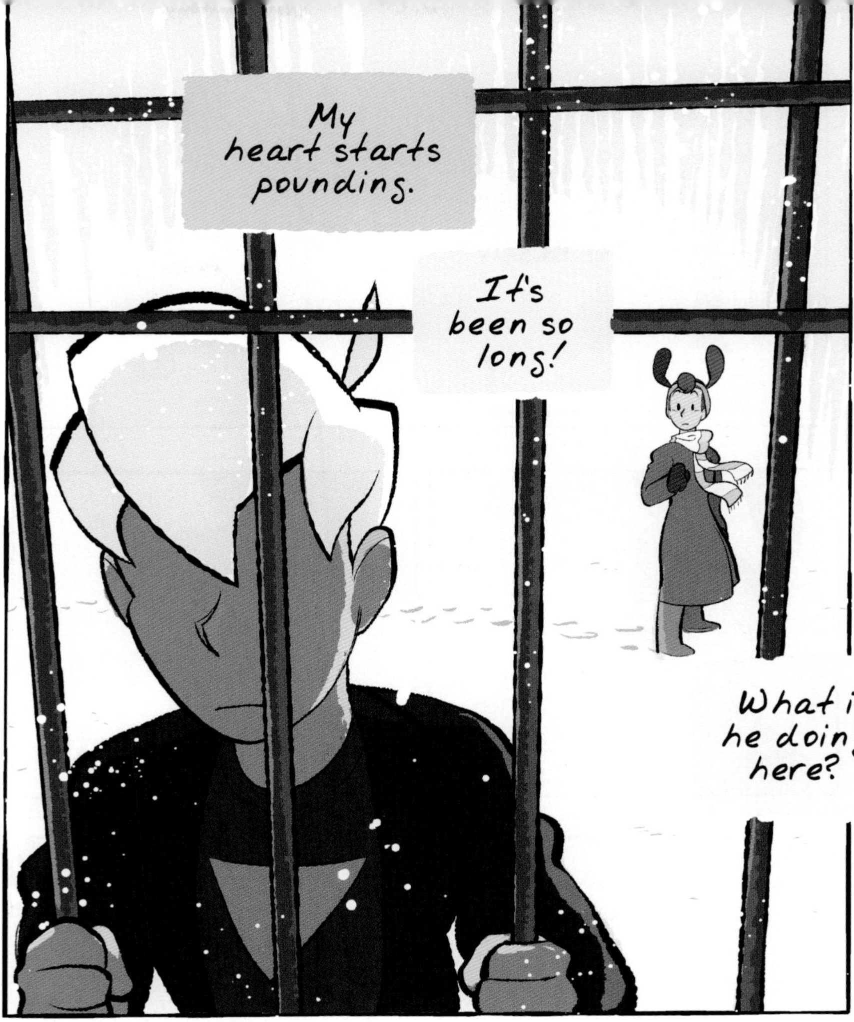
My heart starts pounding.
It's been so long!
What is he doing here?

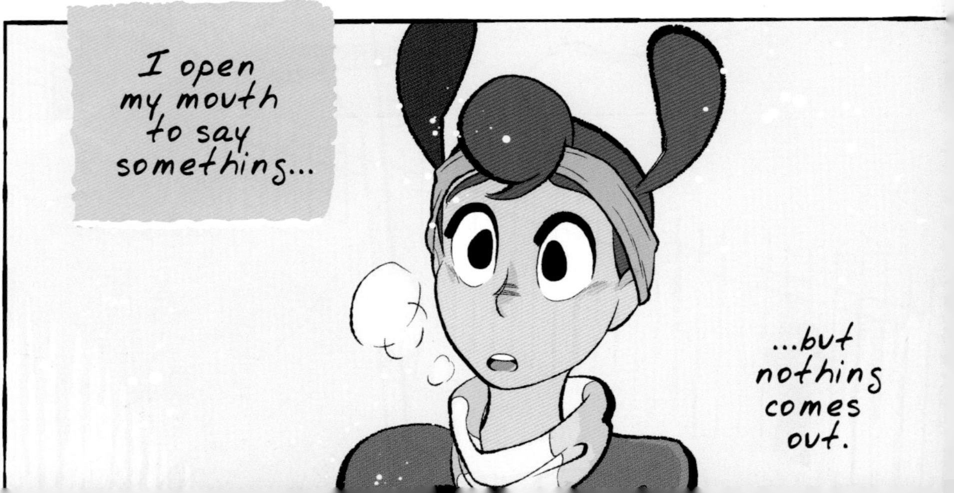
I open my mouth to say something...
...but nothing comes out.

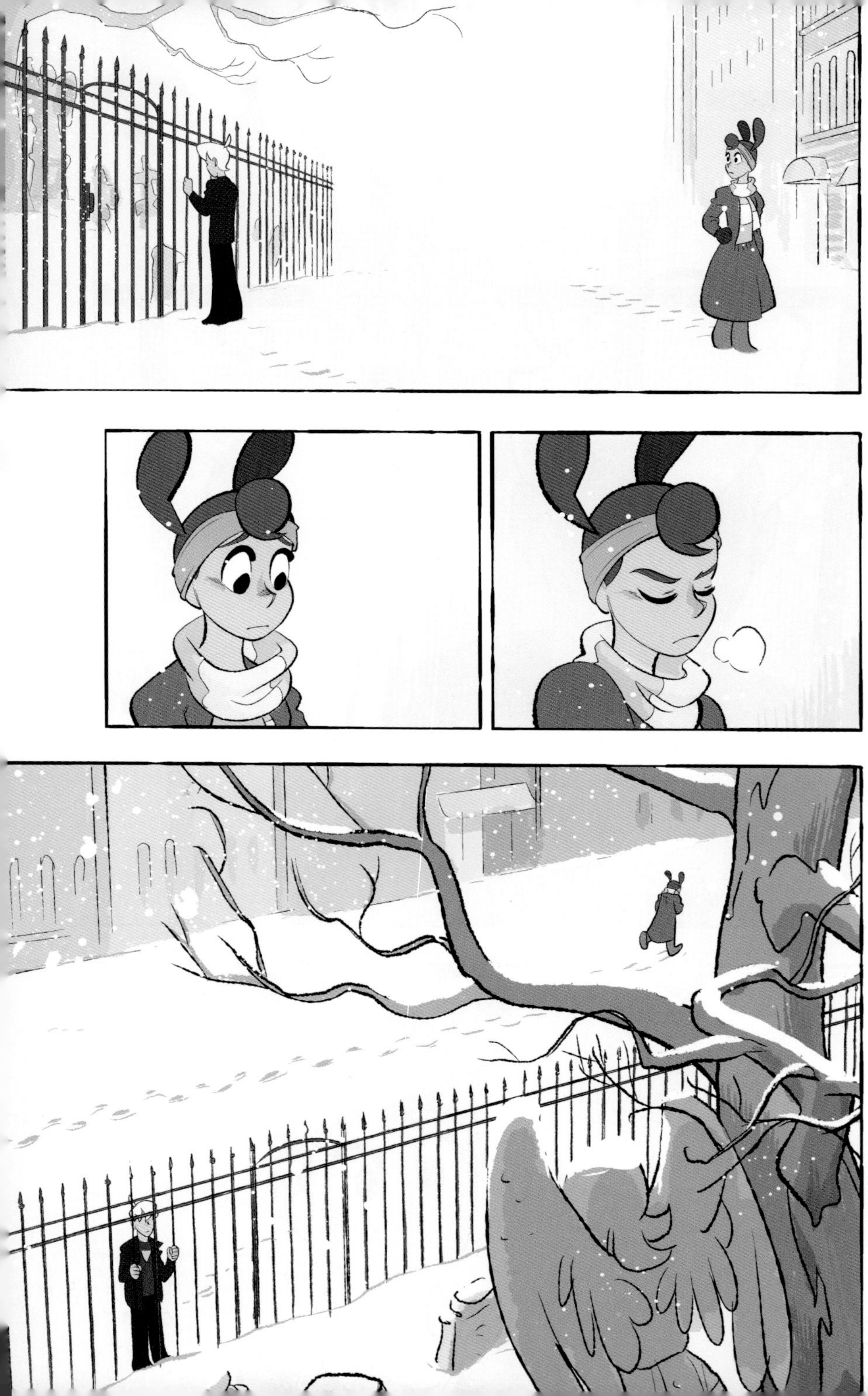

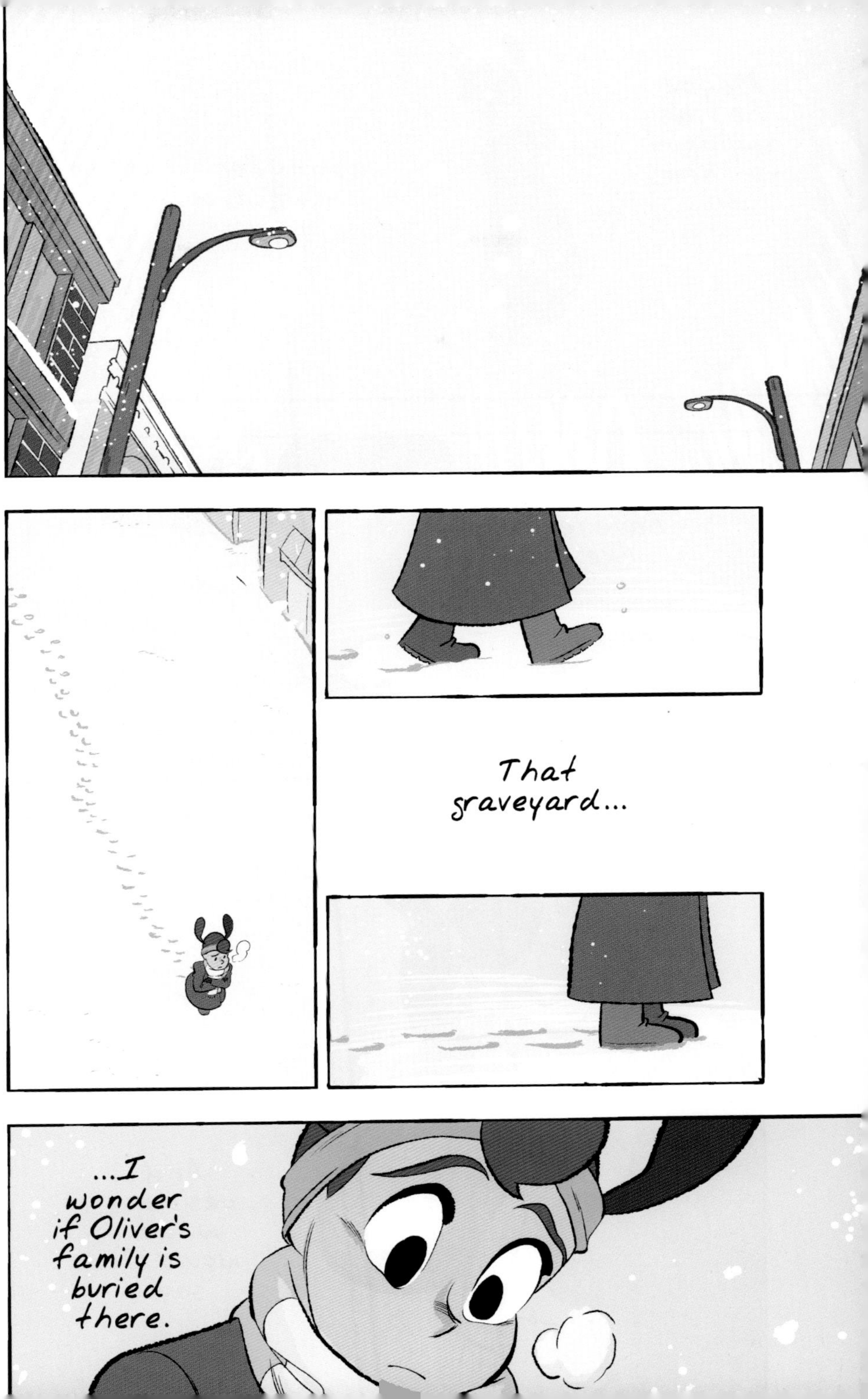

That graveyard...
...I wonder if Oliver's family is buried there.

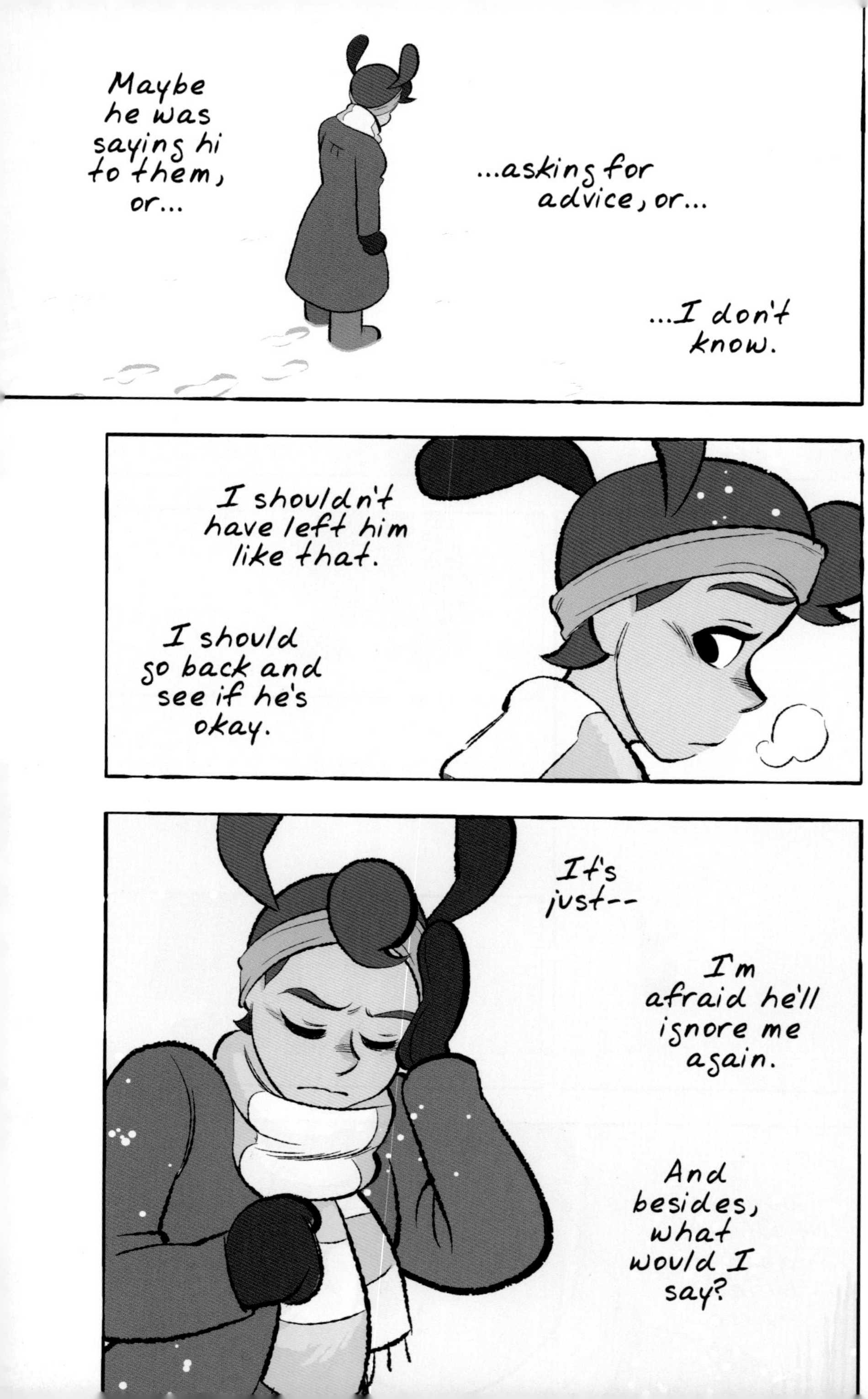
Maybe he was saying hi to them, or...
...asking for advice, or...
...I don't know.
I shouldn't have left him like that.
I should go back and see if he's okay.
It's just--
I'm afraid he'll ignore me again.
And besides, what would I say?

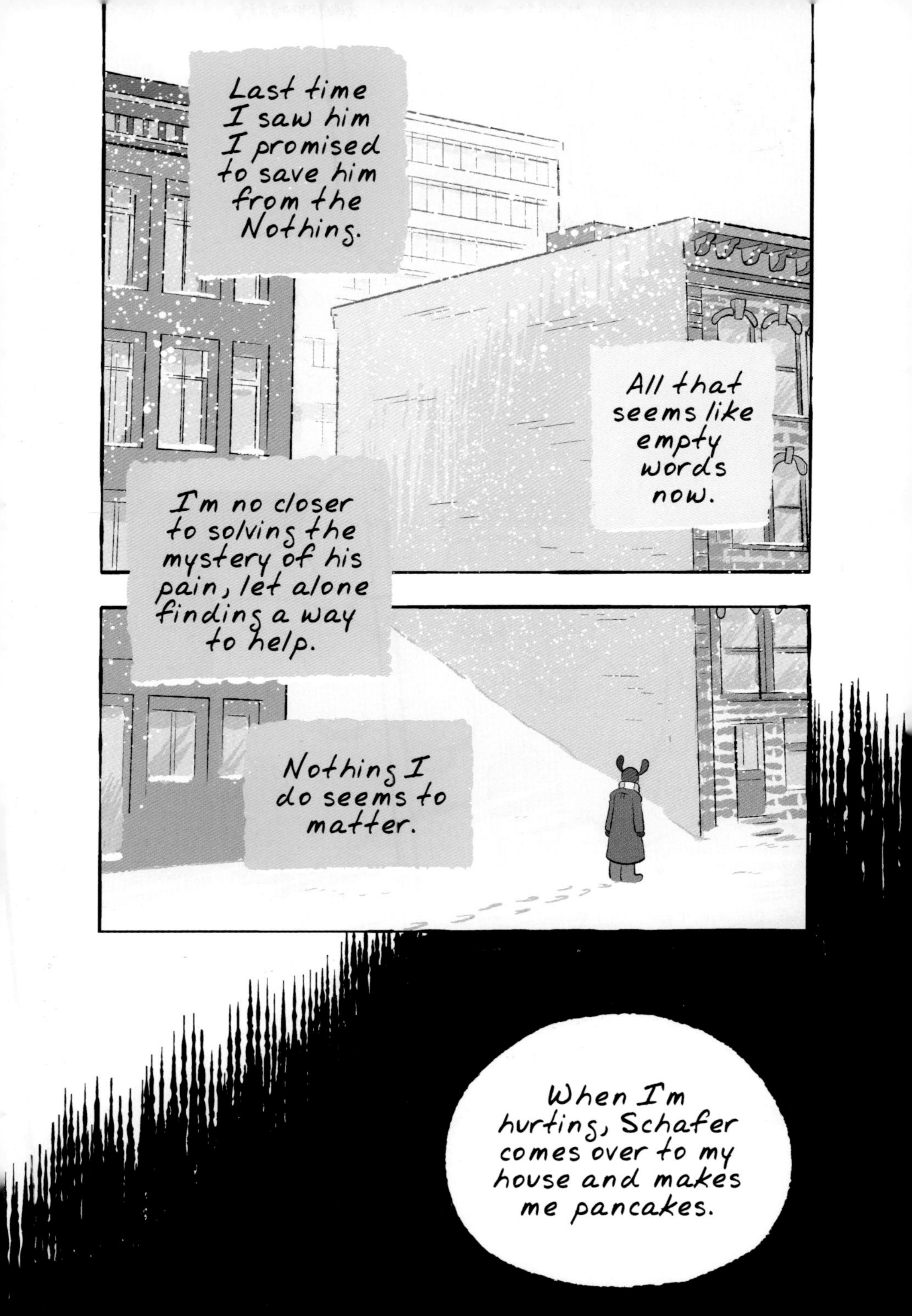
Last time I saw him I promised to save him from the Nothing.
All that seems like empty words now.
I'm no closer to solving the mystery of his pain, let alone finding a way to help.
Nothing I do seems to matter.
When I'm hurting, Schafer comes over to my house and makes me pancakes.

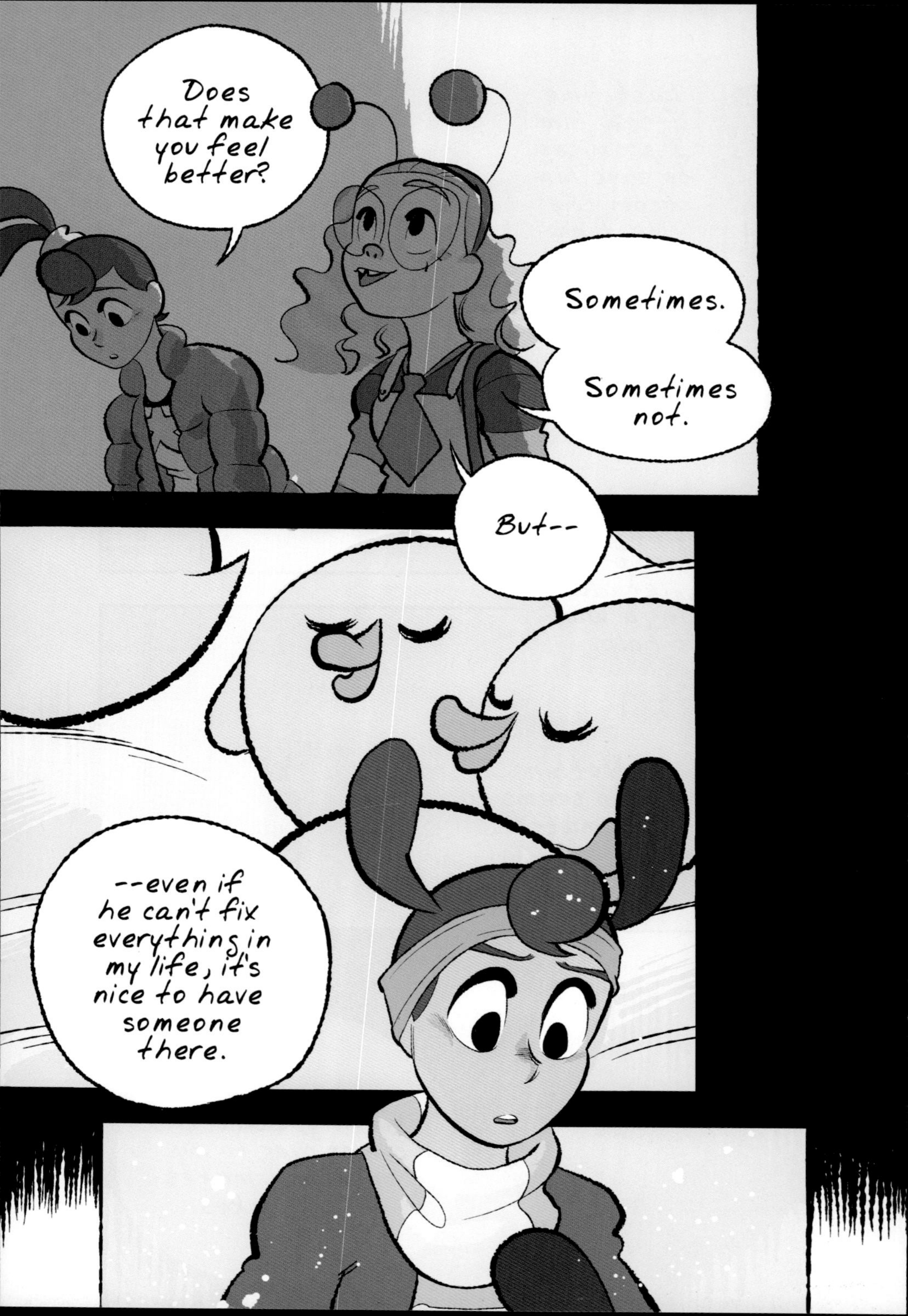
Does that make you feel better?
Sometimes.
Sometimes not.
But--
--even if he can't fix everything in my life, it's nice to have someone there.

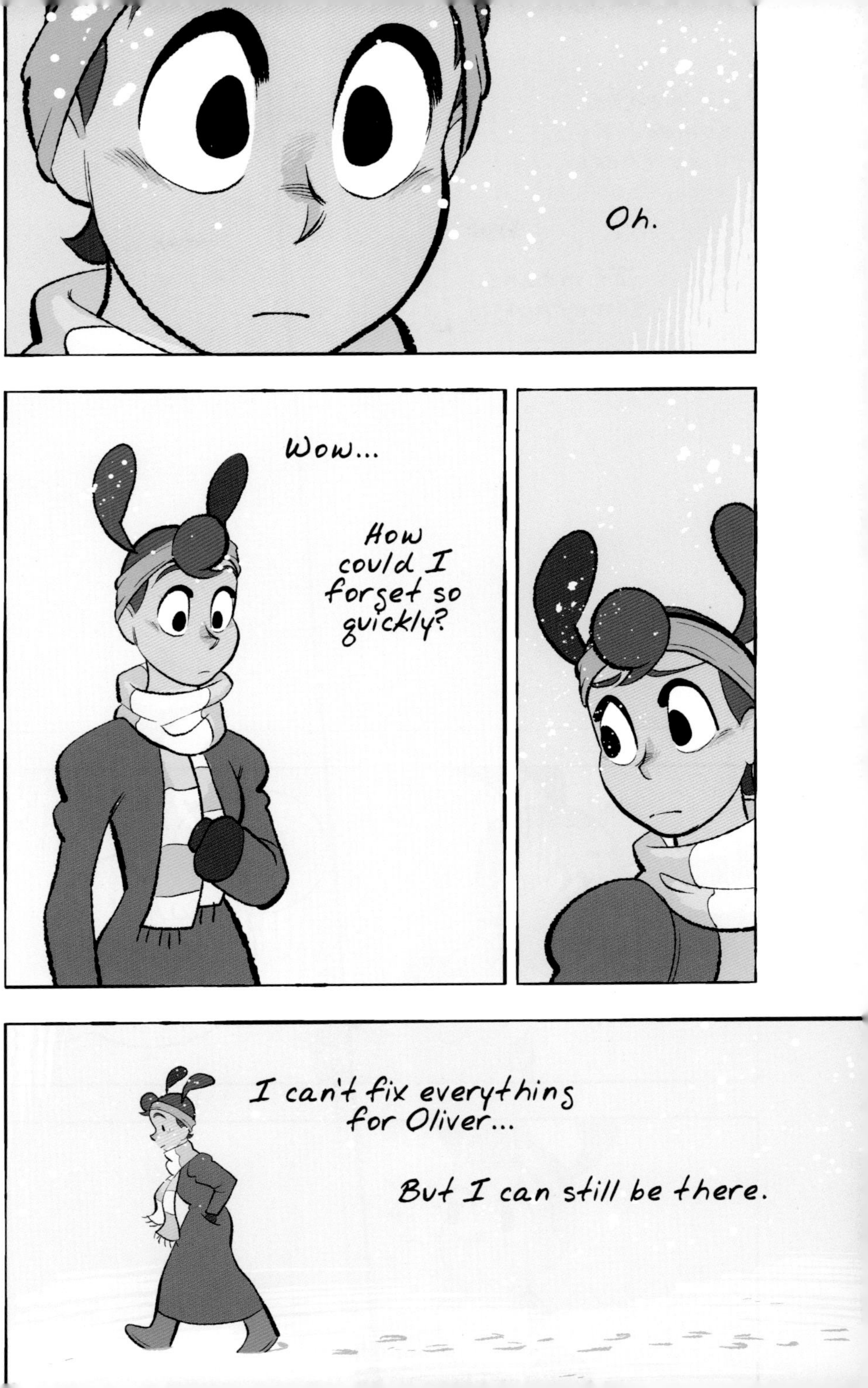
Oh.
Wow...
How could I forget so quickly?
I can't fix everything for Oliver...
But I can still be there.

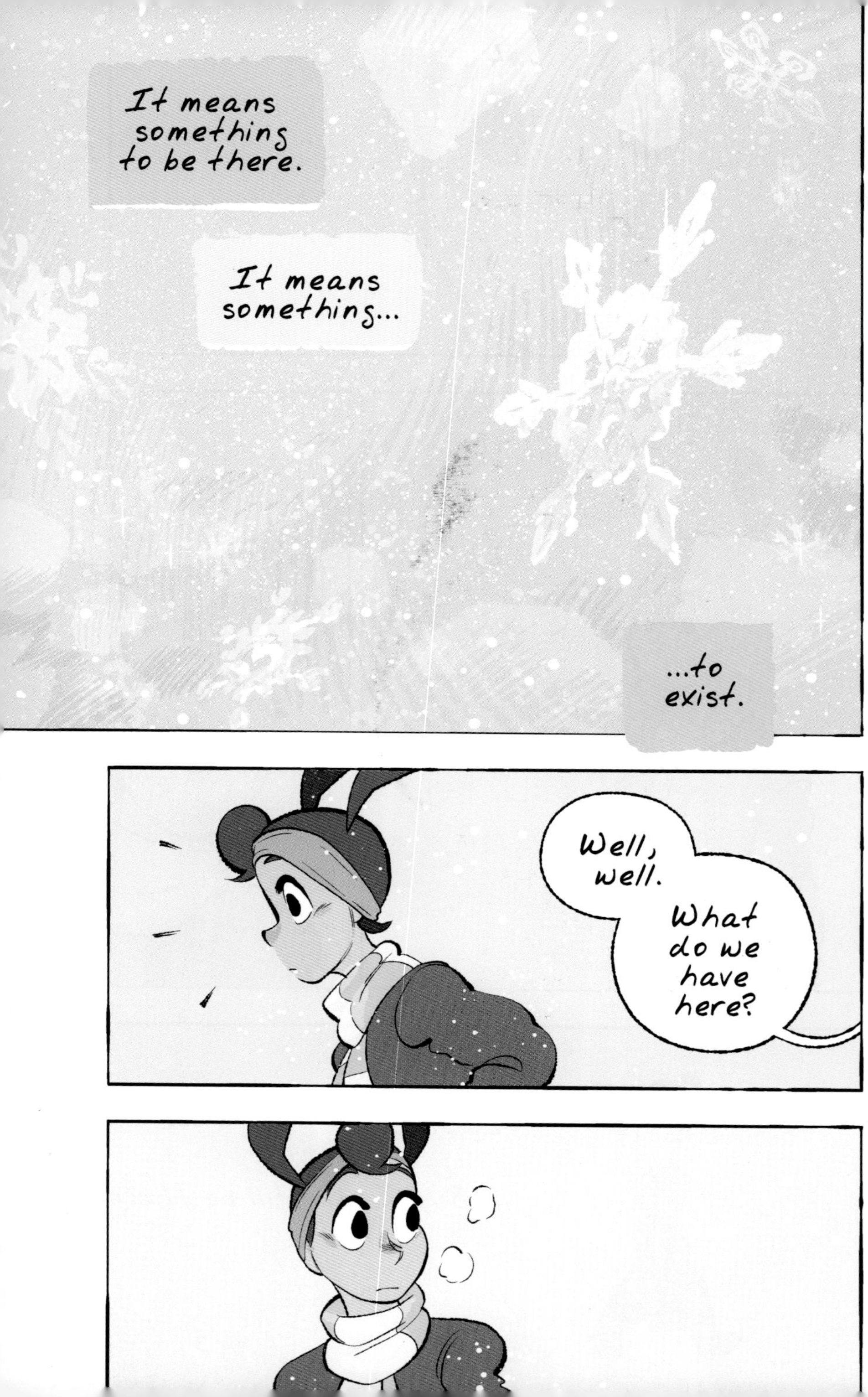
It means something to be there.
It means something...
...to exist.
Well, well.
What do we have here?

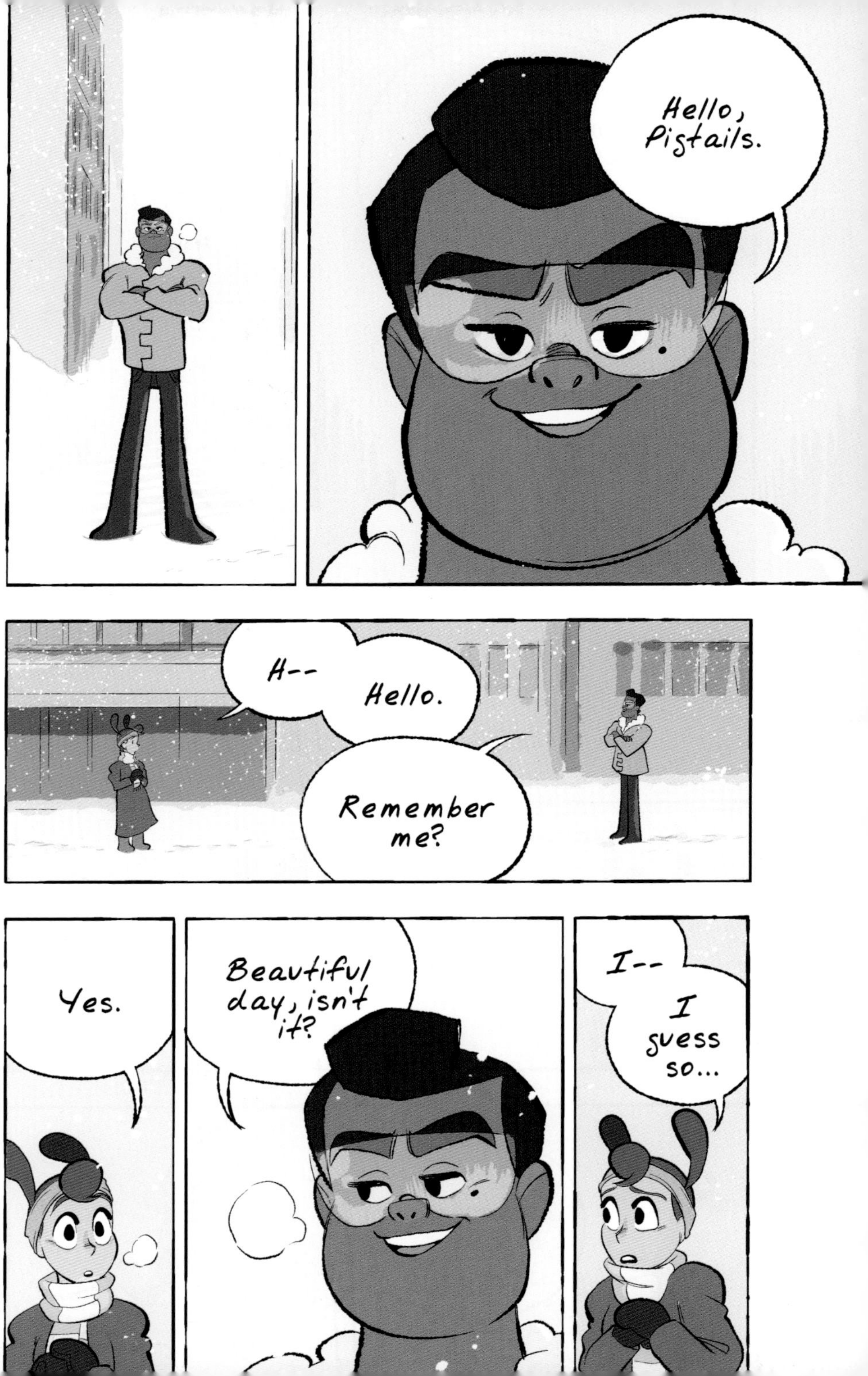
Hello, Pigtails.
H--
Hello.
Remember me?
Yes.
Beautiful day, isn't it?
I--
I guess so...

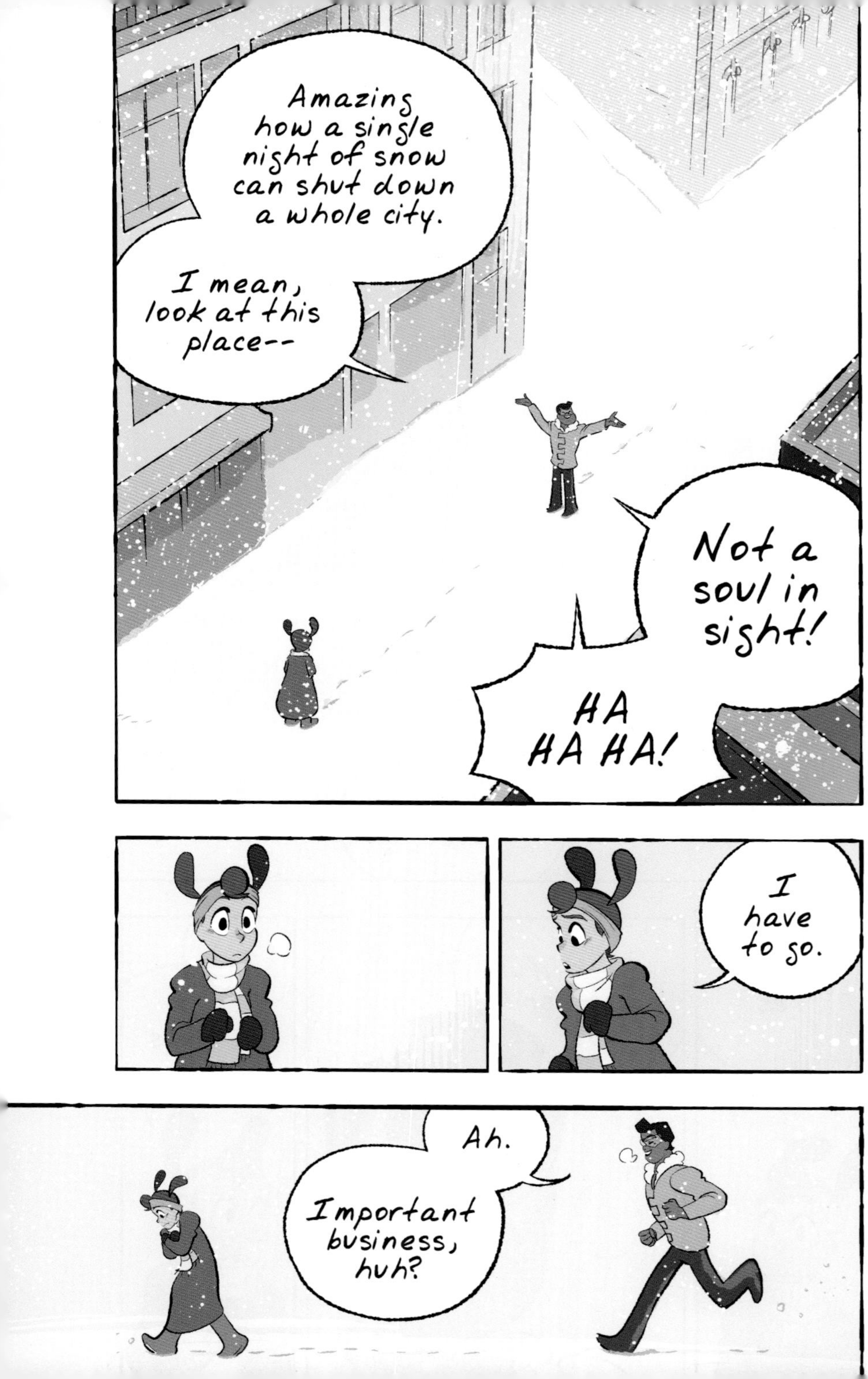
Amazing how a single night of snow can shut down a whole city.
I mean, look at this place--
Not a soul in sight!
HA HA HA!
I have to go.
Ah.
Important business, huh?

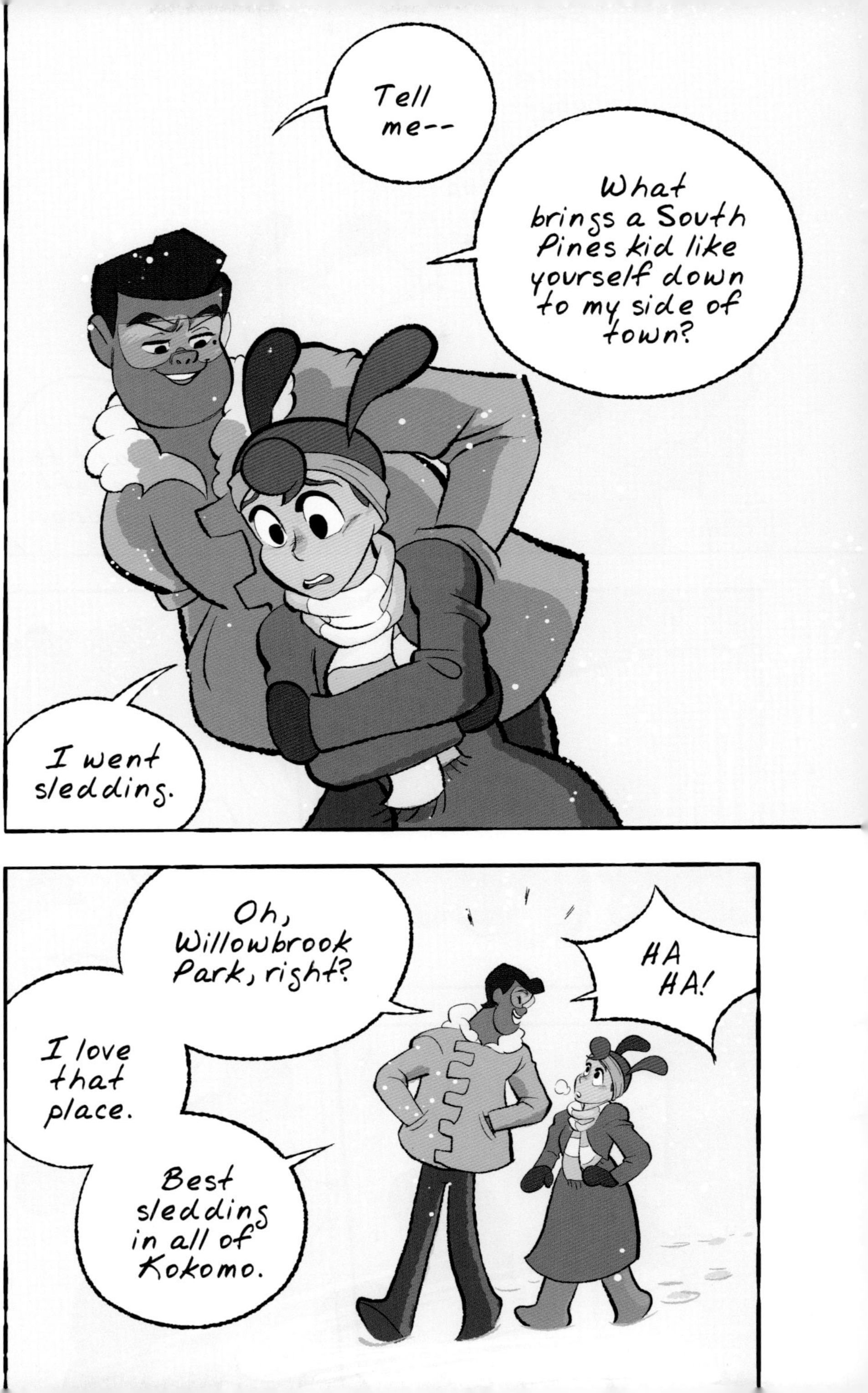
Tell me--
What brings a South Pines kid like yourself down to my side of town?
I went sledding.
Oh, Willowbrook Park, right?
I love that place.
Best sledding in all of Kokomo.
HA HA!

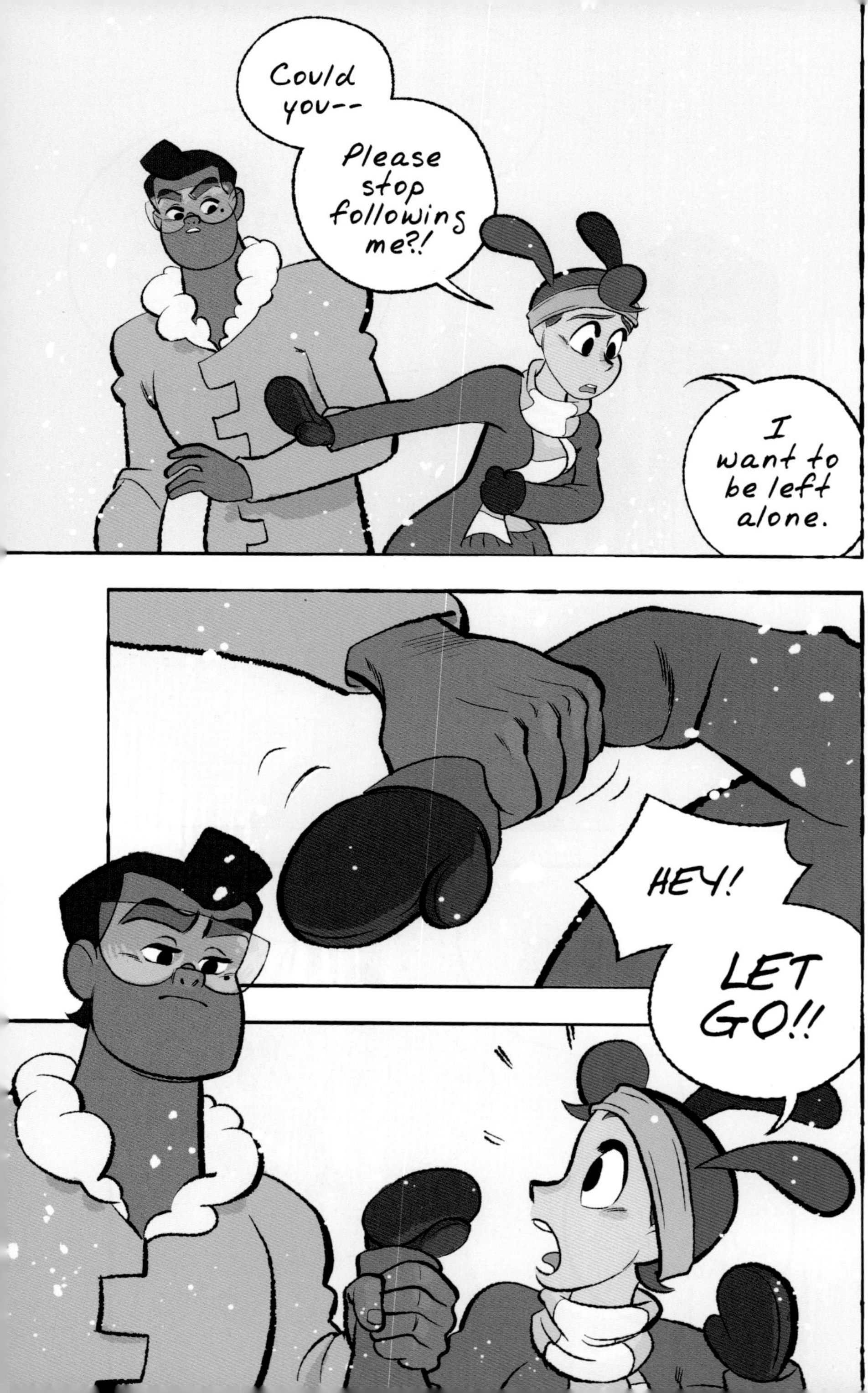
Could you--
Please stop followins me?!
I want to be left alone.
HEY!
LET GO!!

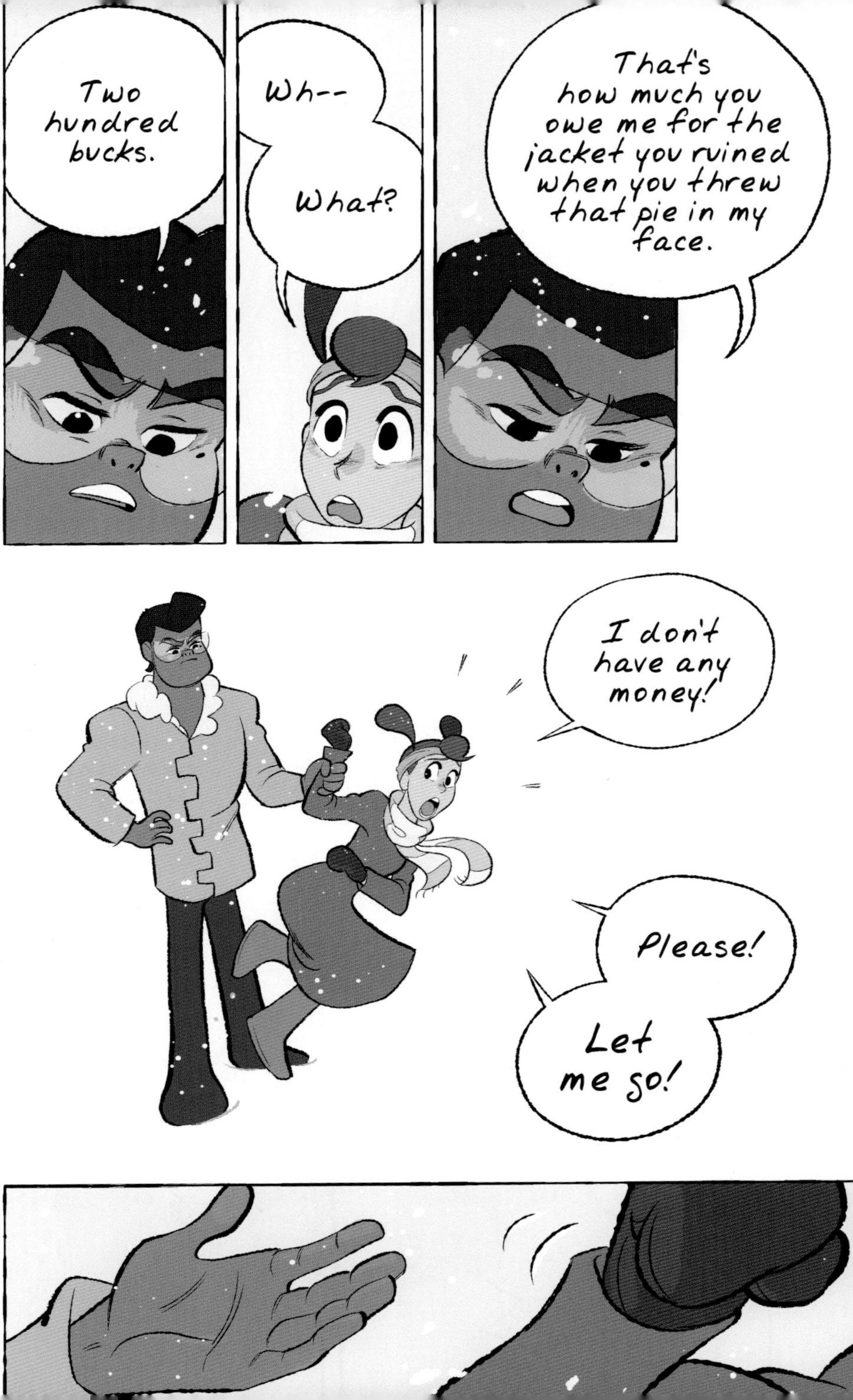
Two hundred bucks.
Wh--
What?
That's how much you owe me for the jacket you ruined when you threw that pie in my face.
I don't have any money!
Please!
Let me go!

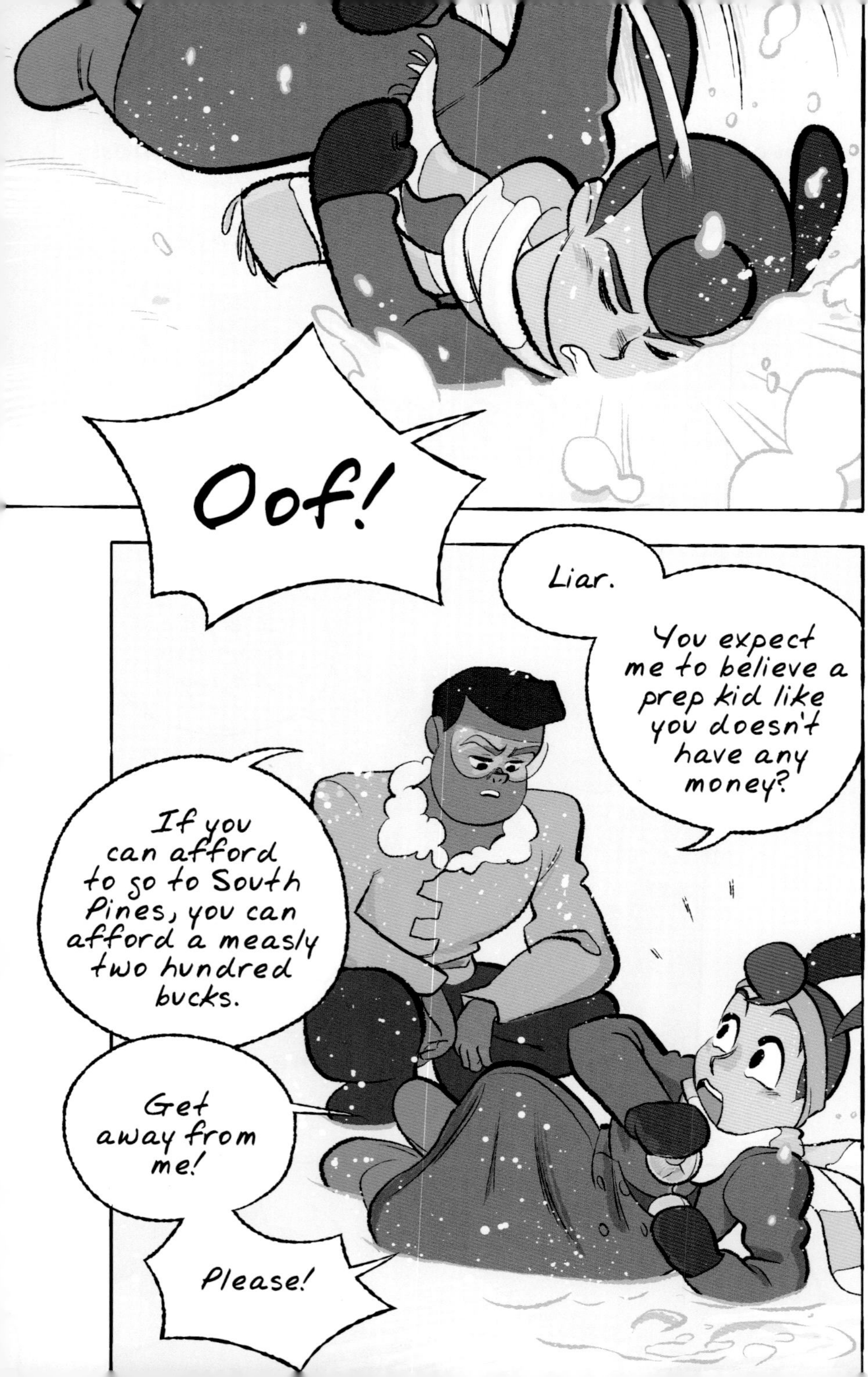
Oof!
Liar.
You expect me to believe a prep kid like you doesn't have any money?
If you can afford to go to South Pines, you can afford a measly two hundred bucks.
Get away from me!
Please!

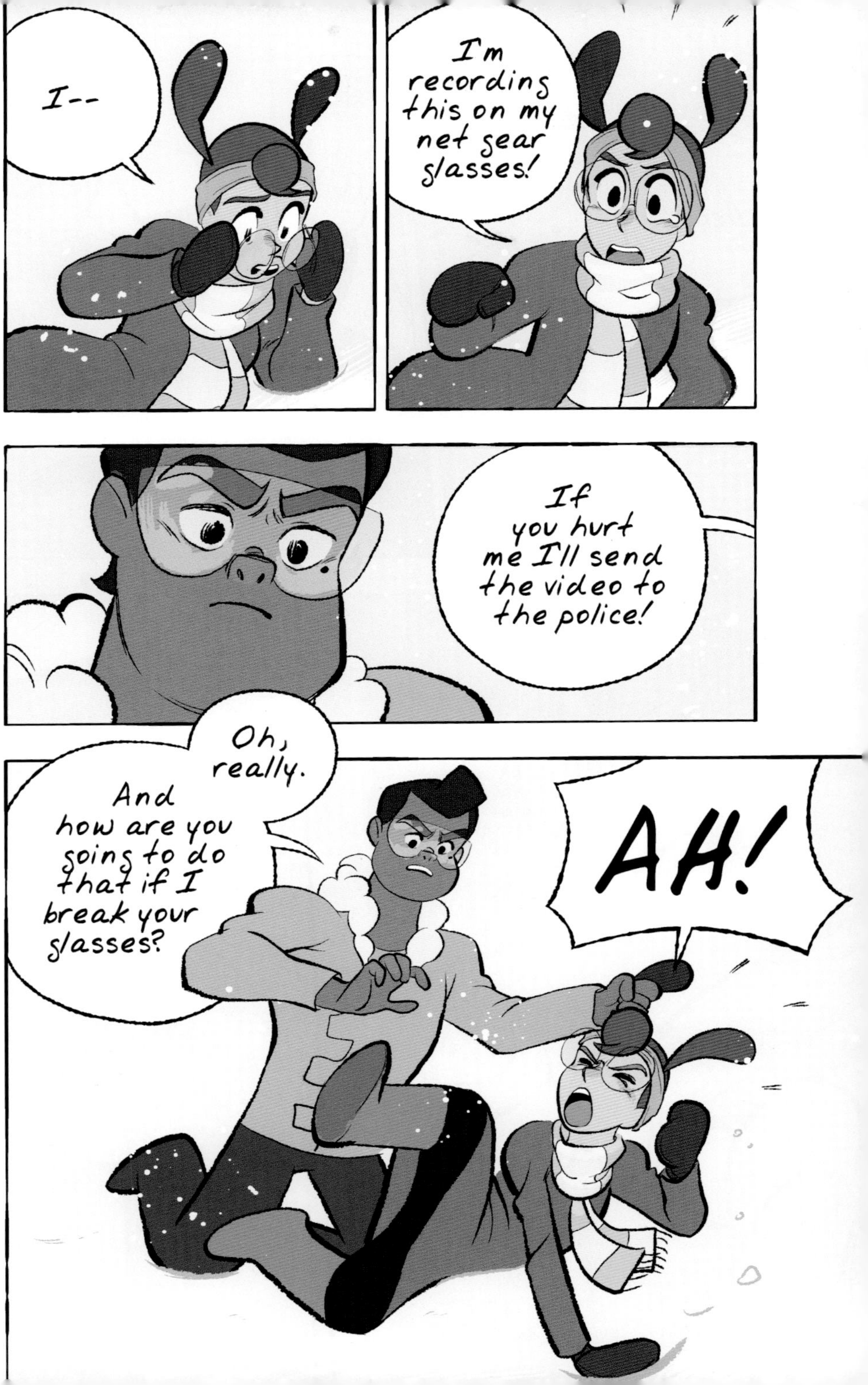
I--
I'm recording this on my net gear glasses!
If you hurt me I'll send the video to the police!
Oh, really.
And how are you going to do that if I break your glasses?
AH!

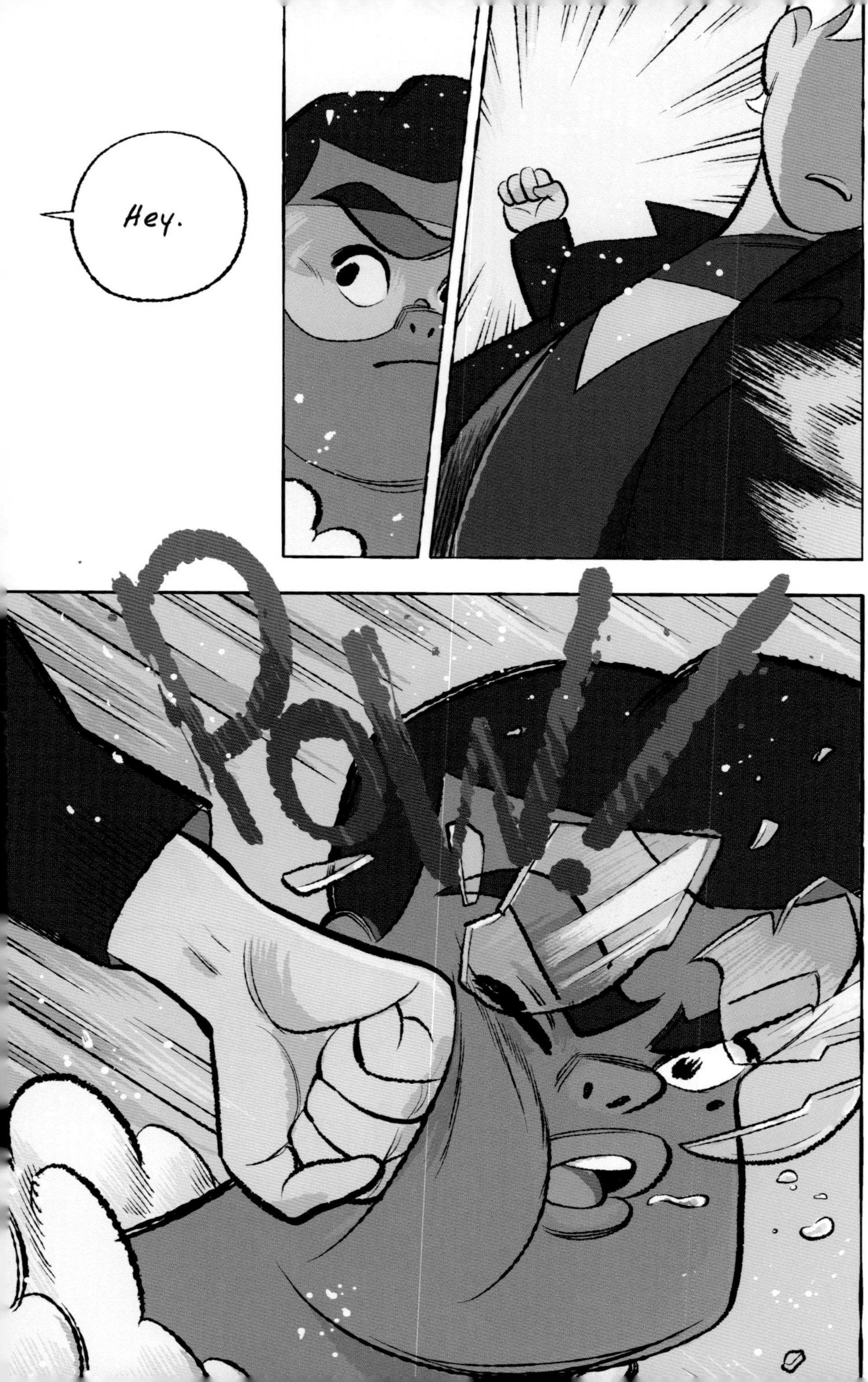
Hey.
POW!

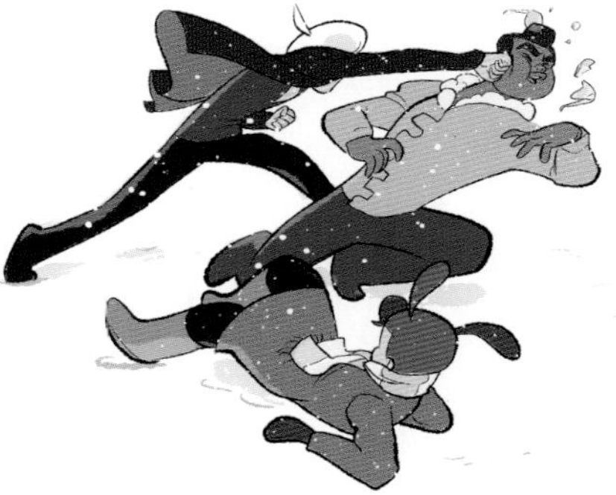

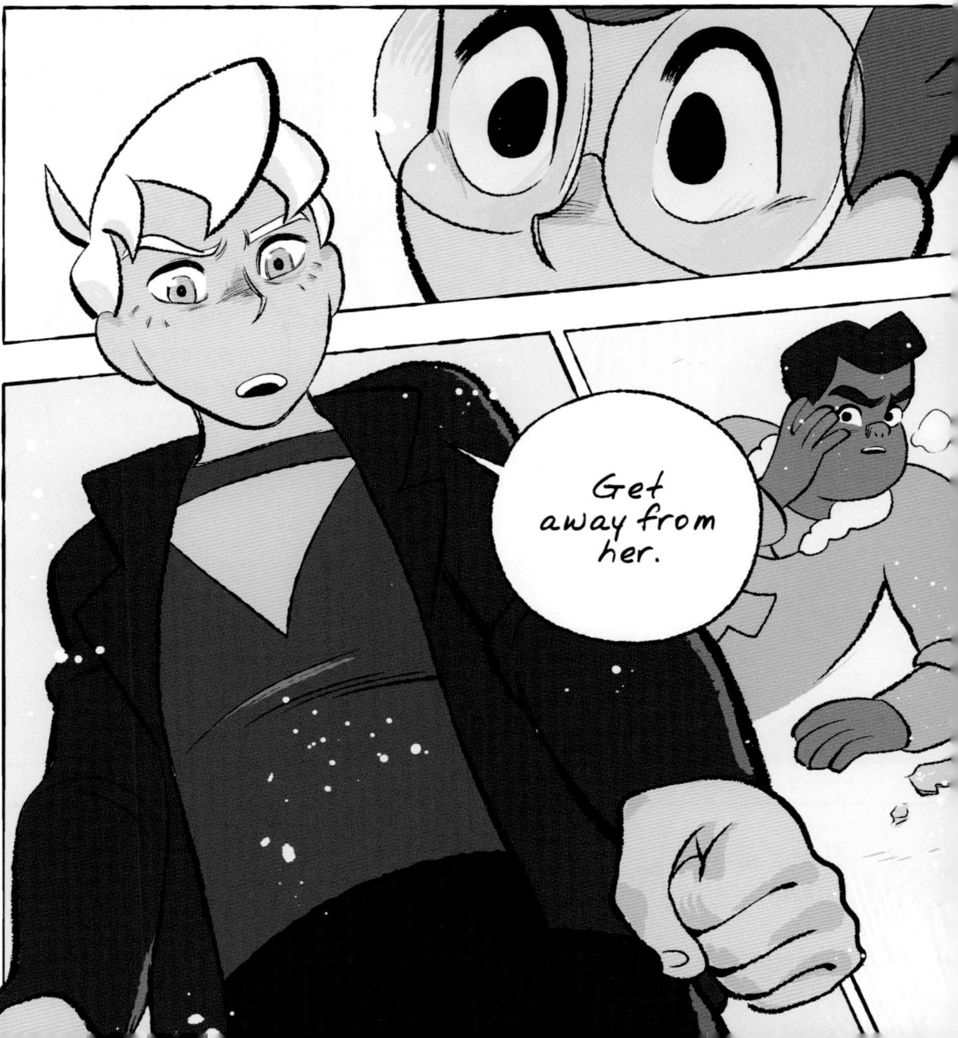
Get away from her.

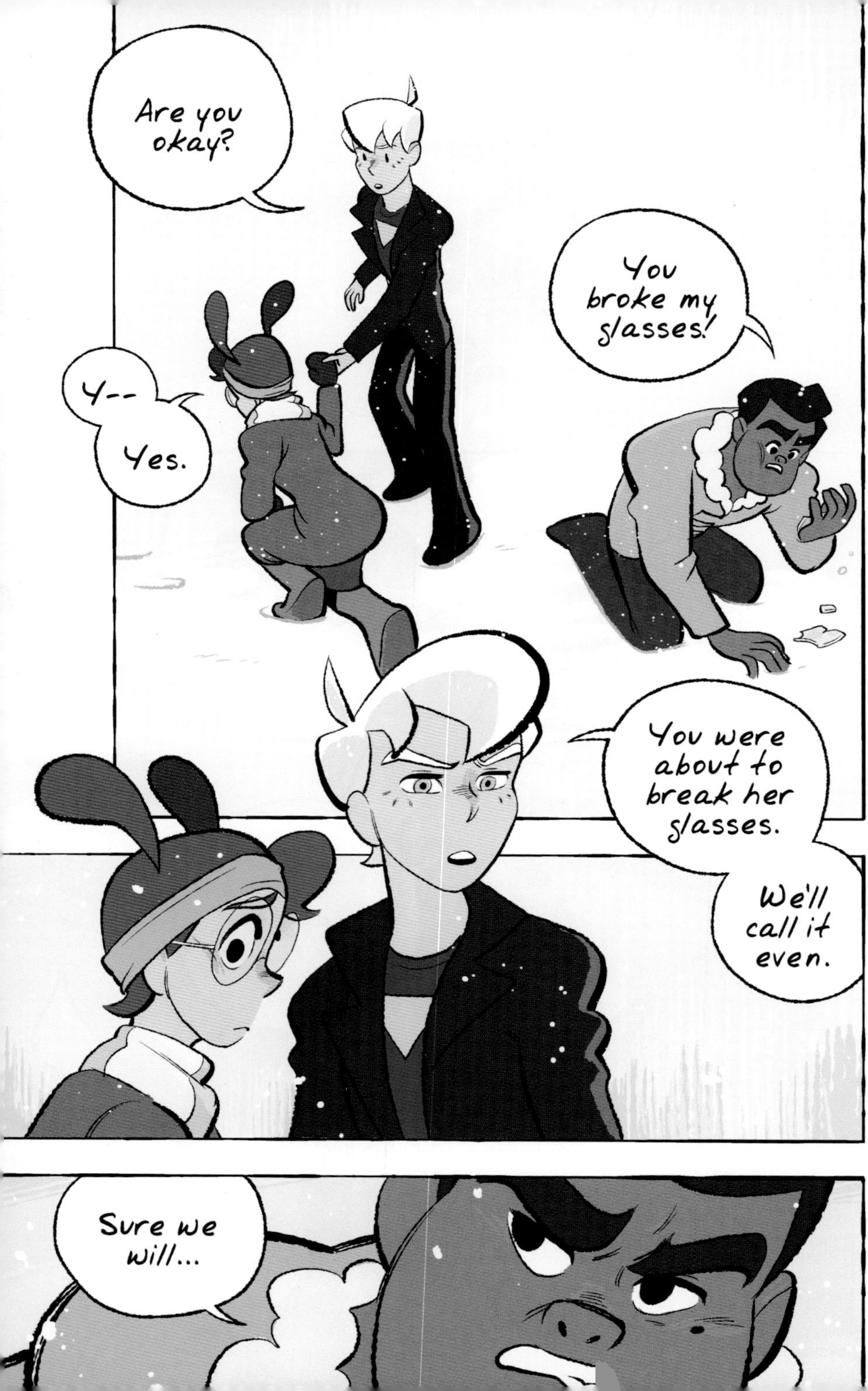
Are you okay?
Y--
Yes.
You broke my glasses!
You were about to break her glasses.
We'll call it even.
Sure we will...

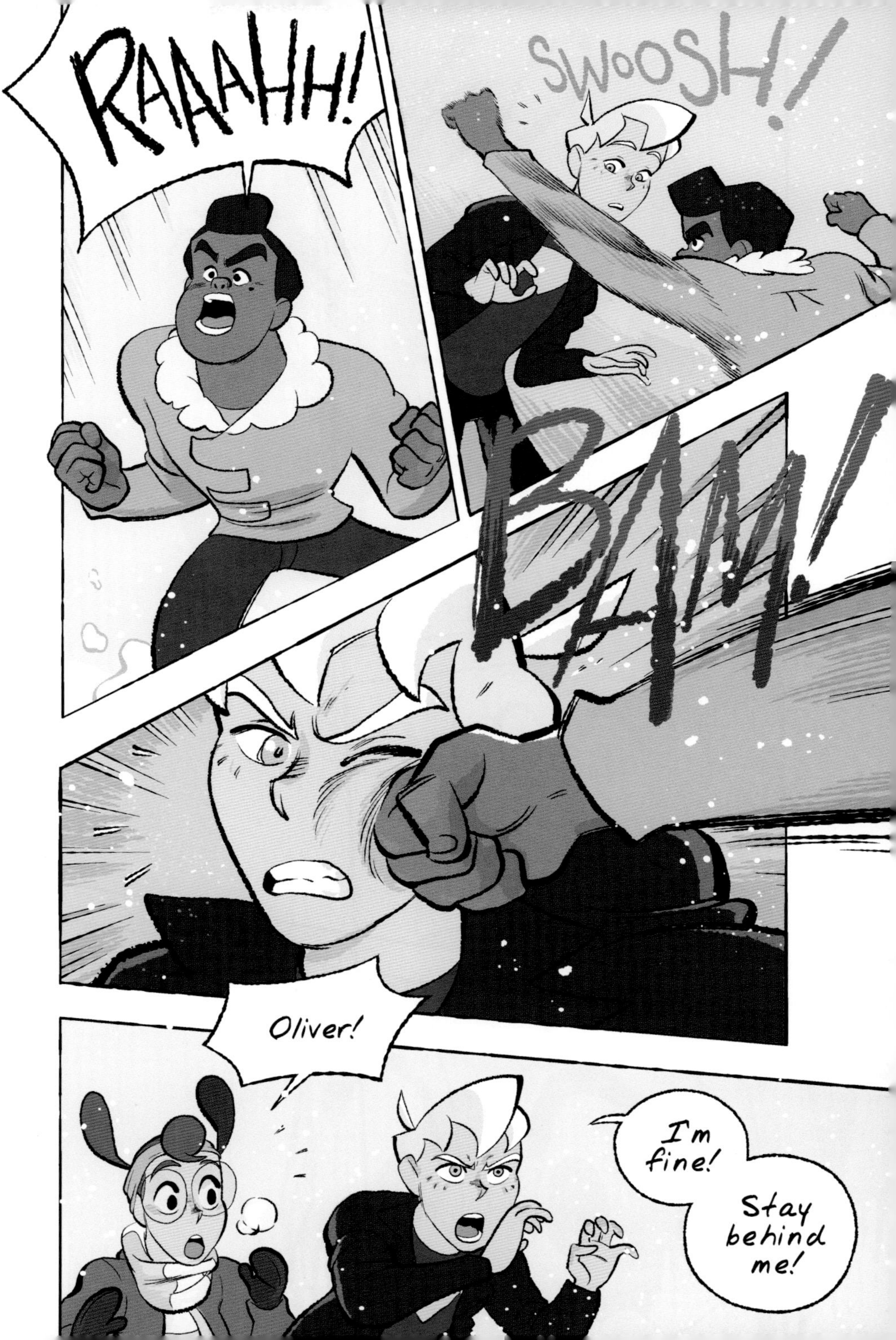
RAAAHH!
SWOOSH!
BAM!
Oliver!
I'm fine!
Stay behind me!

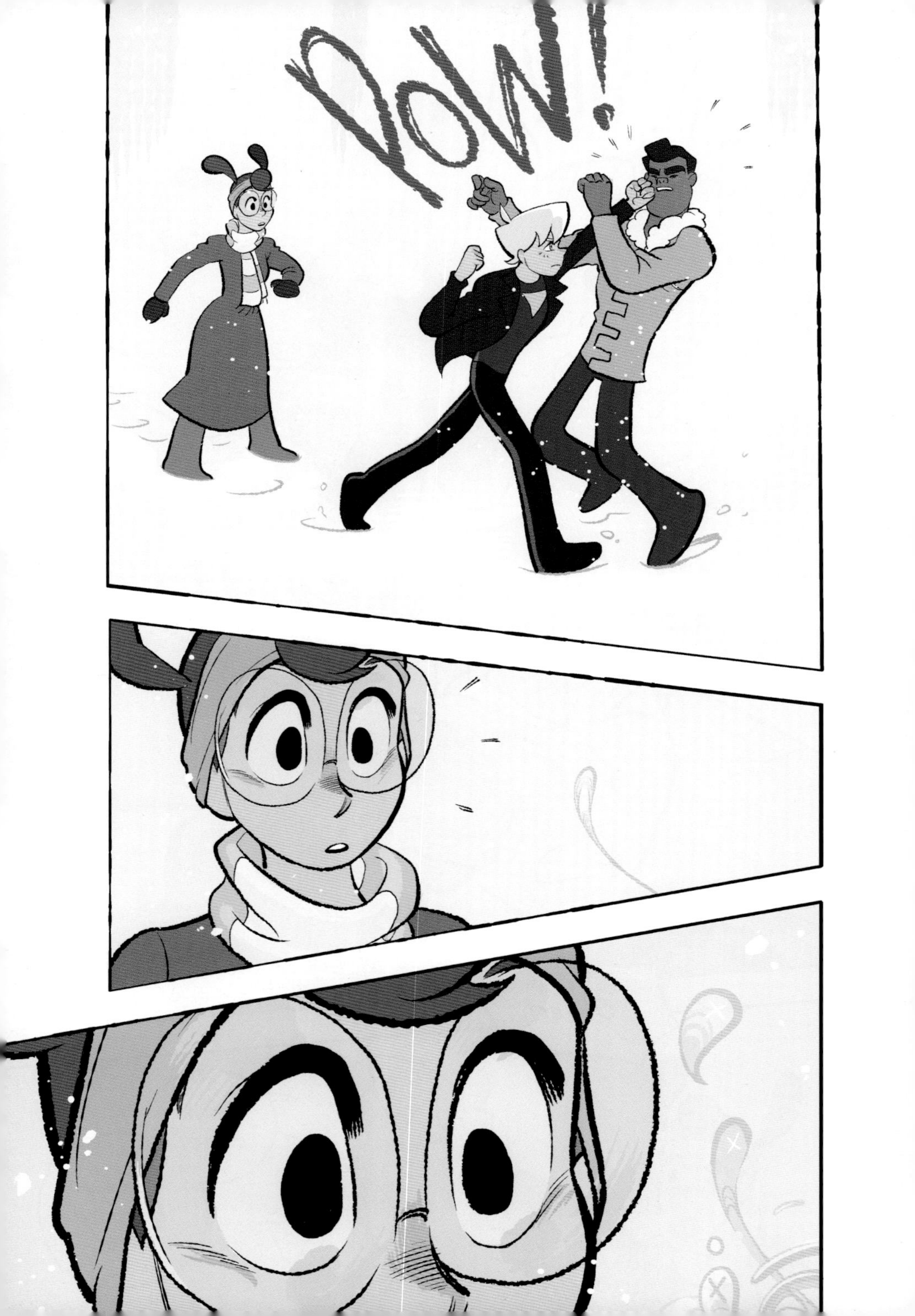
POW!

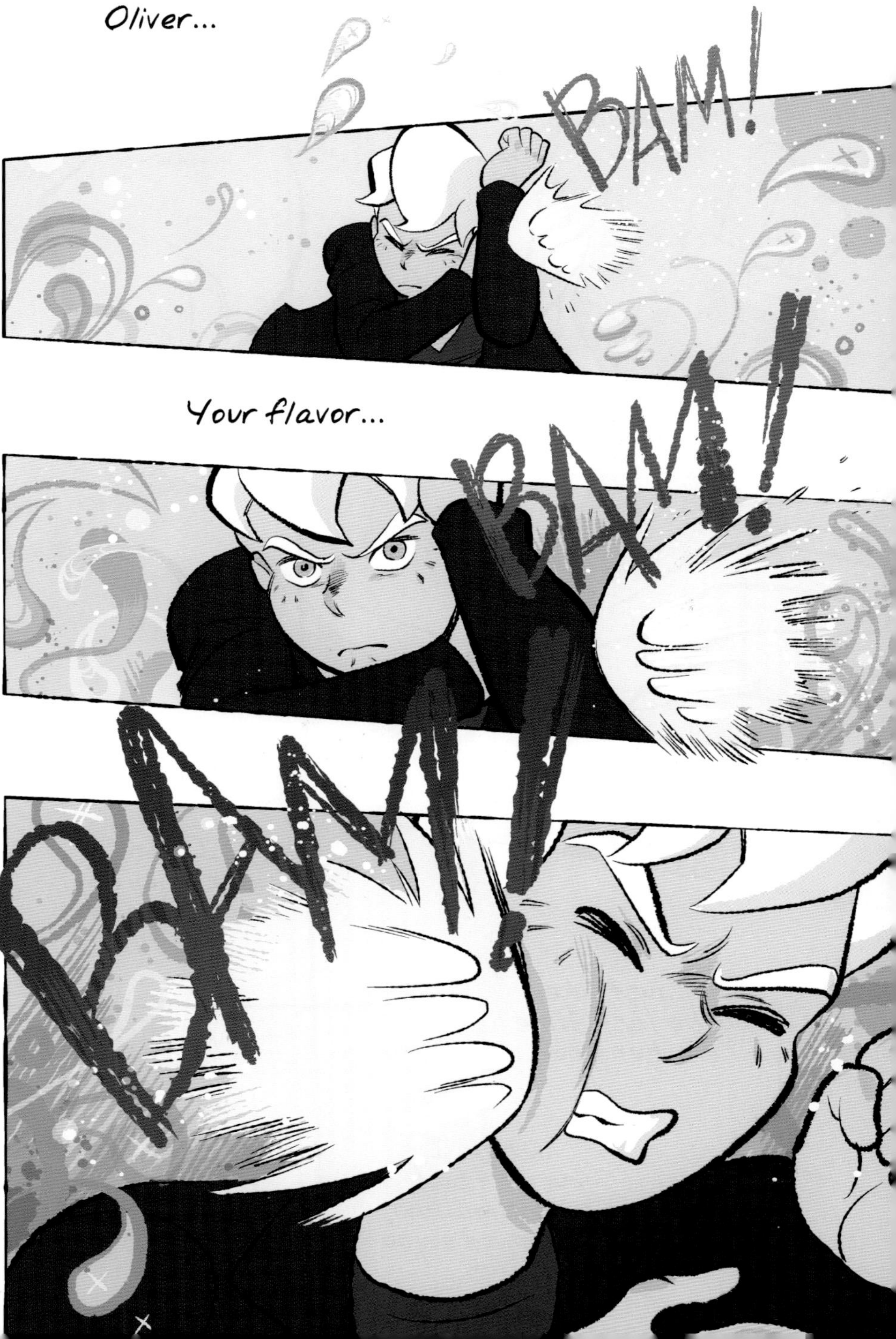
Oliver...
BAM!
Your flavor...
BAM!!
BAM!!

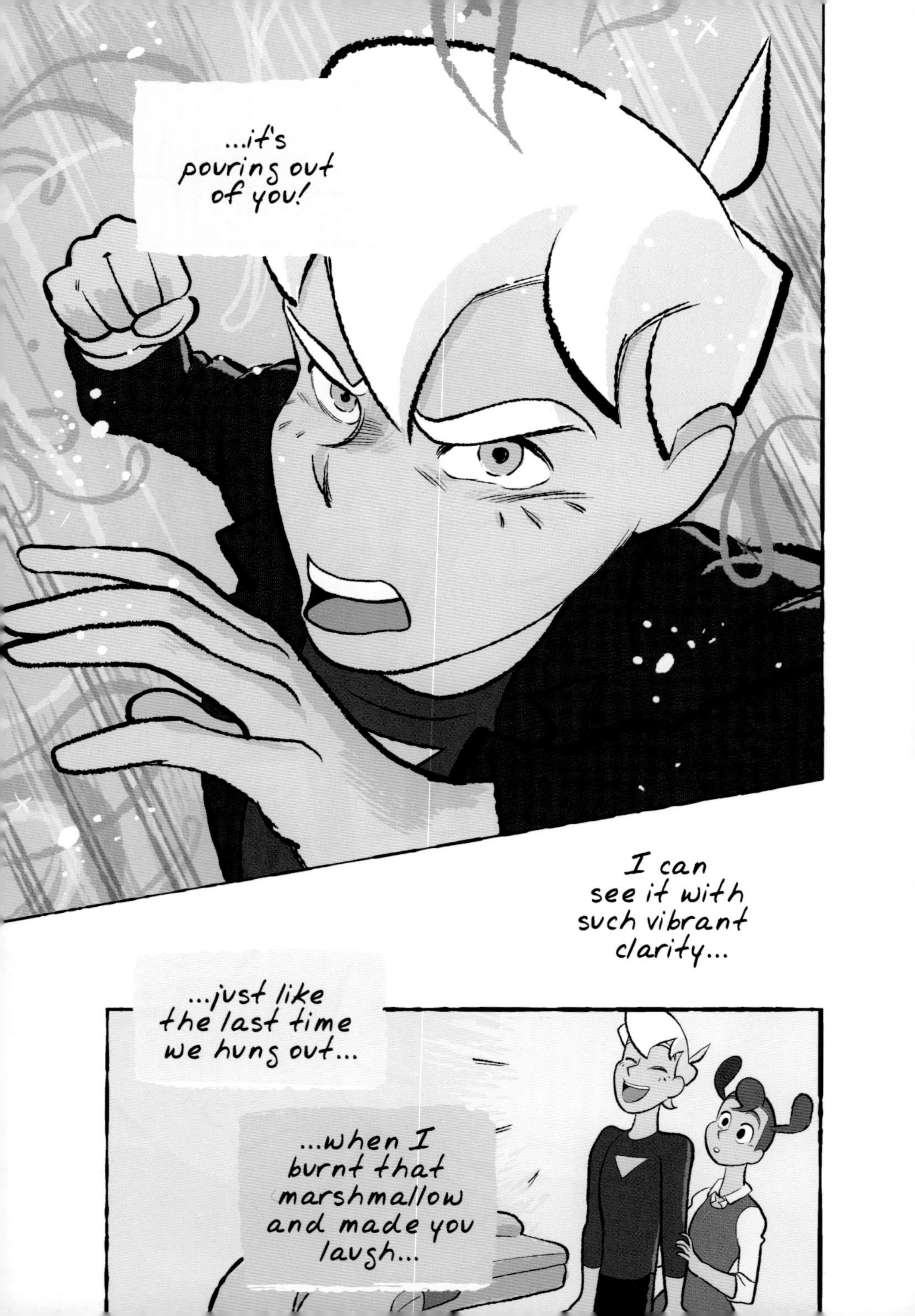
...it's pouring out of you!
I can see it with such vibrant clarity...
...just like the last time we hung out...
...when I burnt that marshmallow and made you laugh...

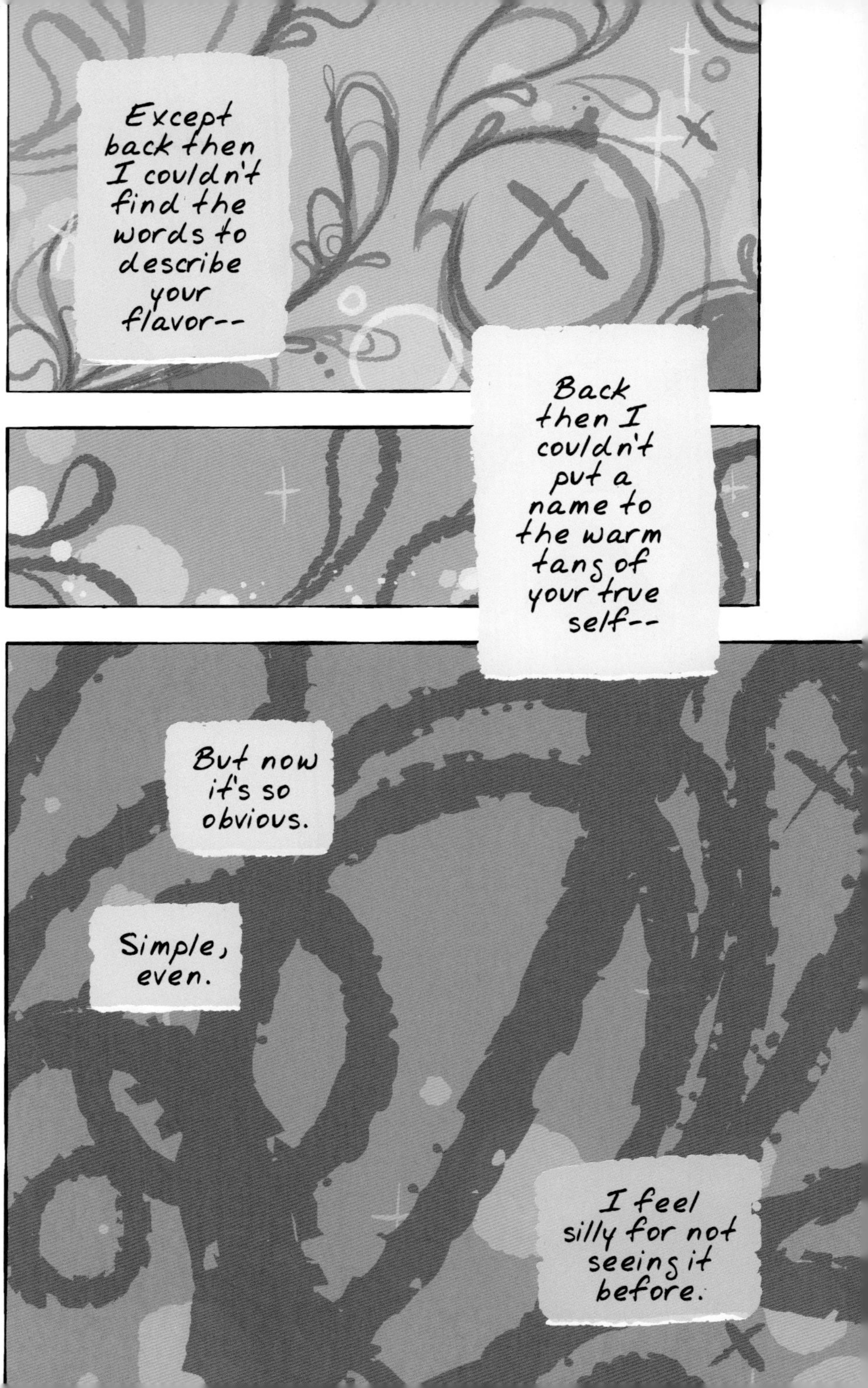
Except back then I couldn't find the words to describe your flavor--
Back then I couldn't put a name to the warm tang of your true self--
But now it's so obvious.
Simple, even.
I feel silly for not seeing it before.

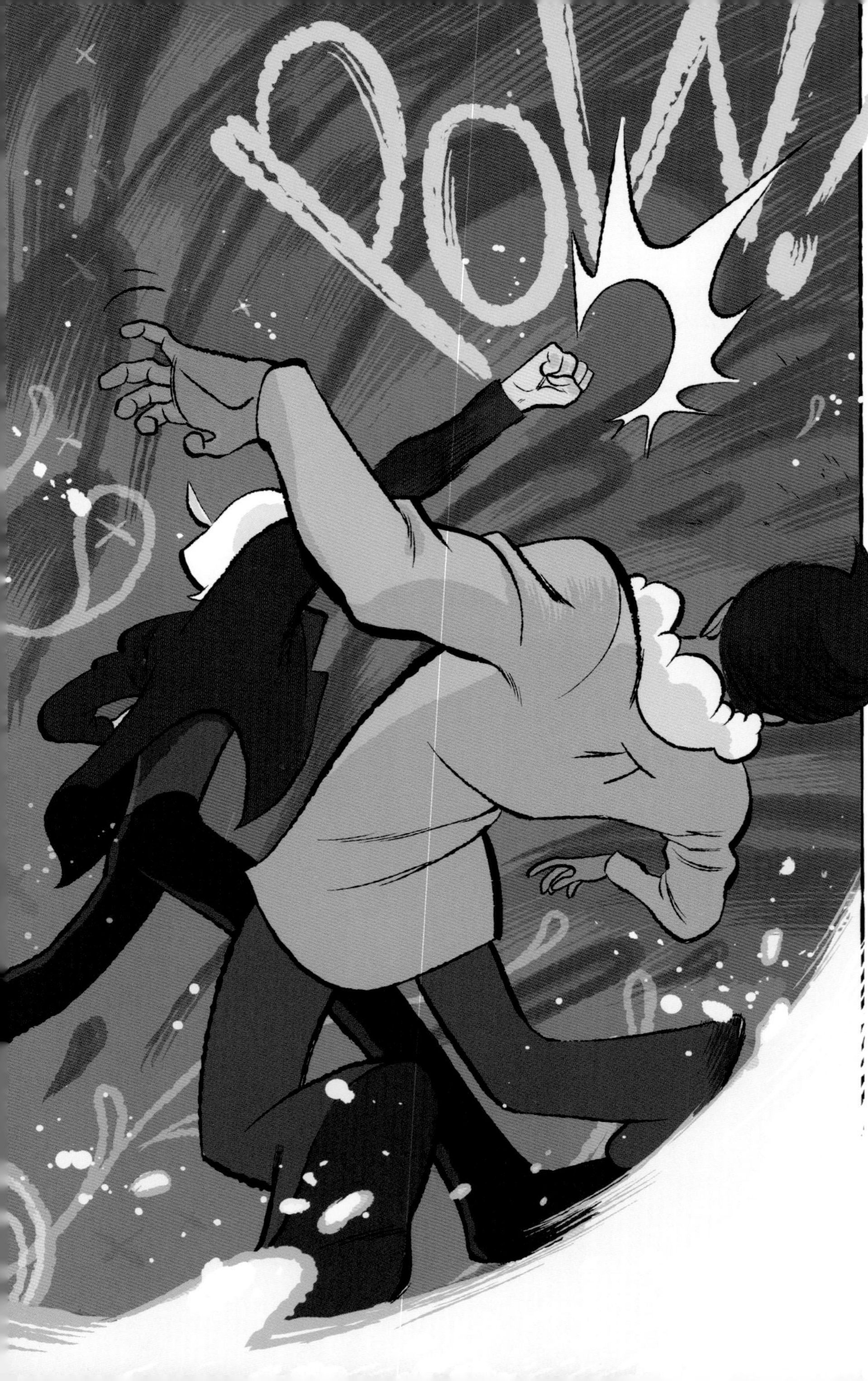
POW!

Orange.

Orange
with a hint
of cinnamon.

That's
the flavor
you've been
hiding.

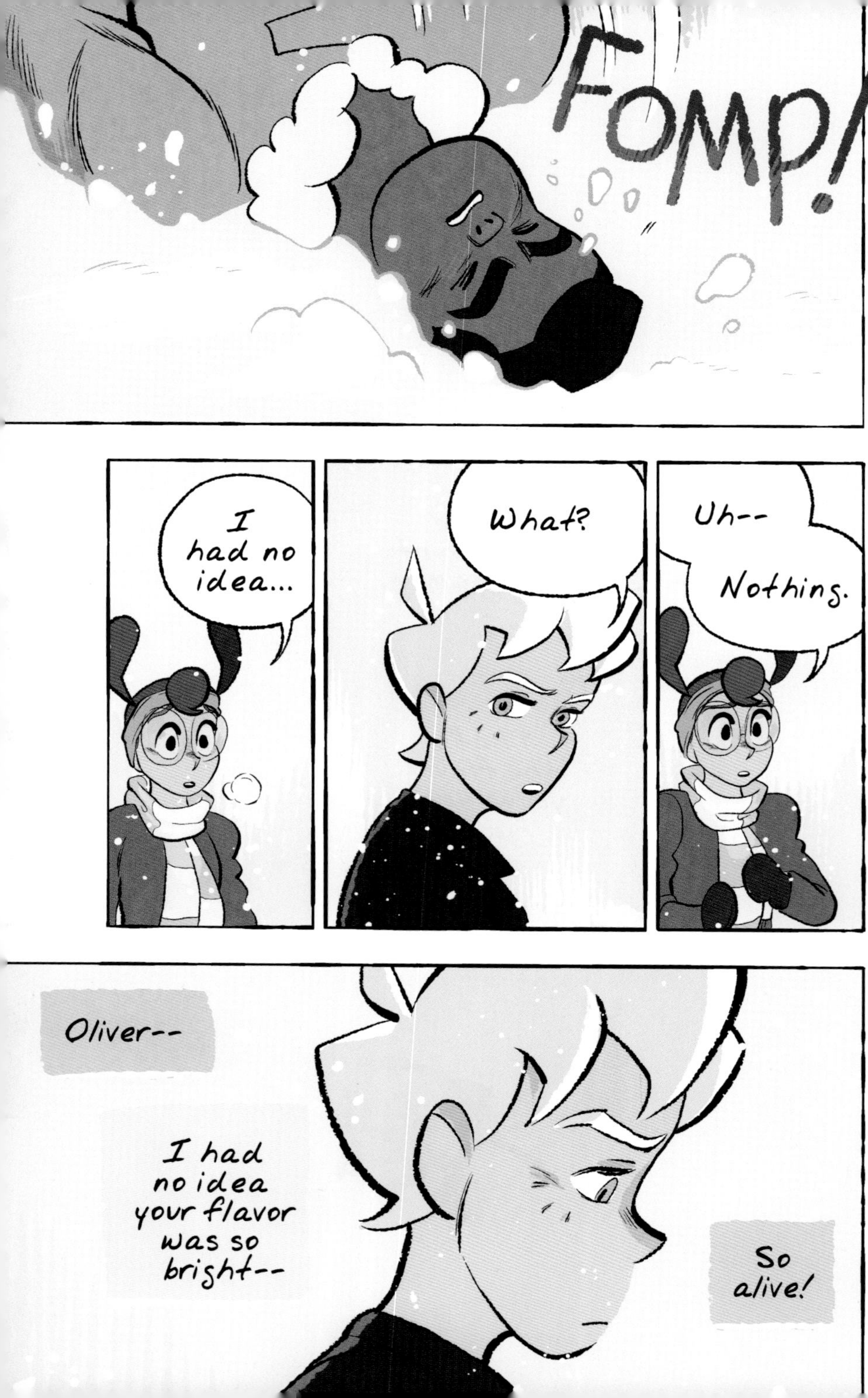
FOMP!
I had no idea...
What?
Uh--
Nothing.
Oliver--
I had no idea your flavor was so bright--
So alive!

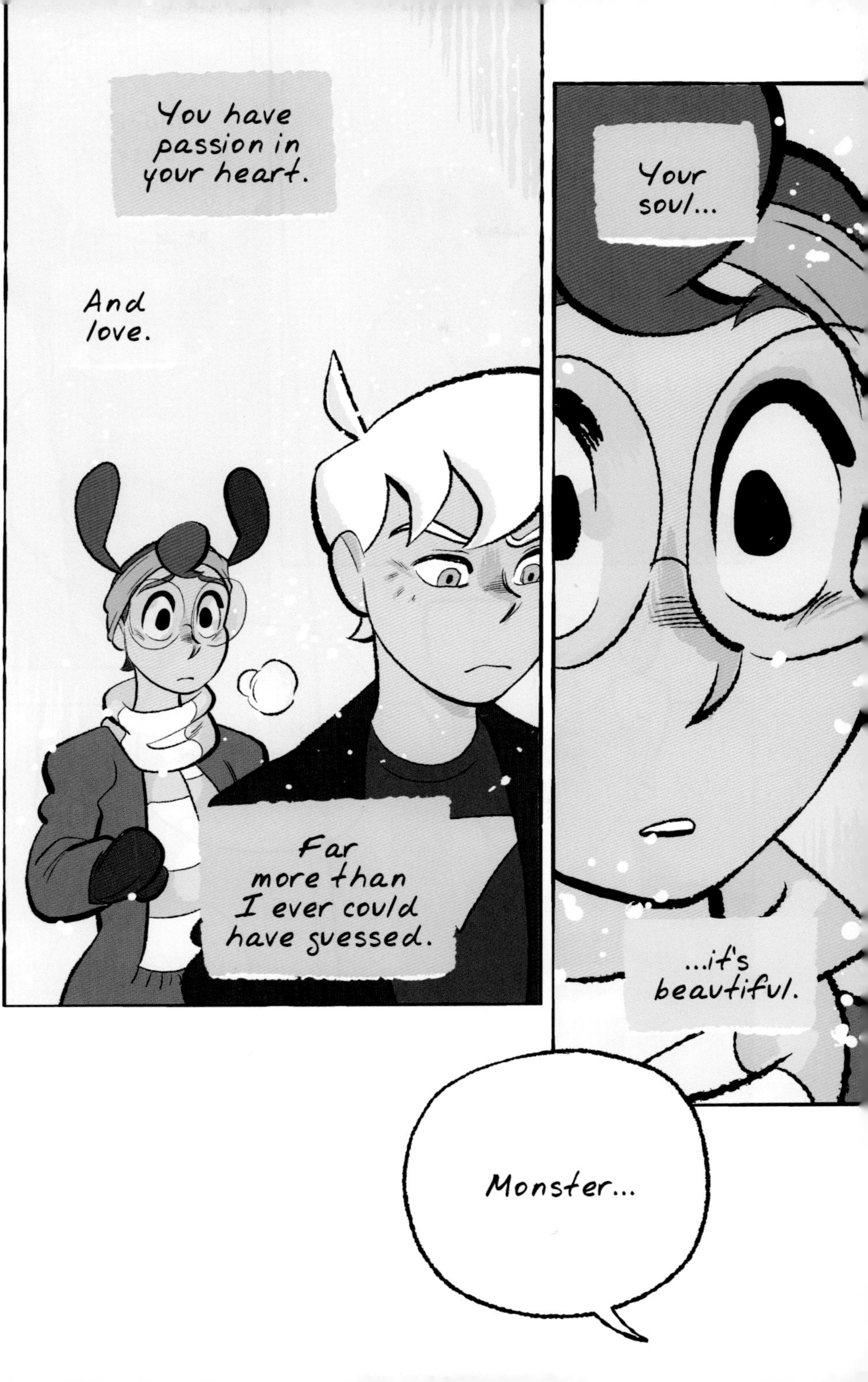

You have passion in your heart.
And love.
Far more than I ever could have guessed.
Your soul...
...it's beautiful.
Monster...

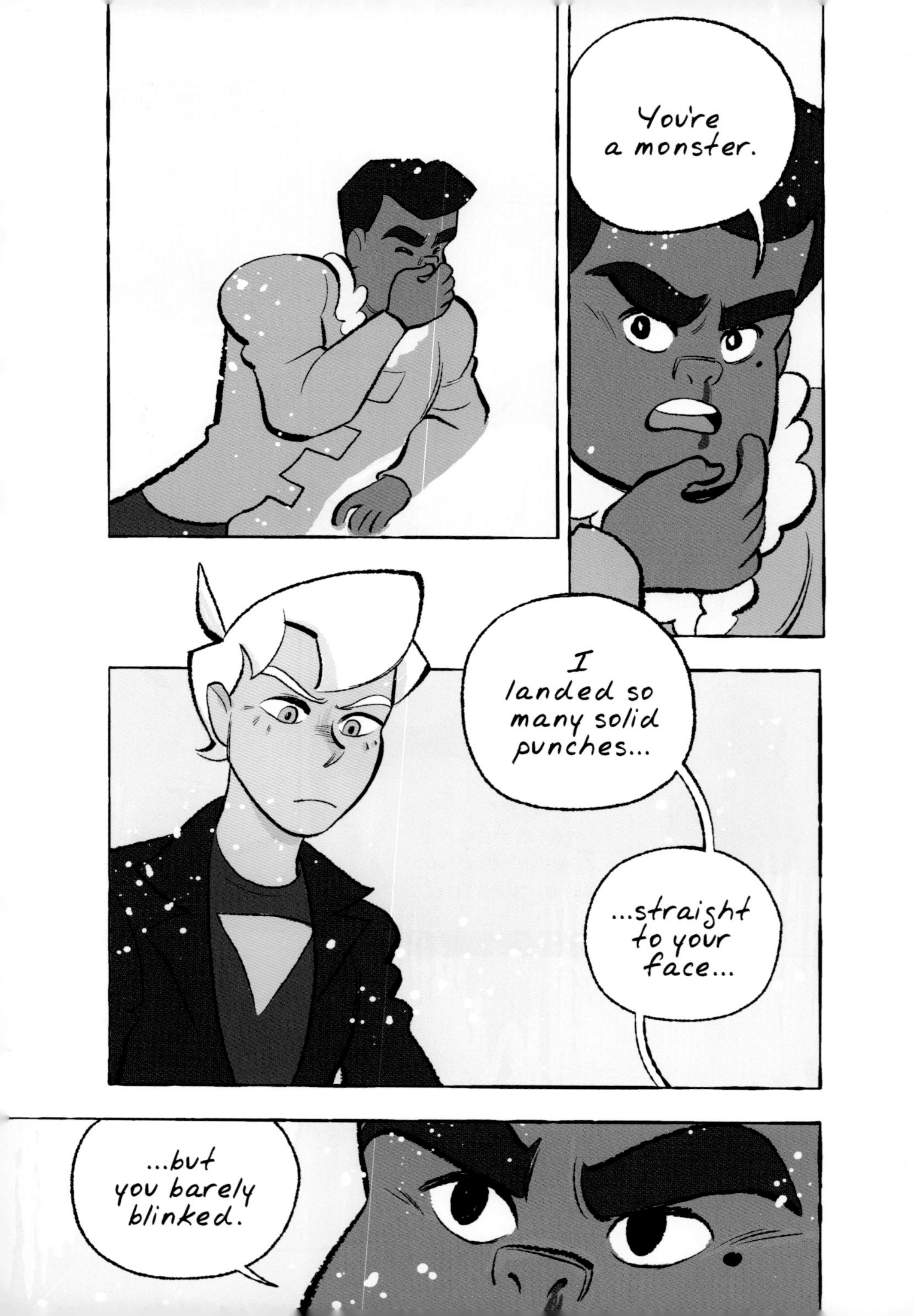
You're a monster.
I landed so many solid punches...
...straight to your face...
...but you barely blinked.

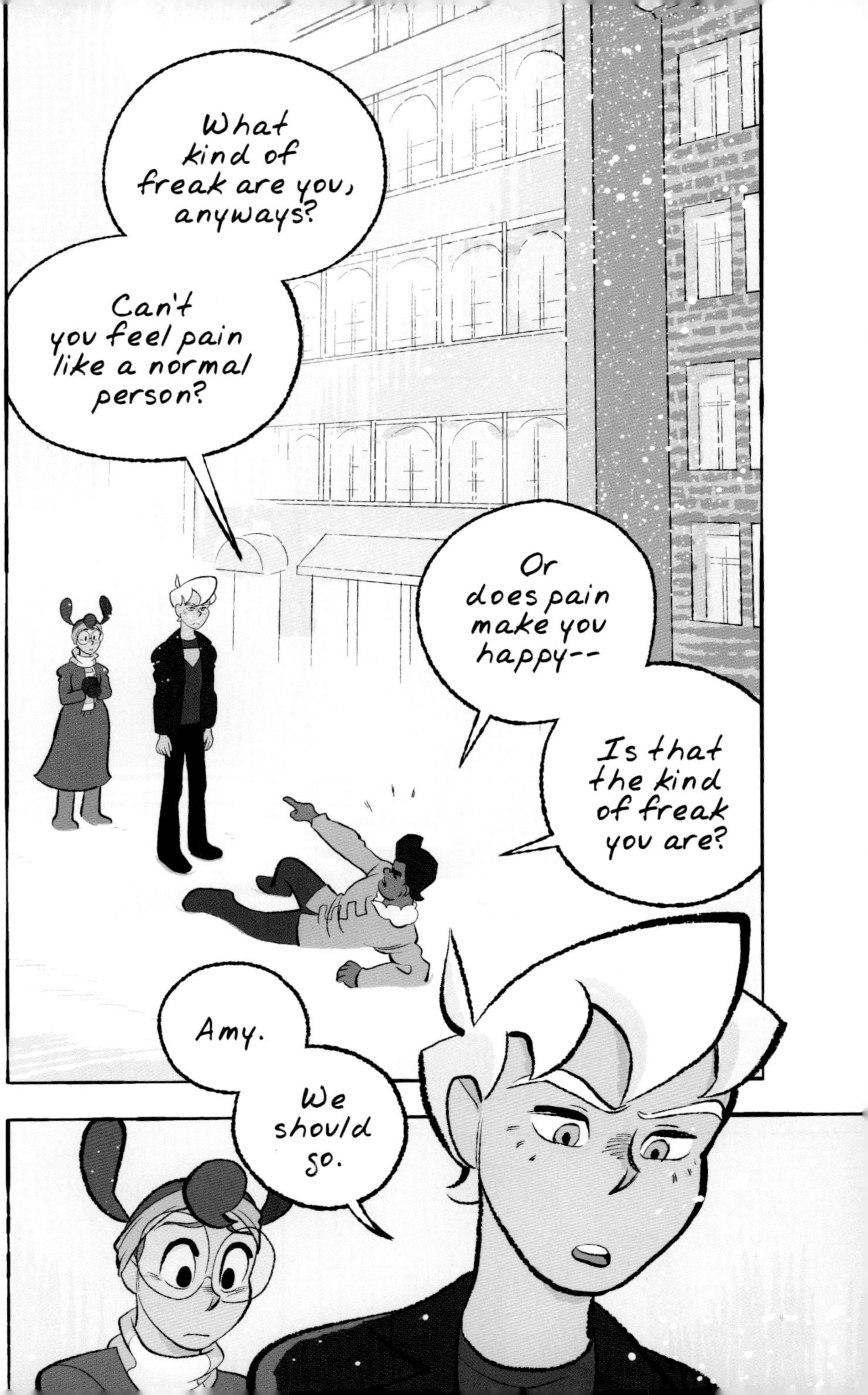
What kind of freak are you, anyways?
Can't you feel pain like a normal person?
Or does pain make you happy--
Is that the kind of freak you are?
Amy.
We should go.

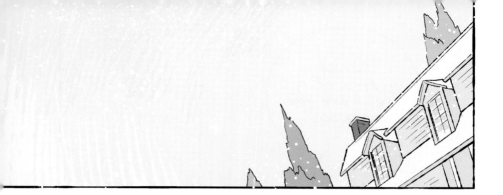

We walk for a while in silence.

I feel numb.

The word "monster" echoes in my head.

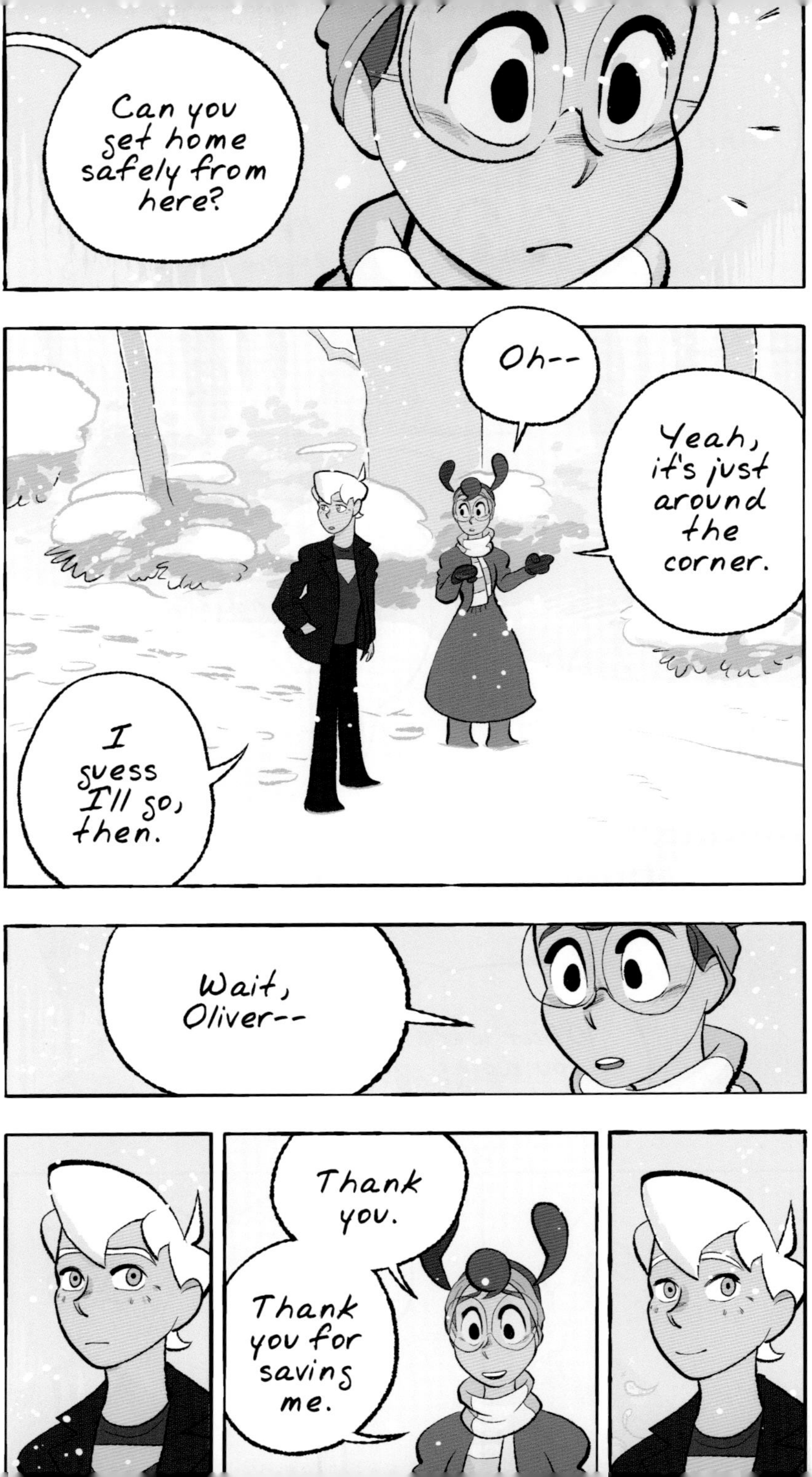
Can you get home safely from here?
Oh--
Yeah, it's just around the corner.
I guess I'll go, then.
Wait, Oliver--
Thank you.
Thank you for saving me.

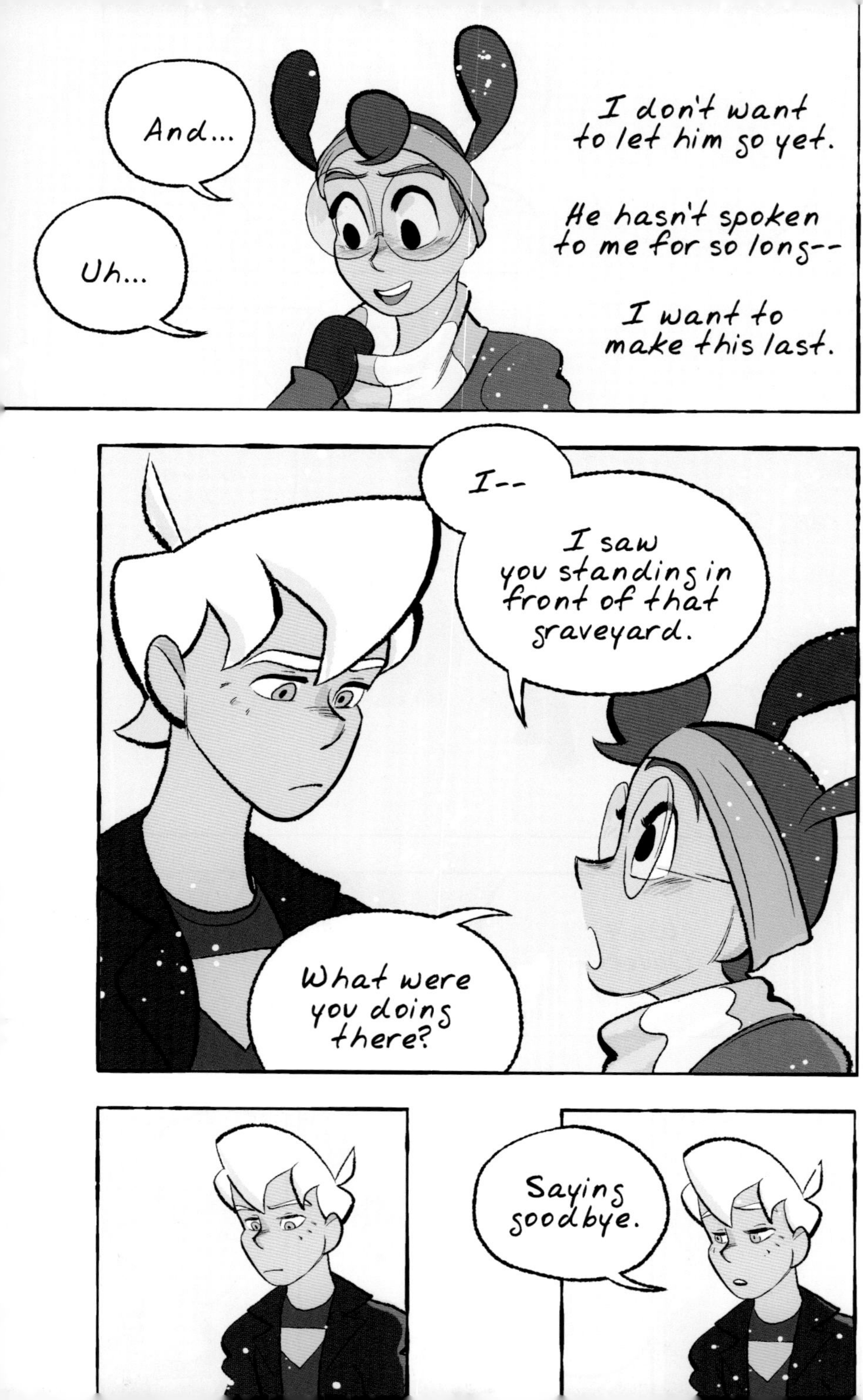

And...
Uh...
I don't want to let him go yet.
He hasn't spoken to me for so long--
I want to make this last.
I--
I saw you standing in front of that graveyard.
What were you doing there?
Saying goodbye.

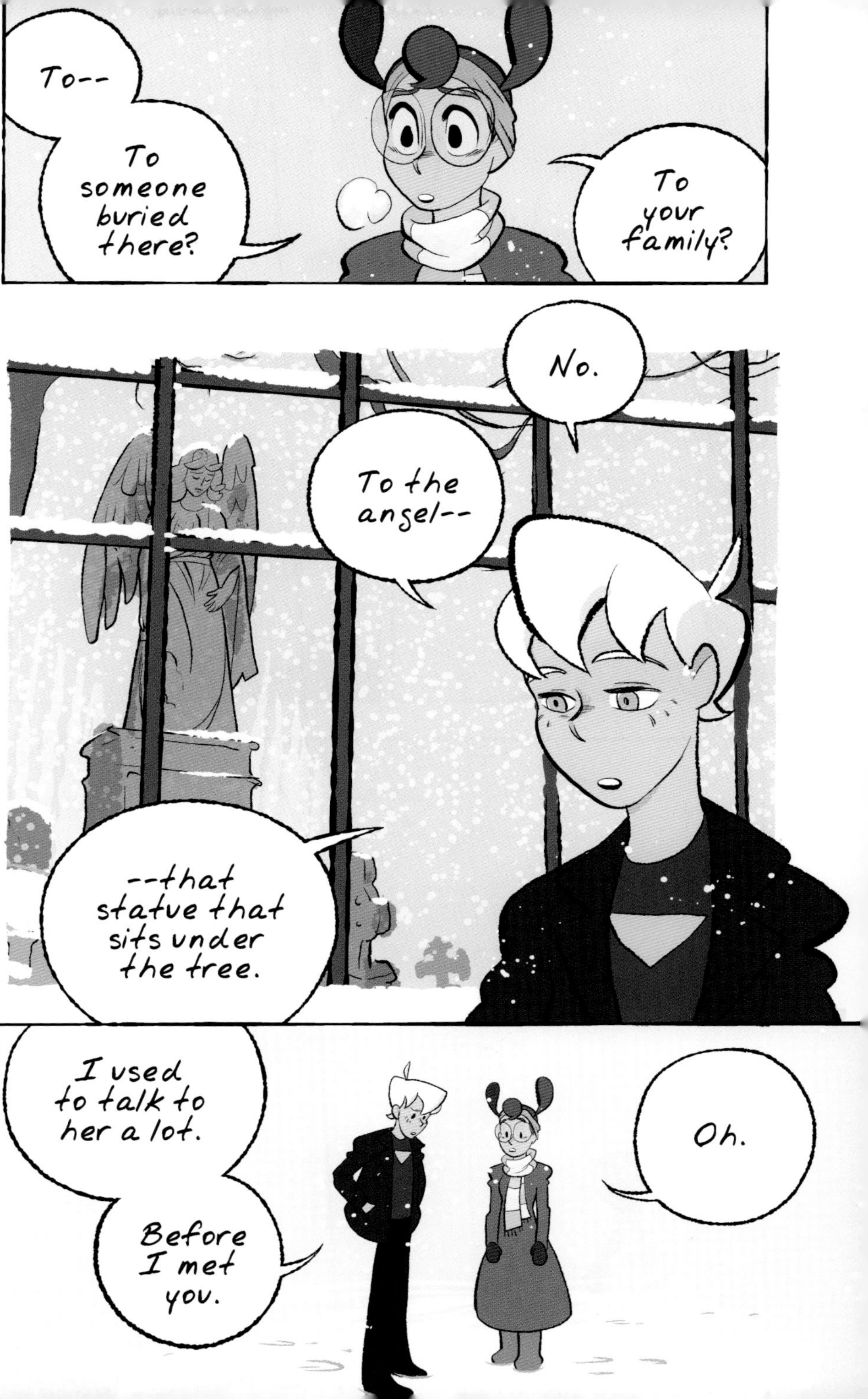
To--
To someone buried there?
To your family?
No.
To the angel--
--that statue that sits under the tree.
I used to talk to her a lot.
Before I met you.
Oh.

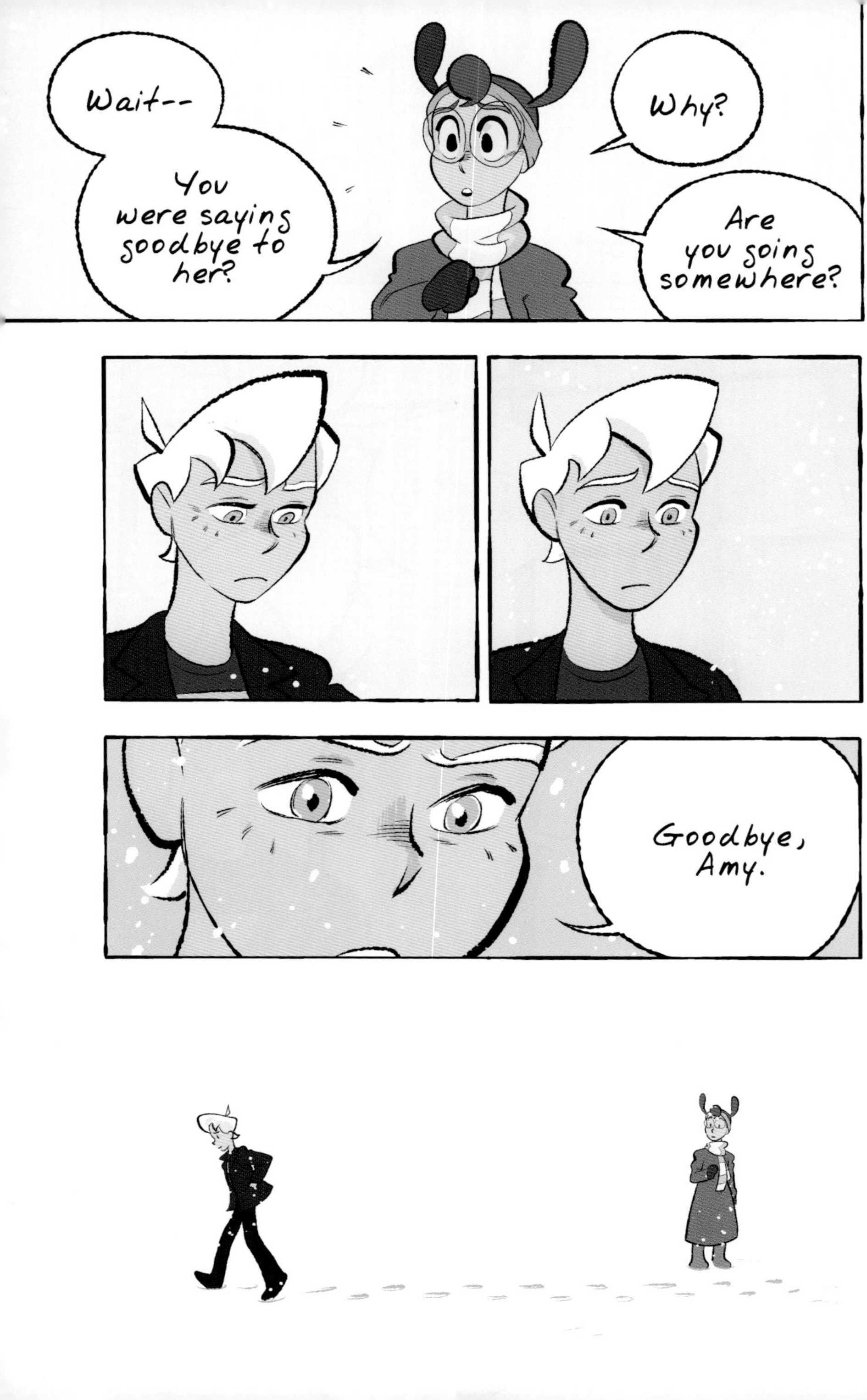
Wait--
You were sayinɡ goodbye to her?
Why?
Are you ɡoinɡ somewhere?
Goodbye, Amy.

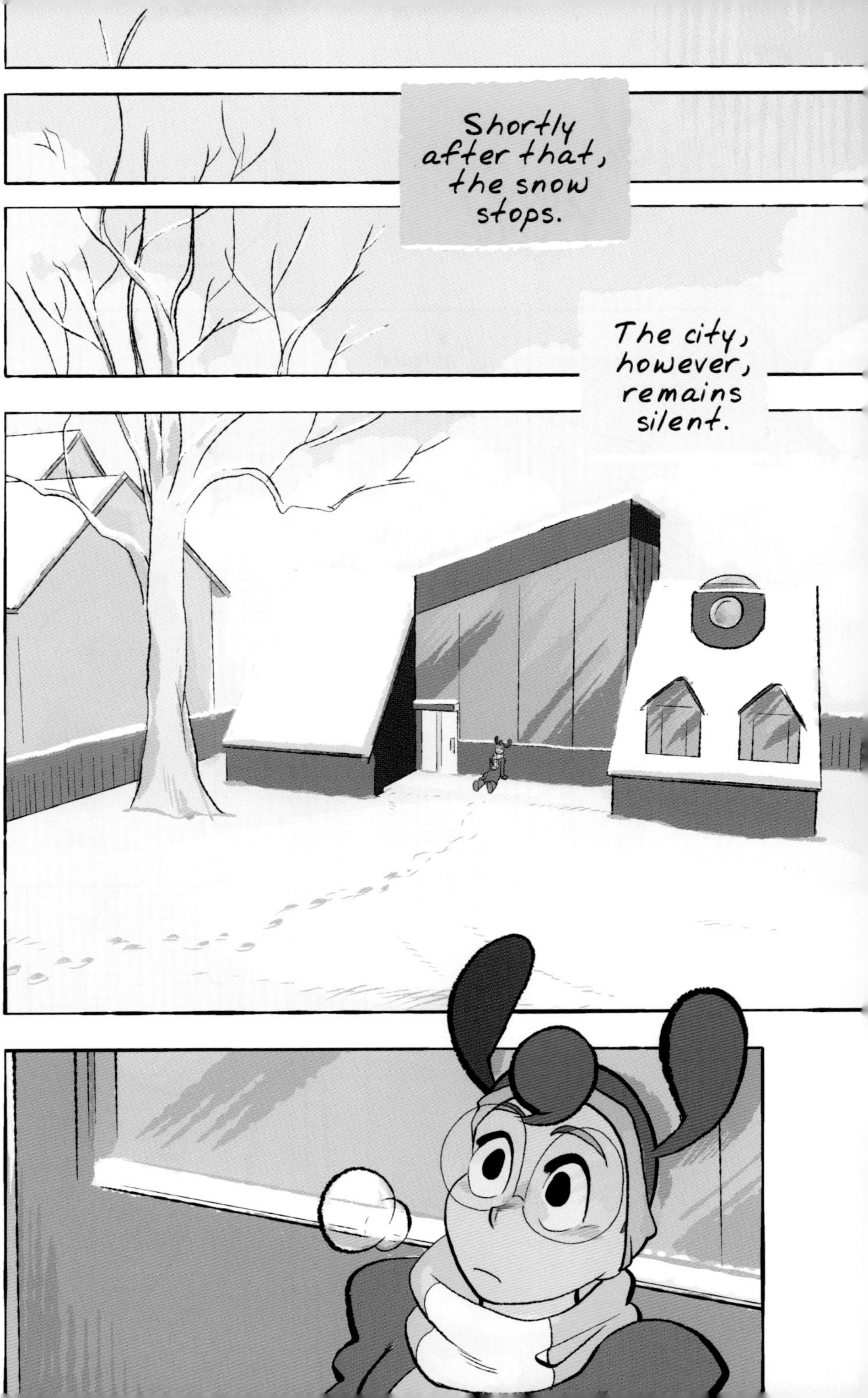
Shortly after that, the snow stops.
The city, however, remains silent.

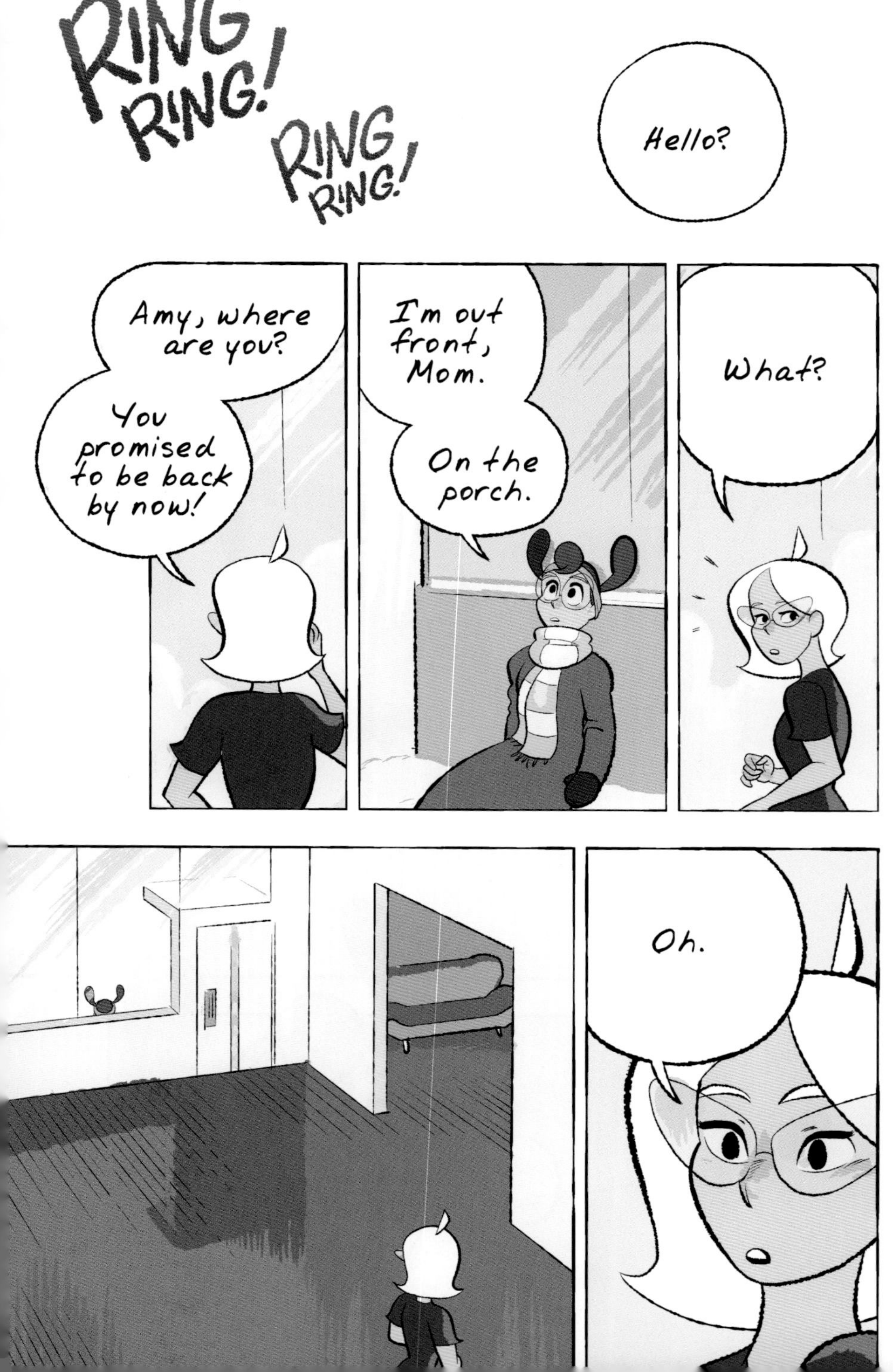
RING RING!
RING RING!
Hello?
Amy, where are you?
You promised to be back by now!
I'm out front, Mom.
On the porch.
What?
Oh.

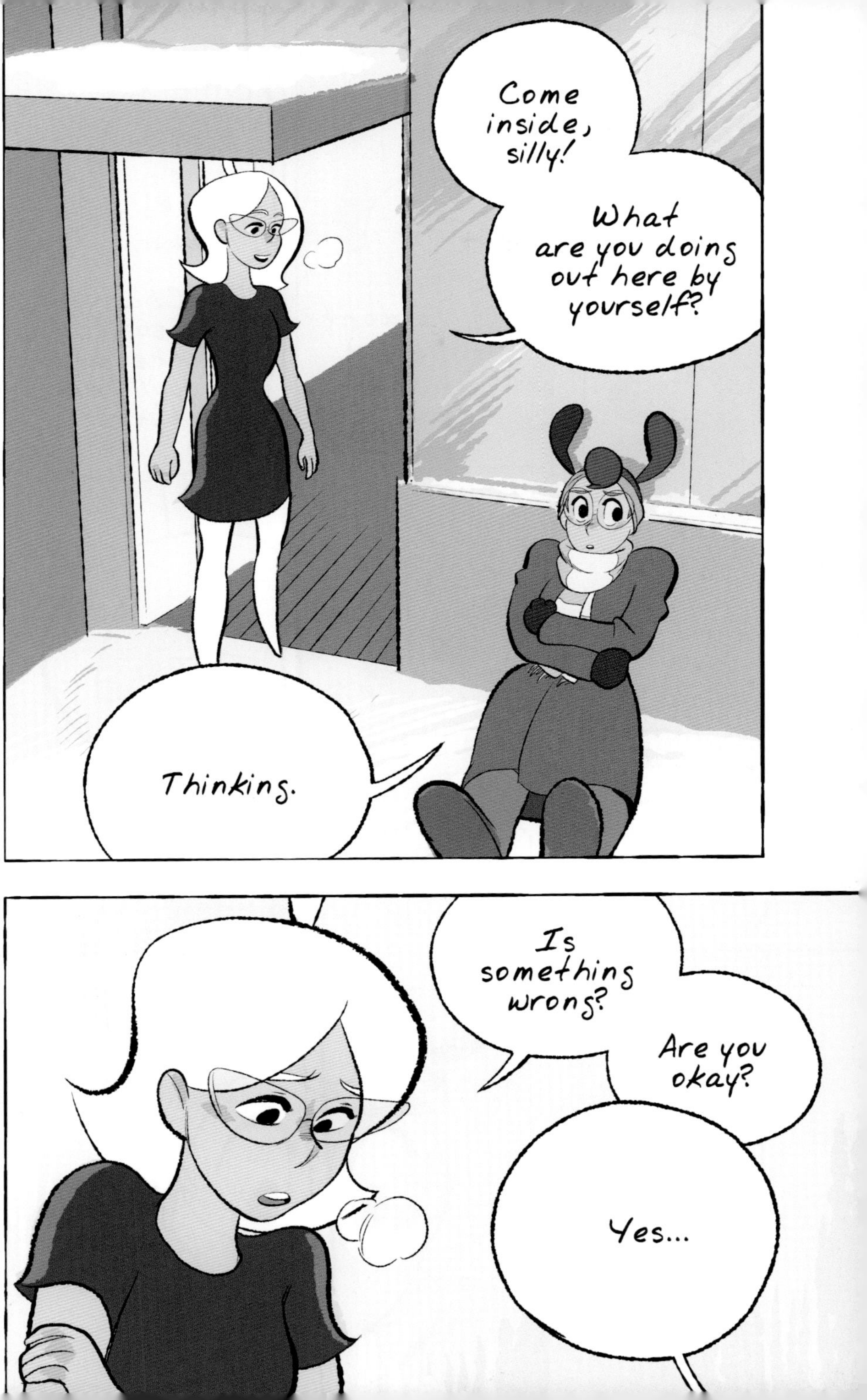
Come inside, silly!
What are you doing out here by yourself?
Thinking.
Is something wrong?
Are you okay?
Yes...

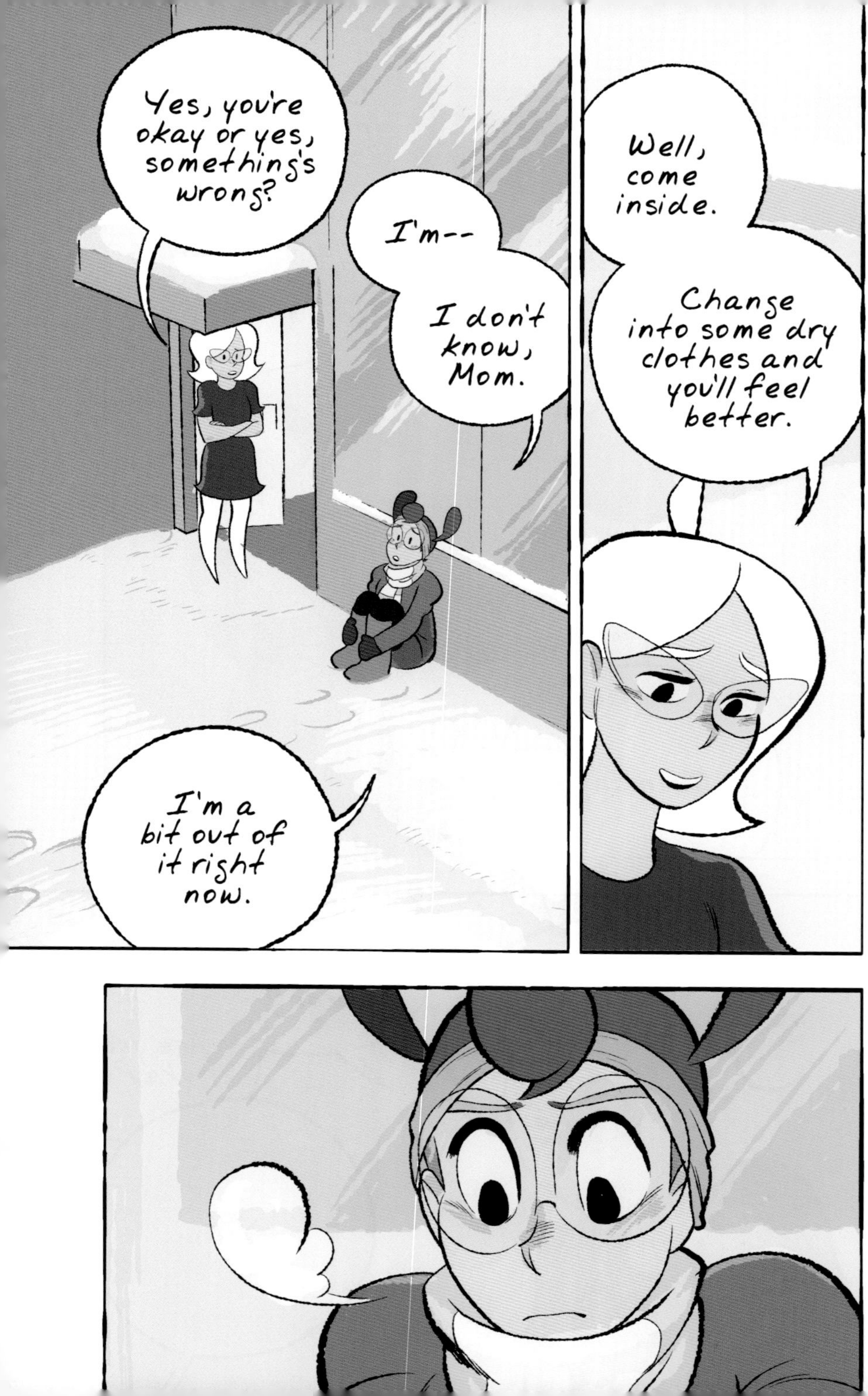
Yes, you're okay or yes, something's wrong?
I'm--
I don't know, Mom.
I'm a bit out of it right now.
Well, come inside.
Change into some dry clothes and you'll feel better.

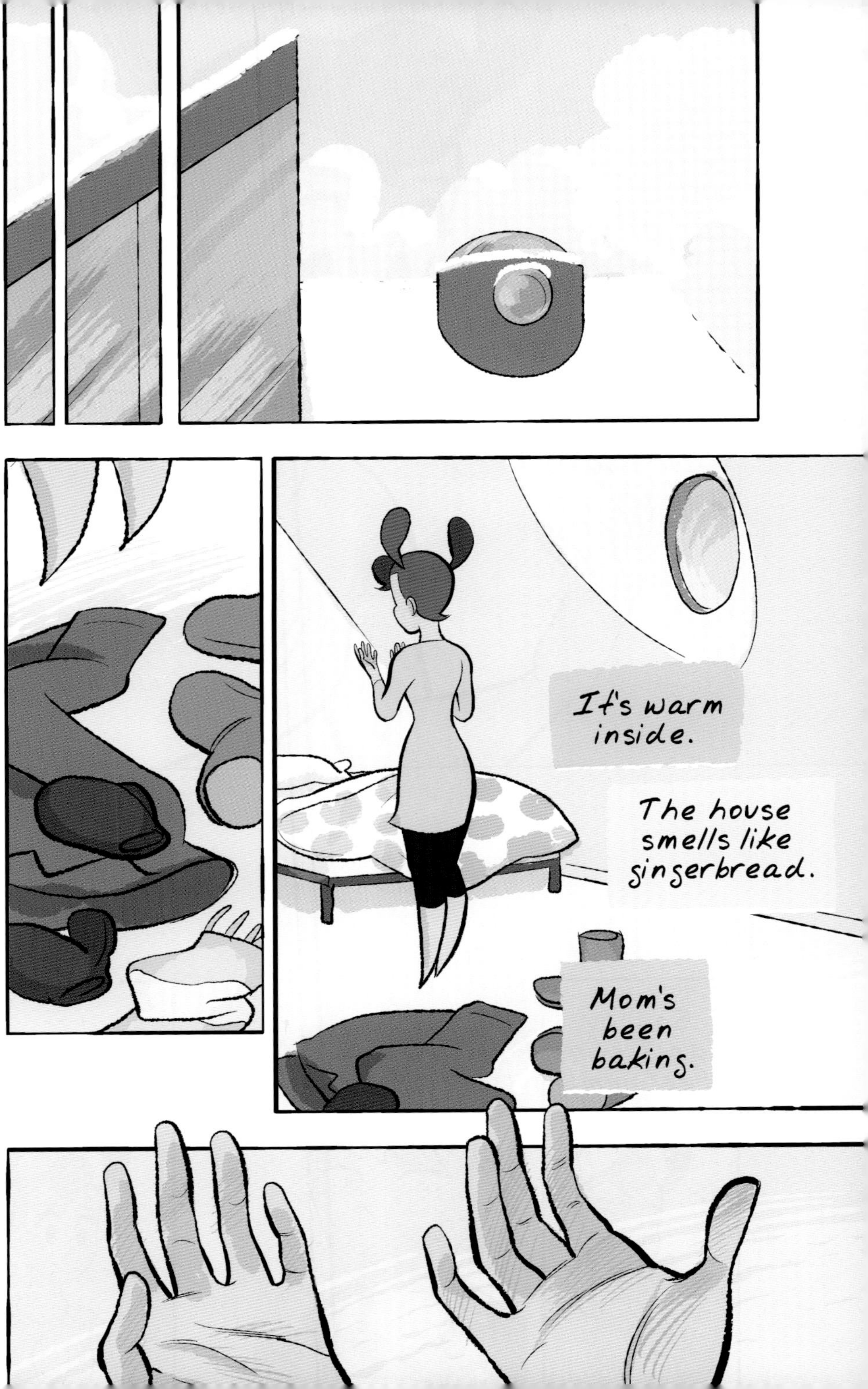
It's warm inside.
The house smells like gingerbread.
Mom's been baking.

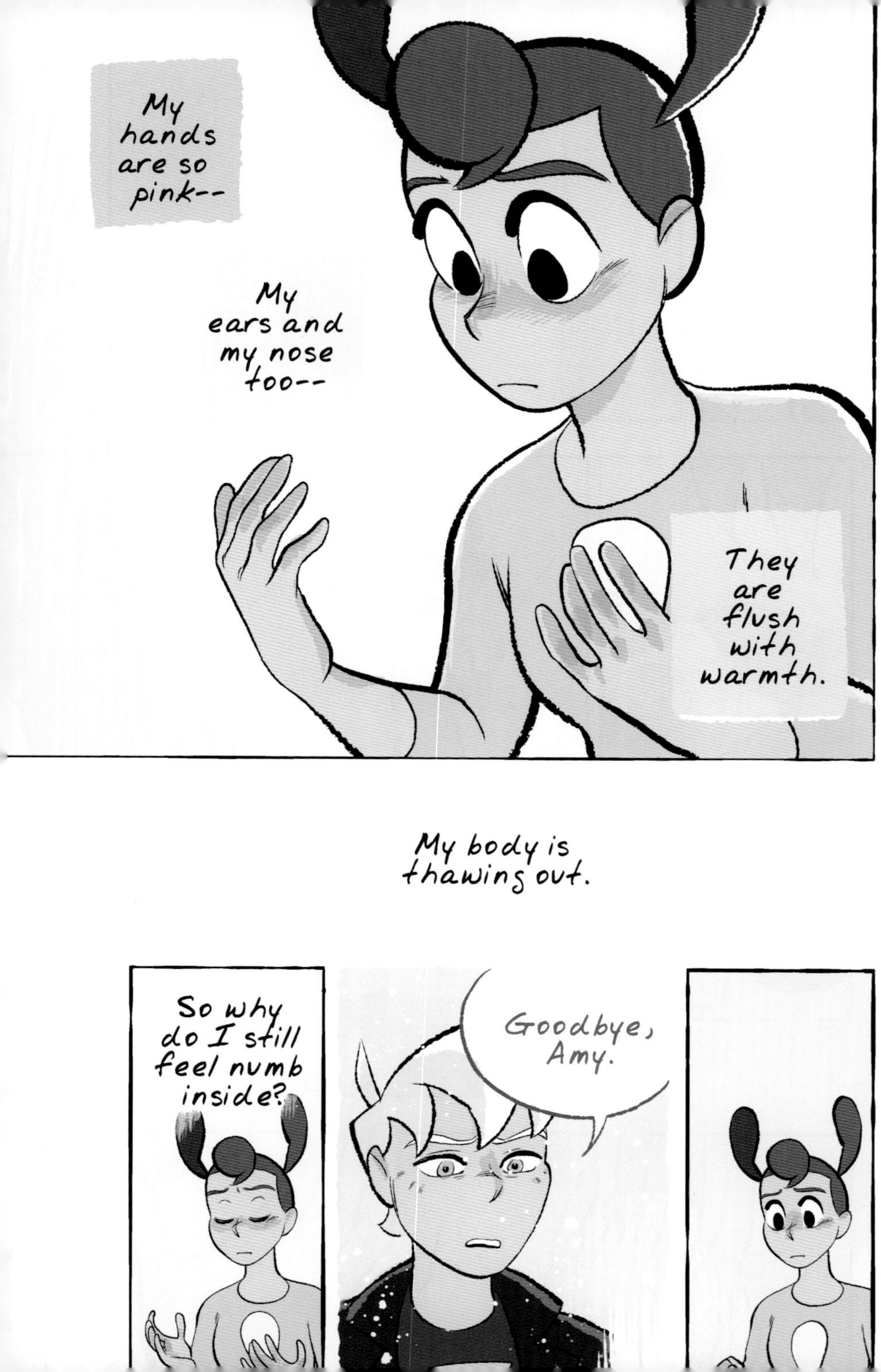
My hands are so pink--
My ears and my nose too--
They are flush with warmth.
My body is thawing out.
So why do I still feel numb inside?
Goodbye, Amy.

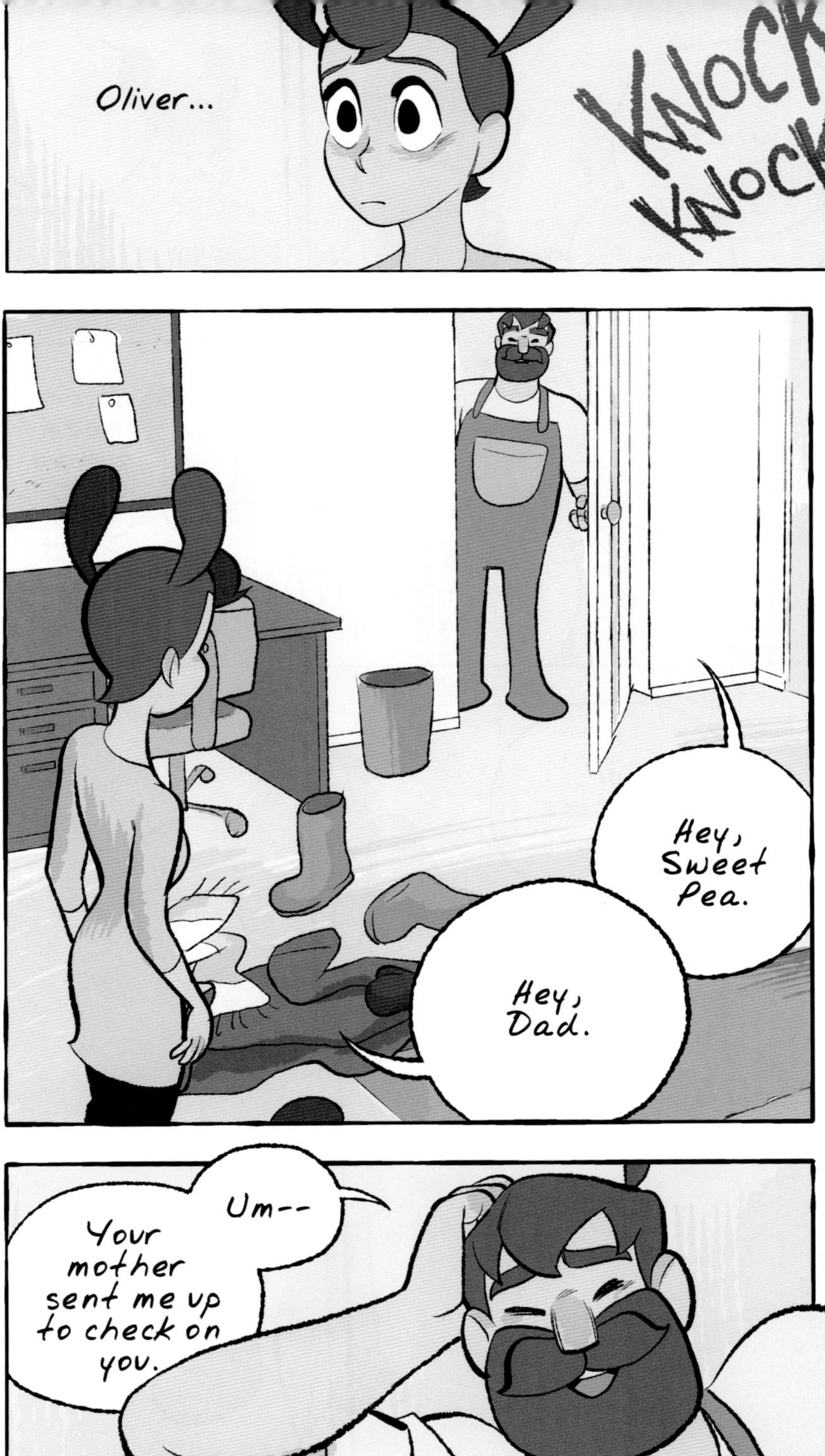
Oliver...
KNOCK KNOCK!
Hey, Sweet Pea.
Hey, Dad.
Um--
Your mother sent me up to check on you.

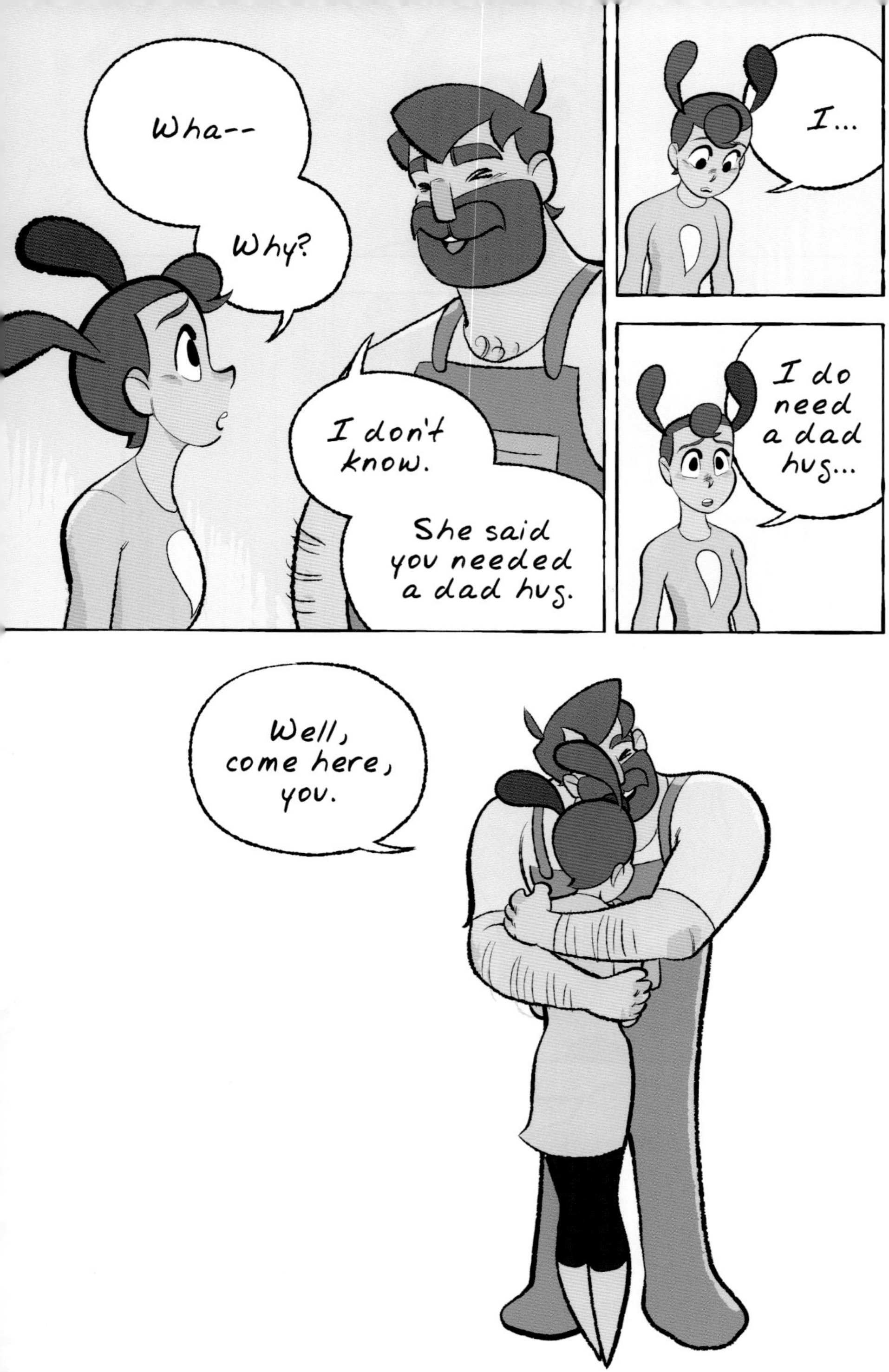
Wha--
Why?
I don't know.
She said you needed a dad hug.
I...
I do need a dad hug...
Well, come here, you.

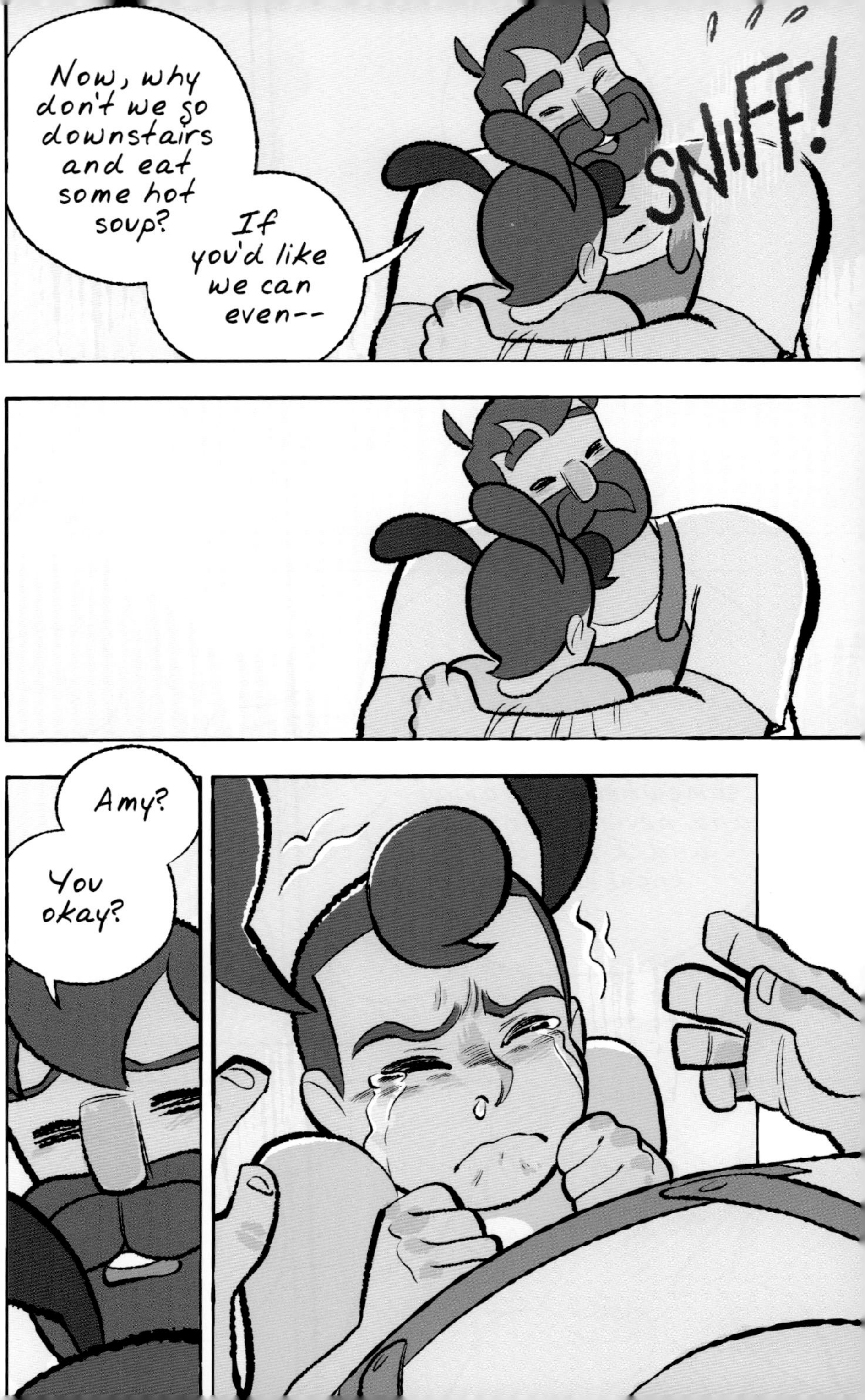

Now, why don't we go downstairs and eat some hot soup?
If you'd like we can even--
SNIFF!
Amy?
You okay?

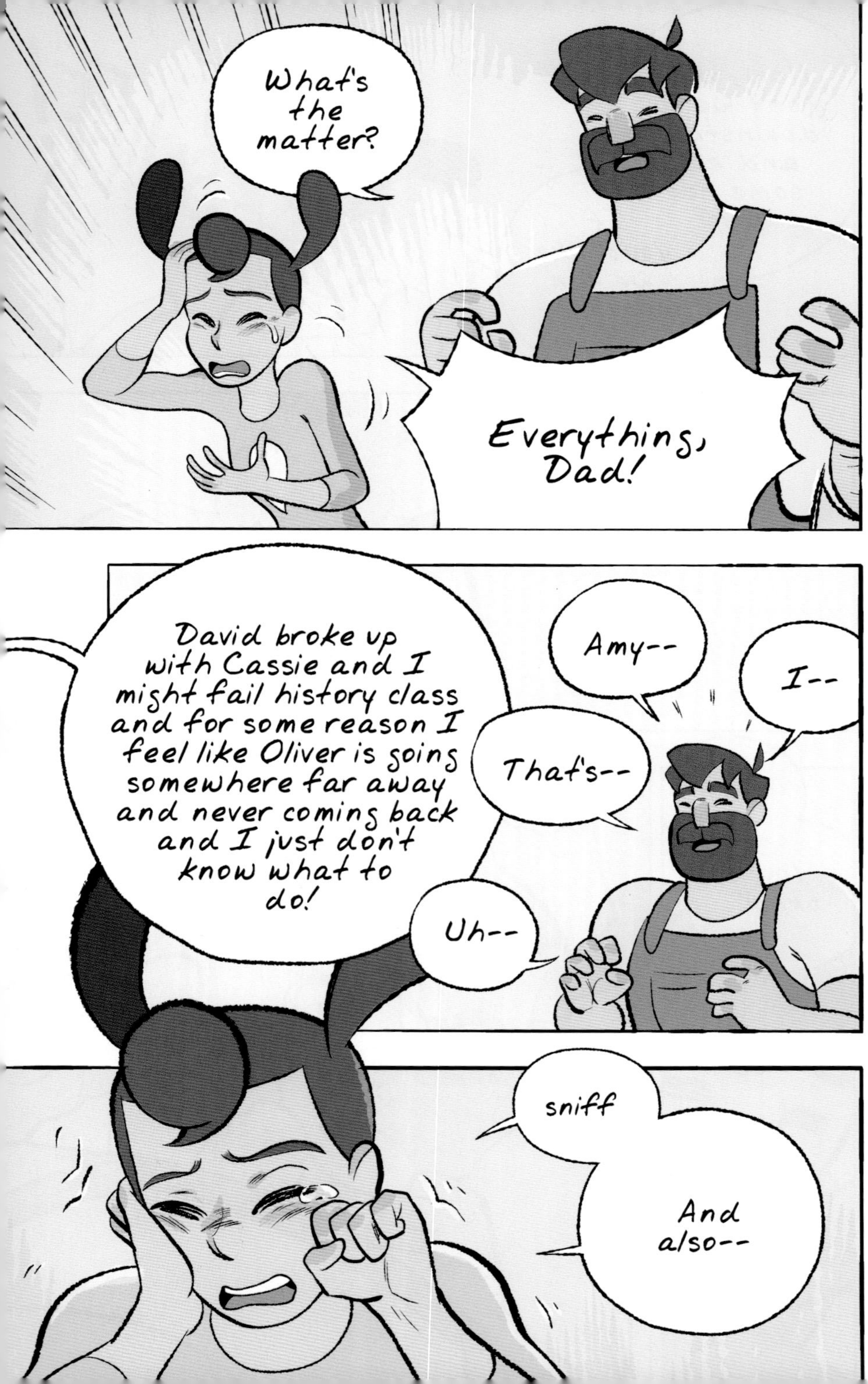
What's the matter?
Everything, Dad!
David broke up with Cassie and I might fail history class and for some reason I feel like Oliver is going somewhere far away and never coming back and I just don't know what to do!
Amy--
I--
That's--
Uh--
sniff
And also--

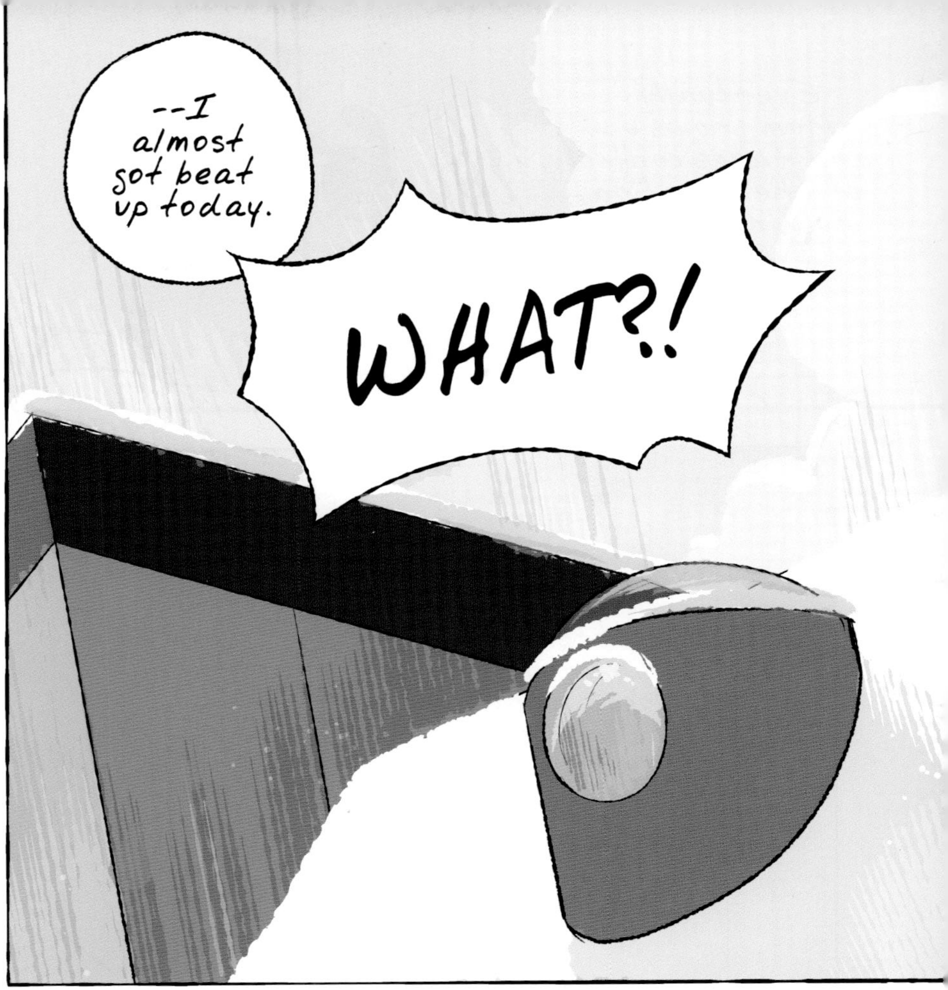
--I almost got beat up today.
WHAT?!

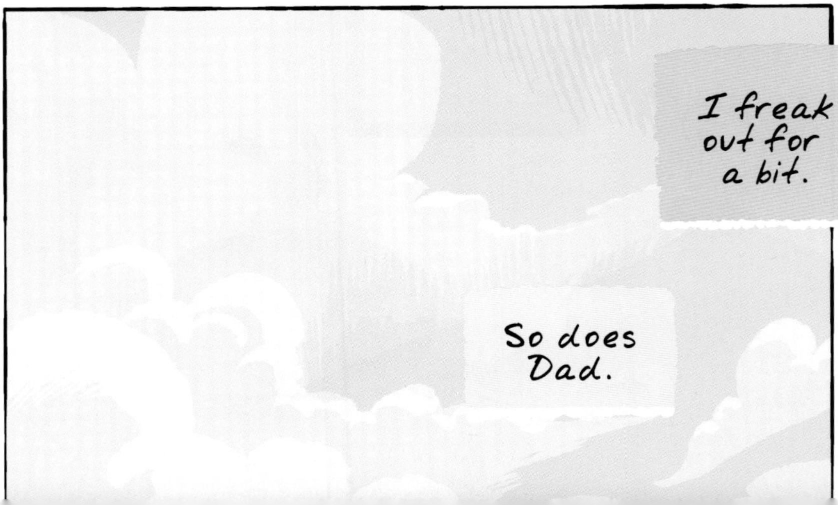
I freak out for a bit.
So does Dad.

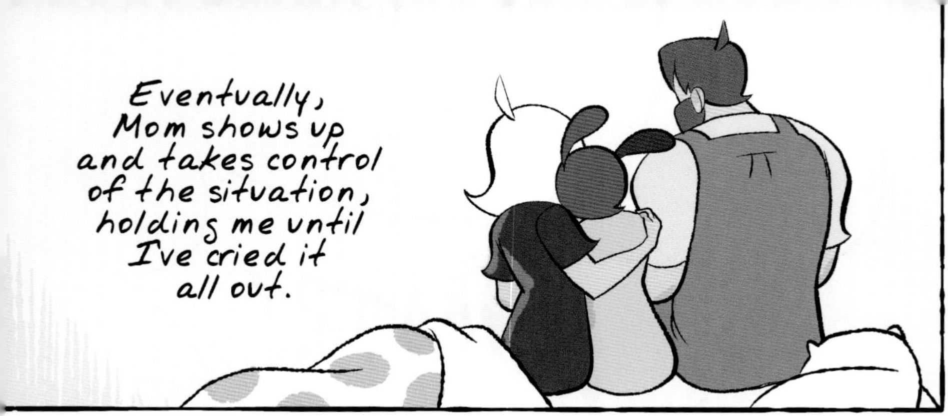
Eventually, Mom shows up and takes control of the situation, holding me until I've cried it all out.

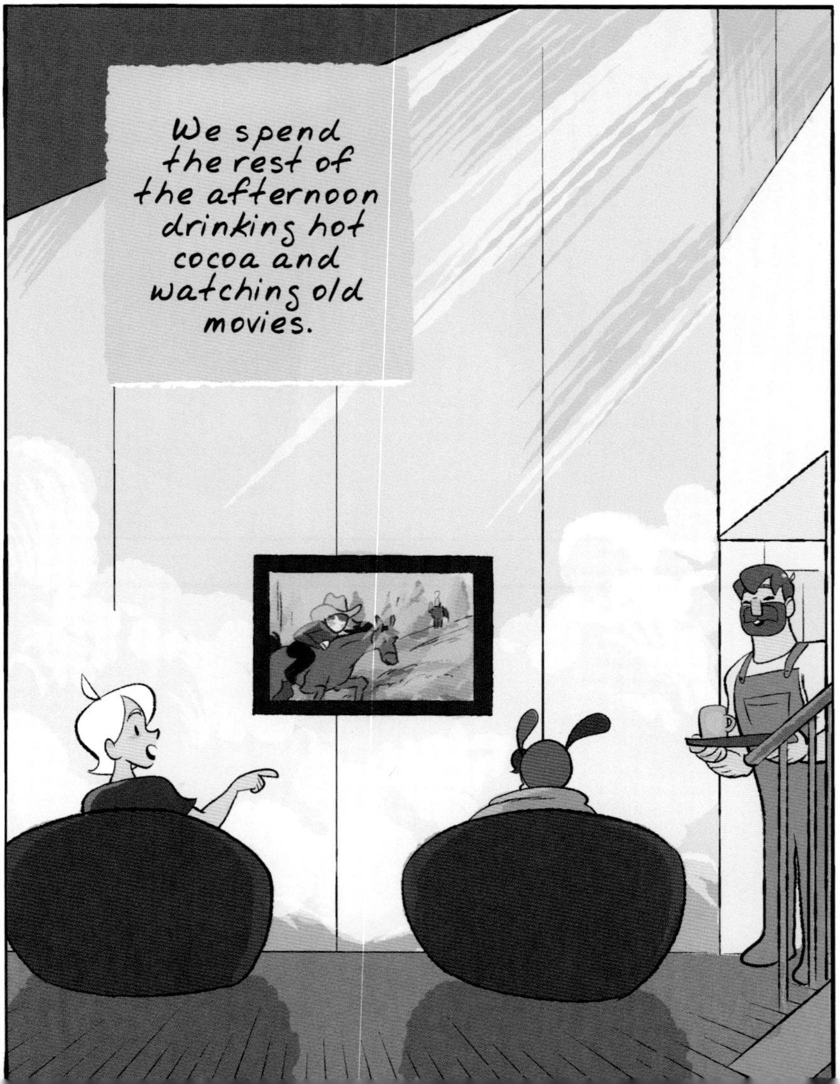
We spend the rest of the afternoon drinking hot cocoa and watching old movies.

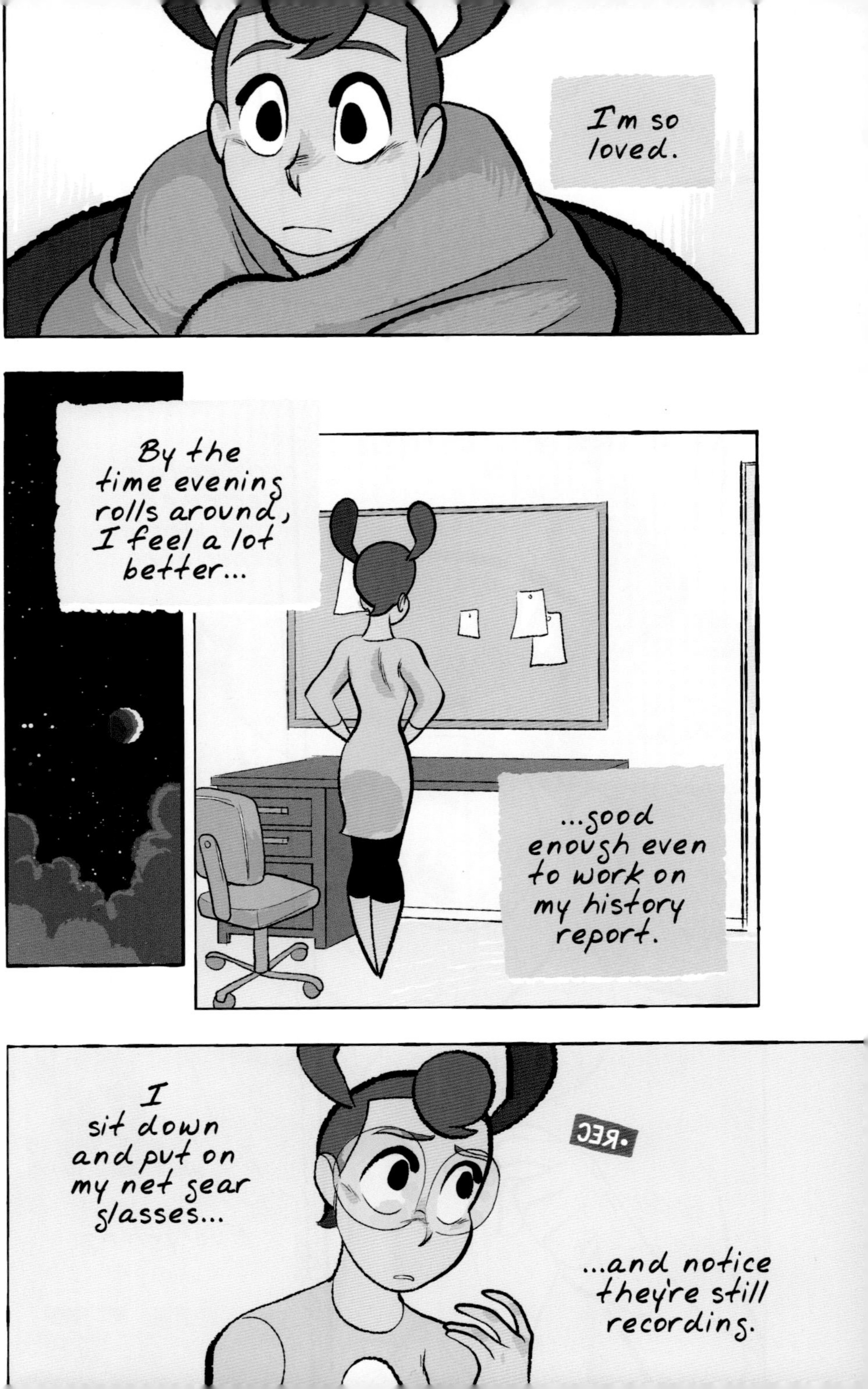
I'm so loved.
By the time evening rolls around, I feel a lot better...
...good enough even to work on my history report.
I sit down and put on my net gear glasses...
•REC
...and notice they're still recording.

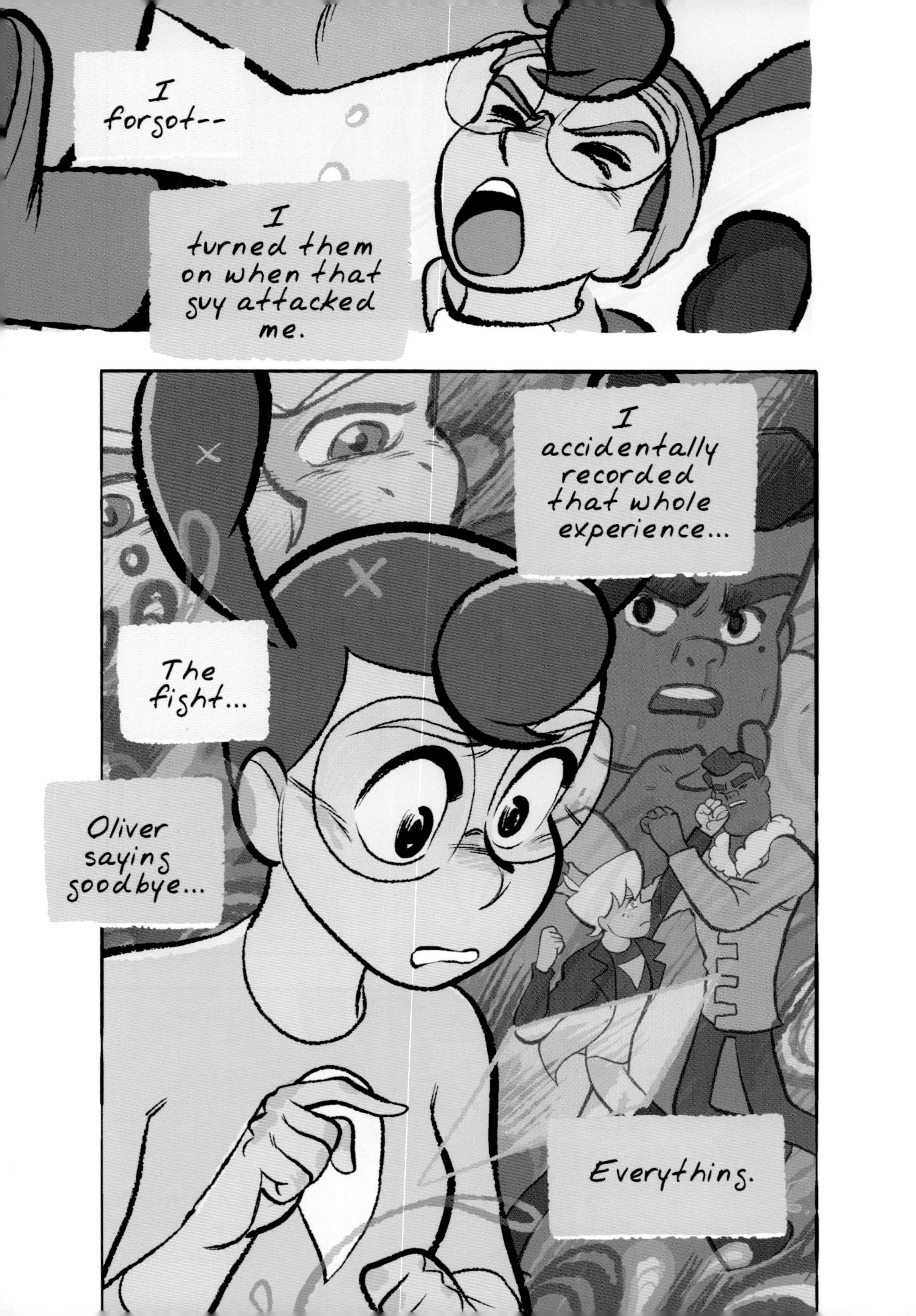
I forgot--
I turned them on when that guy attacked me.
I accidentally recorded that whole experience...
The fight...
Oliver saying goodbye...
Everything.

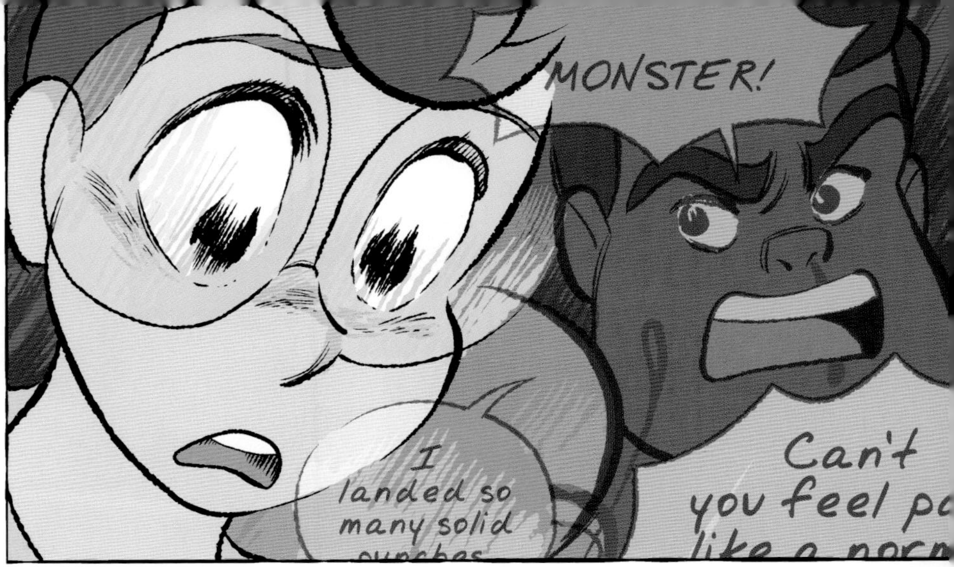
MONSTER!
I landed so many solid
Can't you feel

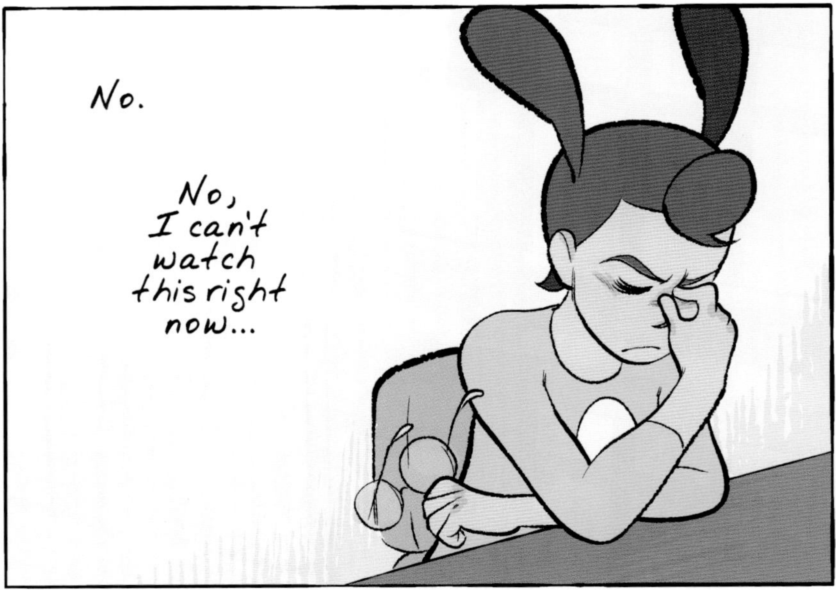
No.
No, I can't watch this right now...

Maybe tomorrow...

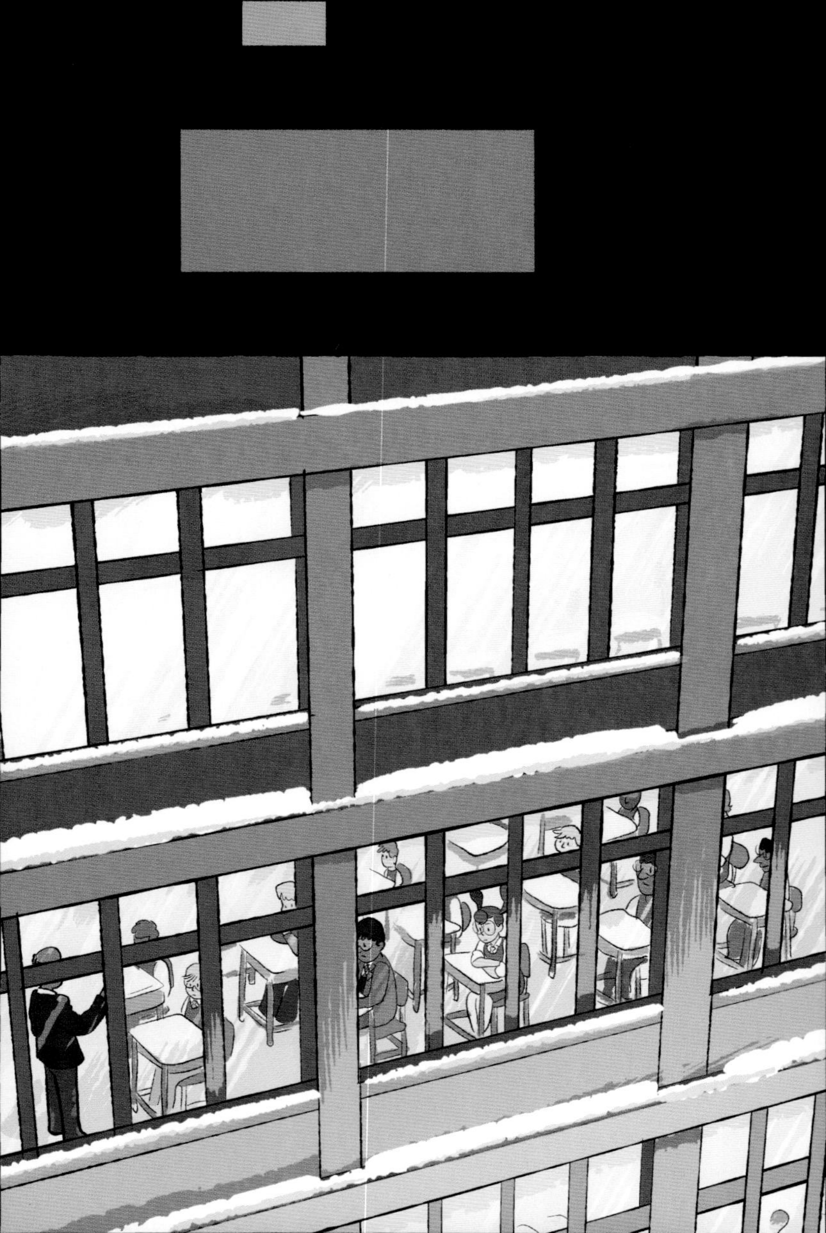

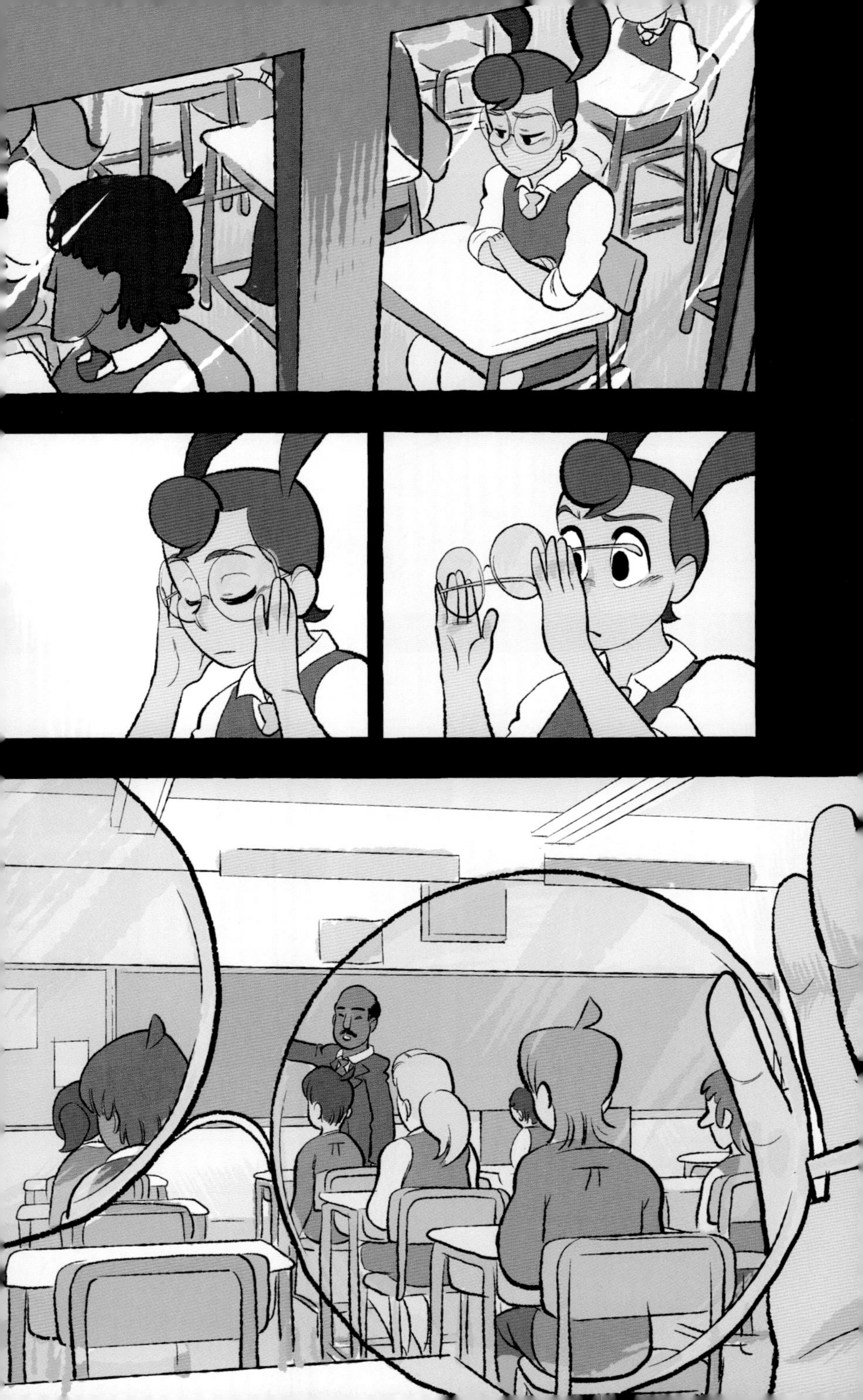

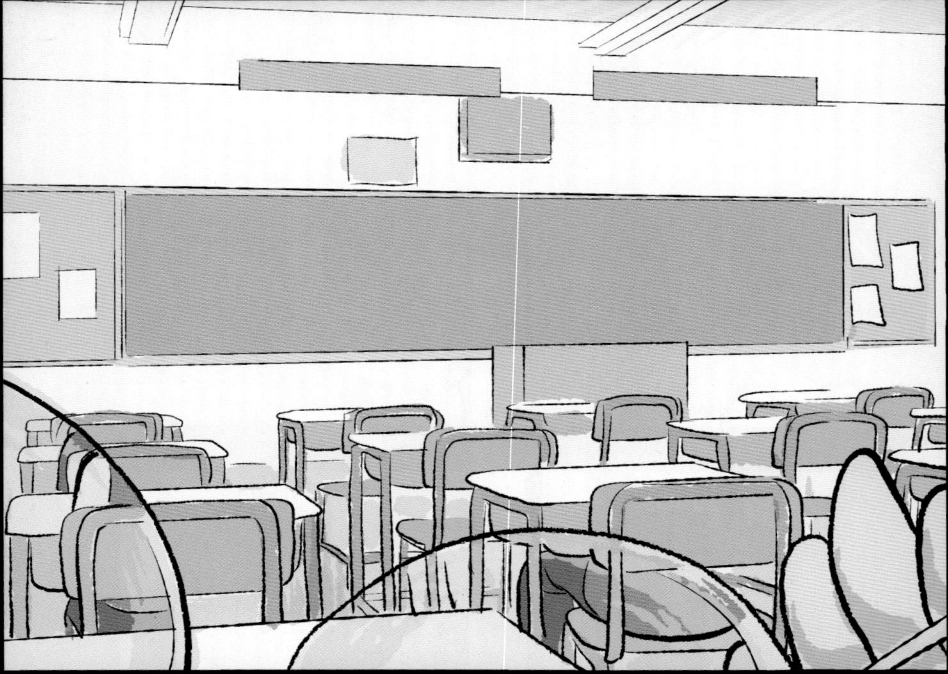

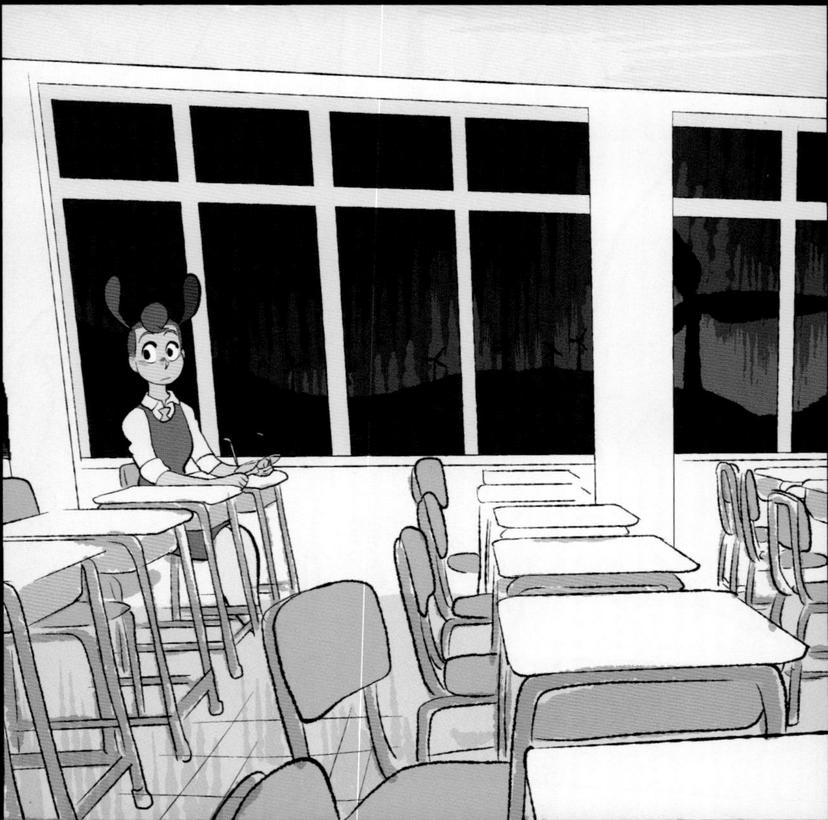

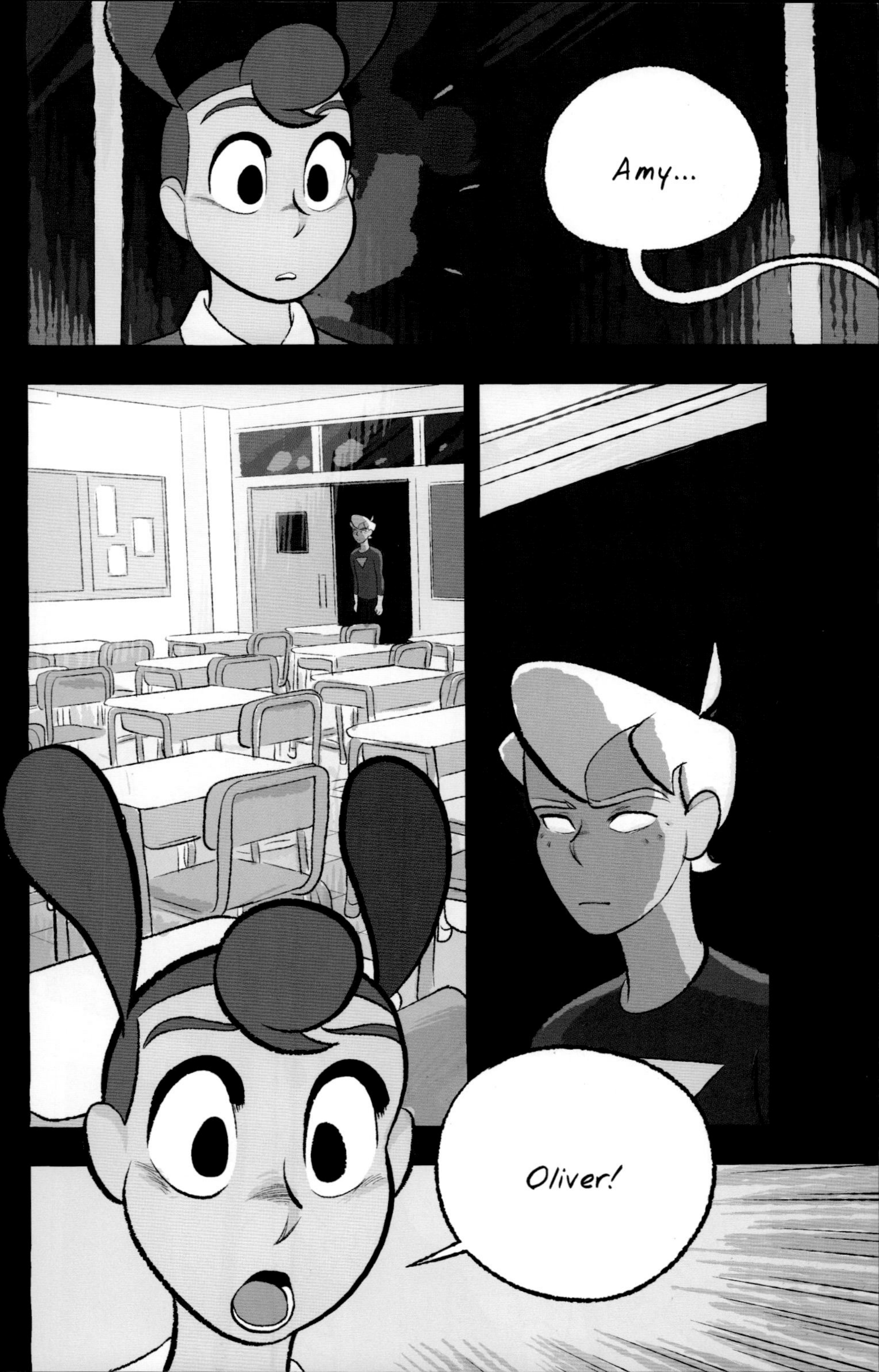

Amy...
Oliver!

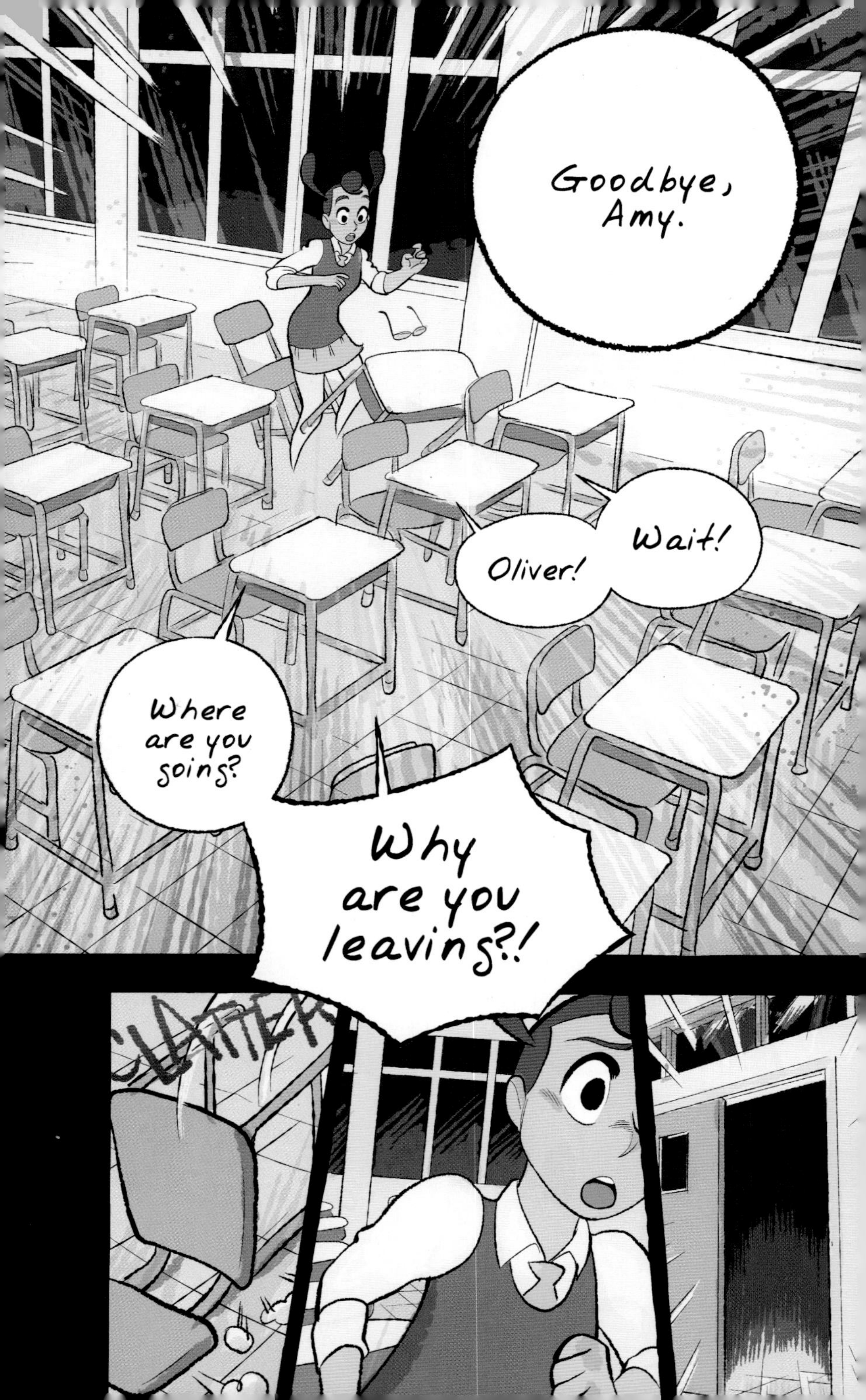
Goodbye, Amy.
Oliver!
Wait!
Where are you going?
Why are you leaving?!

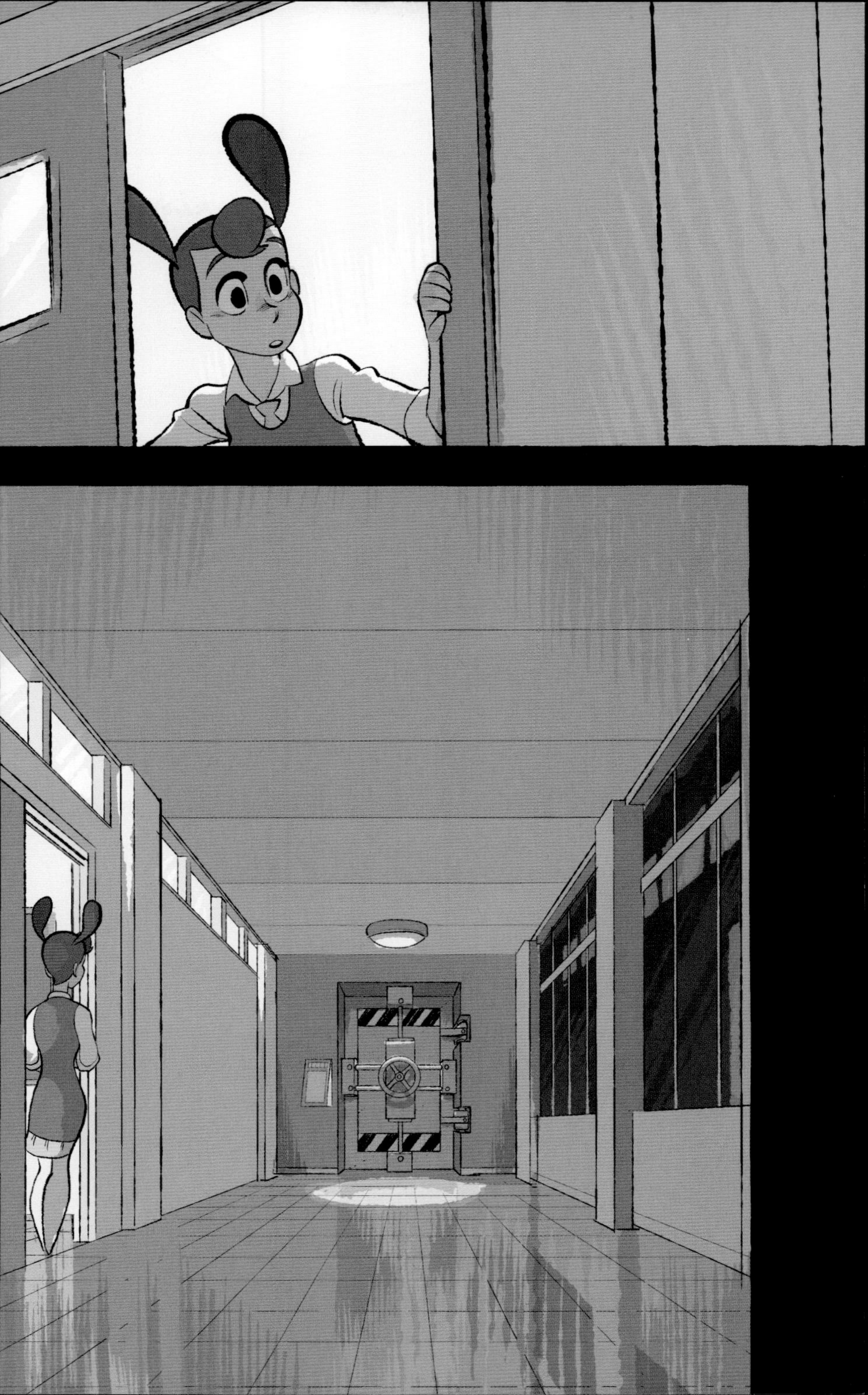

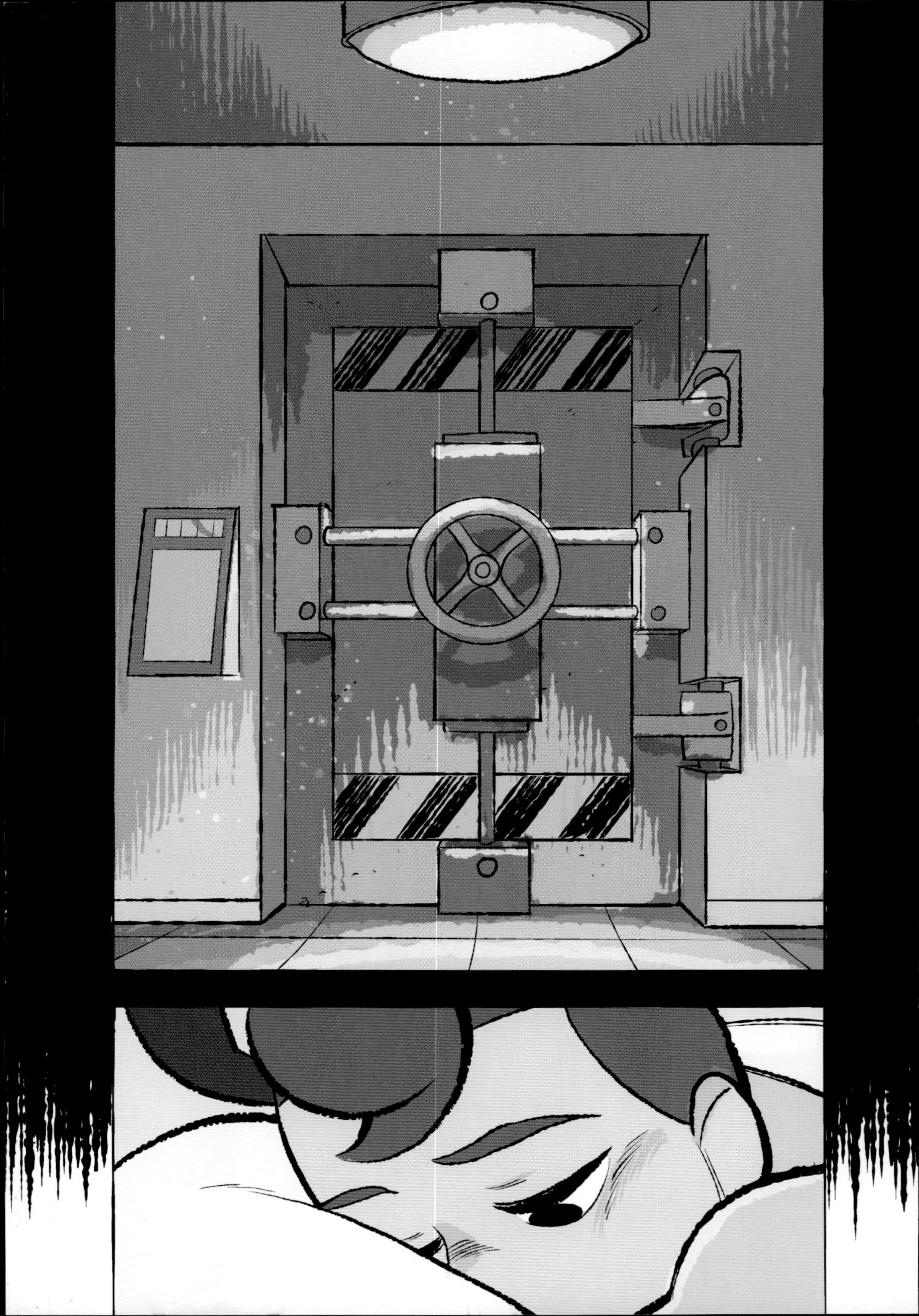

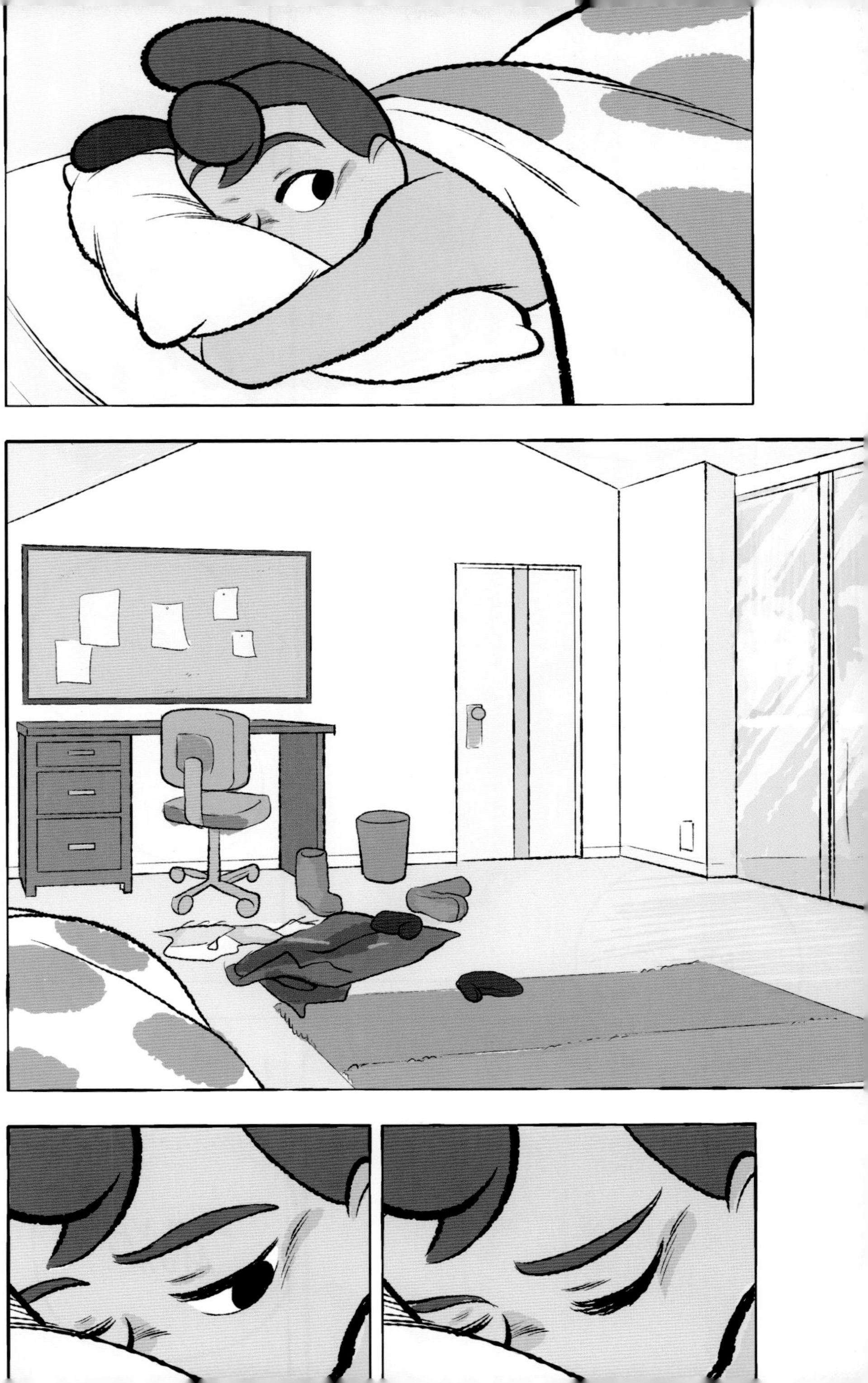

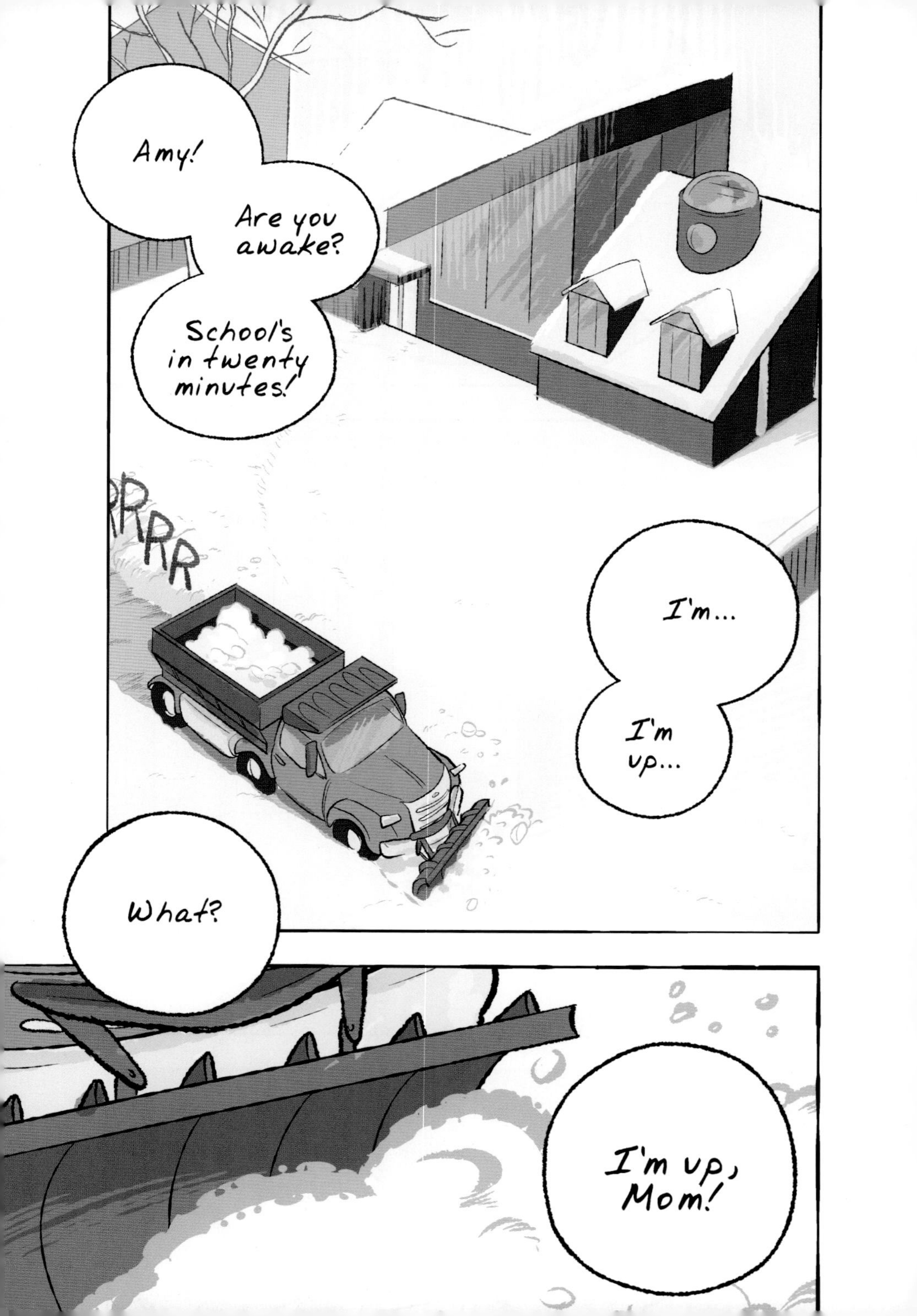

Amy!
Are you awake?
School's in twenty minutes!
RRRR
I'm...
I'm up...
What?
I'm up, Mom!

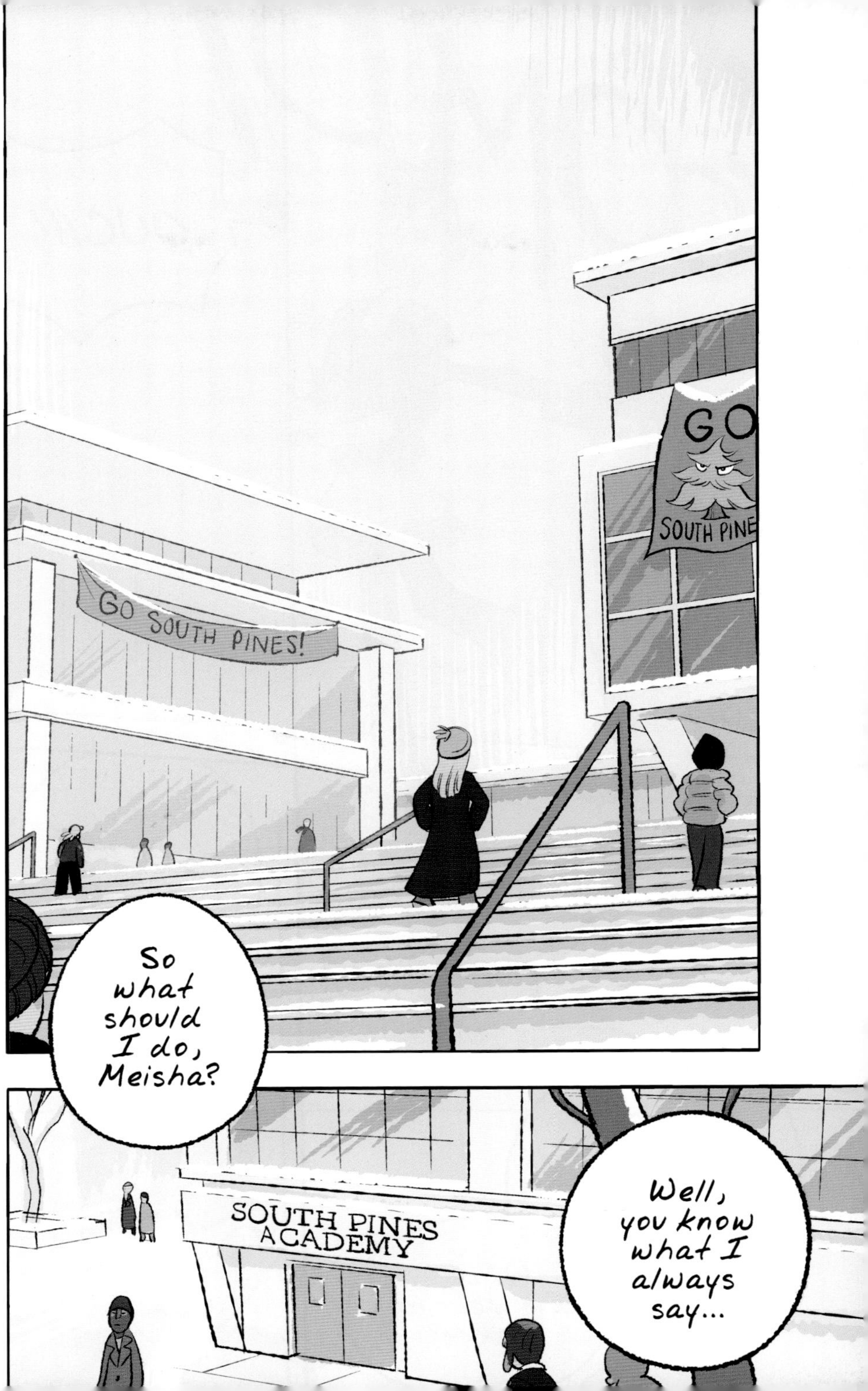
GO
SOUTH PINES
GO SOUTH PINES!
So what should I do, Meisha?
SOUTH PINES ACADEMY
Well, you know what I always say...

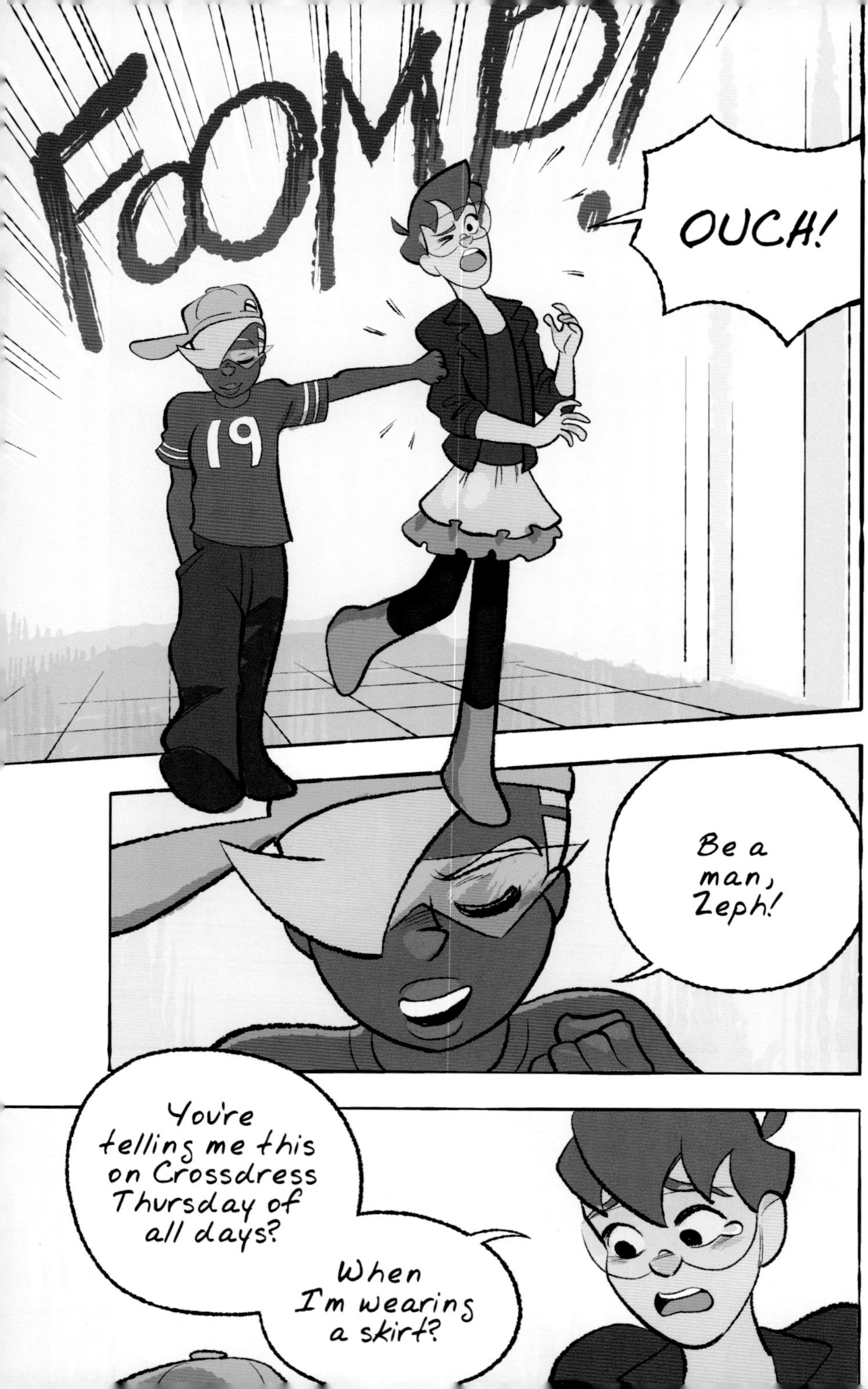
FOOMP!
OUCH!
19
Be a man, Zeph!
You're telling me this on Crossdress Thursday of all days?
When I'm wearing a skirt?

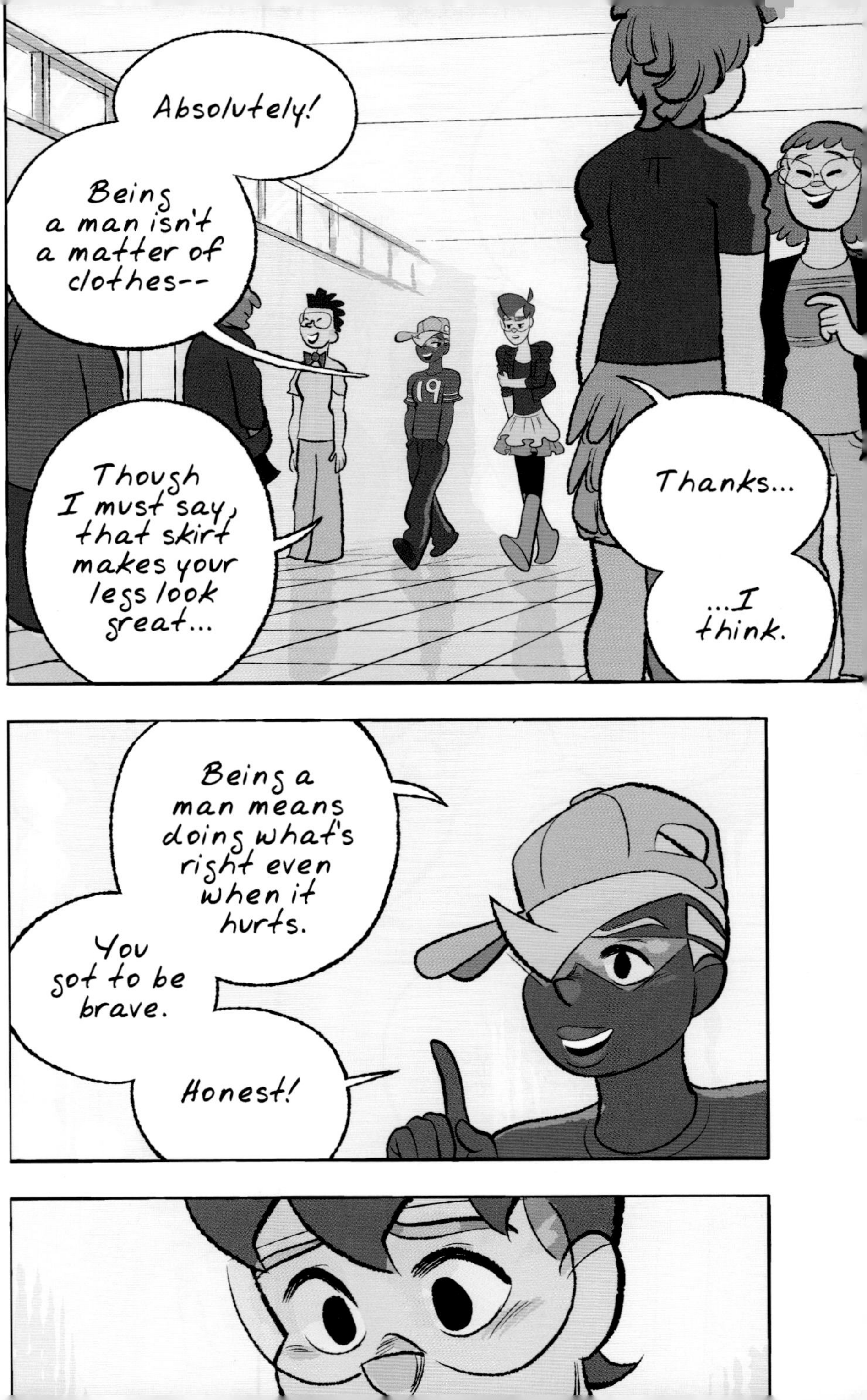
Absolutely!
Being a man isn't a matter of clothes--
Though I must say, that skirt makes your legs look great...
Thanks...
...I think.
Being a man means doing what's right even when it hurts.
You got to be brave.
Honest!

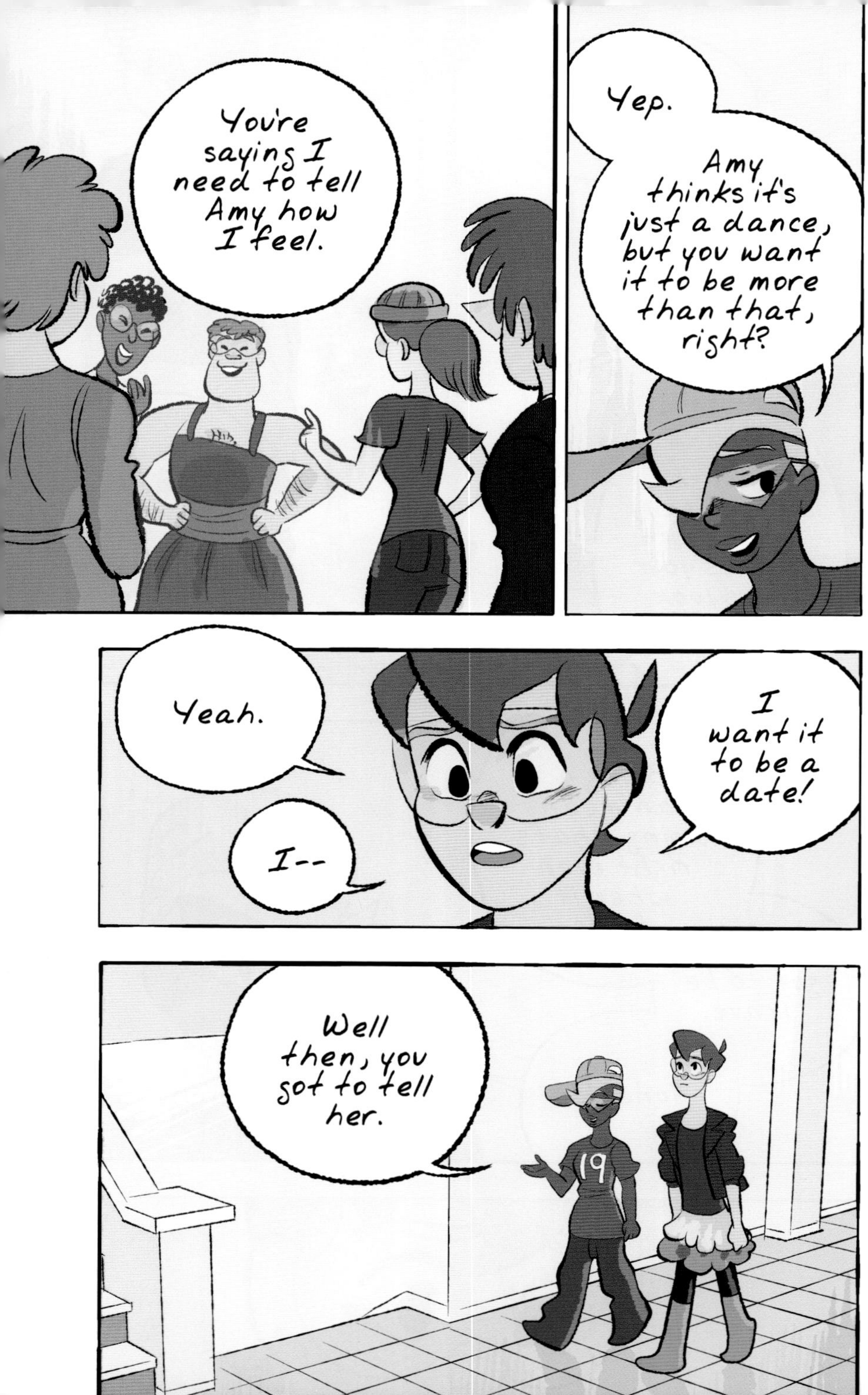
You're saying I need to tell Amy how I feel.
Yep.
Amy thinks it's just a dance, but you want it to be more than that, right?
Yeah.
I--
I want it to be a date!
Well then, you got to tell her.

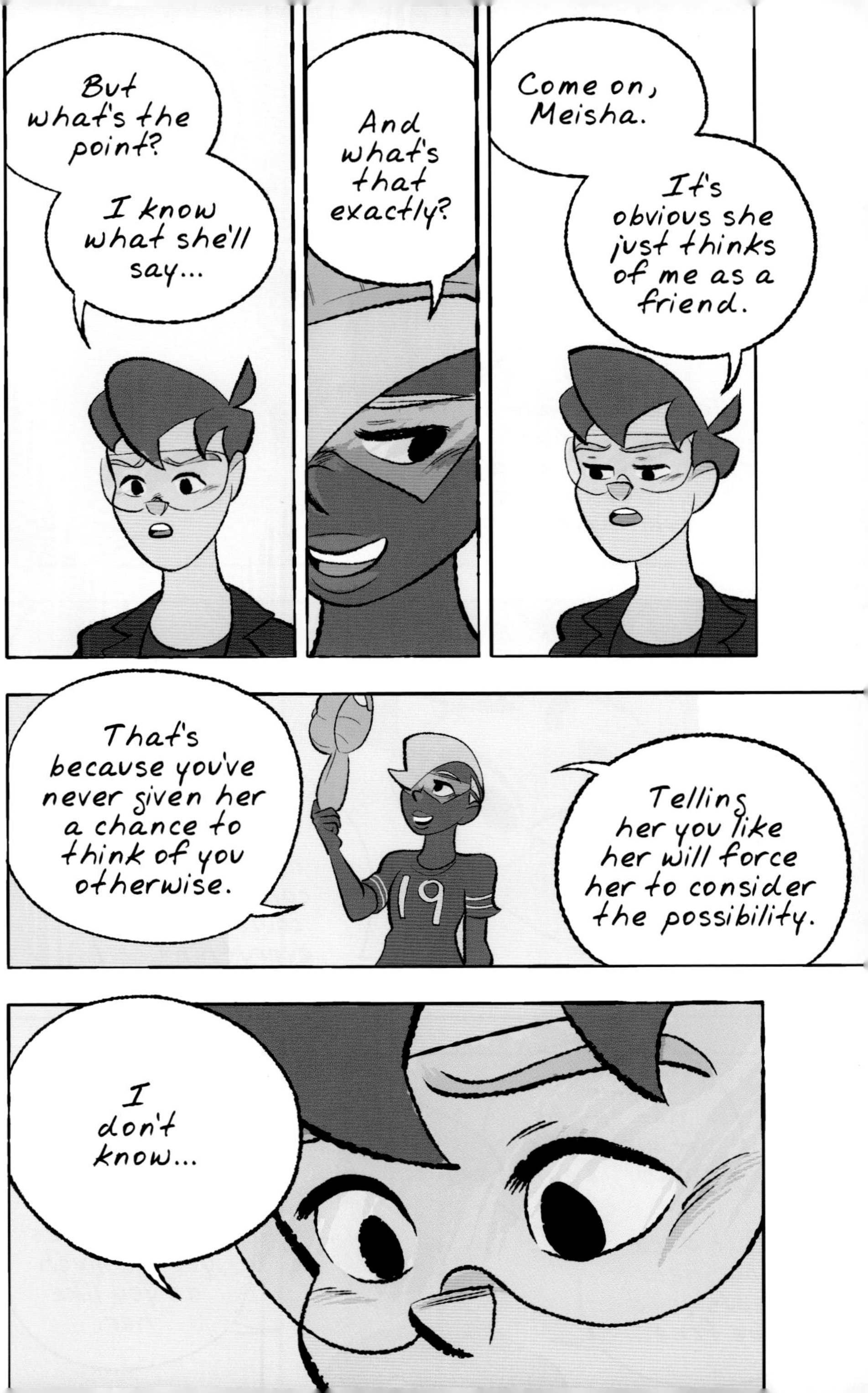
But what's the point?
I know what she'll say...
And what's that exactly?
Come on, Meisha.
It's obvious she just thinks of me as a friend.
That's because you've never given her a chance to think of you otherwise.
Telling her you like her will force her to consider the possibility.
I don't know...

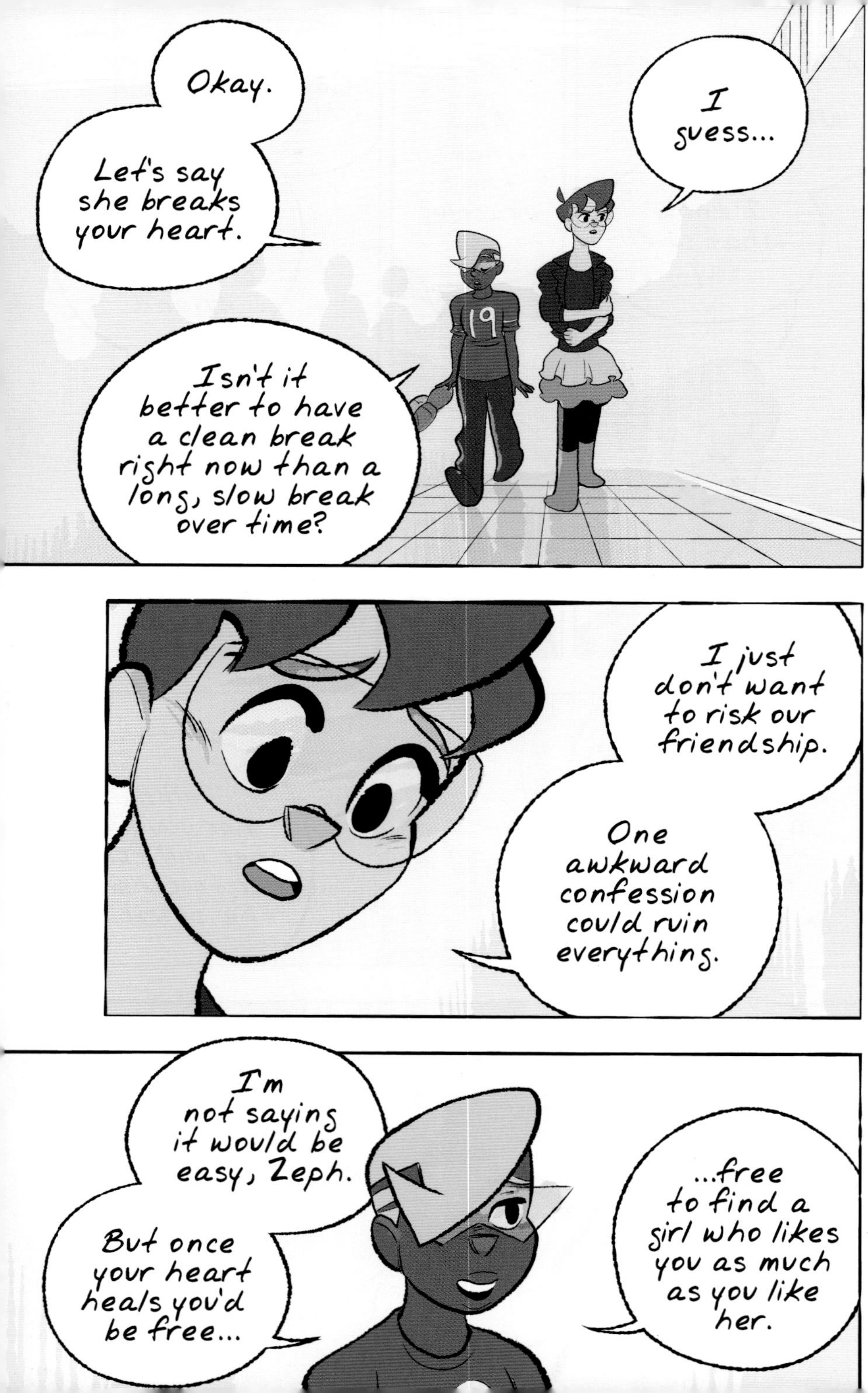
Okay.
Let's say she breaks your heart.
I guess...
Isn't it better to have a clean break right now than a long, slow break over time?
I just don't want to risk our friendship.
One awkward confession could ruin everything.
I'm not saying it would be easy, Zeph.
But once your heart heals you'd be free...
...free to find a girl who likes you as much as you like her.

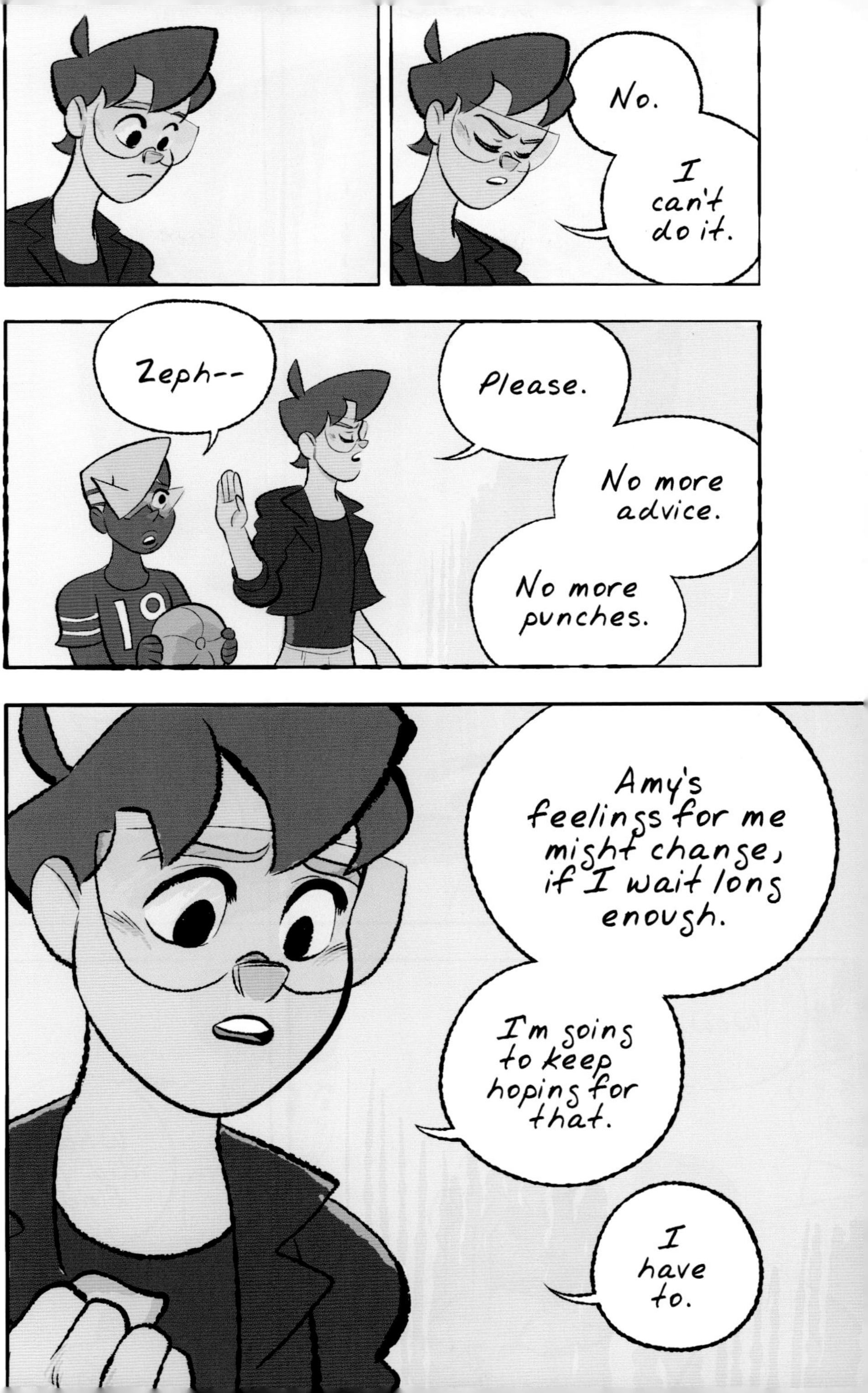
No.
I can't do it.
Zeph--
Please.
No more advice.
No more punches.
Amy's feelings for me might change, if I wait long enough.
I'm going to keep hoping for that.
I have to.

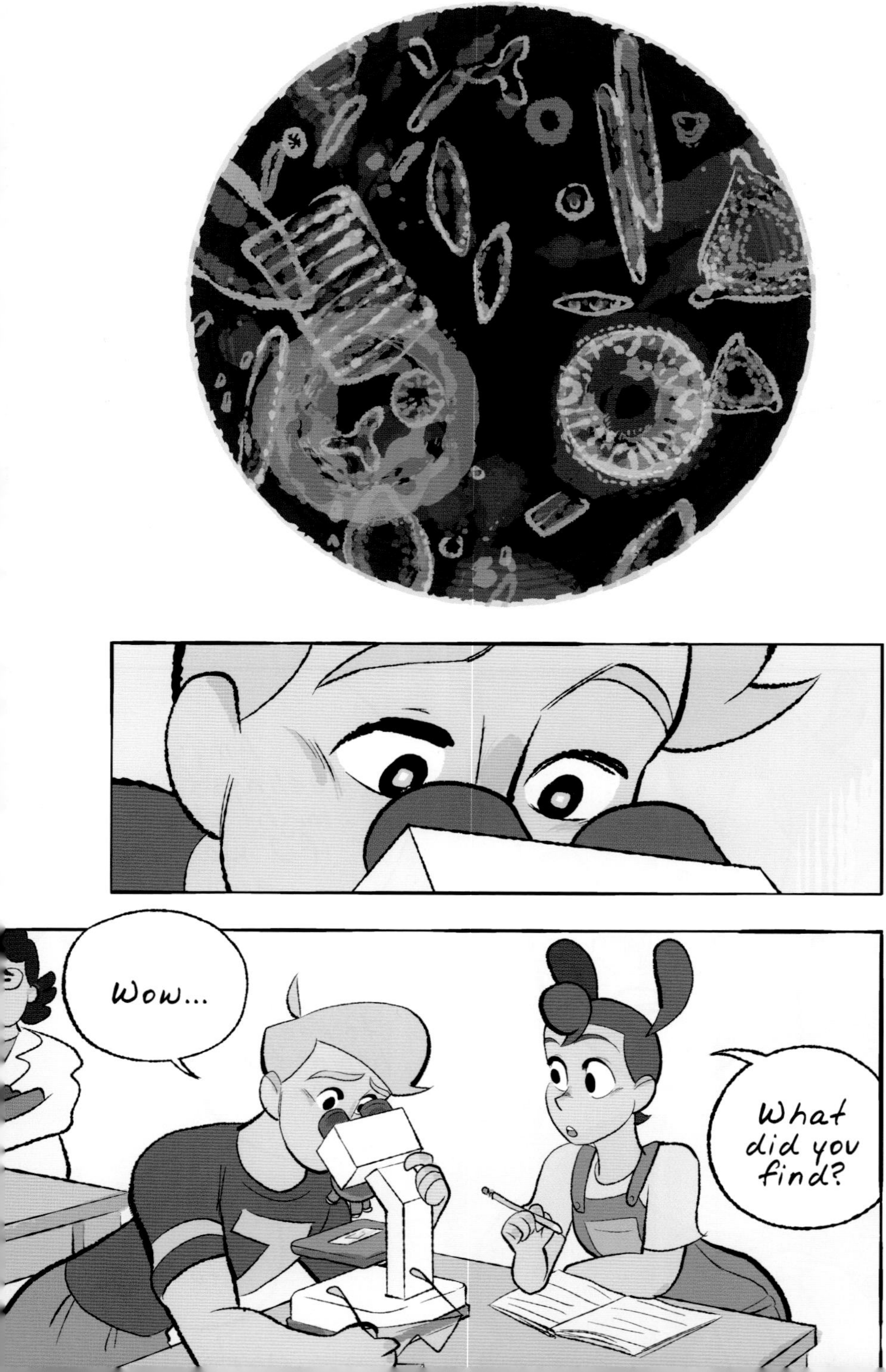
Wow...
What did you find?

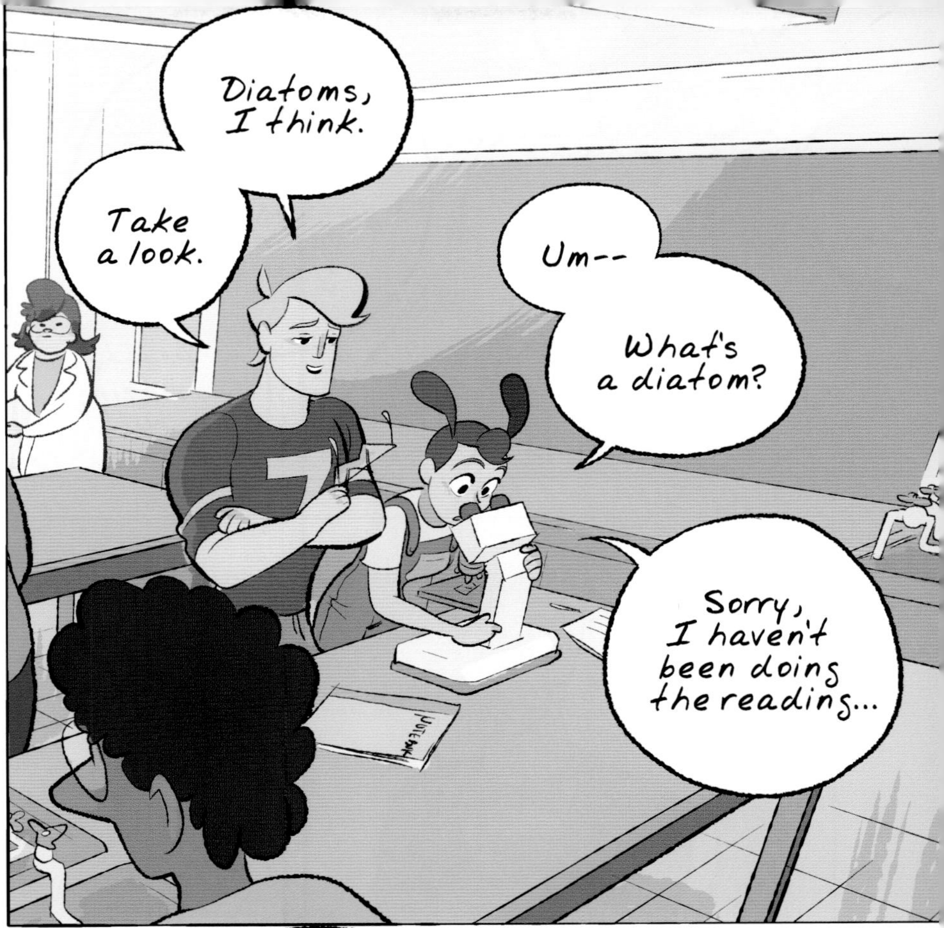
Diatoms, I think.
Take a look.
Um--
What's a diatom?
Sorry, I haven't been doing the reading...

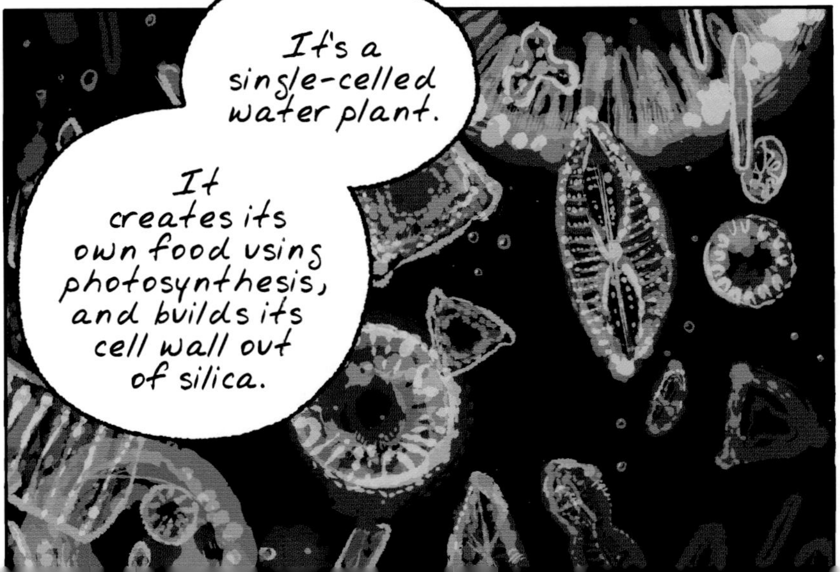
It's a single-celled water plant.
It creates its own food using photosynthesis, and builds its cell wall out of silica.

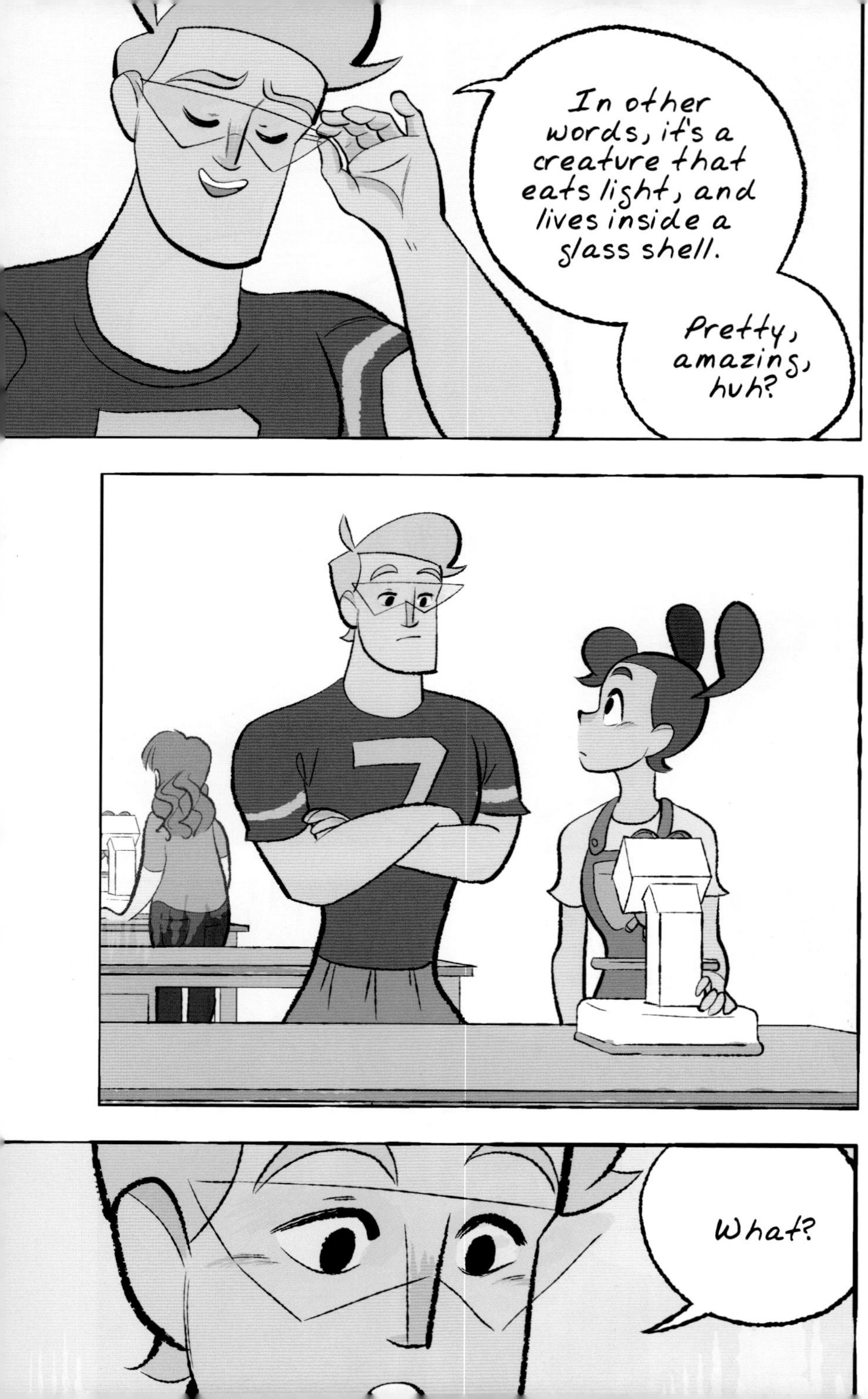
In other words, it's a creature that eats light, and lives inside a glass shell.
Pretty, amazing, huh?
What?

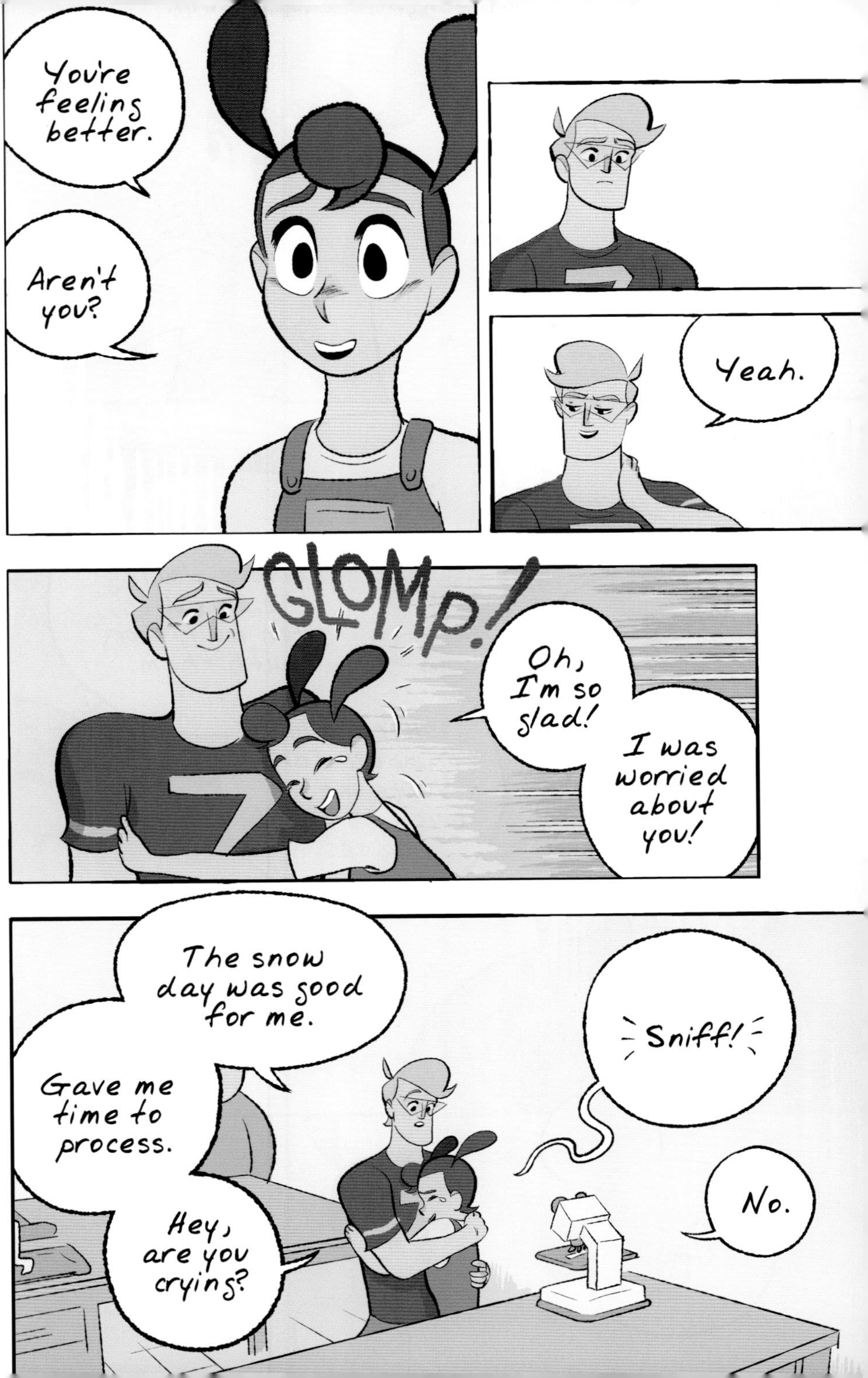
You're feeling better.
Aren't you?
Yeah.
GLOMP!
Oh, I'm so glad!
I was worried about you!
The snow day was good for me.
Gave me time to process.
Hey, are you crying?
Sniff!
No.

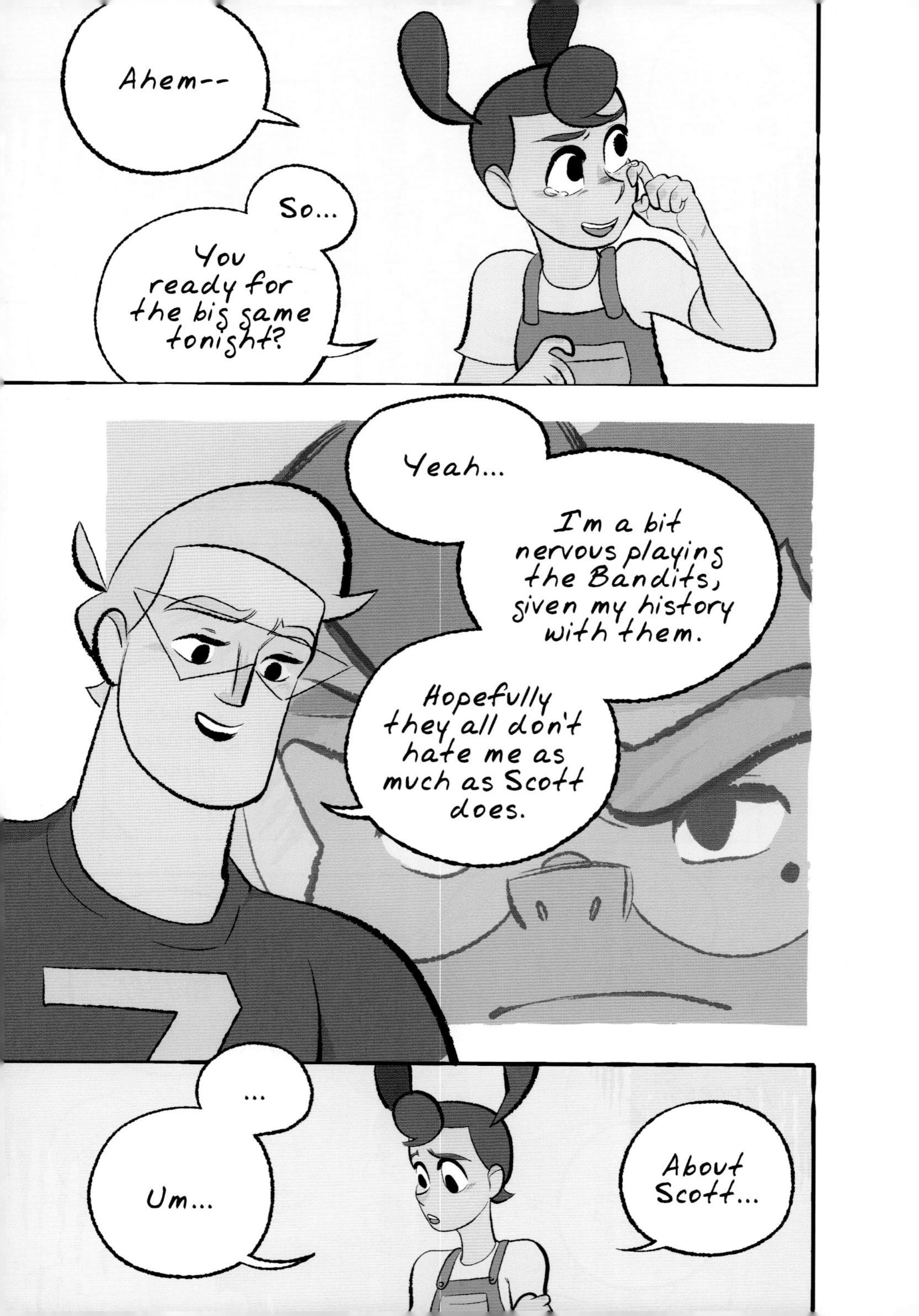
Ahem--
So...
You ready for the big game tonight?
Yeah...
I'm a bit nervous playing the Bandits, given my history with them.
Hopefully they all don't hate me as much as Scott does.
...
Um...
About Scott...

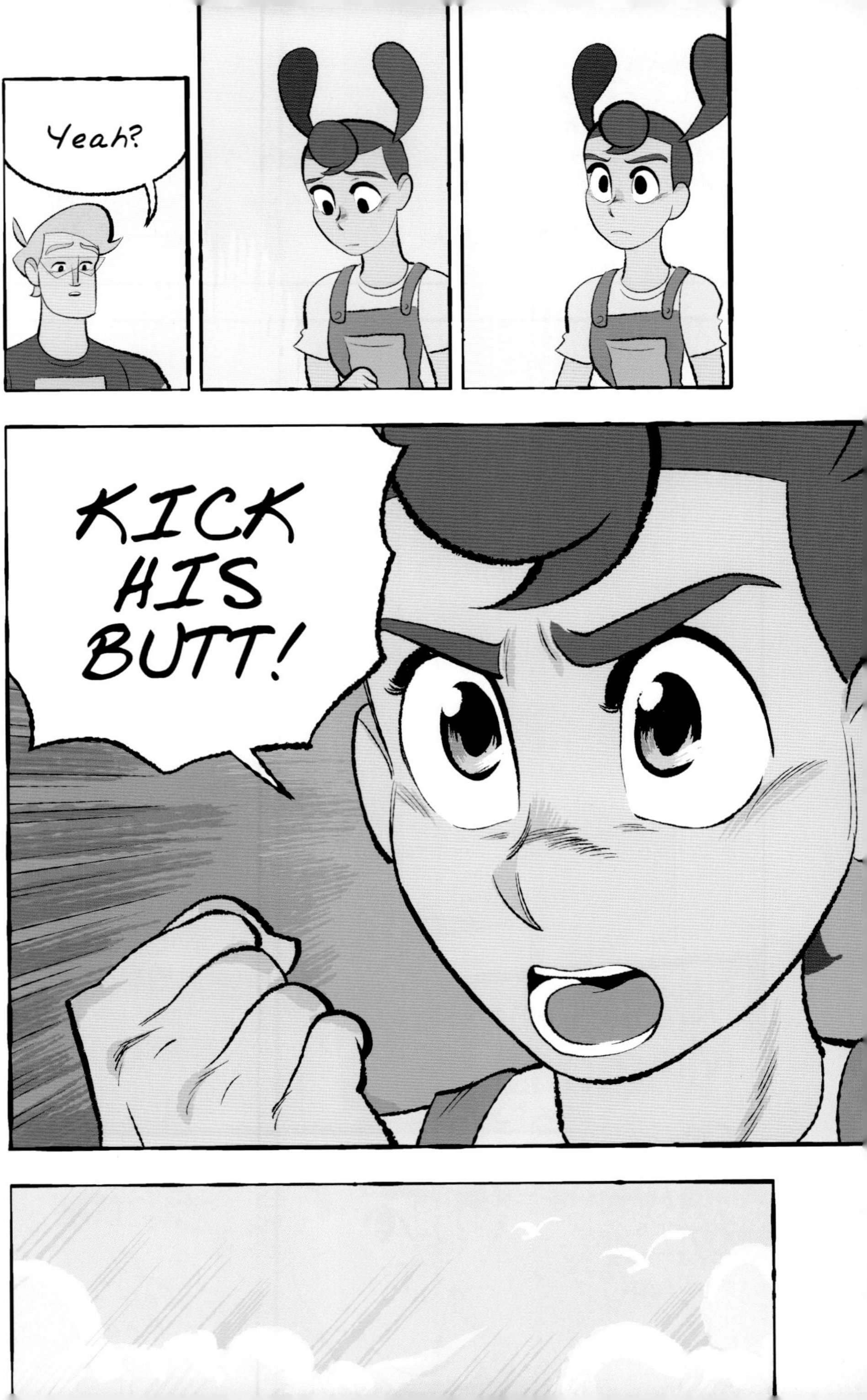
Yeah?
KICK HIS BUTT!

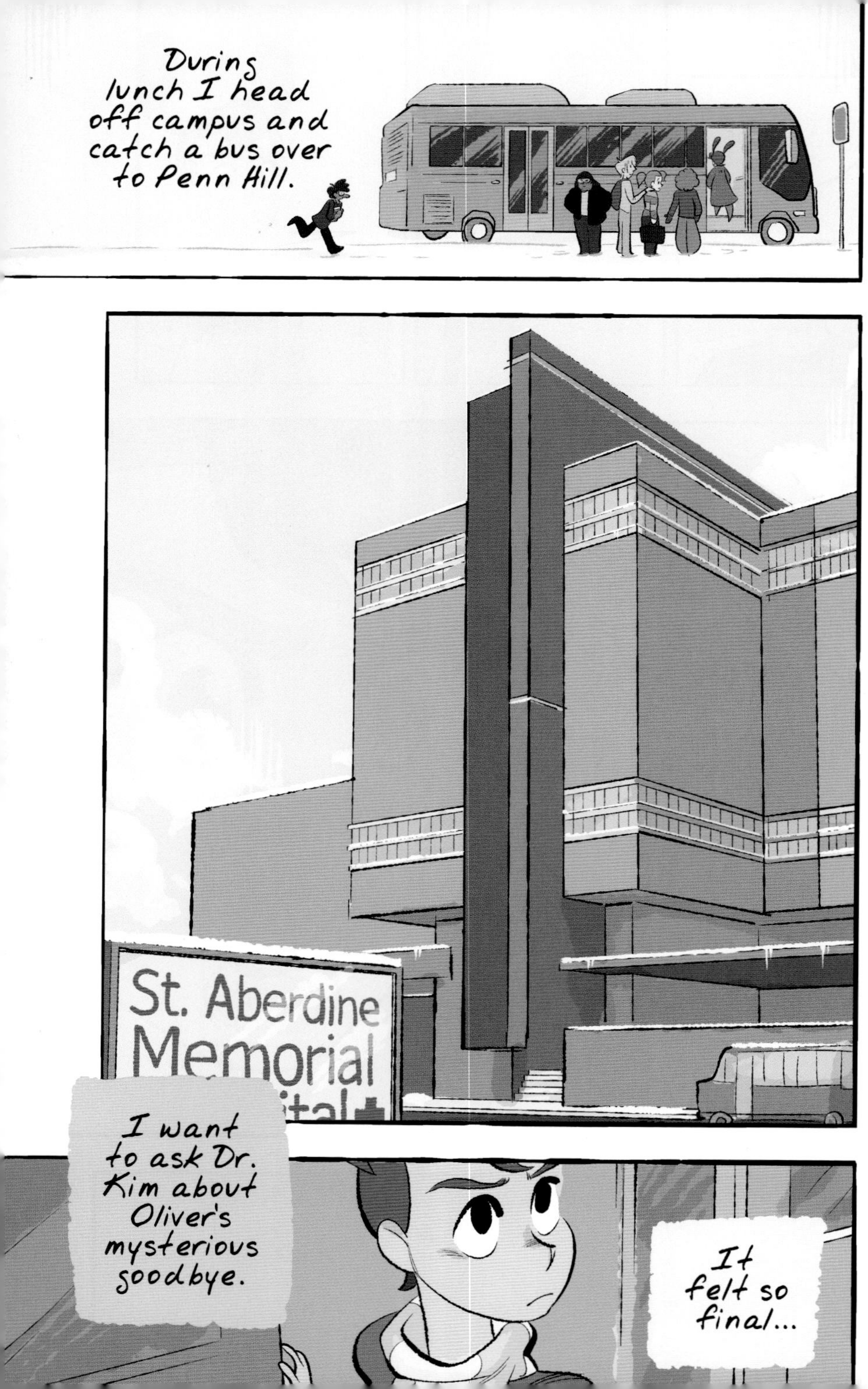
During lunch I head off campus and catch a bus over to Penn Hill.
St. Aberdine Memorial
I want to ask Dr. Kim about Oliver's mysterious goodbye.
It felt so final...

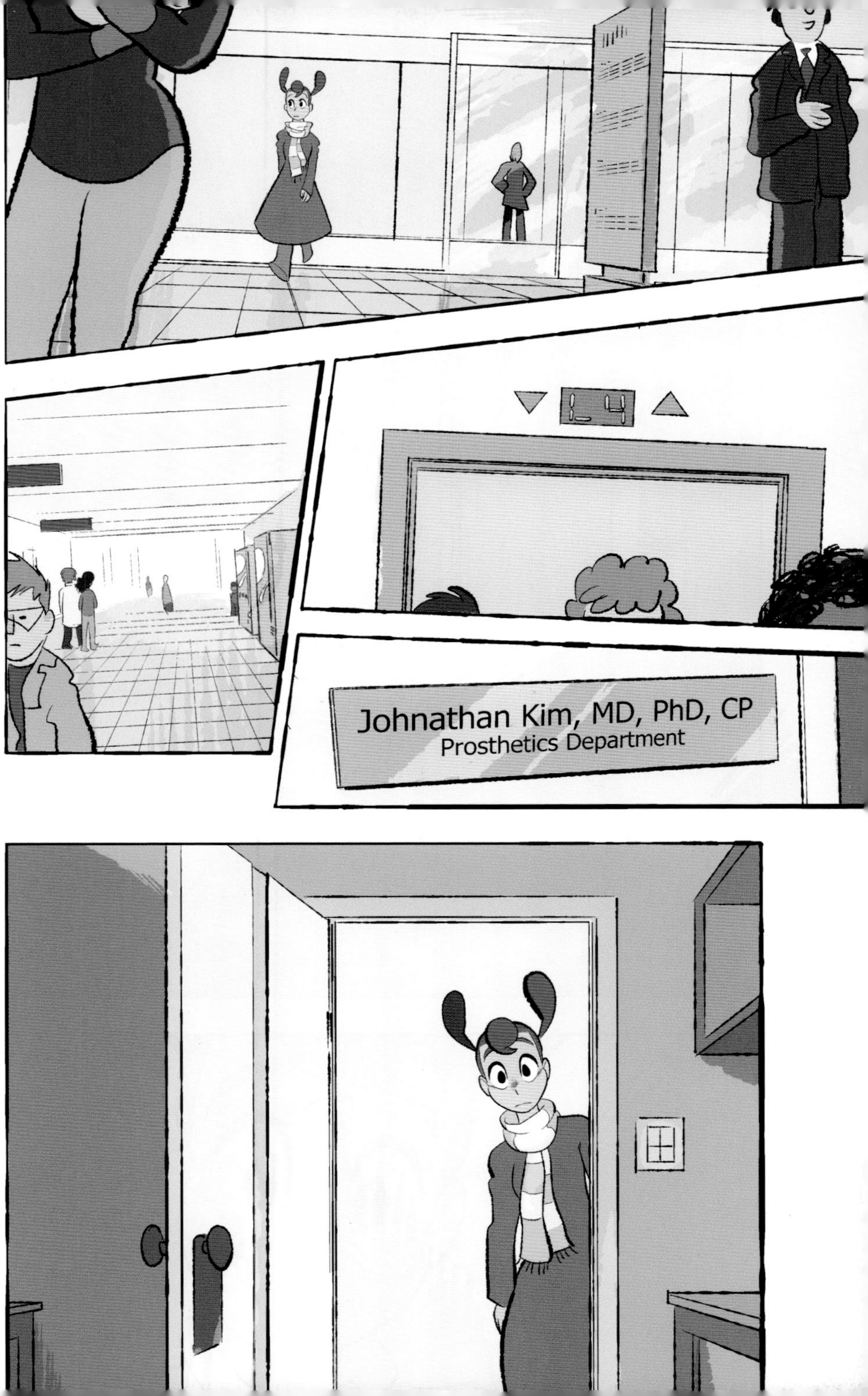

L4
Johnathan Kim, MD, PhD, CP
Prosthetics Department

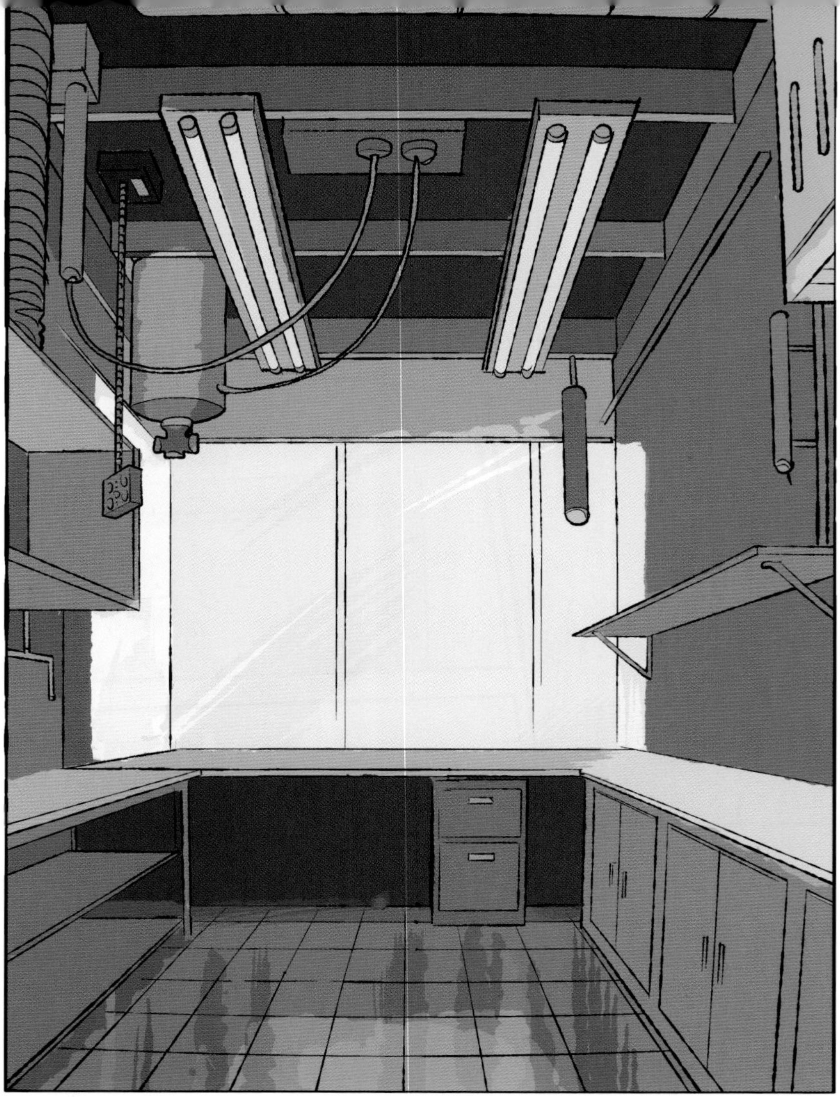

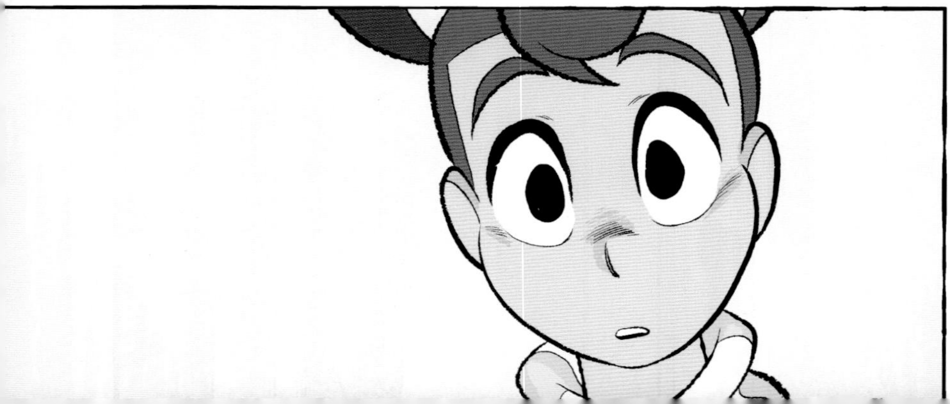

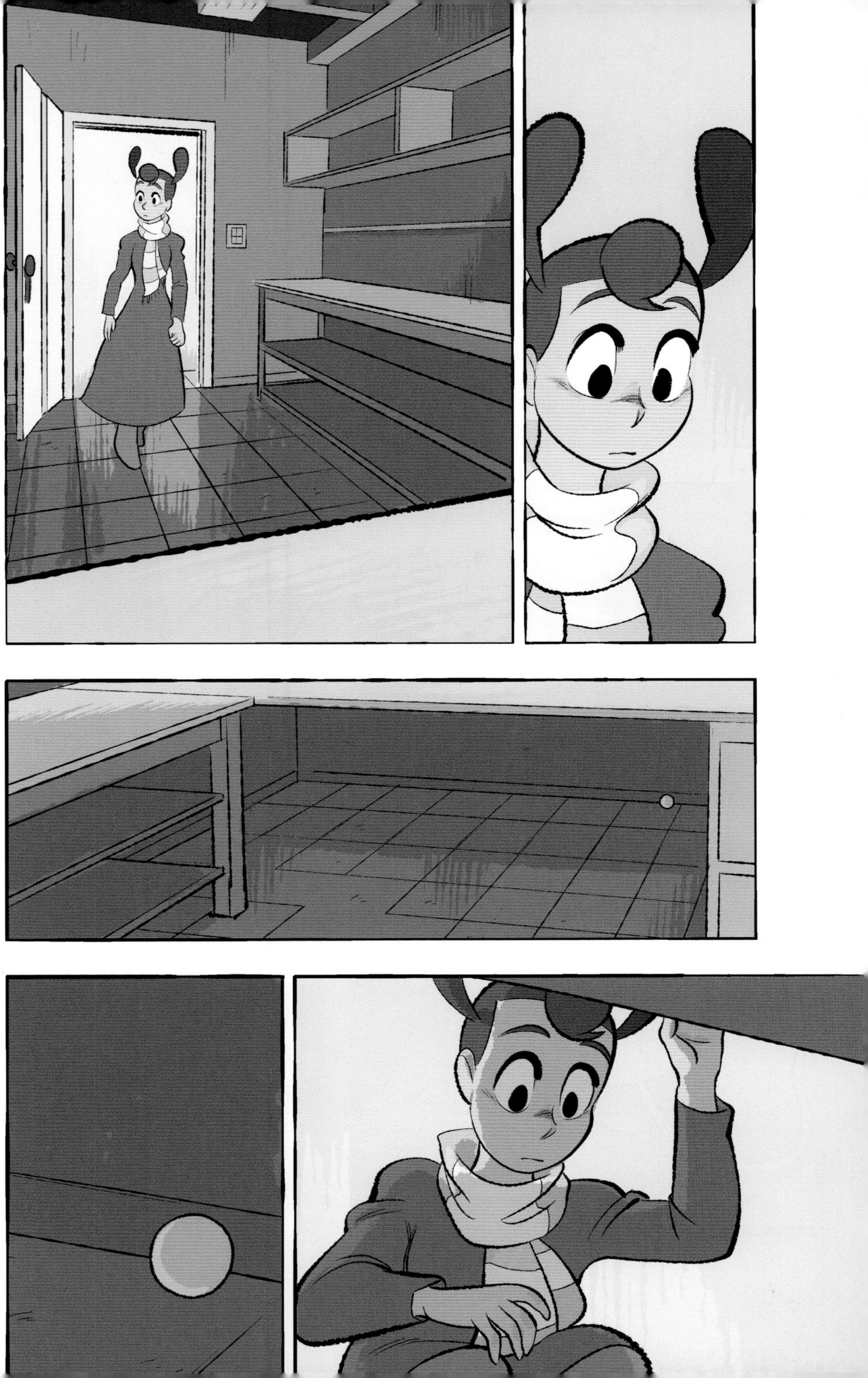

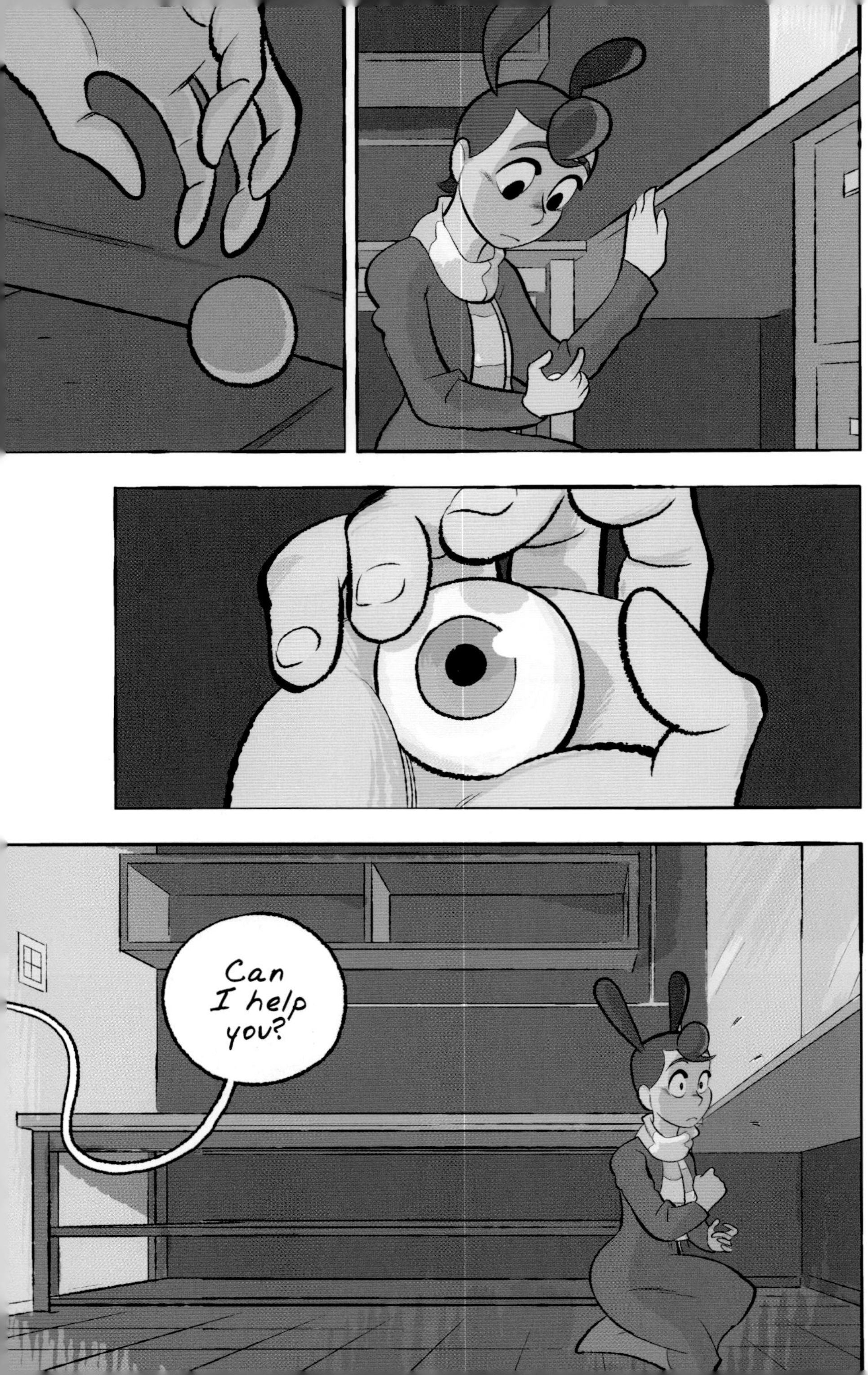
Can I help you?

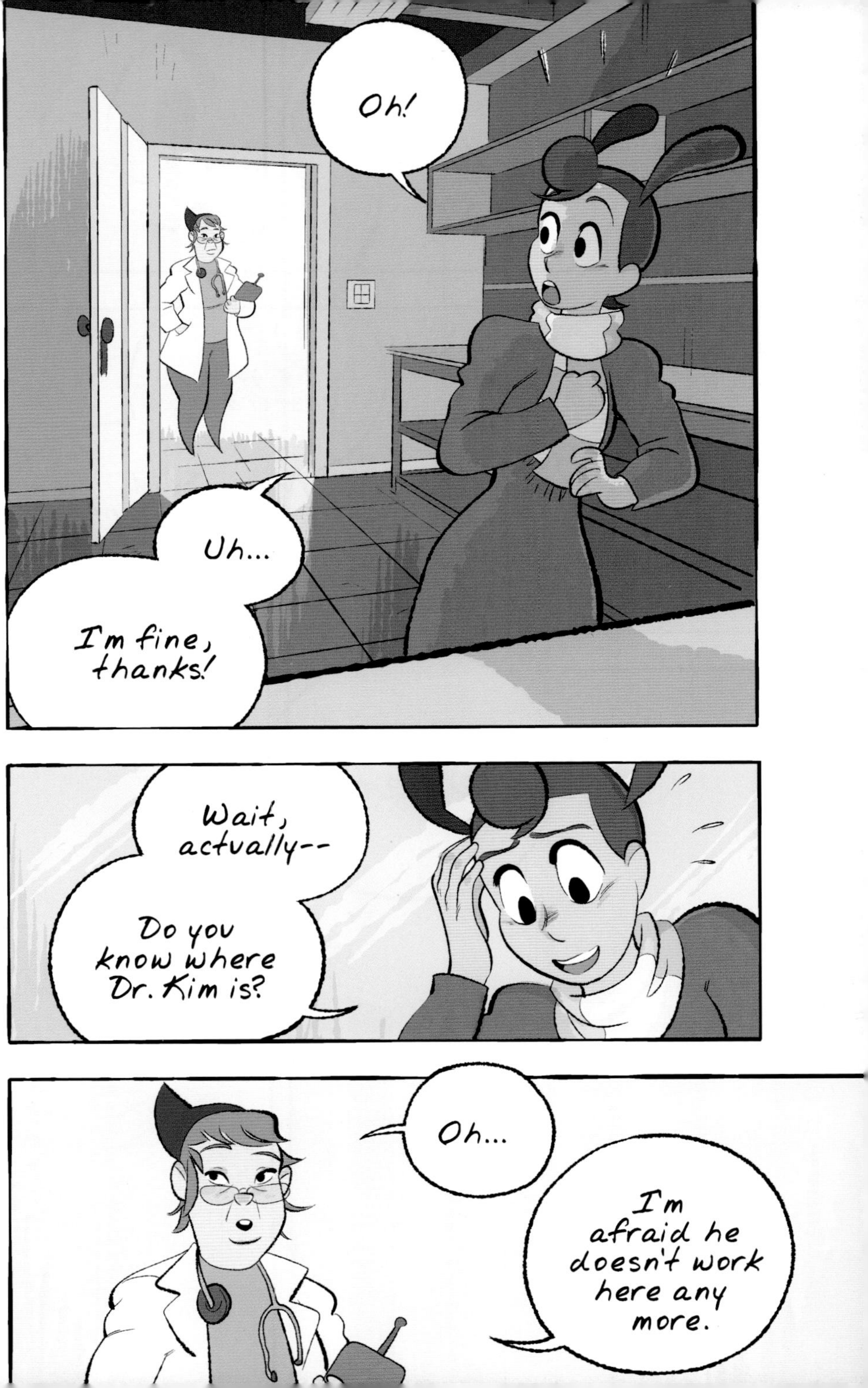
Oh!
Uh...
I'm fine, thanks!
Wait, actually--
Do you know where Dr. Kim is?
Oh...
I'm afraid he doesn't work here any more.

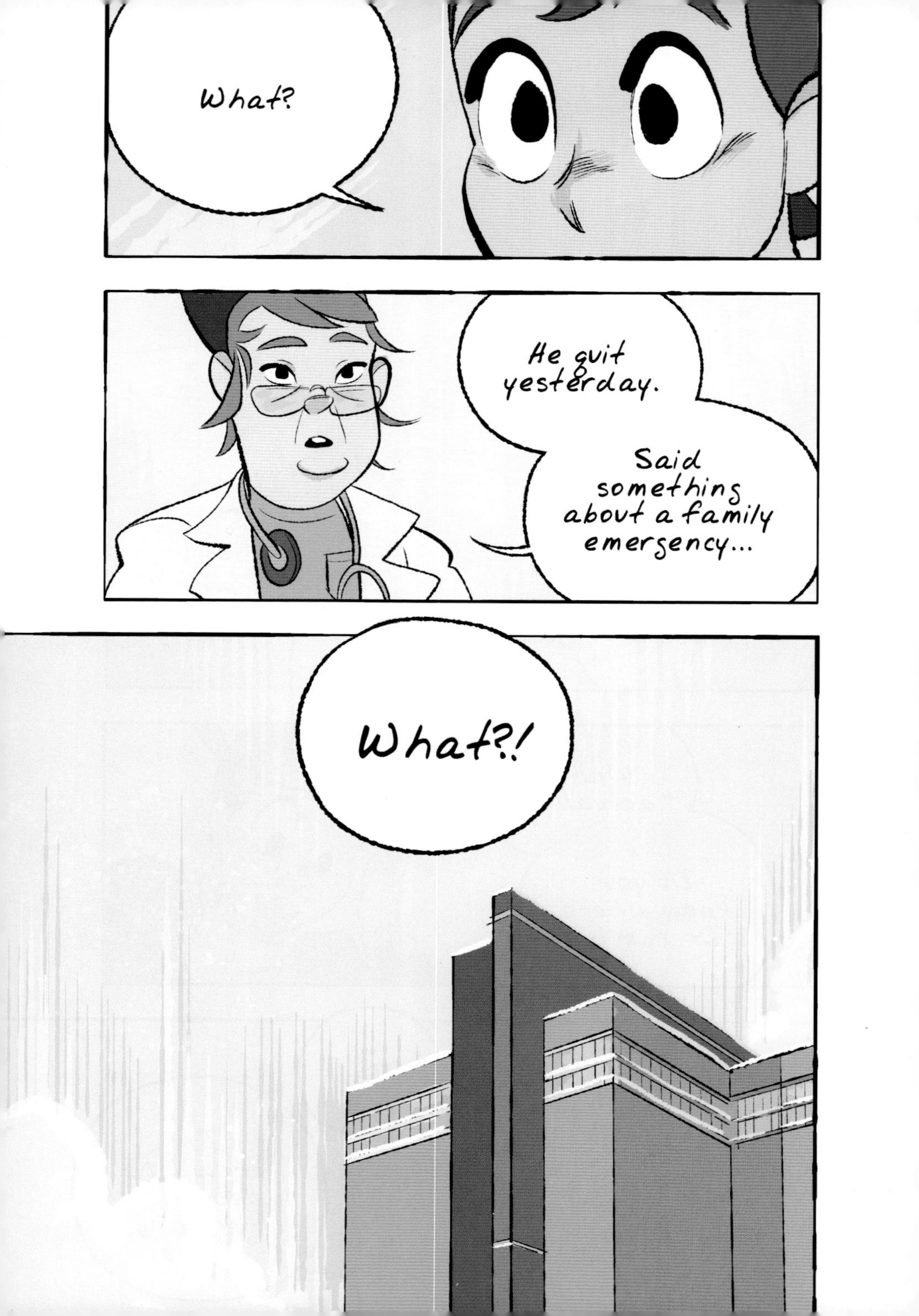
What?
He quit yesterday.
Said something about a family emergency...
What?!

Li'l Amy

by
Stephen
McCranie

Mom!
I'm home!
Amy!
How was your first day of school?
It was good.
What are you doing?
Yoga.
Cool!
It's like you made a little tent with your body!
A little mom tent!
This is the best.
I could live here forever...
My--
My arms are about to give out--

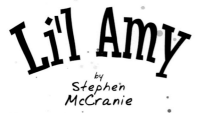

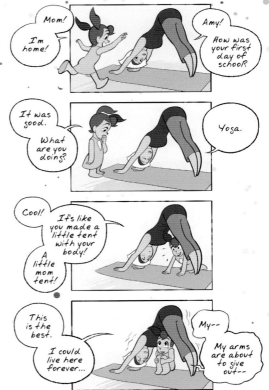

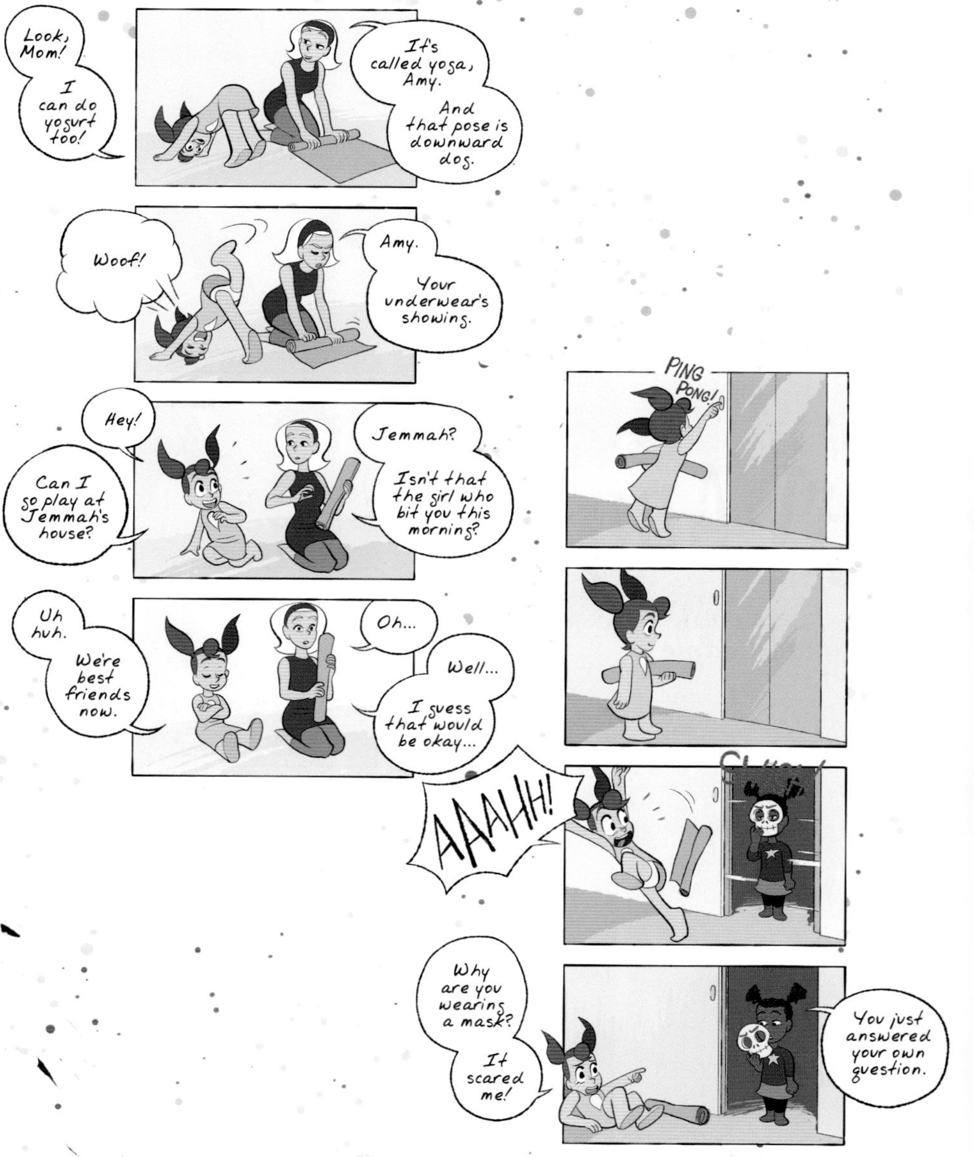
Look, Mom!
I can do yogurt too!
It's called yoga, Amy.
And that pose is downward dog.
Woof!
Amy.
Your underwear's showing.
Hey!
Can I go play at Jemmah's house?
Jemmah?
Isn't that the girl who bit you this morning?
Uh huh.
We're best friends now.
Oh...
Well...
I guess that would be okay...
PING PONG!
AAAHH!
Why are you wearing a mask?
It scared me!
You just answered your own question.

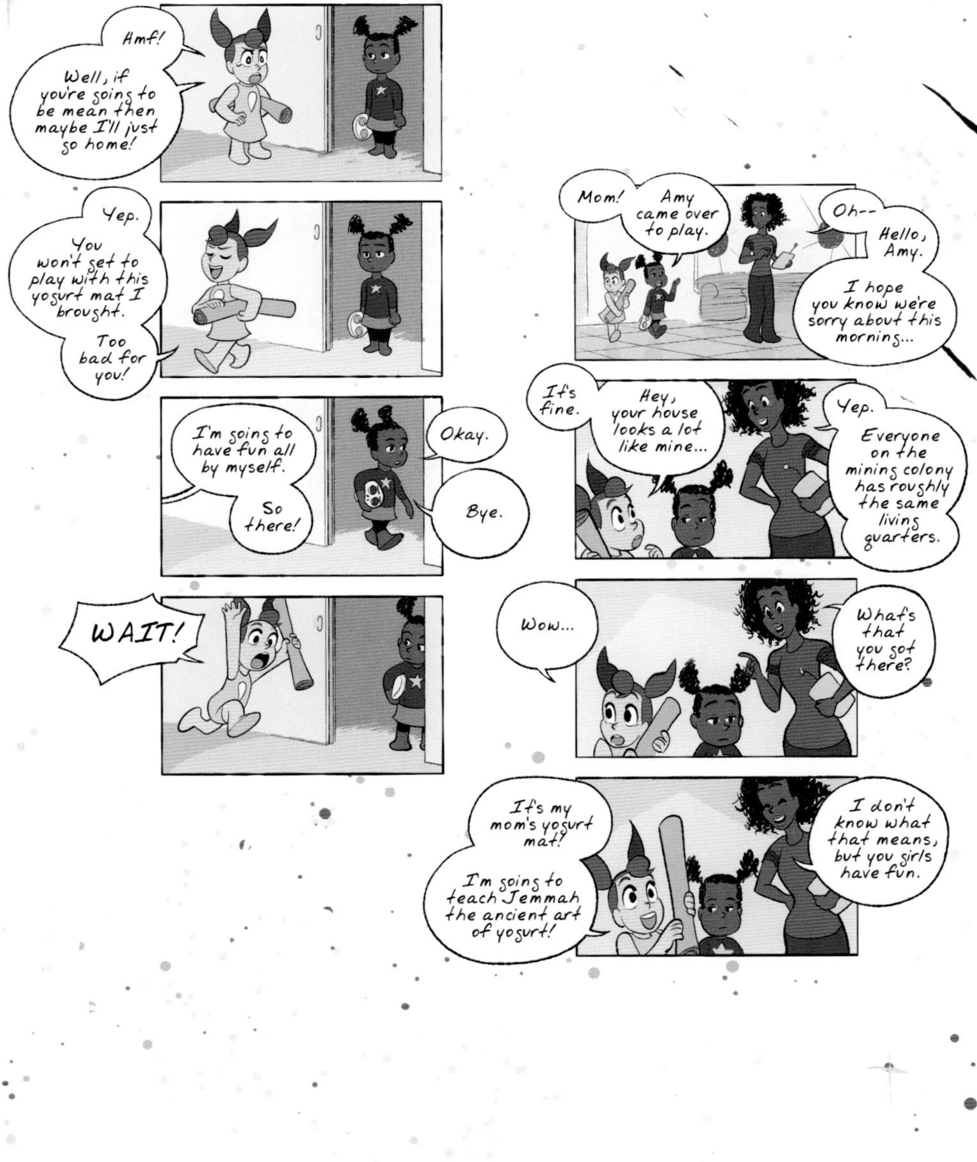
Amf!
Well, if you're going to be mean then maybe I'll just go home!
Yep.
You won't get to play with this yogurt mat I brought.
Too bad for you!
I'm going to have fun all by myself.
So there!
Okay.
Bye.
WAIT!
Mom!
Amy came over to play.
Oh--
Hello, Amy.
I hope you know we're sorry about this morning...
It's fine.
Hey, your house looks a lot like mine...
Yep.
Everyone on the mining colony has roughly the same living quarters.
Wow...
What's that you got there?
It's my mom's yogurt mat!
I'm going to teach Jemmah the ancient art of yogurt!
I don't know what that means, but you girls have fun.

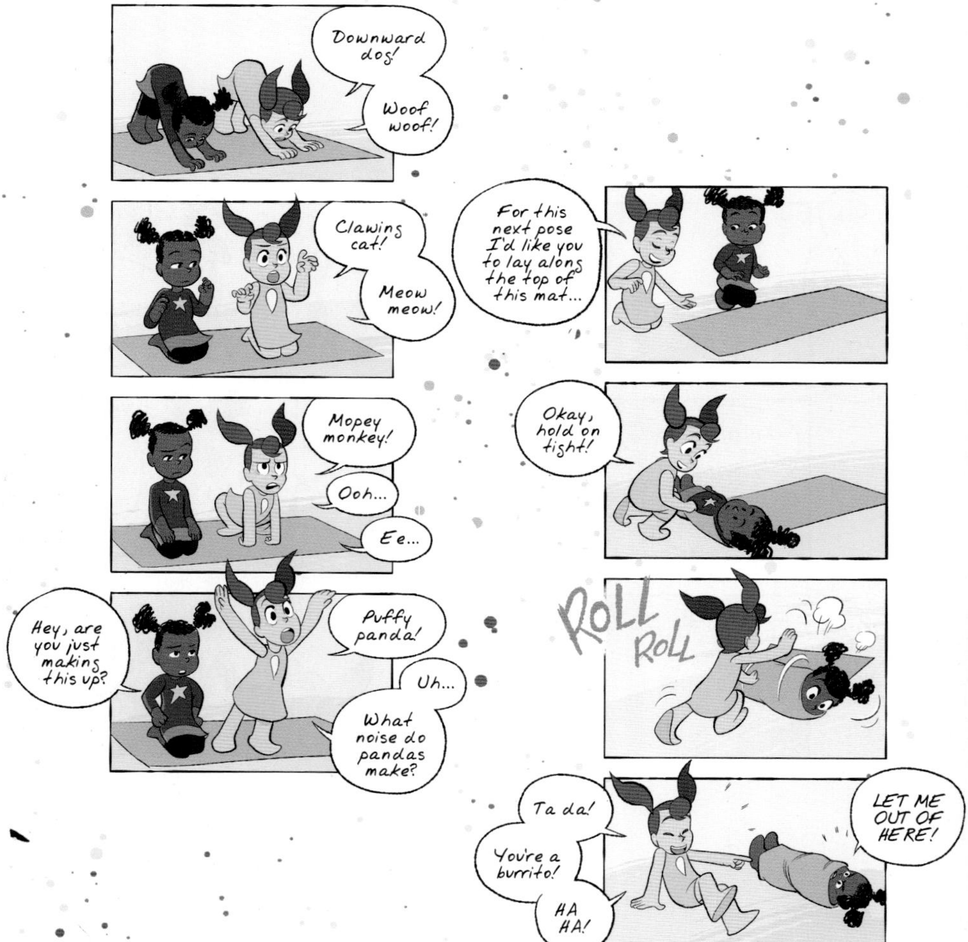

Downward dog!
Woof woof!
Clawing cat!
Meow meow!
Mopey monkey!
Ooh...
Ee...
Puffy panda!
Hey, are you just making this up?
Uh...
What noise do pandas make?
For this next pose I'd like you to lay along the top of this mat...
Okay, hold on tight!
ROLL
ROLL
Ta da!
You're a burrito!
HA HA!
LET ME OUT OF HERE!

COMING SOON . . .

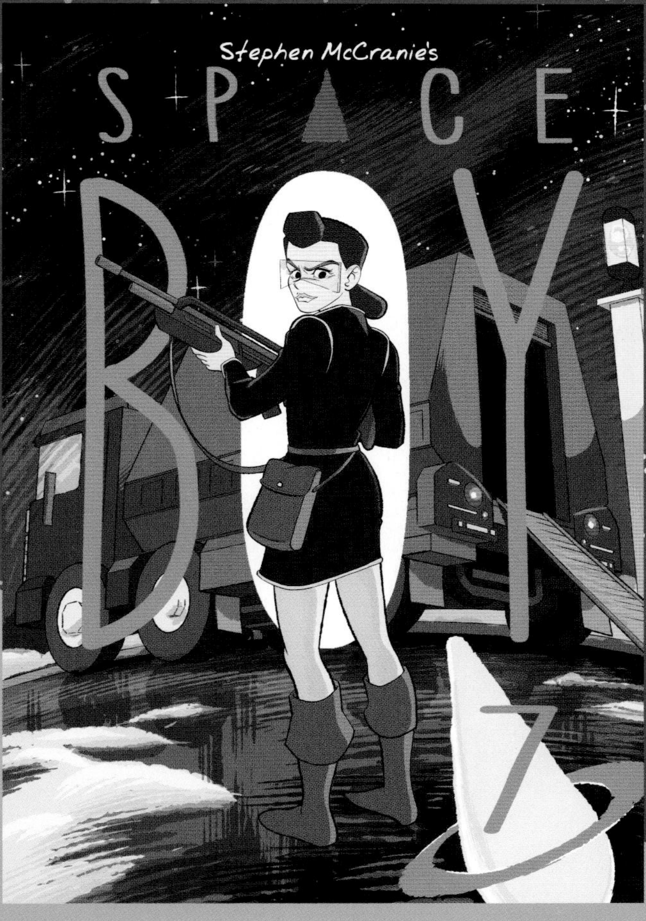
Stephen McCranie's
SPACE
BOY
7

Life is changing quickly for Amy and her friends. A new romance blossoms between Tammie and Schaefer, and Zeph reveals his feelings for Amy. But when Amy discovers startling new information about Oliver and a mysterious military organization, it threatens to come crashing down on her friends . . . with potentially tragic results! Find out more in the next volume, available June 2020!

HAVE YOU READ THEM ALL?

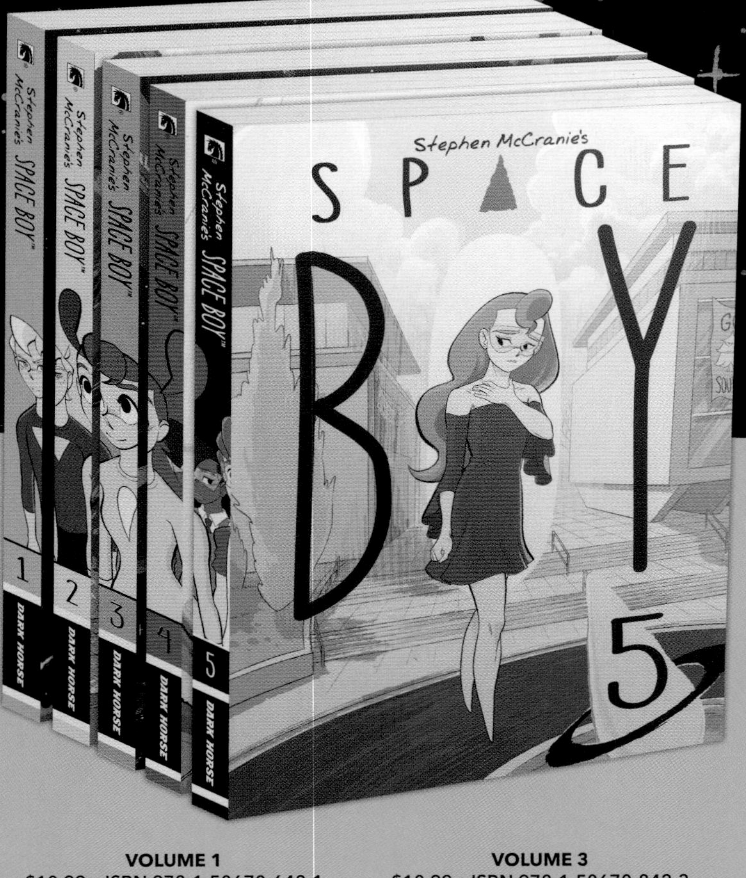
Stephen McCranie's
SPACE BOY
5
Stephen McCranie's SPACE BOY™
DARK HORSE
1
2
3
4

VOLUME 1
$10.99 • ISBN 978-1-50670-648-1

VOLUME 2
$10.99 • ISBN 978-1-50670-680-1

VOLUME 3
$10.99 • ISBN 978-1-50670-842-3

VOLUME 4
$10.99 • ISBN 978-1-50670-843-0

VOLUME 5
$10.99 • ISBN 978-1-50671-399-1

AVAILABLE AT YOUR LOCAL COMICS SHOP OR BOOKSTORE
TO FIND A COMICS SHOP IN YOUR AREA, VISIT COMICSHOPLOCATOR.COM

For more information or to order direct: On the web: darkhorse.com, E-mail: mailorder@darkhorse.com, Phone: 1-800-862-0052 Mon.-Fri. 9 a.m. to 5 p.m. Pacific Time.